FORTUNE'S FOOL

ANGELA BOORD

Impossible Books

Copyright © 2019 by Angela Boord

All rights reserved.

No part of this book may be reproduced in any form or by any electronic or mechanical means, including information storage and retrieval systems, without written permission from the author, except for the use of brief quotations in a book review.

Cover illustration by John Anthony Di Giovanni

Cover design by Shawn T. King, STK Kreations

❀ Created with Vellum

For Andy
Thanks for sticking around.

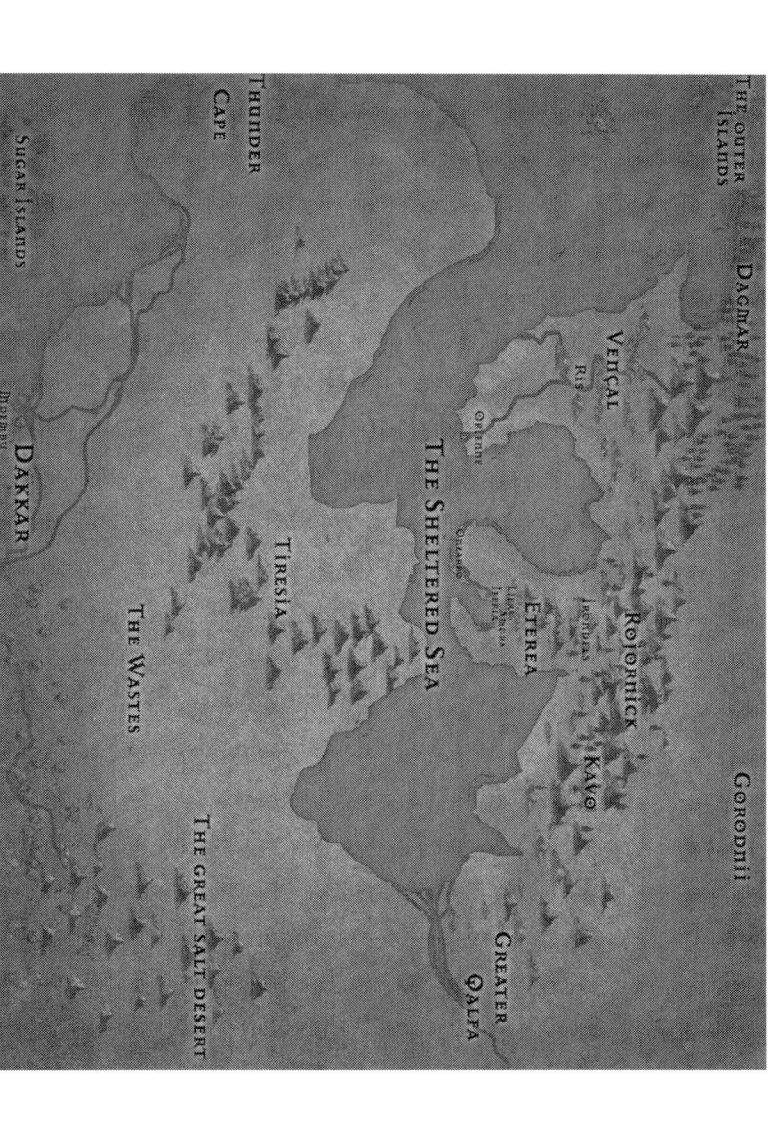

PART I

CHAPTER 1

MY RIGHT ARM IS MADE OF METAL.

A man named Arsenault made it for me, but he never told me its secrets. He didn't have time. He gave me the arm and sent me to safety, then he rode off to die.

My arm shines like silver and withstands all weather and all blows, but it isn't a dead thing. No leather straps attach it to my stump, no belts or buckles of any kind. The metal grows right into my flesh. From the sculpted whorls of my metal fingerprints to the dimple of my metal elbow, it might be the arm with which I was born.

Except that it's not.

That arm lies rotting in a cedar casket in the ground beneath a cork tree, an arm of meat, skin and blood like any other woman's.

Not that anyone can tell I'm a woman. I dress like a man and work as a gavaro, wielding my sword for coin. People know me as Kyris. But the name I was born with is Kyrra. Kyrra d'Aliente, only child of Pallo, the Householder of House Aliente.

My father is dead now, and the name Aliente is no longer my own. I am forbidden to use it, upon pain of execution. I may be the last Aliente alive, but I can't even say so.

The men beside whom I fight don't usually want to know House names anyway. Every gavaro tells his own lies of how he came to this mercenary life. After five years of saying it, I have almost come to believe that my name is Kyris di Nada, and that I sprang full-grown, metal-armed, from the rocky brow ridge of the Irondels.

Kyris No-Name. Of Nothing, Nowhere.

The name with which I was born caused a war. Ask anyone in the city of Liera and they'll tell you, *Kyrra d'Aliente did it. Cutting off her arm wasn't enough.* They know whom to blame for the crumbling walls of their once-elegant buildings, the deep pits left by cannonballs in the stone canal moorings. The tumbled brickwork still clogs the canals maintained by lesser Houses, who can't afford to dredge them out.

As if I might have been somehow more than incidental in the great games of the Houses. The Prinze controlled an entire fleet and a quarter of the coastline of the Eterean peninsula. Of what consequence was my arm to them? They cast it aside and trod over my family the way their horses trampled our land in battle.

I wasn't there for the battles. Arsenault asked me to go north to Rojornick, out of Eterea entirely, and I did. Some would call me a coward for honoring that promise. Maybe they're right.

But now I've come home, and answers are what I seek. About the five years that have passed since Geoffre di Prinze staged his first raid on my father's land. About where Arsenault might be, if he's not dead and buried. Information has become scarcer and more precious even than a black-market gun, snatched for a small fortune from under the omnipresent eyes of the Prinze.

Every new fact is like a shining flake of gold glittering in the waters of a stream. I sift through them, examining each with care. Then I tuck them away along with all my other secrets. My sex. My name. My arm.

Like a pilgrim, I come to Liera seeking truth.

CHAPTER 1

A SAILOR'S INN, DOCKSIDE.

The smell of sweat and perfume, garlic and wine. Glowing orange light and jittery black shadows on board walls, men rattling carved bones in metal cups, swilling wine, kacin smoke swirling white out of worn wood pipes. Light glints off everything: the sweat on the brows of men and women, gap-toothed smiles, silver table knives, the eel-skin wrap of dagger hilts.

"Hey, Kyris!" Shevadzic calls, waving at me from his seat at the kai dahn table. He's been teaching me to play. His Rojornicki accent is somehow comforting even here among my own people; I got used to it during the five years I was away, and didn't realize that I would miss it when I came home. I did a lot of fighting alongside the Rojornicki.

I'm not sure what he thinks about me or if he knows about my arm and or what I'm like in battle, but he treats me with a fatherly kind of respect. Gray salts his red hair.

I thread my way through the crowd and over to the table in time for the next game. "Kyris," a man sitting at the corner says with a grin as I take my seat. He's wearing Qalfan robes, but he's pulled his headcloths down in a casual manner, revealing a thicket of wavy black hair, bronze skin above a stubbled black beard, and that long slash of a grin he's not afraid to use. "I'm winning too much tonight, and Vadz is putting me off."

"Vadz isn't putting you off, Razi," the man beside him says. The glass beads braided into his black hair tinkle when he turns his head. Nibas and I fought together in Rojornick, where he was one of our archers, but when I switched sides and went over to the Kavol, he left Rojornick and headed south, saying he was done with snow and cold and just wanted his native sunny Tiresian drylands. I was surprised to find that he'd gotten hung up here, but happy to see a friendly face.

"Sure, he is," Razi says. "Or else I'd have enough coin by now to head upstairs and find some company."

"Maybe I should thank Vadz for keeping you out of trouble. Every time you go upstairs, I end up hauling your ass out of some fight." Nibas turns to watch Vadz roll the bones and swears. "Vadz. You're a whore. Look at that shit you just threw."

Vadz chuckles as he takes the handful of trinkets—no coin yet—that the men have laid out on the table. "Shit only stinks when you're downwind," he says, grinning.

The men swear while I study the bones he cast. Kai dahn is a complicated game of interpreting number combinations. Vadz's bones have carvings of women on them, too, which give them meanings I'm still trying to remember.

"Do you understand why I won?" Vadz asks me.

I finger the first bone, which lies on its side, showing both a 5 and a woman sitting astride a horse. "Five was in the first position. A lucky number, especially when seven and nine are in the second and third position and twelve is last. The five can therefore be read as a porpoise, a fortunate animal."

"Very good," he says, nodding. "You have a head for this game."

I shrug. "It's just rules, luck, and a little bit of mathematics. There isn't any strategy."

"On the surface, perhaps," Vadz replies calmly, sweeping his bones back into the cup with the side of his palm. "The trick is to know more about the game than your opponent. There are different interpretations. I could call your attention to the three at the sixth position, which alters your reading slightly. The five is not only a porpoise but a woman underneath: a mermaid." He grins.

I pick up the bone and squint at it. The woman on the horse is naked, covered only by the fall of her hair. "Five's a woman, I understand, but why the horse?"

"Kai dahn is a game Eterean sailors stole a long time ago, from one of the lost tribes of the Saien. To these tribes, everything had two sides. The other numbers in this cast make the five a lucky number, a most fortunate number. But cast in a less auspicious way..." He shrugs, a little shrug. "Five can be the worst number. It causes a lot of arguments, on ship. Interpretations differ."

"But the horse?"

"Love and death, she comes the same."

I frown, staring at the bone in my hands. Those lost Saien tribes have hit a little too close for comfort tonight. I had the day off and spent it playing cards on the Talos, the street where our contracts are traded, hoping to hear just one mention of Arsenault that gave me hope. But all I heard were the same old war stories.

"Hey, Kyris, you look like you could use some wine," Razi says. "You're off duty, yes? Time to have a little fun."

"I would if I had any coin."

"Vadz—float him a loan, get him some wine. He's going to ruin our night with that face."

"It's more likely to be your fault if the night gets ruined," Nibas tells Razi. "Stop blaming Kyris."

Razi shoots Nibas a sour look, then turns to me. "Live a little every once in a while, Kyris; that's all I'm saying."

"Eh, leave him alone," Vadz says. "He probably did more work than you did today, Razi. At least, I hope he did, because he owes me rent."

He eyes me hopefully.

I sigh. "Haven't gotten paid yet, Vadz, sorry."

Nibas picks up his own cup of wine. "You still working that job guarding that Caprine girl?"

"That...ended," I say. "A fortnight ago."

Razi laughs. "What he's not telling you, Nibas, is the girl decided she liked him. Probably all that yellow hair."

Nibas gives me one of the small curves of his mouth that passes as a smile. "That true, Kyris?"

I shift uncomfortably. "Maybe."

"And her father tore up his contract right there."

Vadz crosses his arms over his chest and shakes his head. "When were you going to tell me, Kyris?" Then he sighs. "I suppose I can float you another loan. But no more after this. What about that other job you've got?"

"Right," Nibas says. "Weren't you looking for a gavaro? The Aliente captain?"

He means Arsenault. I nod carefully. I've invented this job because I need the information, and it would seem odd and dangerous for me to ask for it outright. I'm definitely not getting paid for it, and I'm not sure how many times I can put Vadz off. "You got any information for me tonight, Vadz?"

Vadz shakes the bones in the cup. "Everyone in Liera would like to find that man, Kyris. But he's probably dead. Most of the Aliente gavaros are."

"You still think he died at Kafrin Gorge."

Nibas was in Rojornick with me during the wars, but Razi and Vadz fought in Liera. Both of them heard the stories of Kafrin firsthand. Razi looks uncharacteristically serious, and Vadz shudders and makes a sign against evil in the air before him. "Yes, I still think he died at Kafrin. If I was betting, no one would bet against me. You know what happened."

"But no one could place him there. And his body was never found."

Vadz shrugs. "Doesn't mean his body didn't burn up in the fire. There were lots of bodies and all of them unrecognizable, down to cinders and ashes—not even bones left. Haven't you heard the stories the Prinze gavaros tell?"

I've heard too many stories from too many people. There aren't that many firsthand accounts, and I'm ashamed to say that part of me is relieved when I don't have to sit through one. Listening to those stories is like having a chirurgeon dig at a rotten wound.

But I make myself shrug. "There are things Vadz doesn't need to know. "I'm wearing a green armband. I don't get a chance to talk to many Prinze."

"Well, they'd be happy if I could lead them to the Aliente captain, too, wouldn't they? They've still got posters up for him. Ten thousand astra on his head, dead or alive. I'd be a rich man if I turned him in."

"As if you would give the Prinze anything, Vadz. I know what happened to your men in the war."

Vadz leans forward on the table and points at me, ready to elaborate on his favorite complaints yet again. "The Prinze had no call to fire on that ship. We were hauling grain."

Nibas shifts in his seat. "Come on, Vadz. How many times can you tell this story? You were hauling guns."

"But they didn't *know* that, did they? They fired even though I'd begun to run up the white flag. The guns were all hid in the grain. They'd never have found them, and we were carrying injured, too, up to the Qalfans in the Quarter."

"So, why would you turn Arsenault over to men like that?" I say.

"I just wonder why you're so persistent in your search for him. What can he matter to you?"

"I have employers who'd like to know, that's all."

"Caprine? That would make a pickle of the peace accords, wouldn't it?"

"If anyone found out. But my employer isn't Caprine. So, you don't have to worry on that account, Vadz."

"Dakkaran, then, maybe," Vadz says sagely. "Didn't your captain have some link to Dakkar? Guns? Kacin?"

The Dakkarans used to hold the monopoly on the guns they smithed and the powdery white drug made from berries from their jungles, a long time ago. But that was before the Prinze stole both from them.

"There might have been some kind of link," I say, hoping I've kept my voice noncommittal. "Guns, I think."

"Whoever your employer is, he doesn't pay you very well," Vadz says skeptically.

"He's paying me for information, isn't he? I haven't brought him much."

In truth, I've found hardly anything at all. It's as if Arsenault has disappeared from the face of the earth. Probably, that does mean he's dead.

Maybe.

Vadz sighs. "Well. If you could use another job, there's been a man in here. Looking for you."

I'm still holding the bone. I lean the chair up so the front legs rest on the floor again, and put the bone down. "What kind of man?"

Again, the little shrug. "A gavaro; how am I supposed to know? Qalfan. He looked hard."

Razi perks up and scans the room.

"Did he say why he wanted me?" I ask.

"He told me to tell you his employer wanted to talk to you about a job." Vadz gestures with his cup. "In the back room."

My eyebrows lift. If you have business you want to keep hidden, you can rent Laudio's back room, but you'd better pay him well and hope he walks away.

"The gavaro was Caprine, then?"

"Not Caprine," Vadz says. "Sere. He wore an indigo armband."

I stiffen. Sere are almost as bad as Prinze, except that they've managed to retain their neutrality, with ties to both Prinze and Caprine, the two rival families around which the lesser families flit, hoping to sip of their nectar. Lieran politics are a morass of kin alliances, but when it comes down to it, the most important question is *Do you stand with Prinze or Caprine?*

The major feat of the Sere is that they've avoided becoming attached to either House and instead have grown their tendrils into both.

Nibas gives a low whistle. "Working for the Sere would put you in coin."

"And is this employer in the back room tonight?" I ask Vadz.

He glances at me out the corner of his eye. "Do you see that man standing just to the left of the Marquis painting? He's the one who's been asking."

"Found him," Razi says. "If he's working for the Sere, I don't know who he is."

I try to look up without looking up. The Marquis painting is a painting of a Vençalan nobleman in his boudoir with a courtesan, while Cythia, the goddess of love, looks down on him in approval. Laudio probably got it cheap.

The Qalfan gavaro looks out of place beside it.

In contrast to the lush greens and oranges of the painting, he is one lean, angular expanse of black. Black—from the leather boots that show beneath the hem of his allaq, the body robes that are usually white, to the urqa he wears wrapped around his face and head. From this distance, I can't even see his eyes, the slit in his urqa is so narrow.

Black isn't a color you see often in Liera. It's the color of ravens, of carrion-eaters—of death.

I wear a black cloak and a black-and-silver tunic. Those were the colors of the Rojornicki boyar I fought for, and I still wear them in honor of him. Arsenault gave me the cloak, but I'm not sure he would appreciate the irony.

But there is a familiarity to the gavaro's stance. He's the kind of gavaro you'd notice anywhere, no matter what he wore. Like he's quick with his sword and knows how to use it. And with his height, he probably has the reach to do some damage.

I push myself back from the table with my right hand, forgetting for the moment that Vadz has seen me most often use my left. Nibas and Razi know about my arm because they've fought beside me, but they also know why I like to keep it secret. Vadz frowns at me slightly, but my right hand looks normal enough when it's gloved. It makes the wrong noise when I bump it against wood, though, not a fleshy sound but a slight metallic *ting*.

I close my fingers against my palm and stand up.

Vadz trades a glance with Razi and Nibas. "You know...the war's over and you're not in Rojornick anymore. Jobs are just jobs. You make your money and you get out."

I pick up my own wine and drain it while I watch the Qalfan. He sees me and straightens. Good. I set the empty goblet down and pick up Vadz's dice. "Jobs are always just jobs, aren't they?" I say, shaking the bones.

"Sometimes, I don't like that look in your eye, Kyris."

I tip the cup, and the bones come rattling out.

A five in the first position again. After that, the numbers are all a random jumble, some of them lying on their sides.

"Dread gods," Vadz says. "I've never seen a throw so bad."

I grin at him. "Death's my job, isn't it?"

⁂

The Qalfan gavaro doesn't speak as he walks ahead of me up a narrow staircase to the room where Laudio keeps his books, not to the back room. But he flashes a glance at me before we walk into Laudio's study. He has light eyes but not obviously blue. The way his brows pull down over them when he sees me up close is somehow familiar too.

He hooks his indigo armband with his thumb, and the gavaros guarding Laudio's door let us in.

"Who are you taking me to see?" I ask as we cross the threshold of the doorway. He doesn't answer, just keeps walking past Laudio. Laudio comes half out of his velvet upholstered chair, putting his kacin pipe down on a leather-bound book of carefully penned figures. The gavaro doesn't raise his head until he reaches the paneling at the back of the room.

"Tell your mistress she'll have the Imisi rosé if she wishes," Laudio says, sitting back down, hands wandering over the cover of the book. The Qalfan—half-Qalfan or a slave, with those eyes—looks back at him and nods.

Laudio bends his neck stiffly but keeps his eye on us.

Mistress, he said.

My hopes die. A man who's looking for me might have been Arsenault at last, but a woman...it really is about a job.

It was probably a stupid hope, anyway. I've been in Liera six months now without a single lead on where he might be, except for dead.

The gavaro pushes the paneling into the wall with the flat of his hand, revealing a swing-door leading to a secret staircase. Clean-burning beeswax candles glow on peeling blue paint, outlined in white—waves for Tekus, the Father God. We're close enough to the water that the passage might once have led to a cave that opened into or above the sea, Tekus's domain. The Etereans riddled the high sections and cliffs of Liera with catacombs and filled them with the bones of their ancestors. Perhaps we walk above them now.

Once down the staircase, the hallway winds around the corner of the building, and the walls become so narrow that the Qalfan's shoulders push against them. He glances back at me once but says nothing. Then out of the darkness ahead of us a door appears, illuminated in yellow light. He raps on it twice before pushing it open.

Mistress.

A woman sits there, waiting for us. The room is over-decorated with gilt and panels painted with scenes of goddesses and carpeted in blue velvet so deep, my heels sink into it. Incense laces the air with the scent of cloves, and the warmth of the fire blazing in the marble fireplace raises sweat on my forehead. My metal arm throbs with the sudden change in temperature.

The woman reclining on the mahogany settee makes the

room look tawdry in her simplicity. Her pewter silk gown shimmers in the candlelight, modest and yet somehow revealing the way it clings to her body. A pair of ivory combs secure curls the color of black-cherry wood in a fashionable sweep atop her head. She wears no jewelry but a lustrous pearl choker, probably worth more than five years of my pay. Her blue eyes are the color of gathering storm clouds. She narrows them on me.

I know this Sere. Her name is Tonia, and she used to be Caprine before she married. I can only hope she doesn't recognize me.

"Kyris di Nada," she says. "My Qalfan was right; it is you." She smiles at me, a cold, fake smile, one I saw often enough on my mother's lips as she welcomed our neighbors into the conservatory for tea. My mother fought her own wars, not of swords but of teacups, waged on sunlit afternoons with women who filled their husbands' ears with secrets when they went home.

The Qalfan slips behind her to sit on the floor, legs crossed, head bent.

Tonia notices me looking at him. "He's no matter. I trust him to keep information where it needs to be kept."

His silence begins to bother me. "Is he mute?" I know he's watching me from under the wrapped cloths of his urqa, but I can't see his eyes.

"Falin? No. But he's smart enough to keep his mouth closed. And he's handy enough with a sword to keep you from getting ideas."

I eye her warily. "My friend said you might have a job for me."

"They told me you liked to get to the point. Yes, I have a job for you. But surely, you'll let me entertain you first. Will you have some wine?"

Warily, with my hand near the hilt of my sword, I edge over to a chair covered in claret velvet. I sit, and she pours wine of the same color—not the rosé—into a crystal goblet.

"I do have a job for you," she repeats. "But I must know that you'll say nothing to anyone of what is said here. I've heard, through various channels, that you're good at keeping secrets, but I need assurance. You must not speak of what transpires tonight. Is that clear?"

Her gaze meets mine again.

I set my glass down on the table between us. "Do you think I'm that stupid? You've brought your assurance. If I refuse to accept your offer, you'll have me killed before I leave the tavern."

Tonia arches an eyebrow. "You can always leave now. Before you hear what I have to say. But there's a great deal of coin involved."

I'm only too aware of my purse hanging limp inside my cloak. But this won't be a simple matter of guarding a few bolts of silk. Not if Tonia di Sere is in charge of it.

"Coin's not all I care about," I say.

"I've heard that you like to take jobs based on ideals... of a sort."

My right hand twitches and my fingers clack together, softened by the leather of my glove. I clench it into a fist and pick up the wineglass with my left hand. "I wonder who you've been talking to." I drink quick, the way a man might. When I set the glass down again, only a small puddle of red swirls in the bottom, the color of blood.

"I have my sources." She adjusts her legs under her skirts and smooths the fabric over them. "I also hear that this job may appeal to you on a somewhat baser level."

She sips her wine and watches me over the rim.

Something in the way Tonia looks at me makes me think she knows who I am. And wants to use me.

I have been used before.

I stand up. "You can keep your gold and your wine and your Householder intrigues. It's a mess to get involved."

"Don't be a fool. You must have known what was at stake when you learned I wanted to meet you in the back room. You did know where my Qalfan was taking you, didn't you? Or have you been gone so long that you've forgotten the ways of Houses?"

I was right. She knows who I am.

She knew I wouldn't be able to resist a job handed out from the back room of Laudio's, and maybe she also knew the kinds of questions I've been asking. But a job based on the tangled skein of loyalties lying in wait for me here in Liera...

"Keep your House ways," I say. "I'm in for something more honest."

I start for the door. The Qalfan rises in one quick motion, but before he can reach me, Tonia blurts, "Cassis di Prinze is at the Aliente hunting lodge. And I want you to kill him."

⚜

"Cassis di Prinze?"

Is my voice steady as I say his name?

Tonia flicks her hand at me. "Go ahead. Walk out that door. My gavaro won't kill you. Maybe you can even see what Cassis does to my family this time. You once had Caprine ties, didn't you?"

"Once," I say, dropping my hand from the doorknob. "But your father sat on the Circle that voted them away."

"And given the chance you'd exact your revenge on him rather than Cassis? Cassis has taken my sister to the Aliente hunting lodge; Cassis oversees the Forza and the Aliente estate. You'd walk away from that?"

No. I can't walk away from that.

A long time ago, I fell in love.

Many ladies had run themselves through on this spear before me, but they hid their wounds in lesser marriages or else moved through the temples, the cripple colonies, silent as a winter chill. I paid them no attention. Instead, I played my scales and worked my embroidery obliviously, hating the frivolous poems my tutor made me memorize about birds and chaste women.

CHAPTER 1

What I wanted was passion.

The summer I turned sixteen, I thought I found it. He walked in like the scent of orange blossoms, immediate and beautiful. His mahogany hair, the same color as his eyes, was caught at the nape of his neck in a silver clasp, and he wore a silver-hilted sword at his side. Here, I felt, was a man who could do what women whispered about over my mother's teacups, whose touch could burn away the chaste bonds that kept me stiff as brocade.

His name was Cassis. The son of a family that had no business treating with mine.

Prinze.

I move slowly back to the chair with the empty wineglass next to it. I sit down and curl my hands around the ornately carved wooden balls at the end of its arms.

"All right," I say. "I'll listen."

※

"Cassis has sequestered himself on the old Aliente hunting lands," Tonia says, rising to pace. "And taken my sister with him. He says he means to have her as second wife."

"And you believe him?" I ask.

"If I did, would you be here?"

"His father will never allow it. But it might be good for you. You're Sere now. Why should it matter to the Sere if a Prinze marries a Caprine?"

Tonia glares at me. "*Second* wife," she says. "If he stoops to that. I am a Caprine by blood and birth, of the main branch, and the wife of a man who lies at the bottom of the sea because of the bloody Prinze; have you forgotten that?"

I haven't. What Lieran could forget how Ricar di Sere died, leaving the Prinze with the sole claim on the gun trade?

I wonder what game Tonia is playing. I've been too long away from the ways of Houses. "If Driese were to marry Cassis, there would be kin ties. The Caprine could buy guns."

Tonia waves my statement away. "At what prices? My father would never debase himself so, and he will never consent to Driese becoming a man's second wife when she could have her pick of suitors otherwise."

Except that the pool from which Driese might choose a suitor has diminished. The loyalty of the Sere, Tonia's in-laws, is somewhat vague, and there are no Aliente anymore. Or at least, I haven't found any yet.

"She could have her pick of suitors," Tonia says again, as if she can read my thoughts. Her expression grows troubled and she starts pacing again.

"I want you to rescue her," she says, without turning around. "Bring her back and kill Cassis."

Do I want to kill him? It's a ridiculous question. Almost rhetorical. The issue has never been *whether* I want to kill him but *how*. Slowly, with poison? Dramatically, running Arsenault's sword straight through his heart? Or perhaps ironically—using only my right arm to bash his skull in?

The options I've entertained over the years have been endless but never more detailed than in the past year. I've acquired much more experience in killing people, for one thing, and for another, it's not just myself I'd be avenging now. Not just my family.

Because if Arsenault *is* dead, there's no one who had a hand in it more than Cassis did.

But I don't want to look too eager. If I'm to take this job, I need to keep my head.

"Perhaps your sister doesn't want to be rescued. And what will happen when Geoffre di Prinze finds his son dead? Who else knows about this?"

"My sister is a fool," she says, "and doesn't know the import of what she does. Would you tell me to leave her?"

"Perhaps not. But you didn't answer my other questions."

Tight-lipped, she says, "No one else knows. Driese and Cassis escaped in secret. She met him at a crossroads, but it won't take long for either of our houses to discover their subterfuge. As for what will happen after Cassis is dead...I expect that you will be sufficiently discreet that the murder is not traceable to me or the Caprine or the Sere, and that no one discovers that Driese was there at all."

My brow furrows. "Won't Cassis's retainers know? Or Driese's maids?"

"Driese has gone in disguise," Tonia says. "She sneaked out with the help of one of her maids under cover of darkness, and my parents are trying to keep the news contained to prevent scandal. I assume Geoffre is doing the same thing on his end."

"How do *you* know where Driese is, then? If Driese took such pains to avoid notice and your parents and Geoffre are hushing it up?"

Tonia brings her head up like a nervous horse. "I have my sources. You don't need to know more."

How often have I heard those words? I spin the wineglass with my right hand and watch the way it throws the light back at the room.

"I'm not a philanthropist," I say. "I lost an arm because of Cassis di Prinze. I'd rather not lay my life at his altar, too. How much will you pay me?"

Some of the color comes back into Tonia's face and she smiles.

"I am a Sere," she says. "The regent of my husband's estate, with all his gold at my disposal. I think we can decide upon a reasonable amount."

"Fifty thousand *astra*," I say abruptly. "And we'll have a deal."

The gavaro against the wall jerks his head up. But Tonia never even blinks. She sits back down on her settee and stretches out like a lioness back from the hunt. Triumph flashes in her eyes.

"Done. Bring Driese back to me safe, and proof of Cassis's death, and fifty thousand astra will be a small price to pay."

I'd do it for free, but I should have asked for more. To kill the son of the most powerful man on the Eterean peninsula?

Tonia pours me more wine. I drink it all at once and it goes to my head.

Just like revenge.

CHAPTER 2

When I leave Laudio's back room, Vadz's kai dahn table is full. He rattles the bones in the cup and spills them across the table.

Five in the first position again, the mermaid. Razi is surrounded by other men and a wreath of smoke. He smiles wide as he scrapes a pile of silver and brass buttons toward himself. "You were born in a fortunate moon, Vadz. You never let me down."

Fortune, I want to tell him, is hardly that reliable.

"Vadz," I say, while he's grinning and piling up his own winnings. "I need to talk to you."

He looks up at me with an expression of mild surprise. "Now?"

"There's money in it."

A faint glimmer of interest lights his eyes. He scoops the bones back into the cup. "Table's closed. I've business to attend to."

"Just like that?" Razi says. "I was winning!"

"Better to quit while you're ahead."

Nibas rises and taps Razi on the shoulder. "Come on, brother. Time to go upstairs."

"Ah," Razi says, smiling. The smile falters when it lands on me, though.

He pauses as he walks past me, and leans down to speak in my ear. "If that Qalfan gives you trouble, tell me. I hear working for the Sere can be dangerous."

"You're not my nursemaid," I whisper back at him.

"No. But there's something strange about his stance."

I frown, considering this. But then Vadz rises and cracks his back. "I take it your journey to the back room was a fruitful one?"

Razi and Nibas are gone, and I step a little closer to him, so I can talk without being overheard. What I have to ask isn't something I want passed on. "I need a gun."

His salted auburn eyebrows shoot upward. "What?"

I study his face. This is a chance I've taken, that I can trust him.

I know someone else I could see about a gun, but dealing with him could be far more dangerous.

"You do know where to get one, don't you?"

"You'll hang if the Prinze catch you with it. They enforce those smuggling laws when they can. Weren't we just talking about my ship? It's at the bottom of the bay because the Prinze thought I was smuggling."

"They'd have to catch me. Can you get me one or not?"

He looks troubled and surveys the room. "Maybe. But it's not safe to talk here." He reaches down for the threadbare green cloak hanging on the back of his chair. "Are you sure you want this? It's deep water."

"I can swim," I say. My hands seek out the hilts of my weapons of their own accord. I always feel better with steel in my hand. Metal seeks its sister.

Vadz studies my face for a moment. "Well, come on, then," he says. "If you won't be persuaded."

CHAPTER 2

VADZ LIVES IN A SKINNY BUILDING ON ONE OF THE NAMELESS small canals that empty into the lagoon. He doesn't have enough money to own it outright, but he's charging me rent on a room at the top floor anyway. When I have the money, I don't mind paying, because the room has its own ladder entry and the money goes toward the medical supplies his wife uses to treat refugees.

Three ragged children are sitting at the table when we walk in. Aleya leans over them, ladling big, steaming spoonfuls of lentil stew into their bowls. They're already chewing pieces of the crispy flatbread she cooks on a griddle in the fire, but they stop when they see us, like rabbits caught among lettuces in the garden.

Aleya glances up, worried at first, but then she smiles for the children. "It's just Vadz and Kyris. Nothing to worry about. Plenty for all."

Vadz catches her around the waist and pulls her into a kiss. I imagine that in her youth, Aleya was the kind of woman who collected suitors, and I've often wondered how she ended up with Vadz. She's beautiful in a different way now with gray threading her black hair, her dusky skin flushed with the warmth of the cookfire. The loose red robes she wears, Qalfan-style, are a bright spot in the otherwise small, rundown room.

Coming back here after dealing with Tonia di Sere makes me nervous, but Vadz is right; if there's a safe place to have a conversation in Liera, it's his kitchen. Authorities and criminals alike know what his wife does, so they leave it alone.

"You're home early tonight," she says.

Vadz darts a quick glance at me before he answers. "I thought I'd quit while I was ahead for once. Thought if my streak held, I'd make it home for a hot meal."

"It does appear that Fortune has smiled upon you," she says. "*After* the little ones eat."

Vadz turns to the smallest child, a girl with tangled brown hair who can't be more than eight years old. "You're not going to put away that whole pot, are you? Got a stomach that goes all the way down in your leg or something?"

The children look at each other as if they can't quite decide whether to smile or not. Or maybe they don't remember how.

Vadz's face creases into a smile for them. "Eat your stew, claim your mittens and a cloak, and you can go next door to sleep. There's space."

"But—" one of the children, an older boy, starts, then stops.

"But what, child?" Aleya asks.

"Is it safe?"

"Safer than anywhere else you'll find tonight," she answers. "And in the morning, we'll check on that sore you've got on your leg, yes?"

The boy nods and they eat their soup like ravenous wolves, then take the rest of their bread plus their mittens and cloaks and disappear out the door.

Vadz and I slide in at the table.

"More strays?" he says to Aleya.

She pulls out two bowls and turns her back to us, sighing as she dips the ladle in the stew again. "The city is full of strays," she says. "It's not like I have to go out looking for them. I took an oath to heal, didn't I?"

"I'm not sure you can heal all of them."

"Oh, like you can talk. Where did you get all those mittens from? And the cloaks?"

"That Garonze regiment will never miss them. You know how hard it is to get supply orders right."

Aleya sets the bowls in front of us with a bemused smile. "Right. Also, I noticed a very large bag of flour sitting in the larder."

Vadz sniffs and twirls his spoon in his stew. "The Lady and the Vine had an extra."

"One day, all the gavaros on the Talos are going to find out why you smuggle," I tell him.

"What—you think it's going to hurt my reputation as a steely-eyed highwayman?"

Aleya laughs and leans against his shoulder, reaching down to play with the hair at the back of his collar. "Robbing the rich to give to the poor?"

"Now, that—that would hurt my gaming table."

"How?"

"Nobody wants a do-gooder as a dealer. A gambler always wants to think he's in the right when he beats the house."

"Well," Aleya says, straightening up to clear the children's dishes, "I see that your own stray has made his way back after a few nights gone. Welcome home, Kyris. Where've you been?"

"Here and there," I say, smiling tightly. I try to hide my impatience by tucking into the stew, for which I would ordinarily be grateful; it's redolent with cumin, a welcome warmth on a cold night. But tonight, I feel like I'm vibrating like the struck wire of a harpsichord.

"It's that Aliente gavaro captain, isn't it?" Vadz says suddenly.

I bring my head up. "What?"

Vadz turns to Aleya. "You might want to be gone for this conversation, love."

Aleya sighs. "What have you got for him now, Kyris?"

Guiltily, I trail my spoon through my stew. "I just want him to pick up a little something extra for me. For a job. When I get paid —"

Aleya rolls her eyes. "I've heard *that* before."

"It'll be worth it," I say, looking up at her. "And I'd rather the money went to your enterprises than to the other networks in this city."

Her brows arch upwards. "The other networks in the city? So, it's a little more than a bag of flour, is it?"

Aleya's no delicate flower. She was Vadz's partner through all the smuggling he did in the wars—the reason he was hauling victims to the Qalfan Quarter for healing in the first place.

But her presence still makes me shift uncomfortably in my

seat. "No, it's not a bag of flour. But I'd rather talk about it with Vadz, if it's all the same, Aleya."

Aleya snorts and pulls up her own chair. "If Vadz is involved, then I am too. Especially if you want the money to go to my *enterprises*. Is this a job that's going to hurt people? I don't want blood money."

"It's a job that will right some wrongs. Let's put it that way."

"What do you need him to get, then?"

"Aleya," Vadz says. "The less you know, the better off you are."

Aleya leans back in her chair and crosses her arms over her chest. "It's a gun, isn't it?"

Vadz breathes in heavily through his nose and sits back, scrubbing his beard with one hand.

"All I want is an extra," I say. "I'm not looking to get hooked up with real gunrunners. I just need a misplaced pistol."

Vadz leans on his elbows. "Nobody *misplaces* a pistol."

"You're good at making it seem like things have been misplaced, though, aren't you?"

"A few cloaks are one thing. A gun's another. I might be able to convince the Prinze a couple of their gavaros have been selling arms on the black market. But it's less likely you'll survive being caught after all those questions you've been asking about that Aliente captain."

"This job doesn't have anything to do with him."

"So, you're not working for any Aliente rebels?"

I stop and stare at him in surprise. "If I was working for a rebel cell, would I want *one* gun?"

"Perhaps not. But I've only heard that kind of hero worship from Aliente sympathizers."

"Hero worship?" For a moment, all I can think of is how Arsenault would react to this conversation. The way his brows would rise and how the corner of his mouth would pull up. Then he'd say something like *That's a dire situation, if you've run out of gods and are using me as a replacement.*

"I think you've misunderstood me," I say. "I certainly don't *worship* the man."

There were many ways I felt about him. That I still feel about him. But worship was never one of them.

He wasn't the kind of man who wanted worship. Or needed it, either.

"Let an old man share his wisdom, Kyris. You've got to be more careful with those questions. You're awfully young to wind up dead."

"Vadz, if I die and do what I've been hired to do, it will be a good death."

Vadz rubs his forehead as if talking to me is giving him a headache. "There are no good deaths. Are you one of those Adalusian idiots?"

Adalus is the Dying God. A while back, an Adalusian sect thought they could change the course of the wars by dying in the name of Adalus. Two hundred young men flung themselves off the cliffs at Iffria into the tortured, pounding surf. Some of them died instantly, smashed upon the rocks, but a great number only suffered broken bones. A Lieran merchant told me the story, wide-eyed, as we both sat in the hall of a Rojornicki boyar. He'd seen it, he said, two hundred men who dove off the cliffs like gannets. No one dared pick up the bodies, so the birds got them. If they did shorten the wars, it wasn't apparent. The fighting went on for two more years.

"Of course not," I say. "My concern is more with vengeance."

"Vengeance," Aleya says. "So, it *is* blood money."

Vadz's gaze strays to my right arm. "What do you have up that sleeve?"

"An arm. Nothing more."

He pinches the bridge of his nose. "Just how much money are we talking about?"

"How much do you need?"

"If you want a pistol...not an arquebus...five thousand astra should cover it. For Aleya's strays..."

"All the gold in the Sere's vaults probably wouldn't cover that," Aleya says, sounding tired. "More people come into the city from the rural estates all the time. The fields and flocks haven't recovered from being plundered and burned. So many children lost both parents. And the Houses continue to maintain their standing armies at the expense of the serfs. They've used up their winter stores, and what little remains to eat is still going to feed householders and gavaros."

She taps her fingers on the table and her dark eyes flash. "And as if all that weren't bad enough—may the gods have mercy on us—when the weather warms, we'll be right into fever season. It's going to be bad this year, with all the crowding on the waterfront and in the Kinless Quarter. The water's already foul there, and it will just get worse."

We're all silent for a moment as her words sink in. Then I start figuring expenses in my head.

"I get half my pay tomorrow," I say slowly. I'll need a horse, probably some different clothes, fare for a ship down the coast, and then...

Maybe enough to get me to Vençal. Maybe Arsenault ended up back there. I doubt it, because I'm sure he would have left me clues. But maybe.

"I can get you ten thousand astra tomorrow. If I can, I'll send you more when the job is done. To help with the fevers. Does that make it worth it?"

Vadz and Aleya look at each other in amazement.

"And all you need is a pistol? One?" Vadz says in disbelief.

"It's a one-person job," I say. "But there's plenty to share. My needs are simple, really."

And also nothing money can buy.

"Isn't working out of the Night Market risky?" I ask Vadz as we walk along the waterfront to meet his contact. The air smells of dead fish and feels like mucus in my lungs. It might as well be made of something solid. I flex my right hand to keep it from stiffening in the wet cold.

"My man doesn't sell guns there. People contact him there and he directs them to his clansman."

Still, I feel edgy, like somebody is watching us from the shadows. But when I turn around, there's nobody there.

The Mera di Capria, the Canal of Flowers, splits a promontory of land that juts out into the Sheltered Sea. On the right side of the Capria lies the Day Market, bustling with merchants, artisans, farmers, peddlers, and ordinary citizens from dawn until dusk. On the left, the Night Market carries Lieran commerce deep into the dark hours from winter until the end of spring, giving restless householders something to do on those long, cold nights.

Paper lanterns bob on wires strung between stalls, flashing crazy shadows as the wind tosses them. A line has formed at the gates, and gavaros wearing Prinze blue and silver check to make sure nothing is smuggled in. The Prinze get a cut of the proceeds from every stall in the Night Market, even if it does violate all the laws of the Charter. They stand at the gates to make sure no one undercuts them on their own merchandise. No guns for sale, and if you bring in silk, there's a hefty markup if it doesn't have a Prinze—or a Garonze or a Sere—seal on it. But they haven't been able to lay claim to the Day Market yet, and their stringent practices in the Night Market will likely lead to fewer and fewer purchases of silk here. My father would swear about it, but my father would be happy to see them shooting themselves in the foot.

The guard makes me open my cloak and show him my weapons, then glances at my Caprine green armband. Both Day and Night Markets are neutral ground. Gavaros don't usually care about Houses. The wars ended only because the gavaros wanted their pay but were tired of getting killed. Battles turned into extended draws, until both sides were forced to sign peace accords with each other. But that was after Kafrin Gorge.

Maybe because of Kafrin Gorge.

The guards wave us in and we enter with a small crowd of people, instantly enveloped by the spectacle of the market. The smell of cloves and cinnamon, the snap of canvas in the wind—each stall brightly painted with House colors or a merchant's design—householders on parade in their masks and velvet cloaks.

In Liera, every night is a festival. Vadz and I stand out with our naked faces.

"We'll buy masks," he shouts above the din, and I nod, edging my way through the crowd after him, but all I have are a few catos, and that won't even buy me an unadorned mask of leather or wood.

"Vadz," I say, "If you could loan me—"

He waves away my embarrassment. "No matter. I had a good night. What about this one?"

He holds up a leather goshawk mask, black with gray feathers glued on at the sides, making it look like a mask on a mask. "I can pay you tomorrow," I say.

He nods absently as he hands it to me. He chooses a fox mask for himself, done not in fur but wood. "And two blue feathers," he tells the shopkeep, "as long as you can find."

The shopkeep doesn't even raise an eyebrow. He has no trouble finding the feathers, producing them from somewhere under the table. Such small signals are commonplace in the Night Market, where intrigues abound. He and Vadz haggle while I slip on the hawk mask and look around. People drift back and forth like the tide, shoring up against the small wooden stalls for a moment before flowing on. There are women here but always well guarded. A woman with a turquoise beak and a cockade of white feathers has a cage of gavaros.

A tall man wearing a gray wolf's head looks my way. Its gray fur ruffles in the wind and lantern light glints on the slivers of glass that form the eyes. If it isn't a real wolf's head, it must have been Fixed—worked with magic, the way my arm was. He lays a fist-sized rock down on the table at an artisan's stall. If he's an artist, he doesn't look it. A man who moves with such economy and wears a sword at his side, he's either a gavaro or a householder. A gavaro wouldn't be able to afford that mask, though, unless he really is a Fixer, and they're all being snatched up by Geoffre di Prinze.

Vadz touches me lightly on the shoulder. I turn around too quickly.

"We're headed for the piazza," he says.

I adjust the mask-strap at the back of my head and plunge into the crowd after him.

Crowds make me nervous, and the mask blocks my peripheral vision and gives the world a curious tinny quality, capping off sounds until they seem thin and dreamlike. Vadz weaves his way in and out and among people, the two long blue feathers bobbing behind him ridiculously. The people we pass all look up at them, trying to read the sign, and turn away when they can't. Snatches of a dozen conversations worm their way into my mask. It's a spy's holiday, the Night Market. I've spent a few nights here myself since I returned to Liera, asking questions about the war, the Aliente, and Arsenault. Maybe Tonia's Qalfan noticed me here.

I've never seen the wolf mask before.

Something begins to bother me about him. Why did he stare at me so directly? Did he know what Vadz's sign meant?

"Vadz," I say, turning sideways to avoid the crimson-liveried guard of a bird of paradise. "There was a man in a wolf mask back there. Have you seen him before?"

Vadz doesn't look at me. His mouth turns down a bit. "There are a lot of men in wolf masks in the Market."

"Not like this one. It's a wolf's head. Looks real."

His mouth turns down a bit more. He glances over his shoulder. "No," he says. "Should I have?"

I shrug. "His mask was a work of art; that's all. I thought you might have seen him before."

"I doubt that's all you think, Kyris."

"I haven't seen him before either."

I catch a glimpse of gray fur over my right shoulder. "He seems to know you."

"Does he?"

I put my hand on the hilt of my knife.

"We'll go sit near the fountain," Vadz says.

The Night Market is set up on a square, as are most public places in Liera, with a fountain at its center. In the middle of the fountain stand massive alabaster sculptures of Tekus, king of the gods, and his son, Erelf, the god of knowledge. They sit on thrones, as if in judgment. Sculpted ravens—the gods' eyes—scatter at their feet and perch on their shoulders. Water trickles out through pipes set into the gods' outstretched hands.

I'd rather sit anywhere but near the fountain.

Geoffre di Prinze commissioned the statue. The statue that used to stand in this fountain was an old Eterean one of Adalus, holding sheaves of wheat in his hands. The worship of Adalus dwindles, though. Geoffre backs the worship of Erelf, and Geoffre is the hand that turns the Circle. Works of Adalus have gone disappearing lately, and even the Adalusians fling themselves into the sea.

People still gather at the fountain, though, the way they always have. Courting couples sit with their chaperones and speak to each other in low tones; bolder, older men and women tryst. Gavaros circle the fountain like the iron spikes of a fence.

I don't know how they ignore the way the ravens hunch forward, as if they're listening in on every conversation. Erelf's knowing smirk always makes me feel as if I've been caught out doing something I shouldn't.

Vadz puts a hand on my shoulder and bends down to speak into my ear. "Too many gavaros. He won't find us in this company."

CHAPTER 2

I start to nod, but a flash of yellow glass catches my eye.

The man in the wolf mask is coming up on Vadz. "Vadz," I say, putting my hand on his arm. He looks at me. "No." I point with my left hand, my knife half out of its sheath and in my right hand. Vadz turns around and the man in the gray wolf mask is right there. He leans down as if to speak, and Vadz bends closer to hear him, his elbow drawing back within his cloak so that I know he has his hand on his knife too.

The man in the wolf mask says something in a low voice I can't hear and points at Vadz's feathers. Vadz frowns.

"What? What did you say?"

He leans forward instinctively. When he does, my arm hums. It knows when there is danger. I start to push Vadz to the side, but during the motion, I see the flash of metal in the man's hand, and I shout, "Vadz!"

But it's too late.

The knife slides deep into his stomach, just below his ribs. The man holds the knife angled up, for killing. Vadz cries out, clutching the knife hilt jutting out of his gut. His knife drops to the ground. The sound of the crowd masks the clatter and his cry.

Metal glints in the wolf's other hand—another knife. One in Vadz, and one for me.

I look up to see light eyes hidden behind yellow glass. Startled eyes. We stare at each other as if neither of us can move, knives out.

Then he drops his. It clangs on the cobbles, a weird hollow ringing in the closed-in space of my mask, and he shoulders his way into the crowd behind him.

The woman in the bird mask screams when she sees Vadz on the ground. "You!" she screams, pointing at me. "Murder!"

I'm surrounded by people. The man in the wolf mask is getting away. Walking fast but not running, and I can't go after him because of this wall of people staring down at Vadz. Vadz's chest doesn't move. His green eyes stare through the holes in his mask unblinking, glittering in the lantern light.

"He did it!" the turquoise bird says. "He did!"

I have my knife out and there's blood on my shirt. Vadz's blood. From when I tried to shove him away.

I look down at Vadz lying there, dead.

Then I run.

※

THE CROWDS OF THE NIGHT MARKET ARE MY ALLIES. I'm still wearing my hawk mask as I shove people aside and dodge through holes between them. Shouts follow me, shrieks, the sound of pounding, running feet, the clank of scabbards. The sound of screaming gets trapped in my mask. I duck through the labyrinth of stalls and loop around in the wolf's direction, but I can't see him. He probably took off his mask. I keep mine on so nobody will see me take it off and tell the Prinze what I look like.

I slow to a quick walk and head for the north wall. People mill around me, gavaros closing in to protect their charges. I just keep walking. Houses and shops huddle against the wall, their low-sloping tile roofs within reach for anyone willing to jump, and I'm not the only one with this idea.

The Prinze can't stop every smuggled good from coming into the Night Market. There are at least ten people going up and over the wall right now, and the maze of shops is a mass of confused, frightened people arranging themselves into small, defensible squares.

"Prinze!" somebody yells. "Prinze are out!"

I clamber up the wall in a hurry next to a little beggar girl. She skins upward faster than I can but slips at the top. I catch her, and she glances back at me, breathing hard, wide-eyed. Then she's over the top and dangling down the other side.

The roofs are a better escape, though. I eye the distance

between the gutter and my outstretched hands. Then, with a prayer to Ekyra, my patron, I leap.

For a moment—too long—I'm not sure if I'm jumping or falling. Then I catch the lip of the rough stone gutter, right hand first, and swing in the air. My shoulders yank painfully in their sockets and my feet bounce against the wall, then I lever myself up. The gutter is full of rotting leaves and soupy, foul-smelling water. My hands and knees splash into it as I heave myself over the top. Below me, feet scuff as the girl drops to the ground and starts running.

I keep low as I clamber to the peak of the roof, my boots slipping on the tile. But I can't resist a look back when I get to the top.

The girl is gone, but the Night Market is like a swarm of insects, the lanterns like fireflies. Somewhere in that crowd is the man who murdered Vadz.

The man who also wanted to murder me.

I slip up over the top of the roof and down the other side. When I hit the ground, I'm in an alley.

I rip off the hawk mask and hurl it away from me as far as I can.

CHAPTER 3

I wander in a daze most of the night, unable to settle anywhere. I see Prinze in every crowd whether they belong or not, feel the breath of that wolf on my neck regardless of what is behind me. I keep thinking about Aleya in her kitchen, waiting on Vadz to come home. How is she going to find out he's dead?

The last thing I want is to lead the assassin to that safehouse full of refugees.

Or maybe the last thing I want is to have to face Aleya. To explain that I can get her the money, but I can't buy her husband back.

I feel like a fool and a coward. Liera won't let me forget any of the debts I have to pay, and now I have another life to account for. Everywhere I go, I see damage from the wars—broken walls, orphaned children, clogged canals, shattered statues of Adalus pulled down by Geoffre di Prinze.

All these threads spinning themselves out like a worm weaving its silk cocoon, not knowing the cocoon will lead to its death—those precious gossamer strands that householders wear like murder incarnate.

Dammit.

I take a deep breath and make myself think.

Who else knows about Driese and Cassis? Who knows who could also want me dead?

It's easy to put a finger on the Prinze. They'd want to stop me from killing Cassis. But they'd have nothing to gain from letting Cassis marry Driese, either.

There might be Caprine interests at odds with Tonia who want Cassis alive and a baby from the match; I don't know which way the Sere would lean. They might want me killed, too.

The man in the wolf mask could have done a good job of it. But why didn't he? Why kill only Vadz?

Perhaps I'm giving too much credit to the spies. Perhaps the man in the wolf mask didn't know which of us Tonia had hired and went for the more obvious target.

But the question remains—how could he have known about Tonia's intrigues so quickly? In order to time it so perfectly, he must have been following us from the tavern. But Vadz and I saw no one.

Unless Vadz had arranged with the murderer to bring me to the Night Market. I scowl as I banish that voice from my mind. It's possible that the murderer might betray Vadz if they were in it together, but why would he have dropped his knife at the sight of me, his true target? And if he was in it for the money, why didn't he wait until I was paid?

Even behind the yellow glass the man's eyes were familiar. The shape of them. The way they widened in surprise when I stared into them.

First Tonia di Sere's Qalfan and now an assassin. Two men who've reminded me of Arsenault in one night. Since returning to Liera, there have been glimpses of men in which I thought I saw something of Arsenault—a flick of black hair, eyes I thought might be gray but on closer examination were blue, a tall silhouette that bore the wrong face. False hope, in every case.

Surely, somewhere there is another man who looks like him, who moves with the same kind of coiled grace. Other men have eyes like that.

And Arsenault would never betray me. Especially to the Prinze.

I find myself picking my way through more and more rubble. The people have changed. This is the Kinless Quarter. Beggars, clothed in rags, smelling of kacin smoke and vinegar-piss, hold out their hands to me as I walk by. No family, no name—I'm just like them. I drop my last catos into their palms, wondering if the twenty-five thousand astra will be waiting for me at the money-changers' tomorrow so I can pay Aleya the blood price I owe her now. Or if the man in the wolf mask will put a knife in my gut instead.

As I move away from the beggars, down the alley, an old piece of paper nailed to a door catches my attention.

Arsenault again. His picture still turns up everywhere, but where is he?

Seeing him like this, now, is like having my heart squeezed in a fist. Loneliness falls upon me so heavily, I can hardly breathe.

I pull out the crumpled poster in my pocket to compare versions in the gray, almost-dawn light. He looks so much meaner in these sketches. They've made his brows too heavy, given him a scowl he rarely wore, and his beard is so full and wild, he looks like a bear. His scar stands out livid on his face. The apprentice who did this sketch has gone beyond what he was paid for, adding a maniacal glint to Arsenault's eyes.

Unable to help myself, I trace the lines of his face with my finger. But the ink just smudges and blurs. I'm afraid that five years apart has begun to blur the memory of his face in my mind, too. Maybe that's why every man I see lately looks like him.

I wipe the residue off on my trousers and look around. It's as good a place to sleep as any, I suppose—just a nameless alley in a part of the city where no one has a name anymore. But it feels somehow safer with Arsenault's picture keeping watch above me. I kick some rocks out of the way and sink down against the wall that still stands, wrapping myself in Arsenault's cloak.

I promise I'll find you if I can. If I can't, I hope you'll find me.

I squeeze my eyes shut. "Arsenault, you idiot," I whisper, "why did you make me go in the first place?"

Tomorrow, I'm going to buy a gun. And then I'm going to ask Cassis some questions.

Right before I blow a hole in his head.

PART II

CHAPTER 4

Arsenault never knew me when I had two arms of flesh and blood. Had I continued in my life as Householder's daughter, I would never have known him. Perhaps there would still have been a war, but without Cassis's betrayal, there would be no Arsenault. It's a strange thought, one I've turned about in my mind for many years and have yet to make peace with.

I first met Cassis on a hot, dry day in the summer of my sixteenth year. When genealogists record the births of babies born that summer, they always name it *Zete*, the Summer of Thirst. In truth, I don't remember being thirsty, though our wells began to dry and the mulberries' leaves turned yellow before their time. But then, my thirst was not for water, and my father's cellars were full of expensive Amoran wines.

I was my father's only child. He could have taken another woman to wife, one who might have borne him a son, but he loved my mother and did not subscribe to the new laws that allowed a man two wives. I wasn't privy to my parents' discussions of heirship, although I know they must have had them; perhaps I would have been named the legal heir to the household, had I not been such a disappointment. Many families now found themselves without male heirs and were forced to divide their lands between their daughters and nephews, cousins, or brothers whom they did not trust. It was a great period of consolidation and rivalries among Houses. But I was sixteen and cared little for politics, except when its spear pierced my cocoon with a girl's most important question.

Whom shall I wed?

I never expected Cassis di Prinze to be among the men who courted me. My mother was born Caprine, and the Caprine and the Prinze were great rivals for the sea trade. Perhaps in another city, my match with Cassis would have been a good one. But the Caprine and the Prinze sought no alliances with each other. Instead, they built up their rivalry the way walls are built around cities, with new bits added by each generation. In the case of my family, my mother's kin ties dictated that our silk ship in Caprine holds and that we pay Caprine fees for carrying it. The Aliente were an old, landed family; we owned no ships, no dye houses, no caravans. Instead, our fortunes dangled on threads so fine and thin, they couldn't be seen in the light—silk, spun from the descendants of stolen Saien worms.

Silk bound us to our land. Because of my mother, the Caprine usually fetched us a fair price. But as the Prinze grew ever more aggressive in their quest to monopolize the sea trade, the Caprine gave ground. Their carrying fees dipped lower and lower, but the number of ports at which they could sell goods dwindled until the savings in carrying fees no longer compensated for the money lost on the silk itself. We had chests and chests of silk held back. My parents argued about it often.

I might have been the solution to the problem, had I married into an Amoran house, or perhaps even an Onzarran one with their overland trade. I had seen envelopes on my father's desk sealed with the wax marks of Rojornicki boyars and Vençalan noblemen, and even the small royal house of the Carrata, who were rumored to have gained a taste for exploration. But my father obeyed the laws of our ancestors. He would make no betrothals before my eighteenth nameday.

CHAPTER 4

And so, when Cassis arrived, the first Prinze to visit our land in many years, I remained in my father's villa, sweltering in the conservatory and picking halfheartedly at the strings of the harp my mother insisted I learn to play. The lorikeet swinging in its wicker cage above me ruffled its blue and scarlet feathers and squawked. I had lapsed into staring out the big windows, and the commotion in the halls that accompanied Cassis's arrival was a welcome distraction. I paced to the door and watched as servants scurried by, bearing armloads of linens and trays of food and wine. After a few moments, I stopped a kitchen girl carrying an earthenware jug.

"Why are you running? Is there a visitor at the gates?"

She looked up at me with wide black eyes. "My lady," she said, "it's a Prinze with his gavaros. He's come to treat with the Householder."

My own eyes grew wide. "A Prinze? Which one?"

"The younger, I think... Forgive me, lady, but they'll be wanting the jug."

I'd seen Cassis at my friend Ila's feast when she'd come of age last spring. He'd attended with his retainers, a group of dark-haired cousins clothed in silks of the most expensive blue and purple. I'd only caught a glimpse of Cassis, but I remembered him to be handsome. The Prinze were normally out of all my considerations, but no Prinze had arrived at our gates since Geoffre di Prinze, head of their House, had visited us when I was a child. It was either a hopeful or disastrous sign that Cassis came now, and I couldn't remain in the conservatory, unknowing. I lifted the jug out of the servant's hands, and she stared up at me.

"My lady—"

"I'll bring it," I said. "You can run some other errand."

She gave me a frightened look. She must have been new in the house and not used to me, but I gave my actions little thought.

The Prinze were in the receiving room, just as the girl had

said, with my mother and father. The men looked as if they'd had a hard ride from Liera. The road wasn't long, but it was steep, a difficult climb in the heat. The gavaros' faces were brown with dust, and their sweat left thin white runnels through it. All of them wore the sky-blue Prinze armband, and all of them were armed with swords and daggers.

In their midst sat a young man dressed in tawny gold silks slashed with orange, his dark hair pulled back with a silver clasp. His eyes were dark and almost too big for the lean face in which they were set, and his mouth was flexible—not a cruel mouth, but surely one capable of a pretty cynicism. In the gleaming silver hilt of his sword were set three large tourmalines etched with tridents. The sunlight pouring in the open courtyard doors flashed blue-green off the stones and made his silks shimmer—a tight weave with the thinnest threads, the work of hundreds or thousands of worms. The breeze fluttered his sleeves and breathed the scent of roses into the room, which otherwise smelled of wine, sweat, and dust.

No one saw me enter. The gavaros' backs were to the door, and they were all big men. My parents sat in front of them. I put the pitcher down on the sideboard and bit my lip as I watched, leaning against the doorframe, blocked from sight.

"The city reels with fever," Cassis said, his voice a pleasant mid-tenor. "The elders say it's the worst they can remember. Everyone takes precautions to save themselves from the night air, but those fools down in the Kinless Quarter breathe their ill humors everywhere. My father is sending his entire fleet from the city before they're stranded. He needs more goods to fill his holds. He sent me to determine if you had kept any silk back from last year."

My father frowned. Liera was more prone to water fevers than we were in the hills, but we weren't so high up that they never reached us. In fever season, we took care with guests. Before he asked about the Prinze offer, my father said, "And you've come from Liera, just now?"

CHAPTER 4

Cassis shook his head. "We've retired to Padera, all the family. Our retainers carry out our business in the city."

"And this offer to buy my silk, with what price does it come?"

Cassis glanced pointedly at my mother, then at his men. "We can discuss the terms at your leisure." He was only three years older than me, but one did not grow up in the shadow of Geoffre di Prinze without acquiring a certain acumen for negotiation.

Finally, he saw me.

I don't know if he recognized me from Ila's ball, or if it was simply that in my water-blue silks, I was dressed far too well to be a servant. But when he saw me, his eyes widened and his hands tightened on the arms of the chair.

My father finally noticed me too. "Kyrra," he said. "What are you doing here?"

"I thought to bid welcome to our guests." I hoisted the jug up off the sideboard and carried it over to the tray beside Cassis. A number of goblets stood there, and I filled them all. Cassis watched me while I poured.

"May I have the honor of an introduction?" he asked.

"My daughter," my father answered, clipping the words in vexation. "Kyrra."

I inclined my head. "I bid you welcome in my father's house." Out the corner of my eye, I caught my mother's tight-lipped expression. But Cassis still watched me. When I handed him the goblet, our fingers touched.

There was a moment of staring too long, a jolt, a shiver. How does one describe these feelings afterward without making them seem boring and cliché? There is that moment when one is young in which all the clichés seem true.

His fingers slid away from mine, slowly. Then he raised the cup to his lips and drank.

"Your daughter does us great honor," he said.

His eyes never left my face.

It is true I was a challenge to my parents. My mother said I was born screaming and didn't stop until I was six months old. As a small child, I drove my nurses wild trying to contain me. Allowed to play in the garden, in a trice I would scale the cherry tree that dipped its branches over the garden wall. My hands and knees bore constant marks from my adventures, and my mother's seamstresses despaired of keeping me in untorn frocks.

As I grew, my restlessness did not ebb. It wasn't enough to ride in the coach to Liera or to watch the city pass by as we floated in the little wicker canal boats; I must be out in it. Once, when I was eight years old, I strayed from my mother's side in the market and wandered all over the dockside before she found me, having befriended a tattered bard who regaled me with stories of the Spice Road and played me a Saien tune upon his harp. The strangeness of the day remained with me long after the cane marks faded on my backside, like the memory of an especially favored sweet.

I drove my tutors mad with my questions. I had a good head for numbers and a talent for languages, and I quickly moved beyond the borders of a lady's education. It was only my father's indulgence that gave me more. I learned to read, to play the harp and the lute, though not well—to speak Rojornicki, Tiresian, Qalfan, Vençalan, and ancient Eter, a language hardly anyone studied anymore. I could converse in most of the dialects of the peninsula. I had maps and poems and made a mess of a dozen canvases in my attempt to learn to paint like the Eterean masters. I never had the patience for sewing, but my mother made me do it anyway, the same way she made me study etiquette and practice the harp until I was sick of it.

That evening, hospitality demanded a dinner for Cassis and his men, and I went early to my rooms to prepare for it. But as I was standing at my bedside, trying to decide between two gowns, one mulberry and the other a soft gray, there was a knock at the door and one of my chambermaids went to answer it. I heard murmuring and the clank of porcelain and silver.

I paid it no mind. Instead, I lifted my curls and squinted at my reflection in the long, silvered mirror that stood beside my bed. "Do you think I should wear my hair up in combs, like this?" I asked my other maid, a woman named Mam who had been brought into our household as an orphan child. She wasn't old enough to be called Mam, really, but everybody did. She said she thought it was short for her long-forgotten given name. At the time, her story struck me as incomprehensible; how could one forget one's own name? But now I wish I could do the same.

She was a round woman with thick, dark hair and eyes the color of mossy wood chips. She put her hands on her hips. "You aren't going to a ball."

"She's not going anywhere," my other maid, Bella, said through the open door to my bedroom. It had been some misguided sense of humor that named her, I often thought. She was small and her doughy features were of the plainest sort, pale and not well served by her lackluster brown hair. She hadn't been with me for as long as Mam.

"The Messera says she's to remain right here."

I turned around. Bella carried a tray on her right hand, a stand for it in her left. A full meal was laid out on the tray—a white porcelain bowl brimming with braised snails and salty pannenda ham; a plate of flatbread and olive oil; slices of orange and yellow melon; glistening black eggplant sprinkled with green basil. They'd be eating the same down in the courtyard, but the indignity of having to eat alone in my own chambers stole all the pleasure from it. Bella jerked her left hand and the stand unfolded, and she lowered the tray down onto it with a sigh.

I frowned at it, then at her. "I'm not a child," I said. "My mother has no right to keep me here."

Bella shrugged. "It's what Utîl said, so it's what we'll do. Likely your mother doesn't want you within reach of that Prinze. Isn't it so, Mam?"

Mam nodded. "And here you are, mooning over your dress, so I'd say she's right. You don't reach your majority for two more years, Lady Kyrra; you can wait that long."

I glowered at them, but they were used to my imperiousness. My mother had made them into my two shadows, but I had failed to sway them to my confidence; they did her bidding, and her bidding alone. "I'm too old for nursemaids," I said.

"And too young for men," Mam told me as she walked out the door and over to the armoire that held the linens. "You'll have your whole life for men and children. Your mother's right to keep you away from Cassis di Prinze, if he's anything like what I've heard."

I had been twisting my hair in my hands, the way I did sometimes when I was annoyed or thinking. Overcome by curiosity, I let my hair drop and walked out into the sitting room, where Bella and Mam busily set the table, tying back the long muslin curtains so I could sit and enjoy the breeze.

"And what have you heard?" I asked.

Bella arched her brows as she ran her hand over the tablecloth to press out the wrinkles. "My cousin has cousins who serve the Prinze in the house, and they say he goes down to the smoking dens."

"Dresda tells me he got a tavern girl with child but she lost it." Mam looked at me pointedly. "And he's Prinze. You never know what they're up to. Weren't the mistiri surprised to even see him here?"

I nodded reluctantly. "But he comes with an offer to buy my father's silk. The Prinze have never offered that before. And anyway, it's his father who's Head of House, not him."

"Acorns," Mam said as she set out the plates, "do not fall far from the tree."

I scowled. "It's not as if I'll seek a betrothal with him. But he is handsome, don't you think?"

"My old aunt in the kitchens told me, 'A pretty face will hide an ugly mind,'" Mam said.

"P'raps I'm lucky, then," Belle said. "One look at my old self and the pretty ones run straight away."

They laughed about it. I could never fathom the humor of servants, so I went back into my bedchamber and stepped into the mulberry gown. When my maids saw what I was doing, they stopped laughing and looked at each other.

"You won't be getting out that door, Kyrra," Mam said.

"My father may yet prevail. How will it look to the Prinze if the Aliente Householder doesn't trust them enough to allow his daughter to eat in their company? Hospitality will be compromised, and my father could never allow that. Do my buttons, Bella. And my hair. With the combs."

Bella and Mam traded glances, frowning, but Bella came. Her sturdy fingers rasped on the buttons as she fastened them. I held my hair up so she could do the ones at the back of my neck.

In the mirror's reflection, I saw Mam standing in the doorway, watching me. She hugged herself loosely and frowned. Then she noticed me watching and eased her expression, turning around.

"You may be right," she said. "But until then, you'll sit and eat your pannenda like a dutiful daughter."

I HAD NEVER BEEN A DUTIFUL DAUGHTER. BUT I KNEW MY father. And I knew the rules of etiquette from the hours of study my lady tutor had required of me. It would be a serious affront to Cassis to keep me locked in my room, an admission that my father didn't trust his guest even though he'd taken an oath of no harm.

I had only raised the spoon to my lips when the call came for me to attend.

Dinner was served in the gardens as evening began to fall, soft and blue, blessedly cooler. The scent of roses lingered from the day, mingling with the beginning of the nightly jasmine bloom. Our table was laid on a patio among the potted lemon trees, where we could watch the sun set over the western hills.

Because the Prinze visit was unexpected and for business, dinner was an intimate affair, only my parents, Cassis, and I. We would join the fosters and gavaros in the hall later, for dancing. Cassis was already there when we entered, and he stood as the servant swept out my chair for me.

"Lady Kyrra," he said, bowing as I sat. "It's a pleasure to be able to dine with you tonight. And your parents," he added, almost as an afterthought.

I smiled at him. In preparation for my season of courting parties, my lady tutor had told me that women should grace their suitors with demure but enigmatic smiles, to entice them into further conversation. She was Vençalan, of course, and didn't understand that our matches were mostly about trade. But I had not expected an opportunity to practice. Madame Vevant said I frightened people with my natural mannerisms, so I tried to make my smile demure and enigmatic.

I must have looked as if I'd eaten a sour candy. Cassis blinked and looked so confused that I lost my concentration on "demure" and instead bit my lip to hide a laugh.

One of his brows flicked upward.

Perhaps men weren't as intrigued by *demure* as my lady tutor wanted me to believe. I put it down as another tick against her and bent my head to look at my plate so I wouldn't start laughing.

Cassis sat across from me in a rustle of silk. All I could see were his long fingers curling around the stem of his wineglass. Another tourmaline flashed on his ring finger. The setting was intricately worked silver, a sea serpent eating the stone. Diamonds edged the serpent's tail, which curled up on the other side of the ring.

"It's been a while since we've visited the city," my father said to him, "What news have we missed, up here in our hills?"

"I hardly know where to start, Mestere. How many months has it been since your last visit?"

"Oh, late winter. It's hard to get away during silk season."

"They've a new theatre in Padera now," Cassis said. "To entertain for the summers. And I hear that the playwright they're employing is extraordinary. He's dug up some of the old Eterean plays, given them a new twist. I hope to see one of his performances after we make this last buying trip."

"Old Eterean plays, eh? So, he's using actors, choruses—not mummers."

"Mummers," Cassis scoffed. "Mestere d'Aliente, only the rabble go to see mummers now. Gavaros, laborers... they'll even let in kinless at some of those shows."

"What plays are they doing in Padera?" I asked.

"Oh, I think...*The Fall of Attrasca.* And *The Doom of Ires.*"

"My goodness," my mother said. "Such heavy plays for summer."

"They say that in *The Doom of Ires,* they pour a river of brandy down a giant model of a volcano and light it on fire."

"I would like to see that," I said.

My mother made a soft, dismissive sound as she unfolded her napkin over her lap. "It's only for spectacle, Kyrra. That's all it is."

"But that's the point, isn't it, Mother? Why go to the theater at all if it's only to see the same old rituals acted out? The dancers paint themselves in white paint and bound across the stage as stags. A man in a deerskin is shot by his brother and falls to the stage." I rolled my eyes. "It's boring. Why not add a little spectacle? I should like to see the volcano."

I looked up at Cassis. He flashed a smile at me—handsome, bright, easy. "Exactly," he said, and my heart stuttered. He gestured with his fork for emphasis. "Tell the old stories in a new way for a new age. That's the philosophy behind the new theater. I've heard that Attrasca actually falls from a great height in the play, into a net, at the end. People who've seen it say you get an excellent sense of what heights the emperor aspired to and the depths to which he subsequently fell."

He turned the fork on a big chunk of melon, slicing through it with the side.

"I hope in the play it's clear that Attrasca was pushed," my father said, frowning. "When Attrasca fell, it was a sad day for the Empire. Probably the beginning of its end, though it took hundreds of years to unravel. But the seeds were planted then."

"Attrasca was your ancestor, wasn't he?" Cassis said.

"The Aliente trace their roots back to him, yes."

"I've always thought Attrasca a fascinating character. All the stories make it sound as if he formed the Empire singlehandedly. And then to lose it all..."

"On a betrayal," I said. "His wife gave him up to her lover, didn't she?"

"No, you're thinking of something else, Kyrra," my father said absently, teasing a piece of snail meat from its shell with a tiny, two-pronged fork.

Cassis looked up from his plate. "It's a fairy story, right? The one they recast as a romance last season. With the prince who leaves his kingdom on a search for knowledge. When he finds it, he wraps it in golden cloth and locks it in a golden casket and returns to his castle, only to find that his wife has taken a lover and they've been plotting to steal this beautiful thing he's brought back."

"And when the wife and her lover try to take possession of the chest, he must have them both killed," I added eagerly, remembering. We had a troupe of mummers come and play the story for us at Midwinter...although I didn't want to admit that part to Cassis. He'd just think me provincial. "But now the castle is hopelessly tainted by the tragedy of their love..."

"...and he rides off into the wood, giving up his throne forever and bestowing the golden casket upon a lowly servant girl..."

"Who, of course, turns out to be a long-lost princess." I

grinned, unable to help it. "There do seem to be a lot of long-lost princesses running around in these stories."

"But it's so romantic, isn't it? I saw it performed in the Amphitheater itself. When the prince ordered his wife taken away to be executed, he actually wept real tears. You could see them reflected on his face in the lantern lights."

I sighed. "I would so love to see a play in a theater. I've never been."

"Mestere," Cassis said, turning to my father. "This is a situation you must rectify. The new theaters are a measure of how far we have advanced. No longer can it be said that one must travel to Qalfa or Dakkar for learning and culture. Liera is no backwater town anymore. We are reclaiming our heritage."

My father traded an amused glance with my mother before he answered. "Interpreting it, you mean," he said.

Cassis paused in the act of cutting his eggplant. "But that is what one does with history, isn't it, Mestere? One must always interpret it. One can't just...lock it in a casket and carry it around under one's arm. It's a different world now than the one the Etereans left us. Why should the Qalfans claim all the navigation tables? Why should Dakkar own the technology that builds better weapons? Haven't our shipwrights built faster ships than the Qalfans? Haven't our engineers discovered again how to build clocks and arches? Why should our playwrights not celebrate the old stories for the benefit of Liera?"

"You know, all of this could have been prevented if more people simply learned to read Eter over the years. Then you would know what was *really* in the texts."

"Aren't the translations faithful?"

"Translations," my father scoffed, and leaned forward to point at Cassis. "This, right here, is the problem. No one wants to know what Attrasca actually said, but what some puffed-up scholar in a university tower *thinks* he's said —"

"Papa," I cut in, before my father could get too far into one of his favorite arguments, "I believe we were talking about the possibility of me going to the theater."

"Perhaps..." Cassis said slowly. "Perhaps it might be arranged...for me to escort you—your family—if you were to visit, Mestere. At least...to show you to your section."

Above my head, my mother and father again traded glances, this time of surprise and alarm. I expected them to react in such a way, given that Cassis was a Prinze. Perhaps he could show my father to his section, but my mother? Me? We both had Caprine blood.

I cast all awareness of their fears aside. My attention was given completely to Cassis, watching as he rolled the stem of his wineglass between his thumb and forefinger, his eyes on the ripple of wine against the sides of the glass.

Then he looked up and caught my gaze. Just for an instant, until my mother turned the conversation deftly back to safer ground. But it was an instant that made me shiver.

"I think the weather may start to turn soon," my mother said. "Already the breeze shifts and grows cooler."

※

"Kyrra, that young man is like a fox among pigeons," my mother told me later that night, as we sat overlooking the sweltering room where our minor nobles and gavaros danced. "He didn't come here just to talk to you about the theater. He's a Prinze; there's something he's after."

I sniffed. "Perhaps the Prinze have realized that fighting the Caprine saps their treasury. Did Father take the offer to ship our silk?"

She faced me, and I had to look at her. "It's a few chests of held-back silk, Kyrra. You are not silk. Be mindful of the chair in which you sit."

She leaned over and touched the arm of my chair. It was a smaller version of my parents' chairs, although theirs were carved with figures of Tekus the Father God and his wife, and mine was carved with figures of the goddess Ekyra, patroness of fortune, for whom I had been named. The chair was meant for the Aliente heir and had been left unfinished for a long time. Some months after I bled my first woman's blood, my father presented it to me, carved with images of my namesake, a winsome woman with long, flowing hair. I had never liked the chair but would never tell my father so; it was uncomfortable, and in every pose, Ekyra's face looked vacant as a wax doll's. I could not imagine a goddess would be so lifeless.

The musicians began to pick out a quick, rousing rhythm. Bootheels rattled on the floor as gavaros and serving women swung by each other in a flash of color. Cassis approached the dais, then held out his hand and bowed to my mother, going down low, almost upon his knee.

"Mistiri," he said, addressing both my mother and my father, "may I request the honor of a dance with your daughter?"

My stomach tightened. My mother looked to my father, whose gaze moved restlessly from Cassis's bent head to the silks he wore—clean sky-blue silks, dyed in Liera for sure, but the work of whose worms? He might not agree with Cassis about the status of Eterean scholarship, but one could see the thoughts working behind his eyes. He wondered if the silk was ours, and what it would mean to the worms in the trays—who were even now being gorged by feeders and guarded by gavaros—if Cassis di Prinze wore Aliente silk.

Arguments about theater were one thing—the worms, quite another.

You are not silk, my mother said, but did that mean I was more or less important?

My father inclined his head, somberly. I couldn't tame my smile, and Cassis smiled back at me when he took my hand. His palm was damp with sweat, not soft but not hard, and he gripped me too lightly. I curled my fingers tightly around his, and he blinked again in surprise.

"I thank you, sir," I said, and he took me into the clomping, whirling throng of dancers, finally away from my father and mother.

"I thought you would never get through them," I said when we were well away, in the middle of things. Our arms hooked and we whirled around the floor, coming close enough together to speak only once every measure.

"Your parents guard you well," he said. "It's to be commended."

A whirl away, then back.

"But surely, I'm not in any danger from you, am I? The son of such a prominent House?"

His eyes narrowed on me, as if trying to gauge my question. I made myself look innocent. Then he laughed. "Tell me, what is the proper answer to that?"

My stomach fluttered. I laughed shakily, suddenly glad that we were in the middle of a good-natured reel.

But then the dance ended and the music slowed.

Perhaps the musicians had noticed Cassis and me dancing together and assumed I was being courted rather than toyed with, as my mother thought. The glow in Cassis's eyes seemed sincere enough to me. But perhaps I can be forgiven for conflating desire with love, an easy-enough thing for women of my station.

As it stood, the lutist began to play his slow, sweet music, and Cassis and I reached toward each other. Our fingertips touched, lightly. My fingers were soft, but his were calloused. We were forced to look at each other directly, keeping our eyes on a level at all times.

His eyes were so dark. I saw myself in them, moving through the flickering candlelight. My disheveled curls, our hands as we made our way down the line, elbows crooked, bodies never touching but close enough that my skirts brushed his leg.

His lips grew soft, and I found myself staring at them.

Then he let me go. Startled, I looked up to see a different

man bowing low. I hadn't expected to change partners, even knowing it was the way of the dance. The man—one of our gavaros—raised his palm, and I darted a glance over my shoulder to see Cassis coming up from his bow to place his hand against the hand of one of my mother's fosters.

But he was looking at me.

<hr />

IN THE MORNING, CASSIS AND HIS MEN LEFT, BURDENED WITH twenty cedar caskets of silk and more than a few aching heads from the wine of the night before. Some of the serving women stood near to see them off, waving scarves. I had spent the few hours between dancing and dawn alone, still feeling the heat of Cassis's palm against mine. My parents didn't allow me to watch his departure, at least from the doors of our villa. Instead, I observed it all at a distance from my window, the cloud of dust raised by the horses obscuring the figures of the men.

When my mother entered my room later, I still sat at the window, staring beyond our hills at the thin, glittering ribbon of sea that lay along the horizon.

My mother snapped the curtains shut. "We are going to make overtures to Felizio di Caprine for your hand," she said, without any greeting whatsoever.

I looked up at her, unsure I'd heard her correctly. "Felizio di Caprine is nearly twice my age and killed his first wife in childbed."

"Felizio is of the main branch of the Caprine and will carry our silk for free if you marry him. He has better alliances with the dye merchants, and his trade contacts lie mainly west, where the Prinze have made fewer inroads."

"The baby was too big; isn't that the husband's fault?" I rose and wrapped myself in my arms. "A marriage with the Prinze would only strengthen Liera. Not just our family, but Liera."

My mother leaned forward. "This is infatuation talking,

Kyrra. A Prinze makes no gestures without a knife up his sleeve. He doesn't want you. At least not to marry."

"You might as well sign my death warrant now, Mother, if I'm to be married to be Felizio di Caprine."

She looked up at the ceiling. "May all the gods have pity on me for having such a stubborn daughter. Felizio di Caprine is best for you and for our House. He'll treat you well and we won't have to worry about words that hide daggers. Cassis will come back with our share of the profits, and that will be the end of him."

"Mother—"

She waved my words away and strode purposefully out the door, slamming it behind her.

Dear gods, I thought, *save me from Felizio di Caprine.*

If I had known how casually a prayer might be uttered and the extent of the damage it might cause, I would have been more circumspect with my words. But I was named for the goddess of fortune, and so I cast my words to the wind.

And the wind took them and cast them back at me.

※

A FORTNIGHT LATER, CASSIS RETURNED WITH MY FATHER'S share of the money. I was out riding, surrounded by a bevy of attendants including three gavaros, both my maids, and one of our falconers, whom my father required to be present when I hunted. I hunted my own birds, two big, black-masked goshawks, but my father didn't trust me to do it myself. They were heavy, and it was only through hunting with them that I developed the strength in my right arm necessary to accept their weight on the glove. But I could do it alone. I was even good at it, though most of the credit had to go to the birds.

I had expected word from Cassis in the intervening period and grew sullen when it didn't come. I argued with my mother in my head, since the only times I saw her were in the company of others, at tea with the women of other hill estates, ones that had been guaranteed free of fever. We were preparing to retire to our mountain lodge, and she couldn't be bothered with my frivolous, naive desires. She didn't speak to me again, but I saw her sharp glances and took their meaning.

Then Cassis returned, arriving when my parents were touring the groves and couldn't immediately be called back.

Instead, he found me.

We met near the mews. My female hawk still sat on my forearm. Blades scraped as gavaros loosened their swords behind me, and Bella gasped.

"Lady Kyrra," Cassis said, inclining his head as his horse stamped impatiently in the dust.

The sight of him startled me into familiarity. "Cassis! Do you come on business?"

"Yes." He flashed me a smile. "And to see you. Do you think your parents will appreciate some good news?"

I laughed, startled. "Truly? You'll be making an offer for my hand?"

He directed his gaze to the dust. "I couldn't get you out of my mind this past fortnight." Then he angled his head up to watch me again and smiled.

A Prinze makes no gestures without a knife up his sleeve. I searched his face for guile but found none. Felizio di Caprine was foremost in my thoughts, anyway; my parents had sent a courier out five days earlier, riding at speed. It only seemed logical that my parents sought to betroth me before the Prinze could act, regardless of how old I was.

But wouldn't this match, Aliente and Prinze, do more for Liera?

"My parents will have no choice but to appreciate your father's decision," I said.

His smile became a long, thin line. "Yes. I suppose so."

At my shoulder, Mam whispered, "Kyrra, this isn't proper."

"I'm chaperoned, aren't I?" I said, without taking my gaze

away from Cassis's face. "I'm in no danger from you, am I, nesters?"

In response, he slid down from his horse and let the reins fall as he approached us. The sleeves of his shirt—indigo satin—fluttered in the wind as he held his hand up to me, where I sat astride my own mount. "I mean you no harm. I'll make your parents see."

In his brown eyes I saw only truth. I cannot say, with the benefit of hindsight, that I noted anything more or less in their depths. I was a girl, and he was beautiful and forbidden, and with these words, I fell in love with him. I would not have seen wickedness in him if he had worn it like a scar across his face.

When he took my hand, my fingers shook. He ran his thumb over my knuckles in a rough caress, then let me go and mounted his horse again.

As he made to turn back down the path, he said to me, "I'll see you again, Lady Kyrra. If not this afternoon, then on the morrow. In this, I won't be stopped."

I thrilled to find myself with a lover who made such declarations.

❦

I WAS AFRAID MY PARENTS WOULD ABANDON CASSIS WHEN WE left for the lodge. But at dinner that night, Cassis announced that he would accompany us. My parents could do nothing about it, and desperate thoughts of Felizio di Caprine flitted in my mother's eyes.

But Cassis pledged that he meant no harm to me or my house, and my father, who abided by the old laws governing hospitality, threw open his doors to him, as a good host does to a guest. Cassis had complete freedom on the estate, could roam as he wished, could accompany us to the lodge...

And could venture into the conservatory, where I played the harp, alone, unguarded.

In truth, my serving maids should have been with me. But I slunk out while they were still attending morning chores, gave a leftover sweet cheese pastry to the young gavaro who stood at my door, and went down to the one place no one would ever expect me to go.

I didn't like playing the harp. But I cherished being alone. I fed the lorikeet some slips of bread I'd secreted in my pockets, and I sat down to pick at the strings until someone came to take me back to my chambers. The muslin curtains swirled over the marble tiles, the hot wind doing nothing to cool my skin. I pulled at the bodice of my dress for relief.

Then I looked up and saw Cassis standing there. He didn't smile. The lorikeet squawked and beat its wings against the cage.

"You're unguarded, Kyrra," he said.

My breath came fast. "I know."

"Have your parents learned that I'm no threat, then?"

I smiled at him. "They will. But today, I'm here on my own. My maids think they hold the keys to my prison, but they don't."

He hesitated. "No one knows where you are?"

"Not yet. Though I imagine they'll figure it out soon enough."

He seemed to consider that. Then he stepped closer to me, so close I could smell him. He was a swirl of scents, musk and sweat, cedar, lavender. "If I did mean you harm, you wouldn't send me away. Would you?"

It was a strange thing to say. A strange thing to explain now, years afterward, that I knew exactly what he meant. For a moment I felt thin, as if he had seen into me. But perhaps he had heard stories about headstrong Kyrra, who never did as she was told, whom men courted only for the worms in her father's nursery.

"No," I said.

He bent and kissed me.

There were footsteps in the hall soon enough. We ducked out the window into the garden, giggling like fools. We darted along the rose hedge and fetched up laughing amongst the lilacs, now green and out of bloom. Small drops of dew still hung from the undersides of their leaves. We rattled them off with our passing and streaked our silks with water.

"You were never meant to be held so tightly," Cassis whispered to me. "Your parents should let you out."

"Oh, it's my fault," I whispered back. "I disobeyed them so much when I was younger."

"Do you regret disobeying them now?"

I shook my head. "No."

He frowned. It wasn't the response I'd been expecting. I drew back a little. "Have I said something? Shall we go back to the conservatory?"

He seemed almost to shake himself. "No!" he said, then more softly, "No. It's too long to wait, to do it that way."

I raised my eyebrow. He sighed and reached out to wind one of my curls around his finger. The gold caught the light and glistened like metal. I looked away from it and up to his face. "Do you blame me for wanting to know you first?"

"No," I said. His finger trailed away from my hair and I shivered. "I wouldn't have come if I did."

He moistened his lips and leaned near me. I met him in this kiss.

It was not like the first, no innocent meeting of our mouths. He pressed his mouth down hard on mine, as if he'd better do it fast, before he lost his courage. But it awakened in me a hunger to match. At first, that frightened me and I tried to push him away. "Cassis," I said, thinking that I hadn't known what *knowing* entailed.

But he gripped my shoulders and murmured, "No, Kyrra, don't," his lips brushing the lobe of my ear, and though I was frightened, I didn't want him to go away, to leave me unsatisfied in the midst of the summer heat. So, instead, I pulled him down and swallowed his kisses with my own.

His lips were hot on my neck. His calluses caught at the silk of my dress and his hands shook as he fumbled at the laces of my bodice. When he pressed his lips to my breast, I cried out and he drew away.

It was the last moment of turning back, one we both cast aside. But it hurt at the end, not what I was expecting, and I bled on my skirts and frantically tried to rub out the spot, sobbing as more blood trickled down my thighs. Cassis ran his finger through it.

"Now neither of us is innocent," he whispered.

⁂

I MOVED ABOUT IN A DREAM FOR THE NEXT TWO WEEKS.

The servants packed up our clothes, soaps, perfumes and shampoos, casks of wine, boxes of books, cases of flour and lard. The gavaros saw it all loaded onto wagons. My father took care of the last details demanded by the worms, and Cassis supervised his own men and spoke with my father. As a declared guest, Cassis bore certain responsibilities, and one of them was that he would not harm the householder's property or his daughter.

But I slipped away and aided Cassis in breaking that rule.

I met him in the conservatory twice. In the garden again, once, and for only a few hasty moments, which left me smoothing my rucked-up skirts in a hurry.

The stables were my favorite. A few stolen moments were all we had, anywhere, but the excitement made up for it, that delicious rush of reckless fear and defiance, the knowledge that we might be caught any moment. That was why I liked the stables best. We only met there twice, tucked under an eave in the hayloft. But it was twice while the grooms and gavaros moved about in the yard and might have entered the stable at any moment. I bit my lip to keep from crying out at the end, digging my fingernails into his back, and he held me so tightly, I thought I would suffocate. Out in the yard, men called to each other, and below us, horses snorted and stamped their hooves.

How stiff and cold and official it would have been with Felizio di Caprine. When Cassis took me to wife, we would make love on the bed or the rug or the table, anywhere we pleased. We would rut like animals if the moment grabbed us, or make love as tenderly as if we danced the gavotte.

But it didn't take long for me to worry that I might become pregnant, and I wondered why I had not been called down to the receiving room, to hear the official courting announced.

"Is my father stalling?" I would whisper, in those precious few moments when I held him in my arms, after he'd spent himself. "My parents don't trust you."

He would nuzzle my shoulder, then roll away from me and sit up, brushing off his damask or satin and pulling taut the laces of his open breeches. "Politics is a delicate art, like dancing. Don't fear."

Sometimes he would touch me, other times not. The last time, I hugged myself, the laces of my bodice still half-undone. "My mother was fertile," I said, and he put his hand on my knee and looked into my eyes.

"And that is a good thing."

Any marriage I made, to Cassis or Felizio di Caprine, was contingent on what the conjure-women and genealogists had to say about my own fertility and the fertility of my family. It was already a black mark against me that my mother had only borne one surviving child and that a daughter, although she'd also once conceived and delivered a stillborn boy. The Caprine were in general the most fertile of Houses, a fact which infuriated the Prinze. Cassis's elder brother had married a fertile woman but so far had produced only two daughters.

It couldn't go on forever.

Cassis had made his way to my window after dark that night. The next day we would finally leave for the lodge; our stay at

Villa d'Aliente had extended because our worms would not eat, though the silk-master coerced them with every trick he knew—harvesting the leaves only under a full moon and soaking them in the collected drops of morning dew, bringing in a lutist. But finally, the worms ate and we were going to leave.

I pleaded a headache that night and retired early. I blew out the candles and waited until the moon had risen a fourth of the way in its path across the sky, the agreed-upon time for our meeting. Then, as quietly as I could, I unshuttered my window and leaned out. Cassis threw me a rope, which I made fast to the leg of my bed.

"Shall I come up for you?" he whispered.

"You'll fall if you have to carry me down. Let me come on my own."

"On your own?" In the darkness, I couldn't see his face. But I heard the surprise in his voice. I took the rope in my hands and let myself out the window before he realized I meant what I said. It was a stout rope, and my flimsy silk slippers made it easy to feel out footholds in the knobby stucco. My nightgown caught on the thorn hedge at the bottom as Cassis lifted me over it. When he put me down, he immediately caught up my hands and stared at them in the thin trickle of moonlight.

I laughed, softly. "I'm on the ground, none the worse for wear."

"I expected I'd have to help you down."

"It's not the first time I've climbed out my window."

He seemed to think about that for a moment, then he put his hands on either side of my face and kissed me. We ran away through the garden, scaled the cherry tree that had been my ally in so many other misadventures, dropped down on the other side of the wall, and followed the path to the stables.

One of Cassis's gavaros stood at the back door.

I balked at the sight of him. Though we had often made love while others went about their business, we had always assured that we weren't seen meeting each other.

Cassis noticed my hesitation and took me by the hand. "Shh, Kyrra. Federico is one of my most trusted men. He won't say anything, will you, Feddi?"

"I'm as one who has his tongue cut out, lady," the gavaro assured me, bowing his head.

"But the candles," I said. "There's someone else in the stable. He'll hear us in the quiet."

"A groom," Cassis whispered. "Nothing more. If he hears, he'll think it's a gavaro tupping a kitchen girl."

I remained frozen for a moment, unable to take another step, but then Cassis pulled me into the stables and we climbed into the hayloft.

My father's prize Ipanzers were housed at one end of the stable. We chose the area above the common horses, the ones gavaros would ride.

I didn't hear my father's boots on the packed dirt floor. I didn't hear anything until he said, "Kyrra!"

I froze, too stunned even for a gasp, my lips still pressed to Cassis's mouth. I looked in his eyes for a moment, but his gaze flickered away, down through the opening in the loft where the ladder was.

My father must have been visiting his horses one last time.

His prize horses. How could I have been so stupid?

But the gavaro should have warned us.

My father stood in the hall below us, a riding quirt forgotten in one hand as he leaned against the ladder and looked up through the hole in the ceiling where the ladder was. The end of the quirt trembled. His face was as waxy as the candles burning in the iron sconces on the walls.

Cassis let me go too slowly. "Mestere," he said. "This is not the way it looks."

"Are you raping my daughter?"

"Papa!" I said. "No!"

My father's expression changed. "Tell me this is only his doing, Kyrra."

I could say nothing to that. I hung my head and pulled my gown together. Tears blurred my vision. When Cassis moved away from me, I didn't watch him. The ladder shook against the loft as he climbed down it.

His bootheels scuffed on the dirt. "Mestere," he began, but whatever else he might have said was cut off by the smack of the quirt against wood. I looked up finally, in alarm.

Cassis backed away. His gavaro stood behind him, sword drawn. My father was only armed with a quirt, but he pointed it at Cassis and said, "Go back to your chambers. I'll discuss this with you later." His voice shook.

Cassis closed his mouth, glanced up once at me, then turned and walked out, flanked by his gavaro.

❦

MY FATHER TOOK ME BACK TO MY ROOM. WHEN HE OPENED the door and led me in, my maids were crying. Bella jumped up and tried to hug me, but I pushed her away. Mam hung back. My father said nothing, closed the door, and left.

"Leave me alone," I said, and went into my room.

The rope was coiled up on the bed. My maids or someone else had found it. They must have shown it to my mother, because my shutters were locked with a contraption of wrought iron. I walked over to the window and rattled it with both hands, but the lock was new, thick, and hopeless, probably meant for the doors of a silkhouse. I uttered a sound that was not a laugh or a cry but contained both—a sound of desperation. Then I lay down on my bed next to the rope and started to cry. But they were stunned little dry half-sobs. My emotions hadn't fully formed yet, and mostly, I felt numb.

Some time before dawn, I fell asleep and dreamed that Cassis came back for me, but ravens filled the stables and I couldn't get to him, though I slashed at the birds with my father's quirt. And I dreamed that my father hit Cassis instead of the stall, and

Cassis pulled his sword and cut my father before I could stop him.

The turning of the doorknob woke me in the morning. I opened my eyes to see my mother standing in the doorway, her hands white with flour, dressed in a plain linen skirt and blouse, a towel at her side. She'd been supervising the kitchens. She did that when she was upset.

"What will you do to me?" I asked.

"I'm not going to do anything to you, Kyrra," she said in a tired voice. "But I do wonder if you've forgotten how to think."

"He'll marry me, Mother. It won't be a problem. He came here to court me."

"Cassis left this morning."

For a moment, her words made no sense. I remember it clearly, the way the sounds seemed jumbled up and the methodical way I had to sort through them. Yet even after I understood, I refused to believe.

I clambered up onto my knees, still on my bed. "No," I said, shaking my head. "Cassis loves me."

"There's a difference between love and lust. I thought I taught you better."

She looked so sad. I jerked my head toward the window so I wouldn't have to look at her. But the window was still shuttered and locked.

"I suppose Papa will cast me off now that he's sent Cassis away?"

"Your father did *not* send Cassis away. He was of the same opinion you were, that a match with the Prinze might be good for all of us." She sat down heavily on my bed, rumpling the linens, and began methodically rubbing the flour from her fingers with the towel.

I stared at her. "It was you, wasn't it? You finally convinced Father that Cassis must have a knife up his sleeve, that his will couldn't be good—"

"And it wasn't, was it?" My mother leaned over toward me. "He seduced you, a girl of sixteen—"

"He came to court me, Mother! He said so!"

My mother's blue-gray eyes were as brittle as a winter sky. I have been told I have my mother's eyes, but the people who said so never saw her behind a closed door, in the privacy of our chambers.

"Then he lied," she said. Her voice was as precise as the blade of a knife. "Didn't he?"

I laughed. It has always been my way to laugh when I should cry. I put my hands to my mouth. "No," I said through my fingers. "No."

My mother rubbed her brow. Her floured hands left faint white stains on her forehead. "Think, Kyrra. If he charges you with seduction, it will impugn the Aliente name, and a marriage even to a minor Caprine will be out of the question, regardless of whether or not the Caprine suspect fraud. They can't afford the association. Our alliances will never be powerful. But what if he's gotten you with child? What will happen then?"

She gazed at me, eyebrows arched, one hand on her knee.

I tried not to see the sense in her question.

The candles had been lit. The gavaro should have warned us.

Reluctantly, I said, "I'll be cast out and the Prinze might lay claim to our lands through the child."

My mother rose. "We'll continue our negotiations with Felizio di Caprine for your hand. We may be forced to bend to the Imisi or the Forza, though. Maybe we can pass off your loss of innocence as a seduction on Cassis's part and have the whole affair written away—although if it's Geoffre di Prinze's intent to break our name, we won't have the wealth or the power to counter his influence. We'll have to go back in stores to get the money; it's been a dry year—"

"Cassis will marry me!" I shouted. "He loves me and will save me from Felizio di Caprine. I won't marry Felizio, Mother—not while there is a chance that we can still negotiate with the Prinze!"

"Kyrra!" my mother hissed. "You've jeopardized *all* negotiations for your hand—don't you realize that? You must stand in the Circle to be guaranteed in marriage. Do you think the name Aliente so powerful that we could circumvent the entire League? There is no magic that will give you back your lost virginity!"

I tightened my arms around myself and turned away from her.

She made an exasperated noise between her teeth. The *scritch* of her hands on the towel told me how furiously she wiped them. "Cassis abandoned you. Geoffre di Prinze will never compromise his standing by accepting a tainted woman, particularly one his son has already discarded. I've heard rumors he's arranging Cassis a marriage with Camile di Sere. If you're pregnant, you've given him an excuse to claim our lands after your father's death without the inconvenience of allying himself to us at all. Without paying anything."

Tears blurred my vision, but I kept them from spilling onto my cheeks, hot as they were. "Cassis would never be so cruel."

For a moment, the room was still. I couldn't bring myself to turn around and face my mother, not with those tears in my eyes. Her skirt swished faintly over the carpet as she walked up behind me and placed her hand on my shoulder.

"Let us hope not," she said. Her hand drifted down my bare arm so she could take my fingers in her own. "For your sake. And for all of us."

❧

MY BODY EVENTUALLY BETRAYED ME.

I missed my courses that month. My usual time came and went, but there was no blood. Frantically, I checked my marking sticks to see if I had made a mistake in counting, the knowledge that I hadn't sitting in my heart like the stone of a fruit. I felt ripe and gravid, but not with the seed Cassis had planted inside me; instead, it was this information, this evidence, that would grow and metamorphose like our silk worms.

Like a fool, I thought I could keep it secret from my mother. But I could not keep it secret from my maids.

My mother surprised me in my chambers again one night, two months on, while I was embroidering by candlelight. Doing my stitches was mindless work, and I needed that because otherwise, I felt as if I were drowning.

She brought me a cup. I thought it was wine. "Mam told me you weren't feeling well," my mother said. "Drink this."

"I don't know what lies Mam has been spreading, Mama. I feel fine."

"Kyrra. *Take the cup.*"

And then I finally understood. I stared at her—her eyes, the slate in them crumbling in desperation; her face, ravaged with worry lines I had never seen before.

I looked down at the cup. A long time. Then I took it up with shaking hands and drank.

It was not wine. It was foul and sulfurous, spelled with some awful, unnatural magic, and I can still taste it sometimes before a battle, at any important moment. I drank it as quickly as I could, but at the end, nausea claimed me and I vomited a mouthful between the fingers of my hastily raised right hand. The red liquid dribbled over my knuckles and spotted my white nightgown like drops of blood.

"I'll help you into another gown," my mother said as she came to take the cup from me and placed it on the table. "You should rest now."

I closed my eyes and nodded. Then my mother's hands were at my sleeves, and I let her undress me and put me to bed as she seldom had when I was a child.

In the morning, Cassis's child died in great rivers and clots of blood.

Awakening to this, I thought I was still in a nightmare. I

knew what must be happening, but none of it felt real. It was as if I stood outside my body and looked down at someone else—some other stupid girl fooled by a pretty smile who was now paying for her actions with the life of her child.

Then the cramps seized me and I screamed.

Mam and Bella ran into my room. Mam hugged me and sent Bella for my mother. Then she pulled off my bloody gown in her gentle way, and she washed my thighs while I held rag after rag to my crotch. After I was dressed again, my mother finally arrived and Bella stripped the bloody bed, and I lay down and bit my pillow when the cramps came too hard. It lasted for a long time and soaked many rags, many sheets.

For days, my thoughts tumbled in a blood-tinged haze. I remember thinking, if only I could travel backward in time and tell myself to stay out of the conservatory. If only I asked the right god, maybe everything would be erased as a frightening dream. If only I could hide in the cupboard, the way I had as a child.

I had always been able to escape any requirement laid upon me. By slipping out my window. Climbing the cherry tree. But I could not escape this.

My mother had liberated a fair amount of gold to pay for the potion and the silence of the herb-woman who made it. But an herb-woman who would brew such potions and take such bribes was vulnerable to selling her silence to the highest bidder. The rumors began quietly, but by late fall, they raged like the brush-fires we all feared at that time of year.

The only remaining mystery was why the Prinze remained silent for so long.

The first snowflakes were falling when the Prinze made their formal accusations, and my father was busy supervising the weaving and dyeing of silk. In such a dry year, there wasn't much. Our revenues would be down. And then me.

My father countercharged Cassis with seduction. But, as my mother had predicted, the Prinze had too much power in the

Circle. And the charge that I had killed a babe in my womb was true.

If only my mother had killed the herb-woman who made the potion. Emotion had no place in the games Houses played; that lesson I learned well.

It was a lesson driven home to me when Cassis testified in front of the full Circle. Representatives from all the Lieran Houses major and minor alike were there, seated on the hard wooden benches that curved along the walls of the Dome of the Gods. A statue of Erelf, the god of knowledge, stood in the center, and Cassis knelt before it when he testified. The ravens on the god's shoulders watched me over Cassis's head.

Carrion-eaters. Not like my hawks. Should I have been surprised that they failed in their service to the truth?

"I was bewitched," Cassis said. "Kyrra d'Aliente spoiled her mother's womb for sons, and she has taken a great hate to all men. She seduced me so that she might also kill my son. Everyone knows that the Aliente grow desperate for new outlets in which to sell their silk, and new ships in which to carry it. But my father wouldn't deal with them, and this is how they take their revenge."

Was there anger in his face, that I had killed his son to save my House? He never looked at me once.

Hate kept me unmoving while three women made me lie on a table in the center of the Circle and proved I was not a virgin, and hate kept me from hearing the words of the sentence all the way through: "Kyrra d'Aliente is hereafter disowned by her father and cast off forever as an unchaste woman. From this day forward, she has no right to either the Aliente property or the Aliente name. If she should be caught using this name, she shall be executed on the whim of the Circle. For deliberately causing the miscarriage of Cassis di Prinze's child, the Houses are in agreement that Kyrra d'Aliente's right arm shall be severed from her body above the elbow."

And so, they took me outside and made me kneel and lay my

arm on a wooden block, and then the executioner tied a leather strip around my bicep and brought an axe down on my arm while Geoffre di Prinze and his son stood to one side of me and watched.

The blade whistled in the air as it came down. Then there was a *thunk*, and my arm lay on the block, still twitching, while they dragged me away to stanch the blood pumping from the ragged stump.

I didn't faint until I had a good look at my arm lying there.

I wanted to remember it.

CHAPTER 5

I MET ARSENAULT ALMOST A YEAR LATER.

It took a long time for my stump to heal, and then I worked in the silkhouses and slept with the girls who combed the silk. They were all unmarried, about my age, but came from families who had lived and died and worked on Aliente land for long ages. Combergirls grew the nails of their index fingers long and notched them, one, two, three, sometimes four times, making their own hands into the most delicate of combs, honing the tines of their nails every night with emery files.

I stirred the big pots of boiling water filled with cocoons, and the combergirls combed them out and fed the raw silk thread onto spindles. Since my ancestors had stolen the first silkworm eggs, silk production in Eterea had flourished until there were several grades of moth raised up and down the peninsula. We raised various species ourselves, but our most-desired silk, the kind for which we were known, was spun by giant moths the size of hummingbirds. When we boiled their cocoons, the thread turned a deep, shimmering burgundy, the color of our House. It turned the water red as blood and stained the combergirls' nails and fingertips. After all the thread had been spun, the dead worms sank to the bottom of the pot, and it was my job to fish them out with a strainer and take them to the compost heap, where they would decay and eventually feed the mulberry trees.

With the heat in the boiling house, I sometimes felt as if I had been sentenced to a life of labor in the underworld.

The only break in my day was to bring water to the gavaros, whose job it had once been to serve me. And all around me every night, girls tended their perfectly matched hands. I preferred it when the girls left me alone, and most of them did. Except for Ilena, the girl who slept beside me.

Ilena had long, notched nails on both hands, and she was haughty about it. Her mother was teaching her to spin—a more skilled occupation than combing—but her mother was demanding and jealous, and Ilena remained proudest of her nails. She used to sit on her straw mattress and spread both hands wide, admiring the way they caught the moonlight. The other girls both hated and loved her, but she saw in me someone she could beat down to make herself appear better than she was.

Ilena saw Arsenault first. We were sitting outside with the other girls and a handful of gavaros, taking our midday meal outdoors. The day baked with a dry heat which was still a relief from the steamy oppression of the silkhouse. My father granted all of us, from the lowliest swineherd to the most valuable silk weaver, the same midday ration—a slice of flatbread spread with a paste made of chickpeas or an onion baked in the fire. Because I could eat this meal one-handed the same as anybody, it was the one time of day I felt as if no one stared at me. But I still tried to maintain my distance.

Ilena's soft exclamation made me look up. My father had come into the parched yellow courtyard formed by the silkhouses, accompanied by a tall, dust-covered man carrying a bag and an axe, a knife on one hip and a sword on the other. He wore the black felt hat with the rolled side favored by most gavaros, and so I understood that like all gavaros, he must bring all his possessions with him wherever he went. But even I was surprised by the axe.

And then there was his scar. He had his good side turned to us at first, and it was easy to see why Ilena was interested in him. He was a well-made man, tall, with broad shoulders and a strong profile. But as he talked to my father, he removed his hat and turned, so we could see his scar.

Even at a distance it stood out, a line jagging from his temple down his cheek into his beard. It must have continued across his scalp as well, because a shocking strip of silver-white streaked through his black hair just above it. Several of the girls gasped, and even the gavaros milled around, murmuring to each other.

"Will he guard the combing house, do you think?" Ilena said.

Ilena didn't often ask me questions as if I were a person, so I thought she was speaking to someone else. I tried to hide inside the veil of my dirty, tangled hair and continued to eat my bread.

"Well?" she said impatiently. "It's your father, isn't it? Have you heard any news?"

Ilena never seemed to understand that I had no dealings with the house anymore. I shook my hair away from my face because I couldn't push it back and hold my bread at the same time. "I don't know if he'll guard us," I said. "My father should have no need of more gavaros."

Truthfully, I wanted nothing more than to see my father gathering more gavaros—to raise an army to crush the Prinze. But deep down I knew that the time for that—if there ever had been a time for it—was long past.

Ilena watched the new gavaro wistfully. "He looks like a foreigner. Maybe even from the north. He's fair-skinned."

I finished eating and licked the traces of oil from my fingers. "He's not so handsome with that scar. Perhaps he's only come to fight the fires."

Fall had lasted an interminably long time. The rains were late, it was hot, and brushfires erupted in the canyons almost daily. Everyone—man or woman—was marshaled to fight them, frantically trying to save the groves of mulberry trees upon which all our futures depended.

Ilena shook her head. "But he's carrying so many weapons. He probably got that scar in a duel."

All Ilena's dreams wore robes of silk. In the spinning houses, the women sat at their wheels, repeating all the popular romances of the time—eager to imagine being carried off by a foreign prince, wearing dresses sewn from yards of silk, unwound and combed from thousands of cocoons. Cocoons were the yardsticks of our lives.

But I was done with romances, myself.

"He probably likes boys," I said.

Ilena shot me a barbed look. "He doesn't seem the sort. I hope he guards the combing house."

"I'll be the one to bring him water," I said for spite, and walked away while she glared.

There was no way to tell by looking at him then that he could do magic. But the aura clung to him like road dust, so even a girl like Ilena could feel it. In the beginning, the other gavaros avoided him, but if Arsenault noticed, he didn't seem bothered by it. I myself paid little attention to him at first, barely sparing a passing glance for him on my errands. I kept my eyes down in those days and had no use for flirting the way Ilena did.

But sometimes, I would find him watching me as I carried water to the men. I couldn't carry the full bucket all the way from the well, so I had to dip it half-full and hook the handle over my forearm. I resigned myself to taking three times as long as a whole woman and endured the gazes and words of the men as they drank.

"Build up that arm, girl; we don't have all day."

"Is it a girl? I thought the Householder sent us a clay golem for a water boy."

"Maybe that Prinze just wasn't picky."

Then they would laugh and turn to their work. But Arsenault never laughed. He only drank. I kept my gaze pinned to the metal ladle. I saw how his knuckles were nicked by dozens of tiny white scars and the way the ladle bumped against his chin, dripping water into his beard, leaving it shiny and black. But I never once lifted my eyes to tell the color of his eyes or if they were looking at me. Once the ladle was back in my hand, I immediately turned from him and dipped it for the next man.

Then one day, the next man was Vanni di Forza.

I should use the word *man* loosely. Vanni was the same age I was, seventeen at that time. He was a foster of my father, one of the many sons of minor families hoping to metamorphose kin ties into a more profitable relationship of silk. He'd lived with us for three years already, flitting about at the edge of my attention like the girls who fostered with my mother. As the Householder's daughter, I had always been kept separate from the fosters. It wasn't deemed seemly for me to fraternize in circles beneath my station.

Vanni di Forza had seemed so small when I lived in the big house, an insignificant speck in my universe of Caprine, Prinze, and Sere. But now that I had fallen, he loomed as large as a stray dog terrorizing the sheep.

As was my habit, I handed him the ladle without looking at him. I didn't even know it was Vanni until he spoke.

"There's not enough water here for me to drink," he said, and poured the water from the ladle onto the dusty ground. Startled, I looked up. I didn't remember him well, but then, a year between sixteen and seventeen can make an enormous difference in a boy; he was taller and broader than I thought he ought to be, with a brown fuzz on his chin as if he were trying—and failing—to grow a beard like Arsenault's.

"I thought you were supposed to serve us, Kyrra," he said. His mouth made a cruel twist some might have called a smile, but there was a glint in his dark eyes I didn't like. A kind of mean amusement.

I brought the bucket up in front of me like a shield. "Is it my fault if you spilled the water? If you'll hand the ladle back, I'll dip you more."

Vanni's eyes flashed. They were a dark brown the color of

rosewood and might have made him handsome had they contained a wholesome wickedness instead of the vindictive humor that lit them now. "This ladle?" he said, twirling it in his hands. "I'd rather have a cup."

"I don't have a cup. The gavaros all drink from the ladle."

"Do we look like gavaros?" he asked the two boys who'd come down with him—both sons of minor clans I didn't recognize.

The boys made negative noises like they were choking on laughter.

"I think we're all householders here, Kyrra. Surely, you won't have forgotten."

I ground my teeth. "Of course not, *Mestere* di Forza." I did my best to curtsey with a spine that felt stiff as a rod of steel, clutching the bucket in my one hand. "If you'll give me back the ladle, perhaps I can find you a cup."

"Sali, why don't you give her back the ladle?"

Vanni threw it to the boy standing behind me. The boy plucked it out of the air and frowned.

Once, on a winter visit to Liera, I saw some boys in a back alley tormenting a dog. It was Longest Night, and the boys had tied Saien sparklers to the dog's tail. When the boys lit the sparklers, a golden fizz of fire and sparks spewed out of the paper tubes, and the terrified dog bolted, streaking down the alley like a big rocket launched over the Mera di Capria. The boys bent over laughing, but all I could think of later was the dog.

"Then I might have to touch her," Sali said. He threw the ladle to the boy beside him.

"Don't look at me," that boy said. "My mother said she's a witch."

He threw the ladle back to Vanni, who caught it easily. "Filipe, you coward. She's not a witch. Everybody knows she just likes to do it in the dirt. I heard she had all the stable boys, too."

My face flamed. Vanni smacked the bowl of the ladle into the palm of his hand and grinned at me.

"Well, Kyrra?" he said. "What are you waiting for?"

"I'm waiting for *you*," I said. "To give me back the ladle. Like a gentleman ought."

All the boys laughed at this.

"Oh, a gentleman." Vanni sketched an overwrought bow, flinging the ladle out with a flourish as if it were a sword he was pledging to the Mistiri of his House. "I must have missed those laws in my tutoring. Where is it written that a householder must be a gentleman to a kinless girl?"

"Where is it written that a householder ought to be an idiot?" I retorted. "You've had your fun. Now give me the ladle. You know I have to hand it back at the end of the day or Master Fenn will have it out of me."

Vanni darted a glance at my rear end and his grin grew. "Out of your backside, you mean?"

Vanni wasn't the only man who assumed that because I'd lain with Cassis, I would lie with anyone. Mostly it wasn't the gavaros; it was the householders. Men who only a year before were competing with each other just for a chance to lift my hand to their lips.

But it made me angry, and I wasn't afraid of Vanni. I lifted the bucket as high as I could and swung it with all my strength at Vanni's head. As it turned out, I still didn't have much strength. The bucket flew from my grasp, and Vanni had all the time in the world to step away from it. It barely grazed his chest before tumbling harmlessly to the ground.

Water sloshed his silk shirt, though, leaving big dark patches on the light blue fabric. He frowned down at it, smoothing the wrinkles with his other hand.

"Now, that was uncalled-for," he said.

"You are a *wretch*," I said, and launched myself toward the ladle.

He jerked the ladle upward, holding it over my head so I'd

have to jump like a dog to get it. With tears of anger and frustration pricking my eyes, I almost did. Whenever I recall this now, I wonder why I didn't just walk away. Deprived of their fun, the boys would have dropped the ladle and gone on to goad me with something else. But it was like I lived my life in a dream then, by dream rules and dream logic. Instead of walking away, I shoved at Vanni's chest.

I couldn't have made a bigger mistake. He grabbed my wrist and pulled me against him with his left hand while he held the ladle out of my reach with his right.

I shouted. Vanni kept grinning his toothy wolf grin down at me, and then he hurled the ladle to one of his friends and put his other hand securely on my backside to ensure that I wouldn't be going anywhere.

Behind me, boots thumped in the dust, and the boys' laughter abruptly died. Vanni looked up and I twisted my head to see over my shoulder.

Arsenault stood in the center of the group of us, holding the ladle, which he had picked out of the air. I don't know how he was close enough to grab it without any of us knowing he was there, but Arsenault was like that. He was a big man, but he could move like a cat when he needed to. In his hands, the ladle looked like a weapon.

"Hey, gavaro," Vanni said. "We're just having a bit of fun. Don't you have other things to do?"

"I've come to retrieve the water girl," Arsenault replied. His accent was strange, all the syllables rolled the wrong way. But his command of the language was good. "She has other chores to do today."

"They can wait, can't they?" Vanni said. "The Householder's fosters have need of her." He looked down at me, the grin making a reappearance, then pulled me in so my pelvis rubbed against his.

I stomped on his foot with my heel as hard as I could. I was barefoot and he was wearing boots, but I put a lot of force into it and he jerked his foot back with an *mmph*, pushing me away from him at the same time, though he still gripped my wrist like a vise.

"It seems as if she takes exception to your claim on her time," Arsenault said. Amusement laced his voice, faintly. It only made Vanni's temper flare.

"I'm a *householder*," he said. "I am in charge of this situation."

"Last I heard, Pallo d'Aliente was in charge of all the situations on his land. I'm sure you could take it up with him." Arsenault's voice was lazy, almost bored. He bowed minutely, adjusting his grip on the ladle. "Mestere."

He looked at Vanni from beneath the brim of his hat. His stance was respectful, but even I could read the message in his eyes. I could read it but I couldn't make sense of it.

I didn't know why he would care what happened to me. When I lived in the big house, I never went anywhere without an escort of gavaros. If Vanni had attempted to touch my shoulder without my permission, they would have drawn steel. But that was only because they were paid to protect me. Arsenault had no reason to put himself crossways with Vanni di Forza, and so I didn't understand why he stood there in the circle of boys who outranked him, jeopardizing his livelihood.

I knew my father wouldn't grant me any special treatment. If my father was caught giving me protection, the Circle would slap more penalties on him and maybe me, too. The Prinze would make sure of that.

Vanni laughed. "You're saying that Pallo d'Aliente cares whether this girl dispenses her water every day?"

Arsenault shrugged and stuck his free thumb into his swordbelt, swinging the ladle up and around with his other hand. "How do I know what the Householder feels? All I know is that he has certain rules, which he expects to be followed. I must confess I'm still learning your customs, but I think one of them is that fosters swear to abide by the rules of hospitality. Which means they do no harm to the Householder's family or his property, is that right?"

The other boys shifted nervously. "He's right, Vanni," the one called Sali said. "She's not the Householder's daughter anymore, but she's still his property."

Vanni looked between the two frowning boys and Arsenault, who stood there unconcerned and not quite deferent. Then he swore and pushed me away. I stumbled backward, almost going down in the dirt, but Arsenault caught me by the elbow, righting me. When I turned to look at him, he brought the ladle up and handed it to me.

"Master Fenn should have this back," he said. "I'll wait for you."

My brows pulled downward. But there was no lie in Arsenault's eyes as he bent and offered me the ladle.

His eyes were gray...but not gray. Gray was the color of an overcast sky or a stormy ocean. Arsenault's were the color of hammered steel. They lit for a moment like light tracing a blade, until I thought that maybe a strange ray of sunlight had played a trick on me.

But then the light faded and he was just a man with an ugly scar, handing me a ladle while I stood barefoot and rumpled in the dust.

❧

AFTER I RETURNED THE LADLE, ARSENAULT BROUGHT ME TO the gavaro barracks.

In my life as Householder's daughter, I hadn't spared a thought to where the gavaros lived when they were off their shift. I didn't expect the low, rectangular building built of mud and straw, painted white to reflect the sun and covered in a wild profusion of fading magenta bougainvillea blooms. Its wooden shutters and huge iron-barred wooden doors were thrown open in the afternoon heat, and off-duty gavaros lounged outside in the courtyard playing cards, wearing their shirts untucked, their feet and calves bare, swordbelts slung over chair backs. Meanwhile, on-duty gavaros walked in and out of the building, fully armed and dressed in their burgundy tunics and black felt hats. Small knots of women formed amid the gavaros, scrubbing laundry in big wooden tubs or hanging it to dry on lines strung between two scraggly pine trees—talking and laughing with each other and with the men. A few children ran around underfoot, most of them too small to be out of dresses, and some of the women wore babies strapped to their backs.

I felt as if I had stumbled onto another world—a world which had somehow been tucked into the folds of the world I knew, like an object kept secret in the folds of a robe.

Arsenault strode past the washerwomen with a long, deceptively easy stride I couldn't hope to match and walked through the large, open oak doors. I put my head down and concentrated on his boots. They were big, dusty, brown leather boots cuffed at the knee, and their hobnailed soles rang on the stone tiles, the only sound in the dim quiet. He greeted several of the men with brief nods as he led me down the corridors, but he said nothing until we reached a small room near the back of the building.

"Stay here," he said. "I'll be back in a moment."

Only gavaros with rank had their own rooms. The raw recruits slept together in a big room in the center of the barracks. Utîl, the leader of our gavaros, had a larger room near the front of the building. Arsenault, as a new hire but clearly a veteran, merited one of the smaller cells at the back.

The shutters on the one narrow window were closed, and it was hard to see after being outside in the bright afternoon light. I could make out a cot on one wall and a table littered with scraps of wood and metal shoved against the other, a chair pushed under it. His axe hung in a rack above the table and glittered in a stray shaft of light.

"You've brought me to your room?" I said with alarm as I turned to face him.

He didn't say anything, just stepped back out into the hallway.

"If you mean to abuse me, my father's laws will prevent you, too!" I shouted after him.

He pulled the door shut behind him. I listened for the sound of a bolt or the click of a lock, but neither came.

It didn't make any sense for him to trot out my father's laws to Vanni di Forza only to circumvent them himself, but I didn't understand what "chores" I could do in this sparely furnished room. The mystery guaranteed I would stay so I could solve it. I threw open the shutters to let in some air and light, and after a moment's hesitation, I drifted over to the worktable, thinking that in case he did mean me harm, I could use a chunk of wood as a weapon.

He had several projects in various states of progress but nothing was finished. A carving of unfamiliar wood striated with bands of rose and lavender in the shape of a fox. A piece of reddened cherry became the sweep of a woman's hair, so natural it might have been real. But the woman's face was unfinished, and for some reason that troubled me. Next to it lay a wolf fashioned of bright silver metal.

I touched the wolf's flank and a light frisson shivered through me. Then the door swung open and Arsenault shoved in a wooden tub with his foot, then followed, carrying two big buckets of water on either arm.

I drew my hand quickly back from the wolf. Arsenault kicked the door closed and poured the contents of the buckets into the washtub.

"What is that?" I said.

Arsenault barely glanced up at me. "What does it look like?"

"I can't say. You told Vanni di Forza I was needed for chores."

"I do have chores for you. But first, you'll take a bath."

"Here?"

"If there was a better place, I'm sure you'd have done it already, Lady Kyrra."

His words stung, but I didn't know how to respond to them. It was true what the other gavaros had said, that I was in danger of turning into a clay golem. But the girls in the combing house all bathed together in the stream that ran through the glade below the combing house, and if I bathed with them, I would have to show off my stump.

I settled on calling him out for using my name. "You may not call me *lady*," I said. "It is against the law."

He shrugged and straightened up from setting the empty buckets down in the corner. "Is anyone here to pass sentence?"

"I don't see how I will bathe here."

"I have a towel," he said. He crossed to the far wall and opened a small chest, from which he extracted a neatly folded, undyed linen towel and a cloth for washing and laid them on the cot. "And soap." A small bar followed, scenting the air with the kind of exotic spices the Prinze and their allies sold in the Lieran Day Market. Cloves and musk and perhaps even tea from Saien, the black leaves called sukong that the men drank sometimes.

An earthy, male scent, completely unfitting for a woman. My soaps had smelled of lavender and citrus and roses.

"Your soap smells expensive," I said skeptically.

"I've traveled." He pulled a small ivory comb out of the chest and laid it next to the towel and soap. It, too, seemed out of place in the small room with his dusty boots and the nicks on his hands.

"I'll wait outside." His gray eyes flickered down over me and he frowned. "I suppose you'll have to hand your clothes through the door. To wash them, too."

That was too much. I knew I had fallen, but the thought of having been rescued from the taunting of Vanni di Forza only to be forced to sit naked in the room of a gavaro...

My eyes felt as hot as my face, and I gathered my skirts in my hand and tried to push past Arsenault to the door. "I see now what *chores* you'd have me do."

He put himself in front of the door and crossed his arms. "I suppose you have a right to be wary of wolves, but just because you're fallen, do you think it means you have to stay down in the dirt?"

His words startled me into looking up at his face, at his arched, aristocratic black brows—such a contrast to the thick ridge in his nose where an old break had healed—and the scar that ran down his temple. In spite of myself, my eyes were drawn to that scar. It was white with age, but the cut must have laid his skin open to the bone.

His mouth—more expressive than I would have thought for a man who seemed so hard—softened and he said, "I'll beg a spare dress from one of the women. When you get out of the bath, put on my clean shirt and tunic. They're hanging on a hook on the wall. I'll knock when I get back, leave you the dress, and take your clothes."

For the first time all afternoon, I realized he wasn't wearing his tunic, just a burgundy armband tied around his bicep. He'd been off duty when he faced Vanni di Forza.

"I don't understand," I said. "Why are you doing this?"

He watched me for a moment. I could almost see him sort his words. Then he said, "You look like you need it."

❧

MAYBE I SHOULD HAVE BEEN INSULTED. BUT IN TRUTH, I wouldn't have been able to stop Vanni di Forza myself, and I did need that bath badly, for more than one reason.

Arsenault walked out and firmly shut the door behind him. After he left, I discovered it could be locked from the inside, so I did. Then I closed the shutters, wrestled my clothes off, and sank naked into the cool water in the washtub.

I tried not to look at my stump. Unlike Arsenault's scar, my scars were still pink and livid. The muscles of my upper arm had shrunk until even the portion of limb that remained looked wizened. Useless. Ugly.

I tried also not to think about my last bath, the night before I left to stand before the Council. That tub was large and copper, and my chambermaids warmed the water with heated bricks. Mam washed my hair and teased out the tangles while Bella soaped my back. Then they rubbed my skin with lavender-scented oils and wrapped me in a thick cotton robe that smelled of rose petals, and Mam oiled my curls and braided my hair.

The memory itself was like a scar, and the worst part of it was not the hot water or the lavender oils, but the way Mam braided my hair.

I couldn't braid my hair on my own now. That was why it was such a tangled mess. The girls I slept with and worked around all wore their hair in braided crowns. Sometimes, they helped each other, but no one wanted to help me, because they didn't know how much help could be given without breaking the terms of my sentence, and I was too ashamed to ask for anything. Once, a girl named Gia tried to help me—picking up the comb from the floor where I'd thrown it in frustration—but Ilena laughed and asked her what kind of *combergirl* she was, if she was headed out to comb the guardian dogs with their matted hair next. Gia was a shy, kind girl and blushed so hot and red that I couldn't find it in myself to let her help me again. So, I gave up on combs and steeled myself to all the barbs Ilena threw my way, about how maybe I ought to be guarding the sheep instead.

The tangles still wouldn't come out, no matter how much I lathered them with Arsenault's soap. I was still scrubbing when Arsenault rapped softly on the door.

"No," I called out. "Not yet."

"I thought you didn't want a bath," he said through the door.

"I'll be done soon!" I answered. But even though the water was cold and the tub small and cramped, my muscles and my mind had begun to loosen. I didn't feel so much like an animal anymore, ready to scratch and bite.

Maybe I wasn't so eager to get out of the tub.

When I felt as if I couldn't scrape another fleck of dirt from my skin, I got out and dried myself with Arsenault's thin towel, then wrestled on his extra shirt and his tunic over that. The hems of both fell past my knees, granting me a basic decency, though they left my calves exposed. When I unlocked the door and let him in, he laid a bundle of clothing down on the bed. I caught a flash of red rolled up in a brown skirt and walked over to sort through it.

The girl he'd found had given him everything—drawers, stockings, chemise, the sleeveless guarnello that all the girls in the villa wore, this one with a red bodice and brown skirt embroidered with yellow flowers. To my relief, the strings of the bodice had been laced already; I thought I could loosen them enough to get into the dress without having to unlace them. I had learned to tie a simple knot with my one hand, well enough that I wouldn't be too embarrassed by the looseness of my dress.

"Margarithe is of a size with you, I think," Arsenault was saying. "She's one of the kitchen girls. I hope…"

His voice trailed away and I realized he was staring at me.

My cheeks fired and I tried to tug the tunic down further. "*Ser*," I said.

He cleared his throat and looked away. "I gave you a comb, didn't I?"

He hadn't been looking at me at all. He'd been staring at the disaster of my hair.

Now my cheeks were red for a different reason. I tried to seem aloof.

"I used it," I said.

His mouth hitched up at the corner. "Which edge?"

I glared at him. "Try to braid your own hair without two hands. The tangles won't come out and I can't do anything to fix them."

The slight smile at the corner of his mouth disappeared. He cocked his head thoughtfully. "You have no one to help you?"

"The combergirls? Why should they want to help me?"

CHAPTER 5

"I don't know. Have you given them reason to want to help you?"

"If you mean have I laid myself down at their feet—"

"No, Lady Kyrra, that isn't what I meant."

"What did you mean, then?"

He looked at me with those odd gray eyes again, long enough that I had to resist pulling the tunic down further.

"Come here," he said.

"I've already said I won't do your *chores*."

"Is that all you think about? I was hoping you'd help me with my shirts and polish my boots."

"Your laundry?" I raised my stump. "I can't even braid my own hair; do you think I can do something as heavy as your *laundry*?"

"Yes, eventually," he said, and instead of waiting for me to come to him, he came to me. With a swift, silent motion, he twisted my hair into a tail with one hand and pulled his dagger with the other. I jerked forward but he held on tight, and in an instant, the blade sliced the tail cleanly off. My curls sprang up to the bottom of my earlobes, and my scalp felt freer without the weight of all that hair pulling down on it.

He cast the sheaf of matted, dun-colored tangles onto the floor.

"Now you'll be able to take care of yourself," he said.

※

"You'll have to pay back Margarithe's dress. We had to burn yours," he said after I had dressed. "Come back tomorrow and I'll set you some chores to do."

"Your laundry?"

"I'm not sure you're ready for laundry yet. I'll have you polish my weapons."

I had been expecting any number of chores, but polishing his weapons wasn't one of them. He was wearing his sword right now. It had a plain cruciform hilt, a dull silver pommel, and a grip wrapped in dark, worn leather. Most householders hired their swords and had no need of wielding their own. In contrast, Arsenault's looked used.

"You jest with me. This is an idiom, a way of saying something unspeakable in your own language."

He laughed. "Is that what you Lierans call it? Maybe you can work on my mail shirt, then. That'll keep you busy a while."

"Your mail shirt?"

"I took an arrow down in Onzarro not long ago. Good thing the mail slowed it down, or I might not be here talking to you."

I frowned. I had spent a long time fighting off fevers after my arm was severed, and I often ran into situations in which I discovered that the world was not what I thought it was. "Are they fighting in Onzarro again?"

"Aren't they always fighting in Onzarro? I picked up a short-term contract with a spice merchant trying to protect his overland trade."

My frown deepened. "From the Prinze, you mean. They're trying to take that trade by sea."

Arsenault brushed something off his sleeve. "The Prinze are trying to take a great many trades these days," he said offhandedly. "I had a horse shot out from under me."

By the Prinze, I thought, and then—I realized I had heard the story.

"You weren't fighting for a spice merchant," I said. "You were fighting for the Camerani. Onzarro's ruling House. That's who the Prinze butted up against. And the Camerani had a gavaro—a captain—who led the charge against the flank and forced the Prinze marines back to their boats. The Prinze ships were manned by archers and the Camerani captain was hit but fought on, down the beach. That was *you*, wasn't it?"

"You seem remarkably well-informed for a serf girl."

"The bards," I said. "They give us our news, then Ilena embellishes it for the benefit of the other girls. I believe she said your black hair gleamed in the sun and you were wearing plate and silks, and when you fell, you said something like, *I will fight on if I have to run barefoot down this beach*."

There might have been a faint blush on his cheeks as he glanced up at me sideways. He cleared his throat. "'If I have to run barefoot down this beach'?"

"Ilena can tell a good story."

"I believe what I said was *Get this gods-cursed horse off me; I've been shot*. But it does sound better the way she tells it."

In spite of myself, my mouth tugged upward. "Did you fight on down the beach?"

He nodded. "That much is true. But I wasn't wearing plate— or mail, either. I got out of that shirt as quick as I could in case we were forced to fight in the water." He cocked his head. "I did manage to keep my boots on."

"So, you weren't fighting barefoot in the water?"

He smiled, wryly. "I try to avoid fighting barefoot in the water if I can. But it didn't come to that. The saboteurs holed the hulls. We sank three ships that day." Then he sighed. "It won't matter in the end, though. The Onzarrans can't hope to keep a monopoly on the spice trade. It's far easier and faster to get to Saien and Hamari by ship than it is by the Spice Road, especially now that the Rojornicki boyars are trying to murder each other. If the Prinze can round Thunder Cape, they'll have the trade from Dakkar, too."

I looked at him with new appreciation. So, he had fought the Prinze and he had a grasp of geography and politics. Perhaps my father did have plans.

Or perhaps... the Prinze weren't just invested in taking the spice trade. They nearly owned it anyway. Perhaps what they wanted now was silk. Silk to trade for spice.

Abruptly, the feeling I'd had, of having an easy conversation with someone, departed.

"I should get back to the combing house. The girls will be wanting water, and I'll need to sweep, too."

Arsenault kicked himself away from the wall. "Sunset tomorrow, Lady Kyrra. Don't forget."

"Sunset!"

"After your chores are done. Then you can do mine."

"But—"

"You'll need to pay back Margarithe, won't you?"

He stopped on his way to open the door and looked down at me. I swallowed the rest of my protests and made to walk past him. But he stopped me with a hand on my wrist. Just a brief touch, enough to make me look up at him again. "Here," he said, holding out the comb, "this is yours."

I didn't know what to say. So, I didn't say anything. I took the comb from him and fled.

⚜

ILENA DIDN'T LET MY HAIR GO UNREMARKED, OF COURSE. IT was the first thing she noticed when I walked into the combing house that night.

"Are you finally in mourning?" she asked, as she wove her own hair into a single broad plait over her shoulder. "Or did you go to the grooms for a trim?"

I pulled my new dress off over my head and stood in my chemise as I laid the guarnello down on my mattress and folded it slowly. "Careful," I said. "I might bite."

Ilena rolled her eyes and the girls around her tittered. But it was easy to see that the change in my appearance made them all nervous because they couldn't explain it. I couldn't explain it either. Maybe Arsenault had only cut my hair to make it easier to comb, but I felt as if part of my past had gone with it. Was I in mourning? What was mourning supposed to feel like? I just felt dry and beaten down inside, like the dirt of the courtyard.

"Where did you get that dress?" Ilena asked. "And the comb?"

I thought of Ilena and her stories of plate armor and silk and the reality of Arsenault standing in his small room with the blush on his cheeks and the worn sword at his hip, and I didn't know what to say. "A gavaro gave it to me."

"He'll want something out of you if he hasn't got it already," she said. "No man gives something for nothing."

CHAPTER 6

I THINK ARSENAULT LIKED TO SOLVE PROBLEMS, AND MY DAILY life presented an endless stream of them. We found no way for me to mend his mail shirt with only my clumsy left hand and a single pair of pliers. Instead, he set me to mending and making clothes. Once, as he was repairing the padded leather doublet he wore beneath his mail, I was struck dumb when he laid the needle down and picked it up again in his left hand.

I watched as he fumbled the long strip of leather through the needle's eye and secured it awkwardly in a slip knot with his thumb and index finger. Frowning in concentration, he began slowly to push the needle through the leather and padding in a row of crooked stitches. At the end, he flipped the shirt, attempted three or four times to make the knot, then lifted the shirt so he could pull the end of the thread tight with his teeth.

"I believe you'll just have to go slowly," he said, "until your left hand learns what you want it to do." Then he leaned back in his chair, kicked his feet up on the table, and switched hands to do the rest of his shirt.

By winter's end, my left arm had grown hard and wiry, and my left hand, while not nimble, was at least usable. But I was no closer to knowing why Arsenault wanted me for his chores. He never expected any of the favors a woman could give, even after I paid Margarithe back for the clothes, and he always asked, never demanded, if I would come back for more work.

I began to think that maybe he did like boys. But one morning very early, I came upon Margarithe herself leaving the barracks, winding her dark hair up with both hands as she went. Arsenault stood watching her, leaning against the doorframe with his hair down on his shoulders and a crooked smile on his face. I had no reason for being at the barracks that day, so I don't think Arsenault knew I was there. I felt strange afterward for wearing Margarithe's old dress, and I wondered what he saw when he looked at it.

But when I wasn't seething over my crooked stitches or growling at the odd damascene carvings in the blade of his sword, which ate polish but would not swallow it, we sat together in his room companionably enough. A small brazier on the table provided us heat while a candle lit up the winter dark, and I would work on a seam while he wrote in the little leather diary he kept. He wrote or sketched in it almost every day.

"What are you writing about?" I would ask him.

Sometimes, all I received was a brief, murmured "Nothing important," but other times, he would tell me.

"The silkhouse roof was sagging from the weight of the snow. We had to shovel it off."

"I'm not sure that's the kind of thing I would commemorate in my diary. It seems like just an ordinary day."

"It was an ordinary day. That's why I want to remember it."

At that time, my memory of *ordinary days* was both sweet and painful. I was growing more used to my new ordinary, but unlike Arsenault, I still wasn't sure I wanted to dwell on it.

"Do you keep track of all your ordinary days?" I asked.

"Most of them." He frowned, his mouth forming a troubled, thoughtful line. "My memory isn't always what it should be."

"Perhaps you're just growing older."

He had not a touch of gray in his beard, but I enjoyed prodding him with the difference in our ages. I had no idea how old he really was.

The stylus stopped scratching across the paper, then started up again. He spoke without looking up. "I imagine I'll only be fit to sit in here by the fire soon. I'll have to send you out to shovel snow instead."

I shook out the shirt I was mending and bent over, squinting to see my stitches in the dim light.

"We'll be a pair then, won't we? The infirm old man and his poor cripple, both up on the silkhouse roof, trying to figure out how to get back down."

Arsenault chuckled. "Shoveling snow reminds me of my home."

"And so, ten years from now, you hope to look back on it?"

"In ten years, I hope very much to be able to look back on it. It's not always guaranteed, you know—a future."

"I suppose that's true," I said. And then, because I didn't want to think about myself anymore, I added, "In your line of work."

He blew away the bone dust that fixed the metal from his stylus onto the page. "You know," he said, "I once shipped on an ice cutter. We fit a metal plow onto the prow of the ship and we would ram the ice to keep the harbor open as late as we could. Twenty-four men on the oars, and eventually, the ice would take over anyway and we'd just retire to the tavern to drink away the rest of the winter. Sometimes, I think about how useless that was, what else I could have been doing."

"I suppose you don't remember *that* winter very well," I said.

He chuckled again, but this time, it had an edge on it and he ran his free hand through his hair. "No," he said. "Nor, to be honest, the following spring. I much prefer keeping up your silkhouses. Yesterday, I fixed a hole in the pigsty."

"Are you a gavaro or a farmer, Arsenault?"

That got a laugh out of him, and finally he looked up and met my eyes. "Perhaps I'm a gavaro pretending to be a farmer."

And perhaps if our evenings had always been that way, he wouldn't have been such a mystery to me.

But then there was the dagger work.

I stared at the dagger stupidly for a long time after he gave it to me, wondering why he would do such a thing.

"Here, let me show you," he said, and came up behind me to adjust my grip on the hilt. It was just a brief touch of his hand on my hand, his arm along my arm, the scent of his black-tea soap too close, and his presence large and warm behind me. It shouldn't have affected me the way it did. But I tore away from him and dropped the dagger, my heart thudding.

He bent and picked it up off the floor.

"Kyrra." He moved as if to come closer, then stopped when I backed away. "I only want to show you something useful. As a trade. You've paid Margarithe back, and I'd like to keep you on. I can pay you coin for your work, but I know that you used to fence and I thought...maybe you'd rather have knowledge? Skill?"

He'd only known me a matter of months and yet he already knew me so well.

"But I'm not allowed blades," I said, trying weakly to force myself back into the position to which I'd been consigned by law. To try and be dutiful, as a penance to my parents.

"It's good to know how to use a knife. Even if you don't own it."

He made it sound so natural to take the hilt. So I did.

❦

ONE MORNING, HE CAME TO THE COMBING HOUSE EARLY TO get me. Most of the combergirls were gone, back with their families for the season, but I remained for Mistress Levin to shepherd. I washed the soot from the floor and walls of the big room every morning, toted in more wood for the fire, made tea in a cast iron kettle, and washed our cups when we were done. After I finished my chores, Arsenault would be knocking on the door, bending low to walk in the doorway and waiting for me to wrap myself in my not-warm-enough cloak spun from the leftover wool of our sheep.

The cold never seemed to bother Arsenault. Not like it bothered me. The ghost of my arm throbbed in the cold. Sometimes, I would wake at night, crying out, my left hand closed on the space that should have been my right forearm. I could do nothing for the pain, and bad nights made for bad days.

That morning, I came out of the combing house rubbing my stump, sloshing through the icy mud in my thin shoes. Patches of snow lay on the land like old scars, and the sun shone a weak and watery yellow in a white sky. The wind rattled tree branches and whipped my hair into my face. I hooked it behind my ears and looked up at Arsenault.

"Here," he said, pulling an ugly green-and-brown knitted scarf from inside his cloak. "Put this on."

"Why?" I asked.

"Because you look miserable. And we're going to Liera."

He put the scarf in my hand. I stared at it for a moment, slowing almost to a stop. He kept walking and I had to run to catch up. Mud splashed the hem of my dress and my worn brown cloak.

"I can't," I said.

"Can't what?"

"I can't put on this gods-cursed scarf myself, and I can't go to Liera."

Now he stopped. "Why not?"

"Because I lack an arm, and I think it's against my sentence. Serfs don't leave the estate."

"Only because they've no one to take them. You have someone to take you."

"The scarf is going to drag in the mud while I try to wrap it."

He took the scarf from my hand, tucked one end into my cloak, and wrapped it twice around my neck. "There," he said. "Now you have no reason not to go to Liera."

He started walking again without waiting for me.

"Arsenault!" I shouted, and jogged after him. The cursed man took one stride for my every three, and he was wearing a good black wool cloak that I had never seen before. His feet were shod in sturdy leather boots, too, while my shoes lacked proper soles and leaked.

"What?" he said when I came to walk beside him, breathing hard in the cold air.

"Stop that. I'll come to Liera with you if you tell me why you're taking me."

"I need to go to the market. I thought you would like to come."

I narrowed my eyes. "But why?"

"Because I thought you would like to come. Do I need another reason?"

"Yes. That's not a proper motive."

Arsenault's eyebrows rose. "We're not plotting an assassination, Kyrra."

"Why *me*, though? Surely, one of the other gavaros would be more useful to you—Verrin, perhaps."

"Would you rather I asked Verrin?"

No, I didn't. It suddenly came to me what Arsenault's offer meant—a chance to be away from the combing house, to go into the city without a retinue or a list of social calls or my mother. A chance to walk the docks, down on the side where ladies didn't go.

But it *was* Liera. I might see an old acquaintance, and beyond the fact that I wasn't sure I was allowed off my father's estate, I didn't think I could bear being recognized. Let them think the fevers killed me or left me senseless and mad. Let them think my father had put me on a boat to a cripple colony, where I lived in my white robes at the mercy of the sea, feeding myself on fish and shriveled oranges. Let them not think I had become a whore to a gavaro, that I was the woman the Prinze claimed me to be.

I gave Arsenault what I imagined to be a stern glance. "You know I'd do anything to get out of the combing house."

Arsenault smiled. "I thought so."

"No," I said. "You knew so." Struck by a sudden thought, I eyed him skeptically. "This is just another way to get me to do something I think I can't, isn't it?"

"I hadn't meant for it to be, but it does seem to be turning out that way, doesn't it?"

I glared at him. He gave me that maddening hook of a smile and quickened his stride, so I could no longer talk and keep up with him. We walked all the way to the stables like that, and when we got there, he stopped with one hand on the stable door's iron handle and reached inside his cloak with the other. He came out with a small leather pouch and handed it to me.

"Keep it safe," he said.

"What is it?" I wanted to open the bag and look for myself, but to do that, I would have to pry open the knotted string with my teeth. If it had only been Arsenault and me in his room, I wouldn't have hesitated, but here, where someone might see, I paused.

Arsenault leaned against the door and tugged the bag open for me, just enough to catch a glimpse of glinting metal, razor edges, and a collection of moons, stars, and spiky writing etched into the flats.

"Blades," I breathed. "Arsenault!"

"The rules against blades only extend to your father's lands, don't they?"

"No. Anywhere. Arsenault, if I'm caught with blades...they could take my other arm. Or my life."

He pulled the bag closed again. "Well, keep them out of sight, then. But they're not weapons."

"What are they then? They've an edge to them, don't they?"

"They're just blades. They're not meant for killing."

"And why are you giving them to me now?"

"I'll need them when we get to Liera. Keep them safe for now."

He twisted the handle, pushing the door open with a creak, and I had no choice but to tuck the bag into my pockets and follow. The smell of horses, straw, and liniment immediately assaulted me and, with it, my old life.

I hadn't been to the stables since I'd lain in the loft with Cassis, and I was unprepared for the tears it brought to my eyes. My woolen mitten scratched my face as I rubbed them away. When I looked up, Arsenault had already walked down the line of gray Ipanzers to where the tease mares were kept. The breeders used them to incite the passion of the Ipanzer stallions, to prepare them for breeding with an Ipanzer female. But the tease mares would never bear a foal of their own.

Householders didn't ride tease mares. They rode Ipanzers.

Serfs walked.

Arsenault draped his arms on the stall door at the end of the aisle and clucked softly at the plain bay mare who nudged his shoulder with her nose. She was the antithesis of the Ipanzer, the lithe gray warhorse that had borne generations of Lierans into battle. Ipanzers were fine animals, sleek, almost silver in the candlelit stables, with thin velvet black nostrils and small, trim ears that swiveled at the slightest sound.

Arsenault reached inside his cloak and drew out a carrot; the bay mare lipped it, then clamped down with her big yellow teeth and swallowed it in jerking bites. He scratched her forelock and stroked her behind the ears, and she whiffled his shirt with her nose.

"She's calm enough," he said. "I think you could handle her."

I stood there for a moment before his words sank in. "You expect me to ride?" I said. "On my own?"

"Unless you'd rather ride with me. But my weight's enough for any horse."

"Aren't we going into Liera for supplies? Shouldn't we be taking a cart?"

"The road's too muddy for a cart, and anyway, the supplies we need will fit into saddlebags. I thought you might appreciate riding on your own again. The groom assured me you enjoyed it once. He even said you were good at it."

The mare stretched her neck out to sniff me, too, and I backed away from her. "Which groom would that have been? The one who testified against me at the trial?"

Arsenault rubbed the bridge of his nose. "No," he said. "That groom has moved on to other pursuits, along with your chambermaid. Are you satisfied?"

I hadn't heard. I wondered where Bella had gone, if she'd married the groom after all. I sniffed and looked at the floor. "Nothing will bring my arm back."

"No. You're right." He swung the stall door open, and the hilt of his sword bumped against the stable wall. "Nothing will bring your arm back. And nothing will bring back your old life, either. It's time you got used to the idea."

"I don't need lectures from you," I said. "Don't you think I deal with the reality every day?"

He took down a blanket from a peg next to the mare and settled it on her back. "I think you mostly live in a world you've created, not the world as it is." A saddle hung next to the empty blanket peg and he took it down, placed it securely on the mare's back, and bent to tighten the girth around her belly. The mare stood calm. She whickered at Arsenault, and he patted her and straightened up.

His eyes were calm too but laced with a metal edge. It made me angry. "If my company irritates you so, why do you want me to come with you?"

"Get on the horse, Kyrra."

"You haven't bridled her yet. I can't—"

"Get on the horse."

I looked down. There was a stepstool at her right side. I gathered my skirts in my left hand and walked into the stall, stepped up on the stool, and let my skirts fall as I gripped the mare's mane. I tangled my fingers in tight. The mare stood for me, placid. It had been months since I'd mounted a horse. But I should be riding an Ipanzer, and all I had now was a little brown tease mare, who bowed her neck and waited for me.

A cripple's horse was what she was.

"I won't," I said to Arsenault. "She's not a real horse, just some stupid mare without any spirit, and you've only brought her here for me because she's easy. I won't have you feeling *sorry* for me."

"Kyrra, get on the thrice-cursed horse. You're not riding to war; you're just going to Liera. You've lost an arm, but you're still alive. Your life might even be more interesting."

"More interesting? What right do you have to say so to me?!"

"Perhaps none. But what prospects did you have before?" He leaned forward, facing me over the mare's neck. He never raised his voice, but it felt like the inexhaustible well of his patience might finally have run dry. "What did you look forward to? Being bred like an Ipanzer mare to produce more heirs for someone else's family? Conservatory afternoons full of negotiation with other women? Would you have gone gentle into that life? Or is that why you're here, because it didn't suit you?"

I was breathing hard. I still had my hand wrapped around the little mare's mane. Passion I had wanted, and passion I had gotten. But not the kind I thought.

"I can't guide the right rein," I said and cursed my voice for trembling. "I'll pull her left too much."

"Use your knees," he said.

Tears muddied my vision. "Damn you. You said this wasn't about doing something I thought I couldn't."

"It's not. You can still ride."

"Why do you want me to bring the blades?"

"Get on the horse, Kyrra."

I yanked the horse's mane as I stepped into the stirrup and swung myself up on her back, crying. I pulled up too hard and overbalanced and stretched out my right hand to cling to the mare's neck and lurched forward because I only had my stump and almost slid off the other side and onto the floor. Arsenault caught me by the shoulder and pushed me upright in the saddle.

"See?" I said. "I can't do it by myself!"

He didn't say anything, just took down the bridle and buckled it around the mare's nose, adjusting the bit in her mouth. I sat on her back, choking down the rest of my tears, feeling her breathe with my legs. Seeing the world from that height again.

Arsenault ducked under the mare's neck and came up beside me. He had a pair of boots in his hands. "The groom didn't give me these," he said, "but I don't think anyone will miss them."

I stared at him. His face wavered in my sight with the last of my tears.

He waited on me.

I levered my shoes off with the stirrup bars, and he put the boots on for me.

❧

We splashed down the path away from the stables, following the Aliente road past the bare gray mulberry groves and the fields where shorn stalks of wheat poked up through the snow. It wasn't long before my thighs hurt and the muscles of my left arm cramped from holding the rein too tightly. My mare kept slowing until I finally learned to relax. I had been a good rider once, and now I clutched at the rein like a girl who was just learning.

The Aliente road joined the old Eterean brick road on the other side of a stone bridge that spanned the northernmost tip of Kafrin Gorge, where the gap was narrowest. I had never liked crossing the Gorge. The limestone bridge was barely wide enough for a carriage. My ancestors had built it when they claimed the lands on the western side for the Aliente, but how they did so, no one knew. On a clear day, one could look down on the tops of the twisted laurels that grew in the rocky soil far below. People said it was built of magic, coaxed from the gray rock that lined the sides of the gorge. Whether or not there was magic involved, Kafrin Gorge was an eerie place in the snow. In the mist created by the warming of the day, the Gorge seemed bottomless, the bridge built to span the clouds.

It left me dizzy with vertigo. I wanted to close my eyes but didn't dare. I always had trouble with vertigo, crossing this bridge. But now it was worse, even with Arsenault riding his black gelding next to me, so close I could touch the sleeve of his cloak if I wanted to.

He let his fingers skim the stone rail as the horses plodded on. It made me sick. "Don't," I said.

Fog obscured his expression. I leaned over my mare's neck so I could be close to something real.

"Hang on, Kyrra," Arsenault said softly. His shoulders twitched as if he might move his arm. "It's an old place, isn't it?"

"The gavaros say it's full of ghosts. Probably from the fires."

He looked over the edge. "I don't think the fires created all the ghosts."

I wondered what he meant, but the wind gusted and I clung to the mare's neck. Out of the corner of my eye I saw a black blur. Then his hand was at my shoulder, steadying me.

"I think I'm going to be sick," I said.

"Wait till we're over the bridge."

I tried to laugh, because I thought it was a joke. But there was no amusement on his face. He held on to my shoulder the rest of the way across.

Then we were on the other side and he let go. His black-gloved hand disappeared in the wind-tossed mane of his horse.

He didn't say anything, but as my head cleared and my stomach settled, I noticed the worry lines fanning from the corners of his eyes. He stared straight ahead and didn't speak again until we were well away from the bridge.

WE DIDN'T ARRIVE IN THE CITY UNTIL AFTER NIGHTFALL. Snow drifted over the old Eterean road in places, and that slowed us down. But it was more dangerous to sleep by the road than to press on into the city. By the time we rode beneath Liera's carved gates, my stomach was grumbling and I was stiff, sore, and exhausted, almost dozing in the saddle.

We came in the Raptor Gate, which led directly to the Talos. The Houses held the Talos in common, and as such, it had developed its own sort of market, a place where the contracts of gavaros were bought, sold, and traded like the rights to grazing land. The steady metallic *clop* of the horses' hooves as we made our way down the brick street joined the general din, and I could do nothing but look around in amazement.

Men sat bundled against the cold under billowing, painted canvas pavilions and watched us pass. They wore House colors, most of them, but you could tell the householders from the gavaros because scribes sat beside the householders, scribbling furiously. Brokers at tables hawked gavaros like livestock. The gavaros didn't have to be present, but some of them were— sitting around small bonfires in the shelter of the mud-brick buildings that lined the street, roasting chunks of lamb and onion on wooden skewers, playing cards and drinking. They seemed more intent on their card games than they did on the tables.

The smell of sizzling fat made my mouth water. "Will we get something hot to eat, Arsenault? Are we going to find an inn?"

"I know someone. He'll put us up."

"Is it safe?" I asked.

"Depends on what you mean by *safe*."

I watched the men sitting beside the buildings, playing cards. Scabbard tips stuck out beneath the hems of cloaks, dragging the ground as they leaned forward to play a hand. One man sat on a rickety wooden chair with his back to the wall of the barracks, a brown glass bottle in one gloved hand, watching me. He toasted me with the bottle, and I turned quickly away, back to Arsenault.

"Surely, we won't be getting our supplies here."

"Best not to talk about it now," he said, nudging his horse past a group of gavaros who stood in the road, ringing a householder clad in a sky-blue cloak. Prinze colors. I ducked low on my horse. She tossed her head at my sudden movement and bumped Arsenault's horse with her haunches. I couldn't help looking backward, my heart thumping, sure it was Cassis.

"It's not who you think it is," Arsenault said in a low voice, leaning over so I could hear him. I looked up at him in surprise. He'd flipped his hood up.

"I know that," I said hotly, and sat up straighter. I wanted to flip my own hood up; my ears were cold and burning at the same time. But I didn't trust my sense of balance yet and couldn't let go of the rein.

My mare edged closer to his gelding, and my leg brushed his. I pulled her away. "Why would it be? There isn't any reason Cassis would be down here, in the dark."

Arsenault shrugged, but he looked troubled. "No," he said. "You're right."

"*Is* there a reason he would be?"

"Your blades would do you little good in that case," Arsenault said.

My cheeks flamed, and I was glad of the cold that had already raised a flush in them. "I wasn't thinking of that."

"Perhaps not now," he said, and turned his horse toward a narrow alleyway that branched off the main road.

I squeezed my knees around my mare's sides, wincing at the pain it caused me, and she followed him. The alley disappeared between two cracked brown brick buildings.

"Arsenault," I said, "where are we going?"

It was dark in the alley. My heart beat faster. There wasn't room for me to ride beside Arsenault, so I had to stay in back of him.

Then he pulled his sword. I knew it from the low hiss it made as it came free of the scabbard, and the flickering orange light from the mouth of the alley reflected in its blade.

"Arsenault?" I said. I wanted to shout and to whisper at the same time. My voice came out as a combination of the two, a loud, urgent whisper that immediately struck me as cowardly. I cursed myself for it, but when he didn't answer, I called again, louder, "Arsenault!"

A shadow moved ahead of us, a rumpled shape I had taken to be a pile of broken furniture. It straightened up into the form of a tall man and stepped off the crooked staircase into the alley in front of Arsenault. I pulled my horse's rein so tightly that I bowed her head and she whinnied at me in distress.

"It's you," the shadow said, squinting up at Arsenault from the folds of a cloak. I couldn't see his face, but he had a deep voice with an accent I couldn't place. Not Eterean. "And you've brought me someone."

"I told you I would," Arsenault said.

"The girl?"

Arsenault nodded, a movement of the darkness.

"Arsenault?" I said. "Who is this? Have you taken me here to give me up?" I pulled the reins so tight the mare danced backward, hooves ringing on the stone.

"She doesn't trust you, eh?" the man said.

Arsenault sighed. "No," he said. "Jon's a friend of mine. We'll stay with him."

"You meet your friends in dark alleys? With your sword drawn?"

Arsenault twisted his sword. The light bounced off it. "It's just that my sword is rather distinctive." The odd carvings on the blade glowed for a moment much too brightly to be lit by the lamps on the street at my back. I looked around wildly for the source of the light, sure that someone else had stepped into the alley with a lantern, but there was no else there. The light winked out when he sheathed it, and he swung his right leg over his horse's back to dismount. The saddle creaked and his bootheels crunched in gravel and broken glass when his feet hit the ground.

The other man grunted. "Best you put that away. There's Prinze about tonight."

"I saw that," Arsenault said grimly. Then he looked up at me. "Come on, Kyrra. We're staying here."

"I don't believe you. Why would we stay with a man you meet in an alley?"

The man laughed, a low laugh that rumbled. "A bit picky for a serf girl, aren't you?"

"I'm not—" I began, then realized I was. I shut my mouth.

"I won't let anything happen to you," Arsenault said.

I made an exasperated noise and traded the rein for the horse's mane. I clutched it for a moment and made a point of not looking at the ground. Arsenault made no move to help me, but eventually, after a great deal of work and almost overbalancing, I finally stood on the ground.

I faced Arsenault. "You just stand there."

"You didn't need my help," he said.

I gritted my teeth and resolved not to say anything. Instead, I raised my hood. The man who had looked like a heap of castoffs stood before me now, tall and broad, with a sword hilt jutting out the front of his cloak. He grinned at me, a flash of white teeth in a face as dark as the cloak he wore, then inclined his head, a subtle movement that was hard to see. "I welcome you to my house," he said. "It's not much, but..." He spread his hands. "...what can one do?"

Inside, the building was surprisingly warm and well lit. A fire blazed in a mud-brick fireplace, and clean-burning beeswax candles littered the dark wood mantel. Strings of dried garlic hung on iron hooks on either side of the mantel, and a black kettle hung over the fire. Whatever simmered inside lent the room a spicy, foreign aroma.

The only furniture in the room was a low table made of wood so dark, it looked like cast iron. It sat on a tasseled red-and-orange carpet that covered almost the entire floor, which was made of worn wood plank. Empty crockery plates and wooden cups were arranged on the table, and large pillows lay scattered around it. On one of these pillows reclined a man in Qalfan robes the color of old ivory. He'd pulled the bottom of his urqa down below his mouth and was smoking a polished wood pipe. When I walked in, his eyes narrowed.

"I thought you were bringing someone for me to read," he said.

"I did," Arsenault said.

"It's a girl," the Qalfan replied.

I wanted to sigh. Wasn't it obvious I was a woman? I wondered why these men had to state it over and over.

"I've already been through that." Jon's voice boomed in the small space as he shrugged out of his cloak and unwound a thick black scarf from around his neck. I was already starting to sweat, and the smell of the food on the fire pained my stomach, but I didn't want to take off my cloak. I wanted Arsenault to say he'd made a mistake, that we were going to stay at an inn closer to the markets, like I expected we would when I'd gotten on the horse.

Four stacks of leaf-wrapped blocks were piled against the wall behind the Qalfan, and I didn't want to know what they contained. I didn't want to know what the Qalfan was smoking in his pipe. Cassis had told me stories of what the Qalfans unloaded from their holds onto Lieran docks after they unloaded the barrels of pickled figs, the cedar logs, the ivory tusks that lined the stalls of Caprian markets. Piles of round metal tins full of crushed black poppy seeds, crackly brown sweetweed, and kacin, the dusty white powder made from the dried berries of a plant that grew in the jungles of Dakkar.

Cassis told me he'd tried it once. He said it felt like paradise but it burned his lungs and his nose, and the next morning, he'd woken with a headache far worse than any caused by wine.

Arsenault began taking off his cloak. When he saw me standing immobile in the center of the room, he stopped.

"Kyrra. Jon has offered us his house."

Jon stood leaning against the mantel, watching me. He smiled again, without showing his teeth this time, and took a pipe out of his pocket, a metal tin from his other pocket. With one large finger he tapped a fine green-black powder into the bowl of the pipe, then replaced the tin in his pocket and reached up for something on the mantel, which he swiped across the wood.

Whatever it was—a yellow wood stick—its end suddenly burst into flame. I stepped backward in alarm, and Jon chuckled as he touched the flame to his pipe and shook out the stick. Then he threw it into the fire, and the fire immediately flared yellow.

"By all the gods," I said.

Arsenault hung his cloak on a hook that jutted out from the wall by the door. "A match, Kyrra. The Saien make them. It's only pine soaked in sulfur."

Jon puffed on his pipe. "Lierans," he said.

"I've never seen one before."

"They've only started to come into the markets." The Qalfan tapped his ashes into a white ceramic bowl. He smiled slightly, most of his face visible in the gap between the layers of his urqa. "It's sweetweed," he said. "From the Yrian province of Greater Qalfa."

"In the blocks?" I asked.

"In my pipe." His expression was flat.

"Take off your cloak and scarf, Kyrra," Arsenault said.

I paused for a moment while all three men looked at me. Slowly, I unwound the scarf from around my neck. I walked to the hook beside the one that held Arsenault's cloak, and I hung it up while the men watched my back. Then, clumsily, I unfastened the rope loops of my cloak. My thumb slipped many times on the wooden toggles, and I was grateful that the men could only see my back. I shrugged out of the cloak and caught it with my left hand before it fell to the floor.

I didn't want to turn around. I knew they were all looking at the severed stump of my right arm. Even Arsenault.

"Ah," the Qalfan said. "I see now why you bring her to us."

I looked over my shoulder. Arsenault, at least, seemed troubled. But Jon and the Qalfan continued to watch me with unconcealed curiosity.

"Now you know why I'm a serf," I said to Jon as I hung up the cloak, and he hitched an eyebrow and laid his pipe in a shallow clay bowl on the mantel.

"The smell of that food," he said, "is making me hungry."

WE ATE FOR A LONG TIME. THERE WAS NOT ONLY THE STEW IN the pot but baked yams and flatbread from the ashes, and pickled figs and dates and candied fruit in tins. The stew was so spicy, it made my eyes water, and full of ingredients I didn't recognize. We ate it over chickpeas and scooped it up with chunks of bread. The stew made me thirsty and I drank too much of the sweet wine Jon served with it. By the time the meal was over, I was dizzy.

The men spoke little during the meal, mostly about shipping and the gavaro market, and how Arsenault's commission with my father went. He glanced at me while he talked about it, but I made a point of concentrating on my food. No one asked me any questions, and I said nothing while I ate. When we finished, Arsenault brought a bucket of water from the cistern and we all washed our own bowls. Then the Qalfan and Jon retired with their pipes, and Jon offered one to Arsenault, and he took it and the sweetweed and lay back on the pillow next to mine, puffing smoke in lazy clouds at the ceiling.

"Why don't you take a look at her now," Arsenault said, smoking. "We'll be spending tomorrow in the market."

"Are you kidnapping me?" I asked. My tongue felt thick. The warmth of the wine was pleasant. The thought of being kidnapped wasn't that alarming.

Arsenault laughed. "Why would I need to kidnap you? You came on your own."

"Because you told me you wanted my company. But I was right, wasn't I? You did have another motive."

"Hah," Jon said. "Smart girl." He got up and walked to the wall where the bricks were stacked and began unwrapping one. The leaves crackled. He discarded the rope and the wrapping on the floor and hefted the white, pressed rectangle in one large hand. Then he peeled off a small strip of the compacted powder with his knife and tossed it in the fire. The fire popped. "Have to sell that cheaper," he said.

I looked at Arsenault. "Only the Prinze sell kacin."

"True," he said, watching the smoke drift up toward the rafters.

He'd brought me to a den of smugglers.

I struggled to get up, but my legs felt rubbery. The pillows were too deep. I scrabbled at the table, but my fingers kept slipping. The room began to spin, a whirl of orange and red like the spirals on the rug.

Words fell out of my mouth. "I don't know why you've brought me here," I said. "I trusted you, Arsenault, may all the gods damn you."

There must have been kacin in the wine. And now the room was full of kacin smoke.

My nose burned and ran. I wiped it with my sleeve. My eyes started to burn, too.

"Arsenault!"

I felt like I was falling, but I was still in the pillow, staring at the ceiling. I thought I saw Arsenault get up beside me.

Then the world drained away, like blood flowing from a wound. I grasped for it but it ran through my fingers, and the night flowed on like a dream.

"If she brought blades," the Qalfan said, "I should see them."

"Give him the blades, Kyrra."

Arsenault's voice. Arsenault's face was all I could see as he bent over me. His scar stood out like a lightning strike. I reached up to trace it.

He pushed my hand back down. "Kyrra, the blades."

I cursed him. Garbled words came out of my mouth. My wrist flopped but I managed to hike it under my skirts and retrieve the leather bag from my pocket. Cold air brushed my legs and there was a tug and then my skirts were down again.

Arsenault handed the bag to the Qalfan, who dumped the blades out all over the floor.

"Those are mine!" I shouted. "Mine!"

"Huh," Jon said. "She fights, doesn't she?"

As if I were a fish on a line. "I'm not a fish!" I yelled at him.

"A swordfish," Arsenault grunted. "Maybe."

The Qalfan ripped open the sleeve of my stump and poked me with one of the blades.

I screamed. Fire rippled up my severed arm, outlining the ghost of it in red and blue curls of light like flames.

The Qalfan dragged the tip of one of my blades down the glowing length of it, and I started to cry.

"She holds on to it still," he said.

"I know," Arsenault replied, as if he was breathing hard.

"Then why do you want me? You can see for yourself and there's nothing I can do."

"Nothing at all? Jon said you're a surgeon. That you've grafted skin."

"Immediately after the severing. And nothing as big as an arm."

"But with the blades."

The Qalfan spat. "Foreign magic. Inferior. Nothing will bring back an arm."

He got up and walked away. I saw him go, passing out of the room the way a reflection disappears when the angle of the light changes. Everything in the room shimmered. Perhaps I was the one in the mirror, looking out.

"Arsenault?" I said, struggling to get up. "He'd put a dead girl's arm on me?"

They said it was half-magic, what Qalfan doctors did, that they would sometimes slice the noses off corpses and attach them to the faces of men whose faces had been mutilated in battle. The price for that was carrying the corpse's ghost on your back for the rest of your life.

I carried one ghost with me already. I didn't need any more.

Arsenault pushed me back down. "Hush, Kyrra."

"Arsenault, it's my arm!"

"Hush. It's all right."

"He can't give me my arm back? There was a chance?"

"No chance," the Qalfan said from somewhere I couldn't see him. "No chance at all."

"You said he was a chirurgeon, Jon. I've *seen* what Qalfan doctors do and so have you. She's kept the line of her arm; you see it too, don't you?"

"So do you, Arsenault. And you see those blades on the floor as well?"

"A dead girl's arm, Arsenault!" I shouted, clutching him by the collar. "Was there a chance?"

"Gods," Arsenault said. "Kyrra, lay back." He pushed me down again and let go of me, then rocked back on his haunches.

"I see the blades," he said. "I've seen them fall that way before."

"Darkness in all four quarters. How often does that happen?"

"You can't take action based on that kind of fuzzy information. You don't know if the cast was for past or present or future."

I heard Jon sigh. "We've argued philosophy before, my friend."

"She hates the Prinze."

"It was a stretch of an idea. She'll have to remain armless. Perhaps you're only trying to exonerate yourself, eh?"

"I've given up on that, Jon. I'm just trying to do my job."

"Going beyond the call of duty, as usual. I wonder why?"

I tried to speak. I looked up at them with my eyes wide open. But I had gone past words. All that passed my lips was a string of meaningless sounds—*uh uh uh*—like a woman who has lost her tongue instead of her arm. I flailed out, and Arsenault caught my arm and pressed it into the pillow. He stared at me for a moment, Jon frowning over his shoulder, and then he sniffed and wiped his nose with his sleeve.

"Damn kacin. Muddles me."

"One day, it's not going to muddle you so much that your gods can't find you, you know."

Arsenault smiled—a cold smile, bleak. I thought it was a trick of my eyes. "We'll hope it's not this lifetime. How far do you trust your chirurgeon?"

"About as far as the door."

"He hasn't left yet, has he?"

"I hired a man to take care of it."

"You trust your man?"

"He needs something from me. The chirurgeon doesn't."

I stared upward in the glassy silence, unable to move. I could have been dead. I wondered if they would know it if I died.

"There must be other ways," Arsenault said. "Beyond grafting on a new arm."

Jon rose, knees creaking. "I'm sure there are. I'll leave it to you to decide whether or not to take the chance. We've more important things to worry about."

Arsenault remained squatting beside me, hands clasped

between his knees. His eyes were red. He reached up to rub his right one, the one next to his scar, then he dropped his hand and looked at me.

"Right," he said softly, and rose. He pulled my cloak off its peg and covered me with it. He got his and covered me with that one, too. Then he brushed a strand of hair from my face and tucked it behind my ear.

I could only stare at the ceiling for a long time after he left, the stump of my right arm twitching at my side.

※

IN THE MORNING, IT WAS VERY COLD. I WOKE TO THE CREAK and thud of boots on the plank floor. There were no windows, so the light couldn't cut into my eyes, and that was good. Everything else did. The whole world was sharper, as if it had grown edges. I put a hand to my brow and squinted at Arsenault standing over me holding a steaming crockery cup.

"Good morning," he said.

I ripped off the cloaks and lurched to my feet. "Good morning? Why is it a good morning? You brought me here so that a Qalfan necromancer could make a ghost of me and now it's morning and I still have only one arm? There is nothing good about this morning!"

My stomach started rolling before I finished yelling at him. I clutched my mouth and closed my eyes.

Arsenault said nothing.

"I'm going to retch."

"Do it in the pot, then," he said, and I heard a clang. When I opened my eyes, a dull tin chamber pot sat next to my foot.

"Bastard." Then my stomach clenched and I fell on my knees and vomited up my entire dinner from the night before.

After that I shook, and Arsenault made me leave with him for the market anyway. On our way out, we passed the remains of the chirurgeon and I retched again, all over the steps.

He was dead in the street, leaned up against the wall of the house with a bottle in his hand. His urqa hung down below his chin and was stained with blood. He smelled, even in the cold. Like meat gone bad after slaughter. The blood had dried black all down his robes.

Arsenault cursed. He walked over to the Qalfan and pulled up his urqa to hide his face. Something shuffled beside him like a rat, but Arsenault lurched to the side and pulled his sword.

A small lean-to built of scrap wood huddled against the other side of the alley. It looked like a pile of sticks, but a man came out of it. He wore a black cloak pulled close around him, and a black scarf pulled up over his chin and the bottoms of his ears, but his head was uncovered. His hair was so black it looked wet, blue-black as raven feathers, and he had high brows that arched over dark eyes. He wore black gloves and black boots. When he saw me watching him, he grinned, the corner of his mouth pulling up, crooked and cynical, above the frayed edges of his scarf. In that moment, the fact that he wore black seemed not so much a harbinger of death as a dangerous sense of irony.

"You knew him, did you?" he said to Arsenault. "Pity. I'm sure his knowledge was considerable."

"Did you do this?" Arsenault said.

The man tilted his head and looked at him. "All I'm willing to say is Jon shorted me on my supply. Tell him to give me the rest of what he owes me, and I'll convince the Qalfan gentleman to take his leave elsewhere. Otherwise, he's got a new job as your doorman."

He sniffed and rubbed his nose with his sleeve. His dark eyes were glazed.

"Jon paid you what he owed you," Arsenault said. His face took on a hard look I hadn't seen before—a careful, masked look that was different from the expression he gave me when he didn't want to answer a question. Arsenault had his hand on his sword, but the other man stood before him, picking at his teeth with a wooden stick as if he was oblivious to the fact that Arsenault was ready to cut him down where he stood.

"I don't think you'll draw your sword right here in the street, will you? I want to talk to Jon."

"Kyrra," Arsenault said, without looking away from the man, "go back inside."

I hesitated, and Arsenault glanced at me quickly, a rapid sideways movement of his eyes. "Kyrra."

I grabbed up my skirts and hurried behind him, clattered up the steps and inside. The door slammed after me, but I could hear their muffled voices.

The other man laughed. "Obedient wench, isn't she?"

"She's no business of yours."

I bent and pushed the door open just enough to allow me a tiny sliver of a view, in time to see Arsenault step forward into the other man's space, his hand on the hilt of his sword and the blade partially visible above the edge of the scabbard. "You'll dispose of the body like you were asked, or you'll join him."

People will say it's a cold feeling, when you realize the danger in those you thought you knew, but it wasn't for me. Instead, it was just a moment of feeling everything around me, all the way through—my shaking hands, the queasiness in my stomach, the scaly frost on the inside of the door, the rickety wood that separated me from two men complicit in a murder.

I knew the sword at Arsenault's side wasn't for show, but for some reason violence seemed much tidier in stories.

The man smiled wide at Arsenault and put up his hands. "I'll dispose of the body if that's what you want. But I'll be talking to Jon."

Arsenault jammed his sword back into its scabbard and stepped away. "You'll dispose of the body," he said, then when the other man didn't move, he added, "Now."

A flicker of heat flared in the man's expression. "You're mad," he said. "With all the crowds in the Talos." But he dragged the chirurgeon away from the wall all the same.

Arsenault shrugged. "It should have been taken care of under cover of darkness."

The man wiped his nose again. "And what would Geoffre di Prinze say if he found out there was a house of sorcerers in this street?"

"In this street?" Arsenault said, looking around. "I don't see one in this street."

The man shrugged, his hand on the dead Qalfan's shoulders. "I hear Cassis di Prinze may be interested in buying my contract. As he's interested in buying the contracts of very many gavaros these days, particularly ones from…shall we say, more foreign shores? Shores that may dabble a bit?"

Arsenault scowled. "And where would you be from?"

"Me?" The man waved his hand. "I'm Amoran. Fallen from the enemy's hands, as it were. But you know, we Amorans have a greater talent at divination."

"You lied, then," Arsenault said.

"You know what the Talos is like. Its talons rip everybody sooner or later. I'd sooner they ripped the Prinze." He grinned, then sobered abruptly. The change was complete; it was as if the kacin-addled blackmailer had fled, leaving something metal in its place. This man had the look of a gavaro. "Cassis di Prinze is being forced into something he's very little knowledge of. I've seen what goes on in your house. It's something Geoffre would pay well to learn."

"Is it, now?"

"And may the gods help all of us if he does. You know that as well as I. I'd rather not have my contract bought by Cassis di Prinze."

Arsenault shifted so I couldn't see his face. Instead, all I saw was the wind snatching at his braid, his cloak snapping against his calves, the other man's face over his shoulder. "And why is that?"

"Because Geoffre *knows* things. Things a man would sooner not tell him. I've my secrets like any man, only I'd rather keep them, eh? And you...well, you down here in the Talos...maybe it won't matter that I'm dragging a dead Qalfan chirurgeon out into the street on the same day the Prinze patrol is in town."

"You're a man who likes to have it both ways, aren't you? Are you trying to tell me that you'll tattle to Geoffre or that you foresee a time when Geoffre will overstep his bounds and step on the backs of people like you?"

The man laughed. "Oh, I'm sure he'd step on me. I know my place."

"Something I'm happy to hear, you can be assured."

The man's eyes narrowed. "Come to think of it...I might have seen you around once or twice. As an accompaniment to Devid?"

Arsenault cocked his head. "You might have seen me in the same establishment. Liera can be a small city."

"And now I wonder where your commission is. Was that girl missing an arm"

Arsenault moved so quickly, I wasn't prepared for it. All in an instant, he clenched the man's shirt in his fist and shoved him sprawling into the sticks of the lean-to, which collapsed in a clatter against the stone street. Arsenault pulled his sword, but so did the man; my heart pounded and I pressed against the door.

Steel hissed and clanged. The swords tied up, then slid free of each other, and in the end, Arsenault stood with his foot on the other man's chest, the tip of his blade hidden inside the man's scarf, resting at the hollow of his throat.

The man's hands were empty. He stared up at Arsenault for a long moment. Then that grin split his face again and he chuckled weakly.

"Pardon," he said. "I didn't know she was yours."

"You'll not threaten her," he said. "That's all. I can be patient with you over the Qalfan, but I won't tolerate threats to her."

"I shall treat her as carefully as if she were my sister."

Arsenault leaned forward, putting more pressure on the blade and more weight on his foot.

The man on the ground lifted his open hands. "No threats!" he gasped. "You've made your point. Get me a commission away from the Prinze and I'll take care of your Qalfan and leave Jon's cheating be. That's all I ask. And Geoffre will never find out what goes on in that house."

Arsenault stepped back and sheathed his sword. "I'll talk to Jon," he said. "Now get this body out of here before it starts to smell."

He turned around the way a wolf might when he's shown himself leader of his pack. I bit my lip, sure the other man would go for his sword, but instead, he sat up and hung his head between his knees for a moment, then collected his sword, sheathed it, and rose to drag the body across the paving stones.

"My name is Lobardin," he said, "and I expect you will talk to Jon."

Arsenault made a noise that could have meant anything, and put his foot on the first step. It shuddered beneath his weight.

I pulled away from the door, looking around the dim room in fright. I ran toward the far wall, my boots pounding on the wood floor, but there was nowhere to go. When Arsenault opened the door, it threw a little more light into the room, but then the door slammed and I was in the dark again, staring at Arsenault.

He stopped just in front of the door as if he were surprised. "Kyrra?"

"You were going to kill him," I said. "You and Jon—you had that Qalfan killed. You're a smuggler."

He shook his head. "No."

"That gavaro *murdered* a man for a handful of kacin!"

The stucco nubs of the wall pressed into my back. I put my palm against them, as if I might feel my way to freedom. But whenever I sought freedom, it seemed to end up like this—just a more dangerous trap.

Arsenault frowned. "He'd already rendered service to the Prinze. Would you let him go to tell what he knew?

His words left a bitter taste in my mouth. I hesitated. "What did the gavaro mean, about Cassis buying contracts? And Geoffre? What do you have to do with that?"

With a troubled glance at the door, Arsenault said, "As little as possible. Geoffre has become obsessed with magic. We keep ourselves to ourselves here in the Talos. I didn't want to see you compromised."

"*Compromised*. What do you mean by that, Arsenault? If Geoffre found out I was violating my sentence, I'd be dead!"

He looked troubled but he didn't say anything.

"I heard what you and Jon talked about last night. I saw my arm. Were you going to let the Qalfan mate a dead girl's arm with my stump?"

He moistened his lips. "It wasn't supposed to be a dead girl's arm."

I laughed, more in horror than anything else. "What—the arm of a live girl, then? Another girl like me?"

"It was supposed to be *your* arm. Your mother had it embalmed using Qalfan techniques. If it was done properly, your arm is still whole and untouched. They sealed it in a cedar coffer, didn't they?"

None of his words made sense. When I opened my mouth to ask him what he meant, all that came out was more laughter like a flock of frightened starlings.

"You jest with me."

He sighed. "It doesn't matter. The Qalfan said it couldn't be done."

"Do you have my arm here?"

He laughed in surprise. "That would be a little...morbid, wouldn't it? To carry an arm all the way to Liera?"

"You must have planned to do so some day."

That sobered him. "I suppose I did."

"How did you find out what my mother did with my arm?"

"I asked her."

"And she didn't think it odd?"

"She told me anyway."

"What are you going to do about that gavaro? Lobardin?"

"Depends on what Lobardin does. It'll probably be Jon's decision, anyway."

"Who is Jon? Who does he work for?"

Arsenault looked away from me, ran a hand through his hair, and scratched his beard before he answered.

"Jon is...Jon. He's a Dakkaran merchant. He has connections to a number of people and he's here to maximize his family's interests. That's probably all you need to know."

It wasn't all I *wanted* to know, but I knew it was probably all I was going to get out of him. I could draw a few more lines on that sketch myself. Since the Prinze were trying to muscle the Onzarrans off their trade monopoly with Dakkar, it made sense that Jon would step light around them, and I could erase Arsenault's word *merchant* and pen in *smuggler* well enough.

"You should have told me what you were doing."

"If you'd agreed ahead of time, it would have been against your sentence. But if I brought you down here unsuspecting...I thought there might have been a chance." The smile faltered. "Well. I suppose I'd understand if you didn't believe me."

I thought about it. I watched him standing there with his hands hitched on his swordbelt, a shaft of sudden light cutting a blade across the wood floor at his feet, and I wondered why he had put a sword to that gavaro's throat only when the gavaro mentioned me.

Finally, I said, "You could have killed me before now. Many times. You could have handed me over last night. I might be in the hold of a slaver right now, bound for Dakkar. Or the Sugar Islands."

His face transformed. It was the first time I'd ever seen him wear an expression he didn't try to school. He looked like I'd wounded him. But angry, too. "I'd never sell you south. I'd never sell anyone south. Do you think so little of me?"

"I don't know what to think of you, Arsenault. Granted that you were trying to keep me innocent of intent, but what was I supposed to do if the Qalfan said the arm would work? And I returned to my father's estate with two arms? Do you think the Prinze would believe I had nothing to do with it?"

He made a noise, a wordless response to what I'd just said. Then he walked over to the fire and kicked ashes over it. It died slowly, a mass of glowing red embers stubbornly clinging to life.

"Will you come with me to the market, at least?"

"If I decided to stay here for the day, would I be safe? Would you give me a knife?"

His jaw twitched. He scuffed more ashes onto the fire with the toe of his boot. A piece of glowing charcoal spilled out onto the bricks, and he kicked that back in, too. "Yes," he said. "You'd be safe."

"Would you let me have a knife?"

Now his jaw clenched. He stood looking at me for such a long time that I got a sinking feeling in my stomach. *No*, I thought, *this is as far as my freedom goes. I am just a chunk of metal to him, to be sculpted as he wishes.* The realization tasted bad in my mouth. I didn't know why I'd expected any different. Maybe I'd just hoped he would be different.

But then he bent and slipped his fingers into the upper of his boot. When he straightened, he held a dagger. It was a thin, wicked-looking blade with a polished wood handle that matched the leather.

He flipped it over in his hand so I could take the hilt.

"I don't need you in the market," he said. "But if you came, I might enjoy the company."

CHAPTER 7

THE DAY MARKET WAS KNOWN FOR ITS FOOD, BUT I WAS TOO queasy from the kacin to eat. Instead, we meandered through the textile section on our way to Artisans' Row. We walked with our hoods up in the chill morning air, so I felt safe, and Arsenault even gave me his arm—his right instead of his left—like a gentleman. It felt strange to be wandering the market with him. To be touching him. His arm, clothed in a sturdy wool shirt, was hard and warm beneath my hand, and his muscles flexed as we walked. Sometimes, my shoulder bumped into his bicep and he would look down at me and an uncertain smile touched the corner of his mouth, and then he would look up again and the air clouded frosty with his breath.

The clenched-up feeling of earlier had leaked out of me enough that when I saw a stall selling guarnellos, I slid away from him and lingered to admire them.

He leaned back against a barrel of sand holding one of the tent poles firm against the wind.

"The blue one," he said.

"What do you mean, the blue one?"

"That's the one you should buy."

I laughed. "Arsenault, I don't have even a cato. How am I supposed to buy it?"

"Well, it's the new moon, so your father paid his gavaros. And they paid me for your sewing. I have the coin with me."

"Pay? I'm a serf. The Householder gives us food and shelter; we give him our work in exchange. There's no pay involved."

"A nobleman's view of the situation if I've ever heard it."

I bristled, clenching the fabric of a pale green guarnello in my fist. "What is that supposed to mean?"

He straightened up again, hooking his thumbs in his swordbelt. "Look. Kyrra. I've been paying you with daggerwork, but the other men are paying you for your work, too. You're not a slave."

"I didn't think I was."

His shoulders sagged. In relief? Had he really been so worried about the situation? "Good," he said. "I'd hoped you stayed by choice."

"That's important to you, isn't it?"

"Of course it is. Why wouldn't it be?"

I shrugged, fingering the woolen fabric of the guarnello. Not so long before, I would barely have given it a passing glance. But now...it seemed like an impossible luxury, to have two dresses. And to be able to buy one myself?

"It's not important to all men," I said. "Nor to you yesterday."

He flinched and looked around. The shopkeep sat far back from the counter with a dress in her hands, stitching with her head down but still keeping an eye on us.

He curled his hand around a span of scaffolding.

"It was still important to me," he said. "I just charged past it. Jon says that sometimes I have a tendency to...overstep a situation."

"Overstep?"

He dropped his hand. "Go beyond what a situation actually seems to require? For good or ill. It's a failing. I've tried to root it out. I built tables for a while. Didn't think I could get into trouble building tables."

I couldn't tell if he was being earnest or just trying to lighten the conversation, but the image startled a laugh out of me. Arsenault with his sword and his scar, building tables. "You were a carpenter? Are you jesting with me?"

He shook his head. "No. It was good work, putting things together instead of tearing them apart."

He gave me a pained smile.

"Why did you stop, then? Couldn't you have gone on being a carpenter forever?"

He rubbed his forehead. "I suppose... I can't quite remember why I quit." The painful smile he'd worn a moment earlier became a dark, puzzled frown. Then he seemed to shake himself and straightened up. "It's been a long time. I'm sure it will come back to me."

"How many winters did you really drink away, Arsenault?"

The smile returned. "Probably too many. Buy the blue one."

"I've never had my own coin," I said. "Do I have enough?"

"I imagine you know how to haggle."

I stiffened. "Of course I know how to haggle. I'm Lieran, aren't I?"

"Well, then, I imagine you have enough."

"I like the green."

"Whatever you like. It's your money."

I stepped back from the dresses to look at both of them. The weave was tight in both, which would make for a warm fabric, but the green was embroidered with white edelweiss, the blue with twining pink roses. There was no difference in the quality.

"The blue's better, you think?"

He shrugged. "It matches your eyes."

He smoothed his cloak over his sleeves and walked over to the counter to call the shopkeep.

He knows what color would match my eyes?

But I had little time to think about it.

He counted out my coin to me and I haggled the shopkeep down so that I had a few catos left, and then he bundled the dress into the bag he wore slung over his shoulder and set off at his usual long-legged pace for Artisans' Row.

I hurried to catch up. By the time I did, he was already wandering among the tables, stripping off his gloves as he browsed the metals. He stuffed his gloves in the bag, too, then laid his hand down on an ingot of silvery metal as big as my fist.

He closed his eyes and brushed the metal with his thumb.

I felt for a moment as if I were intruding on an intimate scene.

"Arsenault," I said, out of breath, coming up to stand beside him.

He blinked, as if I'd startled him. In the space between the flick of his eyelids, his eyes seemed to flash with a sheen like the metal he held in his hands.

Probably it was just a trick of the light. Like his sword in the alley.

"Is that why you wanted to come to Liera? To buy metal?"

He slid a glance at me. "One of the reasons."

I looked back at him sourly, the dress all but forgotten. "Was that the *official* reason?" I said.

"One of the reasons," he said again. "I also wanted some wood. Maybe some good iron, too." He added, almost as if he were talking to himself, "Although steel might be too heavy..."

"For what?"

"For a project your father wanted me to take on."

"What is that you've got there? Is it silver?"

He shook his head. "No. I don't know the name in your language. Tiaannamir."

I stared at him.

He smiled ruefully. "Long name. I know."

"It's not that. I just—I always thought you were Vençalan."

Because of your name. From the Outer Islands. You know—with your light skin. But —"

His brows pulled down and he looked at me with a peculiar expression, then caught himself doing it and almost jerked away to browse the table again. "The Outer Islands. Yes."

"What language is that metal named in?"

"Tulan. It's a northern metal, deposited only in the mountains of the north. Tule, Dagmar. Very strong. Hard to work, though."

"I thought you said you made tables."

"Among other things. I enjoyed making tables. But I've a talent for metal."

"Then why aren't you a blacksmith?"

That odd, pained look returned. "It's a long story."

"Arsenault, are you feeling well?"

"Probably just the kacin from last night." He flashed me a wry grin that wiped away my uneasiness. "Are you hungry yet?"

"I think...maybe."

"Well, I am, so let's give it a try."

He didn't haggle for the metal, just flipped the shopkeep a couple of coins that flashed gold in the sunlight, and slid the ingot into his bag.

He'd paid multiple astra for a piece of metal the size of my fist.

Where did he get so much money? Did my father pay him that well? Why would my father want a chunk of metal from Dagmar?

I had to jog to catch up to him again and almost lost him in the riot of the Eatery.

Arsenault stood in the middle of the chaos, looking from one booth to another, while people walked past us with steaming skewers of meat or rolled-up flatbreads full of olives and cheese. "Well," he said, "I know Dakkaran, Qalfan, Onzarran, and Hamari. But not so much your northern dishes. Just what your cooks feed us in the barracks."

"You don't want to visit the Vençalan booths?"

"I know Vençalan food. I'd rather try yours. Else what's the point of traveling?"

I thought of my father. When I was a child, he would lead me through the jumble of Eatery stalls, past all the strange and intriguing foreign sights and smells, to the set of vendors he liked best—the ones that reminded him of home. He hated having to come into the city, and hated bringing me into it especially. Without his iron grip on my wrist and a contingent of gavaros dedicated to finding me in the probable case that I did manage to escape, I might still be wandering the streets of Liera, unable to find my way home.

"Some people would rather be reminded of home. If they had traveled far from it."

"What good would that do me? I can't go back. And this time of year it's just pickled herring and salted cod. I've developed the taste for a little spice over the years."

"In Onzarro?"

"There, and on the caravans."

"What haven't you done, Arsenault? Where haven't you been?"

"Well, I haven't been to Saien yet. Or Rojornick—I'm almost certain I've never been to Rojornick. Or Gorodnii."

I couldn't tell whether he was putting me on or not. And perhaps I was still feeling a bit vengeful about last night.

"All right," I said. "Come on."

I led him to an open-air stall where a man was cooking with a big pan over a blazing fire. The flames shot up around the bottom of the pan, which the man shook back and forth periodically, making the contents jump. From here, whatever was inside looked like the deep pink and red corms of a flowering plant.

"What is that he's cooking?" Arsenault's brows knotted and he leaned forward to get a better look, sniffing. "Smells good," he said uncertainly.

I walked up to the counter and waved a hand to get the attention of the woman who was working there with the man.

"How fresh are those?" I asked.

"Came from the hothouse this morning."

"What do you put on them?"

"Just salt. Straight from the flats. Finest seta you'll eat in the market today. A whole coneful, only a cato."

Beside me, Arsenault murmured to himself slowly, in his foreign accent, "*Seta*."

I had to admit that I was enjoying dragging this out. "My treat," I said. "I still have a few catos left."

"Save your coin," he said. "I'll pay. But why does *seta* sound like your word for silk?"

"Mmmm," I said, and flashed my fingers at the woman. "One cone, one bottle of wine."

"Three catos," she said, and I turned to look at Arsenault.

He fished the coins out of his bag and laid them on the counter. The woman swept them up and they disappeared into her pocket as she bent and grabbed a bottle of red wine. She set it down, then took a wide piece of paper and began rolling it into a cone. When she turned to the man cooking behind her, Arsenault leaned over to me.

"You've a rather smug look on your face. What am I eating?"

"What's the point of travel, Arsenault, if you never try anything new?"

"Here you go," the woman said, flashing a big smile at Arsenault as she handed him a cone full of crispy red worms.

I grabbed the wine bottle and doubled over, laughing. "Oh, Arsenault," I said. "The look on your face."

"Are these what I think they are?"

"They're silkworms. The Garonze try to compete with us by building hothouses for their mulberries to leaf earlier. But it's still inferior silk. We sometimes eat our worms, but usually the first crop in spring. By the time the mulberries drop their leaves, we're sick of seeing worms, and the trees need fed, as well as the pigs and the chickens. All we need for silk are the cocoons."

He sighed. "And so, you exact your revenge."

"It's not so bad, Arsenault, truly. See?" I held the bottle against my body with my stump and reached across him to take one of the fried worms from the cone. I crunched it theatrically in my teeth before chewing and swallowing. It was salty and hot and nutty-tasting. I pulled the cork on the bottle and took a long swig to wash it down.

"The wine's decent enough, too," I said. "Not an Imisi mark, of course, but it'll do. Well? Are you going to try one?"

He looked down at the cone, his lips pressed tight together, nostrils flaring as he sniffed. Then he sighed. "I suppose I should get this over with."

"I could take my revenge in worse ways," I said. "Have you ever eaten live octopus?"

"No. And I don't care to, either." He picked a worm out of the cone and held it up in front of his face.

"If you look at it, you'll never eat it."

He slid it into his mouth all at once and bit down on it. His face contorted in disgust. "The texture," he muttered with his mouth still full. "Kyrra."

But he chewed and swallowed and then held his hand out for the bottle of wine. I handed it to him and he took a good long drink.

"Arsenault," I said. "They do not taste bad."

He lowered the bottle. "No," he said. "It's just knowing what I ate that..."

His voice trailed away. I looked up at him impatiently, but he wasn't looking at me or the cone or the wine. Instead, he was gazing across the market, a worried frown pulling down the corners of his mouth.

I turned to follow the line of his gaze. I wasn't as tall as he was, so it was harder for me to see through the crowd. But it was easy enough to catch the flash of sky-blue silk and note the way the people swelled out around the group of men who walked through the market like a boat cutting through water.

"Prinze," I whispered.

No, not just Prinze. In the center of the gavaros I caught a glimpse of dark hair and a silver sword hilt, a smile tossed carelessly and bright.

It was Cassis.

❧

"Kyrra," Arsenault said. "Turn toward me. Not quickly. Just as if I've spoken to you."

I was shaking. I didn't know why. I didn't want to be. But I couldn't stop.

I turned toward Arsenault as if I were made of metal gears, like a figurine of a girl on a clock, every movement a creaking jerk.

Arsenault bent down. "Kyrra, look at me."

Somehow, his voice cut through the thick haze that had descended upon me. "Take the wine," he said in a low voice. "We are going to walk away. Just as if we were anybody else. But keep your back to him. I'm going to put my arm around you to hide your right arm against me, all right? Yes? Kyrra?"

He pushed the bottle of wine into my hand. I nodded and closed it around the neck of the bottle, but I hardly felt it.

Arsenault slid his arm around my shoulders and pressed me up against him. I felt as if I must be dreaming. I stumbled and his arm tightened around me, holding me up.

"We're going to look natural," he said, "just like any other gavaro and his woman in the market on a sunny winter day. Nobody will notice. We'll walk back through Artisans' Row and exit into the city, take the long way around through the Kinless Quarter..."

"Hey, they have seta today!" one of the Prinze retainers

called. It wasn't all gavaros, then, but maybe fosters or cousins, too—I didn't recognize the voice.

"Seta," Cassis scoffed. "That's for serfs and farmers, Zio. You waste your money on that. They've got fried squid over here."

I stiffened. I couldn't help myself. Whether it was at the sound of his voice or his words, I couldn't have said. But there was a hitch in my step that caused Arsenault to stumble a little. His arm pulled down on my cloak and the wind gusted and my hood fell down. I couldn't reach up to put it back on because I was holding the wine.

From behind us—too close—I heard Cassis's voice again.

"Wait," he called. "You—do I know you?"

Arsenault cursed softly under his breath.

I looked up at him, just a moment. The expression on my face must have been one of terror. My emotions were like a storm. They didn't take me all at once. The fear came first, like the wind ahead of the rain. But the rain, the thunder—all of that was on its way. I just couldn't sort it yet. Couldn't name it.

And Arsenault was dragging me along.

"You!" Cassis called. "I'm talking to you! Didn't you hear me?"

His voice came from right behind me.

And then—he touched my left shoulder.

I tried so hard to remain looking straight ahead or down at my feet. But I couldn't stop my initial reaction, the reaction anyone would make, which was to glance upward, to see who had touched me.

It was all a whirl. Cassis's dark eyes, the wind whipping his hair in his face—the wind whipping my hair in my face, thank all the gods, tangling it beyond all hope and hiding me behind its screen. I knew I had lost weight and I didn't think I looked the same as I had a year and half before, but what did he see in my eyes when I lifted them—just for that instant—to his?

"Get your own girl, Mestere," Arsenault growled, in a voice even I didn't recognize. "This one's mine."

I snapped my attention to Arsenault.

Arsenault's hood hid everything but a brief glimpse of his profile and a disdainful snarl. His scar was on the other side, but all the danger I had seen in him earlier this morning was on display. He was taller than Cassis by a good handspan and his body was tense against mine. His right hand was free and he could get at his sword now, for better or worse.

"Are you threatening me?" Cassis asked. "There are ten of us here, six gavaros and four householders. You wouldn't stand a chance. Do you want to go with this man, miss? Are you really willing?"

Was he going to be a gentleman? To *me*?

Now the anger rolled up. Instead of answering, I jogged my arm out as if trying to pull away from Arsenault, and I all but hurled the wine bottle down in front of Cassis.

The bottle shattered, spraying glass and wine everywhere. Cassis jerked backward. Arsenault yanked me forward. A crowd began to form, to see what the commotion was, and Arsenault pulled me into it.

"Walk fast," he said. "Don't run."

Behind us, voices, boots, and swords clattered together. Cassis must have rounded up his gavaros, unable just to let it go.

"Dammit," Arsenault said.

"Not that way," I whispered. "Come on."

I couldn't pull him in the direction I wanted him to go, so I just went that way. He didn't know the Market like I did.

To his credit, Arsenault simply followed me—not holding on to me now, so I could go faster. I ducked in and out of people, heading toward the edge of the Market. When I heard the sound of running boots, I ran too.

Behind the wooden stalls were the old buildings of the Day Market, where silk and spices and merchant cargoes still traded. Behind those buildings lay a smaller canal that led to the Mera di Capria and the alley where the Day Market dumped its trash.

There were piles of crates and packing and broken pottery.

CHAPTER 7

Rotted vegetables. Fish guts. A couple of kinless children picked over the rotted food for something to eat.

"Quick," I said. "Arsenault, the seta."

He was still holding the cone in one hand, gripping it so tight, the cone had collapsed at the bottom. He looked down at it as if just realizing he was still holding it and then, understanding what I meant, he held it out to the children.

"Here you go," he said. "There are going to be men here in a moment. Take these and eat."

One of the children—a girl, about ten years old—grabbed it from him and ran, followed by a boy, probably her brother. As they were disappearing down the alley, I squeezed into the close gap between buildings and slid past a crate full of shattered amphorae into a hidden doorway.

Arsenault followed me.

It was a tight fit for both of us but especially for him. He stood bent over and had to slide his left arm around me because there was nowhere else to put it. He thrust his right hand through his cloak, maybe so he could pull a knife sheathed at his back. Then he whispered a word in a language I didn't know.

The air changed—as if it grew closer around us, shimmering and thick as liquid.

Cassis and his men pounded into the alley.

"Did they come this way?"

"Dear gods, what is that smell?"

"Cassis, what do you care about a gavaro's whore?"

"She looked familiar; that's all."

"But you share your tavern girls well enough, don't you?"

Snickers from the other retainers.

Hate welled up in me so suddenly, it felt like a rush of blood in my ears, blotting out sound and vision. Not just hate for Cassis—hate for myself, too, that hope would spring up just because some idiot Prinze retainer accused Cassis of giving me special treatment.

Arsenault drew me closer against him with both hands,

crushing me against his chest. Maybe he thought I was about to leave the doorway and get myself into trouble.

All I could hear for a moment was the rapid beating of his heart.

Best you put that away, Jon had told him when he unsheathed his sword. *There are Prinze about tonight.*

Was Arsenault running from the Prinze, too?

"Zio," Cassis said. "Shut up. I've never hurt a girl, and you know it."

"Well, except—"

"*Shut up.*"

Dear gods. They were talking about me.

Cassis kicked something. Wood splintered and splashed as it landed in the canal.

I flinched. Arsenault put his hand on the back of my head and pressed me tighter against his chest.

Finally, Cassis sighed. "It doesn't matter. If she wanted to be with that bastard, there's nothing we can do about it, is there? Dammit, now all my clothes smell like shit."

The sound of their bootheels on the bricks clicked farther and farther away, until the keening of gulls and the distant noise of the market again formed the outside world.

But my world remained the dark circle of Arsenault's arms, the soft scrub of his shirt against my cheek as he breathed, and the sound of his heart, gradually slowing as time dragged out and Cassis didn't come back.

Finally, he moved. His right hand drifted away from me and he leaned back as far as he could to look out the doorway.

A big breath and most of the tension went out of him. The air around us seemed to spread out again, the way air should.

"He's gone. Kyrra, are you all right?"

"Yes," I said. "But, Arsenault—why are *you* hiding from Cassis di Prinze?"

PART III

CHAPTER 8

Seven years later and I'm retracing my steps from that long-ago trip with Arsenault to Liera. First, I'm going down to the Talos, to meet Razi and Nibas for our regular weapons practice, and then I'm going to hide from the Prinze in the Day Market again.

It's barely light when I step into the practice yard at the end of the Talos. The yard has always been a vacant spot, not too far from Jon's old house. The Etereans built a round here for fights or circuses, and it was too hard to put up any buildings on top of it, so it just remained as it was until the gavaros who were waiting on their contracts put it to good use. Now it's full of gavaros who come to trade gossip and blows in the misty dawn.

Impossibly, Razi's already waiting on me, sitting on a fence in his fighting robes. His urqa pulls into his mouth like he's yawning, but he's covered this morning, not in the sort of situation where he wants to show his face.

"I didn't expect to see you so early," I say.

He pulls the urqa down a little so he can speak without it muffling his words too much. "You get what you wanted last night?"

Damn. I'm not sure I want to admit that Vadz is dead yet. I feel shaky and try to get rid of the feeling without taking the deep breath I want to. "No," I say.

"Vadz couldn't get it for you?"

"He didn't get the chance."

"Did somebody cut out on you?"

I walk over to the wall where all the blunted practice weapons hang in neat rows, provided by the Houses who use the circus to scout for swordsmen. Swords, knives, spears, staves, halberds. Leather gloves and shields have their own space. I grab a pair of heavy, steel-studded gloves, which I pull on over my own thin leather ones, and then I take down a battered longsword. "Where's Nibas?"

Razi gets down off the fence and joins me at the wall. He chooses two short swords, as usual. They approximate the curved watered-steel swords he wears at his side, of which I have long been envious.

"Nibas is coming later. He had a long night."

"Nibas had a long night?"

"There's a courtesan at the Lady he likes. Don't let him fool you, Kyris. He's actually a man under all that growling."

I laugh. "You forget I've seen him drunk. And amid crowds of grateful townspeople."

Razi smiles and chuckles softly. "He's told me some stories. But you didn't answer my question."

I move into one of the marked-off spaces in the ring and fall into the guard stance Arsenault taught me. Razi follows, holding his swords crossed over his chest. He bows.

"May the Magnificent Sun forever shine upon you, Kyris," he says, the same way he begins every fight, but this time when he steps back, he says, "Who did that Qalfan work for?"

I step around the edge of our circle, watching for an opening in his defense. "Sere. Vadz told you."

"Sere don't usually hire Qalfan gavaros at home. The only

ones I know work for their foreign ventures. Where they're more likely to run into the Empire."

He makes a feint that I see coming. I sweep his blades aside with a long stroke of my own. He comes up and under my sword again, fast, and I jump backward.

"I can't give you the details."

"That kind of job, is it?"

He lunges forward with a more serious effort. I have to work hard to turn him aside. He's using short swords, but he's taller than me, so my longsword only puts us even in terms of reach. In terms of strength...

One of his swords whistles down too quick for me to stop. I throw my right arm up to block it.

The blade clangs against it and we both move apart, breathing hard.

"That is an unfair advantage," he says.

"We're fighting. Everything's fair."

"Lieran bastard."

"Whatever it takes."

He comes at me again, pressing me hard, blades whirling at my head. I beat him back, barely. My whole body is still stiff from sleeping in the alley, and I wonder why he wants to know about the Qalfan. Does he know something I don't?

My inattention costs me. I bring my sword up in preparation for a downward cut, but he gets underneath me and slashes my left arm.

The swords are blunt so they don't cut, but when a Nezar hits you with one, it still hurts. You can't tell by watching Razi when he's off duty, but he's trained as one of Qalfa's elite fighters. My left hand spasms open on its own. Taken by surprise, I lose my grip on the two-handed sword even though my right arm is strong enough to use it one-handed. The sword falls to the dirt and I bend over, gripping my forearm.

"Point," he says. "Haven't had your coffee yet, have you?"

"Shut up, Razi."

That blow hurt. I flex my fingers, trying to regain feeling in my hand.

He steps up close to me and leans down. "Does it still work?"

"It will," I say, straightening up.

"You've got something on your mind."

I bend down to pick up my sword.

"I've got a lot on my mind. I have a lot of errands to run today."

"Some people just use Qalfan robes to disguise themselves, you know."

I look up at him.

"It's true. Irritating, but true. It's convenient, if you know how to wear an allaq and urqa. Hide yourself and you might be anyone. Do anything."

"Do you know that gavaro from last night, Razi?"

"I can't see through cloth. And sometimes, slaves do come up into the ranks from other lands."

"It's my business, though, isn't it?"

"Look, I'm just pointing something out. I thought you ought to know. If you're working for the Sere, they'll pay you well, but just—watch your back, yes?"

I nod. "I am watching it."

"Well, good," he says, then lifts his swords and grins. "Because you never know when someone's going to come at you from behind."

❦

AFTER I FINISH UP WITH RAZI, I TAKE ALL MY BRUISES TO THE best place for news in all Liera -- the morning café in the Day Market, where the old men sit and drink coffee and play cards. I've got a few hours until the Sere countinghouses complete their transfers so I can see if I've been paid. A few hours to worry about the man I'm going to have to see if I want a gun.

Jon Barra.

I ran Jon down as soon as I walked off the ship that brought me home from Rojornick. He and Arsenault had a complicated relationship, but I thought that one might call them friends...if Jon called any man *friend*. If anyone would know where Arsenault was, it would be Jon. If anyone had helped him hide...the only man who would have helped him hide...

Jon Barra.

But even Jon thought Arsenault was dead. Or at least that's what he told me.

I've spent the last few months trying to keep out of Jon's long shadow. Jon is either well known or notorious in Liera. Like me, he left when the wars started, and like me, he fought in Rojornick. Unlike me, he maintained a twisty web of influence and income that survived the fighting. As a result, he's one of the few Dakkaran merchants remaining in Liera. Since the Prinze destroyed the Dakkaran royal family.

But I need to hear the news before I see him again.

The morning café used to be held in the expansive halls of the trade buildings during the winter, but now it's housed in a hastily constructed wooden structure that backs to rubble.

The morning hasn't warmed much, and my right arm groans painfully with the change in temperatures as I step inside the cafe. I rub my wrist as I make my way through the tables, looking for an open seat among the old men, gavaros, and merchants who have already claimed most of them. A roaring fire heats the room, which smells blessedly of coffee.

I slide into a tall seat at the end of the service counter where kitchen girls go back and forth, pouring coffee and carrying out trays of pastries. I don't have any money, which means I'm going to have to rely on the goodwill of a kitchen girl for breakfast. Again.

"Kyris!" one of the girls calls out cheerfully. "Be right there!"

I nod at her, forcing a smile I don't feel. The man sitting next to me sets down a sheaf of papers and pushes his chair back.

"Hey, mestere," I say, putting on my best and broadest Rojornicki accent, trying not to think of what Razi and Nibas would think of me if they could hear. "That's the café's paper, yes? Belongs to Ser Carvoli?"

"Yes," he says with a sniff, leaving the papers where they fall and making no attempt to hand them to me. "If you can read." He leaves without otherwise acknowledging me.

"Lierans," I mumble. Put on a Rojornicki accent, and everyone in town assumes you're a barbarian. I grab the paper and press the folds flat against the wood of the counter.

Page 1:

GEOFFRE DI PRINZE TO DEDICATE NEW TEMPLE TO GOD OF KNOWLEDGE

Sketch of an Eterean-style temple with an enormous front staircase, leading up to a giant statue of Erelf with his ravens huddled on his shoulders, looking down on the populace below him.

Page 2:

PIRATES ATTACK PRINZE SPICE EXPEDITION, TAKE NO PRISONERS

Well, that explains itself. If it was Qalfan corsairs, I hope they sank the boats and made off with a fortune in nutmeg.

Page 3:

MADNESS IN THE NIGHT MARKET

A sketch of Vadz lying limply half in the fountain, bleeding out like a sacrifice all over the ground. Standing around him are a host of screaming women in masks...and a man who is supposed to be me, I guess, leering down over Vadz with a knife, the hawk mask making him—me—look like a carrion eagle.

"Damn," I mutter.

The neutrality of the Night Market was threatened last night when a known Smuggler was Viciously Murdered near Erelf's Fountain. The Watch has declared that the Murder was almost certainly the result of a Betrayal among Criminals. The Murderer is suspected to have ties to Aliente Rebels intent on bringing down the peace...

Aliente rebels again. I wish they existed. But if they did, I would have found them by now.

I let out a frustrated noise through my teeth and smack the paper down on the counter, only to find myself looking at a startled kitchen girl.

"Oh!" she says, and jerks backward, the cup of coffee she carries sloshing over the rim. A couple of drops splatter her hand. I leap up from my seat to help as she hisses and sets the cup down on the counter, but she's wiped her thumb with her other sleeve already.

She gives me a pained, lopsided smile and sucks the burn on the back of her thumb.

"Read something you didn't agree with, Kyris?"

"Oh," I say, remembering quickly that I'm supposed to be Rojornicki, "it's only some of your expressions I am having problems with. You have so many dialects, a person wonders why the news cannot be written in Vençalan for everyone to read, yes?"

She laughs. "You're too highborn for us, Kyris. Not everyone reads Vençalan in Liera, but some of us can puzzle out the Lieran, or at least understand it if it's read to us. Here, I brought you some coffee and a bun. I'm on a break right now. Will you read the news to me?"

"Of course." I shake out the paper and pick up where I left off, aloud this time, in my overdone Rojornicki accent. The first time Vadz heard it, he doubled over laughing, but only a native-born Rojornicki would be able to tell that I'm putting anyone on.

> *"The Prinze will increase patrols in the Night Market and in the rest of the city to prevent more Violence from these Gangs who seek to break the Peace and Wreak their Vengeance upon the Good and Innocent citizens of our City..."*

I stop because I'm too angry to read anymore. I take a sip of coffee and a bite of the pastry the girl brought me instead.

I've fooled her completely. Just like I fooled Vadz and Aleya.

She's leaning over the counter now, with her head propped in her hand, frowning vaguely at the paper. When she notices me watching her, she looks up and smiles—a little too hopefully. I've been taking advantage of her hopefulness too often, and the owner is probably going to take it out of her pay soon, if not her hide.

One more person to add to the red side of my ledger.

And damn, but that picture of Vadz lying in the fountain is beginning to haunt me. We weren't fighting a battle, he didn't understand that associating with me was going to get him killed, and neither did his wife. Now he's one more soul for which I'll owe a blood price when I cross over into the realm of the gods, to be judged and sorted at their Tribunal.

I take another drink of my coffee, set it down on the saucer, and make myself smile back at Lise, the kitchen maid.

"Are there really such gangs loose in Liera?" I say.

She shrugs. "People talk about them. Doesn't mean it's true, though. Here, listen to old Liardo over there. He's been going on all morning about how the Sere are blocking the reconstruction by withholding payments from the building crews on purpose."

"Why would they do such a thing? Don't you all need buildings?"

"Because they want to get back at the Prinze but they don't want to come right out and say it. They're supposed to support them, aren't they?"

"I thought all the big Houses were equals."

She laughs. "That's a cute notion, Kyris; is that how it works in Rojornick? Of course, *that's* not true. Or at least not if you listen to all the talk in here. That man Rezzi—you know, the gavaro with the big mustaches?—*he* says the Prinze are blackmailing the other Heads of House into giving Geoffre di Prinze more and more power on the Council." She beckons me closer and then leans down until our heads nearly touch. "They say he isn't content to just lead the Council. They say he's going to bring a vote to reestablish the Doge's seat as ruler of Liera, and then…"

She looks around to make sure no one is listening before adding in a whisper, "And then they say he wants to make himself Emperor."

"Emperor? Like—what was his name, Attrasca?"

She dips her head, and her fuzzy yellow curls scrub mine.

"Is that just a rumor or is it true?"

"Could be either." She's smiling a little, looking at my mouth.

This has probably gone far enough. I pull back and straighten up.

"Well," I say, like the flustered and proper Rojornicki boyar's son I'm pretending to be, and Lise giggles, her brown eyes twinkling at my innocence. "Well, but—isn't there talk about Geoffre's son? Didn't he just lose his second wife?"

Lise leans down on the counter again. "*Well,*" she says in a low voice. "You didn't hear this from me, but one morning, we had some gavaros in here early, and *they* were talking about how Cassis di Prinze's wife had a lover and Geoffre found out and it was right after that she developed her illness…"

"Poison?"

"You didn't hear this from me, you understand? But the gavaros were talking about how they had just hauled an Amoran apothecary down to the holding cells, and you know what the Amorans are known for, right?"

"Mmmm," I say, turning around to look at the room.

It's true; everybody knows what the Amorans are known for. If I was smart, I'd visit an Amoran apothecary myself, ride to the hunting lodge where Cassis is holed up, pose as a lost traveler asking for food from the kitchens, and poison Cassis's meat. That's if my goal was to get in and out and collect my fifty thousand astra.

But a Prinze ought to be killed by one of his own blood-soaked weapons.

In my opinion. Which is the only one that matters right now.

"They *say*," Lise went on, "that Geoffre is looking for another wife for Cassis right now. A fertile wife."

"Getting desperate for a line of succession, is he?"

"Well, if he keeps killing off his sons' wives—" She put a hand quickly over her mouth and looked around with wide eyes. "I shouldn't have said that," she whispered.

"I don't think anyone heard you but me, Lise. And I promise I have no interest in your Lieran Houses. When my exile ends, I'll be going straight back home."

Lies, lies, and more lies. But Lise loses some of her frightened look. "They say Geoffre has *eyes*, though. And *ears*."

"Magic?" I murmur.

She nods. "Just look at all those men he keeps around him..."

The door rattles. I look up to see a tall man in a dark blue cloak sweeping out of it. People stop talking as the wind skirls, cold, inside. I catch a glimpse of dark hair against the blue of his hood, and then the door slams shut behind him.

I'm off the chair in an instant.

"Kyris? Where are you going?"

"I think...perhaps...a countryman..."

I stride around the tables, where the men have all gone back to their conversations, and throw open the door.

The man with the blue cloak is nowhere to be seen.

Instead, I'm looking at the Watch walking down Artisans' Row to the café.

❧

SIX MEN. FOUR OF THEM PRINZE, ONE FORZA, ONE GARONZE.

I open the door behind me and slink inside again, closing the door as gently as I can. I walk back over to the counter, where Lise is waiting on me, still wearing her surprised, confused expression.

"Did you know him?" she asked.

"I didn't get a good look," I hedge.

I smooth out the newspaper page with the picture of Vadz in the fountain and skim the article until I find a description of myself.

> *The Murderer wrapped himself in a Black Cloak and stood over the Dead Man like a Raven preparing to dine on his Flesh...*

Dammit, my cloak. And if they knew Vadz was a smuggler, that means they probably know he was Rojornicki, too, and they might put *black cloak* and *Rojornick* together...

And end up at the right answer after all.

"Lise," I say, sliding out of my cloak just as the door opens again. "I've told you about my exile, yes?"

"Because of the enemies of your family."

"They'd like to hunt me down. I fear...that they may have followed me here."

"Oh, Kyris!"

"No, shh. Can I come around the counter with you? Out the back door?"

She looks back over her shoulder nervously. "I don't know..." she says. "Ser Carvoli..."

I'm already moving. The Watch is standing just inside the room, pushing down their hoods, surveying the tables. I'm carrying my cloak in a bundle pressed against my body by my right arm.

I can almost hear Arsenault's voice in my ear: *We're going to look natural. No one will notice.*

I meet Lise at the end of the counter and smile at her. "I think that man might have told your Watch some lies about me. They don't know he's not telling the truth. We're all crazy barbarians, yes?"

"Crazy barbarians," Lise says, laughing softly as I come up beside her and put my left arm around her shoulders. I'm not much taller than she is.

I steer her back into the kitchen before I let her go. "Thank you, Lise."

I press a quick kiss to her cheek, and then I'm walking fast, in between the pastry chefs and the other kitchen girls, who start to call out at me, *What are you doing in here, where are you going, you're not allowed —*

But I'm out the back door now and walking as fast as I can around the building. Toward the open-air stalls of Artisans' Row and the Textile Section, where I lose myself in the crowd and do a quick trade of my black-and-silver Rojornicki tunic for a plain brown cloak.

❧

"I want to check an account," I tell the Sere clerk, who keeps writing at his desk without looking up at me. His floppy indigo beret looks like a dinner plate about to slide off his head. "I'll need to write down the numbers for you."

CHAPTER 8

The counting house is dim, lush with velvet rugs and draperies. Knots of householder men sit in upholstered gilt chairs surrounded by their servants. Big slate boards line the walls, and more clerks wearing those floppy indigo berets climb ladders to write on them with styluses—ship dockings and departures, the prices of cinnamon and pepper, gold and silk.

I need to get my money taken care of quickly. I lost the Watch in the Market, but that doesn't mean I won't run into them again. It doesn't mean that they won't ask the right questions of the right people. It doesn't mean that the assassin in the wolf mask isn't tracking me down right now, while I stand here.

"Did you hear me?" I say. "I need to check an account."

The clerk finally looks up at me. "A numbered account?" He sounds skeptical, probably because of this brown cloak I'm wearing now, and my white shirt with no tunic. My green armband is hidden.

"That's right. Money should have come into it early this morning. I want to know the total amount, and then I want to deduct fifteen thousand astra and move the rest to a different account."

"Fifteen thousand? There's more than fifteen thousand in that account? For you?"

I glance over my shoulder and then lean in like I'm telling him a secret. "I'm taking a payment for my master. He doesn't want it traced. Do you understand?"

The clerk cocks his head, then nods slowly. Transactions like this happen in Liera every day. "What is the new account?"

"It's a number too. I'll write it down for you if you have a piece of paper. But this is secret, si? It falls under the keep-mum laws."

I reach in under my cloak to hook the green armband on my right bicep. No one else can see but the clerk.

The clerk's eyes widen, but then he schools his face the way he's probably been trained. The keep-mum laws come into play when the Houses trade for power. As my father's only child and the daughter of a silk-growing House, I received the education meant for his heir. I learned accounting and banking laws, and I know how to manipulate the price on a bolt of silk, probably better than the Forza do if that slate is any indication. Invoking the keep-mum laws means that if this clerk divulges any of the information traded in this deal, he'll have his mouth branded.

"That will require a seal," the clerk says shakily.

"I have it."

I dig in one of the inside pockets of my cloak and come out with the seal Tonia gave me. It's a Caprine seal, carved with the image of a bull and a sheaf of wheat. Hopefully, this will gloss the fact that the account I want to move the money to is an old Aliente account, long out of use, passed down only in the Householder's own family as a source of emergency funds. My father kept the seal in a secret alcove in the wall of his study. For all I know, it's still there, but I remember it well enough to recreate it.

The clerk picks up the seal and rises from his seat to walk through a narrow door into the back. I rest my hip against the desk and scan the countinghouse. I don't think anyone followed me from the alley. All seems normal. The householders, smoking and jaded; the clerks, industrious; a few gavaros hanging around the door—bodyguards trading notes.

The clerk returns carrying a book of slips.

"It is as you said," he says in a low voice as he sits down. "I can write you a letter for fifteen thousand astra if you tell me who to make it out to. Ten thousand astra were transferred into the numbered account you provided."

I tilt my head. "Make a letter out to Jon Barra for five thousand," I say, "And send a letter for ten thousand by guarded courier to the Qalfan hospital for a healer named Aleya. The letter needs to be disguised and delivered only into Aleya's hands. Take the fee for that from my master's account. And—I'm sorry, sir, I've just remembered—a hundred astra in coin, five broken into catos—will that be too much trouble?"

"No," the clerk says, blinking as if he's stunned. He reaches for his quill. "No, ser, no trouble at all."

※

From the countinghouse, I pay a boatman to pole me down the Mera to the quay, by far the quickest way to get there, and from there to a smaller canal leading to the Dalza, the area where the ship captains and merchants live. I hop out of the wicker boat onto the dockside and head for the streets fanning up the hummock from the green lagoon.

All the houses look the same—narrow, white stone, red tile roofs. The Dalza escaped destruction in the wars by reason of heavy bribes, and also because most of the fighting was focused on the wharves where the Houses keep their warehouses and the ships come in. Some of these houses still sport gilt lintels over their gates and doorways, and some have elaborate fountains in the front courtyard—nymphs and goddesses mostly, spilling water from their hands. But some of the houses are shabbier, with roof tiles missing and overgrown ivy storming their walls. The house I'm looking for is one of these, all the way at the end of the street. The waves of the lagoon slap against the red brick wall of the back garden, which is wild with bougainvillea and roses not yet in bloom.

I grip the giant iron knocker on the front gate and give it a few loud raps. In a moment, the wooden doors creak open and a tall man scowls at me from the security of his red-and-gold livery. Jon only employs fellow Dakkarans. He earns his livelihood as a trader of rare woods, but he might as well have a Dakkaran legation here on the sly...which seems likely, knowing Jon. His guard has the dark brown skin and the black-dotted cheekbones of a Dakkaran warrior, and I hold my hands away from my weapons.

"I'm here to see Jon," I say.

"Lots of people come to see Jon," the guard says. "Who are you?"

"My name is Kyris."

"Why would he want to see you, Kyris? You don't look that important to me."

"He'll know who I am. Just give him that name."

"You have a purpose in mind?"

"If you tell him my name, that will be enough."

The guard looks skeptical. "Skinny whiteskin boy like you calling on Jon?" he says. "We'll see."

He straightens up and shoves the gates closed. His bootheels thump on the flagstones as he walks away. I lean against the front garden wall and check my surroundings. It's a better neighborhood than the one Jon used to frequent, but the memory of last night keeps me jumpy.

Then bootheels click closer, and the gates creak open again, wider this time.

"Jon says he'll see you," the guard says. "Follow me. Close." If he was surprised by Jon's answer—and I can't see how he wasn't—he's already hidden it. He steps back so I can walk inside the courtyard. Then he closes and locks the gate and leads me up a flagstone pathway to the front door of the house.

From the outside, Jon's house is unremarkable. It doesn't stand out from any other house on the street.

Inside is a different story.

The floor plan of the house is designed for an unobstructed view of the lagoon from front to back. The foyer—tiled in quartz-veined marble—leads straight to a big, open room with a wall of windows.

So much glass. So much silk in the patterned velvet-and-brocade curtains. How much coin did he spend on that wall alone?

The furnishings are similarly expensive, in the careless, simple way of those who have money and nothing to prove. The patterns on the silk upholstery are woven by the most prestigious velvet makers in Liera. Mixed in among the threads I see some burgundy, too—Aliente silk from another time.

Jon himself stands in a corner of the room, looking out at the lagoon. A woman and a man—both of them tall and Dakkaran, their long locks gathered together at the nape of their neck with matching red silk cords—sit in chairs on either side of Jon. They wear traditional Dakkaran robes woven of red Lieran silk, long to the knee and slit at the hips, belted with a gold wrap with big, curved daggers thrust through it. Polished ebony hilts peek up over the cuffs of their boots.

"Kyris, my lord," the door guard says.

Jon doesn't turn around, but he shifts his head to the side. Unlike his guards, he wears Lieran clothes—not red like those of his servants, just a simple spun brown with black trousers—and his locks are twisted into a shorter queue at the back in a Dakkaran version of the Lieran style. If you met him on the street and didn't know him, you would think that the only Dakkaran tradition he maintains is the gold that lines the curve of his right ear in rings.

But it's a front, a disguise, like the tumbledown facade of the house.

"Kyris," Jon says, in his deep, booming voice with the lilting accent. It echoes off the high ceiling.

I straighten up. "Jon."

"You've been scarce."

"Working for the Caprine."

"I still don't have any information for you."

"I'm not here about that."

"No?" Now he does turn around. He looks me up and down. "Have you accepted the truth, then?"

"That Arsenault's dead, you mean? I won't accept that until I talk to somebody who's seen his dead body."

Jon sighs. "Just as stubborn as always, I see. What are you here for, then?"

"Best spoken about in private, Jon."

"Mmmm." The guards in the chairs look up at him for guidance, and he gestures with his chin over his shoulder. "I'll take him to my study. You two stand in the hall."

They both rise and bow with very little expression, their arms crossed over their chests. But as they walk past me, their eyes tell me how prepared they will be if I try anything dangerous.

I show them my open, gloved hands, but I think it just makes them more sure I'm trouble.

Jon extends an arm. "After you." I have no choice but to walk down the hall with Jon at my back. He's wearing his swordbelt, even in his own house, and having him there makes me nervous, but what choice do I have?

He closes the door to his study and sits down at a big teak desk angled into a corner where he can see everything. Then he leans back in his chair and tosses his feet up on the desk as if it's just a table at the Lady and the Vine.

"Now," he says. "What is this *something* you need, Kyrra."

I hook my thumbs in my swordbelt and look around while I think of how to approach the subject. Out of habit, I catalog the strategic qualities of the room. Jon has, of course, gotten me in the weakest position, with my back to the window and the door.

"I need a gun," I say.

Jon laughs. "You always did like to charge."

"Hurts less if you get it over with."

He shakes his head. "It's no wonder no one could ever send you scouting. All you do is rattle the brush and give yourself away. You ought to hedge around a subject like that a little."

"Make small talk, you mean? You know I'm not really interested in the weather. I need a gun."

"You have the coin?"

"I have enough."

"What kind of gun are we talking about here, Kyrra?"

"A dikkarro." A handgun. Wheellock, so you don't have to fool around with matches. Small enough to be carried in your belt or hidden in a cloak.

Jon's brows lift. "Not an arquebus?" he says.

I shake my head.

Jon puts his hands behind his head. "Well," he says. "That's going to cost more, isn't it?"

"More than an arquebus? Jon. If I haul an arquebus out of here for the Caprine, the Prinze will be on top of me and you faster than I can prime the pan. Why should a dikkarro cost more than an arquebus?"

Jon laughs softly. "Why should a dikkarro cost more than arquebus. Don't play stupid with me, Kyrra. You know how much more workmanship it takes to make a dikkarro. You're just trying to bargain with me."

I shrug.

"And if you want a dikkarro, it's not for a military operation, is it? You do the things you can do with a small gun and it gets traced back to me, and then what happens? At least an arquebus, that's maybe to protect your master's land from bandits, possibly that can be overlooked." He eyes me shrewdly. "Depending on who you're working for, of course."

"I can't carry an arquebus, Jon. I need a dikkarro."

"Now I know it *is* that kind of job, and I have to ask myself, do I want to be involved in one of your House games?"

"Like you aren't already involved in a dozen. I'm just a nobody gavaro in most men's eyes."

"That's only because most men aren't looking at you. But some do."

He gives me a sharp glance that makes me think he has someone specific in mind.

"You know, Jon," I say, "I've been running into somebody familiar lately."

"You're from Liera. I bet you know a lot of people."

"Are you sure you don't have any new information about Arsenault?"

"What, you think you've seen him? Out walking around in the city?"

"There was a man who seemed familiar."

"It's wishful thinking. I've been in Liera longer than you have. Don't you think I would have found him by now? Or at least discovered a lead to his whereabouts?"

"Maybe you just haven't been telling me the truth."

"Why wouldn't I tell you about him, Kyrra?"

"Because you're using him somehow?"

"Or because it was that damned promise to you that got him killed?"

"That's not fair, Jon, and you know it. You wanted him right where he was. He was working with you. *For* you, for some gods-damned reason I never understood. So, it was your fault just as much as it was mine. And *you* didn't have to leave him."

Jon drops his feet and sits up straight. "Arsenault was a fool to make you the promises he did. And you were a fool to let him. You knew how he was and you knew how it was going to end up. I tried to convince him to leave them all to kill each other, but he wouldn't. All he wanted was to keep you out of it. And yet here you are, walking right back into the spider's web."

I dig the letter of promise out of my pocket and slap it down on his desk. "Look. All I want is a little gun. I know you can get me one. There's five thousand astra, and if you need more, I can get it."

I won't say his words about Arsenault don't hurt, but he's wrong when he thinks there was anything I could have done to stop Arsenault from making and keeping his promises.

So, fuck him and the blame he's laying.

He leans back in the chair, away from me, darting a glance down at my right arm.

"I'm an honest merchant now, Kyrra."

"You? Leaving the gun trade to the Prinze? You expect me to believe that?"

He gives me a dark look and swipes up the letter of promise. It looks flimsy and small in his massive hands.

"That's a Sere mark," he says.

"And what if it is? The Sere are bankers."

"Sure they are. But what I hear in the Talos is that the widow Tonia di Sere is looking for a left-handed gavaro and she'll pay for his whereabouts. Nobody knows if the widow wants to hire him or...you know." Some of the tension in his jaw relaxes. He grins.

I roll my eyes. "You think this is funny."

The grin flees. "No. Because what I also hear is that Geoffre di Prinze's son Cassis has lost his second wife with no heirs and his first wife lives on barren, and the Sere are upset at her treatment and looking for an excuse to cannonade the Prinze."

"Why would the Sere want to cannonade the Prinze? They've made their fortune being neutral. The wars are over. The Houses have all signed peace treaties."

"And you believe that? You, Kyrra?" He shakes his head. "Your Houses remind me of lions. For a while they sleep, but they're never really at peace." Then he shrugs, a barely noticeable movement of his broad shoulders. "Perhaps the Sere tire of being the power behind and now wish to be the power in front. There's another rumor, too, that Cassis di Prinze has found a pretty Caprine to be his mistress. And who better to blame a war on than a pretty girl in an opposing family?"

The fingers of my right hand tense. I flex them and the metal pings. "My arm is buried, Jon. That's all past."

"Not while the Prinze are in control of the Council and you're still alive." He gets up and walks to a cabinet against the far wall. "You want some wine?"

I try to relax again, but our conversation has me strung tight as a bowstring. The stress thrums in the metal of my arm.

"Not if all you have is that sweet stuff. What about the gun?"

He turns slightly and cocks an eyebrow at me. "What about the gun? The Sere are using you, Kyrra."

I take a deep breath. "I'm a gavaro. Just doing a job."

He opens the cabinet and pulls out a papyrus-wrapped green glass bottle, making an exasperated noise through his teeth the way my mother would have. "You sound like Arsenault. But you've got a choice. Turn down the gold and walk away. Aren't you tired of being used?"

"It's too late. I heard the information and I took the money. If I walk away now, I'll be dead before tomorrow morning." I decide not to mention last night, but maybe he's already heard that news. "If you can't get me a gun, I guess I'll have to go to someone else."

"You don't have anyone else," he says as he retrieves a goblet and pours the wine into it. It's a deep red, the color of blood, and the bouquet is overly, almost sickeningly, sweet. It always reminds me of that night with the kacin and the Qalfan chirurgeon.

"But if you won't be persuaded, perhaps I could find you a gun."

"I knew you wouldn't let me down, Jon."

He picks up the goblet. "No. You gambled that I wouldn't. There's a difference."

❦

I LEAVE JON'S WITH INSTRUCTIONS ON WHERE TO MEET HIM in the morning, but it feels like I got off too easily. Maybe it's the way my arm is vibrating with this weather or maybe it's just Liera, but I feel like I might jump out of my boots. It's a sunny early-spring afternoon and I can see into all the dark corners. As long as my arm is hidden, I don't look distinctive in any way. There's no reason to assume I've been recognized, and yet...

By the time I enter the merchant's section of the Dalza, I'm sure I'm being followed.

Sometimes, it doesn't pay to argue with your paranoia. The smart thing to do would be to try to lose whoever's following me. But I'm still wound tight from my conversation with Jon, and coming off Vadz's murder, being followed just makes me angry. Really fucking angry. I'm not going to let these people think they can run me like a rabbit.

I still don't know who's behind me—maybe it's Tonia di Sere's Qalfan checking up on me, or maybe it's the man who killed Vadz, or maybe somebody Jon set on my tail. At some level, it doesn't matter. I quicken my step and head toward higher ground and the Silk District.

The Silk District saw fighting during the war. This is where the big silk-weaving warehouses stood, founded by a younger Aliente son who couldn't inherit the villa. We sent our raw silk to them and they turned it into the finest cloth Liera produced. Aliente silk made Liera's reputation in the rest of the world.

The first thing Geoffre di Prinze did after the fighting began was to torch the Aliente looms. Caprine forces worked hard to put the fires out, so the remains of the warehouses still stand—full of ghosts, it's said, the leftover souls of the weavers who died in the fire, doomed to spend eternity clacking at the looms.

We Etereans like ghost stories.

The doors are still intact, though, their handles chained together with a rusty padlock. I bring my right fist down on it a couple of times, and the links crack enough for me to pull it free. I push the door open and slide inside.

The fire burned a hole in the roof, so it's lighter inside than it ought to be. I can easily see that someone has been trying to salvage the looms. Of course they would, now that the Aliente are out of the picture. Our big looms were made by master engineers who installed many improvements to make them more efficient and easier to use. The Garonze never had anything like them. It pains me to see them in this state of disrepair—almost like old Eterean ruins, some of them burnt, some dismantled, others just standing forlorn, gathering dust.

I dart into one of the dark, crowded corners, where the warps and creels stand beside the looms. The looms are huge wooden contraptions, taller than a tall man, with ladders that allow top access to fix mechanical problems. I skim up one of the ladders fast and balance in the beams that form the roof of the loom, shrouded—I hope—by the darkness thick in the corner.

The door swings open slowly, and a man steps inside.

He's wrapped in fighting-style Qalfan robes—gray for daylight, the kind that Razi wears. Qalfan fighters prefer to accomplish their masters' orders in the safety of utter secrecy so that neither the fighter or the master will be implicated in any wrongdoing.

My first thought is that he's Tonia's Qalfan gavaro, checking up on me. But he's wearing two cutlasses, Dakkaran-style, so he might have come from Jon. Remembering what Razi told me this morning, I'm aware that beneath those robes, he might not even be Qalfan at all.

He stands in that position, looking for me, for a long time. So, he's patient. And he hasn't pulled a weapon yet, which means he's either got a knife up his sleeve or *maybe* he's just watching me.

But I'm not sure I believe that. Not after Vadz.

I kick at a giant wooden cylinder standing on its end some distance away. The creel, still threaded with bits and pieces of charred silk threads, looks like a giant bird cage hung with toys, the way I used to do for the lorikeet in our conservatory. The creel wobbles, clattering against another loom, and my pursuer's attention snaps over to it.

Now there's the glint of steel in his hand.

So I know.

I ease my own knife out of its wrist sheath and forward into my right hand. I don't have to worry about cutting my metal hand, so I can pull that knife quick, handling the naked blade. He walks forward, toward the creel, his boots making no sound on the dirt floor. He reminds me of a big cat, stalking toward me into the darkness.

I settle myself, waiting for him to get close enough. Then I jump.

CHAPTER 8

He looks up as soon as he hears the clatter of my boots against the wood. He jerks sideways, throwing his knife hand upward. I hit him in the side, driving the hilt into the join of his shoulder. He staggers sideways into the skeleton of the loom next to us, his urqa muffling his shout of pain. But his reflexes are good and he uses my momentum to slam me into the side of the loom. I get my right arm tangled in the threads still knotted there and rip them away like I'm tearing through a spider web.

"Who sent you to kill me?" I say, breathing hard. "Did Cassis buy you away from Tonia? Or maybe it was Geoffre? Or are you working for Jon?"

He says nothing, just walks the circle we're making, both of us staying out of striking distance. In the dim light, I can't tell the color of his eyes, but they're narrowed on me, intent.

I shift my attention to his torso. Don't want him to fake me. My main objective is to tear that urqa from his face. But I have to stay alive to do it.

His lunge, when it comes, is quick and lethal as lightning. I jump back out of the way. He pulls his cutlass with the other hand and steps up quick, sword held back for a slash.

I tear a wooden dowel free of the warp that stands beside the loom and swing it like a club, straight into his stomach.

He folds over, all his breath coming out in an *mmph*, but keeps his grip on his weapons. I grab at his urqa while he's down. But he pulls backward out of my grip. We're close for an instant, though, close enough to lock gazes.

Dammit. In the darkness, it's hard to tell. Light eyes could be blue or green or gray...

He tears away from me and falls back into a guard position, breathing hard. He's got the cutlass two-handed, so I guess he dropped the knife. Something about the way he stands guard nags at me. It's different from most Qalfan and Dakkaran fighters.

I pull my sword, the one Arsenault gave me—the sword that used to be his. It gleams faintly in the darkness, waiting for a stray bit of magic to light it up, and I swing it in a great arc at his legs.

His cutlass meets my blade faster than I thought possible. He turns my strike up and back, and he's pressing an attack, binding the blades. I shove my hilt upward, toward his jaw, and he jerks backward, only to come around again with a blow aimed at my left arm.

He's fast. And good. Really good.

But I want that urqa off.

Instead of coming back with a killing blow, I shove my right arm up to meet his downward cut. Metal rings on metal, but it's not as hard as I expected, and even as I'm stepping into my intended strike, trying to slice off the urqa with the tip of my sword, it surprises me.

He pulled the blow. Why did he pull the blow?

My blade catches the side of his urqa and the sound of ripping fabric fills the room.

I catch a glimpse of a knife-edge nose and dark hair. Then he drops the cutlass and runs.

Why is he running?

I bolt after him. He's heading for the doors on the other end of the warehouse, running down the narrow corridor between the looms. When he senses me behind him, he leans over and hurls a creel into my way.

It almost slams into me. I shove it aside, dodging around it—cursing—and he ducks into a dim space between looms.

I follow, but there's no one there. There's nowhere he could have gone—I look up, but he's not on top of the looms, either—maybe in this thin space between warp and loom—where it feels cold and misty all of a sudden, as if perhaps there are ghosts here and they've been waiting on me—

—and then when I step out of the space, another creel explodes in front of me. In reflex, I bring my sword down and chop it in half. Blood pounds in my ears and the singing rises urgent in my arm.

I catch my breath to fight down the feeling, but by the time I'm moving again, the door bangs and I look up to see my pursuer sliding outside.

When I follow, he's already gone, melded somewhere into the shadows and leaving me feeling as if I've just had a fight with a ghost.

CHAPTER 9

I'VE ONLY MET A HANDFUL OF MEN THAT QUICK WITH A sword. The Qalfan—or whoever he was—wasn't even putting his whole effort into those blows. He might as well have been having a spar, like a cat toying with a mouse.

Arsenault was one of the men I knew who could fight that way. Lobardin, the gavaro who killed the chirurgeon in the alley for Jon, was another. But Lobardin would never have kept his mouth shut when questioned. And anyway, he'd probably rather rot in the underworld than work for Jon again.

It's been almost seven years since Jon made Arsenault bring Lobardin back with him to my father's estate. *Put a viper in a pot and you can watch him*, he told Arsenault, and though Arsenault was unhappy about it, he did what Jon wanted. After watching Lobardin demonstrate his skills, my father hired him on the spot. When he wasn't smoking kacin, Lobardin could be reliable and even charming. But there was always something uneasy that lay underneath Lobardin's charm, something hard and dangerous.

Arsenault himself rose in the ranks until he was in charge of a gavaro patrol guarding the silkworm nursery. Aside from the mulberry groves themselves, the nursery was the most valuable property on our land. As such, it was often the target of bandits in the springtime, who came to steal not silk but silkworm eggs.

Our bandits lived in the northern hills and in other seasons made their living by preying on merchants and travelers journeying to Rojornick and Kavo and other points on the Spice Road.

But in the springtime, the minor silk-growing Houses would often secretly hire them to attack our nursery to replenish their stores, to destroy our supply so we couldn't compete, or to drive up the price of silk. Only the Aliente grew burgundy silk, and it fetched a high price.

The raid came on the night of a new moon following a hard sanval, the wind that blew storms up from the south each spring. Some of the trees were damaged, and we worked hard all day cleaning up the branches, trying to salvage as many as we could for the worms. I helped strip leaves until long after dark. My hand was bloody and sore, and my arm and back ached by the time we were done and the overseers began to remove the torches.

Arsenault rode between the nursery and the nearby groves all day. Lobardin was there, firmly under Arsenault's authority, no matter how much it galled him. He was among Arsenault's men that night in the mulberry grove. I remember the way the air smelled, full of earth and rain. The silhouettes of the gavaros moving through the trees, shivering the branches. Arsenault grew tenser and tenser as the day went on, sitting his black gelding and watching the hills worriedly. But the bandits still took me by surprise when they swept down upon us out of the dark.

We only had a few moments of warning. The wind shifted and a horse's whinny carried down to us from the northeast. Arsenault wheeled his horse and hissed at the men next to him, "*Get them down to the combing house*," and the two gavaros pulled their swords and shouted at us to *move*, and then an enormous number of armed men seemed to explode from the night.

Arsenault had been expecting the raid. Some of his men were disguised as serfs, but now they grabbed pikes and pulled swords and met the bandits that poured down on us on their horses. When we, the real serfs, heard the first galloping rush of men on horseback, we began to run down the hill to the combing house.

I turned around to find Arsenault, and my hesitation caught me up in the chaos.

Chaos was all it was. In the dark, I couldn't tell Aliente from bandit. Horses screamed as they were skewered by pikes. The smell of rain became the smell of blood and shit and vomit. The ground turned to mud. Men screamed just like horses as they went down. Bodies slammed against each other and into trees, shaking water off the branches. Laughter rose above the din, hysterical and high-edged, and I caught a glimpse of Lobardin in the torchlight, cutting through men like a serf would scythe wheat.

Then horses were pounding around me, and a man leaned out of his saddle and grabbed me up by the waist. He was wrapped in scratchy black wool that smelled sour and old, and all I could make out of his face was a few pale smudges and the glint of dark eyes peering out of a mask of dirt. I cried out, kicking and wriggling to get out of his grasp, but he tightened his grip and slammed me down behind the pommel of his saddle like a sack of grain.

"Bastard!" I yelled at him. "Let me go!"

He responded by wheeling his horse around and shoving his hand down on my back.

Then Arsenault came down upon him with his axe.

It whistled through the air above me, just over my head. If I had pulled back farther, it might have taken the top of my hair. The blade sank deep into the man's chest, crunching through flesh and into bone. Blood sprayed outward, warm and soaking into my dress; the man screamed. I looked over my shoulder, through the blowing strands of my hair, and watched the momentum of the axe sweep him off the saddle and over the rump of his horse onto the ground, where another horse—dancing backward—planted a hoof in his stomach and drove him into the mud.

I started to slide off the horse and made a desperate grasp at the horse's mane.

"Kyrra, ride!" Arsenault yelled at me. And then he was plunging into the fray again. I scrambled upright, ignoring the reins, clutched at the horse's mane for all I was worth, and drove it on with my knees, out of the trees and down the path to the combing house.

※

THE NEXT DAY, IN THE AFTERNOON, ARSENAULT CAME TO GET me from the boiling room.

He had turned the raid into a rout, though it hadn't felt that way in the middle of the fighting. We lost two gavaros; the bandits were cut down to a man. The attack in the mulberry grove turned out to be a distraction for a much smaller force that was sent in to burgle the nursery, but Arsenault had been using scouts to watch the area and had suspected a ruse. Utîl remained at the nursery with a well-armed patrol all day, so when the bandits arrived, expecting their distraction to call all our gavaros to the trees, Utîl and his company stepped out of their hiding places and surprised them with swords and halberds.

I ached all over and I hadn't slept much. Poets glossed over the blood and fear when they spoke of battles. They didn't mention the way the screams of horses and men became the same. Or that when you were safe, you would collapse on the dirt floor of the combing house, not feeling safe because there was someone else to worry about. And then, when the doors were flung open, and he strode with those big strides over to you, to kneel in the dirt and take your shoulder in his hand and look down at you with his face smeared with blood...you would begin crying all over again. And then he would give you a shake and say, *Why didn't you run with the others?*

And you would have no answer to that. Not until later, when it was too late to tell him anyway.

He still looked angry when he strode up to the big vat of boiling water and stood in the steam, watching me. He had a scratch on his cheek and his left forearm was wrapped in a bandage, but other than that, he seemed healthy. He glowered at me from under the hair that had pulled from his braid.

I pretended to ignore him, my stick turning circles among the bobbing maroon cocoons in the water. I had to stand on a stool to use a stick long enough to get to the bottom of the vat, so for once, Arsenault and I were on the same level.

"I see that you're well," he said.

"As are you," I answered without looking at him.

"We spent the morning burying the bodies," he said. "The dogs got the horsemeat."

I blinked and stopped stirring. "The dogs..." I repeated.

He let out an explosive sigh. "Kyrra. What were you doing out there? Did you volunteer? So you could be near the fighting?"

Yesterday morning, the thought had crossed my mind, but then I had dismissed it. I didn't want to admit the real reason I had been caught up in the fighting, so I might as well blame everything on Master Fenn. "No," I said, leaning the stick against my shoulder. I put my hand out, palm up for him to look at. "I knew it would be harder than stirring cocoons. Master Fenn rounded up everyone who didn't have essential work. Do you think I would do this voluntarily?"

Arsenault leaned down in the mist to peer at my hand. It was swollen with scratches and blisters. It hurt to hold anything, but I didn't have time to search out bandages this morning or the desire to ask anyone to help me.

"Kyrra," he breathed.

"I didn't mean to get in your way," I said as I started to stir again.

CHAPTER 9

"Put that stick down and come with me. I'll see to your hand. Master Fenn!" he called. "You need another pot-stirrer! I'm taking her away for other errands!"

Master Fenn hobbled up, eyeing Arsenault over the tops of his half-moon spectacles. He was shorter than me, and Arsenault towered over him the way a prince in a fairy story would tower over a woodland faun. "What other errands, Captain?" he said, looking up. "What can she do that's more important than stirring those cocoons?"

"Helping me clean up around the nursery," he said. "You can find another stirrer, can't you?"

"I suppose so, but I wish you'd all decide where she's really going to be assigned. Hadn't she just ought to be moved to the barracks? Do you use her in the kitchens?"

"We're down a girl," Arsenault said, which was a lie. There were plenty of kitchen girls. All the unattached girls on the estate wanted to work in the barracks kitchens. "Maybe I'll see if we can work her in. It's a good idea."

That's all I needed, to get a new job pounding bread dough for gavaros.

"Well," Master Fenn said. "I don't think I can contest you, Captain, especially after last night. Which House bought that raid?"

Arsenault shrugged. "The bandit we managed to save didn't know much, but from what I could piece together, I'd say Garonze."

"The bard who came in last month said they were cozying up to the Prinze."

"Officially, they're still allied with the Sere, but it might be true. Who's to say."

"The price of silk is down."

"But they wanted the eggs," I said. "The caterpillars. If they wanted to drive up the price, they would have tried to destroy the eggs, not steal them."

"If the Garonze are trying to get into the Prinze's good graces..."

"Do you think there will be more raids?" I asked. "Are they going to try again?"

Arsenault's gaze flicked upward to mine. "Probably. If there are more of them left."

Master Fenn shook his head. "There are always more of them left."

"Then we'll have to stomp them out," Arsenault said. "Like killing vipers in a nest."

<hr />

"AM I REALLY GOING TO WORK IN THE BARRACKS KITCHENS?" I asked him after we walked into his quarters and he closed the door. "Are you assigning me work now instead of offering it?"

He'd been promoted to a larger room. His worktable fit better and he'd acquired a mirror, which sat in the corner and reflected the room in a manner I always found sinister, as if something lurked behind it, watching us. If I could do it without him noticing, I always shifted the mirror to face the shutters or the wall.

"I had to say something to get you out of there. Let me see your hand."

I bit my lip and put my hand out. He frowned down at it, then retrieved his chest from the corner of the room and dug in it for a small ceramic pot. He also came out with his sewing kit and a handkerchief.

"What are you going to do with that?" I asked him.

He struck a spark with his flint and lit a candle. Then he pulled a needle from his sewing kit and thrust it into the flame.

"Keep holding your hand out."

He bent my fingers back and punctured one of the blisters with the needle, draining it. I jerked, more in surprise than pain, and he tightened his grip before he did the next one.

CHAPTER 9

"They were causing you some pain, weren't they," he said.

I made an affirmative noise.

He let go of my hand to lay the needle down, then returned to dab it with a clean cloth, smearing the now-flaccid blisters with cloudy ointment from the little pot. It smelled medicinal in a way that immediately brought back memories of pain and fever.

The next thing I knew, Arsenault was down on one knee next to me with his hand on my shoulder, holding me in the chair.

"Kyrra?"

"The herbs are strong. I didn't sleep much last night."

He eyed me skeptically as he grabbed the handkerchief and tied it around my hand. I flexed my fingers. They felt stiff.

"Am I to work in the kitchens?" I said.

"I told you I don't know. I was just trying to find a way to get you out of the boiling house. In case there's another raid."

He stood and turned to his worktable. A leather sheath rested there with a hilt sticking out of it—a medium-sized knife, small enough to be concealed but big enough to do damage. He swept it off the table and held it out to me.

I looked up at him in surprise.

"Here," he said.

I closed my fingers slowly around the hilt, then laid the sheath down in my lap and pulled the knife, holding it up to examine it. The hilt was carved of a deep red-brown wood I didn't recognize and wrapped in calfskin. Small, wicked teeth lined the edge of the blade.

Arsenault made a clatter, dragging up a chair to sit beside me. "It's a basic gavaro's knife. Useful for many situations. But get it up and under a man's ribs and he's dead."

"Why are you giving it to me?"

"I want you to carry it."

I pushed it back into the sheath. "Arsenault, my father's laws—"

"What if I hadn't seen you on that horse?"

I'd been trying not to think about that. When I lived in the villa, bandit raids seemed exciting, the bandits themselves faintly romantic. I never thought what it was like for serfs. We lost serfs to bandits like we lost sheep to wolves. But now I was a sheep.

"My father upholds the laws. I'm not allowed to carry a weapon. 'If we don't have a rule of law, then all we have is a rule of passion.' That's what he always says, Arsenault. You've probably heard him say it."

From the look on Arsenault's face, he had. His gaze shifted to my sewed-up right sleeve. "What if the laws are bad, though?"

I sucked in my breath and stood up. "It wasn't my father's fault I lost my arm."

His eyes snapped, taking on that metal color they did sometimes. Then he leaned his chair back against the wall, folding his arms over his chest. "Perhaps not."

"What is that supposed to mean? My father had nothing to do with my arm! It was Cassis—the Prinze and their backhanded plotting. By the time the Council sent their representatives to our door, he had no choice. Did you expect him to lose all his holdings just for me? To start a war just to save my arm?"

"Do you think he'll be able to avoid a war?" Arsenault got up so quickly from the chair, I had to take a step back. "Dammit, Kyrra, the Prinze are going to have war no matter what he does or what *you* do, trying to fit in with all these damn laws! You did what you did and you took your punishment. Anyone with eyes can see you regret the crime, and now you ought to be allowed to get on with your life and protect yourself!"

I stared at him.

No, I thought. *Not just anyone with eyes can see that. Only you.*

I looked down at the floor. "If the bandits had taken me," I said, almost in a whisper, "so much the better."

He was silent for a moment. Then he moved closer, so that I had to look up.

"Well," he said. "You might make a decent bandit princess, at that."

Anger surged through me, that he would mock me this way... but then I noticed the worry lines around his eyes.

Was he was provoking me on purpose so I'd let it go?

I forced myself to smile and tossed my hair. "I'd enjoy being a bandit princess. I'd carry a cutlass and wear a vest full of knives, and I'd prey on rich householders. The serfs would worship me."

His lips twitched with the ghost of a smile as he leaned his hip against his worktable and crossed his boots at the ankle. "Is there a bandit prince in this story?"

Certainly not the man who grabbed me last night. I tried not to shudder. "I suppose so. There's a bandit prince in every story, isn't there?" I said.

"Most of them."

"I know—I'll find myself an exiled outlaw. A prince accused of a crime he didn't commit. Together we'll rule the rest of the bandits and be the scourge of the Houses."

Arsenault's smile lengthened, but for some reason, his eyes looked hollow. He picked up the knife again.

"Take it," he said.

I laughed. "It's just a story, Arsenault."

"I made it for you."

It caught me by surprise. "You made this blade?"

"I did. I told you I've a way with metal."

"You said it was a long story."

He smiled again but the easiness had gone, leaving it tinged with bitterness and regret. "It is. Not as interesting as the story of the bandit princess."

The silver wolf stood at the edge of the table. I picked it up instead of the knife. The oil from my skin dimmed the shine of its surface, and feeling I'd somehow marred it, I tried to wipe it on my skirt. But my thumbprint still glared at me.

"You made the wolf, too, didn't you?"

A shadow passed over his face. "A long time ago."

"And the woman. Where is the woman? Did you finish her?"

I was unprepared for the pain that appeared in his eyes. It

flashed to the surface and then disappeared behind that careful, neutral expression that always drove me mad.

"Which woman do you mean?"

"*Which* woman? Arsenault, don't tell me that you make it a habit of carving statues of women?"

I had the satisfaction of seeing him put off balance. He straightened up, going pale. "What? No. That—" He ran a hand through his hair. "You meant the basswood."

"Why would I have meant anything different?"

"Forgive me, Kyrra. I've probably had even less sleep than you."

"Who did you think I was talking about? Do you have so many women, Arsenault?"

"Of course not. I try to avoid entanglements."

"Entanglements." I let the word stretch out on my tongue. Then my treacherous tongue betrayed me. "Is that what Margarithe was?"

"Margarithe..." he said slowly. He colored along the line of his beard. "I suppose I shouldn't ask her to take you on as a kitchen girl."

The heat that scalded my own cheeks was so strong and sudden, it felt as if it would char me. "Why not?"

"Because— How did you know about Margarithe?"

It was either beat a hasty retreat or admit what I'd seen. "You aren't the only one who has eyes around here. But I'm happy to know that's how you think of your women, Arsenault. Fodder for your carving, perhaps? Metal to play with and then to discard?"

"If I say I want to avoid entanglements, it's not because I think less of the women—it's because I think less of myself. And if you think you can compare me to a householder who seduces a girl only to abandon her—"

He bit off the rest of his words and the muscle in his jaw twitched. He was angry, really angry. But bringing up Cassis wasn't fair.

"How would you know what it's like not to be considered a person but only an *entanglement*?"

His face went ashen. "Kyrra, that isn't what I meant—"

"I don't care what you meant," I said.

I shoved the silver wolf in my pocket and ran out the door.

CHAPTER 10

"So, you're Arsenault's girl." Margarithe wiped her hands on a towel and looked me over as I stood in the entrance to the kitchen.

I'd spent the night stewing in anger and guilt over my conversation with Arsenault. I'd slunk back to the barracks that morning, intending to apologize, only to find that Arsenault was gone, up at the stables putting together a team of men to lure the bandits out by another ruse—posing as a rich merchant with his gavaros. Lobardin was the one who gave me the news, cheerfully reminding me of how excellent Arsenault was at keeping his secrets, before he jogged off down the hall to join them. And it was Lobardin who told me, grinning, that I would be working in the kitchens. Lobardin liked to flirt with the kitchen girls and they with him, and if I'd had less to worry about, I might have worried about that. But instead, all I could think about was that I would now be under Margarithe's direction.

Her arms were covered in flour to the elbows, her dark hair wound into a plain knot at the back of her head, but it was easy to see what Arsenault saw in her. We may have been "of a size" as Arsenault had said, but she filled the same space with far more curves than I did.

And of course, she had both her arms.

"I'm not—" I began. But then I changed what I had been going to say. "The gavaros pay me to do their mending. But Lobardin said I've been assigned to the kitchens now."

She considered me a moment. "Do you know anything about cooking?"

It was a fair question. I had been taught to play the harp, to dance the gavotte, and to converse with courtiers of many different nations...but as a noblewoman, I wasn't able to dress or eat without the labor of others. Nowhere in my education had I been taught how to assemble even the simplest of meals.

But I did know something about cooking. My mother had always supervised the kitchens when she was upset or worried, and I'd spent my youth darting in and out among the cooks in such an aggravating fashion that they'd begun to defend themselves by putting me in their offense, allowing me to pummel the bread dough into submission.

"A little," I said. "I can knead dough and roll it. Chop vegetables. Stir soup."

Or at least I used to be able to, when I had two hands. But I knew what Arsenault would say if I claimed not to be able to do those things just because I lacked an arm.

Margarithe nodded. "There's a bowl of dough over there ready to be rolled out for ioli. Just touch it with your fingers. Keep the bandage out of it."

I flinched. Her tone of voice was more practical than unkind, but after my conversation with Arsenault yesterday, she could have said hello to me and I would have read more into it. I walked over to the bowl she indicated, on the same battered wooden table where she'd been kneading dough when I walked in. A rack of smooth wooden rolling pins hung on the wall beside it. I pulled one down, then threw a handful of flour onto the table and scooped the heavy mass of eggy yellow dough out of the bowl. It took me a while to get my hand under it, and the dough stuck to my fingers because I had forgotten to dust them with flour. I tried to peel the dough away but without my right hand to help, I didn't make much progress. Finally, I gave up and smashed the dough with my knuckles.

The kitchen girls stared at me, their friendly chatter silenced. For a moment, the only sound was the crackling of the big fire where a kettle of broth was boiling, filling the room with steam and the smell of lamb. I found myself wishing Arsenault had left me in the boiling house, even though the work there was hard, hot, and boring.

Then the *thunk* of knives on wood began again and the kitchen girls resumed their conversation as they chopped vegetables.

Margarithe looked troubled, but turned back to her dough. She pushed both her hands down deep into the mass and leaned on them. "I guess having you work here will make guarding you easier," she said.

"Guarding me?"

"Isn't that Arsenault's commission?"

I had only just managed to flour the rolling pin, making a mess in the process. I pressed down hard on it, but the dough barely moved. "This is the first I've heard of such a commission."

"Oh. I thought he said..."

"You probably know better than I do. I only mend his shirts."

"You seem to spend a lot of time with him, though."

In order to roll the dough into an even square, I had to lean down, almost onto the table, putting all my weight into it. I knew the girls were watching me, but I could see Margarithe watching me, too, pretending that she wasn't.

"He seems to have an endless list of chores that need doing," I muttered.

"Well. He'd need to keep you close, wouldn't he?"

"But the Mestere isn't allowed to protect me."

"I'm just telling you what Arsenault said. When he asked me for my extra dress."

"Thank you," I said. "For the dress. Arsenault said he paid you back."

I tried to shake the sticky dough off my fingers so I could use a cutter to slice the rolled-out dough into squares to stuff with cheese, but it clung stubbornly. I wiped my hand on my apron and some of the dough rolled off onto the floor.

"He bought me a lovely guarnello when he was in Liera last, and a scarf made of rose silk. It was quite thoughtful," Margarithe said.

I wondered when and why he had gone back to Liera. Or maybe I was just trying not to think of the rose silk scarf and the lovely guarnello. That he had bought her as a gift.

Probably because it suited her eyes.

"I'm glad the debt was paid," I said, reaching for the utensil crock though I knew my hand would leave little bits of flour and crusty dough on all the other kitchen tools.

But Margarithe grabbed the cutter and handed it to me before I had the chance. She smiled tightly and then turned away, mercifully allowing me to blush without watching me do it.

Why hadn't Arsenault just left me in the boiling house?

"It must be difficult for him, trying to juggle all the different roles the Mestere wants him to play," Margarithe said. "Do you know where he is now?"

I cut a long track in the dough, concentrating hard on it. "Lobardin said they were headed out to take care of the remaining bandits."

"Arsenault's quite a swordsman. I'm sure if anyone can take care of those bandits, he can. You've watched him at practice, haven't you?"

Of course I had. I'd practiced daggerwork with him, too, in a little grotto behind the barracks, where an armless statue of a nymph stood guard over a spring bubbling out of the hillside. He moved through his strange foreign forms with the ease of molten metal.

But it wasn't the way he swung his axe that had defeated those bandits. It was his ability to outthink them.

Why hadn't Arsenault just told me that my father hired him to protect me? Why would he need to fool me into thinking that he was treating me like he did because it was his own choice and not a commission?

Unless Jon had put Arsenault there to use me, the way he had sent Lobardin there with Arsenault. As fodder for some plan that Arsenault refused to talk about.

I stopped cutting tracks in the dough and looked at Margarithe. She was concentrating on her task, pushing the dough out with both her hands, a dusting of flour smeared white on what was possibly the *lovely guarnello,* a dusky rose color that did indeed suit her olive skin and deep brown eyes.

Well, it seemed that Arsenault had fooled both of us, hadn't he? So, at least I had company.

༺༻

By the time Arsenault's party returned a week later, I had made so many ioli, I felt like I folded them in my sleep. I was sitting on an empty barrel in the corner of the dining hall, nibbling on one of the last fried ioli, when the big doors were thrown open and Lobardin strode into the room grinning, with his arms outstretched.

He was wearing a wine-colored cloak so dark, it was almost black, with a long rip down the back like someone had taken a knife to it. His silk shirt and trousers were smudged with dirt, and a big purple bruise spread across his cheekbone.

"Brothers!" he said. "Let us rejoice, for we are victorious! The banditti are no more, and the Mestere has allocated us all a few extra barrels of wine in appreciation!"

I nearly choked on my ioli. But the other gavaros set up an immediate whoop and began pounding their knives on the tables for him.

"Tell us the story, Lobardin!"

"How did you defeat them?"

"Was there a battle?"

"Patience!" Lobardin called out, laughing. "Get me some food and a glass of wine and a woman, and I'll tell you soon enough. The rest of our party will be in too, and you can mob them with your questions."

A clatter at the door made everyone look up. A few more gavaros entered, looking just as dirty and abused as Lobardin but less brash about it. They wore burgundy Aliente tunics, one of which had an alarming slash down the front, and black felt hats that looked like they'd been smashed into the dirt.

I slid off the barrel and stood on my tiptoes, looking for Arsenault.

Behind the group of gavaros in tunics, two more gavaros were dragging him in.

Margarithe came to stand beside me and put a hand to her mouth when she saw him. The hall went quieter, and Lobardin turned around with a piece of bread in his hand, which he raised in a salute when he saw who it was.

"Ah," he said. "Our fearless leader. Behold our captain, the architect of our victory."

Arsenault grunted. He was wearing almost as much black as Lobardin had in the alley in Liera. He had on his black hat and his black cloak. When his cloak fell open, the strange, foreign-cut shirt he wore under it shimmered black and gold. He wore his regular black trousers, but his left thigh was wrapped in dirty white bandages. The two gavaros in their burgundy tunics helping him didn't look much better; one of them, a young blond gavaro named Saes, sported a gash above his right brow, and the other, a man with curly black hair and a broad chest named Verrin, had the sleeve of his brown shirt ripped cuff to elbow, and a blood-crusted cut winked in the gap.

But they were both grinning, in the manner of men who had

just cheated death. Saes and Verrin stepped away and Arsenault collapsed into a chair.

"Are you going to tell the story or not, Lobardin," he said, closing his eyes.

There was something different about his voice. Lobardin glanced at him, amused, then sketched a bow that would have made any householder proud and climbed the bench to the table like he was climbing stairs.

"We went in disguise," he said, standing on the table like a player in a play. "As a merchant train. Our Captain Arsenault played the role of foreign merchant, and I rode ahead like an idiot householder, my saddlebags full of treasure. We had donkeys and silk and an ancient, creaky wagon stocked with wine barrels. And bolts of silk—oh, the best indigo silk—such a shimmering midnight color as you've never laid eyes on."

I had laid eyes on it. A bolt was worth six months' pay for all those gavaros combined.

"We were irresistible! And just as we made it to Lovers' Pass, they attacked. They came down at us from off the rocks. If we'd been a regular merchant train, we wouldn't have had a chance. The leader was Garonze, with military training, and knew what he was doing. They boxed us into the pass so it was almost impossible to fight our way out."

A true bandit prince, then. The Garonze had long been our rivals in the silk trade, in the same manner that jackals tried to steal wolf kills.

"And then to make matters worse, those treacherous Aliente gavaros *deserted* us, can you imagine? But can you imagine that the banditti didn't give chase?"

"Why would they, when they had your barrels of wine and two rich hostages?" one of the gavaros sitting next to him said.

"Well, we'd already sent Verrin ahead to pay them off to make sure," Saes added in the midst of lifting a glass of wine. "He'd been scouting in the past month and the bandits knew him. It was almost like the captain had planned it all from the beginning."

Verrin scrubbed a hand through his unruly curls and smiled in an embarrassed way when a number of gavaros beat him on the back in congratulations.

"But the captain told me only to pay them to let us gavaros go," Verrin said. "Not those idiot aristocrats. We threw them to the wolves."

"You rotten cowardly bastards," Lobardin agreed offhandedly, glancing over at Arsenault. He took a big bite of bread and gulped down about half of the wine that had been pressed into his hand.

He closed his eyes briefly, as in ecstasy. "Oh, that's better," he said. "Maybe we really did make it."

The other gavaros in the party made wordless sounds of assent, involved as they were in their own version of Lobardin's public play. Arsenault had taken off his hat and put his leg up on a chair, and was taking a huge bite of a sandwich he'd made. Pickled peppers hung out the side. Margarithe stood beside him, leaning against the table and fiddling with loose strands of hair at the bottom of his braid, but he still looked tense, his gaze roving the crowd as he ate.

I'd been so wrapped up in Lobardin's story, I hadn't noticed her go. The hall was fuller now too. Everyone on the estate must have seen them come in. I spotted Ilena making her way over to Arsenault. I wanted to greet him too. But if I was merely a commission, then perhaps I would only be a reminder of more work he had to do. I sat back down on my barrel and lifted my feet up onto the top, trying to curl up so small, no one would notice me.

"So, our worthless gavaros ran off and left us to that ruthless Garonze bastard."

"Is that what happened to the captain's leg?" someone asked.

"Hurt it in the first fighting," Arsenault said. "Damn Garonze cut me when I was still horseback. Backed me into a cleft in the rock where I couldn't maneuver."

"Then we had to convince him not to kill us," Lobardin said, growing more serious.

"Fed him a load of your horseshit, did you, Lobardin?" someone said.

Lobardin flashed him a grin, but it lacked the brightness of his previous smile, and he ran a hand through his hair. "Something like that."

"It worked," Arsenault interjected. "The Garonze bound us and put us in his cave."

Lobardin shuddered. It seemed like a real gesture, and one that he stopped as soon as he caught it. "But they weren't expecting our gavaros to come back and attack them," he said with forced brightness.

"Did you get all of them?" another gavaro asked.

"All of them except one. The Garonze captain is down in the holding cells."

A cheer went up. Lobardin took a big, graceful bow, then jumped down from the table. The gavaros who had remained and the kitchen girls and the other serfs were smiling and laughing, pounding the heroes on the back, drinking to their health.

But the heroes' smiles seemed strained as they raised their glasses.

※

THERE FOLLOWED A FEAST THE LIKES OF WHICH I HAD NEVER attended, made all the more amazing because none of it was planned. Gavaros lived hard and might die at any time, so if they saw an excuse for celebration, they took it. The night turned into a bright frenzy around me. The gavaros pushed the tables, benches, and chairs against the walls for dancing, and the ones who could play went back to their bunks for their guitars and fiddles. The room became a swirl of skirts and laughter and stomping boots. The cooks tapped an extra barrel of wine, and all the bottles of foreign liquors that the gavaros were hoarding made an appearance. I remained in my corner, watching in amazement, but somehow, I always had something to eat and my glass was always full.

Arsenault sat in his chair with his head tilted against the back and drank out of a brown bottle—not wine. Margarithe sat next to him all night, and I couldn't bring myself to walk over. As I watched the gavaros dance with all the girls, I remembered the last time I had danced, that night with Cassis. The memory came back so sweet and painful, it was like the first bite of a candied fruit—a burst of sugar so sweet, it made your mouth water in pain.

I was nearing the bottom of my third glass of wine when a man's knee jostled my barrel. I flailed out to keep my balance, and the rest of my wine sloshed over the rim of the glass onto the dirt floor. I stared down at it stupidly, and then a hand grabbed my arm.

It was Lobardin, looking flushed. "Come on, Kyrra," he said. "You can't hide in your corner all night."

"I wasn't hiding—" I began, but Lobardin was already pulling me out into the dancers and didn't grace my words with a reply. Instead, he whirled me around, away from him, then back up close, his hand on my waist.

"I can't do these dances!" I shouted at him. "I've only one arm!"

"Oh, excuses, Kyrra!" he shouted back, and spun me again. "Have a little fun!"

"Are you drunk?"

"Yes, thank all the gods! Are you?"

"P-perhaps..."

He laughed. "Wonderful! Why haven't you been over there, hanging around Arsenault?"

"Because—"

"You can't be jealous of Margarithe, now, can you? Or that girl Ilena?"

"Why can't I?"

"I suppose you can be anything you like. Are you?"

"No! Why should I have a reason to be jealous? Especially of Ilena?"

"Only that she's draped all over Arsenault like a cheap cloak?"

"He can do anything he likes!"

Lobardin snorted. "I'll tell you a secret. I had to give him my stash of kacin."

I stopped. "What?"

He tugged me closer by the hand, then wrapped an arm around me and brought me up so near that I could smell all those days he'd spent on the road. The bruise on his face took the shape of a man's knuckles, squeezing one eye almost shut. A cut slashed the hand that held mine.

"I've been feeding him my kacin for the past three days."

"Why?"

"Well, as often as I've said I'd like to see the son of a bitch writhing in pain on the floor, his mind was our ticket out of there, wasn't it? His mind and his magic."

"His magic?"

He grew suddenly serious. "Look. I don't know why you were in that house on the Talos with him, but I think you probably know a little more than most. This plan of his, it sounds good when I say it on the table, but—"

"He was hired to guard me," I said.

Lobardin's eyebrows came down in a V. "What are you talking about?"

I don't know why I told him. Maybe it was the wine, or maybe I wanted to be off the subject of magic. My phantom arm thrummed, and I looked down, suddenly aware of how close Lobardin was holding me against him.

"Margarithe said he was just hired to make sure I was safe. So, you see I don't know as much as you think I do."

Now one of Lobardin's brows climbed upward. He had the most expressive eyebrows of anyone I had ever met. "Isn't that a violation of your sentence? Your father hiring a bodyguard to protect you?"

"Yes, I know. But...it makes sense. I don't know why else Arsenault would treat me the way he does."

He rolled his eyes. "Kyrra. You can't be this naive. *You*."

"What's that supposed to mean?"

"You can't believe he's only doing what he does because he's been hired by your father *or* because he's being kind. You just can't."

"Why not?"

He snorted again and looked up at the ceiling. "Perhaps things are somewhat clearer to me now." Then he looked down at me and opened his mouth as if to speak but stopped. It was clear on his face that he realized how close we were standing, too. His hand tightened on my waist, his fingers spreading down over my hip. The room spun around me, making me dizzy, and he felt so warm.

A large hand on his shoulder yanked him backward. Both of us looked up in surprise to see Arsenault standing there, swaying and glowering.

"I told you to leave her alone," he said. "Didn't I?"

"And I told you to stay off that fucking leg, too. Do you think I want to have to sew it up again?"

"Doesn't hurt. Leave her alone."

"With all the kacin and imya you've just had, you wouldn't feel it if I cut it off."

Arsenault's scowl deepened, if that was possible, and Lobardin winced, his gaze flickering over to my stump and then away just as quickly.

"Sorry, Kyrra. That was an unfortunate thing to say."

I ignored him. "Arsenault, he's right. If the wound on your leg is as bad as it seems, you need to sit back down. I'm sure Margarithe..."

"What *about* Margarithe. She told me you were working here all week. But where have you been? I wanted to talk to you."

"About what?"

"About..." He cleared his throat. The thoughts skittered in his eyes and across his face in alarming fashion, and he swayed so much, I grabbed onto his shirt. "That Garonze," he said finally.

Lobardin inhaled sharply. "Here, Arsenault?"

"No, not here. I'd rather elsewhere, but she left me for Margarithe and that other girl, and here *you* are, Lobardin—wasn't it enough for me to hold my sword to your neck?"

"I promised not to *threaten* her, Arsenault."

Arsenault made a strangled sound in his throat and grabbed Lobardin by the collar.

"I'm fine, Arsenault!" I said. "And you can tell my father so!"

He stopped and looked at me in confusion. "Your father?"

"Margarithe told me about your commission."

"My...commission?"

"Why my father hired you."

He continued to stare at me. "I have had too much to drink. I think."

Lobardin laughed a high-pitched, nervous laugh that seemed a cousin to the one I'd heard during the raid. "You think? Dear gods, Arsenault. No amount of drink is going to drown those memories."

Arsenault rubbed his scar. "The Householder wanted them taken care of. They were only going to raid again and again. Why not take care of it for good?"

"For *good*. Was that for *good*, what we did?"

Arsenault swung his head toward me. "That Garonze—not a Garonze. Forza."

"Forza!" I said it too loud, and some gavaros standing near us looked my way. I took a deep breath and pitched my voice lower. "Why would the Forza be raiding us, unless it's banished kin?"

"Not banished. All Forza."

"What?"

"He's trying to say that the whole force was Forza," Lobardin said. "They weren't bandits. They were Forza gavaros."

"Even the man who picked me up during the raid?"

Lobardin turned his dark eyes on me, those brows showing concerned surprise. As the evening wore on, it seemed that everyone had somehow become stripped of their masks.

"I don't know," Arsenault said. "But it was even more important to send a message. Since they were all Forza."

"And what message did you send?"

"He drugged the wine before we left," Lobardin said. "And we knifed them all in their sleep."

❦

LOBARDIN DRAGGED HIM OFF TO HIS ROOM AND I FOLLOWED, feeling numb and wondering if I knew a single thing about Arsenault.

Lobardin kicked the door open and staggered into the dark room with Arsenault draped over his shoulders. Grunting with the effort, he wrestled Arsenault onto his bed. Arsenault hissed as he lifted his leg onto the mattress, and I fumbled around in the dark for his flint and a candle. When the wick flared into light, the first thing I saw was the sheath with the dagger in it. The mirror in the corner reflected both light and shadows, and Lobardin took it firmly in his hand and turned it to the wall.

I looked at him in surprise.

"I don't like it, that's all," he said. "They say mirrors are like windows."

"Eyes," said Arsenault, and we both startled. He was lying back on his bed with his own eyes closed, and in the flickering shadows, his words seemed to take on shape, like something hiding in the dark. "They say mirrors are like eyes."

Lobardin turned on him, his face gone pale. "Who's watching, then?" he said.

"Or ice. Maybe... I get the language mixed up."

Lobardin stepped away from the mirror as far as he could.

I put my hand on my hip and considered the situation. "Arsenault, stop speaking nonsense. What do you need me to do?"

Margarithe and Ilena had both offered to help, but Arsenault had said, *No, I need Kyrra.*

If Margarithe hadn't been jealous of me before, she was now, and Ilena didn't need any more arrows to fill her quiver of antagonism toward me. Perhaps Arsenault ought to live alone in one of the hill caves, as he seemed to create hopeless snarls by virtue of entering a room and opening his mouth. I became aware that I was waiting too long for Arsenault to speak, and Lobardin was leaning against the table with his head nodding.

"Lobardin. Go get some sleep. I'll take care of him."

"Eh?" Lobardin brought his head up, then rubbed his forehead with the heel of his hand. "Right. I suppose I should leave him to you. I did the best I could with needle and thread. The bastard used up my supply of kacin."

"You shouldn't have kacin with you, anyway. My father doesn't allow it."

"And will you tell him, Kyrra? I'm going to use what's left tonight or I'll never sleep."

I frowned. "Doesn't it give you dreams?"

"Anything will be better than what I've been seeing."

"But Lobardin—I heard you *laughing* in the midst of battle. And you killed that Qalfan. For nothing."

He ran a hand through his hair and laughed, nervously. "I'm afraid there's a touch of battle madness in my line," he said. "And I was on kacin when I killed the Qalfan—who belonged to the Prinze and fought back, by the way. Why else do you think he bled so much? But these men..." He sighed. "I was sober, and they were *asleep*, Kyrra. Only Arsenault and I knew they were Forza, the rest thought they were really bandits, but...what manner of man devises such a plan? He can't have told your father."

I let my breath out and frowned. "No," I said. "My father would never have allowed that kind of deceit. But my father would have been dealing with raids all spring. By the Forza. Why?"

"I don't know. Why don't you ask Arsenault? Maybe he knows."

"If he'll tell me."

"Well, he's drunk on imya and kacin now, so here's your chance." Lobardin kicked himself away from the table and headed to the door. "I'd ask you to come see me later, but then I'm a little drunk, too, and he'd probably find out."

"Get out, Lobardin. I've no desire to come see you later."

He sighed, theatrically. Then he disappeared out the door and closed it behind him, leaving me alone with Arsenault.

"You shouldn't speak unless you know a man is really asleep," Arsenault said.

"You really are a rotten bastard," I told him. "What do you need my help for? Why couldn't Margarithe come sit with you? You know she wanted to shower you with sympathy and compassion. Now all you've got is an angry woman and me."

"You're not angry with me?"

"Arsenault, what do you want me to *do*?"

"Pull the stitches first. The wound needs to drain, and then I can burn it with silver."

All the wine I'd drunk made me feel seasick at the thought of pulling his stitches. "But silver doesn't burn," I said.

"Just— Kyrra, come here and help me."

He tried to push himself upright, but it seemed to take a lot of effort—whether from the pain or the drugs or the liquor, I didn't know. I propped a pillow against the wall and shoved him up against it, using my left arm and my right shoulder.

That put me very close to him. His chest was warm and hard

against my arm, and I felt him turn his head so that his nose and the side of his face brushed my hair.

"Mmmm," he said, sinking back into the pillow. "You smell of rose. And lemon."

"I traded some sewing for soap," I said. "I got tired of using yours."

"Probably tired of smelling like me."

"Occasionally I enjoy something more feminine," I agreed. I put my nose down close to his leg, sniffing for the telltale scent of infection. The sick-sweet odor was subtle, not overpowering, so maybe the wound had only just begun to turn. "You could use a bath, Arsenault," I told him, patting his other leg.

"Are you going to haul the water for me?" he said.

"I think you'd look strange wearing my guarnello while I burned your clothes."

He chuckled, but then I began unwrapping the bandages, and he stiffened.

"I think Lobardin was exaggerating," I said. "You'd feel it if I cut off this limb."

He let his breath out in what might have been a weak laugh. "Don't let them cut off my leg, Kyrra."

I tossed the filthy bandages on the floor and reached for the candle. The rip in his trousers had been cut wider to keep the fabric off the wound, from high on his thigh down to the top of his knee. The gash in his leg was almost that long. It was red and puffy, but it didn't ooze. It didn't look anything like my arm had when it was fevered.

"You're not in danger of having your leg cut off. I swear you might as well be a little girl."

"Sympathy begins to sound better."

"You missed your chance. Margarithe would probably enjoy pulling your stitches now."

"You think so?" I pushed at the side of his leg and he grimaced. "There's a bottle of brandy in the chest. Soak the wound in it. Do the scissors and needle, too."

I flipped the latches on the chest and peered into it, my heart drumming in ridiculous anticipation of catching a glimpse of what might lie inside. There was the brandy as he'd promised, and the little pot of ointment he'd rubbed on my hand, and the leather roll of his sewing kit. The book he wrote in, wrapped up with a metal stylus. The carved wooden woman, still unfinished, a few delicate golden daisies, and a long, thin rod that shone in the light. Garnet-colored silk lay folded on the bottom of the chest—a shirt, I thought.

"Did you find it? And my gloves?"

"Yes." I had to take time pulling things out one at a time, but finally I managed all of them and hurriedly shut the chest. When I turned around to collect some rags from the bag hanging on the wall, Arsenault was watching me. The way the candlelight fell on his face, half in shadow, half in light, it hid his scar and made his eyes seem as silver as his metal.

I stuck the brandy bottle securely under my stump so I could pull the cork. "If you're to burn the evil out of that cut, why don't you just flame the blade of your knife?"

"You've had all this done before, haven't you?" he said, moving his leg a little to allow me to get closer to it.

I laid out a rag on the table and soaked a few more with brandy, then ran one of them over and around the scissor blades and the needle. "I don't remember much. Just the iron in the fire. And the pain." When I put the scissors and needle down on the neatly folded white rag, I wanted suddenly to throw up. "The chirurgeon used something that put me to sleep."

If Arsenault was going to require me to burn him, I didn't know if I could do it. I remembered the smell more than anything, the lingering odor of burning hair and flesh.

"I thought your father wasn't allowed to hire a chirurgeon."

"I suppose there must have been a way around it. My parents couldn't visit me. The chirurgeon kept me in a small room at the back of his house, and his boy cared for me. Sometimes." I soaked another rag in brandy and turned around.

"Sometimes," Arsenault repeated in a dark voice.

"Sometimes," I agreed, kneeling beside him. "The Qalfan was kind, but he didn't have a lot of time to spare on a murderer."

I laid the dripping, brandy-soaked rag on his leg and he pulled backward. "A wonder you survived at all," he said, letting out his breath.

"Probably," I replied, folding up the rag and leaving it on his upper thigh. I bent my head to concentrate on tearing out the stitches. It was not like ripping out the seam in a shirt, and yet it was. The thread Lobardin had used was hanging out the end of the cut. I snipped it with the scissors and began tugging at it, as gently as I could.

He shifted. I tried to think of something more to say. Whenever the chirurgeon had to do anything painful that required me to be still, he had tried to distract me by talking, or he would bring in his boy or girl to do it.

"The Forza," I said. "Why would they want to raid our silk? We share profits with them."

Arsenault cleared his throat and tried to sit up, but I pushed him back. He gave way much too easily.

"Changing allegiances, maybe," he said, sinking into the pillows again. "Or bribed by the Prinze." He took a big breath. "Hoped you might know more."

"Have you spoken to my father?"

"He was busy. In the nursery. He said he would hear tomorrow. When— By all the gods, Kyrra, do you have to—"

"Yes," I said. "If you wanted sympathy and compassion, you should have asked for Margarithe."

He was quiet a moment. I had gotten about halfway down the cut, opening it back up, but it had scabbed around the thread, and tearing out the stitches opened the edges wide enough to bleed. The sword had gone in deep; layers of muscle were visible inside it. There was no way to get the stitches out without it hurting.

He shifted again. Then he said, "Margarithe was a mistake."

I sighed. "Affairs largely are."

"I knew it was a mistake. But those nights were so cold. I saw the rose silk in the market and I thought how it would look with her eyes."

I was almost to the end, but this was a bad section, where the sword must have pulled free. The gash widened, as if the blade had snagged on his flesh. "I'm not sure you should be faulted for it," I told him.

"Why shouldn't I?" He sounded bitter. "Nobody deserves to be entangled with me. And yet I break down. Over and over again."

I tried not to stare at him. "Well, perhaps she just wanted a bit of comfort in the dark too. Maybe she doesn't want as much out of you as you think she does. Maybe...she'd just like the promise that if she needs some comfort, it will be found."

He brought his head up. "And was that how it was with you?"

I yanked the thread and made him wince. "No. Not exactly. It was only two years ago, but I was so young then. And chasing desire. But I did hope that it would last. I *thought* it would last. I thought we would be married."

"It's hard not to get tangled up with hope."

"But not for you? Have you given up on marriage, too?"

He was quiet for the space of a heartbeat. Then he said, "My marriage ended long ago."

I stopped with my hand at the very end of the cut and looked up at him, stunned into silence. I suppose I knew he'd had a life somewhere; all the gavaros had their own stories, which they might tell you all at once or in dropped comments here and there, like objects spilling unintended from a load, but I couldn't imagine Arsenault without his weapons, striding through the barracks.

"Your marriage?"

"It was so long ago, Kyrra. Are you done?"

I looked down, flustered. "The stitches are gone. Do you want your silver?"

He winced again as he pulled on his gloves, then nodded. "Give it to me now. The kacin is wearing off. I'll have to hurry."

I handed him the silver rod and he bent his head. The rod began to glow with a bright white light so intense, I had to shade my eyes. When I looked back, the end of the rod had turned a shade of dark gray, almost black, and smoke drifted up from it.

"Take the silver end, Kyrra," he said. "Don't touch the black end."

I was shaking. I remembered the way Jon and Arsenault had talked about magic and giving me a new arm in the house on the Talos like recalling it from a dream. "Is it hot?"

"The Qalfans call it lunar caustic. They form it from silver and spirit of niter. It's not hot, but it will burn and stain your skin. Take that end and dig it in the cut—along the sides and inside. It will burn out the fevers."

His voice sounded strained. Sweat glistened on his forehead.

I willed my hand to stop shaking as I took the silver rod from his hand. I expected it to be warm if not hot, but it was cool to the touch. Taking a deep breath, I turned it down into his wound and watched in alarm as smoke curled up from the edges.

"Arsenault—"

"No, that's what ought to be happen. Just—finish. It's...uncomfortable."

He was breathing fast and sweating more. "Was your marriage so bad?" I said, hoping to distract him. "That it destroyed all hope in future entanglements?"

"You mean, beyond a silk scarf and a cold night?"

I ran the silver stick into the deep end of the cut and winced as he tried to pull away from it. I couldn't put my hand on his shoulder to hold him there, so I had to commit to my strategy of distraction. "Yes," I said. "Because it seems as if life would be... long...that way."

I told myself I was just keeping him talking, but perhaps I was asking him mostly to give me some hope for the future, too, that it wouldn't always be this turning of old pain and new emptiness.

"When one has been married," he said slowly, and with great effort, "there is always a piece of you that you have given away. That you will never get back, because you gave it as a gift. Perhaps there will be hope, one day, but for a long time, you just feel like a ghost. A shade of who you once were, when there were two of you."

I took the stick out of his wound. "And your marriage..."

"Sella died a long time ago."

"How?"

He wiped the sweat from his brow with the back of a rumpled sleeve and his gloved hand. "K-killed. Knifed."

I sat down on the chair beside him heavily and set the silver rod on the table. I didn't want to ask, but I had to. "And...children?"

He let his head fall back against the wall, eyes closed, and nodded. "Two boys. A little girl. Pippa. She had red hair. Redder than her mother's." He took a great gulp of air and began stripping off his gloves. "Kyrra, let's not speak of this."

The pain in his voice cut me. Perhaps I should have shown him more compassion, the way Margarithe would have. "But, Arsenault, you don't seem that old."

"I was...very young."

I knew what it was like to be very young. I stood up, taking the ointment with me, then knelt next to him again. He turned his head in my direction and I scooped the ointment out with my fingers and smeared it on his wound. The medicinal smell again filled my head with memories. For a moment, the only sound was the guttering candle and my fingers rubbing the ointment over his raw flesh—blackened now where the silver had touched it.

"I sometimes wonder," I said, while I concentrated on the glistening ointment, "what my child would have looked like, had he been born. I didn't know, but I always think of him as a boy. With dark hair and eyes. Like Cassis."

For a long, stretched-out space, Arsenault was quiet. Then I felt his fingers against my temple, smoothing back the strands of hair that had fallen past my face. I leaned into his hand and he let it linger there, comfortingly, his thumb against the beat of my pulse.

I wondered if I could make the night stop. If we could sit here like this until the sun came up, with his hand warm against me and his fingers in my hair, and neither of us asking anything of the other except only to be.

But then he pulled his hand away. Slowly.

"Kyrra," he said, and I looked up at him. He seemed as if he wanted to say something but then thought better of it, and instead he said, "Will you write in my book? So I don't forget?"

CHAPTER 11

I wrote as much as I could in Arsenault's book, but after a time, he began to shiver and mumble in his own language, and though I used every blanket he owned, nothing seemed to help until I gave up and lay down beside him. Then, finally, his heart slowed its panicked beating and the chills stopped coming. I must have fallen asleep too. In the morning, I woke up wedged between his body and the wall.

He had shifted so that my head rested on his shoulder. His arm curved around me and his hand lay on my hip, as if he had drawn me closer in the night. One of the blankets covered me, too, and I didn't remember sliding underneath it. His chest moved slowly with every deep breath and his skin was cool to the touch. The silver he'd magicked had worked.

I should have gotten straight up. But it was warm under the blankets on a cold morning, and I had no desire to endure the knowing glances of those who thought they knew what had happened. When I raised my head to look at Arsenault, a heavy pain lumbered through it, and my mouth felt like someone had stuffed a rag in it. I wasn't used to drinking. I wanted to close my eyes and go back to sleep, and curse whatever other people thought; it wasn't like I had any remaining reputation to protect, was it?

But the thought of him waking to find me in his bed gave me pause. I wasn't sure I could bear either a positive or a negative reaction. He seemed to be sleeping deeply now. His unbound dark hair fanned out over the pillow and hid his scar, and he didn't look as intimidating, though his beard had grown a little wild. Instead, he felt...safe. Like a shelter, a place to hide when the world outside was cruel.

I wanted to sink back into that shelter and let the outside world be cruel to itself. But I had learned not to trust what I thought I wanted, so I did the smart thing and got up.

Arsenault stirred and murmured something which might have been my name, but didn't wake more than that. I straightened his blankets, closed up his book and put it back in the chest, and then went to draw water to wash. I was embarrassed to be seen leaving Arsenault's room in the dawn light, but I knew the only cure for it was to get on with the day.

I ran into Margarithe at the cistern.

She straightened up stiffly with the bucket in her hands when she saw me. "Kyrra."

I tried to smile at her. "He wanted me to pull his stitches. And burn out the fevers in his wound. He didn't want to subject you to that."

She looked at me warily. "You don't dance around an issue, do you?"

"Better to meet trouble head on. If it's not going anywhere."

She poured the water into the large urn she carried, then passed me the empty bucket. I hooked it onto the pulley and began turning the winch, sending the bucket creaking downward toward the black water at the bottom. I leaned over to watch its descent and was caught by the shimmering skin on the surface of the water, like a mirror that reflected my face back up to me, the wounded, frightened eyes with the hollows beneath. I looked like a winter-starved doe.

"Kyrra," Margarithe said. "I said, is he all right?"

The bucket broke the surface of the water and I rubbed my eyes. Three glasses of wine had been too much—though, truly, I hadn't felt myself for a week or more. I alternated between feeling light and untethered and heavy as lead, as if I were being pulled down into the soil. And it was so cold—so much colder than it was back in his bed, under the covers. "Yes," I said. "I think he will be. He wasn't himself last night. Lobardin gave him something for the pain. He wasn't in his right mind."

Maragarithe eyed me skeptically. "Are you sure?"

What was I doing, handing out this hope to her, even as I hoped she wouldn't take it?

No, I did hope she would take it, because *I* didn't need any entanglements.

If she was right, he'd been hired to keep an eye on me, the same way my father had hired the Qalfan chirurgeon. And the way he had held me tight to keep me safe from Cassis in the Day Market and touched my face in the dark last night meant nothing, nor did the warmth I felt this morning when I woke at his side.

I could feel my face heating at the thought and I ducked my head to keep her from noticing. "He wasn't," I said, truthfully. "Today he'll be better, and I'll work in the kitchen and sleep in the combing house tonight."

"You slept—"

"He had chills. I stayed to take care of him. But they're gone now, and I think he'll heal fine. You know how men are."

Margarithe smiled slightly. "Do you think he'll be out today, or if he's still in his sickbed, will he let me see him?"

I began to winch the bucket back up, thankful that she hadn't pressed the subject. "If I know Arsenault," I said, "he'll be up and around whether it's a good idea or not."

As it turned out, I was right.

He was up and around by afternoon, limping into the kitchens with a walking stick made of two stout olive branches twisted together. I didn't know where he found it or if he'd made it himself, perhaps using magic. But the wound in his leg didn't slow him down much.

He'd bathed and changed into his Aliente clothes. His beard was neatly trimmed. When he saw Margarithe and me side by side at the table, kneading bread dough, he stopped as if the sight pulled him up short. Then he put his head down like he was charging toward battle and clomped up to the table with his stick.

"Arsenault!" Margarithe said. "Should you be walking on that leg?"

He frowned down at it. "It's fine," he said. "Just sore. It will heal better now it's clean." He looked down at the dough that I continued to knead.

"Your hand's better, Kyrra?"

"It is."

He rubbed his beard, and I darted a glance up at him, trying to read his face. He looked like I'd felt the day after he and Jon gave me the drugged wine.

"Why are you here, Arsenault?" Margarithe said cautiously.

"Well, I thought I might get something to eat," he said. "Since I missed breakfast and the midday meal."

He looked over at me in accusation.

"You seemed to need the sleep," I said.

He made a sound somewhere in between scoffing and agreement, then turned to Margarithe. "*Is* there anything to eat? Something I can carry?"

"Why do you need to carry it? You can have some soup and bread and sit right here."

He shook his head. "I have work to do. Kyrra, will you clean up and come with me?"

Margarithe drew in her breath sharply. I looked up at Arsenault's face to see if he had noticed, but he seemed distracted. His gaze roved over the room, toward the door, as if he was impatient to get on with things.

"Why?" I said.

His attention came back to me. "I have to ask you some questions about your father. And the"—his voice stumbled —"the Garonze."

I kept my eyes from widening, barely. Nodding, I wiped my floury hand on my apron and reached behind me for my cloak hanging on the wall.

"Margarithe, *will* you get me something to eat?" Arsenault said, his voice softening, and when I turned, it was to see his hand on hers as it rested on the table.

She nodded, turning her head to the side almost shyly, and disappeared back into the pantry to collect a lunch for him.

I looked away. It wasn't my business what he did, and he hadn't been in his right mind last night, so maybe he had changed it. He hadn't *asked* me to lie down beside him, for the gods' sake.

I began wrestling my way into my cloak, wishing I could give it a good beating.

He surprised me by pulling the cloak up on my other shoulder. I stared up at him. He hardly ever helped me with anything if I could do it myself. But now he was standing there looking worried, and his expression erased my own irritation.

"Is it important, Arsenault?" I said.

"Your father hanged him," he said. "Before I got a chance to ask any questions."

※

HIS HURT LEG SLOWED HIM DOWN, SO I COULD KEEP UP, BUT he gave no other quarter to his injury. We walked away from the barracks into the gray, windy day while he ate another of those sandwiches he favored, and I hunched up in my cloak, trying to avoid the wind. It seemed colder than it ought to.

"Is something wrong?" he asked.

"What would be wrong?"

"You're...quiet."

"Am I really such a chatterer?"

"No, no, that's not it. I meant, usually you're more... Did I say something? Last night?"

Not last night, I thought, and I wondered if maybe I'd just forgotten pulling up the covers as I'd slept beside him, and maybe he'd never realized I was there after all.

But I didn't voice any of that. Instead, I said, "Nothing to wound me, if that's what you mean."

"It's always a haze with the kacin. Just makes my memory worse."

I squinted at him. "Did you take a blow to the head?"

"No, just the leg."

"Not fighting bandits. I mean before. I know this isn't your first military service. And your nose..."

He looked down at me. "What's wrong with my nose?" He sounded half-amused and half-annoyed.

"There's nothing *wrong* with your nose," I said, trying hard not to sound defensive. "It's a perfectly fine nose. But how did you break it? Maybe the blow affected your mind."

He gave me a strange look, then laughed. "I doubt that. Although a more sensible man would probably have left that tavern before the brawl broke out."

"Then your scar?"

His smile died and he touched the scar the way he did sometimes, self-consciously. "No, not the scar."

"Then I don't understand. Why do you worry about your memory? Not long ago, you recited every verse of 'The Robber King' to me. No one has all the verses memorized, especially the boring bits in the middle."

"Memorizing songs isn't difficult. It's events that I lose." He looked over his shoulder nervously, as if trying to make sure no one would overhear. "It has to do with the magic."

"Your magic eats memories?"

"In a manner of speaking. I have this gift...but I paid a price for it."

"What kind of price?"

"The kind of price I would never pay now, knowing what it was. But all that's in the past. I can usually remember what happened yesterday. Unless I've been drinking or smoking kacin."

"So you don't remember last night at all?" I said.

He glanced sideways at me, then back at something on his other side. "I didn't say that."

Who in all the hells knew what *that* meant, but I was afraid to ask. "Well," I began, "you did say something of Margarithe."

"Did I?"

"You said she was a mistake. And yet, just now, you didn't act like she was a mistake."

"Does that bother you?"

Yes, I thought.

"No," I said. "I'm just trying to discern you, Arsenault. Are you the kind of man who will lead a woman on just to get lunch, or was the kacin talking last night, or..."

"I started thinking about what you said."

"What *I* said?"

"About life being long. And how maybe she just wanted comfort too."

"Oh."

He was facing straight ahead, squinting at the horizon as he spoke. Still not looking at me, thank all the gods. "I'm not in a position to make promises. So, I try to avoid situations where they'll be required. But maybe...it was cruel of me to assume she wanted more than I could give." He took in a big breath. "On the other hand...if a woman needed more than comfort...it would be crueler of me to lead her into thinking I could promise anything more. No matter how much I might want to."

I tried to sort that out.

I knew his touch in the dark had been nothing, and that the warmth of waking this morning was only an illusion. I'd spent a long time telling him I wasn't his whore, hadn't I? But if he sought his comfort with Margarithe and spent his time with me, did that mean he really did think of me as a friend, or did it instead mean I was strictly business?

I had never had a friend, so I didn't know how to tell the difference.

My mother had spent a lot of time trying to teach me how to analyze the behavior of others, but I wished her teaching had extended to analyzing myself. Why had it ached to see him touching Margarithe's hand? Perhaps it was because I knew no one would ever touch me like that. Cassis and I had spoiled tenderness in our desperate rush for desire, and now I would never experience it. What Arsenault had shown me last night had nothing to do with that kind of love. He was my protector, perhaps, my teacher, maybe even my friend, but I was certainly not a woman in his eyes.

I wondered why that thought hurt. It shouldn't hurt. I didn't want to be Arsenault's woman, or anyone else's.

I pulled my cloak tighter over my right shoulder and wished the wind would go away. "Well, I wrote in your book for you, like you asked me to," I said.

He looked troubled. "Yes. I saw that."

"Why was the rest of it blank? Is it new?"

"I hide the entries. With a glamour. It'll wear off eventually, but by then...well, I suppose I won't begrudge anyone reading it."

"You mean it will stay until your death? Or that you have to actively—I don't know what words to use—*set* it? Are there spells or magic words or—"

He chuckled. "No. It's not like stories. Magic's not tied up in anything outside itself. It just *is*. No one knows why it calls to one person and not to another. But the ability to use it is something you're born with—like yellow hair and blue eyes. You don't need any special words."

"I thought you said you had to pay for yours."

He forced a bleak smile that didn't look like a smile at all. "In a manner of speaking. Just because a person is born with the ability to *do* magic doesn't mean that person will actually be able to handle the magic. Magic is like an ocean. It will carry you with it whether you want it to or not unless you build walls against it. Sometimes, walls cost more than you're willing to pay."

"So, how do you hide your writing?"

"It's like building a waterway. I divert the magic with my will, to do what I want it to do. In this case, I've locked the magic into the book with a rune on the cover. But it makes it easier if I write with metal. My magic responds better that way."

"I wondered why you had no ink. I've never used a metal stylus before. It took me a long time to write those words. Not just because I had to use my left hand. Is that also what you did with the silver?"

He cast me a sideways look, then took a bite of his sandwich. When he was done chewing, he said, "Yes. I took something I Saw inside the silver and gave it form."

The way he said *saw* made me think that he was not talking about regular sight. "And is this how you go about the world, Seeing into things and bending them to your will?"

He let his breath out heavily and shook his head. "Kyrra, if I teach you to use a sword, will you stop wielding your words like blades?"

"Arsenault, I was merely *asking*. I wasn't accusing you of any wrongdoing. The only magic I've ever been acquainted with is the kind in stories."

"Really?" He arched an eyebrow.

"Why should I know anything about magic, Arsenault? I have no reason to lie."

"Mmmm." He ate the rest of his sandwich and looked like he was thinking. "No magic at all?"

"None. This is Liera. We're merchants, not sorcerers."

"Geoffre di Prinze thinks otherwise."

"Geoffre di Prinze," I said slowly, "is very much a Lieran. I think that's what my mother tried to tell me, and what I wouldn't listen to. He'll use whatever means he can to further his House."

Arsenault looked troubled. We had come now to the little grotto with the armless statue where he brought me to practice dagger strokes. "I think you're right," he said. "I think he's bought the Forza somehow. But I didn't get a chance to ask all my questions. Lobardin and I rode next to the commander in the wagon on the way home, but I wasn't in any shape to think and I didn't want to give him away to the rest of the gavaros. It's bad enough that Lobardin knows."

I leaned against the wall. "Why did my father hang him, then? Did he not know you wanted to question him? Or did he question the man himself?"

"I don't know. Your father was in his study this afternoon and occupied with accounts. I learned the man had been hanged when I went down to the caves and discovered him swinging on the gibbet." He sat down on the wall, wincing as he lifted his injured leg and rested it atop the wall longways. "Would there be a reason your father wouldn't want me to find out the connection between the Forza and the Prinze, if there is one?"

"Of course. If the Forza have gone over to the Prinze and attacked us and it becomes public knowledge, then my father will be beholden, as Head of House, to declare against the Forza. If the Prinze are allied to the Forza, then the Prinze come to their defense and we have a war. He's trying to avoid war at all costs."

Arsenault looked at my arm and I knew what he was thinking. *Or at what cost?* But he didn't say anything. "You think the Forza were just trying to provoke your father? Does that mean there are more bandits in the hills—actual bandits?"

"There are always more bandits, Arsenault. Just like there are always more gavaros."

He snorted. "I suppose you're right. They come from the same pool of men. Why do you think they tried to steal the eggs, then? Not just for the silk?"

"Maybe for the silk. If the Prinze could grow silkworms, then they could make and sell their own silk. They wouldn't need us at all. And then they have something valuable to trade for spice."

"But they'd need your trees. They're a city House, aren't they? No space to grow mulberries?"

I nodded. "The trees would grow too slowly, anyway. But I think you could probably have figured this out for yourself, couldn't you?"

"I had some suspicions, but I needed them confirmed. And I have something else for you out here." He reached down into an alcove set in the wall and pulled out a long bundle wrapped in fabric.

When I hesitated, he gestured to me with it. "Go ahead. Take it."

Something hard lay within the linen wrap. I put it down on the wall and unfolded it.

A dulled metal sword lay there. A practice sword with a battered, nicked hilt.

"I thought you were joking," I said.

"Why would I be joking? Here, pick it up."

"But, Arsenault—"

"You said yourself there are always more bandits. Do you want to know how to defend yourself or not? A knife is fine, but a sword gives you more reach. Pick it up."

"I'm on the edge of the law here, Arsenault."

"It's a practice sword. It doesn't have an edge."

Hesitantly, I wrapped my hand around the hilt and lifted it.

It wasn't as heavy as I thought it would be. Holding it felt awkward but somehow right at the same time. I turned it so the flat lay toward me, and raised it so I could look at it.

"But why, Arsenault? Why are you doing this?"

He didn't reply. Instead, his stick came whistling upward toward me. In reflex, I jerked the sword down, meeting his stick in a resounding *crack* and turning it aside.

He grinned. "Because it's in you. Like magic."

WHEN I MADE MY WAY TO THE COMBING HOUSE AFTER I helped serve dinner in the barracks, a small leather packet lay waiting for me atop the blankets. Ilena sniffed when she saw it. "Payment, no doubt," she told the others, and they all laughed. I picked the packet up and felt its outlines but didn't open it. I already knew what it contained.

Arsenault might be keeping the practice sword away from me, but he wouldn't take no for an answer when it came to the dagger.

I rolled over and tucked the packet into the straw that formed my mattress. Arsenault had run me through my first lesson in the rune-style swordwork he practiced that afternoon and I was exhausted. I pulled the silver wolf out of my pocket instead. I had been carrying it around with me since I'd stolen it, always meaning to put it back on Arsenault's table. By now, my fingers knew it. Drifting in that place between sleep and wakefulness, wrapped in the musty smell of wool and sweat and straw with the girls murmuring around me, I felt my flanks lengthen and grow strong, my arms—both of them whole—stretch to become forelegs. I grew hairy and feral, burned by the scent of game nearby and blood.

I was a wolf, gray-furred, scarred, loping along a pine-gnarled ridgeline above the pounding surf of an unfamiliar sea. The moon glowed bright on the black water, limning the sea oats on the dunes with its silver light. The tang of salt mingled with the prey-smell quivering in my nose. Saliva warmed my mouth.

I padded down the ridge, out of the trees, and onto the sand. The sand crumbled between my toes and itched the pads of my paws, but I hid in the grass, and the wind masked my passing. The world was murky, but I didn't need sight. Scent gave the world its edges, and I maneuvered it with great skill.

The prey I stalked was an elk, an old male, with a velvet rack of antlers spanning more than my human length. It lay on the tideline, little tongues of waves licking its shins, and kicked feebly at the gulls fluttering around it, diving in whenever they could to steal a piece of meat from its wounded side. It smelled of blood and musk, salt and sand.

I crouched in the sea grass. Then I pounced.

Birds flapped away, squawking. The elk bellowed, raised its head, and bucked weakly. I dodged its antlers, then skittered back to sink my teeth into the meaty entrails the birds had begun dragging from its body. The elk bellowed again, in pain, and I gave my head a fierce shake and tugged away a long, glistening loop.

The elk looked at me. Its eyes were black and human, deep as the cloud-scarred sky above us. I wondered, what color were a wolf's eyes?

And then I was no longer a wolf. I was a woman, and I was not staring at an elk but at a man.

He was old—or young. His gray hair, long and unbraided, blew about in the wind. Lines furrowed his face like the surface of the sea out beyond the breakers. But his limbs were lean and taut as a youth's.

Hunter, he said. *What do you want?*

I looked down at my hands. Both were there, but they were covered in blood, down into the creases of my palms. I rubbed them on the skirt of my dress but the blood remained.

Hunter, why do you wear those clothes?

Hunter, what is your wish?

My wish was to rid my hands of blood. I kept wiping them on my skirt.

Please! I said.

But you are a hunter. He frowned, as if he didn't understand me. *You have eaten the flesh. You have swallowed blood. You have done the things a hunter does.*

No, I told him. *I stole a wolf. It's Arsenault's. He's the hunter.*

And yet you are dreaming this dream, on these shores.

He stepped toward me. I backed away, my bare feet sinking into the sand. He placed his hand on my shoulder and bent down to squint at me with his elk's eyes. The wind tossed my hair into my face, and he pushed it away.

Don't touch me! I said.

You came to me. I was wounded. See my side?

I looked down at the gaping wound in his side. Blood ran in rivers down his thighs, and he pressed against me the way a wounded man does when he is at the end of his strength.

You have taken away, he said. *You have eaten. You are a hunter and you may not go back.*

But I must return; I can't stay here!

He chuckled.

Daughter, things are not always as they seem.

And then he was gone. In his place there was an elk, bounding across the dunes, and a man standing atop the cliff with a bow.

No! I shouted when I saw what the man meant to do, but too late. The arrow was already loosed. It caught the elk in the side, and he tumbled into the waves with a deep, throaty bellow.

In the way of dreams, I looked up and saw the man bring his bow down.

It was Arsenault.

⚜

I HAD DREAMED FOR HOURS, BUT WHEN I WOKE, THE MOON

hadn't yet set and everyone was still asleep. I lay there thinking in the dark, my heart the loudest sound. The elk-man in my dream reminded me of Adalus, the Dying God, the god of harvest and of springtime. I didn't know why Adalus would visit me or what he had to do with Arsenault.

I pulled on my boots, then grabbed my cloak and rose as quietly as I could. I made my way past the sleeping combergirls and out into the night. The cold day had become a cold night, kissed by a winter that did not want to go. I had spent most of the day being colder than everyone else, and now it seemed like I would never warm up.

My feet bore me unthinking to Adalus's shrine, where I was surprised to find my father.

He didn't see me come in. The shrine of Adalus was built around the trunk of an old olive tree. Not even the largest man could span its girth with his arms. The tree rose up through a hole in the roof, and the ceiling around it was painted with scenes of harvest, grain, springtime, death. My father sat on the dirt floor in front of the tree with his legs crossed, his back to the door. Stands of candles on the other side of the olive threw shadows out behind him.

Arsenault sat beside him.

"So, the Forza were trying to steal my worms," my father said. "And you think it's because Geoffre di Prinze wants to start a war."

"He's raising troops," Arsenault said.

I stopped in the doorway, unsure whether or not to enter. The thick wooden doors remained always open this time of year, so the sound of opening and closing didn't betray me. I dodged behind one of them and peered through the crack between the door and the wall.

"And you say he's also been talking to the Amorans."

My father sounded tired, but he sat with his back straight, his head up.

"The word I've had is that Geoffre is going to dispatch Cassis to Amora. His elder son's still out with the fleet. There are rumors that they're rounding the Cape. My contact says they're after guns."

Guns. A hopelessly foreign word then. A new spice? A drug like kacin?

I pressed my face to the door and tried to still my breath to hear better. The oak planks with their big iron nails were rough and cool on my face. My toes began to grow cold and I knuckled them under in my boots in an attempt to warm them.

"Do they exist?" my father asked, turning to face Arsenault. Candlelight rippled down his profile—the straight, sharp-edged nose I had inherited, the waves of his steel-streaked black hair.

Arsenault dipped his head. "They do, my lord. I've seen them."

My father sighed. "And this raid from the Forza... You think the Prinze were going to pay Dakkar with my worms?"

Arsenault winced as he stretched out his leg. "I think it's a reasonable explanation. Dakkar doesn't have the means to produce silk, but they import a lot of it. Right now, they receive most of their silk from the Saien, but you know how jealously the Saien hoard the secret of their silk."

"That," my father said with a wry smile, "is unfortunately the fault of my own ancestor. But do the Dakkarans love silk enough to trade for guns?"

"The Dakkarans like silk enough to trade the Prinze a *few* guns. Enough for your engineers to figure out how they work and build their own."

"Ever the Lieran way," my father said. "To steal the knowledge of others and make a living off it. But you think Geoffre means to turn the guns against me."

"If Devid is successful."

"And will he be, do you think?"

I could only see Arsenault's profile, half-hidden by the metallic strands of hair above his scar. But I heard the way he tried to smooth the worry from his voice. "If we're able to get through a word in warning, the B'ara will fight them. But Geoffre may have other means at his disposal."

"Other means?"

"Magic."

My father waved his hand. "Rumors. We live in an enlightened age, Arsenault. You can't tell me you still believe the old fairy stories?"

"Magic may be dwindling out of the world, Mestere, but that doesn't mean it's gone. Geoffre knows how to find it, and he's been collecting it. For what use, I don't know, but I doubt it will be good for his rival Houses."

My father frowned. "How am I to fight guns and magic then, Arsenault? Perhaps I ought to negotiate now. Geoffre's never lost anything he's determined to have."

"Except your daughter," Arsenault said. "He didn't take Kyrra."

"No," my father agreed, looking haggard in the candlelight. "You're right. He did not take Kyrra."

I caught my breath. My mother told me that Cassis had denied my hand, but had my father denied Cassis instead? Anger and shame flared inside me, and the ghost of my right arm throbbed the way it did sometimes. It hurt so badly and so suddenly, I had to bite my lip so I wouldn't grab at the phantom.

"Nor did he take my wife," my father said.

Perhaps I was still dreaming. What would Geoffre di Prinze have wanted with my mother?

"Mestere?"

Arsenault sounded as confused as I felt.

My father sighed. "Geoffre used to watch Carolla. When she danced with me at the courting dances. He knew he couldn't have her since she was a Caprine, but he wanted her anyway. Maybe he even loved her. And then I married her. I suppose you ought to know it's been personal for a long time. Not only since Geoffre's son dishonored my daughter."

In the quiet that followed, I could hear the sound of flames consuming hundreds of wicks. Shadows seemed to flicker darker over my father's face. Arsenault sat waiting for him to speak again, still and straight as a pike.

Then my father sighed and the night got going again.

"How is she, Arsenault? You've not brought me news in a while."

The ghost of a smile touched Arsenault's lips. "Her temper keeps her alive, as ever." Then the smile disappeared. "I've moved her to work at the barracks. To keep a better eye on her."

"The barracks? Do you think that wise, Arsenault? My daughter among all those men?"

"She's in the kitchens and she can hold her own. I wanted her away from the silk. In case there were more raids."

"You don't think it's because of that foster I sent home, do you?"

"Vanni? If it got out what they were doing, they might try to say so—to put up a smokescreen. But you could easily prove a violation of hospitality. There were enough witnesses."

"It could still be used against me. I'm walking a fine line, Arsenault, asking you to watch out for her. If I step too far afoul of it...Geoffre will have me in the Council."

Arsenault's beard obscured his mouth in the dark. But he didn't bother to alter the scowl in his voice. "You're going to have a fight no matter what you do, Mestere. Wouldn't you rather know your daughter's safe when it comes down to it?"

"Of course," my father sighed, rubbing his brow. "But I have a responsibility to my House, too. Kyrra understands that."

Arsenault made a sound that could have had many meanings. Mostly, it was just a rumble.

"Keep doing what I pay you to do, Arsenault. And be thankful you're not in charge."

My fingers and toes had gone numb with cold. I pulled my wool cloak tight around me and slid down the wall to hunker in that small space behind the door, my icy feet tucked under me.

So, I was just a commission after all. A commission and maybe a tool for Jon.

I fought the urge to take a big breath and looked up at the ceiling instead.

A huge image of the god hanging upside down covered the stucco above me, his antlered head bent backwards, white neck stretched by a cord that tethered him to his own ankles and suspended him from an olive's massive branch. This was the part of his story near the end. Adalus was shot dead by an arrow his brother loosed, and then his brother flayed his skin to make a mantle. After his brother flayed him, Adalus was revealed, and when his brother saw truth, he wept. Adalus, watered by his brother's tears, sank into the ground to rise the next year as a field of self-sowing wheat that gave such a bountiful harvest, it could never be matched.

I had no idea what the story could have to do with Arsenault. Maybe the god wanted me to see truth, too.

The kind of truth that felt like an arrow wound.

My father and Arsenault were rising from their seats, and I tried to become like the fist I made of my hand—small, unnoticeable, closed in on myself.

"See that my daughter has sandals for spring and summer," my father said as they walked past me. "And make sure she wears them. When she was a child, she used to look for any excuse to kick them off and run barefoot in the grass."

He smiled. I huddled in my cloak, pressed as far back against the wall as I could.

Arsenault was standing right in front of me now. "She'll wear her shoes, my lord. I'll see to it."

"You ought to go down to Liera as soon as your leg can take it. I'm sure Geoffre will be expecting you."

I froze like a rabbit.

Was my father using him as a spy? Is that why he had run from Cassis in the Market?

But did my father know about Jon and the house on the

Talos? Did he know about the kacin smuggling and the magic and how Jon had paid Lobardin to murder a Qalfan citizen?

Arsenault nodded, sharp and short, and my father stepped past him and out into the night. Once my father was on the other side of the door, Arsenault looked straight at me.

Our eyes met. There was no pretending he hadn't seen me. I thought surely he would open the door and expose me. I clutched the edge of my cloak so tightly, my knuckles stood out white.

But Arsenault only touched the door as he walked away, letting his fingers trail along the wood.

When I was sure he was gone, I came out of my hiding place, stiff-legged with cold. I touched the place on the door that Arsenault had touched, and stared up at the picture of Adalus that covered the wooden planks of the ceiling.

Then I looked down at the place on the door. There was a runnel where Arsenault had traced his finger, lined with ruddy gold that shone like blood in the candlelight.

◈

THE NEXT DAY PROGRESSED IN MISERY, FROM MISTRESS LEVIN swatting my feet to wake me, to Arsenault finding me hiding in a corner of the kitchen, wrapped up in my cloak and my ugly green-and-brown scarf, dozing when I was supposed to be stirring the soup.

"I don't think she feels well," Margarithe told him with some concern when he asked me to come with him, but he said nothing, just waited on me to slide off my stool and then followed me out the door.

We walked in silence to the little grotto with the armless statue, with me growing angrier and angrier and him watching me out the corner of his eye.

"I'd like to exercise with you today," he said, unbuckling his swordbelt and stripping off his tunic. He set both on the stone wall. "I think my leg has healed enough."

"It looked like it hurt you last night."

"Well, I don't think—"

"You don't think teaching me sword will give it that much exertion."

He rocked back on his heels the way that gavaros did, and scratched his beard. "Kyrra," he said finally. "My leg isn't healed enough to do my usual exercises. You've only just begun. Today, all we're going to do is come in and out of guard."

"You're just humoring me. Keeping me out of the way like my parents used to. Wayward Kyrra, causing trouble again, maybe if we give her fencing lessons..."

Arsenault stared at me.

My mind was wandering the way my feet used to. I felt thick as half-frozen mud. I sat down cross-legged in the dirt, snuggling my knees inside my cloak, and tried to shepherd my thoughts.

"I know you only do what you've been hired to do."

"I've been hired to do a number of things. Which are you talking about?"

"You know *which*, Arsenault. I heard the whole conversation last night."

"If you heard the whole conversation, then you know your father uses me in many ways. Guarding the silkhouse and rousting out bandits, for one."

"Spying on the Prinze?"

He put his hand on the hilt of the practice sword and drummed his fingers against it. "You did hear everything, didn't you?"

"I said I did. And it isn't such a stretch to put it together with Jon hiding in that house on the Talos, and the way you were acting in Liera. When we ran away from Cassis, it wasn't just me you were trying to hide."

"If the Prinze had found only me, I wouldn't have worried. In company with you...that wouldn't have gone well for either of us. Worse for you, though. I doubt if Geoffre's done with you."

"He hates me that much?"

"I think he wants you more."

"If he wanted me, he could have had me. Easily. All he had to do was send Cassis to my father with a proposal of marriage. I would have gone eagerly."

"But you came with the Aliente attached. He didn't want the Aliente. Just you."

"Not *me*," I said bitterly. "Just my fertility. No one wants *me*, do they? No matter how far I'm cast down in the dirt, I'm still the daughter of the Aliente Householder. I might as well be a doll."

I picked up a pebble from the dirt and threw it. Hard.

"That might be how the Prinze see you."

"Dear gods, Arsenault," I said, looking up at him. "Can we not just be honest with each other for once? My father commissioned you to see me safe. The only reason you've kept me as close as you have is so you can keep an eye on me. For pay."

Arsenault's hand tightened on his hilt, even though it was only a blunted practice sword, and his stance took on the look of a gavaro who thought he was about to see action. "Your father wanted me to keep an eye on you. He told me that when I was hired. But it wasn't why I was hired."

"What were you hired for, then?"

"My military experience. I was recommended —"

"By whom?"

When he didn't answer right away, I knew.

I swore and leapt to my feet. I had the blunt practice sword in my hand, but I pointed it at him as if it were real. "If you're playing my father over for Jon, Arsenault—"

"I'm not playing your father over. I signed a contract, and I honor my promises." He ran a hand through his hair. "I'm not playing you over, either."

"When have you not played me, Arsenault? In Liera, when

you drugged my wine? Or maybe that was more honest than when you helped me buy that godsdamned blue guarnello because it matched my eyes! Everything you've done to help me, it was just a way of earning your pay."

He looked troubled first and then angry.

"Your father wanted me to keep an eye on you, but he couldn't hire me to be your bodyguard without violating your sentence." He paused. "And are we talking about the dress you bought in Liera? Can a man not pay you a simple compliment without it becoming a conspiracy? The blue does bring out the color of your eyes!"

"And you were only saying so because my father wanted you to be kind to me!"

"You think your father wanted me noticing the way your dress looked on you?"

"A man might make comments on the color."

"A man notices the color *last*," he said, leaning toward me with his eyes flashing. "After he notices everything else!"

I blinked and stepped backward, taken momentarily by surprise. But then even that made me angry.

"No," I said, unwilling to be baited. "You made me see. I thought my father was so straight for the law. But the chirurgeon he hired for me when my arm was cut off...wasn't that also a violation of my sentence?"

"You said a boy took care of you *sometimes*." Arsenault finished the sentence like he was spitting. "How was that a violation of your sentence? If you'd had real Qalfan care, your arm wouldn't look like it does now. And you wouldn't have spent so long fighting fevers. Months, wasn't it? Is that what I heard?"

The blood ran away from my face. "When have you seen..."

"In Liera. Your stump is ragged and all over scars where that hack bled you."

"He said he had to let the humours out. Because of the fevers."

Arsenault cursed. "He was a hack. I've seen what real Qalfan doctors do. Your father may have hired that chirurgeon, but he did it within the law. The way he'd treat any of his other serfs. If he'd had the balls—"

"It's so simple for you, isn't it?" I shouted at him. "You give your loyalty to whoever pays you. But if you were born to a House, you would know what it feels like to be trapped. To be played like a card and treated like nothing!"

"Kyrra—"

He took my arms. Both of them.

Once, long ago, my mother and I traveled to the seaside to vacation with her Caprine sister. I ran into the waves, only to be knocked off my feet and scoured along the bottom until my uncle hauled me out like a fish.

This was like that. A mad rush of memories and anger and fear. I felt as if I was being pushed down onto the block again with my arm held tight. And then...

Black somersaults.

I have no memory of what happened next. The next thing I knew, Arsenault had me pressed up against a tree. His mouth was at my ear, his breath warm on my skin. "Kyrra," he was saying, his voice low and infused with a shaky calm, "Kyrra, come back up. I'm not going to hurt you."

I turned my head toward the sound of his voice. It was muffled, like he was speaking into a pillow. Darkness fuzzed the edges of my vision.

"Kyrra," he said again.

"What," I answered thickly.

He exhaled and rested his forehead against the tree trunk. He still held my left arm pinned tight against my side. My fingers opened and something hard slipped from their grasp and clanged on the stones. His body lost some of its tension, but his shoulder, chest, and hip kept me in place.

"I will never touch your arm," he said. "Unless you ask me to."

My gaze careened over him. There was a long rip down his

right sleeve. "Arsenault?" I asked, beginning to feel scared. "What did I do?"

The wind tossed my hair around and he smoothed it away from my sticky cheek, back behind my ear with his thumb. My heart slowed in its race toward panic only to stutter for a different reason.

"You were hurt. Badly. Sometimes, memory plays tricks on the mind. A man thinks he's in danger when he isn't. And also...I did See something in you."

"What was that?"

"A talent for the dagger and the sword, like mine for metal." He paused and shifted, turning his gaze toward mine. A touch of humor lit his eyes. "Maybe a predilection for battle, too."

I dredged up a bit of a smile. "Are you telling me I'm a shrew?"

That drew a longer smile from him. "More like a mountain lion."

My smile grew. I felt him relax. But we were still standing there against the tree, our bodies pressed together. For the first time in days, I was warm. The tense fear drained from my body and all my muscles unwound. I sagged into him, letting my head tilt into the hollow of his throat. He combed his fingers idly through my hair and relaxed his grip on my wrist with his right hand so that my fingers could brush his—so lightly, I shivered and raised my head.

"You're cold." He had leaned down, close enough that I could feel his breath on my cheek, the brief, soft brush of his beard on my skin.

"No," I said, scarcely aloud, just an exhaled breath over his lips which were now next to my own.

I looked up from the curve of his mouth to find his gaze rising in the same way to mine, a dark warmth in his eyes. If either of us had made the most minute of movements, our lips would have touched. Instead, we stood there, our hearts beating in wild fright, as if we were deer surprised in the forest.

He backed away from me suddenly, leaving me against the tree and opening his mouth as if he wanted to speak. Then he pressed his lips closed, that unaccustomed flush coming up on his cheeks along his beard, and he turned, limping back to the wall to grab his tunic and sword.

"Arsenault?" I said, stepping away from the tree, my heart still drumming in my ears.

"I don't do what I do because I'm paid to," he said, his voice rough. Then he paused and added, in that same voice without turning around, "But this isn't for us, Kyrra. You're the kind of woman who ought to have a promise...and I can't make you one."

CHAPTER 12

I REMAINED IN THE GROTTO FOR A LONG TIME AFTERWARD. AT first, I couldn't seem to move away from the tree. Then I bent and scooped up a handful of sticks and dirt and hurled it at the armless statue.

Eventually, I left to go back to the kitchens for supper service.

I was just coming out of the grotto into the first curve of the path when the brush rustled. It reminded me of the way the gavaros had moved in the trees before the bandit raid. I whirled, touching the dagger in my pocket. A twig snapped and more brush rustled, and then someone dressed in white and tan burst out of the brush into a run.

Not stopping to think or to pull my dagger, I gave chase. If it was a Forza or a bandit, I would have been in trouble, but that didn't stop me. Whoever it was might have seen Arsenault and me in the grotto and, more importantly, might have heard what I said to him.

I took a shortcut off the narrow path from the grotto to the barracks, yanked up my skirts to jump a fallen log, and by the time I was down on the other side, I could tell I was chasing a girl. In the space of a few breaths, I was upon her. I grabbed the back of her guarnello and threw her down on the pine needles.

It was Ilena.

She stared up at me with wide, frightened eyes and breathed in big gulps, winded by the short run. I stood above her, itching to put my hand on my dagger. Maybe it was just my recent bout with Arsenault, but I found it harder to tether myself to this world in which I was supposed to be living.

"Don't hurt me!" she cried out.

"Would you hush?" I said. "You'll have the patrol on top of us, and I'm not sure you want that if you were spying on Arsenault. What were you doing hiding in the brush?"

"Nothing. Sitting." Her eyes flashed triumphantly as she realized I really wasn't going to hurt her. "Listening."

"You *were* spying on Arsenault."

"I didn't mean to spy on Arsenault," she said. "I only wanted to spend some time on my own."

She diverted her eyes, as if embarrassed to admit her true purpose. I wondered if her mother had been at her again.

"But you and Arsenault were already here," she continued. "With blades. So, what could I do but hide in the brush?"

"You could have turned around and left! Did you hear the conversation?"

"I saw you with a dagger, Kyrra No-Name. You're not supposed to have a dagger."

Maybe she hadn't heard me say that Arsenault was working for the Prinze, then. My insides unknotted a little. Then again…

"When did I have a dagger?" I said. "I had a blunt practice sword."

Ilena laughed in surprise. "He certainly wasn't acting like you were using a blunted weapon. He worked hard to turn you away, and then he got you up against that tree."

My face flamed, and she colored a little, darkly. "He said it was because of my memories," I said.

"It doesn't matter, does it? I can still tell the Householder."

Regardless of what Arsenault said, I knew my father meant Arsenault to protect me. But would he have any choice but to discharge Arsenault if he found out Arsenault had given me weapons? My father dealt a stern justice. I had seen corpses swinging at the end of a rope for fighting a duel. What would people say if my father broke those laws, but only for his daughter?

Ilena had risen and now she was stalking off down the path toward the barracks.

"Wait!" I called. "Ilena, why would you do such a thing?"

She glanced back at me over her shoulder with a dark little smile. "I obey the laws; that's why. There isn't anything you can do."

I knew what the smile meant then. My shoulders drooped. "Nothing," I said. "Not anything."

"Well." She slowed almost to a stop. "Maybe something. Maybe I'd like to leave quarters sometime. At night."

"That's dangerous."

"Will you help me or would you rather take your flogging?"

Did I really care if she ran into danger? She probably wanted to see a gavaro. I just hoped it wasn't the gavaro I thought it was.

I sucked in all the words I wanted to scream at her. "You give me little choice. When will you need to leave?"

"I'll let you know," she said, and swept away like a lady finished ordering her servant.

<hr />

I DIDN'T SEE ARSENAULT AT SUPPER THAT NIGHT OR FOR THE next few days. I wondered if he had gone to Liera or if he was just avoiding me. I spent my time in the kitchens, trying to trade for jobs near the fire. Judging by the clothes everyone else wore, the weather had begun to warm, but I shivered unless I wore all my winter clothes, all at once.

Margarithe worried about Arsenault's absence and she

worried about me, too. She had me read aloud instead of pounding bread dough so I could continue to sit on the stool beside the simmering kettle of soup, and I almost regretted my jealousy toward her. But I couldn't look in her face without my own coloring, and since I wasn't sure who had the right of it, me or her, it only made things worse.

Best to put that moment aside, I told myself, considering that it had no opportunity to go anywhere. But the feel of his body pressed against mine would not leave me alone.

One night, I came back to my cot after supper service to find a pair of sandals on my bed and Ilena sitting on her cot across from mine. She sniffed as I struggled my boots off. I left my wool stockings on.

"Tell Mistress Levin I was escorted to the chirurgeon," she said, turning her head in disgust as I pushed my sock-clad feet into the sandals and bent in half, trying to grab the tie with my teeth.

I gave it up as a bad job and pulled the knot as tight as I could one-handed. "She'll ask the chirurgeon and then she'll know you haven't been there," I said in a low voice, trying to concentrate on my sandals.

"Did I say I *wasn't* going? I've been having headaches."

"Are you meeting Lobardin?"

I had never seen her with Lobardin, but it was a good guess that if a girl was sneaking out in the middle of the night, it would be to meet him.

She flushed. "Did I say I was going to see Lobardin? Perhaps it's someone else I'm meeting." That small, dark smile touched her lips again.

My sandals finally tied, I looked up at her. "Can you keep your nails the way you do if you have a baby strapped to your back?"

Her face grew pinched and angry. "I'm leaving tonight, and you will think up a way to put Mistress Levin off if she becomes too curious. Or I will tell."

CHAPTER 12

"I'll put off Mistress Levin," I said.

"Good." Her smile grew less dark but no less smug. "If Mistress Levin asks after that, you can say I'm practicing devotions."

I laughed aloud. "To which god?"

Her cheeks burned. "I'll see you in the morning, Kyrra."

I can't say I was sad to see her go. Once she was gone, I realized how exhausted I was. While the other girls were talking, brushing their hair, relating the stories of the day, and darning their socks by the light of the guttering candles, I curled up under my blankets. I didn't even bother to take off my sandals.

I was awoken some time later by Mistress Levin, shaking me.

"Where is Ilena?" she asked as soon as I opened my eyes.

"Practicing her devotions," I murmured, still half in a dream —searching that foreign shore for Arsenault but unable to find him. Instead, it was only his name that echoed in my head as I woke.

"I dispatched Evalo for her an hour past and the chirurgeon said she left some time ago."

Evalo was one of the gavaros who guarded the girls' quarters at night. He was an ugly little man with a harelip and a limp. I could imagine Ilena's distress at being tracked down by Evalo.

"The chirurgeon didn't send her off to pray?" I said, sitting up. "She said she expected to make an offering after she was relieved of her affliction."

The mistress snorted. "What affliction? Ilena is as healthy as a horse, and she certainly isn't that pious. Quit stalling me, Kyrra; I must know where she's gone. She's one of our oldest combers, and we need her to teach the younger ones how it's done."

I ran my hand through my hair, mussing it, trying to wake enough to think how I should handle this. "Maybe she took Lobardin for escort," I said.

"Lobardin is at his post. Evalo said the doctor told him she had *your* gavaro as escort."

My gavaro?

What had Lobardin said about Ilena that night in the barracks? *She's draped all over him like a cheap cloak.*

"I thought he was in—" I blurted, then cast my gaze to the floor. "I mean, he's been gone, hasn't he?"

Mistress Levin raised her eyebrows. "Apparently, he's returned."

I clenched my back teeth. "Then she's probably fine. Arsenault can certainly defend her against brigands."

"I don't think it's brigands that girl needs to worry about," the mistress murmured. Then she sighed as if she'd come to a decision.

"All right," she said. "Go. As it's your gavaro, and you're as like to know where Ilena's gone as anyone. I just want to know she's safe."

I got up, shivering as I kicked the blankets off, grabbed my cloak from its peg, and struggled it on. Mistress Levin handed me a half-burned candle, then stepped back and folded her hands serenely. "I'll send Evalo if you're not back soon."

She motioned me out the door and closed it behind me. I was alone in the night, with an entire estate to search, for all I knew. But I thought I could guess where Arsenault might have taken her.

The grotto.

I gripped the taper tightly in my hand as I set off down the path. The candlewick gave off a waxy, acrid smell. The night was windy and cold, and I had to walk backward to block the wind with my body since I couldn't cup the flame to keep it alight. What a sight I must have been. If any bandits remained, I would have been easy prey.

The first fat sprinkles fell as I left the path for the sparse forest that lay downhill from the gavaro barracks. Deer and dogs had worn a narrow trail through the undergrowth. I found it, and then I blew out my candle and waited a moment while my eyes adjusted to the dark. Twigs and gravel crunched under my feet as

I started walking again, but the wind and the patter and spit of raindrops helped hide the sound. Through the trees, the shadows of gavaros rippled on the torch-lit wall of the barracks, but no one turned my way.

The trail ran uphill and I scrabbled my way along it, feeling it out with my hand and my feet, until I came to the edge of the trees where the little grotto bit into the hillside. The gurgling spring made it hard to hear, but Ilena didn't have the sense to keep her voice down.

"Have you really traveled so much, Arsenault?"

I almost laughed, but there was too much bile in my mouth. She'd probably lean against him and swoon when I stepped out of the trees.

I ought to step out right now just to see her do it.

But the low rumble of Arsenault's voice held me back.

I couldn't make out the words, and all I saw were shadows moving, shadows that might as well have been trees bending in the wind. The wind gusted again, throwing rain in front of it, and above the sound of the leaves I heard Ilena's "Oh!"

My heart pounded. I was wet now, it was raining harder, but I couldn't force myself to step out of the trees. Let Evalo retrieve Ilena. I turned to go.

The brush rustled behind me. And suddenly, someone gripped my shoulders and dragged me back through it.

I screamed and thrashed before I realized who it was. Arsenault stared down at me and I stared up at him, unable to make out his expression in the dark, except that he had gone stark white.

Ilena ran up behind him, breathlessly, her hand on her mouth. *Arsenault,* she called, *Arsenault,* the way I had in my dream.

He slammed his knife back into its sheath. "Dammit, Kyrra. I could have killed you!"

"Of all the women you could take up with, why Ilena?" I said.

He stood still for a moment, but Ilena filled the silence. "You idiot! I told you to put Mistress Levin off, not follow me to see where I went! Do you want me to expose the both of you?"

"No one will be exposed tonight," Arsenault said curtly, then he stretched out his hand to help me sit up. "Ilena was trying to bargain with me. Do you know anything about that, Kyrra?"

I dusted my cloak. "No. I don't know why she's bargaining with you."

His eyes lit the way they did sometimes, and he frowned but didn't say anything.

Ilena sniffed. "I'm getting wet. Why didn't you stay in quarters?"

"Mistress Levin sent me. I had nothing to do with her knowing. You won't be in trouble."

"Mistress Levin knows my character," Ilena said. She sounded so satisfied, I wanted to hit her.

"I'd wager she does," Arsenault said. "Or I'd hope so. Come on, Ilena." He stood and put a hand on her shoulder. "Time for you to go home."

It took far longer to reach the barracks with Ilena than it would have without her. She insisted on holding Arsenault's arm the entire way there and as a result slipped often on the wet dead leaves that lined the way. By the time we reached the barracks, the flogging had begun to sound good.

Then Arsenault said to Ilena, "Lobardin will escort you home. Tell Mistress Levin that since it's close enough to dawn, Kyrra will stay here to do her work."

Ilena turned a deep scarlet. Her two long nails clacked together until it sounded like they must have split.

"I do not want Lobardin," she said.

We were still standing in the rain. Saes and Verrin were on guard duty. They watched us from beneath their hoods.

"That's not what Lobardin says." Saes grinned.

Verrin chuckled. "No," he said. "It's not what Lobardin says, indeed."

Arsenault hooked his thumbs in his swordbelt and rocked backward. "Have some manners around the lady."

They looked up at him. The flush in Ilena's cheeks had faded to pale, but at Arsenault's words, her eyes flashed with gratitude and triumph.

"I knew you would see the truth of the matter, Arsenault."

A silly girl playing a dangerous game. I saw her standing between the two gavaros, and my eyes were opened.

Still, I didn't want to torment either my father or Arsenault more. "Walk her back, Arsenault," I said. "I made a mistake. You shouldn't pay for it."

"If Ilena doesn't want Lobardin for escort, I'm sure Saes will walk her back. I'll take your post until you return."

Saes grinned crookedly and cocked his head. "And such a lovely night for a walk with a young girl. Will you take my arm?"

He held it out for Ilena, but Ilena only pursed her lips. "You'll both regret this," she said. "You'll see that I carry through on my promises."

"As do I," Arsenault replied. "Now go with Saes, Ilena. I'm doing you a favor."

Ilena laughed, but there was a flimsy edge to it. "A favor? I am out here walking in the rain, and still you wish to entertain yourself with that armless harlot?" She spit in the mud at my feet. "A witch is what you are. Child-murderer. *Kinless.*"

My trembling palm pressed against the length of my dagger, hidden in my pocket. Ilena leaned forward, but the world had slowed and her words mired in my head as if they were stuck in mud.

Murderer. Witch. Kinless.

Every bit was true. And yet she wanted what I had.

I began to laugh. The gavaros stopped in surprise. Ilena took a step backward, and Arsenault straightened up.

I held my hand against my dagger, and my right arm began to throb.

"Shall I put a curse on you, then?" I said, leaning toward her.

She backpedaled, down the curving path away from the gavaros, whose hands had gone to their swords. "Flog me, for all I care. I've lost an arm and a lover, and taken a life. Will you be my next? I'll hang and be glad, I swear it."

Her face was the color of the moon. The torches lit her up so I could See all the way through her, into her fear and her jealousy. Maybe her mother did beat it into her, never allowing her to feel good enough, but she tended it with the same care she tended the notches on her long, curved nails.

Steel hissed free behind me. "Speak not so lightly of sorcery," Arsenault said, and came to stand beside me. "There's been enough said here already."

His words doused me like water. Ilena burst into tears, and I began to shake.

It started in the hand I no longer had. First, my phantom fingers began to tremble, and then the whole ghost of my arm, a shaking so fierce, the thought entered my head that I would shake it off, it wasn't connected to me so well anymore.

I raised my face to Arsenault. "My arm," I said.

Saes came to get Ilena, took her by the elbow, and guided her away.

"Kyrra."

"My *arm*."

I tried to grip it, to stop it. But then the shaking spread to the flesh of me, the corporeal sections other people could see, and I sank to my knees in the dirt.

Kyrra.

Was that who I was? A woman had been named Kyrra once, but was it me?

Witch. Murderer. Harlot.

I saw through Ilena and into myself.

"Kyrra, come. *Kyrra.*"

But there was no Kyrra. There was only this shaking, nameless woman, who had faced down a serf-girl in the rain.

Arsenault picked me up and carried me into the barracks.

CHAPTER 12

I AWOKE FEELING AS IF MY TONGUE HAD BEEN WEIGHTED WITH lead and swollen to fill my mouth. Perhaps I had been ill, as Margarithe thought, and that was why I had been cold for weeks. Or perhaps Ilena had cursed me. I wasn't cold now. My skin felt as hot and dry as paper fed to a fire.

"Arsenault," I croaked, but my voice didn't sound like my own. The room danced around me like a summer mirage—the silk tapestries with scenes of orange trees and maidens playing lutes, the gold candlesticks, the wrought-iron bed canopied in lace and blanketed in velvet and brocade.

My old room. I closed my eyes and wept for joy.

When I opened them again, Arsenault sat in front of me and the room in which I lay was his.

"Lie down, Kyrra," he said. Tepid water sopped across my forehead, leaving beads that dried too quickly. The cloth blurred; watching it, and him, left me dizzy. I wanted to sink into the pillows until the cool white linen covered me like a blanket of snow.

"Take some water. Kyrra."

The rag swiped my lips. I opened my mouth and licked away the moisture that remained. Sleep might have overtaken me; I drifted in and out for days.

"Drink," he said, sliding his hand behind my head. I did and choked, and then began to shake again, and he pulled the blankets up around me—piles and piles of blankets until I felt like a mole shivering under the earth.

"Is this plague?" I asked.

Arsenault laughed, low and tired. "I doubt it."

"I think I shall die."

"You won't. The first time, everyone thinks so."

"This isn't my first fever," I told him. My teeth started chattering, and he tucked the blankets in tighter around me.

"Your body's at war with itself right now. It will take some time to sort things out."

I felt him touch me, stroking my temple with his thumb.

"Save your tenderness for Margarithe," I said, trying to knock his hand away and roll over.

Arsenault sighed. I opened my eyes a crack and watched him rub his brow. His braid was untidy; both black and silver strands had pulled out of it. The white shirt he wore was stained with tar on one shoulder, and there was a scratch at the corner of his mouth.

"Were you in Liera for Jon or my father?" I murmured.

"Both, I suppose," he said. Pottery bumped a wood table. "Here now, Kyrra. Drink again, only a little now."

I leaned forward with his help to take the cup. This time, I kept the water down better. My throat eased.

"You were spying on the Prinze."

"You might say that."

"You cut your lip."

He lifted the back of his hand to his mouth. "It's not that bad."

"How?"

He looked uncomfortable or perhaps I imagined it. My vision shimmered with fever, and it was worse when I looked at him. A nimbus of light blurred his features, following his hand when he moved it. He didn't speak, but somehow, the answer leapt into my brain in a tumble of images that felt like memories.

"I never visited Liera with Cassis," I muttered, closing my eyes. "Who is that woman?"

"Cassis has taken a wife," Arsenault said reluctantly. "Camile di Sere."

Camile. I remembered her. Dark hair and green eyes. Lips so lush and pink that all the girls at the courting parties were jealous and immediately tried to pinch their own to make them look like hers. She was lush all over, dressed in her indigo Sere silks.

"Of course," I said. "Camile. May they have many happy returns."

I felt like I was choking again. I sank down into the pillow and turned my head toward the wall. Yellow and blue sparks slithered across my dark eyelids like silkworms, and I wished they would spin me a cocoon.

Perhaps Arsenault thought I was asleep. Fabric rustled, and his hand settled on my left shoulder. He rubbed the curve lightly with his thumb, and then his arm folded along the back of my arm and he put his forehead down on the pillow. His hair—silky, cool, and loose—brushed the skin of my neck.

He spoke into the pillow in a low, quiet voice, as if he didn't expect me to be listening. "If only I had been there, Kyrra, to keep you safe. And now—may the gods forgive me for anything I do to you."

He remained as he was for a time that was too short. Then his warmth disappeared from my back. The chair rattled and his boots scuffed the floor as he walked away.

A bottle uncorked.

"Damn you, Erelf," he murmured. "She already has to deal with Ires' battle magic. Why should you claim her too?"

※

I KNEW THE NAME *IRES*. HE WAS THE GOD OF WAR—DRIVEN insane with grief when Tekus and his children killed all his kin and usurped their powers. Only Ires had escaped and that because no one, god or mortal, could defeat him. They could only trick him and shackle him deep within the earth, where he remained, still radiating his strange and horrible magic out into the world of men.

But...*Erelf.*

The name echoed in my head.

I knew no one by that name, no man, no god. And yet the sound of it woke something inside me. I spun long, silky strands of thoughts that held no meaning, and betrayed myself by shouting out his name. Sometimes, I woke myself up, and Arsenault would be covering my mouth with his hand, saying, "Hush, don't call him!" So, I began to know that there was magic in the room and not all of it was in Arsenault.

I fell into dreams and not even Arsenault could call me back.

In my dreams, I was an eagle, circling high above my father's lands. My gold pinions flashed in the sun, and the updrafts ruffled the feathers at my throat as I sent my cry out across the blue. My eyes were as sharp as the sharpest of blades. I dove and climbed, watching as the black shapes of humans crawled about far beneath me, swords flashing in the sun, horses roiling and milling into each other, banners snapping the air. I saw Cassis sitting astride a gray Ipanzer that slammed its hindquarters into my father's horse. I saw the pounding mess the horses' hooves made, how at close quarters they trampled bodies of gavaros I had once known. I saw the stark look of terror on Cassis's face, the mud that spattered his cheeks, the blue and gray threaded through his mail shirt. He'd lost his helm. His brown hair was tousled and wild.

I ached for him, as if I hadn't lost my arm. And I hated him at the same time. I thought I'd put dreams of him out of my head, and it made me angry. I swooped down, talons outstretched, ready to gouge his face, to pierce the mail he wore. My talons were metal, and I was an eagle, eater of the dead.

But something knocked me out of the air before I reached him. I spun, head whirling with the pain of the blow, and fell to the ground. I beat my wings against the mud, trying to rise again, but the mud snared me like a falconer's net.

"Little bird, why do you squander your strength?"

A man stood above me, his face shadowed by a wide-brimmed black felt hat. In his left hand he held a long staff made of two strips of pale yellow wood twisted together. A raven perched on his gloved right hand, watching me out of shiny violet-black eyes. It clacked its beak together and I scooted away from it. I didn't know if I was still a bird or a woman, but it didn't seem to matter. The man wore a coarse blue shirt, a black belt, and leather leggings wrapped with tawny fur strips and beaded in intricate red-and-blue patterns. The hat hid the color of his eyes, but his hair was gray-veined black, and there was a scar on his face in the same place as Arsenault's.

He looked like an older Arsenault. And then again, he looked nothing like Arsenault, nothing at all.

"What do you want of me?" I asked.

"Everything," he said, then grinned. "Or nothing. It's you who's called me; perhaps I should ask you the same question."

"Who are you?" I asked, though I knew the simplest answer to that question—*Erelf*.

He squatted in front of me, and his raven made a deep throaty sound and edged farther up his hand. "Shall I ask you the same? You've dined at my brother's feast. You've hunted flesh; perhaps now you hunt wisdom. Or perhaps you don't. Not everyone is born to See."

"I'm not blind."

"Or so you think. If you had been born without an arm, would you miss it?"

I flushed. "I would see everyone else with two arms. I would know."

"Even so. *Seeing* is somewhat harder to define. Did you like the looks of this battle?"

I shuddered. "No."

"Perhaps you'd rather be blind."

"No!" I sat up. "Without my sight, what would I have? I'd be in the cripple colony for sure. Have you sent me this fever then, to take my sight?"

"To take your sight?" His mouth quirked upward. "Do you see more or less now?"

"More of dreams and less of the world. Is that a trade?"

"Only if you wish to remain here. Some do. Do you?"

"Why would I want to stay in this dream? Just because Arsenault says I have battle magic doesn't mean I want your battles."

At Arsenault's name, the man's expression hardened and formed lines; it made him look far older than I had thought upon first sight. Then, abruptly, he smiled. But his smile did nothing to dispel the storminess of his eyes, which I could now see were a dark, murky blue.

"Battle magic. Little carrion bird. Do you wish for battle magic?"

"No," I told him, "I'm only telling you what Arsenault said. I wish all to be spared a battle. I wish I wouldn't have taken the potion when my mother offered it to me."

"Do you?"

"*Yes,*" I said.

"You would have a child, then. A memory of what Cassis did to you."

Was a child merely a memory of past love or betrayal, a memento of an afternoon rolling around in a stable, the fading ghost of a momentary flash of pleasure?

It seemed wrong of him to say so, even though my child was a memory in truth. He had never been born. And yet he remained with me always, much more than a mere image in my mind.

Sometimes as I lay in the dark, I would imagine my life if I had refused the potion my mother gave me. I would see myself with two whole arms, and a little boy with dark curls resting within them as I snuggled him to my breast. In my imagination, we lived in a hut on my father's land with nothing but a bed and a chair, in which I would rock him and sing him lullabies after I was done with my work.

Sometimes, I put Arsenault into this fantasy, watching him duck under the low lintel of the hut door and straighten up with his smile flashing white in the darkness of his beard.

It was a fantasy that dripped out of me like blood, and it hurt the same.

"Well?" Erelf said.

"I would," I said.

He stood. "You carry ghosts inside you. Nothing else. No matter what Arsenault says. Listen to him if you think he has the right of it. But know that you are blind and unaware that you do not see."

He pounded his staff against the ground. The staff dissolved and from it a flock of ravens rose, their glossy black wings beating the air until it rushed past me. Ravens covered the sky like a blot of ink, and a shadow passed where they flew. Over the field they went, their hoarse calls obliterating even the sounds of battle. Men stopped in the middle of the fighting and stared up at the sky, or else they ran and hid in the trees. The battlefield emptied until only bodies remained, and then the ravens lit on the ground to devour them. I swooped in after them and landed on a man's mailed chest, a man dressed in burgundy and gold, my father's colors.

Flat gray eyes stared past me, blind in death. There was a metal streak in the man's black hair.

I was an eagle, eater of the dead. Lest the ravens have him, I took him instead.

※

"ARSENAULT," I SAID WHEN I WOKE, DAYS LATER, "WHAT DO you do in Liera? I must know. *Tell me.*"

Even Arsenault seemed taken aback. He stood and stared at me for a moment. I looked back at him and realized I must have been lying in his bed for days. He stood as if his leg pained him less, and he wore different clothes—just a plain shirt and trousers muddy at the knees.

"You've only just woken up. Perhaps you'd rather have something to eat."

"Perhaps I'd rather have some answers," I said.

He watched me silently for a moment. Finally, he said, "I

work as a gavaro for the Prinze. Not as one of their military men. I conduct special business for the House. The position allows me to collect information for your father."

"And no one questions you? That you're gone so long?"

He shrugged. "People see what they want to see. It's a special position. The absences make sense."

"How long have I been here?" I hesitated, then asked what I really wanted to know. "Were you out very long? Was I alone?" I hated myself for wanting to ask the question, but it came out of me anyway.

He grasped the back of the chair and sat down. When he answered, he spoke in a soft tone that made me think that he understood why I'd asked. "They brought a new horse from Liera and needed a hand to subdue it. A destrier. Otherwise, you've been here eight days, and I've stayed as often as I could. When I couldn't be here, Saes, Verrin, and Margarithe have all taken turns sitting with you. Lobardin wouldn't be put off either."

"Lobardin too?"

Arsenault looked troubled. "I *think* he was worried about you. But I also think he knew you weren't merely out of your head with fever."

"You should have walked Ilena back," I murmured. "Then none of this would have happened."

"No, it would have happened sometime. I'm surprised it took this long."

I ran my hand over the blankets. I realized I was only wearing my chemise, and I wondered who had undressed me. I blushed and pulled the blankets up higher. "Was it magic? Did Ilena curse me? Or did you—"

Arsenault's eyes lit up angrily. He rose and paced over to his worktable, running a hand through his hair before he turned back to me.

"You think *I'd* curse you?"

I sat up and threw the blankets off, forced myself out of bed, and tottered over to him. "But, Arsenault—these dreams must have come from somewhere—from some kind of magic!"

His fingers drifted to the pommel of his sword and his mouth pulled down. Did he think I was dangerous? The thought alarmed me. Who had infected me with this magic if it wasn't his?

But then he took my elbow gently. "At least sit down while I tell you. Please? Kyrra?"

"And will you explain?" I said as I allowed him to steer me back to the bed.

"As much as I'm able. And then you'll eat. You've had nothing but a few sips of broth in eight days."

I nodded and he took a breath.

"Whatever dreams you dreamed were yours. The magic gave them to you, as it claimed you. But also, it seems"—he let the breath out—"Erelf."

Hearing him say the name aloud made me shiver. He leaned across me to pull the crumpled blankets over my lap. "Lie down," he said. "You've probably very little strength yet."

I grabbed the blankets to pull them up myself. "I saw him," I said. "His ravens."

"Maybe Erelf wants you because you're with me; I don't know. It's hard to know why a god does anything. He likes to keep his plans close to his vest."

"He's a god?" I asked, dumbfounded.

"The patron of Sight," Arsenault replied grimly. "I thought you were lying when you said you didn't know anything about magic. I could See it so clearly around you."

"And is *that* why you've been teaching me?"

"Will you believe me if I tell you?" His voice contained a hint of bitterness. "Partly—at least at first. I just couldn't believe—Kyrra, you attract so much magic, you might as well be a wildfire. I couldn't believe that anyone with that sort of light following her wouldn't be aware of it. When I first heard your story and your father told me he couldn't hire me to watch you but he'd be asking about you all the same, I thought I'd just drawn duty on a spoiled brat."

I flinched. "Perhaps...that was fair."

He shook his head. "No. It wasn't. When I saw you wrestling with that water bucket over and over again until you'd conquered it...I knew you were different. And dear gods, that glow."

He scrubbed his fingers through his beard. Then he sighed. "A man's reasons can change over time, can't they?"

There was something in his eyes I felt too weak to see. So I just nodded. Slowly.

His shoulders relaxed. "There are two kinds of magic. The first allows itself to be crafted and bent to a man's will. The second tries to bend a man to *its* will. That kind of magic will swallow you if you're not careful."

"And which kind is it that I have?"

The way he looked at me reminded me of the way he'd looked in my dream as he brought down Adalus, the elk. That mixture of regret and sorrow.

"Oh." I rolled the frayed edge of the blanket against my thumb. "The second kind. Of course."

He sighed, heavily. "Kyrra, I'd have saved you from this if I could have. The Sight that comes and goes can be a burden. And battle magic..."

"Is that what happened to me? In the grotto?"

I tried to push away the memory of what else had happened in the grotto.

"Mmmm," he said, clearing his throat and looking away. He rubbed the back of his neck. "Yes. I think so."

"We call it battle *madness* in Liera. It comes from Ires. His insane desire for revenge."

"It's still magic. It thirsts for blood and chaos, and it needs a conduit to satisfy that thirst. It finds its easiest course in those who have wrongs to avenge. If you can hold it back, it becomes an asset in battle. If you can't..."

"You don't need to tell me, I guess. I heard Lobardin laughing as he cut bandits down."

Arsenault leaned back in the chair. "Lobardin. Yes. I thought that might be the way of it."

"He came to see me?"

"He brought some broth from the kitchens. And—orchids. From the high road." Arsenault gestured carelessly at a plain pottery cup on the windowsill that had been stuffed full of lavender blooms. "I told him I thought you might like them."

I knew where those orchids grew. Once upon a time, I had dragged my chambermaids out into the fields so I could gather them into baskets. I cut so many, I couldn't find enough vases for them, and so I used our good crystal stemware and arranged the flowers all over my room.

That was the spring before I met Cassis.

Tears filled my eyes before I could stop them, and I blinked them away furiously.

"Kyrra? Is something wrong?"

"No, no, nothing."

But I hardly knew, did I? It could be that nothing was wrong…or that everything was.

"Arsenault," I said, reaching out to touch his hand. "Thank you."

He lifted his head in surprise. "Why are you thanking me?"

"For giving up your bed. And taking care of me. For allowing Lobardin to bring me orchids."

"Well." He shifted in his seat, looking uncomfortable. "What else should I have done?"

"You might have done nothing. You might have sent me back with the combergirls where I belonged."

"No, I couldn't have done that."

"But what will happen to me now?"

He sobered. "You'll have to trust me. I told Mistress Levin you're no longer bunking with the combergirls. You'll be safer here." He leaned forward. "I know how this is going to sound.

But my intentions are honorable. There isn't a room for you in the barracks to have for yourself. So, if you'll have it, I'll put up a screen and a cot, and...you can stay here."

I pulled my hand away from his and drew the blanket up higher. "With you? In your room?"

He looked stricken for a moment. Hurt. Or maybe that pain was directed against himself.

Did he still think of himself as my bodyguard? A gavaro with a commission? Was that why he couldn't make me any promises?

"I'm sorry for what happened in the grotto, Kyrra," he said, his voice earnest and low. "It won't happen again. It's just that if Erelf wants you...I'd rather be there. To stop him."

CHAPTER 13

WHAT NOBODY TELLS YOU IS THAT MAGIC IS A PAIN IN THE ASS.

It's like the dinner guest who always shows up uninvited. It comes too early and stays too late. It ruins your evening plans. It's the mistake you wake up with the morning after.

Hopefully, it will leave me alone tonight.

The day crowds are starting to move out of the Temple District, changing up for night crowd worshippers, which are a different sort of people. Kinless, free class, and householder mix here, along with people from all the Eterean cities and every foreign nation. But the night gods are different from the day gods.

The lantern is hung on Cythia's porch, inviting worshippers to pay homage to the goddess of love. The soft glow of candles illuminates a statue of Lusa, goddess of the moon. Pana, the goddess whose name just means *willing*, does a rousing business at night.

And then there are the dark sides of the major gods, which take ascendance when the light fails.

Though Erelf was exiled to the northern wastes when he killed his brother, Geoffre di Prinze has brought him back and elevated him to the position of Knowledge in the daylight.

At night he's the god of secrets, the way he's always been. The god of magic.

It's been a long time since I let myself think about Erelf. I did my best to follow Arsenault's example while I was off fighting on my own in Rojornick, and I became adept at redirecting my thoughts whenever memories of him came up. My employer's wife didn't like magic, and I can only imagine what she would have said if I'd added *unpredictable dreams of an exiled god* to my list of offenses. But for five years I've managed—somehow—to stay out from under Erelf's nose.

And now I'm planning to walk in right past it.

Razi and Nibas, the only men I trust at this point, are sitting with me at an outdoor table across the street from Geoffre's new temple and its enormous statue of Erelf.

"You can almost see up his nostrils," Nibas muses, tilting his head for a better view of the statue's giant nose. His beads clink together as he moves.

"You think they Fixed the snot, too?" Razi says, picking up a pipe that rests in a large bowl on the table. Half-full wineglasses and a bottle of red are arrayed around it. It reminds me of a drunken clock, ticking away the time until I can meet Jon Barra tomorrow for my gun.

"Do gods have snot?" Nibas says.

Razi shrugs. "How am I supposed to know what your gods have and don't have? Do I care about your gods? Always arguing. Causing trouble. Dooming you all to a lifetime of misery."

He takes a pull on the pipe and closes his eyes, then blows smoke with a beatific expression. "Now, that—that is something worthy of a god. Where'd you get it, Kyris?"

I've been throwing some of my money around since I got out of the silk warehouses. Kacin would work better to dampen my identity than this sweetweed mix, but I still can't tolerate it.

"Got paid finally and went down to Pana's temple," I say.

Razi looks at me like I've betrayed him. "And you didn't get me and Nibas first?"

CHAPTER 13

I lean back with my own pipe. "You think I want to share everything with you and Nibas?"

"Besides," Nibas adds, "last time, we had to drag your ass out because that sacred paste made you think you had ants crawling all over your body."

Razi looks at him blankly. "I don't remember that."

Nibas glares at him. "*I* do, and it's nothing I want to repeat. If Kyris tries to take you back into that place, I'll put an arrow in your back. And his." He turns to me. "What did you get us for? You need help?"

"Just information." I dart Razi a glance and then add, "I'm tracking somebody."

"In that temple?" Razi frowns vaguely and gestures toward the statue of Erelf with his head. "That complicates things, doesn't it?"

Nibas looks at my arm. "No offense, Kyris, but if I were you, I'd think twice about that job."

I have thought twice about the job since this morning, and now I'm even more determined to blow a few holes in Cassis—at least one of them for Vadz. I haven't told them about Vadz yet, and it doesn't look like they know. The smoke has loosened my tongue, but instead of talking, I stick the pipe in my mouth and inhale deeply.

Blowing smoke, I say, "Somebody doesn't want me to find the person I've been hired to track."

"Somebody from the temple?"

"Somebody maybe using magic. I don't know if they were from the temple or not. Does the temple hire Qalfans?"

Razi frowns. "Not that I know of. You were attacked by a Qalfan? The Qalfan from the Lady?"

"I'm not sure it's the same person. I caught him in a silk warehouse but he got away. I think he used magic to do it." I tap out my ashes. "I know you've been asking around, Razi. Did you find out anything?"

Razi arches his eyebrow. "You told me it was your business."

"He wore his cutlasses Dakkaran-style. And fought like one of your brothers."

"A Nezar?" Razi looks surprised. He smokes for a moment, thinking, then says, "Well, lucky for you I did ask around. And I might know someone like the man you're talking about. But he didn't come up through the Quarter, and I don't think he's working for the Sere. All I've heard are rumors, really."

I lean forward. "What kind of rumors?"

"You're talking about that Prinze guardsman," Nibas says suddenly.

Prinze guardsman?

Fucking hells.

I bring my arm down on the table too hard and it clanks against the wood. Both Nibas and Razi look at me.

"Ah," Nibas says. "You've got a grudge against the Prinze, don't you?"

"Tell me the rumors," I say.

Razi shrugs. "A couple of my brothers were working a job providing protection for a kacin merchant. One of them intercepted information that the cargo was being targeted by Amoran smugglers. The merchant passed the information on to the Prinze, and they loaned him a man. He was veiled and wore cutlasses, fought like the very spirit of a sword, but at the end of the night…"

Razi turns toward the big statue of Erelf, looking troubled.

Nibas puts down his own pipe. "Razi. Brother. You know those men like to tell stories. It gets bigger in the telling. Like Kyris's arm."

"I appreciate you bringing my arm into it, Nibas. It's got nothing to do with my arm."

"It's the same as your arm. The first time I saw you use that arm, it was terrifying. But not so much the second time. By the third fight, Tirello had made it part of our regular strategy, and by the fourth, we were using you to win bets."

"What in all the hells did that Prinze guard do?"

CHAPTER 13

Razi taps more of the sweetweed mixture into his pipe. "Things went bad. The Amorans had some kind of potion, gave off a poisonous smoke. The Prinze fighter, whoever he was, made a sign with the sword and…"

Razi looks a little sick. He's had a lot of sweetweed, but I don't think that's the reason for his expression.

"And?"

He faces me, all the handsome good humor erased from his face. "The poison became a rain of knives. May the Magnificent Sun witness every word I am telling you, this is what my brothers said. It can't be true and yet they said it. The knives rained down on the Amorans and shredded them, head to toe."

❧

I DON'T KNOW WHAT KIND OF FIXER COULD TURN POISON into a rain of knives, but if he's chasing me because he's on the Prinze payroll, I need that magicked weapon even more.

I pump Nibas and Razi for more information on the Prinze before I lay my pipe down and stand up. The world has an extra spin to it and I put my hands back down on the table, trying to make sure the wine I've drunk is going to stay put.

Watching me hesitate, Nibas says, "Having second thoughts about going to see that god?"

I've got third and fourth thoughts about going anywhere near that god, but I'm not going to get caught out again, especially when I go to meet Jon tomorrow. I give Nibas a short, cynical laugh to pass it off. "I've got to piss. When I see you two again, I'll have so much coin, we'll be able to melt it down and smoke it if we want to."

Razi rises unsteadily. "We've got nothing to do tonight, Nibas. Why don't we go with him?"

"Into Erelf's temple?" Nibas looks skeptical.

"What, are you two my bodyguards now?"

"I'm just thinking I've never had a magician. Can they use magic in bed?" Razi grins. "I think I need my cock Fixed."

"By all the gods, Razi, can't you ever keep it in your pants? I'm on a job."

"I'm on a job too," he says. "It's just for myself. I'm back on duty in two days."

Nibas sighs. "I guess if Razi's going, I have to see his sorry ass back home."

Damn. All I wanted was information, not for them to come with me. This is why I didn't tell them about Vadz.

"I don't need help."

Razi leans toward me, looking serious but not more sober. "I want to see this Qalfan who's following you," he says. "If he's one of my brothers, I want to know about it. Tell him to lay off." He flips one of my curls and gives me his grin.

A smoked Razi has no preference for gender. I found that out some months ago. He has no idea if I'm male or female and he doesn't care.

I shove him backward. "I can take care of myself, Razi."

"I know that. But if he's a Nezar using magic...that's not the same as one of your magicians in the marketplace, selling truthtelling. That's *poison knives*, Kyris. That's why our magicians were bound long ago."

He has no idea who he's talking to. But it's like Arsenault used to say: people see what they want to see.

And the smoke and the wine are making me dizzy. All I want is to get in and out, and maybe if Nibas and Razi come with me, it will hide me better. Maybe I can get them set with lovers for the night and out of my way and safe.

"All right. But we're in and out. Just to the market, not to the altar. If that Qalfan shows up, we're not engaging to kill, because I want to talk to him, all right?"

"I heard the first part of that..." Razi says.

"Shut up," Nibas says, smacking him in the back of the head. "Let's go."

CHAPTER 13

It's somehow colder inside Erelf's temple, as if the marble had concentrated all the chill of the spring air inside it. We skirt the statue and stumble through the courtyard, avoiding the pens where sacrificial fawns bleat after their missing mothers. The sound makes me shiver. Unthinking, I lay my hand on the hilt of my sword.

"Kyris," Nibas murmurs at my shoulder. "Your sword."

I look down. The hilt has picked up a soft white glow, just from the brief touch of my gloved hand in this temple.

Cursing, I snatch it back.

"Give me the coin and let me do it," Nibas says.

"Why would I do that?"

"Because your arm is going to give you away. You're trying to stay hidden, aren't you?"

"Fucking magicians will probably try to cut it off and sell it," Razi offers, his voice muffled behind his urqa, which he has pulled up all the way to the bottom of his eyes. I find myself wishing I could wear urqa and allaq, too.

"I'll do it," I growl. "You two just watch out, let me know if anyone seems to be following us."

"I'll watch out," Nibas says. "At least one of us is competent."

"For an archer, you mean," Razi says.

I ignore them. I can feel little questing fingers around the edges of my consciousness, like hands trying to nudge aside draperies for a peek inside. I concentrate on finding the staircase that winds down to the lower level, tucked inside the hill of old Eterean ruins upon which this new temple is built.

It seems to yawn down into the darkness without a bottom, and suddenly the smoke and the wine make the stairwell feel too close, too confining, like the shaft of a tomb sunk into the earth.

I tug at my collar to loosen it. I'm having trouble breathing.

Razi curses softly when he bumps his head on a low roof beam. "Don't your northern gods believe in candles?"

"He'd like everything to be sleight of hand," I say, and somewhere, in a far corner of my mind, I hear chuckling.

Hello, little bird...

No, no. I push away from the voice and stumble down the rest of the stairs, nearly tackling the acolyte who stands at the bottom, waiting to greet us.

"Oh," she says, and pushes me back upright. I look up into a pale face, with hair that glints red-gold in the flickering light spilling into the bottom of the stairwell from the room beyond. Her eyes are a light green.

"What can I do for you?" she says with a soft smile.

Dagmari. Or maybe...from somewhere even farther north. Somewhere closer to Arsenault's home.

Nibas and Razi come to flank me.

I straighten up and smooth my tunic. "Show me to the weapons table."

※

HALF A TURN OF THE CLOCK LATER, I'M THE PROUD OWNER OF a magic-forged throwing knife set with a brilliant tear drop of lapis lazuli Shaped to turn black in the presence of magic.

My arm works as a divining rod only imperfectly. It sings for all sorts of reasons, many of them internal. But if the stone in the knife turns black...then I'll know.

Not to mention I need a weapon I can use in situations where I can't draw my sword, which is also magic-forged but much, much more distinctive.

Nibas and Razi stumble out into the clear air of the backdoor temple portico behind me. Razi pulls his urqa down slightly so I can see him flash his smile in the lantern light. "That wasn't so bad," he says. "I don't think I've ever seen so many Dagmari in one place."

"You've got a problem if you think the Dagmari are exotic,

brother," Nibas says. "You've never seen one get mutton stew in his beard."

"Eh," Razi says. "They should braid their beards. But the *women*, Nibas."

"You've never seen a Dagmari woman get mutton stew in her beard," I say. "I thank the both of you, but I think I can handle—"

A jolt twangs through my arm and I clutch it to my side. Suddenly, I feel dizzy, as if the effects of the smoke and wine have grown worse, not better with time.

"They're not going to like it if you puke on their patio," Razi says, coming to stand next to me.

"I'm not—" I begin, but then I realize that he's not paying attention to me anymore. Instead, he's standing up, pulling his urqa back up over his nose.

Nibas comes immediately to attention. "Razi," he says.

"There's your Nezar," Razi says in a quiet voice, and bolts for the low wall that edges the garden.

No, I think, Vadz uppermost in my thoughts. But what if Razi kills the assassin before I can question him? "Razi!" I shout, and run after him, and Nibas follows us both, swearing.

Razi seems to throw off the effects of the smoke as he runs. Watching a real Nezar fight—when he's not attacking you—is a sight. He vaults the wall with his long legs and lands on his feet like a cat on the other side. Before he starts running again, his swords are in his hands.

I'm too short to vault the wall. I heft myself up on top and jump to the ground. Nibas lands beside me.

"Just the one?" Nibas asks.

"One," I confirm.

By unspoken agreement, we fan out to either side of Razi as we run to catch up with him, in case my gavaro veers left or right. We're running through another temple garden, lit mostly by moonlight. Pathways veer through dark, spiky lumps of bushes and the bare spaces of winter-dead flower beds.

"Shit," I say, breathing hard. "Shit, shit, shit—"

Razi steps into the darkness under a tree, and the gavaro who's been following me explodes out of it.

Metal clangs and blades flash, throwing sparks when they bind. Both these men are tall, quick, and lethal. Razi shouts at him in Qalfan.

"L'ilq za Nezari dik allin!"

But he doesn't answer. Instead, he slams his sword hilt into Razi's jaw from underneath. Razi staggers backward, getting his own swords in front of him purely by practiced instinct.

My sword, when I pull it, flares bright blue.

The gavaro fighting Razi stumbles and stares at it. Razi comes around with a slash to his side, and the gavaro jumps out of the way. Razi follows with a downward slash using his other sword...

A sharp *crack*, accompanied by a bright orange flash and a cloud of white smoke, splits the night.

Razi stands still for a moment. The sword drops from his hand. Then his knees buckle and he goes down.

He's been shot.

The gavaro's a godsdamned Prinze.

"Razi!" Nibas yells, and catches him before he can hit the ground.

A sound rips its way out of my mouth. Nothing human, more like an animal in rage. And for a moment, rage blinds me. I swing Arsenault's sword out in a great flaring stroke of blue, aiming for the gavaro's neck. He stumbles backward, and I press my advantage of anger, making him defend. But I'm too full of smoke and wine to be a fitting tool for Ires's rage. The God of War leaves me alone, and the gavaro gets one sword thrust straight through the fabric of my cloak.

When I step back to make sure I'm still whole, his empty hand—the hand that must have held the gun—lifts, starts to make a sign.

I yank my new knife from its sheath on my side and hurl it at him.

It has a good weight and I throw true. The blade slices through the urqa, past his cheek. He hurls himself out of the way but not before I see the dark streak bloom on the fabric of the urqa.

He disappears into the trees. I start to give chase, and then I realize Nibas is shouting my name.

"Kyris! Kyris, damn you, we have to get him back to the Quarter!"

I stop and bend in half, hands on my knees, dragging in the cold night air in big breaths that feel like daggers slicing my lungs.

I look down and my knife is lying there.

The stone is as black as the remains of last year's frost-killed leaves.

CHAPTER 14

"A BOAT!" I SHOUT, RUNNING DOWN FROM THE GARDEN AND waving my arm at all the ferrymen moored on the other side of Cythia's temple—which owns the garden where Razi lies, Nibas staunching his wound with his cloak. But in my plain clothes, none of the ferrymen will look at me.

I shove a couple dressed in velvet out of the way and push myself up in front of a ferryman with a larger, canopied boat. "I need a ferry to the Quarter," I say, out of breath. "Urgently. I have a man who's hurt."

The ferryman darts a glance at the velvet-clad couple and then at me. "I don't get involved in trouble—" he begins, at the same time that the man I pushed says, "We were in line for that boat first, what do you think you're doing—"

I propel him backward with my right hand in his collarbone, and then I grab the ferryman by the collar. "I said, I have a man who's hurt. I'll pay you well enough to make it worth your while, but I am not going to take no for an answer."

"Si, si," the ferryman says. "The boat is yours; where's your man?"

I let go of him and fish in my purse for a coin. I press the astra into his hand, and when he sees the gold, he gasps. "Hold the boat," I say, already starting to run the other way. "If you leave, I will find you!"

Back in the garden, Nibas is still holding Razi with his cloak wrapped tight around Razi's left arm. Razi is shaking, the sheen of sweat on his face glistening in the moonlight.

"We've got to get him down to the canal," I say.

"Razi," Nibas says. "Do you hear that? We're getting you back to the Quarter. But you have to move. You have to stand."

"I'm not important enough for them to come to me?" he says shakily.

I bend to take Razi's other arm, one hand on his forearm, the other curled around his bicep. "Your ability to joke badly is still intact, I see." Nibas eases himself out from under Razi and places himself on Razi's other side. "It's going to hurt, but we've got you."

Razi closes his eyes and nods. "On three," Nibas says, and we haul Razi upright.

He exclaims breathlessly in pain and sags against us. "No!" I say. "No, Razi, don't faint."

"My arm. It's—by the Sun, it's like it's on fire."

"You're going to make it," Nibas tells him firmly. "Now lean on us and let's get out of here."

༺❦༻

WHEN THE FERRYMAN SEES RAZI, DRESSED IN HIS NEZAR'S robes and covered in blood, he looks as if he'll be the one to pass out. I revive him by sliding him another astra once we get Razi lowered into the boat and partially hidden by the canopy. "Keep quiet after we're done and I'll give you another one."

"The blood—"

"I'll clean it up. Just move now. As fast as we can."

The ferryman turns his back to me and shoves off from the canal side with his long pole. He expertly guides his boat through the others glutting the edgewater into the center lane, open for emergencies. Mostly, it's used on a daily basis by important people, but I've paid him enough that we've suddenly become important.

The way he shoots us sick glances every now and then makes me think what he really wants is to just to get us out of his boat.

I crouch underneath the canopy beside Razi. He shivers, his teeth chattering, and with every involuntary movement, he moans in pain. I untie my cloak and sling it down on top of him. I've seen men die of these chills on the battlefield.

"Kyris," Nibas says in a low voice. "You need to look at this."

He's unwound his cloak from Razi's arm to check the wound. I lean over to look. The torches that line the canal give us a very dim light, so it's hard to see details, but the gunshot obliterated the need for details.

"He was bleeding from his side," Nibas tells me, speaking low enough that Razi probably won't even register it. Or maybe he'll remember it later in snatches, the way I remember the chirurgeon talking about my arm. "But I think that's just a gash. I think the ball lodged in his arm."

It's a good assumption. His arm is hardly recognizable. Splinters of bone spike up white through the dark red mass of what was once his forearm. Nibas cut his sleeve back, but there are still bits of fabric embedded in the wound, and where the arm isn't red, it's black from powder and burns.

Nibas looks up at me, and I know what he's thinking, what he can't say if Razi is listening.

They're going to have to take it off.

"They killed Vadz," I say suddenly.

Nibas pauses in the act of rewrapping Razi's arm and looks at me like I've just said something in another language. "What?"

"Last night. In the Night Market. You heard about the murder?"

"I heard there was some Rojornicki bastard..." His voice dies. "That was you, wasn't it. And Vadz was the criminal."

I nod.

"Why the hells didn't you tell us, Kyris?"

"I didn't want either of you getting caught up in that."

"It was Vadz! You didn't kill him, did you?"

"No! Do you think I'm a demon?"

"I think you're an idiot. You should have said—"

"I didn't want you to come into the temple with me. I tried to tell you I'd do it myself. I didn't *want* Razi to go after that Qalfan in the garden!"

Nibas looks like he's tearing his words off with his teeth. "Who killed Vadz, then?"

"I don't know. He wore a mask. I think maybe it was the same man who shot Razi."

"Was it the Qalfan from the Lady?"

"I don't know. Maybe. If he betrayed his mistress."

"Mistress?"

"Just forget I said that."

"It's his godsdamned arm, Kyris!"

"Do you think I don't know that?"

"I'm not going to forgive you if he dies. He's an idiot, but he's a good idiot. He doesn't deserve this."

I sit back and draw my arm across my brow. "Don't worry, Nibas. If he dies, I won't forgive myself."

Nibas's face loses a little of its thundercloud look. He looks down at Razi, who shudders beneath my cloak, his eyes darting back and forth, closing and opening.

"You're arguing about me?" Razi murmurs.

"Hush," I say. "It's nothing you need to worry about now."

"Don't argue. None of us knew he'd have a gun."

He closes his eyes again, grimacing in pain. Nibas and I both regard him silently.

Then Nibas lifts his head to look at me. His dark eyes burn with anger like two coal embers.

"You're going to find that bastard. And do for him the way he's done for Razi."

The Qalfan hospital is the largest building in the Qalfan Quarter. Its gray-white stone towers glow faintly in the moonlight, capped off by tile roofs that in the morning will reveal themselves a striking red. Qalfan medicine is in high demand. It's not going to come cheap, even if Razi is a Nezar, honored and feared among his own people.

Getting Razi out of the boat is harder than getting him into it. He's barely conscious, and we're mostly dragging him up the steps and in through the big double doors.

The lobby is ablaze with candles and bustling with activity, even at this hour. The kinless huddle in cloaks on the floor, hoping to be taken as charity cases. A nurse in white Qalfan robes moves among them, distributing food and water. Householding women dressed in silken finery speak to more nurses sitting at big wood tables. Three young men wearing green velvet cloaks shiver in the corner, clutching their stomachs and looking pale.

They all look up when Nibas and I bring Razi in.

Two nurses appear instantly at our side.

"What happened? Where is he hurt?"

Another nurse runs down the hall, hopefully to fetch a chirurgeon.

Razi rouses enough to watch the women standing before us, their fingers moving in a no-nonsense way to check his arm, his side, the feel of his forehead.

He turns toward me. "Kyris," he murmurs. "Make sure my nurses are good-looking?"

"I can dig the ball out," the chirurgeon tells us as he washes his hands, once we have Razi in a room. Light from the candles reflects off his spectacles. "But it wouldn't do any good. It smashed through his bones. There's no way to heal those."

"Does he know?" Nibas says. "Have you told him?"

The chirurgeon dries his hands on a towel and lifts a heavy leather apron over his head. He's only wearing an allaq, not an urqa. His jaw is lightly stubbled with dark hair, like he's been working for a while.

He rolls up the sleeves of his allaq, looking calm but troubled, too.

"No. Not yet. He's a Nezar. If he gives up his arm…that's his livelihood, isn't it?"

"Kyris," Nibas says. He's always had the disconcerting habit of looking you right in the eye when he tells you hard things, and I know what he's going to say to me now. It would be easier for me if he shouted at me again, but his craggy brown face is as spare as the landscape where he grew up, and as uncompromising.

"You've got to tell him."

❦

"Razi," I say, coming to sit next to him. "They'll be giving you more kacin soon."

"My prayers have been answered," he says in a barely audible voice. His eyes are closed and he's drenched in sweat. But he shivers again and I tuck the covers in tighter around him. "What demon created a gun?" he says.

I remain silent for a moment. I don't know what kind of demon created a gun, but I know the demon responsible for their first use in Liera.

Me.

Arsenault always said I wasn't to blame, but I know.

I shift on the hard seat and seek out his good hand atop the blankets with my left hand. His head moves on the pillow when

I touch him. His dark eyes—dull with pain but lucid—search my own.

"All those times I flirted with you," he says, his voice raspy and raw. "I didn't know it would take a gunshot."

I try to smile, to say something sarcastic back, to keep up our relationship as it has been—to give Razi that comfort. But I can't.

"They're going to take your arm, Razi."

He sighs. Turns his head, just a small shift toward the wall. "Thought so."

"It— They'll take care of you here. It will be a long recovery, but—"

"They're not going to give me an arm like yours, though."

"No. But you'll learn how to get by with only one."

"To fight? To earn my pay? Or am I going to have to be like one of those beggars at the door? My father let the Nezari pick me up because he couldn't afford me."

"The Nezari will take care of you. Nibas—"

"Is Nibas there?"

"Outside."

"Not fair to Nibas."

"I don't think Nibas cares."

He falls silent.

"I learned to fight one-handed," I say. "I never expected to get this arm. You'll still have your right hand."

His mouth curves upward at the corner. "Stop whinging? That what you mean?"

I snort and lean over him. "Right. Suck it up, man. I'll make them take it off below the elbow."

"That comforts me."

"Below the elbow will be better, Razi; trust me."

"Don't want to go back to farm in the dust." Now the faint smile comes back. "Terrible farmer, anyhow."

"You won't have to. Just—stay alive and I'll teach you how to fight."

"The chirurgeon—Qalfan, yes?"

"He's not wearing an urqa, but yes, I think so."

"I want to say my prayers. Then—"

"Nibas and I won't leave you. Stay alive, Razi."

"Fate lies with the Sun. Never really understood that teaching. Until now. Idiot."

"I shouldn't have sought you out. Why'd you have to go after him?"

"Thought I was helping you... See? Idiot."

"No, Razi—"

His fingers tighten briefly, weakly, on my own. "Now I know why you hate the Prinze."

"You don't," I say raggedly. "You don't know. But I'm adding you to the debt they have to pay."

※

IT'S NOT ANYTHING LIKE WHEN THEY CUT OFF MY ARM.

I keep telling myself that, as I stand in Razi's room at the beck and call of the surgeon. Instead of a wooden chopping block—a table with a clean white linen covering and surgical instruments laid out on top. A bed where Razi lies propped up. Rows of candles providing warm yellow light. One skinny window beside the bed where the moon hangs like a pearl in the night.

Instead of an axe, there are two saws—one large, one small. A row of knives in descending order of size. A selection of needles. A spool of silk thread. A pair of scissors.

All the steel gleams in the candlelight.

Instead of an executioner dressed in black like a raven, a man wearing spectacles and robed in white leans over Razi, picking small pieces of fabric out of his arm with a pair of tweezers. Behind him, a nurse pours liquids from a selection of brown bottles into a porcelain basin, and a young man in robes waits by the door. The room begins, suddenly, to smell of roses, and then of pine.

But when the chirurgeon rises from his chair and picks up a long silken cord, I begin to tremble.

Nibas, standing beside me with his shoulders squared, looks at me and says, "Kyris."

The chirurgeon looks up at me too. "Are you going to be able to do this? It's no shame if you need me to find someone else."

They've given Razi so much kacin, he's nearly asleep, but at my name he turns his head to look at me.

"Suck it up, Kyris."

"I am not whinging," I say, and I take a long, deep breath of rose and pine. "I can pin your ass to that bed any day."

"Sounds exciting." Razi's mouth turns up into a long, sleepy smile, but he never opens his eyes.

"Very well," the chirurgeon says. "I need one of you to hold this cord tight around his chest. We'll twist it with this piece of wood to keep it from coming loose. My assistant will tighten the cord on his arm, and the nurse will help me sew up the blood vessels. But I'll also need someone to hold him down."

"Will you burn it afterward?" I say, trying to keep my voice steady.

The chirurgeon frowns and shakes his head. "No. I found during the wars that men I burned did more poorly than the ones I wasn't able to burn. But it will be very important to maintain the pressure on those cords so I can sew up the vessels instead. He still runs the risk of bleeding to death. Do you understand?"

Nibas and I both nod.

An enormous wave of relief washes over me.

This is what Arsenault meant about Qalfan care.

We didn't have this in Rojornick, either. When their chirurgeons took off a hand or a foot or a limb, all we heard from the medical tents was screaming. The scent of burning hair and flesh would drift out on the wind, but we could always tell ourselves it was just the smell of battle.

Still. This is worse than sitting outside the medical tents and listening to the screaming.

The chirurgeon eyes me over the rims of his spectacles. "You have to be strong to do this," he says. "Are you sure..."

I flex my right hand. "I'm stronger than I look."

And then we begin.

※

It's bad.

It's very bad.

The sound of the saw as it cuts through flesh and bone.

The smell of blood, somehow so much worse without battle to accompany it.

Razi screaming and thrashing, the chirurgeon shouting, *"Hold him still!"* and *"Pull that cord!"* and the sound of too much blood pouring into the basin on the floor, splashing the chirurgeon and the nurse and the assistant and Nibas and me.

The memories of being thrown down onto that block and hearing the axe whistle in the air until it hit my arm, and the absolute blooming burning red of the pain.

And then the sound of an arm hitting the porcelain basin and making it wobble on a wood floor.

CHAPTER 15

Could it really have been Arsenault, the man who shot Razi?

My mind skitters away from that thought as I walk alone down the hall away from Razi's room, my blood-soaked clothes stiffening as they dry. The nurse catches up with me before I get very far.

"Ser, you can't go out with those clothes. We are happy to provide you new ones before you leave. It is included in your payment."

I threw some coins at them when we brought Razi in. I don't know how many. They were gold.

"Ser." She touches me lightly. On my right shoulder.

I jerk around, grabbing her by the wrist before I think about it. In her wide black eyes I see a reflection of how she sees me—wild, frightening, smeared with blood.

I step back quick and incline my head, the way Arsenault would apologize to a woman. "Pardon. I'm just a little on edge."

She eyes my arm skeptically. Maybe she felt the metal through the cloth. "We have clothes," she says again, slower now, like she's talking to someone with trouble understanding. "If you'll follow me."

CHAPTER 15

She hands me a plain linen shirt, trousers, and a wool cloak, and ushers me into a draped-off closet to change. I strip off my old clothes and stand in the dim quiet of the closet, staring at my reflection in the metal of my arm.

I thought it would be so easy. So appropriately ironic. Use a gun to kill a Prinze, since the Prinze had made guns the instrument of their supremacy. But now I don't know what in all the hells is going on. Why is that gavaro leaving *me* alone? Why hurt everyone I'm with?

As a warning? To scare me off?

I feel like maybe I'm being played by the gods. Manipulated on a stage, like a player in a play.

It's your move now, little bird. What will you do?

CHAPTER 16

Before the Prinze brought guns to Liera, it was as if we were all dreaming. And then Prinze ships landed in port with their holds full of guns and powder, and we all woke up.

The day my dream ended, I was wearing trousers and lying on my stomach in the grass on a hill overlooking the high road, the one that led up to our lodge in the foothills of the Irondels. I was helping Arsenault make a map of our estate. I lived in a tiny corner of his room behind a blanket that gave me some privacy at night, and he remained true to his word; he never touched my right arm, and my corner remained dark and private until I took the blanket down each morning.

Arsenault lay stretched out on his back with his head propped on his pack, his hat pulled low over his face, pretending to listen to me read from a book called *The Pirate Raid, a True Account of Life Among the Most Bloodthirsty of Men*. It was a warm afternoon in late spring, a year after I'd had my first visions. An enormous cork tree spread its arms out like a many-armed deity above us for shade.

"*Prince Udolfo dropped down onto the blood-soaked deck of the pirate cutter and pulled his sword as he approached the pirate captain,*" I read. "*Some said the captain was the son of a giantess. He stripped naked to the waist when he fought and wore his beard twisted up with Saien sparklers. When he lit them, he became so frightening that many sailors threw themselves over the rail in terror without him ever having to bare his cutlasses. But the Prince's courage was made of stronger steel—"*

Arsenault snorted. Or snored. "Are you listening?" I asked. "You'll miss the exciting part. I believe the pirate captain is about to show Udolfo that he's captured his betrothed."

"The woman who fainted at the sight of the pirate? Dolf deserves better."

"Dolf?" I said.

Arsenault's eyes cracked open and he pushed the hat up with one finger. "Isn't that what his companion calls him?"

"I don't think so, Arsenault."

"Mmmm. Maybe I was confusing the story for another."

"Well, you keep drifting off while I'm reading; that's probably why. Honestly, Arsenault, I think I shall stop trying to share books with you and just read in the hall after supper."

"If I'm drifting off, it's only because it's a warm day, and your voice..." He tugged his hat back down over his face. "Somehow, I doubt the author ever really saw what happened with the pirate."

"It's a story, Arsenault, not a military report."

"How was he supposed to light those sparklers without burning off his beard?"

"Perhaps he soaked his beard before lighting them."

"He's got more balls than I do."

"You've absolutely not a speck of romance in you, do you?"

The hat didn't move. "Maybe his betrothed will make a heroic sacrifice and leave him free to court the pirate princess. How would that be for romance?"

I watched him for a moment, then couldn't help skimming forward in the book.

Finally, I huffed out a breath. "Are you sure you haven't read it before?"

"I must have heard it somewhere," he mumbled.

I narrowed my eyes on him again, but he still didn't move the hat.

"Well, you know what I think *really* happened," I said in a bored voice. "I think his betrothed was a lot sharper than she looked. And while she was alone in the captain's cabin, the pirate princess who is in love with Udolfo crept inside to have a chat with her, and as it turns out, the betrothed didn't want to marry Udolfo either. And therefore, she works out a ruse with the princess to make it *appear* that she's sacrificed herself heroically. But instead, a faithful fisherman pulls her out of the water, and she takes the place of the pirate princess, who marries Udolfo and settles down to become a respectable woman."

I closed the book with a triumphant thump and propped my head on my hand to look at Arsenault.

Finally, he pushed up the hat.

"So, that's how you think it was?"

"No woman of rank is that stupid. It had to be a ruse."

His mouth began to curve upward. "But why would the pirates take her on?"

"Well, because the princess asked them to, and she's beautiful. I mean, I expect she was, the way the author goes on about her long, honey-colored hair. On the other hand...she can run a ruse, so she's probably dangerous. I imagine she's had lessons in poisoning."

"Maybe they were all in it together," Arsenault said.

"What—the pirate captain and the princess and the betrothed?"

"Perhaps Udolfo too. Maybe it was all a ruse."

"You mean Udolfo agreed to get rid of her?"

"Maybe they were just trying to sort things out. Maybe Vara attempted to poison the pirate captain and he found her out, and they had a tempestuous romance, there on ship?"

"Vara—the betrothed, you mean? No, she'd be too smart for that. She'd make him wait. By the time they set the plan in motion, he'd be mad with desire and ready to give her whatever she wanted. Even her own ship."

Arsenault rolled over onto his side to face me. "Mad with desire," he said.

There was a deep note in his voice and a look in his eyes that made my heart stutter, but I pressed on. "Of course. And once she's assured of his good faith…"

He'd shifted closer while I was talking, and I found that I could barely think of what I'd been going to say next. Things like this seemed to happen more often lately, and I wasn't sure why. He and Margarithe had lately had a spectacular argument, completely unlike either of them, the sound of their voices carrying through the walls. Arsenault had emerged from the room looking as wrecked as the landscape after a big storm.

"Once she's assured of his good faith," he continued the story for me, "the pirate captain meets her on the deck of her cutter. After he and Udolfo join in fake battle over her. In disguise so her crew will capture him. And she has him brought to her cabin…"

Arsenault's gaze caught mine. I could feel the warm heat of him inches away. Had he moved toward me or I toward him? My heart began to drum and I brushed his sleeve, at the same time his fingers skimmed my hip and he leaned toward me.

A raven croaked above us.

I had never seen a man react the way Arsenault reacted to this bird. All the color drained from his face and he was on his feet, drawing his sword faster than I thought possible. He pointed the tip upward, but the bird hopped down the branch, making a sound like a frog.

I got slowly to my feet. "It's only a bird, Arsenault. Isn't it?"

"I don't know."

He didn't lower his sword.

I came to stand beside him and squinted upward at the raven. It leaned over, cocking its head and puffing the feathers on its neck so they stood out in a ruff. Then it stretched out its foot, showing off the small leather tube secured to its leg.

"It's a messenger bird, Arsenault."

He let his breath out. The blade of the sword wavered, and then he slammed it back in its scabbard and drew his sleeve across his forehead as if he were wiping away sweat.

"Well, come here, then," he said to the bird as he dropped his arm, "if you've got something to give me."

The bird glided down from the branch to land at Arsenault's feet. He went down on one knee to retrieve the message, and the raven stood patiently while he did so, picking at the streak in his hair with its beak.

"How could one tell," I asked, "if a bird was a spy?"

Arsenault glanced up at me sharply, then pulled the tube off the bird's leg and stood up. "Why would you ask a question like that?"

"I was just thinking of the way you looked at this bird."

His glance shifted to the bird for a moment. "Ravens are intelligent creatures. Be careful what you say." Then he cracked the seal on the tube, shook out the tea-stained parchment inside, and the color that had begun to come back into his face fled.

"Gods."

"Arsenault? What is it?"

He folded the letter in half, then in half again so I couldn't see it. His hands shook as he did it.

"Devid's on his way back." The look in his eyes at first was haunted, but, as his gaze roved over my face, it changed to something I had a hard time identifying in him, something that made my heart beat fast.

It was only later, after we had packed up and found the road again, that I was able to put a name to it.

The look in his eyes was fear.

I followed him a long way down the road before he said anything else. I wanted to ask a thousand questions, but the way he held himself stopped me. It was like he had strung himself together with bits of his wire.

He stopped when we came to the branch in the road that led to the big house, and turned to me.

"I'm going to see your father now, Kyrra." He glanced around quickly, as if he was worried someone—or something—might be spying on us in the trees. "Devid is about to land in port with more guns than I ever thought possible. I underestimated the Prinze."

"But isn't that why my father hired all those new gavaros in the past two years? He knows war is coming."

"He doesn't know *this* war is coming. Not one with this kind of firepower."

"Firepower," I repeated slowly, rolling the unfamiliar word around my mouth as if I could taste it. "Like fire arrows?"

"No. Imagine stuffing a boulder into the tube of a Saien rocket and then lighting it off. Imagine being able to stand over a hundred feet away and still kill a man."

"You've seen these guns?"

"I've used them," he said grimly. "And now, with the number of guns and cannon the Prinze have captured... Kyrra, when I tell you to go, will you go? Will you promise to do as I ask?"

I had been expecting him to say any number of things, but this wasn't one of them. "Why would you ask such a thing of me?"

"You've a natural talent with a sword, and that magic always pushing at you. But promise me you'll go when I ask instead of staying here to fight."

"But *I* am the cause of all their troubles," I said, shaking. "*I* am the reason Geoffre will use us to test these guns. Why should I be saved?"

"Maybe you were the catalyst. But it's not because of you."

"How is it not?" I asked. I needed to hear him tell me it

wasn't my fault, and yet I knew that whatever he said would be wrong, just as I wanted to rest my forehead on his collarbone and have him wrap both his arms around me while he said it but I knew that he wouldn't.

Instead, he touched my arm.

I looked up at him, startled.

"It *isn't* because of you. It began when Geoffre loved your mother but couldn't have her," he said. "When she married your father. The Aliente were neutral until then, weren't they? It was only afterward that the Prinze turned away from the Aliente."

"But my mother was Caprine. The Prinze and the Caprine have always been at odds."

"Why did Geoffre send Cassis with an offer to carry your father's silk then?"

"I don't know. My mother didn't know either, but she suspected treachery." I laughed, but it sounded more like a bark; there wasn't any mirth in it. "*A Prinze makes no gestures without a knife up his sleeve*, she said. I thought she was just being paranoid. I thought things might change in Liera then."

Now I couldn't imagine ever having that kind of naive hope. I might as well have been a hundred years old.

Arsenault sighed and pulled me closer to him, letting me stand in the shelter of his arms. It surprised me more than any news could. "I think Cassis wanted you. Perhaps not to marry... but Geoffre is an opportunist. He needs you for something else. Maybe for your magic, maybe as revenge... There *must* be something else. Something beyond his hatred of your father, for him to do what he's done now..."

I swiped my arm across my nose and he dropped his hand. "And what has Geoffre done now?"

"Destroyed Dakkar," Arsenault replied grimly. "For guns."

I tried to wrap my mind around that. Dakkar was a kingdom. How could one man destroy it? And all for revenge on my family?

"What does it matter the motives when it was my action that gave him the excuse?"

"We all do things we regret when we're young, Kyrra. Doesn't mean we can't be forgiven."

"Do you really believe that?" I said.

I wanted him to tell me yes. I wasn't sure I believed it, but right then, I needed the word.

Instead, the expression in his eyes turned them to two open wounds. He opened his mouth and said, "I —" but it was as if his voice froze in his throat after that.

I spoke again, stammering. "N-not all of us begin wars, though."

"No," he said raggedly. "And maybe it will take a long time to redeem some of us." He took a deep breath and faced me again. "But *you* might redeem yourself. If you stay alive. Far more than if you demand to stay with your father."

"But I *would* fight for my father." I felt shaky as I touched his sleeve and added, "And *you*. You must know that, Arsenault."

He looked down at my fingers on his shirt. Slowly, he brought his hand up to rest it on my forearm. "Is it so hard to understand why I would want you to go?"

I hoped I understood what he was trying to say. I was afraid to hope it, but I wanted it badly. Only not like this.

"Am I such a bad swordsman? Have I not been learning—"

"*Kyrra.*"

"You're a gavaro," I said, with tears in my eyes. "You've seen recruits come and go—"

"*I'm a man,*" he said.

He tightened his hand on my arm, pulled me up against him, and kissed me.

I stiffened for an instant in shock. But then I pressed myself against him, tightening my fingers on his shirt to pull him closer. He crushed me against his chest with his other arm, so tightly that any other time, I would have felt as if I was suffocating. Except now I still felt too far away from him; I couldn't get close enough. Everything neither of us had been able to say was in that kiss—a year or more of waiting, of wanting, mixed now with the fear that everything would be lost.

"Promise me, Kyrra," he said when he pulled away, his voice rough. "Promise you'll go when I tell you to. That you'll do whatever it takes to stay alive."

"But where would I go?"

"Out of Liera. Out of Eterea. Somewhere your Houses don't reach."

"And abandon my family?" The words came out like a mouthful of thorns. "You?"

He lifted his hands to my face and stroked my hair back. "Kyrra. Even if you go, you'll carry me with you everywhere."

He leaned down to kiss me again.

Oh, those unfortunate words.

I wrenched out of his arms. All I could see, for a blinding instant, was Cassis on a moonlit night in the garden, when the heat wrapped our bodies in sweat and dust. *I carry you in my heart when we're apart*, he'd said. *I'll carry you there always.*

"So, you can just use me up and get rid of me, is that it? That's why you've waited till now, when it won't make a difference! You can just send me off and you won't have a single entanglement!"

Arsenault stared at me, that wounded, raw look back in his eyes. I stood there, clutching my stump, staring back at him, breathing fast and hard.

Then the muscle in his jaw twitched, and his expression darkened. "I say nothing to you I don't mean," he said in a quiet voice that was somehow as angry as my shouting. "And if you think I've only waited so I could take advantage of you…"

He reached inside his tunic, pulled out the letter, and threw it at me.

I raised my hand in reflex but couldn't catch it. It hit the edge of my hand and tumbled to the ground. I was still staring at it when his boots crunched in the dirt. By the time I looked up, he was already walking down the path to the big house.

"Arsenault!" I called.

He disappeared around a bend in the path without looking back.

CHAPTER 17

THE FLEET HAS DOCKED, THE MISSIVE READ. *I SEND THIS NEWS BY a messenger you know well. It won't fall into enemy hands.*

My own hand was shaking as I held the letter. I sat huddled in a hollow at the base of a big olive tree, wishing the roots of the tree would reach up and drag me down into the earth.

Since that didn't seem likely to happen, I tried again to read the letter.

Nineteenth day of the Blood Moon, in the First Year of the Reign of the Ibuu Adayze dom B'ara

It was written in ancient Eter, a language hardly anyone knew anymore. Arsenault knew that I had studied it, but I was surprised that *he* knew it. The thought quickly turned bitter. Two and two always added up to five with Arsenault, and I didn't know why I should be surprised at anything anymore.

Ricar di Sere is lost, and three of his ships with him. What they will tell you is that the ships were casualties of a battle, that the powder they carried lit them up like holiday rockets—well, that much is true. They went up in streaks of orange fire and rivaled the fireworks the gunsmiths lit for my father's coronation. But the Prinze captain shot his cannon at Ricar di Sere's ship. My sister was in the tower and she saw it. Do not believe anything the Prinze tell you.

My family is lost. When the Lieran ships first appeared on our shores, my father gave them his protection. The Lierans promised my father trade in silk and carpets, and though my father was suspicious and I told him to be careful, he pledged them safety in his house according to tradition. He gave them wine, kacin, whatever they wanted. He wasn't worried. Why should he have been? Are the B'ara not descended from Lion himself? Why should he worry about a bunch of whiteskins, pasty and weak from the voyage, teeth loose from lack of green food or fruit? What could they possibly have threatened us with?

But sometimes the smallest insect causes the most damage. Think of Siki, the mosquito. Think of the great harm his bite does, the thousands of people he fells with his tiny proboscis every year.

The Lierans were like that. Mosquitoes. They even turned on each other in the end. If it weren't for you, Arsenault, and the services you have already rendered my family, I would despair. But you give me hope. Now you are in a position to seek vengeance.

The Lierans poisoned my father with an unfamiliar substance not even his tasters could identify. His tasters died too. Then the Lierans killed the guards of the armory and began unloading powder and guns. They laid waste to the citadel with the big cannons and razed the rest. We were deep in the dry season, and Mdembu lit like a torch. We were not expecting it. We had grown too arrogant, and it made us blind. By the time we mobilized my father's retainers and their men, the flames were already roaring around us.

My sister and Edo are alive, as am I—but Jemma is dead and so are my boys. What am I to do, Arsenault? I had not seen them for years and now I will see them no longer. I feel as if I have become a wooden puppet animated only by revenge.

Adayze and I pick up the shattered pieces of the royal city and send this bird through the ndabik, hoping it will reach you in time. My sister will assume the throne, and I will leave soon for Liera. The Prinze left behind a garrison, but what is left to govern? Everything has crumbled to ash.

In trust,
    Jonawak dom B'ara

JON BARRA.
    I put the letter down in my lap. Then I spread it out on the ground and folded it carefully into a square again, four corners for each of the Houses now involved in this web: Prinze, Caprine, Sere, Aliente. We were the least powerful.
    But *Geoffre loved Carolla.*
    Arsenault was right; my father had never dealt much with the Prinze. Only in the year or so before my affair with Cassis had he extended his hand to Geoffre, because the Caprine couldn't give the money for his silk that the Prinze could. Did my mother ever wish she'd married Geoffre, who had might and power as well as two sons, when all she had was a headstrong daughter and a record of miscarriages, a stillborn boy buried beneath the cork tree?
    My brother didn't even have a name.

She visited his grave often the first few years, placing armfuls of daffodils atop it in the spring, leaving trinkets she'd found in the market, little silver bracelets and rings and rattles. I used to watch her through the garden hedge, but the sight of her crying frightened me. She stayed in bed for weeks after he was born. My father begged and argued and ordered, but she remained encased in her blankets as if she were trying to spin herself a cocoon.

I turned the letter over as if I could make it form a different shape by changing the angle at which I looked at it. I was six years old when the baby was born. My birthday was at Midsummer. The baby was born in winter—I remembered that, because it was snowing when the Adalusian priests laid the coffin in the ground. I remember the snowflakes drifting down lazily out of the metal sky and melting on the lid of the tiny pine coffin. I remembered his little blue face when they laid him in the coffin, the tuft of his dark hair. My mother wasn't there, and I remember leaning against my father, the warm grip of his hand on my shoulder.

Geoffre had visited us the previous spring, coming from Karansis on his way to Padera in the interior. He brought hyacinths and dried figs. Apricot blossoms packed in a crate with mountain ice. My father welcomed him for the week, but all week his face looked too tight, as if it was a mask he wore and not a real face.

Spring to winter. My mother's face had looked too tight as well. But Geoffre...

Geoffre had always reminded me of a wolf. The way he smiled, the way he walked. The kind of wolf that picked off sheep.

Crunch.

If I had been good enough to fight with Arsenault, I would not have been so absorbed in my thoughts. I would have heard Lobardin approach. But by the time I heard the crunching gravel beneath his boots, it was too late. He stood almost in front of me. The spicy-sweet smell of kacin smoke followed him.

I clutched the letter to my chest and leapt to my feet.

"Kyrra," he said, slurring the *r*'s. His pupils almost swallowed his irises, and he walked with a listing gait. "Fancy seeing you here. Where's Arsenault?"

"With my father," I said. I kept a wary eye on Lobardin. He had a personality like quicksilver, and it was worse when he was smoking. And he'd changed over the past year -- grown more bitter, more anxious, more resentful of Arsenault. The effects, perhaps, of knowing that Arsenault was supposed to use him, but not knowing what for and having to wait an interminable amount of time to find out.

"With your father," he repeated slowly. "So...not here."

"No," I said, stuffing the letter in my pocket. "And I've chores to do, so I'll be going. You'd better clean yourself up before you go back to the barracks."

"What did you put in your pocket?"

"Nothing." I dusted my trousers off. "A list of simples. That's all."

"Arsenault has you replenishing our store of herbs now?"

Shrugging, I said, "I do as I'm directed."

Lobardin laughed in a soft, hazy way. "I'm sure you do," he said, and I tried not to flinch. He let his gaze sweep over me. "Still wearing trousers, are you?"

I stiffened and heat seeped into my cheeks. "I live among you," I said. "And I'm not one of your girls. So, why should I dress like one?"

He cocked his head and kept looking at me. "To be honest, I like the look of a woman when you can see the line of her legs."

I took a step backward. I didn't think Lobardin would hurt me, but I had taken to carrying a large iron cloak pin on the inside of my belt in place of the dagger Arsenault had given me. Carrying the dagger made me jumpy.

"A man needs a bit of an arse to grab, though." Lobardin took a quick step toward me and shot his arm around me before I could back out of the way. I stamped on his foot, tried vainly to get my knee in a position where I could bring it up into his crotch, but couldn't shove him away because he held me pressed up against him, pinning my left arm with his. He jammed his mouth down on mine and forced my lips apart in the second kiss I'd gotten that afternoon, this one much different from the first. With his right hand he withdrew the missive Arsenault had thrown at me.

This letter will not fall into the hands of the enemy.

I went cold, stiffened in fear, not of rape but of Lobardin reading what was written in that letter. Then I bit him, as hard as I could. His blood washed into my mouth, salty and warm, and he pulled away abruptly, stumbling backward, with the sleeve of his right arm pressed against his mouth, the letter clutched in his right hand.

I slid my fingers into my belt and came out with the cloak pin. "It's nothing to you," I said. I flipped the pin open and held it like a dagger. "Why do you think it's your business?"

Lobardin took his arm down from his mouth. Blood trickled over his chin. His blood still lay, warm and wet, on my own lips. I couldn't wipe my mouth with the stump of my right arm, so I just licked it off.

Lobardin's eyebrows shot upward. His face lost its dangerous look, and instead he started to grin, which might have been worse. He shook his hair away and wiped the remaining blood from his lips with his thumb. "If it's only herbs, why hide it from me?" I snatched for it, and he jerked it away. "See? So concerned." Then he looked at the letter and frowned. "Is this code?"

I grabbed the letter from his hands before he had a chance to look at it any more. "It's between Arsenault and me," I said. "Nothing more."

He smiled, lopsided, and crossed his arms in front of his chest. The blood he'd wiped from his mouth left a long red streak down his sleeve. "Oh, but you don't know how much I burn to know what goes on between you and Arsenault, Kyrra."

I flushed a deep scarlet and tried to turn my shame to anger.

"So you try to take me for yourself? If that's all you're about, then you ought to know that I'm Arsenault's page, nothing more."

Lobardin's grin grew wider. "His page to write on, maybe."

I forgot everything Arsenault had taught me. I lashed out with the cloak pin. Lobardin, a well-trained warrior, barely had to move to catch my forearm and wrench it around backward, pinning it against my back.

The cloak pin tumbled to the ground. My muscles burned with pain and I stood, hunched, up against him, unable to break free. Unwilling tears welled up in my eyes and splashed into the dust.

Lobardin spoke into my ear. "Kyrra. You know Arsenault's just using you, the way he's using all of us. Stringing you along, making you think you can take care of yourself so he can get what he wants out of you. But I could have you down in the dirt right here and you'd be able to do nothing about it. Would you." He paused as if I was supposed to answer. When I said nothing, he shook me. "*Would you.*"

"No," I gasped, the truth. I was burning inside now, beyond tears or blush. I bit my lip to keep from saying anything else, to force the hurt back inside me. This was not the same Lobardin who had brought me orchids when I was unwell or danced with me in the hall. This was the Lobardin who had crawled out of the lean-to in the Talos, deep in the grip of his drug. I could smell it with every warm exhalation of his breath at my ear. I wondered if he even knew what he was doing, but I also wondered if it was all kacin, or if the wild magic that claimed both of us also guided his actions. For a terrifying moment, what frightened me most was that I might end up like him.

"Well, I'm not that stupid," he said, shoving me away. My arm sprang back into a normal position as I stumbled and fell on my knees in the dirt. I scrambled to my feet and faced him, my arm pressed close to my chest. He stood with his boot on the cloak pin.

"You're Arsenault's woman, whether you admit it or not, and your father's daughter, and I'd be a fool to anger either one of them. But I want to know what the letter says. Who it's from. Why there's a raven in Arsenault's quarters with a tube tied to its foot."

The raven had flown all the way back to the barracks already? And knew Arsenault's room?

Surely, it was no natural bird.

"Why do you need to know?" I asked. "Jon and Arsenault got you a commission away from Geoffre di Prinze. Isn't that what you wanted? Or is your loyalty still for sale?"

"My loyalty is my only asset. I'm afraid it's always up for sale. But when have I failed your father?"

"Perhaps it's not my father I'm talking about. Perhaps I'm talking about you failing me."

"Oh." His features furrowed in confusion, and he looked down at the cloak pin beneath his boot as if he were seeing it for the first time. Then he looked up at me. "Kyrra. Did I hurt you?"

My heart hammered. How to separate the effects of drugs and magic? Which was it that made him act this way?

"I thought we were on better terms; that's all."

Those expressive brows pinched together, and it was clear that he was struggling to follow my train of thought. "Kyrra No-Name...you aren't suggesting that you *like* me?"

I shrugged. "Perhaps if you had asked me nicely, I might have told you about the letter. I don't want Arsenault to know I took it."

Lobardin eyed me warily, like a fox who's scented a dog. "Can you read it?"

"No," I lied, putting on my darkest scowl. "I can't read a bit of it."

He ran a hand through his hair and left it mussed up. "I don't know how he expects men to fight when he doesn't tell us anything. We all know who our commander will be when the time comes."

Then he crouched down and retrieved the cloak pin from beneath the toe of his boot. When he stood up, he held it out to me in the flat of his palm.

"Arsenault is a fool," he said. "For more than one reason. And you can tell him I said so."

※

I THOUGHT FURIOUSLY AS I WALKED BACK TO THE BARRACKS and set up the washbasin in Arsenault's room to bathe my lips, trying to invent some excuse for my injured arm and hoping the pain would go away. But it didn't, and I tasted Lobardin's blood no matter how many times I washed. I was still standing there when the door opened and Arsenault walked in.

I cursed myself for not braving the pain of doing something as simple as hanging up the damn blanket.

Arsenault walked over to his bed without saying anything. I had left the letter on there, and he stared at it for a minute, then picked up a tallow candle from his work table and lit it with a spark from his flint. He took the letter and set it alight.

We both watched the black smoke, thick with ash, drift up toward the ceiling. Little pieces of paper whirled upward on air currents and then drifted down again like snow. Arsenault held the paper until the fire had eaten most of it, then he threw it onto the dirt floor and stomped the flames out.

"You're satisfied?" he said. His words were clipped, his voice cold.

It seemed safer to focus on the information contained in the letter than on anything as volatile as my feelings as I watched him standing there with his hands on his hilts and that thundercloud look on his face, completely at odds with his voice.

"So, Jon isn't just a kacin smuggler," I said, taking a deep breath. "He's the brother of the queen of Dakkar. What does that make him? A prince?"

Some of the storminess disappeared from Arsenault's expression. "The Dakkarans don't think of it like that. He's secondborn, so he's Adayze's Dagger. Her right hand, out in the world."

"Then why doesn't he use his title?"

"Because it's a secret. He gets more done that way. That's the way things are in Dakkar. The Firstborn conducts ceremonies and diplomacy; the Secondborn does the dirty work."

"And is it your work, too?"

He gave me a sideways look like the raven's, then unbuckled his swordbelt, hung it on its peg, and sat down on his bed. He leaned forward and rested his elbows on his knees, his shoulders slumped, and propped his head in his hands. When he spoke, it was to the floor instead of to me.

"Somewhat," he said.

"What does that *mean?*"

He rubbed his temples. "It would probably be best for you not to know anything about the work I do with Jon."

"Do you really think I'm that naive? Do you think I haven't been paying attention to all the stories you tell? None of them add up! You're not old enough to have done half the things you claim to. Unless your magic is inventing memories for you, you're lying to me about something!"

He rose abruptly and paced to his worktable, where the raven perched, its wings folded. "You think I'm lying, do you? All right. I'll give you some lies. Perhaps that's what I should have done all along. How about this one—I killed a man in a barroom brawl and was banished for it, so I stowed away on a Vençalan caravel and was sold to the Qalfans, who carried me through the Great Salt Desert on a caravan and—"

"Arsenault!"

His jaw twitched. Then he rubbed his scar with his thumb. "Pardon. Kyrra."

"All I want to know," I said through gritted teeth, "is how you came to be in this man's service, and where your loyalty lies. And what you told my father."

"You can't protect your father."

"I have to try."

He glanced at me over the ridge of his knuckles. The little white nicks that spoke of a lifetime of confrontation stood out against his tanned skin. He let his hand drop, and it immediately sought the pommel of a sword that wasn't there. "I came to be in the Ibuu's service because his daughter pulled me off a slaver."

"His daughter. Adayze?"

He looked tense for a moment. Then he nodded.

"I had a cabin on one of the Outer Islands, where Tule and Dagmar send their outlaws. I thought it would be better if I just died alone, but I couldn't take the loneliness. When I couldn't stand it anymore, I came down into the village. Did odd jobs for the widows and the women whose husbands were at sea. One night, we were raided by pirates. They put all of us left alive into the hold and shipped us to Dakkar.

"The Dakkarans have standards for how slaves are supposed to be treated. The captain was violating those standards, so Adayze pulled me off the ship and gave me to Jon."

I stared at him, horrified. "Jon owns you?"

Arsenault glanced up, his mouth twisted into a wry hook. "Well, not now."

"But...Arsenault...why are you working for a man who owned you at any time?"

"Because I made a promise."

"To Jon? While you were still a slave?"

"No. To Adayze. Out of my own free will." He frowned. "I don't— Look, Kyrra, there are holes there. I don't remember everything, but I needed to help my people, the ones who were bought off that ship, and then there was a cabin boy who helped me. I did what I had to do."

"And you don't remember what that was?"

"Jon's a decent man."

"But a man in his position might sacrifice decency in order to do his sovereign's bidding. Isn't that the definition of dirty work?"

Arsenault frowned and rubbed his collarbone in a distracted gesture. "That's thinking like a Lieran," he said.

"I've learned from experience."

He gave me a sharp glance and looked as if he was biting down on something he wanted to say. I shifted uncomfortably as a wash of heat spread through me—a strange mix of guilt and desire. It was clear he wanted to say something about what had happened earlier between us. But he didn't.

Instead, he looked down at the floor and grumbled, "Well, you had good teachers."

"What—"

"I've been chasing the Prinze for a while," he said. "Jon and I turned up some connections to Geoffre while I was trying to find my people. We followed those connections north, and that's how I ended up serving on Qalfan caravans."

"And fighting in Onzarro, where you took that arrow?" I said.

"The arrow..." he said, his brows pulling down over the ridge in his nose. "Oh, the arrow. Yes, right. The arrow."

"Have you forgotten that story, too? What else have you forgotten?"

He leaned back against the worktable and crossed his arms. "If I remembered what I'd forgotten, it wouldn't be forgotten, would it?"

"You're insufferable. You knew what I meant."

He shrugged but didn't say anything else.

I let my breath out. "Who's in charge, Arsenault? Did you fulfill your promise to Jon's sister or is it still binding?"

"I'm free to make my own choices," he said, glancing at the raven. "For what it's worth."

I looked at the raven too. It cocked its head at me, and I couldn't help but shiver.

"Erelf—" I began, and Arsenault made a hasty sign in front of his chest, one I had never seen before.

"Let's not speak of him," he said.

"What hold does *he* have over you?"

"I said, I won't speak of him. That's all. It invites his attention." He shifted against the worktable, angling himself toward me. "But this conflict with the Prinze, it's bigger and longer than you know. I wanted you to see..." His voice cracked and he cleared his throat. "Well. Geoffre's burned a whole city, hasn't he? A whole city and—"

He brought his head up and I saw his throat work.

"You know, Jemma was a beautiful woman. Not so much on the outside—I mean, she was pretty but her beauty wasn't physical. When she smiled, it was like the sun shining through clouds. And, dear gods, did she love Jon and those boys..."

If there was anything that could have undone me more, I didn't know what it was. I couldn't stand to see him in pain.

I went to him. I tried to reach out with my left arm to offer my awkward one-armed hug, but pain shot through my arm when I lifted it, and I hissed and brought it close to my body in reflex.

He straightened up. "Kyrra. Are you hurt?"

His gaze swept over me then locked onto my arm and his frown deepened. "What's that on your sleeve?"

A few short streaks of flaky maroon blood had dried there. Lobardin's blood. "Dirt, probably," I said, forcing a smile. I tried to move my arm to hide the stain, but he caught it and I couldn't bite back my cry in time.

His brow furrowed with worry and concern. His fingers crept up over my bicep to my shoulder, where he pressed down, kneading the muscle. "It's not dislocated," he said in relief. Then he looked at me. "How did this happen?"

"I—"

"Kyrra. I told you the truth. Now you tell me."

I didn't want to admit that I had been stupid enough to be

caught out by Lobardin, but it looked as if there wasn't any getting around it.

"Lobardin tried to read the letter," I said. "But he couldn't. He says you don't tell the men enough. I don't think he's working for the Prinze, but..."

Arsenault scowled. "Where are you cut?"

There was no way around this. "It's not my blood," I said.

His eyebrows shot upward. "Lobardin's blood? You pulled your dagger?"

"No. I bit him."

"You...bit him? Where?"

I couldn't lie. Lobardin's face bore my mark, and he wouldn't try to hide it.

"Lip," I said.

Arsenault swore. He let go of me and walked across the room and took his swordbelt down off the wall.

"Where are you going?"

"To find Lobardin," he growled. The raven on the worktable beat its wings and Arsenault glared at it.

"Be gone with you," he said. "It's no business of yours. You'll be back to take a letter later."

The raven clacked its beak and spread its wings. They seemed to stretch forever, and in a moment of black vertigo, I watched the ceiling spread apart, and the raven took flight through it, up into the blue afternoon sky. I staggered and bumped against my cot.

"Magic," I whispered.

Arsenault said nothing. He belted on his sword, then jerked it from its scabbard and stood in the shimmering afterglow of the raven's passing, inspecting its blade. The runes etched into the steel gleamed faintly. When Arsenault looked at me, his eyes were the color I would later associate with gun barrels.

He jammed the sword back into his scabbard and started for the door. "Stay here," he said.

I lurched after him, grabbing at his shirt though it hurt.

"If it were a man and a man, you wouldn't handle it like this. Haven't you been teaching me to take care of myself?"

He half-turned and looked down at me. I had never seen him so angry. "He forced you, didn't he? Threatened you so you wouldn't tell me?"

"No!"

"Dammit, Kyrra." He tore away from me and swung open the door.

I followed. "Arsenault! Murder is a hanging offense. My father won't bend the law!"

"I'm trying to protect you," he said, grinding the words out between his teeth. "That's all I have ever been trying to do. *To keep you safe.* But instead, you think I'm treating you like that bastard Cassis—"

"I want you to trust me with the truth," I said. "The last thing I need is a man who thinks he's my *bodyguard.*"

He glared down at me. Then he whirled away, yanking his sword from its scabbard with a high-pitched scream that made me want to cover my ears. He brought it down, two-handed, in a brutal overhead stroke into the oak table that sat beside the wall. The table was stacked with empty water buckets. The sword passed through the wood as if it were butter. The table split into two pieces and buckets clattered everywhere, rolling across the dirt floor.

Arsenault's blade quivered like a guitar string but otherwise looked none the worse for wear. He jammed it back into its scabbard.

"Fight your own battles, then," he said as he stalked away. "I can't protect you if you don't want me to."

CHAPTER 18

My whole life has been a series of bad decisions.

After I left Razi at the hospital, I walked for a while, hoping for the gavaro to follow me but dreading it, too. I didn't want to find out if it was Arsenault or that it wasn't him and that my arm and its magic had led me into the kind of dangerous paranoia that got other people killed.

Or lost them limbs.

But now I owe Vadz and Razi a debt to solve this mystery and take care of it. So, I'm crouched on a rooftop, hunched in the cloak the nurse gave me and watching the sun rise over the bay, waiting on Jonawak dom B'ara, the Dagger of Dakkar, to show up and give me a gun he's smuggled from the family that killed his and destroyed mine.

We ought to be allies. He ought to be a man I can trust above all others. But Jon plays a long game. Until I know what it is, he's still a player on the board.

A group of ravens settles on the roof next to me.

"Go spy on someone else," I say, and wave my right arm at them. They hop down the roofline, squawking and beating their wings, but they don't leave.

You know this is going to go badly, a voice in my head whispers. *You don't need Sight to tell that.*

Shut up, I tell the voice. *I get the gun, I leave. No one followed me from the Quarter. There's no one down there but kinless children looking for food.*

But what might have happened when you slept?

I twine my hands together and bump them against my chin as I think. I only slept for a short time in the deepest hours of the night, huddled against the warm bricks of the chimney. Maybe something did happen while I slept, but I couldn't stay awake any longer.

What if you missed something? Do you really trust Jon Barra? Do you really think he doesn't know anything about Arsenault?

It's been five years. Do you really think Arsenault would honor his promise to you anymore?

These voices in my head. I can't tell which god it is anymore, or if it's just the whispering of the magic itself, trying to take me over, to fill me up like a hollow in the ground.

My arm absorbs magic. A long time ago, I was only human. But now there's no way to keep the magic out. It's a part of me.

I stand and beat the grime out of my cloak. It's time to go meet Jon.

※

Jon steps out of the shadows when the first orange curve of the sun appears above the horizon. He walks me down the quayside past one of his ships, which has begun offloading long teak boards onto the dock. The wind off the sea slices knife-sharp against my skin. I huddle into my cloak, keeping my head down, struggling to keep up with Jon's long strides.

"I had a few problems after I left you yesterday," I say, struggling to keep my voice unconcerned.

"What kind of problems?"

"You have any Qalfan gavaros working for you now?"

"I've had too much experience with gavaros," he says. "Now I just employ my countrymen. They don't usually switch sides." He gives me a glance I think I'm supposed to read something into. I guess he means when he worked for the Rojornicki. Maybe he didn't approve when I left to work for the Kavol, even though I did it for loyalty's sake—loyalty to my employer, who was betrayed by his countrymen.

"You know anybody with Dakkaran experience who's switched sides lately?"

"To which side?"

"Prinze." I stop and look at him. "Either that or *you're* trying to kill me."

"Kyris. Why would I want to kill you?" Then he pauses a moment with a slight slowing to his long stride and looks down at me. "Somebody's trying to kill you?"

"Me and anybody with me. Figured you might know something about it."

"I'm flattered, Kyris, that you think I know everything that goes on in this city, but I don't. I didn't send an assassin after you. Is this why you need the gun?"

"No. But I wondered if you wanted me out of the way. Or wanted to scare me out of it."

He laughs. "Kyris, I have often wanted you out of the way, but if I set an assassin on you, Arsenault's shade will haunt me into the afterworld."

"Arsenault's shade. It's funny you mention that."

"Why?"

"I'm probably imagining things. But I bought a Sight Stone. The gavaro used magic. And he had a gun. Do you remember Razi? The Nezar Nibas fights with?"

"Your Tiresian archer? I remember him."

"The gavaro followed me to Erelf's temple and shot Razi. He lost his arm."

Jon falls silent for a moment. For a moment, I think I see a real emotion on his face. "I thought you said the gavaro was trying to kill *you*," he says quietly.

"He keeps getting closer. And he seems...familiar."

"Then you are imagining things. It's that arm, Kyris. It invites paranoia. It's not natural."

I rub my metal elbow. I'd like to tell Jon he's wrong but he's not. "It keeps me alive."

"One day, maybe it's going to kill you. I don't know why you want this gun, but I'm going to tell you again—if it's getting people around you killed, you don't need it. Arsenault would tell you the same and you know it."

"Arsenault wanted to be my bodyguard."

"He wanted to be more than your bodyguard. May the fila preserve me, but why else do you think I've looked out for you these years?"

I laugh. "Looked out for me? Jon. I don't think you can call it—"

"I rolled the cowry for you just this morning. They came up dark, bad luck in four Houses. Which Houses do you think they were?"

"You don't roll our Houses."

He shrugs. "Does it matter whose Houses they are? I've been fighting among you whiteskins for so long, maybe the fila have gotten confused. You don't need this gun."

"You're just trying to rattle my nerves now."

"The fila don't lie."

"Maybe they haven't been among Lierans long enough."

The buildings are beginning to bother me. I like moving around the city by rooftop, where I can see. The farther away from the docks we get, the more the buildings become like canyons, blocking out the sun. Up on the rooftops, you're next to the sky and the stars, up in air you can breathe. But down here, we're deep in the realm of the kinless. Beggars and lepers, thieves without hands, men with branded mouths, armless women hawking the only thing they can sell anymore—the only thing they could ever sell, though when they were whole people, they might have called it "alliance."

My fingers drift toward the hilt of my knife. Jon's gaze flickers down to my hand and he sighs.

"And see here, you're proving me right. Jumping at shadows. But you've never wanted to listen to anyone's advice, have you?"

When I protest, he motions me quiet. We're approaching a tumbledown warehouse. A group of children stands in front of it, dressed in the drab brown rags of those born kinless with no hope of ever gaining a House.

One of the children looks up. He's chewing something, and from his pinprick pupils, it looks like kacin. Smoking requires a sophistication these children don't have yet. "Jon," he says. "We watched it for you. Where's our money, eh?"

Jon frowns. "I see what you spent your last pay on. You remember what I said before?"

The boy looks down at his bare feet and spits on the sandy ground. He's missing most of his small toe, likely to frostbite. "We watched it good," he mumbles.

"No pay unless you watch it sober. You could have bought shoes with those coins, and now what have you got? You think you're warm, but you're not. You chew that *kacin*, you feel safe, but you're not safe. Not as long as you have that pleasure feeling, you're not thinking. Anybody could gut you."

The boy actually seems to be taking account of Jon's words, flushing, but Jon glances over his shoulder at me one too many times while he's talking.

It's the gun.

Do you really trust Jon Barra?

In spite of the discussion we've just had, the answer is no.

I tighten my hand on the hilt of my knife. Jon sticks a key from his pocket in the rusted iron lock binding the doors. It rattles around and then he pulls the chain down with a clatter and throws them open.

Jon Barra is smuggling guns from under the Prinze monopoly.

And I am staring at a group of Prinze guards arrayed in silver and blue, all of them bearing dikkarros.

※

Prinze guardsmen seem suddenly to be everywhere. I run down the boardwalk as fast as I can, cold air knifing in and out of my lungs. A dikkarro fires behind me with a low thud. I throw my arms over my head but keep running. The shot splinters wood, but thank all the gods that the dikkarro is hard to aim. I veer into an alley inhabited by a beggar in rags.

"My corner!" he shouts. "My corner!"

He shoots out a foot and trips me. My knees smack the cobbles, and my right hand splashes into a puddle of piss. I scramble to my feet and swipe my hand against my cloak, and the beggar whacks my shins with his cane.

"Old man," I gasp, stumbling back out of his way, "I am not here for your corner."

I pull myself up onto the sill of a half-gutted window before he can hit me again.

I climb as high as I can and wriggle into a gap in the second floor, where a hole has been patched with boards. It'll be a good-enough place to hide, if the house isn't already crawling with guards. Where have they all come from? They seem to cover the quayside.

Thumping comes from downstairs, but upstairs is quiet except for the scurrying of rats. Fire-blackened kacin pipes and empty wine bottles litter the uneven floor. I slide on its smooth-worn surface as I run toward the door, looking for a way out in the boarded-up darkness. The whole house cants sideways.

"Upstairs!" a guard shouts. "Andris!"

"Andris?" Jon bellows. "You're not even supposed to be here! Cover the outside door! Dammit—*Andris!* You have other orders!"

I smack against the boards in the small back room with my

shoulder—another patched hole. The boards shudder but don't give way, so I smash them with my metal arm. That makes a little more headway, but booted feet already rattle the stairs.

Daylight shines through, but I still can't make it out the hole and it's a long drop to the ground. I batter the wood with my arm again and prepare myself to attempt it anyway.

"Halt! Halt!" someone shouts. "You!"

I jam my elbow through the hole and try to wriggle myself out. The jagged boards snag and rip my clothes, raking my stomach as I hang half in the room, half out, and stare at the ground.

It's a long, long drop.

I'm saved it by a hand on my legs, yanking me back in.

I kick backward. My boot connects hard into flesh and bone—a man's face, probably. He lets me go with an angry, muffled cry.

I bring my leg up into the hole and prepare to jump. But then he lurches forward and grabs my arm.

We both tumble back into the room, a tangle of kicking, grabbing, punching arms and legs. I slam my right arm into his face. Blood gushes from his nose. Guards haul me upright and away from him. He lies there panting on the floor, blood smeared across his face.

A big man. Dark hair. Gray eyes.

Is this the man who's been chasing me? If it is, he looks like Arsenault, but then again, he doesn't.

No scar, no metallic streak in his hair.

I curse myself but manage to keep my mouth shut.

He lies there staring at my arm. All the guards in the room are staring at my arm. The splintered wood ripped my sleeve and now the metal glints through.

One of the other guards, an old man with yellow-gray hair and lips too big for his face, gives me a shake. "You're under arrest."

"What for?" I ask. "I've done nothing."

The guard laughs. "Coming into an illegal arsenal like that? Do you take me for a fool?"

I can't help pulling against his hands. "I was duped."

"You look like a dupe. Where'd you get that arm?"

He eyes it appreciatively but with trepidation.

I clench my jaw and refuse to answer. That earns me a cuff on the face—not too hard, but hard enough. "Here, now. I asked you a question."

"Leave him," the man on the floor says.

"Andris, shut up," Jon hisses.

That voice. I know that voice.

It's him. By all the gods, it *is* him.

"Arsenault!"

I rip my right arm out of the old man's grip and lunge toward him, stopped only by a barrage of guards who grab me by the shoulders and throw me down. My head slams into the floor; silver sparkles swim in my vision.

It's his voice, but why doesn't it look like him? His hair has sunburned brown streaks in it. His face—beneath the blood from his nose—it's too young, isn't it? Is it just that he shaved his beard?

But where is his scar?

He frowns, up on one knee now, staring down at me. His brows pull down over his eyes—those same brows. The same eyes, but...murky. His bewildered expression is more frightening than a whole contingent of Prinze guards. There is no recognition in it at all. Just confusion.

The other guards laugh. "Know this one, Andris?"

The man they call Andris slowly wipes the blood away from his face, his fingertips brushing the clear skin on his right temple where his scar should be.

"No," he says. "But I wager he'll be singing come nightfall."

PART IV

CHAPTER 19

DEAR GODS. THIS IS WHAT HE MEANT WHEN HE SAID MAGIC ATE his memories.

But I don't know that, do I? Maybe he's running a ruse. Maybe he didn't know it was me. Maybe...

There are too many maybes.

The guard with the fish lips and muddled eyes slaps a pair of manacles onto my wrists, and a pair of guards stand at my back with their dikkarros out. Then the guards take me down the stairs and out into the alley. The beggar who knocked me in the shins watches the whole spectacle with an addled expression, and then he starts to laugh. It's an edgy sound, too high. I turn away from him, but then I'm left looking at Arsenault.

None of the guards want to touch me, so the old guard makes Arsenault do it. He holds my arm just above the elbow. Feeling in my right arm is distant; a tight grip usually feels as light as the tickle of insect feet. His fingers feel closer and tighter, but maybe that's because my hip bumps his every once in a while, when he pulls me off-balance, and I can sense him there, big and warm beside me—real and alive.

When I dart a glance at him out the corner of my eye, all I can see is the way his cloak falls back over his arm, how his sleeve lies over the hard curve of his bicep— the wet black bloodstain on his tunic. I can't help chancing a look upward—again and again—but every time, I'm met with the same mix of the familiar and the strange.

It can't be him. I'm imagining the resemblance.

But he still walks with that same long stride. And his mouth pulls down at the corners like I remember. His hair—even though there's no silver streak—slides out of its tail and into his eyes the way it always did, and he twitches it out of his face with his old quick, irritated jerk. Every now and then, his gaze wanders in my direction until he sees me watching him, and then he looks forward again, a muscle twitching in his jaw the way it used to. His eyes are shadowed, and not just because a big black bruise is already forming beneath them, spreading from the bridge of his nose. They're as hard to read as the surface of the sea.

Thanks to my arm and my boot, I can't tell if he has a cut on his cheek left by my dagger last night or not.

By the time we arrive at the Prinze compound, on the high ground of the city, the cold spring morning has grown lighter and brighter, but it hasn't gotten much warmer. The guards marched me the whole way with their dikkarros out—easily aimed at that distance—and Arsenault never let go of my arm once.

It's not like I really wanted to escape. But of course, only Jon would know that. The guards expected him to leave but he hasn't, and from the look on his face, he's still trying to think of a way to save whatever godsdamned scheme made him think hiding Arsenault from me was a good idea.

The sight of the ancestral home of the Prinze hulking above us gives me pause, though. Rooted in the bluff that sets it above the lower city, surrounded by a jagged wall lined with pikes, its weathered sandstone walls glow peach and apricot, deceptively innocent. A row of cannons peeks out between the crenellations, ready to unleash all their firepower on anyone stupid enough to threaten the Prinze, and archers pace the catwalk, to finish off

CHAPTER 19

anyone the cannons leave alive. The blue-and-silver Prinze trident flag whips in the wind.

The holding cells crouch in the shadow of the house. The big oak doors are barred with iron and studded with nails whose heads are as big as my fist.

The gate guards peer at us. "What've you got there?" one of them asks.

"Smuggler," says Fish-lips, and spits in the dirt. "To be held for questioning."

"I hear the Mestere's coming down later."

"And you'll just keep your mouth shut, won't you? We'll have this smuggler put away well before then, and everything will be nice and tight as a drum for our lord Prinze. Now open the gates, man, before we all take our deaths out here in the cold."

The guard winches the gates open with a high-pitched creak, and I'm shoved through the dusty courtyard of the prison and into the guardroom.

We enter in a great clatter of swords and guns. The guards took the daggers from both my boots, as well as my sword and big knife, but nobody has had the courage to search the sleeve that hides my arm. I learned long ago to always keep a small knife strapped to the place where my flesh meets the metal. It's a small comfort, but it's gotten me out of some tight places.

The young guard sitting at the desk looks up, startled, lifting his quill. It drips a big pool of blue-black ink onto the parchment before him. I can see Cassis in his features—the mobile mouth and large eyes, the well-defined cheekbones—but his eyes are a sea-green blue and his hair is almost blond.

Fish-lips leans on the desk. Arsenault tightens his hand on my arm.

"Have we got room for another smuggler?" the old man says.

The young guard's eyes widen at the glint of light that flashes off my arm. "His *arm*," he says.

Fish-lips sighs. "Yes, I know, his arm. Probably lost it in the wars. They cut off enough limbs for gunshot, didn't they?"

I glare at him, thinking of Razi.

The young guard swallows. "What did he do?"

"Tried to buy a gun. Jon led us to him. He's the one Mestere di Prinze said look out for. Do we have room or not? I don't want to have to sit on him all night."

The young guard stares at my arm for a moment, then accidentally looks straight at me. I hold his gaze until he blushes and directs his attention down to his parchment.

"I— Yes, I think so. Wait." He brings his head back up. "Is that the one we've been looking for?"

Fish-lips looks annoyed. "I said so, didn't I? It's your problem what you do with him. I just need somewhere to drop him."

The young guard nods. "Bring me his weapons."

A guard comes up from behind with my weapons and drops them on the desk with a clang. The young guard pulls my sword to look at it and his eyes widen.

The dim light of the room bounces off the blade and shines in the runes. The old man picks it up and breaks into a cold grin. "Don't suppose you'll be needing this anymore, will you?"

I shrug, though the thought of losing that sword twists my gut. I glance at Arsenault to see how he's reacting, but he isn't. His jaw is set in a hard line.

"Huh." Fish-lips' eyes narrow and he lays the blade flat on the desk again. Then he picks up my bag and rummages through it.

"Pouch of willowbark," he says, placing it carefully on the table. "Bandages. Comb." The comb Arsenault gave me. It goes on the table, too. "Needle, thread." The contents of my bag are the contents of every gavaro's bag, except for one thing. The guard pulls it out now, holds it up and squints at it.

"That's a pretty piece of work," he says. "I think we'll have this, too."

Arsenault's wolf.

Arsenault sniffs and stares at the wall. I want to kick him just to get a reaction.

"I'll wager you're dead by moonrise anyway," Fish-lips says. The wolf goes into his pockets.

"That should be turned over to the treasury," Arsenault says.

"Shut up," Fish-lips tells him without turning around. "The treasury'll get the arm; what does a trinket matter?" He grins at me. "How's your arm come off, eh?"

I grit my teeth and clench both my hands into fists.

Fish-lips pushes my right sleeve up over my forearm, and I yank away from him. A crowd of guards comes with me.

"Here, now; none of that."

"We'll have to take the manacles off," one of the guards says.

"Or cut off the arm," another jokes.

Wait. Maybe he's serious.

"He's to remain for questioning," the guard behind the desk interjects. "We have to send a message to Mestere di Prinze. Leave him whole till then."

Fish-lips looks disappointed, but I start to grin. It's a bad habit of mine, grinning under pressure.

But they don't expect it. Nobody ever does.

"Here." Fish-lips grabs my manacled hands. He extracts a key from inside his cloak and sticks it in the lock. The manacles snap free of my wrists, and I flex my fingers. He grabs my arm with one hand and pushes the sleeve up with the other.

"Tekus on high!"

I tug free of the startled guards, grab the blade from my bicep with my left hand, and lunge across the desk for the young guard, the nearest Prinze. I want Arsenault, but he's a gavaro and won't do as a hostage and, in any case, would probably knock me on my backside. A householder—that's another matter.

We go over backward in his chair before anyone reacts. Half the men in the room are still staring at my arm as I drag him up with my right arm around his throat, the blade in my left hand pressed against his side. The guard gasps and struggles, but I press the blade into his ribs just enough to pierce the skin, and he stops.

The guards all have their weapons out now but it's too late.

Arsenault stares at me as if I were as addled as the beggar in the alley.

"You," I say to Arsenault. "Push my sword over here. Hilt-first."

He meets my gaze. We stare at each other for a long moment, but his eyes might as well be stone. Then he flushes an angry red and shoves the sword toward me.

I push my hostage forward, keeping the point of my blade in his side as I reach out slowly with my right arm to grab the sword. I sheathe it as quick as I can, then move my right arm back into a headlock around the young Prinze's neck.

"I'm taking him outside," I tell the guards, who watch me like I'm a demon. "I need an escort. Him," I say, nodding at Arsenault, "and Jon Barra. I think those two will do to get me out the gates. You'll throw my wolf outside, too, old man, if you know what's good for you. Otherwise, I don't mind killing him, and what will Geoffre think?"

"You'd kill me for a trinket?" my prisoner gasps.

"I'm partial to the wolf," I tell him. "Not to you."

Fish-lips glares. Then he takes the wolf from out of his pocket and hurls it into the dust outside.

"Go with ye, then, you prickless bastard. They'll hunt you down again before nightfall."

"Not if they want to see your Prinze alive, they won't."

I drag the young guard out the door, followed by Arsenault and Jon. "Pick up the statue," I tell Arsenault, and when he hesitates, I yell at him, "Now!"

Arsenault does as I tell him, then holds the wolf out to me in his open palm.

"Keep it for now."

He pockets it without a word, looking frustrated. Humiliated.

Who is this brown-haired man? Why did I think he was Arsenault?

CHAPTER 19

"What in the name of all the gods do you think you're doing?"

Jon whirls on me as soon as we're out of the gates, his cloak snapping out behind him. The guards watch us from the arrow slits and towers—waiting for me to let go of the young guard, to back away just for a moment. They'd shoot through Jon and Arsenault, but I stay close to the boy, my knife still pressed to his throat.

He's probably too old to be called a boy, but he looks like one to me.

"I could ask you the same thing," I say, dragging the guard backward, away from the prison. As long as the archers can see that I'll kill their Prinze, they won't loose their arrows, but once we're out of sight, the patrols will burst from the gates like packs of dogs. "You, working for the Prinze? And Arsenault—" He walks grim-faced, to my right. "Do you remember me or not?"

The guard rolls his eyes to look at me. "You all know each other?" he rasps.

"We've been acquainted," I say carefully. "In another life."

"You'll all hang when my uncle gets hold of you."

"Your uncle?"

He shuts his mouth. Arsenault watches me, undistracted by Jon and the guard, or the fact that we're walking. He's got his hand on his sword; I never thought to tell him to throw it down. But now, the look in his eyes and his silence...

"Kyris—" Jon says.

"Drop your sword, Arsenault."

He cocks his head and makes no move to do so.

"Drop your sword!"

Instead, he draws it.

I jerk my arm tight against the guard's throat in reflex, choking him, and Jon says in an urgent whisper, rushing forward to grab my arm, "Kyris! Geoffre's his uncle!" as Arsenault shifts the sword so that the hilt is swinging toward my head—gods damn everything, my *head*.

I tear away from Jon, ducking, forcing the guard I hold to duck too. But the edge of the pommel clips his skull with a low, sick *thud*. He cries out and falls forward, and I move my knife in a hurry, before he can cut himself on the blade. I pull him upright and step backwards into the side of a building, holding him in front of me like a shield. I can hear the shouts of the guards already.

"If either of you would care to make the betrayal complete," I say, breathing hard, "I'd be happy to drive this knife into his ribs just a little deeper."

The guard's eyes are round as a child's but glazed with pain.

"They'll be hunting the whole city," Jon says. "You won't be able to hide here. You've outlawed yourself."

"And who do I have to thank for that?"

"Thank yourself for it! You didn't have to take that job. You didn't have to buy a gun for it. Why did you need the gun, anyway?"

"You know why I needed the gun. You must have heard the story."

In my ears, my words lack the impact and anger I want to give them, because my chest tightens like a fist. I feel like I can barely breathe.

Arsenault shakes his head in disgust. "You're going to topple this peace for a petty attempt at revenge. Didn't enough people die in those wars? Aren't you satisfied with that?"

"I didn't cause the thrice-damned war. You told me it wasn't my fault. Did you change your mind?"

A thousand questions light in Arsenault's eyes.

"Kyris," Jon says quickly. "There are many things you do not know."

"You knew, Jon," I say through my gritted teeth. My hostage stirs and I pull him back against the wall with me. "You knew and you lied to me."

"Look at him, Kyris. Can you see the man he used to be? Can you see him at all?"

"I—"

How wild must I look? I curse myself for faltering.

"The things best hidden are those which abide in plain sight."

Arsenault makes a noise in his throat. "Jon. I'm right here."

I pull the guard along the wall. "Throw down your sword," I tell Arsenault. "*Now.*"

That muscle in his jaw twitches again. But he obeys, to the letter, throwing the sword into a pile of broken terra-cotta with a crash.

"Will you let him go then?" Arsenault asks.

"Why would I let him go? Those patrols will be down on me any second, and I can't trust either of you. He's all that's keeping me alive right now."

"He won't keep you alive long," Jon says. "You don't know who you have in your hands."

Arsenault jerks. "Jon!"

Jon ignores him. Instead he leans over to speak directly in my ear. The sounds of running Prinze guards pass by the opening to the alley, as if we have all somehow been obscured, until there is only Jon's voice, the tickle of the guard's hair against my cheek, and the way his back heaves with his terrified breathing, and standing in front of me—Arsenault, watching, horrified.

"That's Mikelo di Prinze," Jon says. "Geoffre's grooming him for the heirship."

<hr />

Jon says he knows a bathhouse, and now that he's given me this information about Mikelo di Prinze, I trust him to take us there, but not enough to let Mikelo walk without my knife in his side. I'm sure we're being followed by a detachment of

Prinze, but bathhouses are neutral territory and I feel safe enough on the Caprine side of town.

Jasmine Pleasures is a two-story building made of quarried white marble built into the cliffs surrounding the low, swampy lagoon that forms Liera proper. In the afternoon sun, the inlaid carnelian flowers and vines around the doorway spark blood-red, tinting the marble a sickly pink. Bathhouses in Liera are all constructed on a similar plan. The baths, separated by sex, are located underground where the hot springs bubble up in rock pools. The men's areas for eating and business are upstairs, where courtesans are also provided. Wives and daughters do not enter here.

Jon walks in the back door with the easy familiarity of a man who's been here before, then disappears down the hallway. Arsenault, Mikelo, and I stand in the entry, where we're examined by a golden-skinned girl in a dress of jade green silk.

"Andris," the girl says, smiling as she leans on a polished wood stand where a book lies open. "I wondered when you were coming back. Are these your friends?"

She looks us over with mild interest.

Arsenault forces a smile. "Yes. Just bringing them in for the night."

"If you have any ideas about who they might want, let me know. I'd be willing to take the shorter one. He's a little scruffy, but he's cute." She shoots me a smile designed to look innocent.

I turn to Arsenault. "They know you here, do they?"

"They've seen me here before," he answers.

I can't think of anything to say to that. I pull Mikelo closer to me so they can't see the knife I have pressed into his ribs. Mikelo stiffens. "*Bend*," I whisper to him, and try to smile back at the girl.

Jon returns with a girl on each arm. "They have a place for us," he says. "I've told Madame Triente what we need."

Next to Jon, the girls look like tiny porcelain dolls dressed up in crimson silk and diamonds. They're probably kinless or they wouldn't be working in a bathhouse, but they're not kinless like me, because most householder men like girls with arms, and the diamonds mean their company doesn't come cheap.

The whores give me a once-over, the same as they give Mikelo and Arsenault, just a quick sweep of their dark eyes, sizing us up. You can tell they like the look of Arsenault more than Mikelo or me, but they like Jon best.

"They're not coming, are they?" I say.

"Only as far as the door."

They shoot him a glance that says they're disappointed, probably because they know they won't be making any money tonight.

Mikelo stares until I give him a push.

The whole house smells slightly of sulfur from the hot springs, and my big cloak is making me sweat. Our boots sink silent into deep velvet rugs.

More courtesans stand inside the hallway, both women and men, and they watch us walk in, flashing smiles like vendors in the market. Arsenault and Jon both keep their eyes forward, but Mikelo has obviously never been in a bathhouse for anything other than a bath. It would be funny if I wasn't strung so tight.

The girls lead us up the stairs to a room with a nameplate that says *Lora*. Which one, I wonder, is Lora? Jon gives them some coins and they drift off down the stairs in a rustle of silk. The work of so many worms, their dresses, their slippers, these rugs. I wonder if any of it is Aliente.

As soon as I shut the door, Mikelo tries to yank himself away from me. I jam the knife in his side and his eyes grow bigger and wilder.

"What are you going to do to me now? Have I come here to die?"

Arsenault's gaze flicks over to me. "If you behave, you'll probably be ransomed."

"I have money," I say, throwing the bolts on the door with my right hand, keeping the knife out in my left. "What I want is safe passage out of the city and an explanation."

"So, you are going to kill him." Jon sits heavily on a couch too low for him. His knees stick out ridiculously. He bends to unlace his boots, and I become aware that my feet ache. Fiercely.

"Mikelo?" I shrug. "Perhaps." I pull my knife away from him. "That depends on whether he wants to test me."

Mikelo eyes me, his face pale. But it doesn't look like he's going anywhere, so I shove the knife back into its sheath. Maybe he's just as curious as I am about what's going on, or maybe he doesn't want to test my arm. Men attribute all sorts of fanciful abilities to me once they know about my arm.

Jon stops unlacing his boots and looks up. "I wasn't talking about Mikelo."

So, Jon *did* know what Tonia was hiring me to do, and for some reason, he wants to keep me from doing it. But why would Jon want Cassis alive? Why work *with* the Prinze? Why place Arsenault in their ranks?

"Well, that depends too," I say. "But I have a contract."

"Now think. What's going to happen if you honor it?"

"My family might be avenged, for one. For another..." I glance at Arsenault. "I did have someone else in mind when I took the job."

"Who?"

"You know who I wanted to avenge, Jon."

Jon grunts, but he darts a quick look at Arsenault. "Yourself?"

I rub my cheekbone where Fish-lips cuffed me and decide to let it go for now. "Maybe."

"Think it through, Kyris. You take back the girl, kill her lover. Now what happens?"

"Why do you care, Jon? Why do you want him alive?"

"You're going to start a war again and it will be useless. You're not thinking beyond your desire to take revenge."

"Like you're so righteous and forgiving."

A rare flash of anger passes over Jon's face. Then he turns to

Mikelo. "How many householders did you lose in the war?"

Mikelo draws himself straighter. "The Caprine put some of our minor branches to the sword; I don't know if there are any of them left. Half the Garonze. The Forza...well, there was that raid on their ancestral home, wasn't there, after they pledged allegiance to us? If the Aliente captain had kept fighting, casualties would have been worse. He had no honor, wouldn't meet an army on the flat, kept pulling dirty tricks. And in the city, the Caprine were getting guns somehow. Thank all the gods they were never able to smuggle as many as we had."

Arsenault just stands on the other side of Mikelo with his thumbs in his swordbelt, scowling but otherwise showing no sign that he remembers that *he* was the Aliente captain Mikelo is talking about. Mikelo doesn't seem to recognize him either. I'm not sure how they've pulled this off, but Jon has some damn balls.

Jon leans on his knees and arches an eyebrow at me. "You know what that translates into when it comes to gavaros, serfs, servants, and kinless," Jon says. "Do you know where your family is?"

"I don't have a family."

"Psh." Jon waves his hand. "Curse your laws. Where is your family?"

I walk to the sideboard, yank the door open. I grab a bottle from the crystal serving set inside and pour without pausing to sniff its contents. It tumbles clear out of the bottle—imya, then. "Jon. You know that, too. Quit throwing me rhetorical questions and give me some real answers. What game are you playing, you and..."

Dammit, if he *is* playing a game and I give Arsenault away to Mikelo di Prinze, he'll have a problem. My arm begins to shake in reaction.

"...Andris," I finish, and take a drink. The imya burns as it goes down.

"It's not a game, Kyris."

My control snaps.

I whirl and throw the glass at his head, but it misses and smashes against the wall, a hundred glittering shards raining down on the carpet. "I know it's not a game! I will kill Cassis!" I take a deep, dragging breath. "And you know why."

The room goes still. Arsenault has his hands down at his sides like he has other weapons, and Mikelo has edged toward the door, but now he stops. My right arm is singing to me and I grip it with my left, hold it until it calms down.

No, not now, this is not the time.

Jon rises, his gaze troubled and pinned to my arm. He's seen me in battle. He knows what happens to me. And yet he keeps driving this spike of revenge and paranoia into me like he's baiting Ires.

"I'll take the boy in the other room," he says, unwilling to cross the line for now. "Since Andris is the one who wrecked my plans, maybe he can talk some sense into you."

Arsenault throws Jon a sardonic look.

If I could stop shaking, everything would be better. I drop my left hand from my arm. "You think I trust you to take my hostage into the other room?"

"We won't escape. You have my word."

"Your word is worth nothing."

He reaches into his sleeve to remove the smallest gun I've ever seen. "It's worth a life."

❦

I DON'T KNOW WHY I EVER BELIEVE JON. I TELL MYSELF THAT I believe him now because he could have killed me and taken Mikelo back himself and he didn't. He has every reason to betray the Prinze and no reason to ally to them in the first place, unless it's to get close enough to Geoffre to put a knife in his back. But Jon has always been willing to throw away even the most valuable card in his deck if it gets him what he wants.

CHAPTER 19

The gun he hands me is a work of art. Smooth-sanded mahogany inlaid with mother-of-pearl forms its stock, its wheel-lock mechanism and both barrels forged of hard watered steel. No fussing with fuses and matches. The gun is primed and loaded, the wheel already turned, which means that Jon could have blown a hole in my head sooner than I could sink my blade into Mikelo's throat.

He was right; it's worth much more than five thousand astra.

After Jon leads Mikelo into the adjoining room, a girl brings us food, and I drag the chamber pot into the closet so Arsenault won't see me use it. When I come out, Arsenault has cleaned up his face and is sitting on the bed with his boots off and his feet up, his dirty blue cloak slung over a chair upholstered in yellow silk, Prinze tunic thrown carelessly on top of it. In his left hand he holds a roll stuffed with pieces of meat and cheese, and in his right, a metal stylus. The nib scratches over a piece of gritty paper he has spread out on a board propped on his knee, leaving brief glowing tracks of magic that soon turn a deep reddish-brown, almost burgundy. My arm hums with it, but it winks out when he sees me. He puts his knee down, then rolls the paper up and shoves it into a wooden tube that rests on the bed beside him. The tube disappears into his pocket along with the stylus, and the board slides upright against the side of the bed.

If I had any more questions concerning his identity, they have just been answered.

I wash my face and my hands in the basin as calmly as I can and dump the dirty water into the chamber pot. Then I sit down on the other side of the bed and take off my boots.

There are courting rituals less complicated than this.

The tray of food rests on the bed beside Arsenault's knees. I make up my supper from the variety of cured meats and cheeses fanned out on the wooden board. A small jar of sweet-spicy preserved fruit and a basket of hot rolls sit next to it. I pick one up and sink my thumbs into it, releasing the steam inside, and them jam as much meat and fruit as I can into it.

"Where is your book?" I ask, licking sticky purple liquid off my thumb.

Arsenault looks up in the process of making himself another sandwich—avoiding the fruit. "My book?" he says.

I seal my sandwich by pressing the edges together. "You used to write in a book. A diary, I suppose. Do you still have it?"

"I imagine it's been lost or destroyed by now."

"You imagine?"

"Hard to say, with the wars." He folds the bread over the top of his neatly layered meat and cheese. "Almost everything has been lost or destroyed, hasn't it?"

The last bite of my sandwich drips onto the bedspread and I shove it in my mouth and chew viciously. Beside me, Arsenault eats his tidy, dry sandwich like a foreigner, lying back against the pillows.

I pick up a couple of pieces of cheese and cast myself back on the pillows, too.

"Why are you working for the Prinze, Arsenault?"

"Jon could answer that better, probably."

"I don't want to hear it from Jon. I want to hear it from you."

"Jon brought me to Geoffre, though." He looks over at me, finally, just a turn of his head. "You *are* going to start a war, you know."

"Who will the Prinze war with this time? The Sere? They're more powerful than we ever were." I fold a piece of cheese and chew on it thoughtfully. "But Tonia was right. I can't leave another woman to Cassis. Unless he's finally grown a pair of balls, he'll still be dancing to Geoffre's tune, and who knows what Geoffre is up to. Though why I should care what these asses do to kill themselves off, I don't know."

Arsenault snorts. "I don't know that you do. Really. Do you?"

I turn my head toward him. It's so strange to see him lounging there, so close and familiar that I want to touch him… and still so far away that I can't.

"How did you find out what I was doing?" I ask.

He doesn't look at me. "Jon has an informant placed with Tonia di Sere."

I curse softly. "That Qalfan gavaro. I knew he was a weak point. Jon said he didn't send anybody to kill me, but..."

"No one tried to kill you."

"Someone did. Twice. Once wearing Qalfan fighting robes. But instead of me, he killed a friend of mine and shot another." I search Arsenault's cheek again for the cut, and once again see nothing but the evidence of our most recent fight. "I nicked him with my throwing knife, though, last night."

"If Jon sent anyone to kill you, I don't know about it."

"Mmmm. Why have you forgotten me?"

My question startles him enough to make him turn toward me. I find myself studying his face, trying to find a memory in it the way I search for the lines of his scar. My scrutiny must make him uncomfortable. He looks away, turning the half-eaten sandwich over in his hands.

"I've forgotten many things," he says—to his sandwich. He doesn't even pretend to look at me. "Most things, maybe. If I knew you in the wars..."

"It wasn't the wars, Arsenault."

He frowns. "That name. I think a woman might have called me that. Long ago."

"Do you remember what she looked like?"

"Dark hair. Brown skin." His mouth curves a little, almost a smile. "She liked to run barefoot in the ocean."

My heart squeezes like a fist.

Not me.

Not Margarithe, either, though.

I sigh. "It's not your real name, is it."

"Doesn't matter. The man my parents named died long ago." He touches his now-unscarred temple briefly, then lets his fingers fall away as if unaware of what he's doing. "And you. With your metal arm. Can I see it?"

He waits for me. I think of all the stories he told me of his homeland, of ice and snow. In his eyes I can imagine a sea choked with ice, though I have never seen such a thing. Desolation, ships locked in port. I sit, turning toward him, and push up my ripped sleeve, exposing the metal beneath.

He touches the flat sheen of my forearm, then lifts my arm until his reflection ripples over its surface. The brown and red in his hair are muted in this light so his hair looks black, like it should.

"Jon found me in an alley," he says abruptly. "He says his gods told him where I was."

"Perhaps it's so. Jon always says he has no magic, but I think he lies."

Arsenault glances up at me sharply, his hands still on my arm. "Magic. That's a word. Let me see the rest of your arm."

I push my sleeve up the rest of the way so he can see the way the metal joins the flesh. "No hinges?" he asks.

I laugh, startled. "You smithed this arm, Arsenault."

He stares at me.

"No," I say. "No hinges. I think there's more metal now than when you fitted it to my stump."

That makes him frown. He runs his thumb up my bicep to the place where metal meets flesh. My arm was cut just above the elbow, but the metal now runs almost to my shoulder. His fingers skim the join and I catch a whiff of musk and black tea mingled in his sweat, and I can't tell whether it's his touch or his magic that makes me shiver.

He catches the movement and looks up at me. His hand leaves my arm and hesitantly, his fingers settle on my chin. He turns my head to the side to look at my profile.

When he speaks, it's almost in a whisper. "Kyris isn't your name either, is it."

I shake my head.

His thumb tracks down the side of my jaw.

"You're a woman."

How did he not know?

He makes a noise and pulls away, but I catch his hand in my metal fingers. He tugs his hand out of my grip and rolls so that his feet hit the floor, and now he's standing.

"Kyrra," he says. "Kyrra d'Aliente."

But he doesn't say it like my name. He says it the way everybody else says it, like it's an accusation, only he's gripping his half-eaten sandwich in his hand so tight, his fingers sink deep into the roll, and he doesn't seem to notice.

Carefully, I unfold my legs and slide off the bed to stand. On the other side. Far away from him.

"What *do* you remember, Arsenault?"

"I remember burning," he says. "At Kafrin Gorge."

※

THIS IS ALL I'VE BEEN ABLE TO LEARN ABOUT KAFRIN GORGE:

A year and a half ago, the Prinze boxed the main Aliente force in the Gorge and set it on fire.

It was late autumn and tinder-dry. The fire roared up the walls of the Gorge and into the trees beyond, lighting an inferno. It spread through the ancient oak groves and up the pine-scrubbed hillsides and almost took the house. It burned the stables and the barns and some of the silkhouses. Half the mulberries turned to ash. But the main force of the Prinze, arrayed at the mouth of the Gorge, remained upwind of the fire and had already dug in with firebreaks and mostly escaped.

After that defeat, the few remaining Aliente gavaros fled. The new Householder—my father's third cousin—and his entire family were knifed in their sleep by a group of Amoran assassins hired by Geoffre. Any Aliente who remained within reach of Liera and did not immediately take ship for Vençal or Onzarro or Tiresia died somehow; the Prinze rounded up a group of my relatives from up north and put them to the very first firing squad ever used in Liera. My father's serfs and servants were allowed to remain on the land, their contracts transferred to Vanni di Forza's father.

I received the news months after it happened, when Lieran gavaros began to filter north. By that time, so many gavaros were deserting on both sides that the Houses had come to the point of signing peace accords. Some of the gavaros who came to Rojornick and Kavo were Aliente.

Our gavaros had been strangely loyal. Most of the men I'd known from my years as a serf were dead, and it was only after Kafrin that the rest gave it up as a bad job.

A young gavaro hired after I left gave me the strangest piece of information, the one that sent me back south. By that time, I was serving in Kavo, hunting down the Rojornicki boyars who betrayed my first employer, a Rojornicki noble named Markus Seroditch. I remember when the gavaro walked into the dining hall of the barracks, still wearing his burgundy Aliente cloak and the stunned look of one new to warfare. I sat him down with a glass of imya and kept refilling it until both he and I had broken down weeping and I had wrung every last scrap of information out of him.

He told me that my father had ridden into the Gorge with his main force, but Arsenault wasn't with him.

I knew that Arsenault had risen high in the ranks. I knew that my father depended on him.

And I knew that Arsenault would never have ordered that many men into the Gorge.

So, where was he? How long had he been gone? A few hours? A day? A week?

Three months. He'd disappeared after a battle with the Forza on our western border. It was a minor battle, really a raid, at night in the trees. The Forza had thought to flank us, but somehow Arsenault found out and led a small force of fifty gavaros to sabotage their cannons and rout them out at night. The mission was a success; the Forza lost all their cannon to spectacular explosions, their leadership were killed in their tents,

CHAPTER 19

and the majority of the force threw down their weapons when it became clear they were surrounded.

But Arsenault never made it back.

In the morning light, the Aliente gavaros searched the remains of the Forza camp as well as the surrounding wood. They sent alerts back to the big house.

Nothing.

His body was never found and nothing else was ever heard from him. The gavaro I talked to assumed he'd died in the explosions or the Forza had taken him prisoner when they retreated and then killed him afterward.

But I knew Arsenault. When the Kavol decided to stop killing enemies and start killing friends, I took the option on my contract, packed up what little I owned, and began the long journey back to Liera.

And now he says he was at Kafrin.

"How?" I ask. "No one saw you—"

"Do you think I don't ask myself the same question?" He runs a hand through his hair. "But all I remember is the fire. I've pieced together enough to know I must have been there with the Aliente force—"

"Must have been?"

"Supposed to— Dammit, I don't know!" He takes a deep, shaky breath. "I remember the flames. The sound they made. I remember... That's all I remember. The burning."

The gavaro told me there were rumors, never proved...that Arsenault had been seen with Cassis di Prinze around that time, either just before or just after.

"How did you walk out of that, Arsenault?"

He turns hollowed eyes on me. "I don't know. The next thing I remember, it was quiet. The sky was blue. I was walking down the Eterean road. The fire hadn't gotten that far. I stumbled into someone's house and they gave me water. Let me sleep and bathed the burns."

"You've no scars. Not even the one you used to have. At your temple. That was a knife scar, though."

He touches his temple and his eyes flicker closed, just for an instant. "No," he murmurs. "I don't think it was a knife."

For a moment, it feels like he might say more, and I hold my breath. But then he drops his right hand and looks at his left.

"Damn," he says, pulling his fingers out of the mangled sandwich. He shoves the remainders in his mouth and swoops up his boots on his way to join Mikelo and Jon in the other room.

I gamble that the three men won't go anywhere while I put my boots on. I need some time to think about everything I've heard and seen. But it still doesn't give me any answers.

The gavaro I met in Kavo thought the rumors of Arsenault meeting Cassis were just meant to demoralize the Aliente. He had a quick mind, but he was too good-hearted for a gavaro's life, and much too kind to work in Kavo. I hope he's moved on by now if he's still alive. He had served under Arsenault and respected him. Wouldn't entertain the notion that Arsenault could betray my father and the men he fought beside so completely.

I couldn't entertain the notion that Arsenault would betray his men like that either. And I still can't entertain the notion that he would betray *me*, although for all intents and purposes, it seems that he has. Those memories must exist somewhere and there has to be a way to make the magic vomit them back up.

But betraying my father...that's another matter.

When I've put myself together again, I go into the other room.

The men are playing cards and eating from a much better tray of food. The kitchens sent Jon a roast pheasant and a bottle of Amoran red. Arsenault straddles a chair and Jon is dealing him a hand. Indij. I can tell by the number of cards and the pile of

CHAPTER 19

Mikelo's silver buttons that sit in a pile in front of Jon. I've never beaten him. Maybe Arsenault has.

Mikelo gives a start when he sees me. "What are you going to do with that gun?"

Arsenault is busy arranging his hand. You'd never know the subject of our last conversation from looking at Arsenault's face.

"Relax," he tells Mikelo. "It's not for killing you."

I rest Jon's small gun on the table in front of me as I take a seat. "You never know. Maybe it is. Deal me in." Arsenault and Jon never take their eyes off their cards as they scoot over to make room for me, but Mikelo eyes the gun.

It sits there like a dare. Any of us could reach for it.

I wait to see what he does, pretending to look at my cards. He edges closer...but then thinks better of it. He presses his lips together tight and squints at the cards in his hand. When he leans forward, his hair falls in his eyes the way Cassis's did.

Why have I never heard of Mikelo di Prinze? He's too young to have been one of my suitors, but I would at least have known his name.

"Pull," says Jon, and we all lay cards on the table—not the whole hand; that's not how indij is played. We only play the cards we think will beat our opponents.

Indij is a game of both strategy and luck. It's not like kai dahn. You don't always play your strongest card first. Sometimes, you hold it and lose for a while. Then you pull it out when the deck's gone down and you know how your fellow players are playing their lords and ladies, generals and jesters.

The jester is the strongest card in the deck, which means Lierans didn't invent it. Someone else's sense of humor. Gavaros love it.

Jon has three lords, a general, and a page. A very strong hand, but he and Mikelo have been playing a while. Probably he could guess what Mikelo held—a lady, two generals, a farrier, a captain. Not so good, but it's all he has left. Jon's beat him handily. But in the fan of Arsenault's cards lies a jester.

He half-smiles. "Now, there's luck for you. Pay up."

"I think you bend luck your way," I say.

"If only I could." He scrapes all Jon's winnings over to his place on the table. Jon sighs and I dig a few coins out of my pocket, and Mikelo frees another of his silver buttons, this one from a pocket on his coat.

"I don't understand," Mikelo says.

Jon raises an eyebrow. "The jester laughs at all of us. Only one in a deck. You've played before."

"Don't you want to tie me up or something? What *are* you going to do with me?"

I reach past the gun for his cards and shuffle them into the deck. My turn to deal. "For starters, I'm going to try to take that last button off your coat. Then I imagine I'll torture some information out of you."

He turns pale as a fish belly. Jon shoots me a reproving glance and shakes his head. "Kyrra. That wasn't nice. Mikelo, she's joking."

So, we've dropped the fiction.

The color comes back into Mikelo's face fast. "He's a *woman*?"

I sigh. I've gotten better at seeming like a man so it doesn't happen too often anymore, but Mikelo's response is so predictable, I want to thump him with the deck of cards. "Just be grateful you've got some buttons to lose. Draw."

Mikelo's hand shakes as he takes a card from the deck. But to his credit he's trying to concentrate on the game. "My uncle won't pay you. He doesn't deal with gavaros. Not like this."

"But you're in the line of succession."

"It won't save you. His son's about to wed a fertile wife; she'll have sons, and I'll be useless. You ought to let me go."

"Now, how do you know that?"

"It's knowledge all over town."

"Sounds a little desperate, Mikelo."

He flushes. "My uncle won't bargain with an armless woman."

I grin at him and lay my right arm on the table so he has to look at it. "I'm not armless. Am I?"

Arsenault stares at my arm for a moment, then turns abruptly to his cards. "What are you planning to do in the morning? If you're not going to give him up?"

"I'll tell you in the morning," I say. Thank all the gods I'm playing indij. Curse the gods that Arsenault and Jon were looking at me when I said it.

"You know you'll have to deal with Geoffre," Arsenault says.

"He'll either show up or he won't," I answer, and start chewing my lip.

What I want is to talk to Tonia di Sere again. To break into her bedchambers and haul her out of bed in the dark and ask her why she didn't know her servants better.

Three ladies, a captain, and a general. What in the name of the underworld does a person do with a hand like that?

I brush the stock of the gun with my right hand as I draw another card.

But would Geoffre want his own sonless son killed? In favor, perhaps, of an unknown Prinze missing a few silver buttons?

Does Mikelo *want* the succession?

My head hurts from playing this game. "Pull," Jon says, and I make a quick decision—three ladies, the farrier I drew, and the captain. The general is my strongest card, and I want to keep it.

Even Mikelo beats me this time, but it's best to get rid of your weak cards so you can draw stronger ones the second time around.

Banging on the door.

I leap for the gun in the same instant that Jon, Arsenault, and Mikelo do, which tells me something, but I'm closest and I have a metal elbow, so I win. I wrench back the dog with its chunk of pyrite into firing position and pull the gun on Mikelo.

Jon and Arsenault fall back.

"Answer the door," I tell Arsenault as I edge around the table, closer to Mikelo.

Arsenault scowls but walks to the door, puts his eye to the spyhole, and lets his breath out through his teeth. "Prinze," he says in a low voice.

"Guards?" I ask.

"Yes. And Devid."

Mikelo doesn't relax. Odd. Jon stands on the other side of him, hands at his sides where I can see them. His expression and Mikelo's are almost twins—tense, like they're both clenching their teeth.

"See what they want," I say.

I wonder how Devid has managed to track us down so quickly, but probably his guards weren't that far behind us or he has spies in the whorehouse. That's likely; whores are the best spies.

But Jon might have sent word.

Arsenault opens the door and stands behind it.

I make sure that all the Prinze can see the gun I have pointed at Mikelo's head.

The girl in front stops in surprise, fear flitting over her face. She's a pretty little thing, all black curls and blue eyes, wearing a diaphanous gown of sapphire silk.

Behind her, the guards stand at silver-buttoned attention, Devid among them. Nine years older, but he hasn't changed much. A few creases furrow his sea-browned skin, and a handful of silver threads sparkle in the dark hair that runs down the Prinze line. He looks more and more like his father. I wonder what Cassis looks like now that he's grown from boy to man, if his shoulders are broader, if any lines are beginning at the corners of his eyes.

The girl stares down at the carpet. "These men request a conference. They have been instructed that this is neutral territory and have agreed to shed no blood. We require a similar promise from you." She lifts her gaze hesitantly, her eyebrows smooth black arches. She can tell I'm a woman, I think. Maybe that's what surprised her.

Everyone looks at me now. I settle the gun against Mikelo's temple. The dog is pulled back, the wheel still set, and my finger rests against the trigger. He goes that fish-belly white again.

"As long as we're only *negotiating*," I say, "there will be no bloodshed. But I'll keep hold of this gun and Mikelo all the same, I think."

"My father wishes to speak with you," Devid says, pushing past the girl before she can tell me whether my "promise" is acceptable or not. "He has a room on a lower floor. I'm instructed to lead you there."

"You're just a messenger, Devid?"

He frowns, taking in my velvet-ribboned queue, my not-quite-flat-enough chest. "I serve my father," he says, "the House-holder of the House di Prinze. He's come to negotiate for your hostage, which is an honor he doesn't usually extend to extortionists. I'd suggest you take it, or he'll see you hanging by four different ropes."

"I've been threatened with worse," I say. "Tell Geoffre he can attend me here." I tug back on the dog to make sure it's settled in place, and it makes a loud click. Mikelo flinches, violently. "Or not," I add.

Devid swears under his breath. "My father doesn't bargain with gavaros."

"Then he won't have an heir, will he?"

By the look on Devid's face, it's a true guess. Devid should, by all rights, be the next Householder. But Devid has only girls, and so far, Cassis hasn't managed any children at all. It's only natural that Geoffre go out ranging for other kin, but how Devid must hate it, to share Geoffre's love with anyone else.

As if Geoffre has love to share.

"Don't bait my father," he says. "You'll lose. I'll lead you downstairs, and all of you can parley. Your two turncoats included."

Arsenault's eyebrows go up at this accusation. *Who is turning which coat?* I want to ask. If I don't know which side they're on, then at least neither do the Prinze. That's one thing.

"We don't want to parley downstairs," I say, in what I hope is a neutral tone. "For all I know, you've an entire detachment of guards out there in the hall waiting to ambush me. You bring your father up here and we'll talk. Otherwise, why don't you just go home and save everyone the trouble. Get yourself another heir somewhere else." I pause. "If you can."

Arsenault gives me a look that says, *You just don't know when to stop, do you.*

Devid stands stiff-legged straight for a moment, then abruptly inclines his head. He looks like a child's toy soldier, spit-shined in his silver and blue, wooden with anger. "As you wish," he says, biting off the words. Then he turns on his heel and flicks his hand at his guards. They whirl out of the room, their cloaks a splash of sky blue against the flowered wallpaper. The girl bows, then follows them out. Mikelo starts to shake as soon as they're gone.

"My uncle won't bargain for me. I don't know why he's come, but he won't bargain. He'd as soon let me die."

"You must be worth *something* to him. He's come here in person."

"I don't know what he's doing," Mikelo confesses, looking at me straight for the first time, "but Devid gave up much too easily."

Arsenault leans against the wall and folds his arms across his chest, looking more like his old self. "He has a point."

"Whose side are you on?" I ask. "Truly?"

He straightens up. "Mikelo's."

His answer surprises me. "So, you side with the Prinze."

"Did he say that, Kyrra?" Jon interrupts, sitting back down in his seat at the card table. He picks up his cards again and begins casually to rearrange them. "I heard him say he stood for *Mikelo.*"

Now, there is information I can use. "You said you rolled

cowries. What did they tell you? Do you stand for Mikelo too?"

Jon looks up from his cards. "I do," he says. "I suppose you should know that. The cowries told me nothing about you except darkness, and here you come in, threatening my ideals."

"You only have ideals when it's convenient, Jon."

"You're not accusing me of being Geoffre, are you?" Jon says mildly. Then his voice turns serious. "Ask Arsenault what he saw."

"Geoffre will be here—"

"Ask Arsenault what he *Saw*."

Saw. Different from mere sight. I turn slowly to face Arsenault, but his jaw has settled into that old expression of when he'd rather not answer. Some things don't change. "Jon misleads you. I can no longer See as I used to. Or so people tell me."

Jon frowns, his brow wrinkling.

"Who else knows you?" I ask.

Arsenault rakes a hand through his hair. "I'm not about to lead three people to their deaths just because of some godsforsaken dream."

"But you trusted Jon to place you with the Prinze. Your dreams must have told you enough that you *stand for Mikelo* now."

The look he gives me is a haunted one. "Maybe," he says. "Whatever I was like before, my Sight now is jumbled and confusing. But Jon's a gambler." He folds his arms across his chest.

This was ever the problem with him. "And how is withholding information going to help any of us?"

"I stand for Mikelo." His gaze is level. "If you don't kill him right off, he's safer with you."

I think about this for a moment, until Mikelo starts to laugh. "Safer with her? She's got a gun at my head."

"But Geoffre di Prinze is your uncle." Jon folds his cards on the table. "Don't you think he'd pull the trigger himself if you weren't of use to him?"

Mikelo falls silent at that. It's obvious that he knows Jon speaks truth. "I didn't know I had a patrol gavaro and a smuggler for my bodyguard. Truly, my uncle thinks highly of me."

"Many people think you're their best hope, Mikelo," Arsenault says softly as he puts his eye to the spyhole again. "And many people would protect your life."

Mikelo chews his lip. Jon says, "We'll see what your uncle has to say, won't we?"

So, Jon and Arsenault will switch sides and risk their identities and their lives to protect this skinny, pale-skinned, shaky boy, who can't be more than two years past his majority. Devid hates him, that I could see, and Geoffre deigns to leave his fortress on the bluff to wheedle or threaten him away from me.

I thought fifty thousand astra was an enormous sum, but now I find in my possession something so valuable, I don't know if I want it anymore.

"WE SEEK SAFE ENTRY!" THE GIRL CALLS OUT AGAIN FROM outside the door.

"Granted," Arsenault calls back without waiting for me. I grab Mikelo and shove him behind the card table, then duck behind it myself. Jon joins me, and Arsenault opens the door from behind it again.

We all know better than to trust Geoffre di Prinze.

But he walks in with no guard ahead of him. His hair is full silver now, but the years haven't diminished him. He still stands as straight-backed as if he were cast in bronze. He wears a cloak of crushed blue velvet adorned with silver clasps and edged with silver brocade, and his trousers are rare indigo silk. On his right, Geoffre wears a black holster out of which protrudes the twin of the gun I hold against Mikelo's head. On his left, he wears his House's sword, Kin-Stealer, its hidden blade etched in sapphire serpents, the emblem of a seafaring house.

CHAPTER 19

Geoffre's lips twitch in an expression too cold to be called smile or snarl. Like the reptile that represents his house, the movements of his mouth are merely rearrangements of scales.

"So," he says. "The infamous kidnapper, and those whom I thought were my allies. Yet you hold no weapons on them. I am betrayed."

The cold smile hardens. We are not playing indij any longer.

"Shall we sit?" Geoffre takes the armchair against the far wall—the most defensible position, the seat of power. Arsenault ghosts by him, wary as a cat. The only other chairs in the room are at the card table. Jon sits, then Arsenault, but it is a long moment before I can force myself to pull Mikelo down and sit next to him.

Geoffre rests his leg on the opposite knee. "Hello, Mikelo."

"Uncle," Mikelo whispers, tight-lipped.

Geoffre watches Mikelo for a moment, considering, then turns to me. "You think you can demand that I negotiate. I've a squad of guards out there with dikkarros and orders to use them."

"The dikkarro is notoriously hard to aim," I say. "With that much shot flying around, you'd be more likely to hit Mikelo than us. And anyway, my gun is closest."

Geoffre taps his chin. "How much money do you want?"

His presence alone probably means I could ask for a quarter to half the sum my father grossed every year for his silks. But even if I got the money, I wouldn't make it out of the city.

But his assumption that I can be bought makes me want to spit.

"I don't want money," I say.

Geoffre's eyebrows peak. "A gavaro who doesn't want money. How extraordinary. I wonder, did you capture Jon and my guard or did you bribe them away?"

"We've been escorting Mikelo," Arsenault says, then adds, bowing stiffly from the shoulders somewhat after the fact, "My lord."

Geoffre snorts. "So you were. Fine lot of good it's done. I had the rest of your detachment flogged. And Jon." He shakes his head mournfully. "I did think we had an understanding."

Jon shrugs. "Such as it was, my lord. I've gone beyond the terms of our agreement. I delivered the gavaro, and it was your guards that lost him. I thought maybe you wouldn't want your nephew dead, so I came as escort when I was demanded to do so."

"Demanded, were you? A stick of a boy like that demanded the both of you, and you went?" He squints at me. "I don't even think it's a boy. I think it's a woman." He pauses. "Well? Which is it?"

I remind myself that I am the one with the gun.

"I have your nephew. Since your sons are both impotent, may I also assume that he's your heir?"

Devid makes a noise in his throat and steps forward, stopped only by Geoffre's outflung arm. I smile at them. "I forgot. At least Devid is a girl-maker."

Arsenault gives me that look again.

But Geoffre starts to laugh. "I believe you are a woman. Only women know how to deal in insults against themselves. Curious, a female gavaro." He leans back in his chair and regards me from eyes which must twin the serpents' on his sword—a glittering stormy blue. "I do wonder where Tonia dug you up."

He cranes his neck over the back of his chair. "Devid, if you'll make sure the corridor is secure."

Devid jerks. "Father, we left a guard on the door."

"I'd feel more secure if I knew my own son was guarding it."

Devid's fingers twist at his side. White-faced, he inclines his head. "As you wish, Father," he says, then turns on his heel, motioning to the rest of the guards in the room and sparing a seething glace at Mikelo. The guards all follow him out, but the little whore remains. She comes to stand behind Geoffre's chair and puts a hand on his shoulder.

Geoffre reaches up to clasp it. "You go, too, Lusinda. I don't think I'll be in danger."

Lusinda shoots us a dagger glance as she leaves, and I wonder if a real knife hides beneath those thin layers of blue-green silk. How Devid must feel, spurned for a minor relation and a whore.

"Now, then," Geoffre says, leaning forward, "we can get down to business."

"Are you sure your son will protect you?" I say, like a tongue probing a sore tooth.

"My son is no concern of yours. Or at least not that one. I understand you've been hired to retrieve a certain Caprine from the care of my second son, and I have to say I wish you luck in that endeavor, though I don't think I can allow you to kill him. He does have some use yet." A brief frown passes over his face. "I'm not quite sure why my smuggler chose not to inform his guardsmen that they were to bring you to *me*, but I'll have to seek that information another time. Perhaps tomorrow," he says, turning to give Jon a wide smile that is nothing more than veneer on his intentions. Jon shifts beside me and stares at the wall.

Maybe Jon didn't send that assassin to take care of me, but I think he might have meant to hang me.

A hollow spot inside begins to ache fiercely. I tighten my grip on the gun and press it harder against Mikelo's fair hair. Mikelo flinches and sways aside, but I yank him up out of the chair so we can both stand. Geoffre's eyes widen, a show of alarm from him.

"I'm not doing anything for the Prinze," I say. "You can keep your gold, your spice, and your ill-gotten silk. But you'll give me safe haven till we're out of the city or else I'll leave you heirless. And you can spend your time in the arms of your whore, knowing she'll have your empire when you die...or the Caprine will."

Geoffre's expression goes flat. He takes a deep breath through his nose. "This is not an acceptable position," he says.

"Do you think you can bully me into doing what you want? I'll have what I want, and then we can deal for what you want."

"I have fifteen guardsmen waiting in the hall. If you should—"

"And none of them will be able to pull their triggers before Mikelo is dead."

Geoffre's eyes narrow. "You're just a girl. You won't kill him."

I pull my hidden dagger left-handed and drive it deep into the flesh of Mikelo's neck where it meets his shoulder, just above his collarbone. Blood wells up and he cries out, his knees sagging. Geoffre, Jon, and Arsenault all jerk forward, but I pull Mikelo hard against me.

"Are you willing to test me?"

"I know who you are," Geoffre says suddenly. "You're Kyrra d'Aliente."

He throws his head back and laughs. "So, all the rumors were wrong, were they? The guards were frightened by your new arm, they said. Now I know they were only trying to save themselves. That you could be a witch. You're just an armless girl."

But he gives me a look and I remember what Arsenault thought, a long time ago, that he knew about the magic passed down in my family and that he wanted me for it. Mikelo's my strongest card, but he's already on the table. If I were playing indij, I'd need another strong card in reserve, and I hope it's my arm. Geoffre might think I can See, but he doesn't know about Ires, and he doesn't know about my arm.

But I've tensed up too much. A vibration shudders through the metal. This is a problem I have—the hate and energy of battle, the metal begins to sing all through me, and I start to shake. Sometimes, it's impossible to stop. I can't ease up on the trigger, but if I don't stop shaking, I'll blow Mikelo's head off.

I take a deep breath and calm it down right before my finger twitches the trigger too far.

"Give me safe haven, and a way out when I'm finished with the Caprine girl. And then you'll get your heir back."

Jon says, "You can't trust her. Wasn't she the woman killed your son's child?"

"Yes," Geoffre says, his voice and face hard. "She was."

Because you made me, I think. *I would have married Cassis, settled down with him, raised a whole family of grandsons for you. But you didn't want me. Whose fault is that?*

"That heir is long gone, and this one's in front of you. I can kill him now or you can give me a chance to let him live. Or perhaps...we could play kai dahn with the heirship."

I point my gun straight down at Mikelo's crotch.

"The dikkarro's a hard aim; do you think he'd be able to make children or not?"

I put on my best grin.

Mikelo makes a soft sound of fear. Geoffre looks like a dog, ready to bite. He rises from his chair and takes a step toward me. I jam the gun into Mikelo's groin and haul him backward, almost to the wall.

"Uncle," Mikelo whispers, trembling as blood runs in a thin stream down his blue-and-gray tunic. "Uncle, she's serious."

"I know she is, you fool," Geoffre says, his thin mouth pulled down in a long scowl, hand on his sword hilt. "Fine, then. You're granted your safe haven as long as you keep my nephew alive and get that witch out of my son's bed. But I don't trust you. You'll take the guard with you. Andris. I hear he was the one who caught you in the first place." Geoffre leans forward to point at me. "If I hear that you have so much as blemished Mikelo's skin, the loss of an arm will be but a passing twinge compared to the pain I'll give you. It's my forest between here and there, and its eyes report what they see to me."

He straightens and adjusts his sword in its scabbard. "I have nothing more to say to you. All I want to hear now is that you've delivered my nephew safe to my doorstep, and Driese di Caprine's arm wrapped up in a bag as proof that she's dead." His mouth twists. "Do you think you can accomplish that? Severing an arm?"

I don't answer. I just stare at him, and he stares back at me.

He turns to Jon before I turn away. "You'll have fifty lashes in the morning, smuggler, and wish you'd never disobeyed me. Get out."

Jon's eyes spark. He turns once, to glance at me from the corner of his eye, and then he walks, straight-backed, to the door. Geoffre rises and follows him.

"My nephew will be *safe*," he says once again as Lusinda puts her hand on his arm. Then the door slams and I'm left alone with a man I'm not sure I can trust anymore and the heir to the most powerful House in Eterea.

<hr />

"Jon will make a bad enemy," Arsenault says when all the guards are gone from the hallway.

I laugh shakily. "Do you think I don't know that?"

Mikelo slumps in a chair, his head in his hands, still trembling. Blood drips down his shirt. Arsenault grabs a napkin and holds it against Mikelo's collarbone.

I didn't want to hurt Mikelo, but my other option was to shoot him and that would have been worse. I don't think the wound is that bad, but it looks like it pains him.

I pace from the sideboard to the card table, a crystal glass of imya in my hand. The clear liquor slops against the side of the glass, and I pause to take a long drink that burns my throat. My eyes water, but I throw back the rest of the glass.

Arsenault holds out another napkin and I oblige him by soaking it in alcohol. When he puts this napkin against Mikelo's skin, Mikelo hisses and jerks backward.

"Jon wanted me dead," I say, going back to pour myself another glass and Mikelo one, too. "Shall I pour for all of us?" I look up, the bottle in my hand, to find both Arsenault and Mikelo staring at me. "Shall we celebrate our victory?"

"Victory?" Mikelo says, coming half out of his chair. "This is no—"

"You're not on my side," I remind him. The barrel of the gun

CHAPTER 19

left an impression in his hair that hasn't come uncrimped yet. He runs his fingers through it as if he needs to shake it out, and then Arsenault bumps his arm and makes him hold the napkin against his wound himself.

"Do you really believe my uncle?"

I hand him a glass of imya instead of answering. His hands shake as he takes it, and he gasps after he drinks.

"What *is* this stuff?" he says, swiping his sleeve across his mouth.

"Imya. The Rojornicki drink it. They say it's fortifying."

Mikelo stares at the empty glass, then holds it out for more. Arsenault's frown grows darker.

"Aren't you going to drink?" I ask him. "I managed not to get Mikelo killed, and what did you expect about Jon? He was supposed to call in Geoffre, and instead, he called in your contingent of guards. Should I give him my scarf for his troubles? A dainty red rose, perhaps?"

Arsenault looks at me for a moment, then grabs the bottle I've left on the table between us. "I don't know what Jon thought he was going to do. But you don't understand."

I try to arrange my face. Dear gods, but it feels strange and awful to play these games with him. "Then enlighten me, o wise one."

"Say you kill Cassis and let Driese go. Then what happens?"

I swirl the imya in my glass. One can hardly see it in this crystal. Mikelo looks at the bottle like he wants another drink, but Arsenault doesn't relinquish his grip on it. He begins fanning out cards instead. His long fingers play over the ornate illustrations of generals and ladies. It's a habit he seems to have, ducking his head when others speak. Listening.

"The Prinze monopoly depends on its insularity. Now think what would happen if Cassis were to sire a son by a Caprine."

I turn one of the chairs the wrong way and sit down, resting my arms on its back and my head on my arms. "Do you mean if the Caprine get hold of her or the Prinze?"

"Either case, I suppose."

I take a deep breath. "In the case of the Prinze...Driese di Caprine would live long enough to have the child. Then Geoffre would have her killed, make Cassis his heir until another, better, more legitimate heir could be produced, and then kill the boy. If it's a girl...Geoffre doesn't need girls and he doesn't need kin ties, so both Driese and the girl are killed in childbed."

"You think that Geoffre would have Driese killed right away? Why wouldn't he allow her to live to see if she could produce a boy? If she's fertile?"

"Because he wants me to kill her now, before she's pregnant in the first place. And anyway, that assumes that Cassis would be faithful. By any definition of faithfulness."

"If she's fertile."

"Well, that didn't matter with me, now, did it? They still sent me to the Council and took my arm. They didn't want me for any reason."

"But you cheated them."

"You make it sound like playing cards."

"Isn't that how you Lierans treat it?'

I need more alcohol to keep this conversation going. But he still has the damn bottle.

"The Prinze and Jon, maybe," I say angrily. "It's a woman's *life* we're talking about, though. The life of her child."

"But you," Mikelo says shakily. "You're Kyrra d'Aliente."

I lift my head. There's no avoiding that indictment, the fear that shows on faces when people learn that I took the life of my own child. The guilt remains inside me like a piece of shrapnel in a closed-up wound. Perhaps it doesn't show on the outside, but every word makes it twist, drawing fresh blood.

Instead of answering, I turn back to Arsenault. "Now, say I rescue Driese and kill Cassis the way I've been paid to do. How does that not fit into Jon's plans, if he wants Mikelo named as Prinze heir? Perhaps Driese is pregnant and perhaps she's not, but with Cassis dead, at least he's removed from your damn card game."

Arsenault pours himself a hefty shot of imya and his gaze flickers over to Mikelo. The hot currant scent fills the room as he tosses it back, then sets the glass down hard again on the table, grimacing.

"What if Driese is pregnant," he says, sitting down and pouring shots for all three of us. "And you kill Cassis. What then? What will the Caprine do?"

"Hard to say. Maybe they'll send her and her child into exile. Maybe they'll have them both killed to keep them from the Prinze. Maybe..."

I let my voice trail off, but we all know what I mean.

"Tonia wants you to take her out of Liera."

"Women generally want to avoid my fate."

Mikelo looks up from his cards. "If you kill Cassis, your life will be forfeit. My uncle will have you hunted and killed as soon as you put down the gun."

"That's why you're the lord up my sleeve, Mikelo. You'd best be more afraid of your uncle."

Mikelo fingers the ragged edge of one of Jon's cards—the other general. The bastard had it all the time.

"I am more afraid of my uncle. I don't mind telling you that, either of you. You can't trust his guarantee of safe haven. You ought to just give me over and have done with it."

"The voice of reason. I wonder why Geoffre himself came to bargain for you if you're meaningless. Or why Arsenault stands for you."

"Arsenault," Mikelo says. "You keep calling him that. Wasn't that the name of the Aliente captain?"

Arsenault goes still.

No, I don't think he's lying. Maybe the magic did eat all his memories.

But...every memory?

I thought it hurt before, thinking he might be dead. But in

some ways, this hurts worse.

"It's a trap," Mikelo goes on. "My uncle doesn't mind sacrificing me as long as I serve a purpose. He's pinning his hopes on Cassis; that's easy enough to see."

I take a deep breath and twirl the glass in my hands. "Were you so afraid that you ignored everything that was said? Geoffre wants you as his *heir*. At least until someone better comes along. Before we go any farther, I want to know who you are."

"He was bluffing."

"He wouldn't have walked out of here if he was bluffing. He would have let me shoot you."

Mikelo thumbs the jester card hard enough to bend the corner, then slaps it down on the table. "I'm his nephew, dammit, in his dead brother's line. I'm in the succession but far enough down that it doesn't really matter who I am, and there is really no reason to risk my life because you're on some idiotic mission of vengeance!" He shoves himself back from the table. "If you are Kyrra d'Aliente, then you're the woman who started this whole war! If you'd just birthed my cousin's child—"

"I would have birthed that child," I tell him, leaning toward him so that my face is in his face, "but I was a pawn, just like you."

His jaw twitches. I can feel mine do the same.

"Is Geoffre playing you again, then?" Arsenault says.

Damn the man. He sits there with his flat gray eyes, watching me. Waiting to see how I will answer.

I feel like I'm full of knives, and they're all cutting me up as slowly as they can. But until I know what's going on, I'm going to have to play this game with Arsenault.

"Since Geoffre assigned you to me, I must assume that you're spying for him," I say.

He wraps his hand around the neck of the imya bottle, leans back in his chair, and puts his feet up on the table like he always did.

"It's a fault," he says. "Assuming."

CHAPTER 20

After we're sure Geoffre has left, Arsenault and I spend some time thinking about the best way to get out of the bathhouse, sketching maps on an extra sheet of writing paper he pulls from that scroll case he carries with him.

Half-full glasses of imya hold down the corners. Mikelo took the bottle over to the bed, where he is grimly drinking himself insensible. It was the only way I could keep him from fretting himself into a panic.

"The bathhouse is built on top of old Eterean ruins," Arsenault says. "I suppose it's not so different from any other bathhouse in that respect, so if you know the usual layout of a bathhouse…"

"Not from the men's side," I said. "Only the women's."

Arsenault nods. "The rooms on this side are built in a rectangular pattern inside the cavern. The Etereans must have used magic to scoop out some of that rock, but what it means for us is that the baths themselves use the natural cavern system but the Etereans made it more logical. Some of the pools are natural and some are fed by a central aqueduct. It brings hot water from deep in the back of the cavern to the front. Then side channels direct the water to different rooms."

He sketches as he talks, making a big rectangle full of oval pools, bisected down the middle by the central aqueduct.

"The steam room is over here. The pumps that bring the seawater up to fill its pools are housed here...and the channel that directs the hot water flows through this natural gap right here. Once you're past it, there are only two more pools on your right before you reach the door to the kitchens. You'll know you're near because they perfume the water with sage. If we're going to try to get out through the baths, there are three ways we could go—the kitchens, the front door, or the women's side." He lifts his eyes to look at me. "I suppose you might exit through either side. But Mikelo and I would stand out if we tried to leave through the women's area."

I chew my lip and study the map. "You must spend a lot of time here," I murmur.

"I've had a few jobs," he says.

"Jobs?" I raise my eyebrow. "Really."

He catches my gaze briefly, then looks back down at the map. "Jasmine Pleasures is a little too high-end for my salary."

"Mmmm. Well. Your memory for places seems good. This is an excellent map."

He's still leaning on the table with both hands, letting his gaze flick over it. "I suppose the ability to make maps doesn't affect the quality of my life much."

"That's a strange thing to say."

He straightens up, so I do too.

His shoulders move in what might be a shrug or a stretch. "Perhaps I've developed a sense of irony since last you knew me."

"No. You've always had that. But it used to be less cynical than mine."

He smiles bleakly. "An innocent, was I?"

It seems strange to think of it that way. But... "Perhaps we both were. In a way."

His brows pull down and he regards me oddly for a moment, as if my words have challenged his opinion of me. My fingers

CHAPTER 20

itch to touch him. The impulse leaves a dull hurt in its wake, almost as if I've lost another limb.

We spend the rest of the night pillaging the whores' closets.

There are the expensive silk dresses, of course. The beribboned corsets and lacy chemises. The frilly white nightgowns. Wigs. But there are also, hanging tucked against the wall in their own section, a number of other outfits which some gentlemen prefer.

An enormous red felt hat festooned with a peacock feather. A peasant's guarnello. A Tiresian girl's blouse and split skirt. Two entire suits of men's clothing tailored to a woman, one a sober chocolate brown, the other carefully crafted of extravagant lavender silk.

I can't resist pulling it out and holding it up to see how it fits. Arsenault is leaning into the closet at the time, but he turns to eye me up and down, brows lifting slowly. Then the corner of his mouth pulls upward.

"That would be quite a daring escape."

I sigh as if in disappointment and hang it back up. "Sadly, I think you're right."

It's hard to remember to be careful around him and all too easy to sink into old patterns. The strangeness of the situation is like a burning in my chest. I try to focus on thinking my way out of this bathhouse, but I'm constantly distracted by the small details of him at my side. The cuts and bruises on his knuckles as he carefully pushes a silk gown out of the way. The rise and fall of his chest as he stands and examines another. The sight of his fingers resting lightly on black lace stays, which he calmly sets aside.

Every part of me aches. My muscles, my arm, my mind, my heart.

I finally throw two dresses onto the bed beside Mikelo, who has fallen asleep or passed out, his hand still curled around the imya bottle.

"Still can't decide?" Arsenault says. He stretches out the skirt of a long pewter-gray gown and eyes it critically.

"One's for me," I say. "And the other's for Mikelo." I pause and eye him. "But I don't think that gown will do for you. Although it does bring out your eyes."

"I thought the plum silk would make me look a bit of a tart," he shoots back, missing the reference completely or at least ignoring it. Either way it hurts. "I'm making an urqa. What are you going to do with Mikelo?"

"Well...*you* might not be able to pull it off, Arsenault, but I believe Mikelo will make a credible scullery girl."

We both look down at him sprawled on the silk bedspread. He seems so very young, with those long, sooty black lashes closed against his cheek. Cassis had long lashes too.

"You know, if you keep poking Geoffre, he'll bite."

"I'm not doing it to poke Geoffre. But I do want to give myself a head start, and I don't trust Geoffre to honor his promises. Do you?"

Arsenault rubs the edge of his jaw, which has begun to darken with a shadow of black stubble. "Geoffre will send spies. But he won't risk you killing Mikelo. At least not right off."

"Why not?"

Arsenault shrugs and his gaze drops to the rumpled skirt in his hands. "He has a limited supply of heirs."

"He's not too concerned with Devid and Cassis."

"He's in marriage negotiations regarding Mikelo right now."

"Is it who he thinks he can get for Mikelo that makes the difference?"

"Perhaps." Arsenault draws his knife and begins to slice open the seams of the dress. I can tell by the way his mouth pulls down that I'll get nothing more by pressing. Not now.

"Still," I say. "I think I'd like to put as much distance between us and Geoffre as possible."

"What do you think Mikelo is going to say to all this?"

"He doesn't trust his uncle either. He'll do what he has to."

CHAPTER 20

Arsenault's knife rips through the silk again. "I suppose that's all any of us are doing."

There doesn't seem to be an answer to that. We both fall silent and turn to our work, pulling stitches, sewing, stitching, and hemming until the night is very far gone. Then, by unspoken agreement, we push our finished costumes to the side and find places where we can sleep, him sitting on the floor at the foot of Mikelo's bed, one of his boot knives in his hand, and me facing him with my back against the door, his sword in my lap and the index finger of my left hand pushed lightly through the trigger of Jon's gun.

※

In the morning, Mikelo wakes with red-rimmed eyes, watery bowels, and a bad case of the shakes. He can't spend more than a few minutes away from the chamber pot, and Arsenault makes him drink water. He throws up the shot I give him for health. By the time we get around to negotiating about the dress, serving girls are clattering about in the hallway outside with breakfast dishes.

Mikelo doesn't want to go along with my plan. Predictably.

"It's a ruse, Mikelo, not forever. They're going to be looking for a Prinze guard and a young gavaro, and instead, we'll leave through the women's dining room underneath the bathhouse as two kitchen girls."

"And what about Andris?"

Andris—Arsenault—shrugs. "The girls won't think it strange if I say I've taken a Qalfan job. I know some Qalfans. The robes will make it easier later on."

I shoot him a sharp glance, remembering what Razi told me about men wearing Qalfan robes to hide. "Do you often take Qalfan jobs?"

"No. But I've experience on the caravans and the girls know that."

"How do you remember—"

"There's no rhyme or reason to it. Jon helped me fill in the gaps." He touches the gray silk folded over the back of a chair, seeming to concentrate on his thumb smoothing out a wrinkle. "At least for that part of my life."

I'll wager he did, I think, but I bite my lip to stop the words coming out.

"Why can't I just robe as a Qalfan down in the baths?" Mikelo asks.

"Because if I go out as a woman, we won't be able to walk out the same door," I say. "Unless you want me to pretend I'm your whore."

Mikelo looks at me in defiance. "Well, why not?"

I lean back on the sideboard, crossing my arms and my ankles. "Are you paying me a compliment?"

His face turns brick red. "No! I mean, I—"

"The other girls will notice a new courtesan. They'd stop us in a heartbeat to find out who I was. And that would lead them to find out who you were."

"Couldn't Andris just...*bribe* somebody to let us out? I mean, if the girls *know* him..."

I stare at him, unable for a moment to accept that he has suggested what he's just suggested. Maybe there's more to Mikelo than I thought.

Arsenault is leaning against the wall with his shoulder, his ankles crossed like mine in that easy gavaro stance. But his eyes, underlined by the violent purple bruise, do not look easy. He straightens up against the wall. "I'd rather not. If it's all the same to you."

Who is this man?

What happened to him in those years I was gone?

"No," I say. I try to keep my voice on a level, but I'm not sure how well I manage. "You're going to put on a dress, because it's just a piece of clothing."

"I don't look anything like a girl."

I take his chin in my hand. "Well, you've got that pretty Prinze mouth. And those eyelashes and cheekbones."

Mikelo jerks away from me, glaring.

"It's just a piece of clothing," I tell him again. "Some paint on your face. It doesn't change who you are inside. It's just a ruse you wear in order to stay alive."

"You're trying to keep me alive now?"

"Well. A long time ago, I promised a man I'd stay alive however I could. I've taken that promise seriously until now, and I don't see any reason I should stop. If you'll keep me alive, I'll keep you alive."

Slowly, some of the suspicion seeps out of Mikelo's eyes. "So, you're not doing this just to torment me?"

"No."

He looks down at his hands in his lap, then gives a short nod. "All right. I'll do it. If it will get us out of this room."

Some of the tension inside me unwinds. A gun against a man's head only works for so long. Eventually, he'll dare you to use it, to see if you're serious. If you aren't, you'll lose him, and if you are...you'll lose him, too, but it will be worse.

Arsenault's shoulders relax their stiff line.

"Keep close to me when we get to the baths," I say. "Remember, I'm armed."

Mikelo nods in a defeated way, and Arsenault moves away from the wall to help me gather up our clothes.

※

I CHOSE A SET OF LINEN PETTICOATS AND AN UNREMARKABLE brown skirt for myself, a loose, long-sleeved chemise, and a set of leather stays that lace in front. It won't be quite like wearing armor, but the leather will give me more protection than a flimsy guarnello.

Before we leave the room, I take off my shirt in the closet and unwind the binding that presses my breasts flat against my chest. I haven't had it off in days, and my ribs were beginning to feel as if they'd been crushed. I allow myself one long, slow, deep breath and a stretch before I slide the chemise over my head and tuck its skirt into my trousers like a long blousy shirt. Then I pull on the stays and lace them up. With my tunic and my cloak on, I doubt anyone will notice my chest as we walk downstairs, but it will cut down on the amount of clothing I have to carry and dispose of.

I can hear Arsenault talking to Mikelo through the closet door, which I left open just enough to shoot him if he tries to escape. I push it open and step out, fiddling with the blousing chemise. I'm not sure it's going to look like a shirt.

"You'll talk to the bath attendant," Arsenault is telling Mikelo. "I think Geoffre is probably trying to keep this situation hushed up..."

His voice drifts off. I look up and he's staring at me. Mikelo, who was frowning in concentration, glances up to see why Arsenault has stopped talking and stares at me too.

I suddenly feel naked. I haven't worn women's clothing in five years.

I put my fists on my hips. "You expected a demon?"

Arsenault clears his throat and his fingers tighten on the veil he's holding. His gaze lingers a little too long on my stays, long enough to bring up the heat in my skin, then flickers suddenly off to the side. "You still walk like a man," he says roughly.

I'm not sure I remember the way a woman is supposed to walk. In the space of a few moments, I'm going to have to unlearn everything I learned over the past five years. Perhaps what I told Mikelo is a lie. Maybe you don't remain the same underneath the ruse. Maybe the ruse changes you until you become the thing you were only pretending to be.

Take Arsenault, for instance. Lobardin was right; he was always a devil with a ruse, which never made any sense given how recognizable he was with that scar and that bright metallic shock of hair. But he never played a role that didn't seem believable, and he never attempted too much disguise. Mostly, he let other people believe what they wanted to believe.

His bruised gaze tracks over me again, like he can't help it, and I pretend I don't notice him do it.

Does he remember me more now that he can see the shape of me, or is it just surprise?

Mikelo says with some horror, "*I'm* not going to have to wear stays, am I?"

Arsenault turns toward him and laughs, shakily. "Dear gods, I hope not. I don't think we could lace them that tight."

I kneel down quickly in front of the jewelry safe so they won't see me blush.

"What are you doing?" Mikelo asks.

"Cracking the lock." I give it a twist and a squeeze with my right hand and it breaks. I open the door to reveal drawers full of jewelry, which I grab and shove into my pocket for later. There's also a slim steel dagger folded up inside its hilt.

"Oh, you dear girls, you're all spies," I whisper, and hunching over the safe, I ease the wooden busk out of my stays and slide the dagger down the slot between them instead.

In another velvet-lined compartment lies a set of silver hatpins. When I first saw the hat, I knew there would have to be hatpins, and I can't hide my grin. The hatpins are half the length of my forearm, and their sharp ends glitter in the dim light.

I shake my hair out of its queue, then twist it up and push the hatpins into the knot to secure it. Now I feel better for being well armed.

When I stand up, Arsenault is still watching me but like he's trying not to.

It's been a long time since a man looked at me like that. Knowing I was a woman.

A knock at the door makes us both jump.

"Would the gentlemen like breakfast?" a young voice calls. I grab my swordbelt and tunic, then rise and join Arsenault in front of the door. He's looking out the peephole.

"A girl," Arsenault says in a low voice. "With a tray of food. No one else in the hall that I can see."

Mikelo groans. "Food. No." Then he takes a ragged breath. "But coffee...coffee might be welcome."

I struggle my tunic on over my head and begin buckling on my swordbelt. "Let her in," I tell Arsenault.

He swings the door open, but he keeps his body in front of it. Through the gaps, I catch a glimpse of a girl in a beige guarnello holding a tray heaped with pastries and buns. There's enough food there to feed an army of gavaros, not just the three of us, and a steaming pot that smells comfortingly of coffee.

"Hello, Andris," she says as Arsenault steps aside to let her in. "The girls in the kitchens sent up your favorites. And for your companion, Cook made some of these Rojornicki buns special. I don't know what they're called."

Arsenault smiles down at her, but I'm watching his face and his eyes are troubled. "Hello, Clara," he says. "Which are the Rojornicki buns?"

I move up beside him to look at the tray. "Kefli," I name them, pointing to the flaky crescents filled with almond paste and soft cheese that Markus and his wife ate every morning. Kefli rarely made it down to the barracks; we lived on buckwheat groats. My mouth begins to water, but there's an off smell somewhere. I sniff, trying to place it, as the girl walks over to the sideboard with the tray.

She's a thin little thing with dull brown hair in two neat braids over her shoulders, and she has to lean backward to lift the tray up onto the sideboard. Arsenault grabs it from her and puts it down himself. The girl smiles at him anxiously, and he smiles back in a manner designed to put her at ease.

"Would you like something, Clara?" he asks. "You ought to have a reward for carrying that all the way up here."

Her smile falters and she shakes her head firmly. "Oh, no, Andris, I couldn't. The girls told me I mustn't. Or—"

"*Or*," he repeats, in that dark way I heard often enough when he registered some injustice done to me. I let my gaze sweep over the girl, checking for bruises, but her skin seems clear. She lowers her eyes to the floor and begins backing out of the room.

"We hope you enjoy your breakfast," she says, not looking up until she steps through the doorway and out into the hall. Then she drops a quick curtsey and bolts away as quick as she can.

Mikelo slides off the bed as Arsenault pushes the door shut. "Maybe my stomach will settle if I put something in it."

Cardamom buns. That's what the girls sent up for Arsenault. Also stuffed with almond paste.

I lean over the tray and take a big sniff.

Lots of almonds on this tray, and there's just a hint of bitterness beneath the sweet.

Mikelo stands at my shoulder, not quite touching me. "Oh," he says. "Raisin twists. My favorite."

There are no almonds in raisin twists.

I look up to find Arsenault also leaning down. We lock glances.

I jerk the tray off the sideboard with both hands and swing it around, heading for the window.

"What are you doing?" Mikelo exclaims.

I brace the tray against the wall and shove open the sash with my right hand, then slide the tray out into the air. It sails downward and hits the cobbles with a great metal clangor. Sweet buns and coffee explode into the air in all directions. People walking below cover their heads, shout, and look up.

"Why did you do that?" Mikelo's voice shakes.

Arsenault comes to join me at the window. A flock of pigeons wings over from the fountain across the street and settles upon the buns, pecking and cooing.

One by one, the birds begin to career around as if they're drunk. One by one, they shriek and collapse and die, shuddering, on the stones.

"Oh," Mikelo says. "Oh."

"It wasn't for you," Arsenault tells him. "Just for us."

"But what if I wanted to share?"

"I guess that's a risk Geoffre was willing to take," I say.

Mikelo backs away from us toward the bed with his hand over his mouth. He's so pale, his cheeks have a greenish cast to them.

I don't have time to deal with him right now. "The girls will be here soon. That poison would have worked fast."

Arsenault nods. "Let me deal with them."

"No."

"They know me."

"They don't know you well enough to refuse to kill you."

"They work for Geoffre."

"This bathhouse is supposed to be neutral. We're on Caprine ground," I say.

"Don't you think the bathhouses in Prinze territory have their share of Caprine spies?" he asks.

Mikelo still looks pale. "Will they take me back to my uncle?"

"Get your shirt straight," I tell him. "We don't have time to make you pretty. We'll throw the guarnello over your shirt and trousers. Get that blond wig."

"What? I thought I was to go down to the baths!"

"What are you planning?" Arsenault says.

"Just do it."

Arsenault growls. "*What are you planning?*"

Instead of answering him, I draw my sword and stand in front of the door, settling my heels into the carpet—my feet clad only in my stockings—in the guard stance he taught me.

A key snicks in the lock.

"Dammit, think!" Arsenault hisses, grabbing my left shoulder.

The door pushes open and my arms move of their own accord, sweeping the sword out in an arc that takes both women standing in the doorway straight across their stomachs.

Blood spills onto the carpet like it was poured out of a bucket. The women make a high, wheezy pain sound as they fall.

I step forward before even Arsenault can react and draw my sword backward across their throats to silence them.

But, oh gods, there's so much blood. Blood everywhere, like I've just sacrificed a couple of sheep.

I swipe my blade clean on my trousers and shove it back in its scabbard. The room smells like blood and shit now, mingled with the odor of almonds and Mikelo's vomit. He's throwing up again, all over the carpet. Arsenault is cursing me. I drag the first girl into the room by the shoulders and her head lolls, the wound in her neck gaping open like a second mouth. He grabs the second girl and pulls her in, then shoves the door closed with his shoulder.

"Who taught you?" he says, furious.

"You did," I say.

For half an instant, he looks taken aback. Gray. His hand comes up to the temple that used to be scarred and he shoves his hand through his hair. Then the grayness floods with color and his eyes snap. "That could have been Clara standing there," he says.

"You knew it wouldn't be. She was only a delivery girl. It was Geoffre's spies who needed to confirm their kill. You knew it and I knew it."

"The *blood*. You should have let me handle it!"

"And give them another chance to knife us in the back? Mikelo, get your clothes on. Come on, Arsenault, if you're coming; we're leaving now."

I undo the laces on my trousers right there in front of him and Mikelo. The chemise falls down past my knees when I yank my trousers down. I unbuckle my sword belt and tear my tunic off over my head, then put my swordbelt on again over the chemise.

"Move!" I yell at Mikelo, and he jumps, looking frightened and miserable. Shaking, he grabs the guarnello I altered for him and struggles it on over his shirt and trousers. Arsenault curses loudly as he wraps his urqa with practiced, vicious movements.

I tie on my skirts the same. Feet in my boots, and I'm looking over at Mikelo, who is still fumbling with the laces on the guarnello. His hands shake too badly to tie them properly. "Wait," I say.

I walk over to the bed and pull a pillow out of a pillowcase. Then I stuff the pillowcase down the chest of the guarnello and I jerk his laces as tight as I can, levering my foot against the side of the bed.

"Kyrra!" he gasps. "I can't breathe!"

I pull them as tight as they'll go, and I tie them off quick. He's still trying to gulp air but his chest looks better. I grab a neckcloth and make it into a sash for him instead, trying to give his waist better definition. Then I settle the blond wig on his head and attach it quickly with hairpins.

In spite of the Prinze mouth and cheekbones, his face framed in all those golden curls looks oddly as if I am looking into the other side of a mirror. He makes an awkward girl possessed of a kind of boyish beauty, as long as you don't look too close. Or maybe the vulnerability I see on his face comes only because he's shivering.

Arsenault looms in over my shoulder. He's wrapped head to foot in shimmering gray silk, the kind of gavaro a rich man would keep beside him as a guard.

Everyone is going to notice him.

"Done?" he says.

I'm starting to shake in reaction too, but my reactions tend to run toward violence and paranoia. I start to worry that Arsenault was in league with the girls, that he'll turn on me once we get downstairs. If he keeps that urqa on, he might as well be dressed in a surrender flag.

How am I ever to know if I can trust him or not? He wears the urqa and allaq so casually and well that I know it's not the first time he's put one on.

He doesn't remember me.

He'll try to stop me.

It doesn't matter that I saw the first glimmers of memory in his eyes right before the girl came in with the poisoned pastries.

"Kyrra?"

I'm staring at him, at his eyes, the same color as the fabric of his veil and just as complex as the silk.

"Done," I say. I pull the gun with my right hand and throw the cloak over my forearm to hide it. "Come on, Mikelo, move. And swish your hips a little, unless you want people to recognize you dressed as a woman."

❦

Arsenault takes the back stairs at a pace that makes me fear Mikelo will slip off a riser and break his neck. He shoves the door to the baths open and we follow him inside, white steam curling around us like smoke, surrounding us with the smell of sulfur as if we've just stepped into the underworld.

He falls back finally and bends to murmur in my ear. "Do you remember the map I drew you?"

"The door to the women's side is past the bathing pools and the steam room," I answer.

"I can't follow you. I'll meet you outside the door to the kitchens."

I catch his arm before he can move off. "Arsenault...I just want to know, before we try this ruse, do you still not remember me? At all?"

His eyes and his brows are the only parts of him visible in his robes. His brows pull down over the bridge of his nose and his gaze roves over me, troubled. At least he's lost some of his anger.

"I... This isn't the time to speak of this."

I nod. His not-an-answer is as good an answer as I can have right now. I had forgotten about deciphering him, but it comes back to me now.

"You're right. We'll meet you. Outside."

I move Mikelo away from him, and he turns aside to go his own way.

Bathhouses are the only place in all Liera where House allegiances aren't immediately visible. There are no colors in the baths. Everyone here is naked.

I can't tell at a glance who is allied to whom.

I haven't been in a bathhouse since I had two human arms. When I dressed as a man, I avoided public baths the way I avoided being taken by the enemy. The only other situation as fraught with danger for me was pissing in the woods. None of my fellow gavaros ever understood why I was so private about my habits of bathing and elimination. But if any of them had ever caught me washing or urinating or changing my cloths when I bled, that would have been the end of my disguise. The Kavol would not have dealt well with me, the Rojornicki better only because Markus Seroditch, the boyar who hired me when I came down out of the high peaks, was an honorable man. A man like Arsenault.

I poke Mikelo in the side to remind him to move his hips and keep his legs closer together, and he closes his eyes briefly and takes a deep breath. Then he does move, subtly, but enough. Men in the bathing pools watch us walk by.

One of them down at the end watches us a little more intently than the rest. In the steam, it's hard to make him out, but I hear a splash and catch a glimpse of a tall man levering himself out of the water, a flash of the white robe he ties on as he walks toward us.

Mikelo's breath catches.

"Keep walking," I whisper to Mikelo. I try to keep myself calm. Maybe the man isn't coming for us.

But my prayers aren't answered. He puts himself in front of us and forces us to stop.

"Hello, girls," he says. "You're from the kitchens?"

I look up at him. And then my breath catches too.

It's Vanni di Forza.

CHAPTER 20

I knew this would happen some time. I was so careful when I was dressed as Kyris, and I could control where I went and where I didn't. My paths lay low anyway, down the streets and alleyways householders don't frequent.

But now I'm dressed as a woman and looking straight into the face of Vanni di Forza, and I can tell from his eyes that he knows who I am.

Vanni himself looks different but not. He's bigger, of course—a man now, not a boy, with a stubbled face and broader shoulders. But his hair is the same lank brown, his dark eyes still the sort that might have made him handsome had they not also been cruel...and his smirk is made meaner by the scar he's picked up at the corner.

"Well," he says, sweeping his gaze up and down me and then up and down Mikelo. "I was going to ask you for figs and apricots, but perhaps I should ask you for water instead?"

Useless to pretend I'm not who he thinks I am. "Of course, if you'd like water, I'll retrieve it for you, mestere." I try not to talk through my teeth.

"And who's this with you? Another new girl?"

He reaches up to finger the curls of Mikelo's wig. Mikelo's eyes go wide.

"We've both been hired in the kitchens," I say. "We'll get you some figs and apricots, Vanni, if you let us go."

Mikelo glances at me in alarm, finally realizing I've been recognized.

"No." Vanni rubs his thumb along Mikelo's chin. "I don't think I want figs and apricots now."

Mikelo looks like a bird caught in a net. He doesn't know what to do. Should he pull away and possibly give himself up? Who is Vanni and who does he work for? Would a woman submit or not? You can see the thoughts on his face.

"Leave her alone, Vanni," I say. "She's new and just a kitchen girl. She's not a courtesan."

"What's your name?" he asks Mikelo.

I want to curse. I want to use all my curses, right now.

Mikelo makes a noise to hide the fact he's clearing his throat. When he speaks, it's a decent attempt to make his voice into a husky female voice like mine. "Kela," he says.

"Kela," Vanni repeats. Then he swings around to look at me. "Kela and Kyrra. Hmmm. What are you doing down here, Kyrra? Our best intelligence had it you must have died."

"I was the subject of intelligence?"

"Given the circumstances of the last time you were seen...it was hard to give much credence to the stories. People said you must have died."

I shrug. "I don't know what the stories said, but"—I gesture with my left hand—"here I am."

"Here you are. Not on your father's estate."

"No. But my father's estate is no longer my father's, is it?"

"No. It's my father's. The Aliente serfs—the ones who still lived—were all transferred to my father. That means you should have been transferred too, Kyrra, according to your sentence."

"You don't think the war disrupted that? How many other serfs ran off?"

"I don't know. Some of them stayed."

I don't want to ask. I don't have time to ask. But the word comes out of me anyway. "Who?"

"I don't have any dealings with serfs; how should I know? I'm living in Liera now, and I have a higher station. Let my father keep the lands. My older brother will inherit. But I'm working with Geoffre di Prinze."

"Working *with* him or *for* him?" I say. "He'll grind you under his heel, Vanni, if you get in his way."

"I'm not getting in his way. He told me I could take you back to the villa, as long as I gave him back his nephew."

Shit.

Mikelo groans. "You knew?" he says. "You knew all along?"

Vanni lets his gaze rove over Mikelo. "You make a pretty girl.

CHAPTER 20

But seeing you with Kyrra...I knew who you must be." He takes Mikelo's chin in his hand before Mikelo can move away.

Mikelo jerks backward. Vanni chuckles and drops his hand slowly, turning back to me. "Do you know how embarrassing it was when I was sent back home before my fosterage was over?"

I can see how this is setting up. I'm going to have to get rid of him, then run for it.

"No," I say.

The gun will be too loud but would be the most effective. It would take too long to grab the knife from my stays. I could go for my sword...

"It was your fault. And that gavaro's. At first, my father wouldn't even talk to me. But I got your gavaro back, didn't I?"

My gavaro.

"He was only doing his duty, Vanni."

"He could have looked the other way."

"What did you do to him?"

Vanni looks smug. "Oh, you'd like to know, wouldn't you? I heard that maybe it was a bit more than his *duty* he was doing, wasn't it?"

I want to hit him, but then I'll never get any more information out of him. I smile at him sweetly instead. "Perhaps he was just more of a man than you were."

The smirk turns into a scowl. He steps toward me. "Not at the end, he wasn't. He broke just like anybody else."

His words make me go still inside. The raid Arsenault led against the Forza before Kafrin Gorge. Was Vanni there?

"For you?" I say.

"For me. For everybody."

"I don't believe it. I don't believe you were the one who broke him in the first place. You just swept in like the vulture you are and picked up the pieces."

"You think you're invincible, just like he did, don't you, Kyrra? That rules don't apply to you. And then when you run into somebody who breaks the rules better than you do..."

"You? You couldn't even have me when I was a serf girl armed with a *ladle*."

He grabs me by my left arm. "There's nobody to save you now, is there?"

"Ah, Mestere Di Forza," a timbrous female voice says behind me. "Have my kitchen girls displeased you?"

I glance back, quick, over my shoulder.

A middle-aged woman stands there, dressed in a spectacularly simple gown of indigo silk that shows off her still-handsome figure, her chestnut curls—threaded here and there with silver—piled on top of her head. Her arm is woven tight around Arsenault's, holding him so close that their hips slide against each other.

He doesn't have a relationship with the girls. It's with Madame Triente, the proprietor of the bathhouse.

Impressions swirl around me in the steam—the way the Madame's fingers stroke his arm; his gaze, struggling with recognition of Vanni; the way his veil sucks into his mouth with a quick breath; Mikelo with that rabbit look again, wondering where he should bolt; and Vanni, gripping my arm harder, staring at Arsenault and then down at my right sleeve which should be empty and is instead supporting a cloak.

"Kitchen girls?" Vanni says, beginning to frown at my arm. "They're not kitchen girls. Didn't Mestere di Prinze let you know?"

He looks up at Arsenault. "You're the one they call Andris, aren't you? I think I've changed my mind." He shoves me backward, toward Arsenault. "Andris, you can take care of her. The Mestere wants her alive but taken down a notch. Mikelo, the Mestere is waiting for you in the kitchens."

Arsenault catches me with his free hand, but he avoids my right arm, instead stopping me with a hand to my back. Steam curls up from the pool, blurring my vision.

"Si, Mestere," he says. "I'll take her outside—"

"No, here. Now. In front of me."

Arsenault still has his hand on my back. I feel the madam pull him the other way. "Not in my bathhouse," she says. "Do you want to run all my customers off?"

"The Mestere di Prinze wants it witnessed. Somebody's got to make sure she's incapacitated. Maybe a little more than incapacitated."

What I wouldn't give to wipe that damn smirk off his face.

"Then can't you go outside?"

"I'll witness outside," Mikelo says quickly. "I'll tell my uncle."

Is he trying to save me or Arsenault?

"No. Here. Now. Andris."

Arsenault's fingers begin to tremble. Does he remember Vanni? Did he really break? Does Vanni know who he is? He begins to tug away from the madam on his other side.

I thumb the dog back on my gun and pull the trigger.

It fires with a loud *crack* and a cloud of smoke. The recoil kicks me back into Arsenault, who rips his arm away from Madame Triente and catches me with both hands. Vanni cries out and staggers in the opposite direction. He slips on the tiled lip of the pool and falls backward into the water.

My cloak ignites with the sparks from the pan.

"Damn dikkarro!"

I throw the cloak at Vanni's gavaros, who have materialized from the shadows with the gunshot. I jam the spent pistol into the waistband of my skirt and grab Mikelo's arm, yanking him with me.

He stumbles into me, then gets his feet in order. He's coming. Even without the gun. "Where are we going?" he gasps.

"Not the kitchens!" I tell him. "Not the kitchens! *Not the kitchens.*"

I'm babbling, trying to stem the black tide that wants to pull me under. I need to be able to think to get out of here. But the magic wants me, and if only it was the kind of magic I could use to bend the steam into a cloak, but it's not.

Arsenault's ironshod boots slide on the stone floor behind us.

I don't want to believe he'll haul me back, but I don't want to put him in that position. Because I didn't kill Vanni, and Geoffre's in the kitchen.

There are gavaros everywhere, Prinze and Caprine, getting in each other's way, milling up as they try to protect their masters. It's chaos. This is too much like battle, and I'm going to go down.

I throw all my remaining willpower into visualizing Arsenault's map. I was an easily bored student but not a bad one; my memory isn't perfect, but it's good.

Mikelo and I are running back toward the stairs. But the steam room should be to our right.

There. Disappearing into the wall is the small channel that takes hot water and spills it into the cold salt water pumped into the steam room. I can smell sage from here.

I pull Mikelo with me. He looks up, startled and frightened, as I yank him toward the narrow opening in the wall where the U-shaped channel disappears. "Come on! This will slow them down."

"But—Kyrra—I don't think I'll fit..."

The opening is small, but I think Mikelo's slight enough to make it. The steam room will be connected to the dressing room and then to the receiving room and out the front door, if we can manage it.

"You'll fit," I say.

"You don't have a gun," he says. "You can't make me—"

The hot, knee-deep water smells so strongly of sulfur, it makes me dizzy. I shove him toward the dark cleft. "If you start to become a liability, I will kill you. Now move."

He stumbles into the blackness. "Oh, gods, Kyrra."

"Keep going. Are you claustrophobic, too? Come on. Your shoulders aren't that broad..."

"I'm going to get stuck. I'm going to get stuck."

Behind me, men curse. Standing at the opening, unable to follow us in. Arsenault can't follow. He's too big. Do I hear his voice, too?

I draw my sword to hurry Mikelo along. He stiffens when he hears the hiss of steel. But the runes on the blade flare and streak up my arm, lighting the slick wet darkness.

"Kyrra?" he says, sounding young and terrified. "What is that light?"

"It's magic, Mikelo. Not long now."

"There's an opening. It drops down. And the steam…"

"Drop," I say. "Into the water."

"Into?"

I shove him and he falls, feet-first, flailing his arms, about five feet down into a pool that's covered in a sheet of steam. When he splashes into the water, a figure obscured against the side moves violently.

"What?" a man exclaims. "What are you doing?"

I jump after Mikelo. The cold water is a shock after being so warm, and thank all the gods it only comes up to my chest. My metal arm screams with the change in temperature.

The man tries to clamber out of the pool. I lunge forward and drag him back down with my left hand, swinging my right fist into his temple. He crumples and slides under the water.

"Mikelo!" I whisper. "Hold him up!"

Mikelo grabs him. I pull myself out of the water, grab the man's shoulders, and start hauling him off.

"What are you doing now?" Mikelo says.

"Hiding. And then we're going to steal some clothes."

❦

I RIP THE WIG OFF MIKELO'S HEAD AND DRAG THE MAN INTO the hallway, where I cast the wig down and make wet footprints leading toward the dressing room. When he wakes up, he'll get help and show them my misdirection, or the guards will find him and see it themselves. Then I run and slide back into the pool with Mikelo, who's shivering with his arms wrapped round his chest.

Gavaros are coming down the hall now.

"Under, under!" I whisper, and I pull him down with me, under the water.

We hunch down, balled up in the water. I look up to the surface coated in steam and I might as well be inside a mirror, looking out.

Looking down at me is Arsenault.

His face shimmers, the years erased. The scar flickers in and out with each ripple of the surface. My breath burns in my lungs and I want to reach up to him, to touch his hand.

Then I blink and it's not Arsenault at all. Another man with dark hair walks the rim, not looking down. He ushers his fellows out quickly.

When the room empties, Mikelo and I burst up to the surface. Mikelo gulps air. "They didn't buy that," he says. "They must be waiting for us."

"Maybe." And maybe Arsenault did have something to do with the gavaros passing us by, the same way he had something to do with Cassis and his gavaros passing us by in the Day Market all those years ago when I hid with him in a doorway. I tilt my head back to catch my breath and look up at the ceiling.

It's covered in a mosaic of ravens. Their obsidian-chip eyes glint in the dim candlelight of the chamber.

Watching us.

THICK COTTON ROBES HANG ON HOOKS LINING THE WALLS, and Mikelo and I strip off our wet clothes and change after the man in the hall comes to his senses and staggers away, calling help. Nobody returns; they all think we've gone back upstairs.

"Quick, now," I say, keeping my sword and gun bundled up

inside my robe. I fish out the rings I stole from my pockets and hang my old clothes on a hook beneath a robe.

"Are we to go naked?" Mikelo says.

"We'll retrieve clothes from the dressing room. Come on."

"They're going to recognize me. And you."

"We're thinking on our feet, Mikelo. Arsenault always used to say if you act like you belong, people usually won't look twice."

"Arsenault. Andris. Would he have hurt you?"

"I didn't want him to have to make that decision."

"The man you shot mentioned a gavaro..."

I let my breath out. "Arsenault. Look, Mikelo, something very strange is going on, and Arsenault and your uncle are at the center of it. I don't know what's happening, but I'm going to find out. It would be easier if I didn't have to threaten you to come with me, but you're still my insurance."

"Insurance." He smirks and flips his wet hair out of his face. "Yes. I do always seem to be of use to someone, don't I?"

"Would you rather be of use to me or to your uncle?"

He puts both hands in his hair and musses it up. "Neither. I don't know what to do, Kyrra. I don't want to be in line for the heirship. Five years ago, I barely knew I had an uncle."

"I'll make your decision for you, then. You're coming with me."

"Will Andris meet us outside?"

"I'm sure he'll follow us."

Mikelo turns and narrows his eyes on me. "Are you getting rid of him?"

I laugh. "You don't know him very well, do you? I'm not going to give him away to Geoffre, in case he's running a ruse or..."

In case he really is broken and that's what's wrong with his memory.

I stutter back into my sentence. "... in case he's telling the truth. About his memory. But I'm sure he'll follow us. Whether he's ordered to or not."

Mikelo frowns. "I'm not sure I trust you without him."

"I've only been honest with you, Mikelo. You know exactly where you stand with me. Can you say that for your uncle?"

His frown deepens and he rubs at the healing wound where I stabbed him last night. "I suppose you have a point. But I don't understand why you're leaving Andris. If he was *your* gavaro."

Every action I've taken over the past three days has been like playing a game of indij I'm losing. This one is a big gamble but I hope to make it pay off.

"If they all have to chase us, somebody is going to reveal his hand."

"So, you're still going to kill Cassis?"

I take a deep breath. "I don't think I have a choice now, do I?"

CHAPTER 21

By sunset, Mikelo and I are on the deck of a Vençalan caravel bound for Iffria. Geoffre expects us to take the hard road through the hills, but after we slid out of the bathhouse wearing our suits of stolen clothes, I visited a countinghouse to change my stolen jewelry and bought passage on this ship. We'll take the road that hooks around the southwestern edge of the Aliente estates. From there, it climbs through the lower pass to enter our game lands from the west. It's actually the easier route, though somewhat more roundabout.

I wonder if Arsenault thought we would take the hill road too, or if he remembers enough about the routes to and from my father's land that he tried to search for us on the docks, expecting us to take this ship instead. We slunk out through a hot, angry crowd, gavaros facing off with steel drawn, Geoffre patrolling the edges, Madame Triente standing on the front steps with her arms outstretched, trying to calm everyone down. I expected to see Arsenault among her circle of gavaros, but I didn't see him anywhere…only felt the protection of his magic in the sword at my side, helping me stay hidden the way it often did. Or maybe that belief has merely become a superstition. Sometimes, it's hard to tell.

I hate leaving him. But if I'm going to learn where he stands, this is the way to do it. I'm confident he'll track us, but where will he meet us? Will he bring Geoffre's spies down on us or will he show up alone?

I hardly know how I feel anymore.

Mikelo braces his hands on the gunwale and squints out over the grass of the wetlands on the coast. Bands of pink and orange streak the western sky—harbinger of a warmer season maybe, or just the false light preceding the sanval's warm, wet, howling kiss. He's wearing a Caprine green cloak and tunic—both irony and disguise.

"Have you ever been away from Liera?" I ask. He's been quiet all afternoon, walking grimly beside me, doing what I tell him but offering me nothing. Now that I've got him, I need more information.

"My uncle only moved me to Liera after the wars started. Before that, I lived in Baleria with my mother."

I search my knowledge of geography. "Where is Baleria? I've never heard of it."

"A long way from here. It's small. Quiet. Mostly farmland. There's no reason why you should know it."

"Is it Prinze?"

A householder's daughter is an expert at lineages, almost as good as the genealogists the Houses employ to keep correct kin records. If I've never heard of Baleria and I've never heard of him, then both might as well have been conjured from the air.

"No. It's where my mother lived. If she had any House ties, she never told me what they were."

I'm surprised. I've been leaning on my elbows on the gunwale, watching the gulls wheel over the marshes, but I turn to face him now. "Your mother was kinless?"

He stiffens and looks down that proud Prinze nose at me. "I don't think my mother was Lieran. She wasn't kinless."

"Then who were your kin? Where did she come from?"

"She... It's not important. She didn't name names when she talked about her past."

Fallen from somewhere then.

"And your father didn't live with you?"

"My father died. Before I was born or when I was very young."

I try to remember what happened to Geoffre di Prinze's younger brother. He did die, some years ago, when I was small. A fever, I think. He made Geoffre's scouting voyages for him, searching for new sources of cargo, and would have had the opportunity to father a few bastards in exotic ports.

"If you're Renzo's son, then you have brothers ahead of you —his legitimate sons. Doesn't he have two?"

"Two sons and a daughter," Mikelo says. "But Georji is a drunk, and Zio ran off to Vençal two years ago after the Sere found some money and one of their servant girls missing."

"He's ever been the black sheep," I say. Zio was the sort of boy who was always in trouble for some sort of harmless social transgression the rest of us wished we'd had the courage to make. It didn't surprise me that he'd been forced into exile.

Mikelo tightens his hands on the railing and watches the black water lap the ship's hull. "Well," he says. "I'd put my faith in their claims before mine, but it appears I may have been mistaken."

For a moment, it's quiet. Most of the sailors have gone ashore. We're left here with the skeleton crew, who talk to each other in low voices and only when they need to. The Vençalans don't care much whom they carry; they try to stay out of Liera's politics.

"So, you really did leave him," Mikelo says abruptly. "Didn't it bother you?"

"What?" I tear my gaze away from the mirrored surface of the water, startled by the change in subject.

"Andris. Arsenault. Whatever his name is. I didn't think you would leave him, but you did."

"I told you why."

Mikelo leans on the railing. "I didn't know whether to believe you. Andris never spoke of his life before the wars."

"No," I say. "He wouldn't have."

Especially since he doesn't seem to remember it.

"I didn't know he supported my claim. As far as I knew, he was just a guard." Mikelo shifts awkwardly. "You have to believe me when I say I never knew my uncle wanted me for heir. He gave me a host of boring jobs. I always thought an heir would be treated better."

"He was probably keeping you alive, out of the fighting. But I imagine more people knew. Maybe even Zio. He probably wanted to be in line for the succession less than you do. Were you allowed to call him *brother*?"

Mikelo glances at me, but it's hard to read his expression as the night grows darker. "I wasn't allowed to call him anything at all. My uncle kept me away from him. I only met him once, when I first came to Liera. I was introduced to him and Georji and Laila in the receiving room of their townhome, and what Zio said was *Oh, thank the gods there's another one*."

"Did Renzo have more bastards?"

"If he did, I've never met any. I think Zio was talking about males in the line of succession. He seemed relieved."

"I imagine he would."

"You sound as if you don't mind Zio."

"Except for the way he looks, he's hardly Prinze at all. And harmless. He's probably a gavaro now."

"But he's forsaken his duty."

"Are you doing yours?"

Mikelo is quiet for a moment. Then he says, "Andris fought for your father. Didn't he."

"Yes. A long time ago."

"I think my uncle was wrong to hire him. I think you were wrong to leave him. Word will get out that I've been kidnapped.

The Caprine might try to kidnap me themselves if they think they can prod my uncle that way."

"It would be foolish of them."

"Still."

I smile a little, in spite of myself. "Are you trying to convince me to let you go?"

He grips the gunwale so hard, his knuckles turn white. Then he releases it and hangs his head. "I don't know what I'm trying to do," he says. "I don't know who to trust. I don't know that I can trust anyone."

I lean down beside him, folding my flesh arm over my metal one. "Welcome to Liera, Mikelo."

Mikelo and I disembark the Vençalan tramper at the village of Cales, halfway between Liera and Iffria.

In Cales, the trade is for relics. The road from the coast to the hills is an old one, lined with crumbling shrines full of ghosts and traversed in the spring and summer by flocks of pilgrims. At the hills' feet, the apricots are in full bloom and flowers fill every stall in the market. Interspersed with the flowers are votas—amulets of amber and iron, talismans of twisted human hair and bone, and little wooden hands, arms, and feet with conjure spells written on them, for healing. As the season warms, the number of pilgrims will grow until they peak at high summer, when it's proof of dedication to brave the fevers in order to prostrate oneself before the gods at Sybal, Tekasius, Sefrana, Karansis.

I decide that we, too, will walk to Karansis, where we can join the old Eterean road into the mountains. Some of the richer pilgrims go on horseback, in litters, with retinues. But I don't want to call attention to the two of us. Just in case Geoffre's spies have picked us up, I change my clothes again—a rose silk gown with dark patches where the stick caught in the dye and another set of leather stays where I can hide my dagger—and then we sell our fine cloaks and buy plain brown ones, dried fish, biscuits, and wine.

Then we begin walking.

Cales is built on a small sliver of flat land that hugs the sea. The road climbs suddenly, as roads often do on the eastern Eterean coast, winding its way through jagged black cliffs that stand off from the shore like obsidian blades. At the top of the ridge, one can look out over the water toward the misty coastline of Amora and back up the coast to Liera. To the northwest stands Mount Kosemi, its peak bare and brown, the only peak in this section of the range unwreathed with snow; instead, gray steam plumes from its crater, leaving the sky above it dingy as an unwashed scrap of cloth. The black, lava-scarred slopes of Mount Kosemi bear lush orchards of figs, olives, almonds, and apricots, but at a price; the orchards are only fifty years old, the previous trees having been destroyed in a powerful eruption in which Kosemi blew most of its north side. They say that long ago, Ires, the god of war, was shackled deep inside Kosemi by his fellow gods when he lost his mind. From Cales the mountain looks slumped, like an old warrior in defeat.

The second day out, Mikelo and I sit in its shadow to eat our biscuits and drink our wine. No one else is around, but I begin to itch in my shoulder blades, as if someone stands behind me.

If I turn around, will it be Arsenault or the man who killed Vadz and shot Razi?

"Tell me what Cassis looks like now," I say to Mikelo, to take my mind from the feeling, and to break the silence, which gnaws at me. "Tell me what's become of him."

Mikelo sits with one knee up, his hand with its biscuit resting atop it, squinting out to sea. In that pose, he reminds me too much of Arsenault, so I follow his gaze to see what he's looking at. Caravels, trampers, carracks, galleons—from this height, all the ships look nearly the same, like small bits of driftwood heaved at the shore.

"He looks much the same as he always has, I suppose. He

hasn't injured himself, or contracted any plagues, or managed to disfigure himself in any other way. How long has it been since you saw him last?"

The last time I actually got a good look at him was in the Market that day I tricked Arsenault into eating a silkworm. "Seven years," I say.

"I suppose he just looks older. He's twenty-eight, not old."

I'm twenty-five. I wonder what Cassis will think of me when he sees me. How have I aged? I'm not the girl I was, and I've spent the past five years trying to hide any part of me that might appeal to man or woman, although that didn't always work. My fellow gavaros wondered why I threw myself into battle the way I did, but battle was safe. It was recreation that was dangerous.

Mikelo is watching me. Over the past five days, I've become familiar with his quiet ways and his sea-green eyes that hide more than they reveal. I'm beginning to wonder if he's playing a ruse too, biding his time for Geoffre. Does he see spies I don't? Maybe an assassin?

Perhaps it's just the emptiness of the road that makes me paranoid.

"And Cassis's wife?" I ask.

Mikelo relaxes and smiles. "Camile. A beautiful woman. She has long, dark hair, eyes the color of agate..."

"And she's barren," I say before I can help myself. My shoulder blades itch again, but when I turn around, all that meets me is the sight of Mount Kosemi, cloaked in its perpetual gray haze.

Mikelo doesn't reply but continues to watch me. He finishes his biscuit and dusts the crumbs from his shirt.

"What are you looking for?" he finally asks.

I sniff. "Nothing." I begin rolling my pack up, getting ready to leave.

"You've been doing that for some time now. Have you heard something? Is it Andris?"

I cock my head, listening for the crunch of gravel or the

patter of voices. But there's only the screech of an osprey riding the winds above the surf, and the distant crashing of the surf itself. "No."

"You seem nervous."

"I'm not going to let Geoffre's men just walk up on me, now, am I?" I rise and shoulder my pack, then kick the crumbs into a pile for the birds. "Come on."

The road follows the lip of the cliff. An old stone wall stands at its edge, crumbling in a dozen places. No telling who built it, but it isn't much protection. Mikelo runs his hand along it as he walks.

"You really do think he's following us, don't you?"

"Of course I do," I say testily. "I said he would, didn't I?"

"Would he know the route you would choose?"

"Maybe."

"How well did you know him? Before."

I squint at the sea. The air is sharp atop the cliffs, cool, but not too cold. I tighten my grip on my pack.

"Well enough."

"So, he might guess that you would come this way."

"He certainly knew all the routes to and from my father's lands. Probably better than I did. He traversed them regularly. But he's become a different man since then."

"Surely, you didn't have a gavaro after you lost your arm."

"He wasn't *my* gavaro. He was my father's gavaro. A gavaro on my father's land, where I was a serf."

"Gavaros switch sides," he says.

"They do. But Arsenault made my arm."

The knowledge rattles him. It's easy to tell; he has such an open face. He glances at my right hand, but I'm wearing gloves—kid leather, the way a lady might. I bargained the seller down, though the price was still too high. But I had to have them.

"Arsenault had a talent for metalworking," I say. "He could See the truth of things. And people. What lay inside them. But that was before Kafrin Gorge."

"Jon brought him to us. 'You've need of a swordsman, don't you?' Jon asked Devid, and by all the gods, Andris could fight." Mikelo turns to me. "I saw him. He defeated all our best fighters, but not Devid himself. He pulled on the last stroke."

"Devid's not the kind of man who respects those who can beat him."

Mikelo shakes his head. "No. Perhaps that's why Geoffre prefers Cassis."

"If Geoffre prefers Cassis, it's only because he knows Cassis is better at manipulating people and easy to rule." My voice is more bitter than the air, but I can't help it. "It was always so."

"Not so much now," Mikelo says.

"That remains to be seen. Which leaves you. Why does Geoffre like you, Mikelo?"

Nothing fills the silence but the crunch of our boots on the lava rocks, the whistle of the wind through the crags that drop away beneath us, the pounding drum of the ocean. Mikelo stares at the ground while he walks, his brow furrowed, carrying his pack as if it weighed a hundred stone. Then he says, "I don't know. If he thinks I'm a better choice than Cassis, it's only because Cassis has rebelled and chooses his own consort. I told you, I don't want the succession. I wish I was never in line for it."

"Devid would have had you killed had you stayed in Liera. Sooner or later."

"I'll do my duty to my house," Mikelo says tightly. "If I have to. But I'm not sure my uncle wants me for that."

"What else would he want you for?"

Mikelo's eyes grow troubled. He turns away from me to stare once again at the scenery.

"Do you know why Jon Barra supports you?"

"No. Do you?"

"I've an idea. I'll wager he wants to break the Prinze monopoly on the gun trade, empty your coffers, and drive all your kinsmen from his country into the sea. He must think you're easy to rule, too."

Mikelo's face darkens. "He's only a smuggler."

I adjust my pack on my back. "They say he's a prince in his country. And Jon has his ways. He was pinned once by a Kavol army on the low ground. But at the end of the day, it was the Kavol who were running away in retreat."

"Jon said when he delivered Andris to Devid that he'd fought with him before, and you say that Andris fought for your father. Jon must not have been able to defeat the Prinze so easily."

"Arsenault commanded my father's forces. Jon had little to do with it."

"It's true then. Andris was your father's second-in-command. That's why you call him Arsenault."

I nod, warily, with the feeling that I have just stepped onto a pocket of unstable snow.

"There are portraits of your father's captain," Mikelo says, and looks at me sideways. "But Andris doesn't...quite...look like him, does he? The portraits all show a man with a nasty scar and a silver streak in his hair. A broken nose. Andris has none of that."

"Perhaps you're right, then. Perhaps it's not him."

"But you believe he is. Why?"

I take a deep breath before I can stop myself, and I scan the rocks that rise above us. Lots of places for men to hide up there.

How to explain to Mikelo all the little things that remain the same—the way he moves and sits, his expressions, his eyes...his taste for sandwiches? And should I?

If Mikelo has come to think of himself as less of a prisoner, I have too.

"I can't tell you why," I say finally. "But I know he's the same man. So does Jon."

"If anyone had recognized him, he'd be in pieces. I think many of my kinsmen hold him personally responsible for many of our deaths in the war. The story goes that he used to work for Cassis but then turned traitor."

"What did he do for Cassis?"

"As I understand it, at first he was just a retainer. But then it came to be known that he had ties to Dakkar, the Caprine, and the Aliente, and he was used mainly for information. Some of it probably resulted in the guns we were able to acquire."

Damn the man.

Arsenault was always a briar patch of secrets. I knew he'd spied on the Prinze for my father, but perhaps we were wrong? Had he not been spying on Geoffre but actually spying on my father for Geoffre? Working his way up the ranks. Working his way...through me?

Or had he gone over to the Prinze after he sent me away, after he stayed to fight with my father though by then, he disagreed with my father on almost everything important?

I can't believe it.

But Vanni said he broke. So, if he betrayed my father, maybe he didn't do it...voluntarily.

I swallow. Mikelo is watching me, waiting for me to say something. "Do you know what happened at Kafrin Gorge?" I ask him.

Mikelo frowns thoughtfully. "Kafrin Gorge was the battle that crushed the Aliente. Afterward, your family members banded only in small groups..." He glances at me hesitantly. "...which were summarily wiped out. It's my understanding that at Kafrin Gorge, my uncle made to parley with the Aliente forces, to allow them to offer surrender. His forces stood down, but the Aliente forces charged and my uncle had no choice but to order the gorge set afire. Your father's forces were caught in the fire and suffered a crushing defeat. Almost none of them lived."

He's talking about my father and gavaros like Saes and Verrin whom I once ate and drank with—of my cousins and uncles.

"And you believed Geoffre so innocent?"

Mikelo stares at me. "It was his word," he says.

Your uncle's word means as much as the dirt we walk on, I want to tell him. But I'll gain no information by trading recriminations. "You said, 'almost none of them lived.' Was there a record of who survived?"

Mikelo's expression is deceptively neutral as he says, "Your captain was rumored to live, but no one knew where he was. Everyone that survived was badly burned. Our troops collected most of them and executed them afterwards. They did them a mercy, as I understand it."

"And Arsenault?"

He shrugs. "His body was never found. To be honest, no one knew if he was at Kafrin or not. I don't know who was commanding the Aliente forces. There were a lot of rumors swirling around by then, and whatever bodies remained after the fire were too badly burned to identify."

"My father died there," I say. "Didn't he?"

Mikelo turns away to stare at the mountain. "Yes."

So, I have it confirmed.

We walk silently for a moment. Then Mikelo says, "Arsenault failed your father. Do you really think he'll follow us?"

Deceptive youth. I look in his eyes and see his uncle, not his cousins or his wastrel half-brothers.

"You fight to wound," I tell him.

"Is there another way?"

※

THE ROAD LEVELS OFF ONTO A PLATEAU OF ROLLING HILLS, greening with grass to be cut and baled for hay. Soon, small green olives will begin to swell on the silver-gray branches of the olive trees and tiny chartreuse bunches of grapes will speckle the hexagonal plantings crowning the hills. But right now, the lavender spikes of blooming orchids thrust up through the grass, and hedges of quince and lilac breathe their perfume into the air.

Near twilight, we veer off the road to search for wild asparagus. I hunt through the bracken to discover the stands of thin purple and green stalks, then harvest them with my knife. Mikelo finds a few mushrooms, beige with gray gills, growing under the cypress trees that form the hedgerow. He opens his hands to show me.

"Aedamma," I name them. "Good to eat." I follow him into the trees and take the few handfuls of forage from my skirt and place them on a large flat rock. Mikelo squats and lets his mushrooms tumble onto it. They bounce like buttons, and I put my hand up to stop them falling off.

"You seem to know what grows here," he says.

"Not so different than our villa. We used to hunt mushrooms in the woods. It was a pastime."

"We didn't eat mushrooms in Baleria. When I joined my uncle at his hunts, we sometimes went into the woods for icini. It was the first time I'd eaten fungi."

The asparagus is so green and tender, I don't even need to strip the stalks. It crunches when I bite into it. I sit down by the rock and stretch out my feet.

"Aren't we going to build a fire?" Mikelo asks.

"No. There are horses coming behind us."

Mikelo stands and looks out between the fans of cypress that screen us from the road. The cypress trees stand straight in a long row, their bulbous shapes like unlit torches. "You knew they were coming?" he says. "From so far away? I didn't see them."

"There's dust in the air. Look again."

He peers out between the trees, parting their branches with one hand. Hard to see in the twilight now, but with the horses, that party should have gained on us. He lets the branch drop back into place.

"I see them," he says.

I take another bite of asparagus. "I think you probably saw them earlier but were waiting to see if I noticed. Do you still harbor thoughts of escape?"

"Don't you?" he says, a tight smile pulling at his mouth.

I pull a rope from my pack. "Eat anyway. It's not too bitter."

He glances at the trees again, a long glance, then comes to sit by me. "How far to the lodge?" he asks.

"A few more days on foot to Karansis. We'll take horses from there. Then...it will depend on whether or not there's still snow."

"And after you take Driese and kill Cassis—what then?"

"That will depend on the circumstances," I say, watching him. "If I don't need you anymore, I'll let you go. I suppose you could go anywhere you wanted. You wouldn't have to go back to Geoffre."

"And you'd just leave? You think it's going to be that easy? You're not going to have to deal with my uncle, or Andris, or Jon?"

"You asked what would happen if I fulfilled my contract. I suppose I'd let you go. Unless you were still useful to me. Then perhaps you could come with me. I've had enough of Rojornick; I'd probably run for southern Vençal. Somewhere sunny and warm."

He holds my gaze for a moment. Still weighing the benefits of escape, the wages of whatever he perceives to be his duty, whether or not he believes I'll do what I say. It's easy to track the course of his thoughts; anybody would be thinking them. He picks up a mushroom and turns it around in his fingers.

"Do you think Andris rides that horse?"

"Hard to say. It could be him..."

"But you don't think so?"

"Pounding in on a horse where everyone can see him isn't Arsenault's style. But it might be your uncle's."

"You know, in Baleria, all the mushrooms were poisonous. Some of them grew big and round as ostrich eggs. We kicked them like balls. I ate one once and nearly died. And here, you tell me mushrooms are good to eat, and I have to decide to trust you or not. From all I've known, fungi are death."

I show him my open hands in a gesture of helplessness. "All I can tell you is that I'll keep you alive as long as keeping you alive keeps me alive. But if killing you will keep me alive, I'll do it. That hasn't changed. I'm a gavaro, Mikelo, and that's as much an offer of trust as I can make."

He frowns at me. "And would you keep from killing a man because of anything else, except that his life supported yours?"

The horse on the road—*could* it be Arsenault? Bringing a Prinze patrol with him? Gooseflesh crawls up my back. I want to go to the trees and keep watch. Instead, I meet Mikelo's gaze, dark in the fading light. "I would," I say. "I have."

His frown deepens, and he rises and walks to the trees instead of me. He looks out once more at the specks the other party makes behind us. "Escape is tangled," he says.

"Trust is tangled too." I uncoil my rope. "Now eat, Mikelo, and then I'm going to truss you so I can sleep for a bit."

He eyes the rope, then me. "I think you're the only person who has ever been completely truthful to me," he says.

He bites into the mushroom and chews it slowly.

❈

AFTER WE EAT OUR SUPPER, I BIND MIKELO'S ARMS AND ankles. This has been our routine. I think he'll stay, but I can't take a chance on trust. If the pilgrims behind us should not be pilgrims but Prinze...

Mikelo rolls away from me in the leaf litter. His fingers wriggle against his back.

"Are your bonds too tight?"

"No." His hands still and in a few minutes, his chest begins to move up and down in a steady, slow rhythm, and the sound of his breathing joins the wind in the trees. He's not used to walking this much, and in truth, neither am I, not after wintering in Liera. My feet are all over blisters.

I ease my boots off and rotate my ankles so they pop.

"What was that?" Mikelo asks sleepily.

"Oh, probably a brigand," I say.

He brings up his head. "What?"

"Honestly, Mikelo. It was nothing. You're too nervous. Sleep for a little while, and if it will make you feel better, I'll wake you when I'm tired."

He settles his head back on the ground, hesitantly. Then he says, "You aren't tired now?"

I am, but I can't sleep. The feeling of being watched hasn't subsided. "No," I say. "I'll stay awake a little longer."

That seems to satisfy him. He goes to sleep, for good this time, and I sit with my back against the tree and pull my boots back on because my feet are getting cold. I watch him and think about things for a while.

I think, why would a Prinze heir receive a commission to tally prisoners?

I think, why would Jon want to hide Arsenault beneath the noses of the Prinze, and why would Arsenault let him do it?

I think, how did Arsenault come to remember my name but so little of anything else?

I know it can't be him on that horse but I wish it would be.

The night air grows cold and I huddle in my cloak, staring up at the stars through the leaves of the trees—patches of night sky like a quilt. The trees interrupt the constellations, so I can't trace them. There are a million stars out in the clear spring sky, numberless in the way of things that are full of numbers. A million times a million, my tutor used to say, more millions than the Sere have in their vaults. And yet, my father countered, the silk our worms spun could cover the sky.

Imagine: a net for the stars woven of silk, every spider-thin strand invisible against the darkness. Stars would spill into it like fish, and our silk would snare them until we bundled them up and they became a brilliant blaze, unified from multitudes into one blinding flare, suspended by one strand of silk like a pendant, a teardrop, pregnant with all the tears one ever might have cried.

I must doze, dreaming of starlight, because the pounding of

hooves catches me unaware. I lurch to my feet, hand on my sword, pulse drumming in my ears.

But the horse passes by in a clatter of steel and conversation, a wind that rustles the cypresses. The horse's rider is running it, but not for urgency; a woman's laugh floats on the breeze, and a man's deep baritone voice.

Then they're gone. I'm left standing in the cold air, my breath puffing out of me in clouds. Mikelo lies in a puddle of moonlight, breathing hard and scared but watching me.

I want to tell him, *Go back to sleep.* But instead, I sit down, my back against the oak again, and close my eyes. On the inside of my eyelids, I see the imprints of stars.

Their lights flare and die, until I am left in darkness.

CHAPTER 22

Five years ago, when Arsenault left me to handle Lobardin while he pursued whatever double life he lived in Liera, I woke late after a cold night that would not be my last, my eyes gritty from restless sleep. My arm was better but still sore from where Lobardin had twisted it. I winced, stretching it, and rushed through my morning wash.

I didn't think anything of Arsenault's absence because he was often absent. Having him gone when I woke up was both a relief and a disappointment. My emotions distracted me as I hurried to dress and get out to the yard, where I was sure I would find him.

I almost ran into Lobardin in the corridor. He stopped me with a hand on my shoulder, and at his touch, I jerked against the wall, breathing hard.

I had caught him in the dining hall the night before. Put my dagger to his throat in front of the other men. I knew he'd been embarrassed, and I also knew that by then the kacin had worn off and he hadn't remembered much of the afternoon at all.

I didn't know if Arsenault had witnessed any of that or not.

He chuckled nervously. "Calm, Kyrra; I meant nothing. I've just a few tasks for you today."

I frowned. "I'll have to do the chores Arsenault left me first."

"Arsenault isn't here today," he said, looking down at his shirt. "Which leaves you to me." He smiled. "I'll see you at the trash pit at midday. By then I expect you'll have most of it buried, eh?"

I clenched my left hand, and my nails bit into my palm. "This is my reward for keeping Arsenault from killing you?"

One black brow arched. "He found out, did he?"

"I couldn't move my arm. I had to tell him something."

Lobardin looked distressed. "Truly, Kyrra, I'm sorry about that." He rubbed the back of his neck. "I don't— It's been hard. Lately. Maybe you understand?"

He tilted his head and looked up at me sideways from under a thick strand of black hair. His dark eyes seemed earnest.

"I don't understand why you smoke kacin, Lobardin. It's not allowed and you're going to get caught one day. My father does not allow exceptions to his rules."

Lobardin's face fell. "So, that would be no."

I exhaled and looked up at the ceiling while I thought about what to say next. "I think we share a common problem," I said finally. "Regarding magic. But I don't think your solution to the problem will work out in the long run. Is that better?"

"Mmmm," he said, and straightened up, as if he were pulling himself back together. "Well. You've still got midden duty."

I pushed my breath out through my teeth.

"It could be worse, Kyrra. There are other ways I could be seen saving face."

"I don't deserve revenge. You were in the wrong, Lobardin, and you know it."

"It doesn't matter whether I know it or not, dove. All that matters is the parts we have to play; haven't you figured that out yet?"

I glared at him and tried to start walking. I needed to eat if I was going to cover that godsforsaken midden by midday.

But Lobardin moved into my way again.

"I hear Arsenault has gone to meet with your old lover. To

talk to him about some cargo his brother's supposed to be bringing in."

"And how do you know that?"

"A little bird told me."

"A little bird?"

"A bird who sings most beautifully to anyone who'll listen. What I hear is that our beloved captain is also a retainer to Cassis di Prinze, and how do you think that works? Do you think the Householder put him up to that—a gavaro, with his loyalty for sale?"

"All of this is news to me," I said, trying to hide behind a mask like Arsenault's. "Why shouldn't the Householder use Arsenault as a spy?"

"It won't look good to the men, will it, if it's spread around?"

I narrowed my eyes. "What are you suggesting, Lobardin? Is this your attempt at coercion? You couldn't force me, so you'll pretend I came willingly?"

"Ah," he said, and a surprising blush came up on his cheekbones. "No. What I really want is information."

"Why?"

"So I can pass it along."

"I don't believe you."

"And you believe him?"

"He's given me no reason not to."

Lobardin watched me for a moment. "He's pledged himself to Cassis di Prinze, too, you know. Just as he pledged himself to Pallo d'Aliente. Which is the stronger pledge? And have you thought that he might be getting to you because Cassis or Geoffre put him up to it?" He stepped closer to me. "He wouldn't be as blatant as Cassis. No, not our Arsenault. He'd be subtle. He'd invite your trust because he'd know that little birds with broken wings do not trust easily. He'd wheedle it out of you until you thought it was safe again. And then what would he do? Do you know how much Geoffre hates you?"

"You don't know any of that. You're making it up."

"I'm trying to warn you, Kyrra. You have some inkling about what Geoffre is like, but...you don't *know*. Not like I do."

"And you don't know Arsenault like I do," I said.

I shoved past him and started walking down the hallway, fast, so he wouldn't catch me again.

"Just have a care!" he called after me. "Think about it while you're shoveling that midden!"

He was wrong, I told myself. Wrong beyond any shadow of a doubt. Arsenault had told me his story about Jon, and Jon had just had his entire family destroyed by the Prinze, and Arsenault was not trying to keep me close but send me away, and not just away but out of Eterea entirely.

But Lobardin was right, too. Arsenault was cannier and capable of subtlety in ways that even Lobardin probably wouldn't understand, and though I'd suspected it, I hadn't known that when Arsenault said he was following the Prinze, he really meant Cassis.

But again—I thought of the way he had looked beneath the olive trees before he kissed me. There had been honesty in that kiss. Hadn't there?

"Damn you, Lobardin," I whispered as I shoved my way out the back door, and crossed the yard to the kitchens.

I paused long enough for a cup of coffee and a bun, which I ate while attempting to trade small talk with Elinda, the kitchen girl who had a stormy on-again, off-again relationship with Lobardin. It was currently off-again while he—for some reason I couldn't fathom—dallied with Ilena. Elinda was in a foul mood, and she was complaining about how the boys had not come in with wood until late this morning, and that Margarithe had left with all her belongings, saying she was going home to Carrazone.

Because Arsenault told her to go, too.

I was glad she was leaving, that she would be safe but also that she would not be there anymore—a feeling that shamed me —but it probably didn't shame me any more than knowing I was jealous that he would exact the same promise from her that he had from me.

She hadn't been an ass about it, either.

I took a rag to wrap around my face as I worked and prepared to attack the trash pit.

We dumped most of our waste in pits that had to be covered with dirt when they were full. Gavaros dug them, hoping not to put their shovels into a plot of land that had already had a full pit dug into it. The pit was home to all the refuse the barracks created that couldn't be burned or turned into compost—bones with little pieces of muscle and gristle still clinging to them, chicken heads, broken crockery and glass, empty liquor bottles, the contents of all the chamber pots. It stank even on the coldest days.

Serfs covered up the trash pit. Gavaros didn't want to deal with it. The dirt saved from the digging of the pit formed a huge cone next to it, and the trick was to climb up on the pile of dirt and toss shovelfuls down, using the dirt as something of a shield. That way, you didn't have to get too close until it was nearly covered, but you also had to have strong arms, to heave the dirt that far.

Covering up the pit was the hardest job in the barracks for me.

The pit had warmed under the sun until the sick-sweet-dead smell made me want to vomit. I wrapped the rag around my face and tucked in the ends to secure it without tying—which I couldn't do one-handed—and picked up the shovel that stood in the dirt.

My tactic was first to scrape as much dirt as I could from the closest side of the pile, then, when the trash on my side was mostly covered, to shovel the dirt onto the other side. That, at least, might cut down on the stench and speed the process.

I settled my feet securely in the small runnel of pebbles and clods of clay at the bottom of the pile, and stretched out with the shovel to knock a spill of dirt down onto the trash.

Splashes and pattering marked the dirt's descent. I looked down to see how far the dirt would spill, and to gauge how much dirt I might have to shovel onto the other side. Then I stood there still, staring at what lay, half-buried in dirt and sausage casings, on top of the mound of trash.

An arm.

At first, I thought it was real, the arm of a woman cut cleanly above the elbow, then tossed carelessly in the waste pit. But when I looked more closely, I could tell it was made of wood—light-colored, striated with bands of pink and lavender. I hesitated a moment, then knocked the debris from it with my shovel. A leather harness with dull metal buckles gripped the end, where it would attach to the bicep. The hand bore long fingers the same size and shape as my own.

I drew back from the lip of the pit, shaking, and looked up expecting to see Lobardin. But no one was there. It was just me and this arm.

Had Lobardin known about the arm? Was that why he assigned me the task?

I was shaking so badly, I could barely hold the shovel. I tried to make myself bury the arm, but I couldn't. In the end, I dug it out of the trash and left it on the ground beside me as I worked. I buried all the rest of the trash and then I took the rag from my face and wiped off the arm and wrapped it up and took it down to the stream with me to wash.

Then I went back to the barracks and laid it on Arsenault's bed.

And I waited for him to come back.

※

But Arsenault stayed gone—longer than he ever had before. I began to wake in the night, my heart racing, sure that Cassis had caught him out in Liera and killed him. Then I would look wildly to his bed only to see the wooden arm lying there, its buckles gleaming in the moonlight, and the shadows of ravens ruffling their feathers outside the window.

Finally came the night when the dry, southwest wind blew, laden with the heat of far-off deserts, and Lobardin walked in with news in triplet: Ricar di Sere's death, the guns, and my father's announcement that he would take a second wife.

Lobardin delivered the news about the guns and Ricar first. He had a pike in his hand and he thumped it on the floor, loudly. "I've news!" he said. "The Householder informs me that we are in a period of mourning for Ricar di Sere, who was lost at sea off the coast of Dakkar. The Householder will be attending his funeral, so many of you lucky bastards will get to be part of the escort he brings with him into the city. And we shall all wear black for a week."

"What was Ricar di Sere doing off the coast of Dakkar?" Saes said in a low voice, leaning over me so Verrin could hear.

"Well, you know what Arsenault thought," Verrin said.

"The Householder shouldn't have him on these damn fool errands now." Saes's green eyes flicked in my direction. "Apologies, Kyrra."

I trailed my spoon through my noodles. "I have no say in my father's affairs."

"Did Devid make it back?" another gavaro asked Lobardin.

Lobardin schooled his features. "Devid did indeed make it back," he said. "And he brought ten galleons full of guns with him."

Ten galleons. I clenched my spoon and stared, as did everyone else in the room. I didn't have to feign surprise; Jon had mentioned no numbers in his letter.

"They can't be selling all those guns."

"To foreign markets. Not to us."

"They'll turn the guns against the Aliente."

"Now's the time to check your contracts, looking for an out."

Nervous laughter rippled through the room. "I've never seen

a gun," said one of the green recruits. "Can't be worse than arrows or pitch fire."

Lobardin laughed. "My friend, you're an innocent. Once, I saw an Onzarran merchant shoot a man with a gun only as long as your arm. The ball went straight through his stomach and out the other side from thirty paces away. When the man hit the ground, I went up to see what the wound looked like. The hole was big enough to put your shoe in."

"Bullshit," Verrin piped up. "Thirty paces, Lobardin? What could do that kind of damage at thirty paces?"

"Well," Lobardin said, resting the pike against his shoulder and beginning to roll up his sleeve, "I've a scar in my arm that will prove I know all about guns. I was shot by one once. Rather irritated husband. Ball just grazed me, but that was enough."

He flexed his arm so everyone could see the mark on his bicep, a U-shaped scar that could have been from anything.

"Why didn't it go all the way through you, then?"

Lobardin pushed his sleeve down. "Guns have range, just like bows. I was already running away. The man the merchant shot didn't have the sense."

Saes snorted. "If you had any sense, Lobardin, you wouldn't have been messing with the wife of a man who could afford a gun in the first place."

"Enough." Util pushed his chair back with a screech and stood up. Silence immediately fell over the hall, but I wondered why he'd let the conversation go on as long as it had. "Lobardin," he said, "if you've more news, get on with it, but I'll not have you inciting rumors in my camp."

Lobardin bowed, a gesture just short of mockery. "I do have other news, as it turns out." He straightened up. "The Householder wishes to let it be known that he will take another woman to wife, and that the engagement is effective as of now, to the daughter of Haral d'Imisi. The marriage will take place on Fortune's Night, on these grounds. His wife, the current mistress"—Lobardin's gaze darted to me—"will not step down as

Messera. We are to prepare for guests and will be allowed at the feast."

There were whoops of joy and relief; for over three years, everyone had expected my father to take another wife, to get another heir, and the worry engendered by his stubborn and inexplicable resistance had wormed its way through every part of the estate.

But I sat, stunned by the news. Claudia d'Imisi was younger than I was. She was pretty enough, with her long, golden-brown hair and her pink-pinched cheeks, and she had a head on her shoulders, too, which would be something my father would look for in a wife. Yet...she wasn't a *wife;* she was only a *girl*. A girl I had known when we wore our hair in twin braids and dressed in lacy pinafores and played with dolls.

I put my spoon down. "If you won't be needing me, Verrin..." I said.

His brow furrowed with concern. "No. I imagine we'll be drinking tonight. Play a hand of indij, Kyrra, if you'd like."

I shook my head. "I think I'll have my drink alone this evening," I said, and he nodded.

"And perhaps Arsenault will be back in the morning," Saes added.

"Perhaps he will," I said, not smiling, and left the table.

My hands began to tremble. Everything I had heard screamed war. But Utîl cared nothing for the future. His contract was up in a month.

What had my father done, charging Arsenault with not two but three jobs?

I went to the kitchens and liberated a bottle of gazpa from the shelves. Gazpa was our own special liqueur, brewed with the mulberries from our trees. My father had sometimes let me take small sips from his glass. I couldn't help thinking of him as I took the bottle back to Arsenault's room and stared at the arm on Arsenault's bed. The first drink I took was hesitant, the way I had sipped the rich red liqueur from my father's glass. But its warmth was so welcome, I took the next swig from the bottle like a gavaro.

What use was the arm, anyway? I couldn't even put it on by myself.

I wanted, suddenly, to be not alone. I wanted the arm, any arm, something to make me feel as if I didn't exist in a space by myself. I wasn't a gavaro, and I would not be invited to the wedding feast. I would eat leftovers in the barracks kitchen, and this was what it meant to be kinless.

I stoppered the bottle of gazpa and walked with it out of the barracks. Eventually, my feet carried me to the grotto with the armless statue.

I clambered up the rocky hillside above the spring and the statue and set the bottle down carefully on the rock ledge. From this vantage point the pockmarked limestone statue looked small and pathetic. I boosted myself up beside the bottle, then stretched out on my back on the narrow ledge, careful not to kick the bottle of gazpa.

Slowly my heart stilled as I lay there, thinking about the armless statue. How old was it? What man had carved it? The Etereans had erected many statues near springs, marking them as holy places or ghost-founts. The mist that spilled up from the bottom of the spring, where the water splashed on the rocks, looked like a ghost. Its cool gray fingers wrapped around my feet, then my legs and my severed arm.

The mist rose to the sky and I began to imagine figures in it —birds, wolves, horses, men. It spread until the moon was a watery rippling of light, the stars mere wavelets of silver, as if the sky had become a vast, deep pool, its waters too black to show any reflections.

The images grew in solidity the longer I watched. Claudia, her long hair falling around her shoulders, wept as my father turned away from her; my mother fed the lorikeet in the conservatory, her mouth a hard, straight line, with her back turned to my father as he stood in the door; the cold white marble tiles glared in the sunlight spilling in the window.

Muslin curtains fluttered in the wind, in a different conservatory. Arsenault stood beside a woman playing a harpsichord, her long, white fingers flying over the keys, raven hair unbound, her shoulders round and small under the fabric of her thin muslin nightgown. She looked up at Arsenault with cat-tawny green eyes and smiled. *I know it's not my husband's fault. He got a child on that woman. I'm the barren one; come, no one will ever know—my husband avoids my bed these days and seeks his entertainment elsewhere.*

Arsenault frowned as if considering her offer. She let her fingers trail down his arm. His frown deepened. The wind ruffled his shirt, lifted the silver strands of hair that had pulled free of his braid. He wore a blue silk tunic over his white shirt—Prinze blue.

He hesitated. Then he leaned down and pressed his lips to the lady's brow. She smiled and closed her eyes, her hand tightening on his. But then he straightened up.

Not today, Camile.

Her eyes flew open in surprise. Hurt and jealousy were green colors, lodged there. When her smile returned, it formed a bitter hook at the corner of her mouth.

Perhaps it's as they say. No one wants a barren woman. Not even a gavaro.

You're married to my lord, Lady.

Which makes me your lady, too. Do you not find me attractive, Arsenault? Perhaps if I called it a duty?

He laughed, low and surprised, in his chest. *If you're that desperate, Camile, go ahead.*

She flushed and turned back to the harpsichord. Her arpeggios were vicious, mangled. Not looking at him, she said, *I saw you the other day. You were with that Dakkaran smuggler's man.*

Arsenault's expression became veiled and careful. *Your husband has his appetites,* he said. But Camile didn't look at his face. She scowled down at her fingers pounding the keys of the harpsichord. In the corner of the room, a parakeet squawked, swinging back and forth on the perch in its bamboo cage.

All the Prinze have their appetites, she said bitterly. *They'll devour you no matter how hard you try to avoid their jaws.*

Arsenault hesitated again. He laid a hand on her shoulder. Her back, so slim and fragile, trembled as she put her face in her hands.

Then there was a crash, the sound of shattering glass.

I sat up with a jerk to find that I had kicked the bottle of gazpa. It tumbled down atop the statue and leaked liqueur over the statue's shoulders, the stumps of its arms.

In the darkness, it looked like blood.

⚜

Two nights later, Arsenault came back.

The moon was waning now, no longer full but still bright. I had left the shutters open for the breeze, but there was no relief from the heat.

At the door's soft creak, I awoke immediately. I opened my eyes but didn't move, frozen with my hand clutching at the mattress. The scuffing footsteps didn't sound like Arsenault's.

He came into the room with his back to me, wearing no tunic or armband, just a plain white shirt. He made his way carefully to his bed. Then he stopped and cursed when he saw the wooden arm.

"I found it in the trash heap," I said. I kept my voice low but it sounded loud in the dark. Arsenault whirled, hand immediately going to his sword. He stood for a moment, then let his breath out in one long exhale.

"Lobardin had me work the midden; he must have seen it, too. It happened the day you left. It's been two cycles of the moon now that we've been waiting for you. Where have you been?"

He pushed his unbraided hair back from his face and sat heavily on the bed, shoving the arm out of the way.

I watched in growing alarm as he began untying the laces of his shirt. None of this behavior was like him. "I knew I didn't hide that arm deep enough. I half-hoped you'd come to your senses, found it, and left. You could have passed yourself as a boy."

"Where would I have gone? With Margarithe?"

"Thought you might have sympathized with her."

He pulled his shirt over his head and threw it into the corner of the room, where it caught on the edge of his worktable and fluttered in the sick breeze.

"You should close the shutters when you sleep," he said.

"But it's so hot."

"Worse things than heat roam the night."

I laughed. "A bandit would have to have balls the size of my fist to walk up to a barracks full of gavaros. What could he gain?"

Arsenault stared at me.

I blushed.

"It's no matter," he said. "I've only been around too many women lately."

"Arsenault."

He sighed. "Forgive me, Kyrra; I'm just not myself tonight, that's all."

Then who are you? I wanted to ask.

He started to lie down on the bed, bumped into the arm, grabbed it and pitched it out the window. It crashed into the trees on the other side of the path. Then he lay down and stretched out, folding his hands behind his head, shirtless but still wearing his dust-covered boots.

I watched, more than a little stunned.

Though we lived in the same space and I often saw him working in the yard, I had rarely caught even the briefest glimpse of him without his shirt. He was always careful to dress and undress only when the blanket was hung, dividing the room.

CHAPTER 22

The only other time he went shirtless was doing manual labor with other men in the heat.

But now the moonlight slid along the rounded silhouette of his shoulders and outlined the hard planes of his chest and the leanness of his stomach. His trousers had pulled down past his hip, exposing the notch of his hipbone.

A heat that had nothing to do with the weather rose within me.

But diverting my attention to the clothed parts of him was hardly better, given the way the silk trousers clung to his thighs.

I made myself step back and consider the larger picture. Big, light-colored splotches of dust mottled his trousers. He must have ridden hard to reach the estate before daybreak. Why had he risked himself riding at night?

I swung my feet onto the floor, and his head shifted toward me, hair slinking down the side of the pillow. "What are you doing, Kyrra?"

His voice sounded thick. Sleepy.

"Where do the Prinze think you go when you come back here? Do they know you work for my father?"

"No," he said. "And I'd like to keep it that way."

I noticed that he didn't answer the other question. I took a deep breath and pressed on.

"Why did you ride so hard to make it back? You've been gone two months. Do you have news for my father? Were you worried about being discovered?"

He looked in my direction for a moment, then turned away. In the dim white light I could see he'd closed his eyes. "Little bird," he murmured. "You ask too many questions."

Little bird. That was what Erelf called me. Not Arsenault.

I eyed him warily, then I stood and walked to his bed.

"Did Camile di Prinze finally break you?"

He opened his eyes. His pupils were too large, like they had swallowed the gray.

Kacin, then. That was why he was acting so oddly.

"What do you know about Camile di Prinze?" he said.

I folded my arms, a gesture I hadn't made in a long time, then dropped my stump and held it behind my back so he couldn't see it. He wasn't the only one being careless tonight; I had forgotten I was only wearing my sleeveless shift. I suddenly felt exposed with my arm out of its covering.

"Nothing," I said, turning around, cradling my stump before me. "I only thought she might have been one of the women you spoke of, down in Liera."

The bed creaked and dirt crunched behind me as Arsenault sat up and put his boots down on the floor.

"She was," he said. "Cassis smokes his nights away and lies with other women. If he's still able to father children, he'll have ten bastards by winter unless Geoffre has something done about it. But Camile remains barren and loveless."

"I saw it," I said. "In a dream. Down by the grotto."

My admission didn't seem to surprise him. He sighed. "She's insistent."

I bit my lip. "Perhaps..." I said—grudgingly, forcing myself, "perhaps you should have lain with her. Does she suspect you?"

"I don't think so. It won't matter if she tells Cassis about my associations with Jon, because Jon supplies him with his kacin. That's where he thinks I go when I'm gone—to guard Jon's runs. He and Jon have an agreement."

"Still," I said.

"Did you *want* me to sleep with Camile?"

I let all my breath out and stared at the floor. "No. I was just trying to think like a householder."

"To be ruthless, you mean." Arsenault paused. "I left Liera like I did because otherwise, I was going to knife Cassis."

"What?"

I looked over my shoulder but I didn't turn around. Arsenault was looking out the window.

He faced me. "All I can think about when I watch him work is what he did to you. And then, if he's not dragging me with him to a bathhouse or smoking den, he wants me back at his townhouse, 'guarding' Camile. Bastard. He's trying to turn me into a whore."

I turned around slowly. "Cassis...*wanted* you to sleep with his wife?"

"I couldn't take it anymore. But if I put a knife in his back and got caught...Geoffre would be able to turn his cannons on your father unmolested, and I'm no closer to learning what he really *wants*. The only ones left in his way are those damn Caprine spies fooling themselves that he doesn't know who they are."

"Are you sure the Prinze don't suspect you? Maybe it was a test with Camile and you failed it."

"Right. See what happens when a gavaro is caught in bed with the wife of a Prinze in the line of succession." He breathed out raggedly. "And I won't say I wasn't tempted. Camile's a beautiful woman. A very lonely, very beautiful woman."

I looked down at my bare toes on the dirt floor and tried to wriggle them into the hardpack. "Camile was always the most beautiful among us. A real prize. Cassis was lucky to get her."

For a moment, Arsenault didn't speak. Then he said, "Kyrra. Cassis is a bastard with a pretty smile. You would have broken him in two. And Camile is like a porcelain doll that's been cracked." He leaned forward, putting his elbows on his knees so he could hang his head and rake his hands through his hair. "You deserve so much more. More than a liar like me can give you, that's sure."

What could I say to that? I didn't say anything.

"Jon thought I ought to make the arm," he said finally. "He wanted me to give you something that would make you look like anybody else. He thought you probably hated the Prinze enough to do anything he asked, to get back at them."

"What did Jon want me to do?"

"I don't know, exactly. He's floated me a number of ideas, and I've harpooned all of them. The first was to put you out among the Prinze serfs, but they'd recognize you in a heartbeat. Then he thought maybe he'd put you among the Sere...which wasn't quite as bad. But still, what are the chances they wouldn't know who you are? In our latest letter, he put forth the idea that you could disguise yourself as a boy, sneak into the house, and kill the family yourself."

I felt as if time had stopped, leaving me standing alone in the middle of the room.

What if I disguised myself as a boy and became an assassin? I could learn to use poisons. I would use something slow-acting on Cassis. Something to humiliate him in public before it killed him.

"I told Jon you'd be dead before you got out the door. But Jon..."

Arsenault stopped and rubbed his eyes with his thumb and forefinger.

"Devid di Prinze and Ricar di Sere razed his home. His father is dead, his wife is dead, his children..." Arsenault shook his head. "Since I didn't see it happen, it doesn't seem real. They called me Ari, you know, all the boys did—Adayze's Edo started it. Jon's boys used to climb all over me when I came in the house. I would turn Dayo upside down and swing him around like a sack, and he'd shriek with laughter. Biyo, I just let hang on my back, and he would pretend I was a turtle and he was the shell. And yet they were twins."

His voice grew hoarse. I knelt in front of him. Hesitantly, I put my hand on his knee.

He brought his head up, lowering his hands.

"I don't fault you or Jon for thinking of using me. I just don't know why you would risk yourself like this for a man who was once your master...or for pay."

"Jon fights my fight more than I fight his in many ways."

"What fight is that, Arsenault?"

"Against Erelf." He sought out my hand, entwined his fingers in mine, and stroked along the edge of my thumb with his thumb. Then he put his other hand on the back of my head and pulled me in closer to him so he could tilt his forehead against mine.

"I've had too many dreams of you, Kyrra," he murmured. "I think they've begun to suspect."

"To suspect you work for the Aliente?" I asked. Could he hear the tremble in my voice? His leg was warm beneath my hand, the steady caress of his thumb on mine maddening.

"No. To suspect that I can See."

"But how would they know?"

"Geoffre's dedicated himself to the god."

"What does that mean?"

"It means the god works through him. He's directing the Prinze not just for their benefit or his. He's doing what Erelf wants him to do. That must be why he's collecting magic."

"What will he do with it?"

"I don't know. Too hard for me to find out without the god finding out. If Cassis hadn't smoked so much kacin, Geoffre would have had me."

I edged forward and leaned into him, sliding my hand farther up his leg. He still had his other hand in my hair, and that thumb moved absently down the curve of my ear.

"It's too much to risk. Stay here, Arsenault. Don't go to Liera again. Util's contract is coming up. My father must see that you ought to remain with the men."

"I wish I could," he whispered. "I wish I could take you away from all these games. But for now, the games define us."

"Only if we let them. Why don't we stop. Just for tonight."

I disentangled my hand from his and moved it up his thigh again. Smooth, slick silk, damp from his sweat, brushed my fingertips. The muscles of his leg tensed.

He lifted his head. His face was very close and his eyes searched mine. "I'll be myself again in the morning," he said in a strained voice.

"That will be too long."

Now that the words were out, I couldn't unsay them. But I didn't want to. I wasn't the same girl Cassis kissed in the conservatory. I was a woman now, and I made my own choices, knowing what they were.

I inched my hand up farther, feeling along the cords of his muscles, as far as I dared.

"You've been gone too long," I whispered. "I've missed you. I don't want to keep missing you."

His gaze roved over my face and settled on my mouth.

"Kyrra," he breathed, like something inside him had loosed. Then he brought his lips down to mine.

It was not like the kiss beneath the olives.

It was not like kissing Cassis.

Cassis and I had always been in a rush. It was a race to get each other out of our clothes, and then everything was over much too quickly. In spite of that, there had always been an artful aspect to Cassis's kisses which puzzled me, as if he were kissing according to a guide.

But Arsenault was not like that. His mouth was warm and soft at first, in invitation. And when I accepted, he drew me against him, kissing me so thoroughly that I felt like I was full of him—his scent of tea and musk, the wiry brush of his beard against the corners of my mouth, the faint taste of ale.

The room had seemed so empty and quiet without him.

His lips sought the corner of my mouth, the skin of my neck, my ear as he pulled away. There was a hungry light in his eyes when he spoke, finally. "Will you stay with me, then? Tonight?"

I let my fingers run through his hair, his beard—over his scar, the lines of his face, well-loved.

"Yes," I said.

⁂

HE HAD TO TOUCH EVERY PART OF ME, AND I HIM—EVERY nick and scar, every evidence of past hurt and sorrow. He lay back on his bed and carried me with him, and there was a moment when the end of my stump brushed the soft, curled hair on his chest and I pulled away.

"No," he whispered, drawing me back. "See yourself as I see you."

He ran his hand down the phantom outline of my arm, and it lit up in spirals of red and blue light. As the light spread from my missing arm to the rest of me, the red shaded out of it, leaving only blue and then a bright white. When he touched my phantom fingers, the light flared and lit the room, then faded to a soft glow he held in his hands.

And for a moment, a few hours of darkness, tangled there in the sheets with him, I was as whole as I had ever been.

CHAPTER 23

I WOKE TO THE SOUND OF POTTERY ON A TABLETOP AND THE strong light of a well-developed morning. Outside, birds and insects chittered in the trees. Distantly, blades clashed and someone shouted, *Move your ass, greenie, unless you want a ride on this pole!*

I barely remembered Arsenault easing his arm from around me as he rose. Now he sat on the bed dressed in his regular clothes and his burgundy armband. His black hair gleamed wetly in the morning sun, the light streak a tidy strip that pulled back from his temple and hooked over his ear.

He smiled. "I brought you breakfast."

He'd set a plate of food on his worktable for me. He must have been to the big house, because the plate was full of buns, figs, and nectarines. Next to the plate he placed a steaming mug of coffee.

I pulled the sheet up over my breasts and tried to wrap it around me as I sat up. "Didn't the kitchen girls wonder why you were taking such a late breakfast back to your room? I'll be behind on my chores, and Utîl will be looking for me."

"You're due a day of leave."

"What did you tell Utîl?"

CHAPTER 23

"I told him I was back, and he didn't ask any questions."

It was difficult to wrap yourself in a sheet one-handed. Arsenault leaned forward and took the end from me, finishing the wrap and tucking it in at my side. I looked up at him and he at me, and I blushed and felt awkward.

Were we still the same people after a night together? What did one say to a man upon awakening in his bed?

Cassis and I had never made love in a bed. Only in secret, illicit places, as quickly as we could. We'd torn at each other's clothes, bruising our lips with the force of our kisses, fucking each other with the reckless abandon of the young and rebellious. But that's all it had been: fucking. Maybe it was something we'd both needed, until Geoffre persuaded his son to navigate our relationship into more treacherous channels. Or maybe it was just my own version of running away like a princess in a fairy story.

But this was Arsenault. He wasn't a boy, and though a small voice in my head urged caution, knowing he was a spy working the murky depths of loyalties, I refused to listen to it. Not with the sun spilling through the beech trees, dappling the floor with patterns of light and dark.

He remained watching me, a hopeful yet half-afraid expression in his eyes.

I laughed anxiously. "I hardly know what to say to you now."

A smile, somewhat embarrassed, flitted across his own lips. "It does seem...different," he agreed.

I took a slice of fig from the plate. "Surely that isn't the way of all relationships. As soon as a man and a woman take a tumble, they cease to talk to each other as if they were the same people. They've instead got roles. Lovers. Man and wife."

I slid the piece of fig into my mouth and picked up the coffee, regarding him over the rim of the cup.

Arsenault frowned thoughtfully as he carved a nectarine into pieces with his knife, then leaned against the wall to eat one of the dripping slices. "No. I remember my mother and father having many long conversations. They were friends more than anything. I think they grew more pleased by each other's company as time went on, not less."

"Was their marriage arranged?"

He shrugged. "I think so. But we came from a small place. They'd known each other since they were children."

"Tell me about them, then. Did you grow up in a great house or a hut? Did you have nursemaids, or—"

He snorted in the middle of eating his nectarine, then laughed. "Nursemaids. Dear gods, no. Our house was small by your standards, but my father built good ships. Men respected him. He had men who worked for him. My mother was able to hire a cook."

"So, your mother...she was responsible for raising you?"

"When my father was at sea. In order to cut timber for ships, he had to sail to the mainland. There weren't many trees on our island. He and his men would lash the logs together into rafts and drag them back. But in the winter, ice locked us in and he stayed home and built boats. And we went ice fishing."

He got a faraway look in his eyes and smiled. "Gods, that was cold. I remember huddling around the fires with my spear in the dark and thinking my toes would shatter if I tried to stand up. The men kept themselves warm with liquor, but I was too young for that."

A shadow of regret passed over his face, so quickly had I not been watching him, I never would have seen it.

"Why did you fish at night?" I asked.

That hook of a smile came out on his mouth, and to my relief, the sadness disappeared. He chuckled. "We didn't. Or—in the north, winter is night, and night is winter. The sun goes to sleep a little more every day in the fall until midwinter, when it only peeks above the horizon for a brief moment around midday. But this time of year..." He smiled and leaned past me to purloin another slice of nectarine. "The sun never goes to bed. It's just one long, never-ending day."

I wrinkled my nose. "That sounds exhausting. Think how much work there would be to do."

His smile grew easier and his laughter a little deeper. "My mother used to say the same thing. I think she was joking, but then we all noticed that some nights, she hung the curtains very early. I always remember her wielding her spoon like a sword." He demonstrated with an imaginary spoon, making feints at his worktable. "*To bed, you heathens! Little humans are not bears; if you stay up all summer, you won't be able to make it up in the wintertime.*"

He leaned back against the wall again, smiling ruefully. "You can't imagine the bitter wailing we set up. People were still talking and laughing outside the window."

I laughed too. "How many of you were there?"

"Five. Three older sisters. And—" His voice stuttered suddenly, and when he recovered, the happiness had gone out of it. "One brother. A younger brother."

His eyes looked hollow. He put the slice of nectarine in his mouth slowly. A cold wind seemed to have reached in the window, in spite of the summer sun.

I set my coffee cup down. "You know, I only meant I want you to treat me the same as you've always treated me. I want to wear trousers in the hall and keep learning to use a sword."

He looked up at me as if I'd pulled him out of a dream. His brows lowered in puzzlement. "Why wouldn't you?"

I'd never seen him look as baffled.

I started to laugh. "Forgive me, Arsenault. Truly, it's good to have you back."

The baffled look gave way to a smile. Not the familiar, slight hook of his mouth but a true smile. It transformed his face, crinkling the corners of his eyes, easing the violence of his scar. I watched him in fascination, but looking at his mouth only made me want to kiss him.

So, I put my breakfast down and crawled over to him and I did.

He wrapped his arm around me and reached up to fumble

the shutters closed with the other. And then he laid me down amid the remains of breakfast, and we allowed the day to grow later together.

❦

Afternoon saw me dressed in my trousers with the leather sheath of my knife cold against the skin of my hip, riding past the edge of my father's property to see a woman about some conjure-magic.

Her name was Isia, and Verrin's woman, Etti, told me about her. Etti always walked into the barracks wearing a toddler on her back and a baby in a sling on her front, leaving her hands free to hold on to the older two, a boy and a girl. When they caught sight of Verrin, they would bolt away from their mother and leap into his arms.

One day, I was standing in the hall when she came in, and while Verrin allowed his older two children to climb him like a tree, I helped Etti get her toddler down.

"Ohh," she said, as she put her hands to the small of her back and stretched. "He's getting so big. I'll have to let him walk soon, but I don't have enough hands!"

I bounced her little boy on my hip and made a funny face at him. He giggled and threw his head backward, his black curls bobbing like springs, and then snapped it back up so I would make the face again.

"One of the older two could hold on to him," I said, wrinkling my face up at her son again. "You could make a chain."

"I suppose we'll have to." Etta sat down on a bench and began unlacing her guarnello so the baby could nurse. "My moonblood's back, so I imagine Verrin and I will have to have a discussion soon. The midwife thought I ought to have a little extra time after Zellie. Her birth was so hard. It took me a while to get around again."

I let her little boy down to run to his papa. "What will you use?" I asked.

"Use?" she said, cocking an eyebrow at me. "I'll tell Verrin he has to stay away from me for a while, is what I'll do. And then I'll do my best to watch my cycles after that until I feel stronger."

"Isn't that risky, though?"

"Well," she said, and I noted the way she darted a glance at my empty sleeve, "everything has its risks, doesn't it? I'd rather risk having a child than the effects of those herbs or conjure-magic spells. I mean, a child isn't really a *risk*, is he? A risk is just a fear and a child's...a child."

"And you're not afraid..."

She sighed. "Well, of course, Kyrra. I'm tired and it was a hard labor last time. Sometimes, it goes badly. But you can't live your life *assuming* it will go badly, can you?"

"I suppose not."

She laughed. "You sound skeptical."

I didn't want to tell her how frightening my miscarriage had been, how I had lain in bed and prayed for the potion not to work and to work at the same time. How was it possible to want such opposite outcomes simultaneously? Perhaps I had once lived my life as boldly as she did, but no longer.

Etti rearranged her guarnello over the curve of breast the baby had exposed when she moved.

"Some of the girls in the shop see Isia," she said. "She lives just beyond your father's boundaries on the high road. Her magic seems better than most, but it's still twisty. Better off if you've a reliable man who'll give you an oath."

She gave me a hard glance, and I knew she was talking about Arsenault.

It had been easy to ignore her when I wasn't sharing his bed. But when Arsenault left me to dress, the worry I'd been shoving away suddenly overtook me. I had been lax in counting days when I lay with Cassis, only sixteen years old and expecting to be married to him. Since I had become kinless and knew worse food and more work, my courses had grown more irregular and it was harder to predict which part of my cycle I was in. But usually, my courses came within a week of the full moon.

How many more days would I have to wait to know if I was pregnant with Arsenault's child? And what would I do if I was?

I didn't want to think about it. I didn't want to avoid his bed after this, and if I was being honest, I knew that if I was pregnant this time, it *would* be different.

But war was pressing down on us. Just thinking of Etti and all her little ones brought a pain to my heart, and I resolved to tell her—or Verrin—that she ought to think about packing up and moving on if she could.

I didn't know how Arsenault would feel about what I was doing. So, I didn't tell him.

The shadows had begun to lengthen along the road by the time I reached the stand of trees at the edge of our lands. I slid off the bay mare I'd ridden to Liera, and looped the reins around the forked trunk of a hawthorn. A door banged and a woman came out, shading her eyes with her hand and looking in my direction. I waved to her and started up the path, and she put her hands to her hips.

I had expected an ancient, warty strega of the kind who turned up in stories to cast love spells for maidens locked in towers. But this woman was my mother's age, her thick black hair streaked with long, wiry gray strands and pulled back in a knot at the nape of her neck. She wore a clean, cream-colored apron stitched with red birds and green tree branches, and a simple brown dress beneath it. Only her hands showed that she might be older than she looked. Her fingers were bent, knuckles protruding like the mountain ridges that loomed behind us in the summer haze.

"Bona giurn," I called out. "Are you Isia?"

She eyed me cannily, out of eyes the color of clover honey, and I began to feel as if I were naked and she could see through me.

"Bona giurn," she replied. "Who are you?"

It had been a long time since I'd been around anyone who didn't know me. I never had to say my name since becoming kinless except for *Kyrra*, and whoever had asked me could generally fill in the rest.

"Kyrra," I said. "Kyrra No-Name."

"Everyone has a name, Kyrra No-Name, and so do you."

"But I'm not allowed to use mine."

She squinted at me. "Ah. Well. You'll have to find another. I know who you used to be, but some of us live more than once. Why have you come to see me?"

I flushed, suddenly embarrassed to say the nature of my errand. "I come to see you for the same reason many women see you."

"Do you, now? I'd have thought you'd have learned your lesson."

The flush in my cheeks became a flame. "I have learned my lesson. I've learned not to leave myself in the hands of herb women. Anyway, I'm already fallen and I can do what I like. Nobody's going to fight over the bastard of a gavaro."

"Depends on the gavaro, I imagine," she said, her mouth twisting. "Are you with child?"

"I hoped you could tell me."

She cocked her head. Then she bent and put one gnarled hand on my belly, just above my navel. Warmth stretched through me, like the tendrils of a plant growing toward the sun. I squirmed and she lifted her hand away.

"No. You're not pregnant. You're due for your moonblood in the next few days. An auspicious time for stupidity."

"Stupidity?"

"You can't go around making yourself miscarry every time, you know. Regardless of what it does to the child, think of what it does to your heart. And one day, a babe will latch on like rose thorns and refuse to give you up. You're still fertile."

I balanced myself as if I was ready to deliver a dagger thrust and gazed straight at her. "That's why I came to you," I said. "So that I would no longer have to worry about my fertility."

Lines appeared on her face, making her look as if she'd aged before me. She twisted the edge of her apron in her hands.

"That's why they all come to me, isn't it?" She turned back toward her hut and shuffled toward the door. Without turning around, she said, "Well, come, if you're that eager for it. I'll not ask twice."

※

The hut had no windows. The only light flooded in through the door when she opened it. The grass smell of the thatch roof mingled with the scents of drying herbs and dirt floor to make the room smell like a meadow. A stone fireplace was built onto the far wall of the hut, and in it lay cold black ashes. She took a poker down off the wall and nudged the pile. Hot red embers turned over with the rake of the hook. She pushed them away, then bent and picked up a piece of charcoal. Dust crumbled from it, sprinkling the hearth like pepper.

"This is not something to enter into lightly," she said, gripping the charcoal. She leaned on the poker, and its point sank into the dirt. "This is not like drinking a goblet full of a potion."

"It's not *easy* to drink a potion, and I won't do it again. If that was all you were offering, I wouldn't be here."

"But do you know what you ask?"

"Etti said you could make me barren. For a while. So no seed could take root in the first place."

"Magic isn't precise. It reworks us in its own fashion. Sometimes, we can't predict the outcomes, so I don't know if your barrenness would be 'for a while' or instead 'forever.'" She leaned closer to me. "If I write these marks on your body and invite the magic to move through you...there is a possibility that you will never have a child. Ever. And there may come a day when you're older, that you will long for the touch of a small hand in yours and a fuzzy head tucked under your chin."

"Maybe one day I will," I said. "When that day comes, maybe magic will move me the other way. But for now...I'm picking up a warrior's life, and a warrior's life is no place for a child. There will be battles, and—" My throat burned as I realized that in spite of myself, I would go wherever Arsenault wanted me to, if he asked it of me. I swallowed. "Well, you see how I've performed my duties to my House. A gavaro's life will suit me."

"You think becoming a gavaro will leave you no consequences? That you'll develop no ties? No loyalties? It's to be you and you alone, is it?"

"A child needs more than I can give. I haven't the knowledge or the ability to take care of a child, and you said yourself it's only a possibility that I'll be barren forever."

She waved her hand in the air. "Possibilities, possibilities. They flutter here and there, like birds. You must know what you risk before you risk it, Kyrra. I tell everyone the same. Maybe you weren't fit to be a lady, but how can you ever be a man? Just because you wear trousers and carry that knife?"

The blood drained from my face. How was she able to tell that I carried a knife? I had made sure my trousers were baggy enough to hide it.

"If you want to refuse me, just say so."

One of her eyebrows hitched. "Did I say I would refuse you? The decision comes from here." She reached forward and touched my chest with one of her knobby fingers, just above my breast where my heart pounded. "What puts you most at risk is what you truly wish for, inside yourself." She leaned back, putting both hands on the handle of the poker. "I facilitate the flow of the magic—I conjure the channels that exist within you. But you are the gatekeeper. You've got a lot of magic already swirling inside you, but this is the magic of the body, of wishes. Some of these wishes are our hearts singing to us; some of them are just the songs of others echoing in our emptiness. Be sure which yours are before you lie down on my floor."

Her speech was too well done to be a serf.

But what did I really wish for?

I could keep myself to myself and stay out of Arsenault's bed. He would teach me daggers and the war would come, and...what would happen then? To any of us?

I could not think beyond that point. The future was a hazy place, like the blue strip that wavered just out of sight on the horizon. I could never reach the horizon, so why did I think I would reach the future?

I stepped forward. The hut was small, but now I was standing in the circle of Isia's presence, across that line that separates one person from another. "I will lie on your floor," I said, quietly, "and you will mark me. Only tell me what price I have to pay."

She held my gaze for a moment, her honey eyes like hardened amber. "I will take a price," she said. "But I won't name it yet. If you promise to pay my price, then I'll mark you."

"How am I to know if your price is fair? In all the fairy stories, the price *is* the child. Is that the way magic works?"

"Who knows the way magic works. If you should ever bear a child, I won't take it from you. Will you promise me or not?"

I saw myself sitting in a hut much like this one, my belly swelling like a ripe pear, and the armies of the Prinze marching up the Eterean road from Liera.

"I'll pay your price," I said, and knelt on the floor at her feet. "Go ahead; mark me."

※

THE COLD CHARCOAL WAS A FLAME ON MY NAKED BELLY. IT left a black burn in its wake as Isia drew her strange, looping designs. Contractions rippled over my stomach, but I only gave birth to pain.

My right arm was on fire when I left. Isia asked me to stay the night, to recover, but I knew Arsenault would be out looking for me when he should be roping Lobardin back into line or knocking some respect back into everyone.

I thought maybe I was beginning to realize why Jon was the man in charge. Arsenault wouldn't have made a good prince.

I scrabbled up onto the mare in the purple twilight, and Isia watched me go. She stood, a dark silhouette with her back to the sun before the wind-waving trees—no doubt thinking how much a fool I was to be abroad so late, when I wouldn't reach the barracks until after dark.

But these were my father's lands, and I had lately begun to feel more at home with the darkness. It made me jumpy in a way that tingled my skin. The wind tangled my hair and made it hard to see, but I ran the mare anyway, less in any desire to be back quickly than for the sheer joy of running.

I thought I would fall off at any moment. And that was part of the pleasure of it. It was almost the same as bedding the son of a merchant House on the floor of the conservatory. I wondered how much of my desire had been sparked by any sort of desire for Cassis.

It was full dark when I finally clattered into the stable yard. After I finished taking care of the horse, I walked back to the barracks in the moonlight and slid quiet into our empty room.

The charcoal lines were still imprinted on my skin when I clumsily unlaced my sweat-soaked shirt and worked it off over my head. They had bled black through the white fabric and I spread the shirt out on my bed and stared at their blurry outlines, in the moonlight that spilled through the open window.

The door creaked open and Arsenault came in.

For a moment, he just looked at me. Then he said, softly. "You went to a conjure-woman."

"It's for the best, Arsenault."

Hesitantly, he stepped toward me. He raised his hands as if to touch me but stopped just short of it. He bent his head and let his gaze skim the lines written on my belly. My skin tingled. I felt the urge to cover myself, but I didn't.

"Conjure-magic is wild," he said.

"It's what my mother should have used."

His brows pulled together. "She didn't? It's woman's magic."

"The herb woman made me a potion. It was different."

He was quiet a moment. Then he said, "It's not my province to ask after such things."

"It would be your child."

He wetted his lips. "Did you not want—"

"That wasn't why I did it, Arsenault. But now is not the time for me to bear children."

"I shouldn't have taken you to bed."

"Do you think this whole affair depends on you? Lobardin says you've sworn yourself to the Prinze and have only been seducing me; is that the way of it?"

Anger rolled over Arsenault's face. "Do you honestly think—"

"Of course not."

He closed his mouth hard on whatever he'd been going to say. The anger eased, but tension still strung his shoulders.

"Your name should have something to do with *nettle*, Kyrra."

Then his shoulders slumped.

"Jon put Lobardin up here so I could keep my eye on him, and Pallo sends me back into Liera for two months. Lobardin ought to hate Geoffre, but..." He turned slightly away, as if embarrassed to say what came next. "Geoffre has a way of using people."

I sat down on the bed and wrapped the shirt around my shoulders. "And how did he use Lobardin?"

"I don't know all the details. But I worry..." He brought his gaze around to hold mine. "Geoffre is coming for Fortune's Night and your father's wedding feast. I can't be here when they are."

I stared at him, unable to comprehend the words he'd just

spoken.

"Geoffre is coming here?"

He nodded. He didn't come to sit on the bed next to me. I sat there alone, staring at my charcoal-blackened fingers resting in my lap, the mass of black thorns that adorned my belly.

"Did my father invite him?"

"He couldn't refuse him."

"Who is Geoffre bringing with him?"

"His wife. Devid, Devid's wife. Their oldest daughter." He paused. "Camile. Cassis."

I rubbed my black fingers together. Then I laughed. A worn-out laugh, without much breath behind it. "I should have known."

"I'll be gone, Kyrra. You could be too."

"Where will you go?"

"You could be farther away."

"You're lying. You'll be there, in disguise." I glanced up at him. "Will you kill him?"

He sighed and sat down beside me. The bed shifted with his weight and his thigh brushed mine. "Geoffre or Lobardin, do you mean?"

I pulled my shirt tighter around me, staring at my boots. "Either, I suppose. I expected you to kill Lobardin a long time ago. What does Lobardin have that is so valuable? Didn't he tell Jon all he knew?"

"Lobardin has a certain...value to Geoffre. Call him a hook. Or maybe bait. Our greatest danger is that he will wriggle himself off."

I looked up at Arsenault in confusion. "Geoffre took Lobardin as a lover?" I asked. I'm sure the bewilderment showed on my face. Not that Geoffre wouldn't take a kacin-addled gavaro for a lover, but that anything might hinge upon it.

"Not precisely. Geoffre's main interest these days lies in the magical."

Arsenault rose and paced to his worktable, where he bent to

pull out the bottle of brandy from his chest. He uncorked it and drank, then held it out to me. I rose and took it from him.

The shirt slipped down my shoulders and I couldn't catch it while holding the brandy. I had almost forgotten I was naked. But I remembered when Arsenault's brows lifted and his gaze tracked warm down my body.

I lifted the bottle to my lips and drank anyway. The brandy burned sweet and hot as it slid down my throat and into my belly. Trust Arsenault to favor a liquor that felt like molten gold.

I put the bottle on the table. Arsenault handed me the shirt and I adjusted it over my shoulders again. "So, Lobardin might betray you to gain his own escape. That's what you're risking, aren't you. You need to be here to see that Lobardin does what you and Jon want, and not what Lobardin wants."

Arsenault's silence stretched out a long moment. He turned away from me and stared at the shutters that barred the window.

I'd remembered.

"You could leave tomorrow, Kyrra," he said. "You could use the wooden arm."

"You said yourself that arm is dead. Will you let Jon treat me like Lobardin?"

He took my chin in his hand, tipping it upward so I had no choice but to meet his gaze.

"I will never betray you to Geoffre di Prinze," he said. "Or anyone. I have made that mistake before."

I was a startled bird he held in his hands. I wanted to ask what mistake he'd made, when he had made it—if he had made it with a woman. Jealousy flared inside me, irrationally, turning the charcoal lines on my belly to glowing embers.

He put his mouth down on mine, and his kiss swallowed all my thoughts and fears. His hand swept over the flesh of my stomach, and the black lines rubbed off on his hand. Every touch of his fingers became a pinprick of desire.

But still I wanted to know—what mistake?

Whom had he betrayed?

CHAPTER 24

Mikelo and I walk the road to Karansis for four days, joining now and again with small groups of pilgrims. Every face seems to be Arsenault's before I look at it closely, every crunching footstep his boots on the path until I turn around. But the world goes on as it always has. Spring unfurls around us as we walk. By the time we arrive in Karansis, groves of wild plums wave pink flowers at the ends of their slim branches, and bowers of white cherry blossoms lose petals in the wind like snowflakes.

It would be easier to enjoy the beauty if there weren't so many people. Karansis is like a spider with roads coming out of it like legs. Down them ride jangling groups of men on horseback—householders from Liera, Amora, Consel, even as far away as Onzarro—to seek vitality in this, the season of youth. Mikelo flips his hood up, and I wish I had some of Jon's magic, whatever it is that lets him slide by unnoticed.

The town of Karansis sprawls at the headwaters of the river Ransi. Ransi's story begins as a youth, when he caught the eye of Tekus, father of the gods. A beautiful youth with hair the color of a raven's wing and eyes the silver-green of olive leaves, Ransi's destiny was unfortunately to be the object of everyone's infatuation. When Tekus saw him, he turned himself into a spring and swept Ransi away, down to his undersea realm, where he hid the boy from his wife. Of course, this situation could not go on forever. Tekus' wife Ahra was experienced in her husband's bad behavior and soon discovered Ransi. She had him cast out naked on the beach, where he was stolen by pirates and sold to a jealous merchant who became convinced that Ransi had betrayed him with *his* wife. The merchant killed him on what would later become known as Murderer's Ridge, within sight of Ransi's home. The hill is covered in big, black basalt murder markers, for Ransi and all the youths who lost their lives at the hands of jealous lovers.

Now the murder markers stand for battles fought and lost. The area surrounding Karansis saw heavy fighting, since it borders both Aliente and Caprine holdings. Arsenault might even have fought here, though I don't know for certain that he did. But it's possible that the town is full of men who might recognize him, who fought not against him but on the same side in the wars.

Ransi's own story had a somewhat better ending than that of my family. Bereft at Ransi's death, Tekus bestowed on him eternal youth, in the form of the thin ribbon of silver water which tumbles from the base of the hills. From here, the Ransi flows down crags and through gorges to hurl itself spectacularly into the sea from the cliffs at Iffria. Men come to bathe in its water, here at the source and in the fall at Iffria, asking the god to grant them Ransi's vitality, and then they go home to make children with their wives. The women who come to Karansis are mostly looking for work, but there are a lot of men, and a lot of jangling metal and horses.

The night before we come into Karansis, I trade my silk dress to a serf girl for her plain gray clothes, and we enter the village in a big group of Conseli householders wearing cloaks with patches of sienna, gold, and emerald. We keep our heads down and the men don't notice a young man and a serf girl on foot. They can't see my sword. It's under my cloak.

"Could we at least have a bed tonight?" Mikelo asks once we're in the city.

I finger the coins sewn into my skirt. "Supper, I think. And new supplies. But I'm afraid the bed will have to wait."

"Does it do us any good to sleep on the road? We're not getting there any faster."

"I'll see if I can find some horses."

The marketplace is full of horses. They crowd the narrow paths between the stalls and tents of lesser merchants, jostling each other, turning the courtyard into a slick mess of trampled dirt and manure. Not a gelding among them, and certainly not any mares. This is about male vitality, not sensibility. Stallions are foul-tempered and bite and kick at the slightest provocation. Two men begin shouting at each other over the behavior of their horses. I expect to see steel drawn, but one of the men makes a rude gesture at the other and rides off through a hole left in the general mass.

The whole place stinks of horseshit.

"We'll hide better if we stay away from the inns. The road from here out belongs mostly to shepherds. People say the dead walk the other sites."

Mikelo makes a face. "I don't fancy waking any ghosts," he says as he scans the rowdy glut of vibrantly painted stalls in the bazaar, lit by the flare of torches in the deepening twilight. A queasy conglomeration of smells blows past on the wind—horse and manure, sizzling lamb, roasted onions and garlic, the faint whiff of bread.

He looks back to me. "Where will we 'find' these horses?"

"There might be a bargain at an inn's stable."

I shift my pack and slide my arm around his to keep him close in this milling crowd, pressing down on his forearm with the fingers of my right hand. He places his hand absently atop mine.

"Where did they all come from?" he asks.

"Three main roads lead to Karansis; ours is only one of them. Some follow the river itself. There's a path along the ridgeline big enough for a line of horses if they ride single-file."

"I suppose you know the inns, then, if you've been this way before?" He watches the ground with concentration to avoid the horse droppings. At the edges of the throng, shovelers wearing Imisi green and yellow toss the day's load into wheelbarrows to carry off as fertilizer for their olives.

"They're all near the spring."

"You're an only child," he says thoughtfully, clearly trying to understand why my family would visit Karansis.

"Yes. My mother had pregnancies, though. She wasn't truly barren."

"So, the spring helped your father?"

"As much as it helps anyone, I suppose. My mother had four miscarriages." I pause. "And one stillbirth. A boy."

"Are you first or last?"

"First."

My mother said I must have spoiled her womb. The midwife pulled me out in a torrent of blood. It stained the tiles of her bedchamber so badly, my father had to have them cut out and replaced. She was confined to her bed for weeks with fever.

"I'm my mother's only child too," Mikelo says.

The inns crowd together where the dirt of the marketplace gives way to brick roads and red-tiled roofs. I choose the one on the end, farthest away from the inn where I stayed as a child. The Beautiful Youth looks as if it might cater to a somewhat lesser clientele.

I let Mikelo walk up the rickety wood steps first. He opens the door and I step past him into the room.

Two big windows on the far wall give a good view of the midden. The spring is invisible in the dim light except for the bobbing of candle flames like fireflies that mark its course. Votas of Tekus and Ransi line the common room, for sale if you've got

CHAPTER 24

the coin. The little statues seem to be keeping watch over the patrons.

Three of five big trestle tables are occupied, and the men who eat there joke noisily with each other and the "beautiful youths" who serve them—both male and female.

Mikelo leans down and murmurs, "Shall we choose another inn?"

I smile because the innkeeper has seen us—a middle-aged woman in a modestly cut scarlet wool dress, wiping her flour-speckled hands on a towel. "No," I say. "This one will do."

He stiffens, but smiles tightly when the innkeep approaches us.

"Loosen up," I whisper.

"Have a seat," she says, giving me a skeptical smile as she eyes my clothes. "We don't see many women in here, but I'm sure if the lady and gentleman prefer—"

"We won't be needing a room," I say. "Just supper."

She raises her eyebrow. "Well, then, you're free to sit wherever you like. But I'd ask you not to dawdle if we fill up. If you're only having supper, we may need the room."

"Fair enough. But..." I hesitate for a moment as if unsure of myself, rattling the coins in my pocket. "We should both like to look."

"Ah." She smiles, more genuinely. "Then you can see that, in spite of our humble surroundings, I only employ the finest-looking youths in Karansis. Some families trace their origins all the way back to Ransi."

"Of course." I tug at Mikelo's arm. "Come, brother. Let us enjoy our dinner."

I lead him over to a table. He sits down and leans forward, whispering at me, "What do you think you're doing? Couldn't we eat in a respectable establishment?"

"You're in Karansis. All the establishments are like this. This one's just cheap."

He stops and looks around. "They're all like this?"

I roll my eyes. "The town's founded on the quest for male vitality. If you were any stiffer, Mikelo, you'd be cast in bronze."

"I think you just enjoy tormenting me."

"It provides me some amusement, I must admit."

He flushes. Then he says, "I think you're lying to me. Why would a father bring his daughter to this town?"

"Because it was a good place to stop over on our way to Iffria. We didn't eat in the common room. The servants brought our supper straight upstairs."

Before he can continue our conversation, a server strides up to stand at his elbow, a slender young man with a clean chin and long ale-colored curls. The kind of man I'm often taken for. He leans past Mikelo's shoulder to speak to us, and Mikelo jerks away from him.

"I'm sorry, sir," the server says. "I didn't mean to startle you."

"It's all right," Mikelo says, forcing a smile. "I was just watching the devotees out the window."

"Ah." The server smiles, but it doesn't light up his eyes, which are almost the color of twilight. "Yes. Devotions are carried on at all hours. Will the sir be attending any tonight?"

Mikelo glances at me. "No. I think we'll just be moving on. After supper."

"Shall I waste my time, then?"

I laugh. "You might earn an extra coin or two."

The server smiles. "One earns one's living."

"One does," I agree. I lay some catos on the table. "We'll eat what that brings us and take some hard food from your stores. And send a woman over here to wait on my brother. He needs his vitality restored."

"Don't they all," the server says with a sardonic smile as he slides the coins into his upturned palm. He bows when I chuckle, then turns and walks away.

"I don't wish a woman to wait on us, either," Mikelo whispers when he's gone. "I don't wish anything."

"You're a man, aren't you? Act like one."

CHAPTER 24

Mikelo grits his teeth. "I am acting like a *householder*. It doesn't do for us to consort with whores. All that produces is kinless bastards."

I raise an eyebrow. "You shouldn't speak so about your mother."

He half-rises, the color in his face telling me that for once, I've struck deep. Then he sits down. "I forget who you are sometimes."

I tap the index finger of my right hand on the table, and the metallic *ting* it makes is muffled but unmistakable. Mikelo pales at the reminder. "It won't do to forget that."

Then the door opens and a man comes in.

Tall. Plain brown cloak, hood up, the tip of a scabbard barely visible at its hem. Not so different from all the other men I've seen today.

The innkeeper smiles as she offers him a table. He bends from the shoulders to speak to her.

"What are you watching?" Mikelo whispers.

"Nothing," I say.

The innkeeper gestures at the room. The man turns his head imperceptibly. Dammit, I still can't see his face.

"You *are* watching someone," Mikelo says, turning in his chair.

"I told you before, I'm not likely to let Geoffre's men sneak up on me."

"Is it that man, in the brown cloak?"

"I'm just keeping an eye on who's going in and out."

"He's coming this way now."

The man in the cloak sweeps away from the innkeeper, toward us. He keeps his head down until he puts his hand on the back of Mikelo's chair.

Mikelo comes half out of his seat, looking at the cloaked man in fright. But then the man tilts his head upward.

It's Arsenault. It really is Arsenault this time.

I feel like I don't have enough air.

The hood of his cloak shadows his face, and he looks so strange without the break in his nose and the scar. It's like the lost memories in his mind have erased the memories that should exist on his body.

"Andris," Mikelo breathes.

It was supposed to be me and Arsenault on the road, where it would be easy to see if he had led Geoffre's spies to me or if he had followed me only to protect Mikelo. Or if he followed me for some other reason I daren't even hope for, sitting in this inn. But the fact he chose to reveal himself here and not sooner tells me something I'd hoped would be different.

I'm going to have to be careful now. Careful and determined.

Before we left the bathhouse, it seemed as if he might have begun to recognize me. I don't know how his magic works or if it's anything like mine. But if it is, and if the memories of me are in the magic, then what he needs is to be pushed.

To be pushed, hard.

Mikelo sits back down, but Arsenault doesn't even look at him. "You left him free."

"He seemed to think I was a better choice than Geoffre," I say.

"And you trust him so far?"

"He hasn't run yet. Have you, Mikelo?"

"If my uncle truly wanted me back, I think he would have found a way to kill you," Mikelo says.

"Well? Did he send you to kill me?"

Arsenault sits down in the empty seat next to Mikelo. "My orders are still the same—to protect Mikelo and make sure you do what Geoffre wants."

"And did you bring Geoffre's spies along with you?"

"No. I'm alone."

"They're probably waiting outside."

"You would've been able to track a group following you on the road, wouldn't you?"

"Which road did you come?"

CHAPTER 24

"The same as you."

"You always did let people jump to their own conclusions. There's more than one road."

"You disembarked in Cales," he says, leaning back in his chair so he can cross his arms over his chest and stretch his legs out. "Traveled up the coast road to Karansis. You've been keeping Mikelo tied up at night but otherwise not. You traded that rose-colored dress last night for a serf girl's skirt."

Dear gods, he's been watching me sleep.

How could he track me like that, so silently? Anxiety sings through me and the magic shoves at me like someone trying to force open a door.

I struggle to push the magic back. I have to keep my head for this.

"Did you follow us from Liera?" I ask.

"I—" he starts, and then his voice dies.

"You didn't, did you?" I say in triumph. "You knew that I would come this way even though no one thinks it makes any sense."

"The hills will have snow."

"The only reason you know the hill road is harder is because you remember riding up it. You know all the routes to my father's hunting lodge because you've been there before."

He drops his arms onto the table and leans forward, gritting his teeth. "I studied them on a map," he says. "I could figure out about the snow, and I didn't think you would be an idiot."

"Why not?" I say, as innocently as I can.

"Because—dammit, *are* you an idiot?"

"*Have* you led Geoffre's spies to us?"

"No!" His tone is low but urgent. Then he drags in a big breath. "He has them out, though."

"What kind of spies?'

"What do you mean, *what kind of spies?*" Mikelo says. "Is there more than one kind of spy?"

"That Geoffre could use? Of course."

The serving girl sets down a pitcher of wine on the table between us. Her eyes are painted in the style of the cheaper courtesans, with little flakes of glittering mica embedded in a paste of ochre. It gives them a swollen look, which is probably meant to be alluring.

"Your food will be out shortly," she says, smiling at Mikelo. "You're in luck; tonight, we're serving roast fowl with pandieti, the little noodles, and it will be coming to you hot. You've arrived at just the right time."

She turns her smile on Arsenault now, clearly sizing him up as a better patron. Or maybe just a better-looking one.

"Will you be eating, too, ser? Staying the night or going on?"

"We should stay the night," he says, looking not at the girl but at me.

"No," I tell him. "We'll be moving on."

He lays a few coins on the table. "For my supper," he says. Then he puts another down. "And for yourself."

She arches an eyebrow. "That isn't enough for entertainment, ser."

"I'm not asking for entertainment. I'm giving you a tip. For serving us. And letting us speak in private."

Now both her brows lift. "Oh," she says. "Of course." She leans over to collect the money from the table, and her breasts are right in his face. His gaze flicks downward, probably not even voluntarily. I reach in my pocket for more coins and catch her sleeve as she straightens up.

"Here," I say, pressing them into her hand. "Take these and give them to that pretty boy who met us when we came in, the one with the curls?"

"Silva?" she murmurs in surprise. "But—"

"Tell him *I* should like some entertainment."

"Kyrra!" Mikelo says. "What are you doing?"

"Hush," I tell him. "Maybe he'll give you some entertainment, too."

CHAPTER 24

I put on my best smile and let my hand trail down over the girl's sleeve as she walks away.

When I turn to face the men on the other side of the table, Mikelo is staring at me and Arsenault has two spots of red high on his cheekbones.

"You're just trying to devil me," he says.

"You might have been entertaining yourself while we were apart, but I didn't have the inclination or the opportunity. Well... that's not true. I did sometimes have the inclination, but I couldn't pursue the opportunity or I would have given myself away."

I smile at him sweetly. He's staring at me with his brows pulled down in that V over the bridge of his nose.

"So, I suppose now that it doesn't matter..."

Mikelo leans over and clamps his hand on my left wrist. "Kyrra, you said we were *leaving*."

"We are. I haven't paid him enough for a night. Yet."

Arsenault makes a rumbling noise. When I look at him, he's poured himself a glass of wine and is taking a long drink. A very long drink.

He sets the glass back on the table and swipes his arm across his mouth. "You're doing this to torment me."

"*Does* it torment you?"

"Why should I care how you keep yourself entertained, as long as it doesn't put Mikelo in danger?"

"You shouldn't. So, if I want a kiss with dinner..."

"I *told* you we should have eaten somewhere else," Mikelo says. "There must be somewhere decent in this town—"

"You could at least give me a chance to prove myself, mestere, before you go telling people I'm not decent."

The serving boy is standing behind Mikelo.

Mikelo shoves his chair back and stands up. The boy—he's not really a boy, I just can't help thinking of him that way—darts out of the way. Mikelo is left standing nose to nose with him.

They both look startled in that position, though the server recovers first.

"My sister wasn't clear..."

"It's me," I say, draping my right arm over the back of the chair. "I'm the one who wants you."

Silva looks down at me, bewildered.

I roll my eyes. "Isn't this how you men do it? You pay your money and receive your services."

"But—"

"But? I paid my money and now I want my services. Or are you going to toss me out for being a woman? In spite of the fact I've traded you coin?"

"Kyrra," Arsenault grinds out. "You're going to cause a scene."

"Nobody will even notice." I pat the empty seat on the other side of me. "Silva's your name, right? Come here."

For a moment, I'm not sure he'll cooperate. Maybe he doesn't want to be ordered around by a woman. Or maybe he's just tired of being a pawn in the dramas staged by householders with money. He looks away from me at the two men, his glance lingering on Arsenault for a moment too long—probably because Arsenault's expression has begun to edge toward the volcanic—but then he bows his head stiffly.

"All right." He slides around Mikelo and Arsenault, giving Arsenault a wide berth, and into the seat beside me.

I position myself where I can keep an eye on Arsenault. Then I lean over with my left hand on Silva's leg for balance and I run the fingers of my right hand up through his curls. I get a firm grip on the back of his head, and he looks at me in surprise. Up close, his blue eyes have rings so dark, they're almost black.

"Your hand," he says, not quite in a whisper.

"Shh," I say, and pull him down to kiss me.

In truth, it's been a long time since I've kissed anyone. But his lips are wooden on mine.

CHAPTER 24

"Really," I say, pulling back. "If that's how you kiss, I think you're going to be out of a job soon."

For a brief instant, his eyes snap. But then he glances over my shoulder at Arsenault.

"Well, if your man over there wasn't looking at me like that."

"He's just jealous I've got you all to myself."

Arsenault makes another noise I can't interpret and pours himself a second glass of wine.

Silva's brows pull down in a confused expression, like he's studying Arsenault but can't quite understand what he sees. A little twinge of uneasiness passes through the metal of my arm. Instead of stopping to consider it, I lift my metal hand to Silva's face and push it back in my direction.

"I'm the one who paid you, though, not him."

"To be fair, sera, I'm considering whether or not the money will be worth it."

I can't help laughing. "Ouch. That sword thrust made me bleed."

"Maybe you should leave off, then," Arsenault says.

"I meant, are you sure you're in a situation—" Silva begins.

"It's like you're daring me now," I say.

I reach out with both hands and pull Silva back toward me, pressing his mouth against my own. Once he gets over his initial shock and puts some effort into it, he's not a bad kisser, although he's still a little awkward. I'm sure it would be a better experience if we weren't both trying to keep an eye on Arsenault.

Arsenault's gaze is pinned to us and getting darker all the time. Mikelo looks like he's on fire from the inside.

All right, then. I paid for a little more than this.

I come up out of my seat, hooking my leg over Silva's and preparing to slide into his lap.

He fumbles me into a clumsy embrace.

The sounds of wood slamming onto the table and a splintering snap make us both look up.

Arsenault broke the stem of his cup. The bowl hits the table with a *thunk*, spilling wine everywhere. He and Mikelo jerk away from the table on one side, Silva and I on the other, all of us getting up out of our chairs.

Cursing, Arsenault grabs the end of his cloak and starts mopping up the puddle of wine, which spills over the edge of the table like a waterfall.

Silva draws his sleeve across his mouth but I just lick my lips.

I try to sound bored. "Watching affected you, did it?"

Arsenault looks up at me with an expression I can't describe. Anger, desire, jealousy, confusion...and an ache that makes me feel like I reached into his chest and squeezed his heart with my metal hand.

I can't do this. Dear gods. I can't do this.

But I must.

I turn to Silva. "I've more coin. What are your rates?"

Arsenault sweeps his cloak angrily over the table, splattering Mikelo with wine.

"Andris—" Mikelo begins.

Arsenault growls inarticulately.

"I didn't think you would care so much, Arsenault," I say. "You seemed to have a good relationship with many of the girls in the bathhouse."

"You like to stage dramas, don't you, Kyrra?" His gray eyes might as well be daggers.

"You're the one who thinks this is a drama."

"And was it the same with the whores? Vanni di Forza? I imagine you don't consider those events dramas, either."

"Were you going to kill me? Or no, wait. Geoffre wanted me alive, didn't he?"

He looks down at the red-soaked hem of the cloak in his hand. "I—I would have figured something out," he says.

"Surely, I don't matter. Vanni gave you an opportunity. You could have killed me and gotten Mikelo back."

He rubs the back of his hand across his brow. "Then Mikelo would have gone to Geoffre," he says.

CHAPTER 24

"But you're working for Geoffre," I say.

"I... No. Yes. But—Jon, I'm working for Jon."

Finally, some truth. I take a deep breath.

"And Madame Triente? Who is she working for?"

"Whoever will guarantee her best interests."

"Are you one of her best interests, Arsenault?"

He flinches and his eyes flicker toward Silva. "The Madame and I...have a relationship."

"Oh," I say, unable to hide the sarcasm in my voice. "A *relationship*. I'm sure that's different than me throwing a few coins at a serving boy. How much does she pay you?"

His chest heaves in and out. The flush comes up high on his cheeks again.

Dear gods. When I flung that spear, I didn't know how well it would hit.

He leans on the table with both hands. "It doesn't matter how much she paid me. She trusted me enough to get you out from under Vanni's orders, but instead, you blew a hole through his thigh. And then she found out you killed two of her whores upstairs, and she went right to Geoffre. He knows you don't intend to obey him now. I'm not sure Mikelo will even be a grant of safe haven"—he whirls to look at the room, his cloak swirling after him—"and gods damn you, Kyrra, there are too many people listening to us!"

There are. The men who were distracted by serving girls and boys are looking up at us. Silva watches us without the alarm or surprise I would have expected, maybe thinking about that name *Geoffre* in conjunction with all the things Arsenault accused me of doing. Courtesans are trained to keep secrets, but he doesn't look like he's had the same training. His cheeks are flushed.

We're in Karansis. Close to Aliente lands.

Another twinge sings through the metal of my arm.

The girl is coming back with the innkeeper, whose hands are white with flour dust. For a brief flash of a moment, I see my mother standing in my room, wiping her flour-dusted hands on a red towel that fluttered limply in the breeze, the ghost prints of her hands upon it waving to me as she told me, *Think*.

But then Arsenault comes close to me again, close enough that he can lean down and say quietly into my face, his words vibrating with the emotion that he seems to be keeping under wraps with iron bars. "You are going to get all of us killed."

I am not immune to emotion either. But my control isn't made of iron. The magic surges up in me and I shove him backward. It's just a reaction, one I can't help. He got too close. He stumbles, one step, then stares at me with his hand on his sword hilt.

"And how was I to know about this relationship?" I say. "I want to trust you, but how can I?"

The expression on his face is raw. But I still can't read it. He takes a quick step toward me with his hand on his sword, and the innkeeper shouts out behind him, "I'll have no trouble in my establishment! If you wish to accost the lady, do it outside."

I gather my resolve again. That stupid, reckless grin twists at my mouth. "Do you wish to accost me, Arsenault? If so, by all means, let us leave."

A fight would be honest, and I've had enough talking. To pit steel against steel, then we might know where we stand. If he'd cut me down, I want to find out so we can get it over with.

My heart beats so fast, it makes my breath come short.

Mikelo says, "Andris."

"Where did you go before Kafrin?" I say, steeling myself for this, too. "Did you go over to the Prinze then? That would have been like you, to stage everything until all the players were in their positions...and then abandon them at the last moment. Did you maneuver my father into that gorge, Arsenault? Did you abandon him in spite of everything I asked you?"

He's wrong about me and dramas. I'm no actor. It was supposed to be a ruse, to press him, but now it isn't. Now I just want to know.

He leans forward. "I don't *remember* what I did before Kafrin

CHAPTER 24

Gorge. I don't remember working for the Prinze or not working for them. All I know is what I am doing now, in this moment. If you wish it to be a fight—"

The innkeeper says, "Get out!"

"Gods, yes, Arsenault, I wish it to be a fight! I want to know who you are now. I want to know if you killed Vadz and shot Razi!"

The words rip out of me, but, gods, the look on his face.

He did it.

He was the assassin.

He whirls around and almost runs toward the door, the cloak smacking wet and red against his calves and the legs of chairs he knocks into as he goes. Men look up at him, but he doesn't stop. He shoves the door open and disappears into the night. The door slams after him, loud in the lull we've created.

I dart around the table and Mikelo grabs my arm. "Who are Vadz and Razi?"

I jerk away without answering. Mikelo comes after me.

The innkeeper shouts at her employees to get back to work.

"It's an argument," she shouts. "A simple argument. Keep your seats. Silva, back to work."

Silva hesitates, then jerks the towel out of his belt and throws it down on the table. "I'll be back in a moment."

"It's only a woman!" the serving girl calls out. "Silva!"

"No, Meli," he calls back. "It's him, it's finally him."

Silva's words almost don't register on me as I shove the door open with my right hand and clatter down the steps. Arsenault is nearly running down the street. I watch him veer into an alley, and I run to follow him, with Mikelo and Silva chasing after me.

Arsenault stands beside some crates, bent over, with his hands on his knees like he's been hit and now he's just trying to breathe.

"Go back inside," he tells Silva.

"No," Silva says, his voice taut with emotion. "I've been waiting for you ever since the Prinze burned our village and took our women. I vowed I'd never be caught so helpless again. I'd never let them take another woman."

I start to laugh, but it's right on the edge of crying. "Even the godscursed serving boy thinks he's got to protect me from you now. Why did you do it? Did Jon tell you to?"

Arsenault stays bent over, breathing hard.

"I knew Jon was lying—" I begin.

"It wasn't Jon!" Arsenault says, and stands up so suddenly, I take a step backward, dragging Silva with me.

"Then who—"

"It was me. I heard what you said to Tonia. I followed you."

I drop my hand from Silva's arm. "In the Night Market? And the silk warehouse? And—Razi?"

He nods.

"He lost his *arm*, Arsenault! I had to hold him down while they cut it off!"

"Oh, gods," Mikelo whispers behind me. Arsenault stares at me, his hand on the hilt of his sword, his face sheened with sweat.

"It *is* you, isn't it?" Silva says suddenly. "I wasn't sure when you walked in, and I got distracted by *her*, but I'd remember your face no matter how much you tried to change it. You're the traitor captain."

Arsenault's sword scrapes out of its scabbard with a strong steel hiss, and he levels the tip at Silva. My hand goes to my own sword in reflex.

"You've no part of this," he snarls. "I don't know what the Prinze did to your village. This isn't about old wrongs. War is war."

Silva's face screws up in anger. He moves closer to Arsenault. He's young and willowy, shorter than Arsenault and unarmed as far as I can see. That doesn't seem to matter to him, though. "You're the man who sold out the Aliente. You could have helped us *and* your men! But you didn't. You just let the Prinze burn everything."

CHAPTER 24

Arsenault stares down at him for a moment, the muscles in his face rigid, the same way I'm staring at him. What in all the hells does this boy know?

But then Arsenault whirls away from Silva and faces me.

The words I say next seem to be pulled up out of me without my consent. They're just pain, bubbling up like hot mud in one of Kosemi's pits. "You said you would never betray me, either, but you hurt everyone around me. Why?"

Arsenault edges backward. He still holds his sword.

"My father burned. That was your fault, too, wasn't it?"

Beads of sweat on Arsenault's forehead glint in the torchlight. "Pallo said— He ordered— Geoffre told me he was moving the army up the other side..."

He shakes his head groggily. The blade of his sword wavers and dips.

"*You made me a promise, Arsenault.*"

"Silva!" Mikelo shouts.

Too late. I swing around to see Silva lunge at Arsenault with a knife. I put my hand to my sword, but Arsenault is closer; he whirls around to face the boy, his sword swinging down in a reflexive blow that Silva can't hope to block. The boy's painted skin goes white beneath its pasted-on colors.

I throw my arm up into the arc of Arsenault's sword. The impact rings up my shoulder, through my collarbone, and into my back. Pain blinds me for a moment, and with the shaking in my bones, I can hardly tell that I've gone down on one knee in the dirt. The metal of my arm and all my bones are singing like fire bells.

I lurch to my feet, groping for my sword. Mikelo grapples with Silva, yanking him backward, trying to get a grip on his wrist so he'll drop the knife. There's something wrong with my right arm. It's out of balance. On fire. My fingers finally spasm shut on the hilt and I pull the sword out of its scabbard.

"Arsenault," I gasp. "Why were you in that gorge?"

Is that horror on his face? "Do you think I haven't asked myself that question? For whom I really fought?"

For whom I really fought.

The singing won't let up. It wraps me in its cloak of pain and fire. I can hardly see Arsenault through its shroud.

I hear the words come out of my mouth like someone else is speaking them. "Were you my father's spy or Geoffre's? He sent you into Liera, but you led him down into that gorge. Didn't you. You shot Razi because you've always worked for the Prinze."

Those nights we were on the road, I practiced saying words that would push him, like a lawyer at a trial. I gambled that he would chase me and show his hand. I gambled that if I could keep playing my part, if I kept pushing him, that maybe I could lay him open. Maybe he would see it was all wrong and I could recover the man at the bottom.

But the singing in my arm grows louder, and I fear that I have miscalculated. I suspected but didn't believe that Arsenault had killed Vadz and shot Razi. I didn't want to believe it. And I did not factor Ires and his magic into my equations. This blinding need of the god to find and repay betrayal.

And now I have let the god into my head and the god's words are coming out of my mouth instead.

Arsenault swipes a hand across his forehead. "I don't know," he says. "Kyrra, listen to me: *I don't know.*"

The singing wells up inside me. I can smell the odor of bodies burning. The salt tang of fear-sweat. Words come out of me, but are they my words? "You made me believe you. You made me promises, but they were just as worthless as anyone else's."

"Kyrra," he says. "*Kyrra.*"

You knew he was ruthless. You knew your father was wrong to trust him, because he sold his loyalty. Why would he have any loyalty to the Aliente? To you? Was there any reason?

Which god is talking now?

I didn't factor Erelf in, either.

These two rotten gods, tearing me apart, trying to use me for their own purposes.

Arsenault is speaking, I think. Maybe Mikelo too. But I don't hear them. I hear only this one voice.

He sells his loyalty. He's lied to you before.

No. They weren't lies. Not exactly. They just weren't entire truths. Why would he have given me this arm? Why would he have sent me off into safety? Why would he have made me those promises?

Vadz lost his life and Razi lost his godsdamned arm.

A Fixer picks and chooses what he'll shape. Why did he choose your hate? He might have chosen your capacity to love. He made you what you are, Kyrra.

Doubt drags me down, wrapping me in its net. There is a part of me that flounders against it, but that part is distant, the part of me that calls *Arsenault! Arsenault!* but is never heard. The part of me that did not go into the making of my arm.

"You broke your promise when you hurt everyone around me. You betrayed me after you said you never would."

This is not going in any way like I planned. I only wanted to push him, but now I've pushed myself until I no longer know what I believe. And I see that there is a part of him that is struggling too, like that part of me that says, *Stand down!* Except that Arsenault made me this way, and somewhere in my bones, I know the voice that is not mine speaks truth.

Then that sliver of recognition in his eyes is submerged by the rage I know, distantly, is mirrored in my own.

"I never betrayed you," he says.

His blade twitches.

Without thinking, I bring mine up to block it. Our swords scrape and clang together, and in an instant, we both look into each other's eyes, as if in surprise that we have come to this moment.

The last strip of my vision snaps and darkness engulfs me. I fall into its embrace, and the singing inside me rages in triumph.

Efsag, irdmar, jorn... The stances sing through my head, buried in my muscles. These movements I once made with this man, the closest we ever came to dancing. Efsag, irdmar, jorn... The words lose all meaning in the battering of swords. I block blows with my arm that would cleave an arm of flesh, and the sound rings out into the night and into my head.

But I am not here.

I am somewhere in the dirt, swept down the tunnels of my own veins, adrift in my own blood. I should be bleeding on the ground by now. He's a better swordsman, but he doesn't have my arm. And he doesn't fight the way I do.

It's always like this. The darkness catches me like an ocean wave and tumbles me along its bottom, scouring me in the sand until I don't know where the surface is. And I awake to find myself standing on a battlefield, bodies strewn at my feet.

Arsenault was wrong when he called it battle magic. It is a madness, an infection in the mind—vengeful, mad Ires reaching out from within the earth to satisfy his rage. It seeks any available tool, and if it finds one, it swings it like a hammer.

I can hear my own lunatic laughter as if someone else is laughing. Arsenault grunts as he struggles to block the blows I pound him with. I'm only strong when I'm fighting because it's the magic, not me. I'd be stronger if I didn't struggle against the blackness, but I bob up and down like a cork in the tide.

I think Mikelo tries to stop me, but I fling him away. I don't hear him scream, so I think he's still alive.

Kyrra, Arsenault says, *stop.*

I can't, I answer him.

Is it this arm he made me? Did he open up this channel so that it would grow wider and wider and harder and harder to close?

Everything goes black again, and when I come up from it, I have him against a wall, pinned, with the point of my sword at his throat. He stares at me the way a man does when he knows he's about to die—except there's something else there, something quiet on his face that lets me know he's already dead.

"Go ahead," he rasps. "Do it. Take your due."

I look at him in confusion. "My due?" My throat feels too swollen to speak, and I don't know what he means. My due? For not protecting my father? For what he did to Vadz and Razi?

The blade wants his neck, but I run my thumb down the hilt, fighting it off. Metal and metal, my arm and the sword do not understand the thoughts that clog my heart.

In that moment of hesitation, Mikelo cries out. A wolfish howl from someone else begins, and I swing around to see a blur of gold, the glint of a knife, a body that shoves its way into me.

Silva hits me before I can react. Arsenault jerks his sword, but not in time.

Silva's blade plunges into his chest.

It grinds past a rib and sinks deep. Silva's fingertips meet Arsenault's flesh. He wiggles the knife back out, and blood gouts up around the blade and spills over his fingers.

Arsenault's sword slips from his hand and clangs on the pavement. The battle-dream ends. Ravens caw from the rooftops above me, shrieking in delight.

I hurl Silva out of the way to get to Arsenault.

Mikelo comes running. He grabs Silva by the shoulder and punches him in the face. Silva makes a *hunh* sound and drops the knife with a clatter. Blood from his nose spatters me, but my hands are coated in Arsenault's blood anyway. I can't hold his weight and he slides down the wall, listing into a stack of crates that rattle on the stones of the alley.

Mikelo stands behind me, breathing hard. "Is he dead?" he asks.

My words have left me. It doesn't seem real, what's happening. Arsenault looks down at the knife wound in his chest, then up again at me. But this time, he lifts his hand to my face. His thumb scrubs past my cheek.

"Kyrra," he whispers. "How has it come to this?"

My heart snags and then begins to drum. There is something new in his eyes and his voice...

I catch his hand before it drops. "You remember me?"

"I knew you couldn't be dead. That memory I had about the serf girl, it was the wrong girl. Just Erelf tormenting me with false information, but I couldn't quite remember..."

His eyes flutter and his chest heaves. "Arsenault!" I shout, squeezing his hand tight in mine, as if I am not the reason he sits propped up in an alley with a gaping hole in his ribs.

"I always remember in death," he whispers again. "All of it. Everything." The muscles of his hand bunch with effort, just to twine his fingers with mine.

In his grip, the metal fingers of my right hand burn, a bright flaring pain that makes me lurch forward into him, catching myself on his shoulders.

"Mikelo," he gasps. "Get Mikelo."

"Why?" I ask. "What use is Mikelo to you now?"

"Don't argue," Arsenault whispers. "Just get him."

"Mikelo!" I call, and Mikelo leans down over me, there all along.

"You came for me," he says to Arsenault. "I thank you."

Arsenault waves his fingers weakly, in dismissal. "I need you to heal the wound."

"What? How? I—"

And then I understand.

Mikelo must be a Fixer too. What else would make him more valuable than Geoffre's own sons?

"Heal him!" I say. "If he says you have the ability, you do!"

Mikelo's face is ashen. "What? What?"

"Mikelo, don't pretend you don't understand. Do you want him to die?"

Mikelo trembles. "No. But, Kyrra, magic..."

"I won't die," Arsenault says, touching the wound with hesitant fingertips. His mouth hooks in a bitter, painful smile. How

CHAPTER 24

much pain must he be in, or is he numb? When they cut off my arm, the pain was bigger than the world. "Erelf bars me from the afterworld. But he'll take all my memories. It's how he tortures me. He's the god of knowledge."

"You didn't trade them for magic? Arsenault!"

"I wasn't lying. Just couldn't tell you the whole truth." His mouth twists into a bleak smirk that quickly disappears. He lifts his hand with great effort and rests it on the back of my head, pulling me down so that my forehead rests against his. "Don't let him take you away again, Kyrra. Please."

I close my eyes, his breath faint against my face. "If you let this man die, I will kill you, Mikelo," I say without moving, "and I care nothing about the price Geoffre has on my head. Do you understand?"

"You were bent on killing him a few moments ago," he whispers.

Was I bent on killing Arsenault? It's hard to remember now. And it doesn't matter. I can't be the cause of his death.

I disentangle myself from Arsenault so I can stand and grab Mikelo, then shove him down to the stones in front of Arsenault. Mikelo's knees smack the pavement, but I am through with words. I try to tighten my hand on my sword hilt, but it isn't there. It's on the ground beside Arsenault.

"Andris," Mikelo whispers, crawling forward on his hands and knees, "I've never done this before."

"Your uncle trained you for it."

"But it was only teaching."

"Do it!" I shout. "For the gods' sake, Mikelo!"

He flinches, then closes his eyes and takes a deep breath. He holds out his hands, close to Arsenault's chest.

"What do you see?" Arsenault whispers.

"Blood," Mikelo answers. His voice is strained. He's sweating. "Blood and bone and tissue and..."

He turns aside and retches on the pavement. "I can't do it," he says, wiping his mouth with a trembling arm. "I can't."

"Mikelo," Arsenault says, his voice scarce, hoarse. "Go deeper than that. What do you see?"

Mikelo takes another deep breath and closes his eyes again. "Heart," he says, his voice wavering. "Lungs." He opens his eyes. "Gods, Arsenault, my uncle didn't teach me about this; there wasn't—"

"Mikelo!" I say.

"Ah," he says, a strangled sound, and squeezes his eyes shut. "Heart, lungs, veins, arteries, blood, blood, blood..."

"Deeper, Mikelo," Arsenault gasps. "Hurry."

"Deeper than what?" Mikelo shouts, his eyes still closed. "That's what makes you up; that's what you are—"

I go down on one knee beside him. "We are more than blood and bone, Mikelo. When you See, you See *through*."

"Through?" His voice takes on a helpless note. Arsenault stares up at the ravens hovering on the rooftops, breathing in short, sharp gasps that make his wound quiver.

"Through," Mikelo says, breathing deeper himself.

Hesitantly, he touches the wound. His fingers slide in the blood.

Then his eyes fly open. He stares at Arsenault in surprise, but Arsenault is looking up at the sky, and his breathing comes farther apart now, more shallowly. He is sliding. Dying.

I expect something, some kind of light or music or fanfare, while all this magic is being worked. But at the most there is a soft glow, as if twilight had become wedged in this alley, trapped in Mikelo's hands. He looks on Arsenault in awe, then lays his hand upon Arsenault's wound as if he were taking and shaping a lump of clay.

Beneath his palm, new flesh ripples over the gash like water, covering it top to bottom.

Flesh ripples the same way metal does, when it's newly a part of you.

Arsenault writhes beneath Mikelo's touch. I put all my weight into holding his shoulders, pinning him against the wall.

CHAPTER 24

He throws his head back and bites his lip so hard, blood flows from it, trying not to scream.

I remember that screaming. I lean into him, harder, and Mikelo makes one more pass with his hand, down the right edge of the wound. The wound bucks. Arsenault grasps at the crates that lie next to him, but he has no strength to hold on.

Then Mikelo falls forward onto Arsenault, sweat running down his face. Arsenault sinks back against the wall, groaning and closing his eyes.

I can't quite make myself let go of his shoulders. "Mikelo," I whisper. "Did it work?"

"I don't know," he says.

His hair glints gold against the deep wine-colored strips of Arsenault's shirt.

Arsenault is wearing burgundy.

PART V

CHAPTER 25

Arsenault's breathing flutters and skips but doesn't stop. Night deepens on the streets, and I am faced with the problem of how to move him, and where to go.

We can't go to an inn. Duels are a fact of life in Karansis, but innkeepers still call the Guard if they think the duel will be one that isn't good for business. In most places, a good fight will only draw customers, but we have been political. And politics, in this land of close boundaries, is never a good idea.

Mikelo tries to stand up and retches again. He can't help me carry Arsenault; he can barely carry himself.

That leaves Silva.

He lay stunned in the alley while Mikelo healed Arsenault, and now I stand with my boot securely pressed down on his chest, the tip of my sword at his neck. He can only twitch because if he tries to get up, the point will go straight through his throat.

"Did your serving girl go get the guards?" I ask.

He stares up at me, his violet eyes wells of fright. "I don't know. But if she did, so much the better. If he's not dead already, let him die in prison!"

"You're not entitled to his life!"

"But you—"

Every befuddled accusation is like a tongue probing at a canker. I jam my foot down harder on his chest.

"I'd kill you right here, but you'll have to help carry Arsenault."

The boy's face transforms. "I'm not going to carry him! He deserves to die."

"How do you know what he did?"

Something rustles at the mouth of the alley. I turn quickly without moving my sword. If it's the Guard, I'll have some explaining to do.

The serving girl from the Beautiful Youth stands there, cloaked, her hood thrown back. She stops when I turn around, then steps forward with trepidation.

"The Guard is coming," she says. "But I didn't call them. The mistress did." She glances over her shoulder. "She sent a runner as soon as you left the building."

Mikelo curses, from the wall near Arsenault. "Kyrra. We can't move that fast."

I don't want anything to do with the Guard, though we could probably just let them have Silva. Mikelo's the problem. He bears enough Prinze features that word would get out about a Prinze involved in a duel in Karansis, and by process of elimination, the family would figure out which Prinze it was.

And Geoffre knows how to spread word faster than mouths might carry it.

"We'll have to hide him, then, and talk our way through it." I glare down at Silva. "I'd give you up, but you'll be helping me carry Arsenault, won't you?"

"Go ahead and give me up," he says. "I don't care."

"Silva?" the girl asks, her voice rising in fear. "What did you do?"

"I killed our traitor," he says with a note of pride. "Like I promised I would."

I bend down past the hilt of my sword. "He's not dead yet.

And you'd better help me hide him quick. Unless you want to hang surrounded by Aliente and Prinze."

Surprise crumbles his mask. "Who are you?" he asks.

My thin smile becomes a grin. "I used to have a name, but now I'm nobody. And I've got nothing to lose. When I let you up, you will help me move Arsenault. Otherwise, I have no problem running you through and saving the guards the trouble."

He looks at me with the utter understanding of one who has seen war. "Go ahead—" he begins, but then the serving girl interrupts: "Silva!"

His eyes flick in her direction, and something changes on his face. "Yes," he says. "I understand."

I wish my Sight didn't come and go. But I don't have a choice, so I let him up.

Between the two of us, we manage to drag Arsenault down the wall and cover him with crates. His chest moves so slightly, I have to put my cheek to his mouth to feel his breath on my skin.

His stubble rakes my cheek as I draw away. I wrap his cloak tighter around him and arrange a few more crates around his legs. Mikelo half-crawls into the pile and sinks down into his cloak until he looks like a heap of trash in the darkness.

I wonder who else has been teaching him.

The Guard clatters down the road in a jangle of tack and steel horseshoes on cobblestones. The low, burbling noise of the river, which drops down in a series of small falls from the town, hides the sound until they round the corner, but when they do, the sound explodes; it's like the whole Night Watch of Liera has come down on us.

The girl shrinks back to stand beside Silva. I step between them, and she looks up at me in surprise.

The front riders ride past, until an observant rider in the middle of the pack shouts, "Ho!" and they all come to a clattering stop.

Horses snort and whinny. The captain of the guard rides at

the rear. He swings down from his horse, long black mustaches flopping, and draws his sword before he approaches us.

"We had a report of some trouble," he says. "A man arguing with a woman?"

"A man tried to accost me," I say. "A gavaro hired by my husband, who felt cheated out of his wages. My husband is running him off. I expect he'll return shortly."

"Is your husband likely to have trouble? What's your House?"

"Cari," I say. A Conseli house.

He looks skeptical. "The gavaro followed you all the way here?"

"He was an obstinate man."

"And these two?"

"Only came to help."

The captain narrows his eyes and looks between them. Silva glares back sullenly, and the girl looks down at the ground.

"If they've run off and you don't know where they've gone, there's nothing I can do. But, my lady, a woman shouldn't be going around alone at night. Your husband should be chastised for abandoning you."

I smile a little. "Sometimes, he may let his emotions get the better of him, but truly, he has my best interests at heart. And I've learnt a little of how to take care of myself, on our travels."

The captain's eyebrows lift. "Well," he says, and salutes me with his sword. "Good evening to you, then. And get out of the night as soon as you can. It's safer inside."

He walks back to his horse and mounts. The other riders—five of them, in a pageant of house colors—have been staring at us, and now they wheel their horses, nudging them into a trot. None of them spare us a glance as they ride away.

As soon as they're gone, Silva tries to bolt. I grab his forearm with my right hand and pull him backward.

He cries out in pain. "What do you have on your arm? It sounded like metal when you blocked that blow."

"It is," I say. "Mikelo, they're gone."

CHAPTER 25

Silence. Then the crates slide over each other and rattle on the pavement as Mikelo straightens up.

"Get the crates off Arsenault," I say. "I'll hold the boy and make sure he helps us acquire our horses."

"And why should I?" Silva asks. "Since you're only going to kill me after I'm done?"

The girl moves quickly in front of me so I have to look at her. "He'll help you with the horses," she says in a soft voice. "I'll pay you for his freedom after, whatever you want, if you just let him go."

"Meli!" Silva says. "Let me make my own decisions. It's my life."

"It's not yours to throw away," she says urgently, leaning close to him. "Do you think it will change anything if she kills you? It might take away your grief, but it will just make mine worse. I know you were just trying to right the wrongs done to us, but you're not going to do that by throwing away your life. Do what she tells you, Silva. Please."

Mikelo moves crates while she speaks. I try to recover my divided attention and tighten my hand on Silva's arm. He stares at me, eyes wide. I'm squeezing too hard. He's going to have bruises.

The shape of Arsenault begins to assume itself in the night. Mikelo puts a hand to Arsenault's chest and hangs his head in relief. "He's breathing," he says.

It's like a miracle, every instant that Arsenault is not dead. Everyone can feel it, Silva most of all. "How is that so?" he asks me. "I drove the knife into his chest this deep!"

He tries to hold up his hand and I jerk it down, unable to avoid the way Arsenault's blood gleams black on his knuckles.

"And I still might kill you for it," I snap.

"It's the captain they've got, Meli," Silva says, "the Aliente captain, the traitor. Now tell me I shouldn't have tried to kill him."

Gods. Who is Arsenault, really?

In the night, the flecks of stone that limn Meli's eyes look like tears. "The war is over, Silva. Let the man be. You were only a shepherd boy; how could you have known what happened?"

"Because I was there! Just like you were! Half of Karansis probably has a story to tell about this man."

I want to shake him until he gives up his story, but this is getting out of hand. I give him a shake anyway. His head snaps backward, and his other hand comes up to claw at mine. I throw him down on the ground.

He gasps and squints up at me through watery eyes, cradling his arm against his chest.

"Enough of this talk. We need to get Arsenault to a bed."

"I've a bed," Meli says quietly, her eyes shining. "And a place for him to recover. Don't hurt my brother, and I'll get you some horses and lead you there. You won't have to steal them."

"Why are you dealing with them!" Silva shouts. "I know how you're going to get the horses, Meli!"

"It's for your life, you idiot!" Meli snaps, whirling on him. "I've lost everyone else; do you think I want to lose you, too?" Then she turns back to me. "Don't you hurt him. I'll give you everything you ask for, anything you want, but if you hurt him, I'll find a way to tell everyone I know about your man there. You'll either have to keep both of us alive or kill both of us."

She stands off in front of me with flat determination in her eyes.

Dammit. The more the battle rage leaks out of me, the more I've lost my taste for killing. I'd run this boy through as soon as he's done helping with Arsenault for what he's done, but we need the bed and I don't want to kill her, too. I can't stomach killing her right now.

"Fine," I say like I'm spitting, and she nods and runs off down the alley.

CHAPTER 25

When she returns, she's leading a rangy chestnut stallion by the reins. The horse towers over her but plods along easily enough—tired, perhaps, or not as high-strung as some of the other breeds I've seen on the streets. Straw clings to Meli's cloak. A small smudge of black or purple lines her cheek—dirt or a bruise.

Everyone can see how she got the horse.

She looks me level in the eyes, though, and hands me the reins. "We have the horse for a few hours only. The owner will be back from devotions after midnight."

I nod. "Thank you." Then I turn to Silva. "Help me get Arsenault into the saddle."

Sullenly, he walks over to Arsenault, who shivers beneath a pile of our cloaks. The ravens are back, lining the gutters above. I pick up a rock and throw it at them. They scatter, croaking, the movement of their big black wings like ripples in the night sky.

The horse shies, hooves ringing on the pavement as he dances sideways. Meli puts a hand on his neck to calm him.

We prop Arsenault up on crates, but we have to stand on crates ourselves to lift him onto the horse. I lash him to the saddle, and Mikelo mounts behind him to assure that the ropes hold, then covers him with cloaks. He looks like a bundle of blankets strapped on a horse, except that his boots dangle off the side.

Meli leads us to a narrow building at the edge of town that is crumbling into its weed-choked garden. The entrance is unlit. There is a hole in the upper story, where the bricks have caved in. "Here," she says, standing in front of the doorway. I can hardly see her.

"Meli," Silva says softly. "No."

"It's the only place," she replies, and pushes open the door. It screeches on old hinges. Her soft shoes make slipping noises on the floor as she walks inside, and then light flares, illuminating a small room with black scorch marks on the brick walls.

The house is a casualty of war too.

Meli comes back out. "We need to go down into the cellar," she whispers. "The rest of the floors are occupied. But don't worry, I'll tell them all some story. You won't see anyone till morning, and I'll tell them to stay out of the basement."

"Who are 'they'?" Mikelo asks, leaning down from the horse.

"*They* are the people run out of their homes by the war," Silva says. His chin juts out when he speaks. "They have nothing to do now but pick pockets and bed men for their bread."

"Charri carves votas," Meli says in an even, soft tone. "She knows some conjure magic. She doesn't have to sleep with anyone to fill her stomach. You and I chose this path." She turns to me. "I'll tell all of them your man there has been injured in a duel and banned from Karansis, and they won't ask questions. We're all running from something." She darts a sharp glance at Silva. "If you'll get him down now, I'll open the cellar doors. It'll be a tight fit, but the stairs aren't long."

Mikelo and I trade glances. Then he slides off the horse, careful not to jostle Arsenault, who shifts anyway and sucks in a pained breath.

The cellar stairs *are* narrow. The cellar was obviously the larder for this townhouse, and the staircase is only wide enough to roll a barrel of wine down. Somehow, we get Arsenault down the steps, Silva holding his arms and me carrying his feet, but Arsenault's sleeves still snag on the walls.

The cellar smells musty and leaks in a corner, a steady *drip-drip-drip* that will drive me mad if we have to stay here long, but otherwise, it's been transformed into a surprisingly snug living space. Narrow windows up near the ceiling, some of them still intact, reflect the light of Meli's stubby candle. A fire, unlit, is laid in the corner in a makeshift hearth of broken bricks, probably scavenged from the wall upstairs, with a hole cut in the floor above to let the smoke out. Two cots stand in the corner where the ceiling doesn't leak, against a wall of shelves holding a few crocks and bottles, a string of sausages, a braid of garlic.

Mats woven of rushes cover the dirt floor to keep the bugs out. They crunch under our boots as we carry Arsenault into the room.

"We can't afford to live in town yet," Meli says, as she goes to the fire to light it. "But we do well enough." She forces a smile. "Someday. Lay him on the cot there by the wall; that's mine."

Silva and I are both sweating by the time we lay Arsenault down. His legs slip through my hands and I almost drop him. Then I sink down the wall beside him, flexing my fingers again. My right arm has started up a queer ringing in my head. Without thinking about it, I pull off my glove and push my sleeve up to examine it.

Meli is in the midst of blowing out the candle, but the light flashes on the metal for a brief instant before it goes out, and Meli's soft cry and Silva's sharp intake of breath tell me that they've seen it.

"Dread gods," Silva says, "what is *that*?"

There's a depression in my forearm.

A dent. In my arm.

I run the fingers of my left hand over it, feeling the little dip, like a worn place in a rock where rainwater gathers. A little rut, right there in the middle of my forearm.

I can't answer Silva. Instead, I breathe in and out, and Mikelo answers for me.

"It's her arm. It's made of metal."

Undentable, unscratchable, indestructible metal. I block blows all the time, and it's always held up. But now—a dent. Something I have no idea how to fix.

What will Arsenault's new scar look like?

In an instant, as I've wondered before, but this time it's different—I wonder how he got the scar on his face, the one that's disappeared now. How many lives has he moved through? I remember reading that story about Prince Udolfo and the pirates on the hillside and how he got all the names wrong but wrong in the way of fond nicknames, and now I wonder what he really knew about Vara, the betrothed, and if he figured into the story anywhere himself. Because what I need right now is a faithful fisherman to pull me out of these cold, angry waters that are threatening to drown me.

It's a painful, old road to trod, and one I am only going down right now because I have this dent in my arm and he is lying there with a dent in his chest, and I don't know if anyone can fix either of us.

The world always falls apart as soon as you sit down.

"Kyrra," Mikelo is saying. "Kyrra, are you all right?"

I lurch to my feet. "Fine. Hungry."

But if I'm standing in the dark with only the low fire for light, I can't tell if Arsenault is breathing or not. I sit back down beside him and burrow my left hand under the cloaks to rest my palm on his chest.

Dried blood and torn fabric snag on my fingertips. The wound is hot, the new skin as smooth and soft as a newborn's. The old skin is crusted with blood and wiry with hair.

"Kyrra," Mikelo is saying again. He bends down over me so his face is close to mine. His eyes form bright, gleaming pools in the darkness. "You should eat something. We have biscuits in the pack. Meli has jerky. Icini and cheese. It's Andosino."

"They eat well down here," I say, forcing a smile. "Andosino cheese."

Mikelo hands me a piece, and clumsily I find his hand in the dark. Our fingers brush, and I squeeze the cheese too hard with my metal hand and it crumbles to the floor. I can barely feel the smear left on my fingertips. I put my fingers in my mouth and all I taste is the tang of metal.

In spite of myself, I begin to cry.

Mikelo's eyes widen. Still I am crying—wheezing, choking sobs with little noise. The noise has all gone out of me already.

I put my hand to my face. Cold metal against my hot, salty skin. Mikelo's boots scrape on the dirt as he backs away. I hear him sit.

"What—" Silva begins.

"Hush," says Meli. "Leave her alone."

Any of them could kill me, but my walls have all been breached already; it almost doesn't matter.

I lie down over Arsenault's legs and close my eyes, still weeping.

❧

I SLEEP A BLACK SLEEP. IT SEEPS IN SO SILENTLY, I HARDLY know I'm asleep at first, and then I know nothing else until Erelf stands before me.

Ravens flutter down the stairs, alighting on everyone sleeping around me—Meli, Silva, Mikelo. Their scaly talons knead flesh as they walk the line of hips and torso, back and shoulders. Big black shapes swoop into my face, and I try to chase them off with my arm, but I can't move, so they land anyway. Three more ravens, one on my arm, the other two at Arsenault's head. The cot creaks and Arsenault shifts, but the ravens remain, settling their wings at their sides.

The raven's claws shriek against my metal arm as it adjusts itself.

Erelf winds his way through the sleepers and comes to stand beside me and Arsenault. The moonlight gives his face a silver cast, as if he might be made of metal himself. "Trying to be his protector now, are you?" he says. "Fancy yourself in that role? Would you like to see yourself as you really are?"

Inside, I'm thrashing. But my limbs lie perfectly still.

Erelf smiles. "Here," he says. "Let me bequeath knowledge upon you." A fog rises from his palm, whitening the room. In that fog are shapes of men, horses, battles—

I heave my right arm up. It takes all my strength. The raven launches into the air, cawing, and I sit up. "I know what I am," I gasp. "I'm a Render, a Destroyer. One of Ires's Chosen. But it's nothing Arsenault made me. It's just who I am. I went down that path as soon as I lost my arm."

Smirking, his eyes flat and hard, Erelf says, "So, the sparrow has found her voice. Well. And she thinks she's special. Little sparrow, that is all you are. Misguided, mismade little sparrow, playing at being an eagle. How long do you think you'll survive in company such as this?" He gestures at Arsenault. "Him, with his guilt, constantly making bad decisions such as the one that gave you that arm. And Mikelo. Shall you delude yourself any longer that you control Mikelo?"

My sweat turns clammy on my skin. "I think Mikelo is too smart to be taken in by your lies."

Erelf raises an eyebrow. "Do you? Well. We'll see. His judgment in compatriots seems a bit lacking"—he looks askance at Arsenault—"but it might be forgiven him, since his uncle was attempting to woo Arsenault to his side. A process I'm sad to see end, for it gave me much entertainment. But the tides of magic grow and ebb like those of the ocean. Who knows where these currents will carry you. Or him."

"Why do you torment him so?" I ask. "A god, so wrapped up in the fate of a human. Why don't you leave him alone?"

"Oh. So, he didn't tell you that, either?"

"He didn't want to invite your attention!"

"Just as every criminal wants to stay out from under the eye of justice," Erelf says, and then he smiles, bleakly, his teeth the white of bleached bone. "But consider—if not for me, he wouldn't be alive for you now, would he? He'd have burned at Kafrin Gorge like the others. Or died in other ways—oh, dozens of times by now."

I open my mouth to speak, but thought fails me. What do I say to that?

Erelf's smile grows more genuine, more wolfish. "If you fly too close to the truth, sparrow, you may get your wings burnt. Did you See into him when you had your sword at his throat?"

Go ahead, Arsenault had said. *Take your due.*

CHAPTER 25

But what had he meant?

"In this life, he courts death. He's miserable. He has no memory, no friends. Did you condemn him to more of that when you could have released him?"

"Killing him wouldn't have solved anything, especially if you won't let him die. He would only have forgotten me again."

"The woman who killed him?"

"Men regain their memories!"

"Who's to say I wouldn't have taken pity on him with the next life and left him whole? Or maybe I would have finally let him cross the barrier and die." His gaze runs up and down me, head to foot. "Perhaps I'd rather have you. You could have taken his place. But now you've just condemned him to more torment."

I catch my breath. "If I thought you were telling the truth, I would do it. But nothing you say comes out straight."

Erelf shrugs. "Truth is rarely what it seems. Ask yourself another question: what are you going to do with Mikelo? And another: what do you mean to do with Cassis? Will it be what Arsenault wants you to do? I'll tell you another story about Cassis and Arsenault if you like, about the entertainments Cassis holds and Arsenault's role in them... Cassis is jealous, Kyrra, and more so now. He might have dozens of bastards, but he hasn't. In the summer, he'll be casting off his wife, and whom will he marry? Do you think it will be Driese di Caprine? Do you *really* think so, Kyrra?"

I don't think so, but I trust nothing Erelf says. "What entertainments?" I ask, and it occurs to me that Erelf said *more so now*, and that means... "Cassis and Geoffre know who Arsenault is? And they still employ him?"

I feel sick. Like I'm lost in a snowstorm, different truths swirling around me, blinding me. It all seems to be true, but maybe none of it is. Or only some of it. I grasp for something solid only to find that it all melts in my hand. If this was a game of indij, I'd be lost by now, penniless.

I've never played any game so badly.

"What does Geoffre want Arsenault to do for him?" I ask.

"Down to asking me questions, are you? Perhaps you should ask, *What does Geoffre want Mikelo to do?* Perhaps you should ask yourself, *What am I going to do now?*" He chuckles. "This battle is too complicated for you, little bird. You've alighted in the middle of the field, and now you're caught, about to be trampled by the hooves of a thousand horses."

I know he's a god but I can't help saying, "If you see truth from all sides, how did you let Arsenault slip past you? He must have bested you, for you to hate him so much. And he's done it again, hasn't he? Slipped right through your hands. Mikelo did that. Did you not see Mikelo coming, either?"

I push myself up off the cot and stand on my own feet, with my dented arm naked in the moonlight glinting like a sword blade.

He takes a step backward—a slight step, no more than a shift of his heel.

"Do you really deal in truth, Erelf, or is it only lies when it comes to yourself? What is the truth about you?"

He pales in anger. Then he leans down so that I fall under the shadow of that damn black hat that looks so much like the ones that gavaros used to wear...the one that makes him look so much more like Arsenault.

"Look to yourself first," he says. "What are you going to do now, with the knowledge that you've stolen a man whose magic Geoffre di Prinze has shaped to do his bidding? That whatever you do to Cassis will be the wrong thing? That no matter what you might tell yourself, *with any action you might have taken, you gave Arsenault up to death?* Whether it's the death of the body or of the mind, it makes no difference, because you are responsible for both of those. Ask Arsenault about those entertainments. Dig in those holes in his brain and see what you find at the bottom. See if you can find Geoffre there, and then ask yourself again, *What am I going to do about it?*"

CHAPTER 25

He straightens up, tips his hat, and smiles. I don't like that smile at all.

"And think about what I said, too, about a trade."

He holds his hands up and all his ravens lift into the darkness until they blur together, a blackness rushing into his palms.

Then the darkness swallows him, too, and all that is left is a shimmer in the air.

※

I EAT IN THE DARKNESS WHILE EVERYONE SLEEPS, BUT THE cold, hard sausage tastes foul to me, the peppers in it too dull, the meat nearly rancid. I don't know if it's because the sausage is bad or if my taste for food has fled with my courage.

I fumble about the shelves for the unbottled wine. My metal fingers thump on the wooden keg in the corner, and I can't seem to close them on the tap. My metal arm is curiously without feeling this morning.

Dirt crunches, then Mikelo reaches around me to push the tap down. "Here," he says softly. Wine splashes into my wooden cup, sloshing onto my hand, the front of my dress.

I've forgotten I'm wearing a dress. I suddenly want, very badly, to bathe and change. I want my trousers, clothes familiar and brave.

I push the tap handle back up myself. "I need to talk to you." The darkness out the windows is graying. I can almost see him, but I feel and hear the way he steps backward more than anything.

"About what?" he asks.

"Mikelo."

Silence for a moment.

"I hardly know who to keep secrets from anymore."

"I suffer from the same affliction. Is there a cistern outside? Anywhere we can get water?"

Mikelo nods. "Meli said so, last night. You were—"

I don't want to be reminded of how I was. I wave his words away.

"Where is it?"

"In the yard, by the far wall." He hesitates. "I'll come with you."

"You won't," I say. "You'll stay here with Arsenault. Do you think I trust that boy and his sister?"

"Do you trust me?" Mikelo says softly.

What would be trusting him more—to have him sit with Arsenault or to send him up to get water alone, to give him the chance to escape?

"I trust you with Arsenault," I say.

"What are you going to do about Silva?"

"I don't know. The smart thing to do would be to kill both of them as soon as Arsenault can move. I don't like relying on either one."

"But...in cold blood..."

"Tender heart, Mikelo." I sigh. "Sit beside Arsenault. Make sure they stay in the basement. I'll be back in a moment with some water."

"Can you carry it? It looked like something was wrong with your arm."

"I'm just going to go up by myself. Where are the buckets?"

"Here," he says, and hands me one.

I take it and head up the stairs. The wood floor creaks beneath me though I try to be quiet, but the house seems to be uninhabited. I push open the door and walk out into the night.

The sky looks like a pierced piece of silk fabric, the last few stars still visible against the midnight blue to the west. In the east, layers of cloud stack, bright bloody red.

A sanval morning. The storm will move in by nightfall. I wonder how badly the ceiling will leak when the winds howl and the rain pours down.

At least we'll have more water. The cistern, a thick stone cylinder that sits on the undamaged side of the house, half-

CHAPTER 25

hidden by clumps of thistle and overgrown bougainvillea, is low. A stone pipe runs down from the gutters of the house to sluice rainwater from the roof into it.

I fill the bucket and wash my face and my left hand. Smears of dried blood have left black spots on the gray wool of my dress. I dip the end of my skirt in the water and scrub at them. But blood stains. I'll never be able to rub them out.

Sun-yellow forsythia bushes line the path. As I walk slowly by carrying the bucket, their fronds brush the top of my head and drop petals in my hair. The flagstones are littered with yellow, nearly gray in this early light. Blue plumbago creeps in the shadows of the forsythia, and daffodils sweep into the turns in the walk. Tall favas grow jammed against the house wall, already dangling tiny, speckled pods.

Life continues as it always does, amid the ruins.

What have I accomplished by going out to get the water myself? Probably nothing. I go back into the house, back down the dark staircase, back into a place that's almost like night.

"I don't know how they live here," Mikelo whispers to me when I come back. "It's so dark."

"They sleep in the daytime," I tell him. "They're awake all night. Their mistress should have given them permanent rooms."

"Why would anyone choose to live here instead?"

I shrug. "To get away, maybe. To feel like someone else for a while."

Mikelo sits on the floor beside Arsenault, leaning against the wall, his long arms draped across his knees. "Because of their job."

"They need to eat," I say as I kneel beside Arsenault, who shudders in his sleep. I use my knife to cut off a piece of skirt for a rag, then dip the rag in the water and lay it on Arsenault's forehead. Water streams down his temples. "But they don't want to be defined by that role."

"Perhaps I can relate. I needed to eat too. So did my mother."

"That's right; you're a bastard, aren't you?"

Mikelo winces. "It's a harsh word. But I suppose in some ways, it's not so different than being a refugee lucky enough to find a wealthy patron."

He's quiet for moment, watching as I swab Arsenault's hot forehead with the wet rag.

Then he goes on. "When I was a young boy, my mother lived with a merchant who rode the caravans. He was a man of no particular House…not exactly kinless, you understand, but his origins were in some question. My earliest memory is of sitting on his saddle, clutching the pommel as we swayed in a line, heading a train of donkeys down a rutted, narrow road. I remember the way the dust swirled around us. And for some reason I remember his hands—he had fine black hairs on his hands that curled over his knuckles. But I don't remember his face well. Just his big black beard.

"My mother lived with a number of men over the years. She never made me call any of the men father. None of them looked anything like me anyway. To be fair, my mother looked nothing like me either—she had long dark hair and dark eyes. I always thought she was beautiful, but then, she was my mother."

The ghost of a smile touches his lips, then disappears as he continues his story.

"This merchant was as close to a father as any I've ever had. That's why the memory is one of my fondest—just sitting in the saddle with him while he pointed out the different birds and plants along the way. By the time we reached Dakkar, my memories are much more vivid. It took us two years. We lost much of the caravan to raids and fevers. The merchant himself died, but my mother found another to take her in, one who rode further to the front of the line. He was cold, but he had a lot of money, and when we got to Dakkar, he had even more because he was one of the men who traded with the B'ara for guns—just arquebus and not many of them, but somehow the networks managed to smuggle them north."

He looks at me for the first time. "I learned that later, of course."

"So, Baleria is in Dakkar." It seems somehow an inadequate thing to say, and yet I feel I must say something. Mikelo nods.

"In the northern reaches. That's where we settled, my mother and I, until I was thirteen. On the day I turned thirteen, I received a missive from my uncle. We lived further back in the interior then, alone on a small homestead. My mother often told me I had a wealthy uncle who might one day call me back to Liera, and she prepared me as best she could. I learned how to wield a sword, how to read, how to write. Nothing more extraordinary than that. She taught me a few symbols that seemed peculiar—to protect myself, she said. But that was it. And this missive came."

"Into the interior? How old was it? How did it reach you?"

"By bird. In a very strange manner." He laughs a little, low and anxious.

I smooth my skirts, remembering the raven Arsenault sent off into the beams of the ceiling with a wave of his hand. "I've seen that sort of flight," I say.

"I'm not surprised," he says. "You seem to have seen almost everything."

"It's not a life I'd have chosen."

He doesn't answer for a moment. Then he dusts a piece of rushes from his leg. "My uncle called me back to Liera. He told me to go down to Mdembu, the royal city, into the garrison there. He told me I'd find my family, and it was time for me to come home and serve my House. To tell you truly, I often wondered if my mother was making him up. She chewed kacin and her habit grew worse as time went on. But we had settled into life there. I knew a girl in the village the same age as me. I had it in my head that some day I would negotiate her bride price and come to live in the village. She used to tease me about how easily I sunburned. Her skin was the darkest umber."

He smiles and closes his eyes. Then he sighs and opens them

again, looking at me. "But all that's behind me now. I went to the garrison, alone, to find that my family had destroyed the city and that my uncle was so wealthy, he could buy even the lives of his kin. I'm nothing but a tool to him. I'd forsake my duty to my House if my House was only made up of him, but it isn't."

I can almost see myself reflected in his pupils, my tousled hair, the ruined gray dress. And Silva and Meli, awake now and watching us.

I wonder how much they heard and what they'll do with the information. Will it put Mikelo in jeopardy?

I push myself to my feet. "It's a fanciful tale, Mikelo. But Arsenault always did say that the best lies contain a grain of truth."

Mikelo remains staring at me for a moment, his expression open, wounded. Then he sees Silva and Meli, too. Understanding gradually lights his eyes, and he begins to laugh.

―❦―

MIKELO AND I SPEAK OF NOTHING ELSE IMPORTANT FOR THE rest of the day. Instead, our attention is occupied by the two courtesans whose room we share, Arsenault lying still unconscious on the bed, and the sounds of people settling above.

The house changes with the rays of the sun into a nest of people, like a rookery full of roosting crows. We look up at the first creaking footsteps. Dust trickles down through the cracks in the floor and rains down on Arsenault. I curse and wipe it from his face.

"I think it's healing," Mikelo says, squinting at Arsenault's wound as if he's dizzy. I move behind him in order to catch him if he falls, but he doesn't. When Arsenault breathes, the flesh stretches and I imagine I can see inside him, the muscle and bone, blood vessels like blue writhing worms, the warm wet red of him. And from there I imagine I can see through him, but all

I run into there is a shifting wall of gray fog, the same as it's always been.

Arsenault shivers and his eyes crack open. I lurch forward, hoping he'll awaken and hoping at the same time that he won't; the *won't* wins, and I'm disappointed. He sinks into something that might be sleep, except a chill seems to have entered the room, and I wonder if he's fighting his own battle with Erelf, if, on some green plain that shelves off into a silver sea, he wields a sword against the god...or if perhaps his weapon is only knowledge, which the god may turn against him.

I realize my right hand is still on his chest and I stand back up quickly, pressing it to my own chest with my left hand.

Mikelo says, "I don't know what to do about the dent."

Mikelo says, "Go upstairs, Kyrra. Meli's going; maybe she can get you some clothes."

I don't want to go upstairs with Meli and leave Silva down here with Mikelo and Arsenault, but I don't want to leave Meli on her own, either. I don't like Mikelo giving me things to do, but I've begun pacing, my fingers twitching at the hilt of my sword. I pull it and examine it in the overcast light from the window.

Silva says, "What are you going to do with that?"

There are no dents in the sword. I think it's made out of the same metal as my arm. If there are no dents in the sword, why is there a dent in my arm?

Perhaps the dent is in me.

"Nothing," I say. I should give the sword back to Arsenault. It isn't mine; it never was. The runes inscribed on its blade are different from the sword stances. I can't read any of them.

Except the one near the tang. *Sanctuary.*

I run one of my flesh fingers over its lines, feeling its ridges the way I have so often over the past five years. Then I hand the sword to Mikelo. He looks up at me in surprise.

"I've my knife," I say, unbuckling the swordbelt and letting it fall to the floor. I'm still wearing the hatpins in my hair, too, though I've almost forgotten. "Don't use it unless you need to."

Mikelo nods jerkily.

Be safe, I wish Arsenault. Then I turn to Silva. "I won't hurt your sister, and you won't hurt Arsenault. Understood?"

<hr />

UPSTAIRS IS FULL OF PEOPLE, MOST OF THEM ASLEEP—ROLLED in blankets, tucked in next to each other. All of them look young.

A woman with terra-cotta skin and pale eyes sits on the steps, stripping long slivers of wood from a stick the length of her arm. Her knife blade flashes as it moves in and out of the light. She doesn't look up even when we let the cellar door close. Her black hair is braided in rows in the Tiresian manner, strung with glittering glass beads of blue and red. They clink together when she turns her head, making a kind of music.

"Charri," Meli says. "We've a visitor. I wondered if you could spare an extra skirt or shirt."

The woman named Charri cocks her head and looks me over for a moment. Her gaze lingers on the bloodstains that mar my bodice.

Finally, she turns back to her carving. Her slim, hard hands guide the knife in a steady rhythm with no shaking. The curls of yellow wood spill off the end of the stick and fall to the floor in a pile. "I found some clothes down near the market the other day," she says, without looking up this time. "They might fit you. Looked like some woman got picked up, threw out her old servant clothes. You think you could wear old serf clothes?"

"I'll take them," I say. "Do you have any men's clothing? Enough for two men?'

"Two men?" The woman eyes Meli. "Why would you need clothes for two men, too?"

Meli tenses. Her smile, when it comes, doesn't have much

ease to it. "Because we have two men in our basement. This is Kyrr—"

"Kyrri," I interrupt, trying to smile myself. "My name is Kyrri. My husband's a gavaro. He was hired to ride with a band of Conseli and there was a robbery and he was wounded, trying to run off the bandits. But the Conseli blamed him and cast him out, along with another gavaro who stood up for him. Meli took pity on us and gave us the cellar until my husband recovers. We've enough skills between us so you won't want for food; I noticed some rabbit runs in your garden when I went to the cistern this morning."

Charri strokes the hilt of her knife with her thumb. Smooth wood, like the wood she carves. A leg, I think it's going to be. Or an arm.

"So, we've got two gavaros in our basement and a gavaro's woman up here, do we? Do we want that kind of trouble, Meli?" She turns to me. "If those Conseli had enough money to hire your husband, they might want what he took enough to send out the Guard."

"He didn't—"

She waves her knife. Is it her house, I wonder? A woman could make a tidy sum if she was good enough at carving votas. Does she make small figures of Ransi that bleed real blood from the heart? She looks as if she could. It's in her eyes.

"All bandits say they're innocent," she says.

"I tell you, we won't be here long."

She sets the knife down on the step beside her and holds the piece of wood up to examine it more closely.

"You'll bring us food?" she says.

I begin to nod, but I'm interrupted by a banging at the door. The sleepers awaken, and those who need to burrow down in holes find them quickly. The cellar doors lift up and slam, once—twice—three times, and I swear under my breath.

Charri and Meli trade glances and then Meli goes to open the door.

A brown-haired man wearing blue and silver, the trident crest of the Prinze embroidered on his breast, waits there. A dark slate-blue sky frames him as he stands on the brick steps.

I fight not to put my hand to my absent sword. Instead, I move slightly away from the door and begin unbuttoning my bodice as quickly as I can. Butchering chickens or rabbits wouldn't lay this much blood on me, and bigger animals—if we had them—are men's work. The fingers of my right hand are stiff, though, and it's hard to push the little white buttons through the holes.

My chemise lies beneath, and I can only hope that it won't seem strange in a house such as this to see a woman with her bodice hanging open and the scalloped neck of her underdress showing.

"Ser," Meli says. "What can we do for you?"

Her voice sounds all right, but her face is ashen and her lips are tight.

The gavaro bows. "We're looking for two men who might have passed through here." He unrolls a sheet of parchment. Lines of pen and ink reveal a face nearly like mine, but more male. Below the sketch of me there is one of Mikelo, but surely, he's never looked that young.

I'm almost done with the row of buttons. Eyes stare at me from the darkening gloom in the corners of the room. The wind gusts, rattling the parchment and swirling through our hair, bringing out gooseflesh on my bare neck.

Sanval.

Charri frowns at the gavaro and Meli glances at me—one quick glance, then down at the floor. But the gavaro notices all the same. He looks straight at me.

The lines of the rune slide through my head, shining the way they do on the sword. *Sanctuary.* One straight line knotted with two loops. I can trace their formation with my thoughts the same way I do with my finger and watch the glow spread...

My right arm thrums suddenly. I try not to wince.

"Have you seen these men?" the gavaro asks.

"No, sir, I haven't," I say.

"Are you sure?"

"If I'd seen them, I'd be sure to tell you, wouldn't I?"

He looks surprised at my manner. Then the surprise turns into fluster, and a wicked gust of wind slams against the house, tearing the parchment from his hand and hurling it at the beams of the ceiling. The paper bobs and dips like a cork at sea, and the gavaro swears and grabs at it, but the paper eludes him. The wind sends it spiraling up the staircase, into the upper story of the house.

"Damn everything," the gavaro mutters, and runs up the stairs to catch it. His ironshod boots shudder the whole staircase.

The wind whistles through the doorway with a vengeance. The hole in the upstairs creates a natural draw up the staircase like the flue of a fireplace. The wind tugs at the ends of the gavaro's hair as he comes clomping back down with the parchment in his fist. He ducks beneath the lintel as he comes to the bottom of the stairs and squints at the sky.

"I think I'd rather spend the afterlife in eternal torment than face that storm," he says as if he's talking to himself, then gives us each a forced smile. "Thank you. I'll be away now, I think."

"Hurry out of the rain," Charri says as he inclines his head again and runs for the horse tied in the street. Leaves, green and brown, skirl around him, and dust hazes the air. He mounts his horse and rides away in a clatter.

"It was you," Charri says softly at my back as I stare out the doorway after him, the wind snatching my hair and throwing it in my face. "Wasn't it. And one of your gavaros."

Can I deny it? "The Conseli," I say, trying a middle ground.

But the footing there is treacherous. "A magic was worked," she whispers. "Complicated. Dangerous. I could feel it."

I turn to face her. "I didn't steal anything," I say. "And neither did either of those gavaros in the basement."

"Magic is like the sanval," she says. "Wild. Be glad it sided with you just then." The wind lifts her braids, and the beads sound like chimes. "I want you out as soon as the storm lets up."

"Fine. But I still need those clothes. I'll pay you for them."

She pushes the door closed, then sits down and picks up the vota and her knife again. She makes one long cut down the length of the wood and holds it up so I can see it. It's an arm with a fist at one end.

She throws it at me. I put my right hand up in reflex to catch it. My arm creaks and the dent twinges, a faint frisson of pain. My fingers spasm shut around the wood anyway. But my sleeve pulls back and in the gap between the cuff and the bottom of my glove, a thin strip of silver gleams in the burgeoning storm light.

She sits there with her knife in one hand, looking at me for a while.

"No payment," she says. "You ruined a vota, and it's yours now. If you pay me, that means I accepted something from you, and then I've got a link between you and your magic I don't want. I'll get you your clothes for free. But you leave soon, hear?"

I nod dumbly, looking at the piece of wood in my hand. Something seems to be curled in the fist, but I can't tell what it is.

It looks like it might be a heart.

A thick red stream begins to ooze from it. It drips down the square-cut fingernails, the tendon-outlined wrist, the forearm. It drips on the floor and spatters on my boots.

⁂

DOWNSTAIRS, THE CELLAR IS A PANIC. THE SOUND OF MILLING voices fills the stairwell as I heave open the cellar door. I haven't stopped to button up my bodice again, and the damp air of the cellar chills the nervous sweat on my chest.

Meli follows me, pulling the door shut over her head. "There

CHAPTER 25

are many, many more people here than you said," I whisper at her.

She lifts her chin. "I didn't say how many people were here, did I? It changes day to day." She picks up a tallow candle from an indentation in the wall and sweeps past me, her skirts gripped tight in her other hand. The light from the candle jitters on the stones as I follow.

I'm still carrying the vota in my right hand. It seemed wrong to leave it on the floor upstairs. Maybe I'll bury it in the garden. Or throw it in the river, the way other people do. I don't know how to get rid of the ill will of a piece of wood.

Three new people are standing in the basement when we get to the bottom of the stairs: three boys, too young to have soldiered in the wars. Mikelo stands with Silva next to Arsenault's cot, and Arsenault is on his hands and knees beside it.

The hilt of his sword lies under one of his hands, pressed into the dirt.

I throw down the bleeding vota and run across the room.

"Kyrra!" Mikelo says. "What happened? These three came downstairs and—"

I fall down on my knees in the dirt beside Arsenault and put a hand on his shoulder. "*Arsenault.*"

Gods, his skin is pale. His hair hangs down in sweat-soaked strings.

"Kyrra," he says, his voice barely a breath.

"You're going to hurt yourself. Get back on the cot. Lie down."

"I thought there was a guard upstairs," he says, a little louder but still strained. "Something. The knot."

He means the rune.

"A Prinze gavaro came to the door. But he's gone now. You should have stayed on the cot." I force the words out, like walking in a direction I don't want to go. But let the truth be told now, and we can find out where we've fallen, if he's forgotten everything again or if, perhaps, he really did switch sides.

He shakes his head, then his lips curve in what might be a smile. "A talent for desperation you have. Always."

I wonder if the language is escaping him. Past and present seem mixed up. Or... I lean down and look in his face. "Who are you, Arsenault? Do you remember?"

He laughs—a wheezing laugh, but a real one. "I'm the man who got knifed in an alley by a table-boy," he says. "And yes, I remember. Gods, you— I *remember*."

CHAPTER 26

THE STORM RAGES FOR FIVE DAYS, BEATING RAIN AND WIND against the high-up window in Charri's cellar and leaking water into all the cracks in the walls.

I have a lot of time to sit and watch Arsenault as his body grapples to incorporate this new flesh, this new memory of an old body. While he heals, I sit and remember too.

The month that followed the announcement of my father's impending nuptials and Arsenault's return passed in a flurry of activity that encompassed not only the serfs and house servants but the gavaros as well, since they were often sent on errands into the city, to acquire luxuries my father didn't keep on the estate, or as escort to my mother, who rode out often as well.

It was a cruel twist of fate that, as manager of the household, she had to plan my father's wedding feast. That it would be held on Fortune's Night only made her job harder. Fortune's Night was Ekyra's yearly festival. Much care was always taken with the festivities, to ensure good fortune for the next year. There were traditional decorations to make and foods to eat and greetings to trade, and the guests would expect an even more lavish outlay than would normally accompany a wedding—the rarest wines, silk table cloths, roasted boar and stuffed peacock...

It would be a feast fit for a king, the gavaros said who hailed from lands where kings ruled.

I couldn't help thinking that it should have been my feast—a bride's feast on her name day. Three years had passed since the severing of my arm. I had turned twenty at midsummer and I was now even older than I had thought to wed.

I wondered what my mother was thinking as she marshaled the estate into action. I saw her sometimes, from a distance as she went back and forth to Liera, Lobardin riding as escort on the high seat of her coach next to the driver.

One day, I was standing at the door to the barracks when I saw her coach stop. Lobardin opened the door and jumped to the ground, then offered her a hand to step down. I put my hand to my brow to shade my eyes, and Arsenault, who was overseeing some work on the roof of the barracks, saw me watching and came down from his ladder to stand next to me.

My mother bent over to inspect the roses by the wall that I had only recently pruned, and the wind snapped her pale mauve skirts behind her. Her long, braided, white-streaked hair slipped over her shoulder and fell against the blooms she held up to her face.

I dropped my hand in surprise. "Her hair," I said.

Arsenault wiped his hands on a rag. "It's been that way for a while. The fiction of dyeing it became too great a task."

"She's letting Lobardin guard her."

Arsenault looked troubled and tucked the rag into his belt. "This trip isn't one that's been planned," he said, and walked away from me down the path toward her, sword swinging at his side.

I wondered if I should go down to greet her too, if three years had been enough time—if perhaps she might welcome it, with this marriage looming over us. Then again, perhaps the marriage meant she wouldn't want to see me at all. In the end, I remained where I was and watched as Arsenault approached her, bowing slightly.

I couldn't hear their words from where I stood. But as it turned out, I didn't need to.

Instead, she came to me.

When she started up the path, my heart began to pound. Arsenault flanked her on one side, supporting her with his arm, and Lobardin flanked her other, keeping his face carefully polite, though as he got closer, I could see the fury in his eyes.

It took me aback to see him display that much emotion. I looked to Arsenault to see if he, too, had gauged the depth of Lobardin's resentment toward him, but he wore his warrior's face —blank, neutral.

Sometimes, he seemed more like a statue than a man.

"Kyrra," my mother said.

Her voice took me by surprise, and I was startled into looking straight at her.

She looked much older than she had three years earlier. It wasn't only the white hair that had nearly conquered the blond. It was the weight she'd gained that left her cheeks plump and jowly with deep furrows under her eyes. Her stays helped trim her waist, but the flesh on her arms sagged.

She looked like a different woman, except for the hard blue-gray eyes I remembered.

"Kyrra," she said again, not smiling. "I know it's you, even in those clothes."

I moved my stump somewhat behind my back and finally found the presence of mind to nod. "Mother."

"Lobardin tells me you've become quite comfortable in the barracks."

Lobardin put on a smug look that mostly didn't infiltrate his eyes. Arsenault looked a little troubled, but nothing more broke his composure.

"The men are kind to me," I said.

The words made me cringe inside, the more so when my mother's brows lifted and so did Lobardin's.

But what else was I supposed to say? If I had known she

wanted to speak to me, I might have donned a mail shirt and come out armed with Arsenault's sword.

As it was, my fingers itched for the hilt of my knife, for security.

"The men are kind to you," my mother repeated. She looked me over for a moment, then pursed her lips. "And what duties do they have you perform?"

I flushed. "I perform the same duties as any servant in the barracks. I'm comfortable here."

Her eyes softened somewhat. "You look as if you might be. You were ever a challenge, Kyrra."

I laid my hand on my side, where my knife hid inside my trousers. It went there of its own accord, but it was only in my mother's presence that I became aware of the small habits I'd picked up. I rocked back on my heels when I did it, just like a gavaro settling himself for battle.

"I'm no longer your daughter," I said. "Surely, that has made me less challenging."

The words just came out of my mouth. But it was like watching a knife blade pass over someone's arm: the cut opened first, and then the blood welled up.

My mother laughed.

"You might think so, wouldn't you? Just dash you away with a swipe of the pen, and my life would be easier? But do you truly see how *easy* my life has become?"

Gods. I hadn't spoken to my mother in three years; I didn't want our conversation to begin where it had left off the day I put on my serf brown and went with the summoners to have my arm severed. So, I did what any gavaro would do when faced with an onslaught he didn't want to meet.

I retreated.

"This battle doesn't need to be fought here," I said, trying to make my voice soft. "I know the straits you're in."

She laughed again, more bitterly this time. "You can't begin to know what place I'm in, Kyrra."

CHAPTER 26

"Then why did you come to see me? Only to disapprove of my clothing and the place where I sleep? Arsenault must have told you about me. Or has Papa kept his designs from you, too? Is that what this is about?"

She went pale, and I felt sick. I wanted to look at Arsenault, to see how he had reacted, but I couldn't. I had to look at my mother. "You don't know, Kyrra," she said again, viciously. "You've spent three years down here on your own, outside of the Circles. The plotting that has gone on behind this wedding would astonish you. Your father wanted me to let you know that you will be under the eye of all, no matter that you no longer bear the name Aliente. To warn you."

Oh, blessed gods, Mother, please not in front of Lobardin.

My alarm must have shown, because she closed her mouth and turned to Arsenault. "You will bring her to the house this evening. Make sure she's dressed appropriately." Then she turned to Lobardin. "Help me back," she said, and he inclined his head to her while looking sideways at me.

Arsenault said, "Go easy on the way home, Messera."

She paused for a moment but didn't turn around. "I will ride as I see fit."

Lobardin held out his arm to her, and she took it and turned her back on me. As they picked their way down the path, my eyes began to burn. Accidentally, I lifted my stump to wipe the burning away.

"What does she want me to do?" I said as I hurriedly swiped my eyes with my left hand. "What is *appropriate* dress? I don't belong in that house."

Arsenault sighed. "No," he said. "You don't. Come on, Kyrra."

I looked up, my vision blurring while I willed myself not to weep. I would not declare that kind of surrender, not while Arsenault was standing right in front of me.

"Why?" I said. "Will you dress me like a doll and deposit me back in my mother's arms for the evening? Surely, it won't take that long for me to muss my hair and put on a skirt."

"Your mother's warning is well heeded, that's all."

"*Well heeded?*" I watched Lobardin help her into her coach. "Lobardin heard it. If he still fights for the Prinze, it won't matter where I am or what I do—they'll find me out, though I don't know what else I can do that will hurt my House." I looked up at Arsenault. "Is there anything else?"

He shrugged, but he looked troubled. "Just come with me, Kyrra. The gods help those who help themselves."

With that, he walked inside, and I knew it was because of the workers on the roof. But I couldn't help wondering, knowing something of his relationship with gods, which gods would be the ones to help us.

※

HE LED ME THROUGH THE BARRACKS, STOPPING ONLY TO PICK up a cloth-wrapped bundle from the chest in our room. Then we were out the back door, avoiding the throngs of servants washing and beating linens, and gavaros cleaning their own uniforms, shining their boots and their swords. Both groups probably wondered why I wasn't with them, but Arsenault's presence was enough to make them shut their mouths.

Had I suggested to my mother that I made my own way in the barracks? It wasn't mine. My way lay always in Arsenault's wake. I'm sure she'd seen that.

I felt like weeping again.

Arsenault didn't stop until we came to our little grotto. The armless statue stood in the spray from the spring, watching me blandly out of its pockmarked face.

I turned to Arsenault. "Why are we here?"

In response, he set the bundle down on the wall and unrolled it.

It was a sword. It was nothing as fine as his sword but still well made. The blade was short and plain, and the hilt wrapped in supple brown leather. I would be able to wield it one-handed; I saw that in an instant.

"It's mine?" I asked.

He nodded. "I had it made for you some time ago."

"And you've just given it to me now? What part of my mother's warning are you heeding by giving me a sword?"

I stepped forward and ran my finger down the flat of its blade. There were no etchings as there were on Arsenault's blade. Just cold, smooth metal.

"I don't understand why I matter to the Houses anymore," I said.

"The Prinze will be here. That's why your mother was warning you."

"It didn't sound like a warning. It sounded more as if she wanted me to step back into my place."

Arsenault flipped the sword around, offering it to me hilt-first. "That might be where your mother feels you're safest."

I clenched my left hand into a fist. "What right has she—"

"Take the sword."

I closed my fingers around the hilt reflexively as he put it in my hand. "You want to spar? Now? This sword is edged."

"We'll run through the forms so you can see how it behaves. It's different than a blunt."

If I had ever had an edge in a battle with my mother, it had long since dulled. I hefted the sword in my left hand. "It's a risk to have me come to the house. If my mother wants us to look proper."

"Trim up your stance." He pushed my shoulder back with one hand, my hip sideways with the other, then tapped the back of my knee with his foot. I bent it in response.

"Why are you giving me this sword now?"

He moved away from me. "Do you have to ask?"

Is war so close? I wanted to say. But I didn't.

He knew, and I knew, and my mother knew. I imagine

Lobardin knew as well, and it frightened me to have left him alone with my mother in that coach.

"You let Lobardin go," I said.

"Bend your elbow," he told me.

I bent my elbow. "Is he working for the Prinze?"

"Recite the runes."

"Dammit, Arsenault!" I let the sword drop and came out of my stance. "Will you answer my questions or not?"

He pulled his sword. It sang out of its scabbard and flashed in the sunlight. "I said," he replied, in a calm, unshakable voice, "recite the runes."

I knew them in my muscles now, but I could also see them in my head as I had learned to write them, a smudged row of black spikes, intertwined.

"Efsag, irdmar, jorn," I began in frustration, reciting the first three of twelve. "But I don't see—"

He came at me. It was quick and unexpected, the fluid movement of a man to whom such movements were embedded in the flesh.

I barely got my sword in front of his. The blades caught and rang with the blow.

"Arsenault!" I shouted.

"Come on, Kyrra," he said to me over the blades. "Follow the runes. Don't think."

Then he brought his sword down, and I had no choice but to follow him.

If I say it was like a dance, I will sound tawdry; every poet describes swordplay thus. Swordplay is not like a dance. You move not with your partner but instead to overpower him. But blood was not our end, so perhaps our swordplay was like a dance—a dance born of anger, not love.

The two have ever been entwined for me, anyway. Angry at my mother, I spent it on Arsenault, and he was there to meet me. I was never under any illusion that he didn't know exactly what he was doing, giving me the sword on that day.

CHAPTER 26

He finally knocked me in the dirt. When I hit the ground, it was like waking up. I noticed the bruises and scratches that marred my skin, and the sweat that dripped from my forehead into my eyes. Arsenault stood above me, grinning, breathing hard, sweat dampening his brow as well.

I sat there, aching for a moment, trying to remember where I was.

Then I laughed. "By all the gods, Arsenault, my mother said I was to look *appropriate*."

His grin caught a twist of wryness. "This isn't appropriate for you?"

He sheathed his sword, then put out a hand and helped me up. I hurt all over.

It was a glorious feeling.

Then I saw the bruises on my arms and ended up staring at my stump.

"Less than a month," I said.

Arsenault was silent for a moment. Then he said, "You're as ready as many gavaros I've trained. More than some. Some of them only come in with fencing lessons."

And it hit me, what my mother's invitation meant. What Arsenault's gift of a sword meant. I had known it, but I hadn't understood. Now comprehension pierced my heart.

"Less than a month," I said. "You think the Prinze will attack in *less than a month*."

He put a hand on my left shoulder and then slowly, mindful of his promise, also on my right. "I wish you would go. There's no reason for you to stay here."

"No reason?" I said. "How can you say there is *no reason?*"

And then I did weep. Finally, viciously.

I let the sword drop to the ground and he held me against his chest. For a long time.

My parents wouldn't see me in daylight. As the day progressed, my bruises grew sorer and sorer, until by evening, my left arm was so stiff, I could barely move it without wincing. But the waiting was far worse.

Arsenault and I attended our own chores in the early afternoon. I went back to our room for the sontana nap, but Arsenault didn't meet me there, and I spent most of the time pacing, drinking his brandy, and sweating, wondering what I ought to wear to the villa. But finally, the drink and the heat put me to sleep.

I awoke with an aching head that didn't make the evening any easier. I put off the decision of my appropriateness until after I'd bathed and washed my hair. I came back to the room in the purple twilight to find Arsenault waiting for me.

He sat at his worktable, dressed in doeskin trousers the color of coffee with cream. His hair gleamed black and wet and hung loose over his shoulders. The armband of burgundy Aliente silk shone in the lights from the candles dotting his table. The candles illuminated the lumps of metal scattered on the tabletop and made them glow, too.

He held an ingot of that odd whitish metal he'd bought in Liera. It looked different in the candlelight, as if it had been shaped. He closed his fingers on it and stood up.

"Are they having us to dinner?" I asked.

A faint trace of amusement flickered in his gray eyes. "Have you decided to wear your robes, Eterean-style?"

I'd snuck in the back door still wearing my towel. Now I stared at my blue guarnello with the pink roses on the bodice and then at my trousers. The dampness from my bath turned to sweat while I stood there, and the shutters rattled with a hot wind that brought no relief.

"You're not donning armor, Kyrra."

"Would that I could," I murmured.

He was no help at all. But I had determined not to ask him for his advice in this matter. I made my own decision.

I put on the trousers. I had a white linen shirt to wear with them, but no armband.

"Do you want me to braid your hair?" Arsenault said when I was finished dressing.

Braiding my own hair was still the only thing I hadn't learned to do. With his help, I usually kept my hair cut level with my chin, but when he was gone for so long, I hadn't asked anyone else to do it, and now I had enough for a short, gathered braid.

I shook my head. I would wear my hair loose in the manner of men attending fashionable dinners, the way he did.

He said nothing but smiled, running his hand through my curls as he bent to kiss me. Then he belted on his own sword, and we went together to the big house, he with his sword on the outside, me with my knife hidden inside my trousers, in the sheath against my hip.

I felt as if I were marching to war.

***

A MALE SERVANT WHOM I DIDN'T RECOGNIZE MET US AT THE door. My appearance seemed to take him by surprise; he stared at me for a moment, then bowed hastily and showed us inside.

"Bona sorro. The Householder and his wife are waiting for you upstairs in the drawing room. If you'll follow me..."

He turned and began walking down the uncarpeted tile hallway. Arsenault made to follow him, but I couldn't help staring at the floor.

"Where did the carpets go?" I asked.

The servant glanced at us nervously. "They've all been sold."

"Sold?" My eyebrows arched. "These carpets were woven by Salafin himself."

Arsenault put his hand on my shoulder and leaned down to speak in my ear. "Many things have changed. Just go."

He flicked his fingers at the servant; relieved, the servant began walking again and Arsenault after him. I had no choice but to follow, the sound of my bootheels echoing hollowly off the bare stucco walls.

Mosaics were now visible on the floor, chipped gold medallions older than my oldest great-grandfather, tile that had been laid fresh beneath the soles of Eterean sandals. Frescoes I'd never seen revealed themselves on the bare walls—the faded gray-green outlines of olive groves, the line of a deer strung up by its heels.

Adalus.

Hidden in the disappearing foliage of olives stood the faintest imprint of a man with a bow, taking aim.

I'd never known Erelf inhabited our very house.

For his part, Arsenault looked straight ahead, his gaze fixed on the servant's back. I don't know if he saw the frescoes or not, but probably—I had to remind myself—he had seen them before. It felt strange to know less of my birthplace than he did, but he belonged to it now and I didn't.

My parents sat on the veranda outside the drawing room, illuminated against the night by a bronze candelabra that gave off a soft yellow glow. More candle flames guttered and shook on the stone abutments of the balcony, but these had an acrid smell —herbs to drive off the mosquitoes and other night insects.

"Kyrra," Arsenault said softly, putting his hand briefly to the small of my back. "They're expecting us."

I gave a start at Arsenault's touch, gazed up at him like a deer, then nodded and followed him across the room.

The servants disappeared and the door closed with a *snick*, leaving us alone with my parents.

"Kyrra," my father said. I stumbled on the division between the stone floor of the balcony and the tile of the drawing room as I turned around. My face burned as I straightened up.

My father visited the barracks from time to time, so I'd been able to track the changes in him, even if we'd never spoken. His hair, once black streaked with gray, was now more gray-streaked black. I wondered what Claudia d'Imisi would think of him.

CHAPTER 26

My mother said, "At least you came."

I couldn't see her face well in the candlelight. There were too many shadows. But I couldn't mistake her disapproval of my appearance. My father looked upset too, a troubled frown pulling down his mouth.

"Didn't I give you instructions, Arsenault?" my mother said.

He stood with his shoulders a straight line. "I brought Kyrra here as you requested me to, Messera."

"So you did," my father said. "And I'm grateful for that. But, Kyrra, you do realize that all the Houses will attend this wedding, and that you may come under disapproving eyes?"

There were no greetings, no niceties, not even a formal kiss. Not even the acknowledgement a servant could expect. Instead, it was as if I'd walked into the middle of a conversation already in progress.

"What matter is it that they disapprove of me now?" I said. "They've always disapproved of me."

I could feel the way my parents stared at my stump. I'm sure they didn't mean to, because both of them turned abruptly away, looking not at me or at each other but instead at different points in the setting: my mother into the night; my father, the base of the candelabra, where wax dripped in thick pools.

"Camile di Sere is barren," my father said. "And Geoffre blames you for cursing his son. If he sees any hint of favoritism from me..."

"He wishes me dead, Father. He'll call anything more than that *favoritism*."

"No." He rose from the table to lean on the balustrade. "He wants you alive, and he wants to observe me favoring my only child, so that he may accuse me of treason in the Circle and legally have all my lands. All the Heads of House will be here, and they will be waiting to catch me in a misstep. The Caprine want me removed and Lisano elevated in my place—do you remember Lisano, my cousin?"

"Just because I'm no longer your daughter doesn't mean I've forgotten all my blood ties, Father."

"Mind your tongue, Kyrra," my mother snapped. "Why don't you sit and eat, and we'll discuss this after we've taken some nourishment. Otherwise, I don't believe I'll be able to stomach it."

My father sighed and sat down. My arms and legs stiffened, and I looked to Arsenault for a cue as to how I should react.

In truth, I only wanted some escape. But he didn't provide it. Instead, he pulled out a chair for me and waited for me to sit before he sat down in the other chair.

I tried to serve myself, but my mother took the spoon away from me and did it. Startled, I looked up at her, but her mouth was pursed tight and she kept her gaze on the spoon as she ladled out a bowl of stewed eggplant, then passed us a cheese board with a fan of thin ham slices above the cheese. There was a platter of sliced melon and a loaf of bread, but the oil that accompanied it didn't have the fruity olive taste I remembered, and the wine was mediocre. The best wines were being saved for the wedding, and maybe the olive oil too.

We ate in silence for a moment, the only sounds the wind in the trees and the *clink* of our silverware. We had small silver forks to pick up our food. The gavaros said forks were becoming the fashion, even among the lesser Houses who could ill afford it.

I ate little. The melon wasn't quite ripe, the ham too salty, and I couldn't seem to swallow with my mother and father watching me cut one-handed, then put down my knife to pick up my fork.

I began to be grateful that I wouldn't have to endure the endless courses of the wedding feast, where hundreds of little silver forks would be laid out in rows.

"Does your arm still pain you?" my father asked.

I stopped trying to spear a chunk of eggplant and looked up at him. "Sometimes," I said.

"The chirurgeons did their best sewing it up. I did all I could."

The corners of Arsenault's mouth turned down into his beard and I knew he was trying not to scowl. I laid down my fork. "It isn't the stump that hurts," I said.

My father's brows lifted in nervous surprise, and I looked away hastily, picking up my goblet and finishing off the dregs of my wine.

My mother sighed. "We can dispense with this, I think. What's done is done, and there's no use trolling back over it. You seem to have healed well, daughter." Her mouth quirked as I put the goblet down. "With your rebelliousness still intact. But I tell you, Kyrra, you *must* obey us in this."

"In what, Mother? If you wished to make it seem as if I enjoyed no favoritism from you, then you shouldn't have invited me here. The servants saw us; they'll talk."

Arsenault cleared his throat. "The servants don't entirely know who you are, Kyrra. Most of them are new."

"They've heard the stories. They've seen me and my arm. Who else lives on this estate without a right arm?"

"My suggestion is still to send her away, Mestere," Arsenault said. "Let her go, someplace she'll be safe."

I frowned. "I told you I would stay, Arsenault. You're staying, aren't you?"

"I fail to see how whether Arsenault stays or goes has anything to do with it," my mother said, leaning back in her chair. Her eyebrows formed twin arches. She steepled her hands and pressed the tips of her fingers to her mouth.

It was a question. More than a question. I battled down a flush and held my head up.

"Arsenault is in much more danger than I from Geoffre di Prinze. If Geoffre were to find him out—"

My father frowned at Arsenault. "I knew she was in the barracks, but what have you told her? Do the other men know?"

Arsenault drew himself up straight, and I cursed myself.

Then the tension in his shoulders eased and he fingered the rim of his goblet, spinning it as he spoke. "No," he said. "Though they might wonder, as often as I'm away. They all know why you hired me, Mestere." He stopped spinning the cup. "One of the reasons, anyway."

My father hunched over his food, arranging his forks. "Would that I could send Kyrra away. But where would I send her? The only place that would satisfy the Prinze would be one of the cripple colonies—"

"And you are of no use to us there, daughter," my mother said as she leaned forward. "No matter how they've tried to sever your ties to your House, you still exist within its confines. We want to show that you have become, in truth, a serf, in body and soul. Then the Prinze won't be able to make any legal claims against us in the Circle. They'll have no evidence to stand on."

"Do they need evidence?" I said. "They'll make it up if it doesn't exist. All they have to do is expose Arsenault and they'll know you've been spying on them."

"As if they don't have their own spies everywhere?" my mother said, waving her hand in dismissal. "It's not illegal, spying."

"But Arsenault is a trusted member—"

My father slammed his fist down on the table so that the dishes rattled. He sat up against the table's lip and said, "Arsenault. *How much have you told her?*"

Arsenault had been following this exchange with an increasingly stormy expression, and now he clearly struggled to bring it under control. I saw the warrior in him as he matched my father's anger with all the give of a steel blade. "I told her only as much as she discovered for herself, Pallo. You can't expect me to carry out all these tasks and have none of them overlap."

My father rose and paced behind the table. "You were supposed to keep her safe. But how is she safe with all this information in her head? In the barracks, with sword and dagger? I thought she was just playing at something, the way she's always done. But do you mean to tell me she *knows*?"

Arsenault clenched his jaw but remained seated. "She knows how to use a knife. And a sword. You told me you couldn't give me any instructions but you wanted to see her safe, so I should protect her in the way I saw fit. That's what I've done. I've protected her in the way I Saw to do it."

I shivered, half in anger, half with the crackling feeling that came into the air when Arsenault spoke of his magic—as if he'd called it to himself. His eyes glittered in the candlelight.

I stood up. "I'm not a child," I said. "I'm a woman grown, without ties to House or kin, and I can choose as I please. If I choose knowledge, then let it be my own responsibility."

They all stared at me, my father, my mother, Arsenault. Magic thrummed in the night air. I could reach out and take it if I wanted.

If my father knew there was magic in the air, he didn't show it, but my mother narrowed her eyes shrewdly.

"Knowledge bears a heavy price, Kyrra. It makes it doubly important that you not give yourself over to Geoffre."

I sat down. "I know far less than he'd be able to get out of Arsenault. Geoffre has no reason to suspect that I know anything."

"Only if you give him no reason to suspect it. But don't think he won't try to dupe you into giving up your information, one way or another." My mother laughed, bitterly. "If he knows you can use a knife, he may even have you attempt to kill his son. Then he could take you on the spot and send his troops down on us all at the same time."

To my mother, it was a jest. But Arsenault's fingers stilled on the table. He looked like a statue, gray, unmoving.

There was fear in his eyes.

I found my hand at my side of its own accord again, and I looked up to find my father looking darkly thoughtful and my mother, torn.

Geoffre loved Carolla, Arsenault had told me, not long before, and I had counted back from a birth to find the month that Geoffre visited us...

Seated across from her, with the magic swirling around me, I Saw the truth.

She had lain with Geoffre and hidden it from my father. Had she done it of her free will? I couldn't tell. But I could see that she knew Geoffre better than anyone.

How naive had I been? I felt like an old woman now, and a dupe.

Arsenault said, his voice rough, "Let me send her away, Pallo. I know a place where she'll be safe. I can send her by boat to Vençal. I know a man there, and I'd trust him with her life. *Mestere*."

My parents had to see what Arsenault and I had become in his plea. I didn't understand how they couldn't.

But they said nothing. The tone of Arsenault's voice might have passed by like the wind, forgotten as soon as it was gone.

"You've done enough, Arsenault," my father said. "I think it's time for you to relinquish your role as bodyguard. You won't be able to perform it, anyway, in the times to come."

Arsenault cursed and stood up, leaning on the table with both hands. "So, now, when your daughter is most in danger, now is when you'll give up her protection? You'll just throw her to the wolves?"

"I am the Householder. I am responsible for the entire Aliente family and all our holdings. *We* are responsible for the safety of every single person on this estate. I am not asking Kyrra to do anything I wouldn't ask of myself."

Arsenault looked like he was grinding his reply in his back teeth. Then he straightened and bowed, stiffly. "Pardon, Mestere, if I misunderstood. I didn't realize that you would stand in her place if need be."

"Do you think I enjoy this, Captain?"

"No, Mestere. But you've refused to listen to all the alternatives I've presented you."

My father gripped his own sword hilt. "Because all your alternatives involve war, damn you." Then he dragged in a heavy breath and turned to me.

"You'll be a serf, Kyrra. You'll trade your sword for a skirt and sleep in the combing house until the wedding has passed, and Lobardin will check in on you."

I came out of my seat. "Lobardin! Father, Lobardin is in Geoffre's pocket! He'll betray you if he thinks he can save himself!"

"What?" my father said, his brows crinkling. He looked as if he'd just been slapped. He turned to Arsenault. "Arsenault—what is this about Lobardin?"

He didn't know. Arsenault hadn't told him.

"Gods *curse* Jon!" I said, shoving my chair away from the table. "You didn't tell my father what you knew? Gods curse you, too!"

Arsenault's expression went flat. I could have forgiven him if he had put his arms out to stop me, if he had been less of a warrior, if he had said, *No, please, you don't understand...* But he did none of that. The pain in his eyes was such that I might have cut him, but the emotion was quickly gone, submerged in that sea of murky gray.

"Arsenault," my father said. His voice shook. "You will tell me what my daughter is talking about. Now."

Arsenault let all his breath out. "Lobardin di Cozin is the youngest son of Trescan di Cozin, the lead householder of the Amoran Circle. He was banished from the city of Amora several years ago for running Prinze ships under the barricade for payment, and when he got to Liera, he went running to Geoffre. But Geoffre used him for another purpose."

"Which was?" My father's mouth was one hard line. My mother clenched the tablecloth in both hands.

She'd trusted Lobardin too but had trusted Arsenault more.

Arsenault rubbed his brow. "Sorcery. Geoffre accepted Lobardin into his household, then made him into a sort of magical experiment. Magic comes in many guises. It can be used for many things—Sight and Fixing primarily—but there are other purposes, fouler, most of them lost. Even Sight can be an evil thing, turned to the wrong ends."

He looked up, his face drawn. "Geoffre had Lobardin See into himself. This isn't a trial to be taken lightly. In my homeland, it was the supreme test of a haukdal, one to whom magic comes willingly and well. It isn't meant for anyone unwilling or for those who only call wild magic. Especially not those whom Ires uses. Most men, when faced with their own darker corners, flee."

As the shadows flickered on his face I thought, *He's been through this trial.* But what had he Seen? Had he fled or had he stood?

I couldn't imagine Arsenault fleeing.

He went on. "Whatever Lobardin Saw, he hates Geoffre now." He turned to me. "It isn't so much that Lobardin is in Geoffre's pocket, Kyrra. It's just that he knows he's caught between two Houses that want to use him, and nobody else wants to hire him because of who he is. Lobardin loathes Geoffre, and I think there's a good chance he could assassinate Geoffre while he's here."

The table went quiet. My father moistened his lips. "We'd have the entire Prinze force down on us in a trice."

"But it would be disorganized. Without Geoffre, who will head the Prinze? Devid? Cassis? They're both weak men. Neither has the strength to marshal the kind of fear their father does. And they have no heirs."

"What you've said courts war," my mother said, tight-lipped. "It invites the Prinze to war with us."

"We'll have war no matter what we do, mistiri," Arsenault replied, looking at my mother directly, then at my father. "Better to have it on our own terms."

"What does Lobardin think of this plan of action?"

"I haven't broached it with him yet. But he knows I plan to use him for something. And he knows it involves Geoffre."

"But why do you fear that Lobardin will betray us?" I said. "If he hates Geoffre, what would be so hard about killing him?"

My father frowned at me, but I ignored him. Arsenault frowned, too, but for a different reason. "Lobardin is also terrified of Geoffre," he said, "and Geoffre wants him because of what he's Seen in him. The risk we take is that Lobardin isn't strong enough to oppose Geoffre."

I thought about Lobardin and his many faces—his mocking public persona full of bravado, and the way he became meaner and more dangerous when he smoked kacin. But I'd also seen what I thought might be the real man inside, and knowing now that Geoffre had used him, perhaps his behavior made more sense. I had no doubt that he could kill Geoffre, and no doubt that he possessed more strength of character than most people credited him with.

But if he recovered his strength...would he perhaps choose to destroy both our Houses, to seek redemption from his family in Amora?

"How do you know about this, Arsenault?" my mother said.

"I had it from him and a man I trust, who knows the truth."

He still wouldn't betray Jon. It made me uneasy, but I held my tongue.

My father rubbed his chin. Then he sighed. "I can't let you do this, Arsenault. There are too many risks involved, and we may yet avoid war."

Arsenault blinked. "Pallo," he said. "Mestere..."

My father waved him quiet. "No. In this I will hear no dissent. I would avoid war at all costs. I will not have the lives of my people based on a man of questionable loyalty. If Lobardin fails, what happens? The Circle hears a case of attempted murder, and the trail leads itself back to you and by extension me, my lands are forfeit, and we submit to the Prinze."

"You don't have to submit to the Prinze," I said viciously. "You could fight then, too."

He held up a hand. "I submit to the *law*, Kyrra. I said I will hear no dissension in this."

"Pallo—" my mother began.

"It is my decision to make!" my father shouted at her. We both recoiled. I had never heard him raise his voice to her in my life. Then he clamped his mouth shut, and his throat worked as he tried to bring himself under control.

"I have said all I am going to say on the matter. Lobardin will be banished from these estates, Kyrra will go back to the combing house, and you, Arsenault—you will keep me *informed* of matters as they stand and when they happen. Is that clear?"

"Si, Mestere." Arsenault inclined his head in respect, but his jaw was strung taut and he had his hand on his sword. He held the hilt so tightly, his knuckles stood out.

"We will not invite war," my father said again. "I am taking a wife to avoid it. Do you think that makes me happy?"

He and my mother shared a long, tortured look, and I could barely breathe.

All of this was my fault.

I clenched my shirt at my side as if everything could be made better if I only had a sword, but there was no way out of this mess. My father came to stand behind my mother and put his hand on her shoulder, and I realized that we were dismissed.

"Father," I said, bowing, "I'll do as you say."

He didn't look at me. Instead, he just waved me away.

I turned around with tears in my eyes. Arsenault adjusted his sword and started after me, bowing, too, but then my father said, "Arsenault," and he stopped.

"Si, Mestere?"

"Send my daughter away after the wedding. Don't tell me where she is. I'll not want to know."

CHAPTER 27

On the fifth day of the storm, when the weather finally begins to clear, Charri comes down the stairs to tell us to get out. After five days of being cooped up in a cellar with Silva and Meli and their companions, it's a relief to be kicked out.

But when we go, we bring Silva with us. As a hostage for Meli's silence. Trapped down in the basement for five days with nothing to do but tend to Arsenault, I learned a few things but not what I most wanted to know.

Silva knows what happened at Kafrin Gorge.

I promise to send him back after we're well away. Meli watches me like she's trying to decide if I'm lying or not. I've tried to talk myself into killing her, but I can't. Two mornings ago, when I woke from another fitful sleep on the floor beside Arsenault's narrow cot, she had gotten him up and given him a wet cloth to wash his face, and was helping him with a bowl of broth. When his blanket slipped off his shoulders, she pulled it back up and kept up a soft one-sided conversation about the weather so he would stay alert enough to eat. When his head began to dip, she caught the bowl and helped him lie down again.

After that, I knew I wouldn't be able to wield the knife. And if I couldn't kill her, that meant I'd have to keep Silva alive somehow, too.

After a lot of struggle, Mikelo, Silva, and I get Arsenault to the end of the street. A burned crescent of forest curves past a shattered house and its courtyard. Broken frescoes litter the blackened tiles, and tiny, weedy saplings force their way up through the stones of the garden paths. Red poppies overrun the garden, spilling over every crumbled stone and garden paver, their vaguely narcotic scent heavy in the air.

Storm wrack—broken branches and shredded young leaves—is scattered everywhere.

In the midst of this riot of life and death, Mikelo and Silva grunt as they help Arsenault to the ground. He breathes hard and blinks sweat from his eyes, then leans against a wall leveled to the height of his shoulders. The bottom strip of a fresco remains intact on the plaster—a row of bare feet, the knees of a kneeling man.

"Kyrra," Arsenault says, rubbing his chest. "Where are we going?"

He isn't quite himself yet—whoever that may be. Today is the sixth day. A hazy pain glaze still floats in his eyes and he's been rubbing his chest a lot, as if he might scratch the new skin out. If my experience is any pattern, he'll clear tomorrow, but he'll be weak. He hasn't eaten much, though sometimes he's awakened as thirsty as a man in the desert.

"I'm going to buy clothes for you," I say, "and some horses. I'm taking Silva with me. Mikelo will stay."

Mikelo and Silva both look up at me in surprise, and Arsenault looks troubled. "You're taking Silva?"

"I can't leave him with you. He's going to help me in the horse market."

"Then you're still going to finish Tonia's job?"

I rub my forehead. I've had five days to do nothing but think, and I still haven't figured out what's going on. I can't imagine we've slipped out of Geoffre's sight, which means he must have wanted us to get at least this far, and if that's so, what is his true goal? Does he want me to kill Cassis? Or does he merely think it entertaining to set Arsenault and me against each other?

"Kyrra," Mikelo says softly. "I could ask my uncle for asylum—"

I let my hand drop and turn to face him. "Your uncle won't give me asylum. He wants something else out of me, but I don't know what it is. The only way to find out is to play the game."

"Is it?" Arsenault says.

Something in his voice makes me turn. His gaze catches mine, and I remember the last time we talked about games we had to play and my naive assertion that we could escape. There is something different in his eyes now since Mikelo healed him, less confusion but more question. I suppose my behavior with Silva at the inn didn't help.

A flush comes up on my cheeks and I look down at the pavers.

But then Razi and Vadz are between us, too.

"You could leave," I tell him. "If you wanted to. But I have to do this."

For the five years I allowed him to fight these battles on his own. For not doing what Jon thought I could do, long ago. If Arsenault hadn't tried to protect me, I might have killed the family then and stopped the war before it started. Then Vadz could have gone home to Aleya and Razi would still have his arm.

Arsenault's expression darkens. "I'm not a coward."

"I meant I'd save you from this fight. It's mine now, and I know you think I ought to stop, but I can't."

The tight line of his lips softens. "I won't leave you," he says.

I nod, a sharp dip of my chin, but inside I am more relieved. What would I have done if he'd said yes?

I turn my attention to Mikelo and Silva. Troubled lines mar Mikelo's face, and Silva looks stormy, left out, unable to follow what I've been saying.

I rise and grab Silva by the arm. "Come on. We'd best be off."

※

"Why don't you just kill me and get it over with?" Silva says after we turn the corner onto the street.

I made him dress in his finest clothes before we left so we could fit in with the householders in town. He's wearing a sky-blue shirt of medium-grade silk given to him by a patron. Not fine enough to be spun from Aliente worms, but silk nonetheless.

"And risk your sister going to the Town Guard?"

"We both know that you've managed it to so you could kill me and she'd never know before it was too late. Meli's a soft touch."

"I don't think she's as soft as you think she is."

"So, you use me before you kill me, then make your escape. If you want me to trade services for horses like Meli did the other night, you can do it yourself."

"I don't think your services are worth a horse, Silva."

Silva laughs—more of a cynical bark. "Oh, that's fine. Go ahead and throw barbs. See how easy it is to perform with a man like your captain looking daggers *your* way."

"Aren't you supposed to be trained for those situations?"

"For situations in which a woman with a metal arm hires me to taunt a wanted traitor responsible for the deaths of hundreds or thousands of men? I'd like to know the madam farsighted enough."

"About that..." I say. With a flick of my wrist, I have the knife out of my wrist sheath and in my right hand. His eyes widen at the sight of the naked blade, and then he looks around wildly as if searching for an escape. But I've led him into an empty street that ends in a box with a collapsed wall. Our only company is a flock of pigeons and a couple of cats, poking through the trash.

"You're mad," he says in a strained voice. "You're just mad."

"Have you figured out who I am?"

He looks startled. "Your name is Kyrra. You're not the only Kyrra in the world."

"True." I push up my sleeve so he can get a good look at my arm. I bound my right hand with linen rags before I left, in place of my gloves. But the rest of my arm is covered only by my sleeve.

His eyes widen, and I let my sleeve fall back into place.

"Arsenault fought for my father," I say.

Silva stares at my arm, then at me. His eyes grow even wider, and his voice shakes when he says, "You're Kyrra d'Aliente."

"Shh," I say, putting a linen-wrapped finger of my right hand to my lips. "No one goes by that name anymore."

"Then why—" He wipes his mouth with the back of his hand and lets it fall. "Your father's captain—he was treating with the Prinze..."

"How do you know that?"

Silva bolts. But I'm ready for him. I lunge with him, catching him by the shoulder with my right hand and slamming him against the wall of a crumbling building. He gasps in pain. I settle my knife against the hollow of his throat.

"I said, *how do you know that?*"

"I saw him with Geoffre di Prinze."

"And what made you think that Geoffre wasn't holding him prisoner?"

"I saw him come out of the Prinze tent. He had no escorts, no guards. He walked out of the camp just as the Aliente troops started moving down the gorge. He was gone when the Prinze lit the fire."

"When they lit your village?"

"The camp. We were shepherds. We had grazing rights on Imisi and Aliente lands. That village was our camp in late summer. It was there, so we used it."

"At the south end of the gorge." I'd hardly call those buildings a village. Lean-tos were set up in the ruins of old Eterean buildings. A common thing, in the Eterean countryside.

"The wind blew up from the south."

"You think Geoffre let Arsenault go because they had a deal. Arsenault would desert my father in his time of need, and my father would lead his troops himself, directly into the way of danger. Is that it? Or do you blame Arsenault for more? If he was in Geoffre's tent, what do you think he was doing there?"

Silva's eyes darken. It's interesting how his eyes change color, blue to indigo—such a dark color, like a twilit sky. "I don't know what he was doing there. But I can tell you what he wasn't doing there. He wasn't doing anything for us. The Prinze torched the buildings, slaughtered our sheep—took the women, my mother, my sister—"

His voice closes off. But it doesn't matter that he stops talking. You can see it in his eyes what happened.

Men don't think at such moments. Neither villains nor victims. I stood in the middle of one of the worst massacres in Rojornicki history and it was the same. The thinking comes after. In dreams and odd moments, when the crash of thunder becomes the exact sound of a cannonball crushing the wall of your room, or when the clank of table knives sends you scrambling for your sword.

"So, you wanted to kill him for that?" I say. "For something the Prinze did to you?"

"He was in Geoffre's tent! He walked away! No one stopped him. They were setting the torches as he went. He was the Aliente captain. He had a responsibility to do *something*."

"Where were you?"

"Roped to one of the buildings. I tried to drag my sister away from one of the Prinze gavaros, and his friends beat me and tied me there. Then they forgot about me." His chest heaves. "I saw everything."

I take a deep breath.

"Arsenault's greatest talent was in making himself trusted,

and my father used that talent to its utmost. My father would never have led his troops into that gorge himself. There must have been something else at work there, something you weren't privy to. There must have been something..."

Something Geoffre did to Arsenault in that tent.

Something someone told my father.

Silva shifts and I jam the knife back against his throat, but he leans forward anyway. "If you believe the best of him, then what happened in that alley? He attacked you!"

"I only wanted to know where he stood. What game he was playing, if he was playing one."

"And that's why you used me to taunt him? What made you change your mind?"

"He wears burgundy," I say—the simplest explanation. Silva wouldn't understand the rest, and I'm not sure he needs to know anyway.

"And that's enough for you?"

"It means more than it seems."

"You just wanted me for my story. And now that I've told you, you're going to leave my body in the dust." He closes his eyes and tenses, in preparation for the wound. "Go ahead, then. I'm ready."

"Do you believe what I said?"

He opens his eyes in surprise. "I— I've not seen anyone wear burgundy in Karansis," he stutters. "The Prinze have banned it."

"It would have been daring if he was only wearing it to fool me, wouldn't it?"

Silva's eyes flicker and his brows pull down, like he's coming to a conclusion he doesn't want to make. "Suicidal. The Prinze would have hauled him into jail and hanged him in the morning."

"You've heard stories about his magic, haven't you?"

Silva eyes me warily. "Stories."

"They're true. Sometimes, magic gets out of hand. The fight we had in the alley was magic getting out of hand. Burgundy is the truth."

"But he did nothing in the Gorge! He just walked away—past the soldiers!"

"Do you think maybe he was trying to take his place beside my father so he could save everyone?"

Silva falls silent.

I slide the knife back into its sheath and drop my arm. "Help me buy the horses. Then you can leave."

Silva's brows arch. "Just like that?"

"Look," I say, "maybe your sister is a soft touch, but she's had enough pain in her life without you causing her more, don't you think?"

"What are you saying?"

"I'm saying that if you make me kill you and force her to carry through on a promise of revenge, you're going to ruin her life. All that work she's ashamed of, all those hours she puts in so she can save some coin are geared toward getting the both of you out of Karansis. Not just her, *you*. You're the only family she has left, yes?"

"Yes, but—"

"And so, not only does she have to work on her back to get you out of here, she also has to keep you from haring off on some damn fool mission of honor to avenge something *she's* just trying to put in the past so she can move forward. And here you are, fixating on it so she can't forget it either."

"But what else am I supposed to do?" Silva says in anguish. "I couldn't do anything then, and you're telling me I still can't do anything about it? I might as well have never been untied from that building!"

"Haven't you been listening to a word I said? Go back to your sister and let her know you've decided to drop your quest for vengeance. Make your money and take her out of here. That's how you help her best."

I'm aware of the irony of what I'm telling him, but just because I can give good advice doesn't make it the kind of advice I can take myself.

"But I can't go back to the Youth. And none of the reputable houses will hire me. I've tried." He runs a hand through his hair, tousling his curls as he stares at the ground. "I make a poor courtesan."

"Your technique did want a bit," I'm forced to admit, and I watch his expression sag even further. For some reason, I feel the urge to cheer him up. "But there are men who like the passion you do have, aren't there?"

He gives me an odd look. "My patrons don't care about me, as long as I play their games. Just like you. Sometimes, I'm not good at playing along."

Those kisses I paid for have given us an intimacy I wish we didn't have.

"Well, then," I say. "Help me buy my supplies and maybe you can try your hand at something else."

"Like what?"

"I don't know. Show a little initiative. Sell ghost tours around the murder markers on Murderer's Ridge."

He darts a glance at me and then, as if he's doing it against his will, he laughs. I smile in return. People eventually fill in the gaps around us as we walk out of the alley and toward the market, and there is no opportunity to speak anymore. Nothing has been resolved, but something has at least been patched.

He'll leave us alone. I don't know where he'll go, but I won't have to worry about the Karansis Town Guard barring our exit on information they got from him.

Mikelo is still there when I get back. He scrambles to his feet at my approach, clutching the sword in both hands. The horses dance behind me as I pull them to a stop, and one of them—a sturdy bay who reminds me of the horse I left in Liera —whiffles my hair.

Over the ridge of the wall, Arsenault looks up. His skin is paler than when I left.

"Where's Silva?" Mikelo says.

"I let him go." Mikelo looks startled, and I add, "He won't tattle on us."

Mikelo gets that rabbit look again. "You didn't—"

I tug the horses over to a willow tree. The new green leaves wisp past my shoulders as I loop the reins around its slim trunk. "Do I look like a woman who's spent her morning hacking a man to pieces?"

Mikelo takes a step back, and Arsenault surprises me with a chuckle. I watch him through a screen of drooping willow branches as I finish tying the horses. The bay mare bumps me with her nose, and I absently snake my arm under her head to stroke her opposite cheek.

"I suppose you don't," Mikelo says—grudgingly.

"He told you why he wanted to kill me," Arsenault says.

It's a statement, not a question. I push the willow fronds aside and walk over to them. "Something like that," I say.

"You believed him."

I sweep aside a pile of fractured terra-cotta and painted pieces of plaster with my boot and sit at a right angle from him, cross-legged, arranging my skirt over my knees.

I don't know what to call the light that glimmers in Arsenault's eyes. It might be amusement or merely curiosity. The color of his skin looks worse, sheened with sweat and pricked red along his cheekbones, but his eyes have begun to seem like those of the man I knew five years ago.

"He told me what he saw at Kafrin Gorge. I told him what I thought about what he saw. Then I told him what an ass he was being for causing his sister this kind of trouble. He seemed to understand, so I let him go."

Arsenault idly scratches his chest with his right hand, then winces. "And what did he see at Kafrin?"

"You. Leaving Geoffre's tent."

Arsenault laughs, shakily. "That's why he wanted to kill me?"

"It wasn't the only reason. He said you walked out of the tent unmolested and thought that proved you were colluding with Geoffre. He said the Prinze did terrible things to the shepherds. His mother is dead. Some Prinze gavaros had their way with Meli. He was tied to a building."

Both Mikelo and Arsenault wince when I mention Meli. It's one thing to know such a thing has happened to a woman without a name...and another to know it has happened to someone who handed you a bowl of porridge in the morning or covered you with a blanket when you were sick.

"He thought I was involved with that?" Arsenault asks.

"No. He thought you could have done something to stop them and you didn't. Or that you *should* have done something to stop them and you didn't."

I pick at the frayed ends of the linen around my right hand.

"He also said you deserted my father and stayed in the camp until the fire started, and then you walked away."

More silence. I unwrap my hand and flex my fingers. Pebbles crunch against the broken stones, and when I look up Mikelo is getting to his feet. He places the sword beside Arsenault. "I think I'll find some water."

He walks away without waiting for an answer.

"You've stopped thinking he'll escape," Arsenault says.

"I don't think he'll leave you."

When Arsenault doesn't reply, I say, "I didn't know what to believe from you. But I thought if I pressed you hard enough, I could find out the truth. And maybe you would remember it, too." I pull on my sleeve, trying to make it cover more of my arm. "I didn't want to believe that you were the assassin following me, but I think I knew, deep down. You seemed so familiar, even in disguise."

"I haven't seemed familiar to myself for a long while now. I have dreams. But when I wake...they're only dreams."

"What kind of dreams?"

He tips his head back against the wall and closes his eyes. "It's a strange state. Having died enough to recover some of my memories without dying enough to lose all of them. It's only been—how long?"

"Since Kafrin? A year and a half."

"A drop in an ocean. It feels as if I've only just awakened. I wandered...I don't know how long. Everything that mattered, I had lost. I decided I would just drink myself to death and start over. For some reason, I thought you were dead. I had it in my head you were a commission I'd had, and I'd failed at my charge. I couldn't remember anything but your name. But I remembered a serf girl... I couldn't quite recall her face..."

He brings his head back up and opens his eyes. "This is how the god torments me, Kyrra."

"But why? How?"

"Long ago, I made...a mistake." He curls his hands into fists and looks darkly down at them. Then the expression crumbles, and he opens his hands and shakes his head. "No, that's not honest. I committed a terrible crime. And I was sentenced for it. By the gods, since it involved one of their own. I was put at Erelf's mercy for as long as he wanted to have me. He hasn't given me up yet."

"Arsenault. A crime involving the *gods*?"

Shakily, he rubs his chest. His skin has gone waxy and it makes the black stubble on his face stand out. "It was a long time ago, Kyrra. The gods were closer to the world then."

"And Erelf steals your memories? That's your sentence?"

"No. My sentence bars me from the afterlife for as long as Erelf's vengeance isn't satisfied, and he's allowed to do whatever he wants to torment me. He's the god of knowledge. He twists what I know and what I don't know. Takes the memories I want to keep and leaves me whichever ones he thinks will torture me most. But I have to die first."

I sit for a moment, trying to sort my way through his words. A hundred questions buzz in my brain at once—what crime, how long has Erelf's vengeance lasted—but only one makes it past my lips.

"You really had forgotten all of me? Except my name?"

I curse myself for sounding so small and young—so like that girl I once was.

"No," he says. "My plan was to kill you, too. But I couldn't bring myself to do it. So, I tried again. And again." He glances at me. "That Nezar I shot—Razi? He was good. Protected you well. But when you pulled that sword and I saw it flare with my magic, it startled me so much that all I could think was that I needed to end things and get away. So, I pulled the gun and shot him."

"Damn. If I hadn't drawn my sword..."

"No, Kyrra. Don't blame yourself. Blame it on me. And on Erelf."

We're sitting an arm's length apart. I can smell him—that musty cellar scent and the sick-sweet smell of spent fever. His wrong-colored hair is rumpled and dirty, and his smooth, unmarred skin and the straightened line of his nose have taken years off his age. But it's him. He was down there after all.

It's a deep gulf to reach across, though. I lean toward him, hesitantly raising my left hand to touch him, and he moves toward me, catching my hand in his.

The crunch of footsteps makes us both look up, over the edge of the fallen wall.

It's not Mikelo. It's Silva, held by Mikelo, his arm twisted around behind his back.

※

"Dammit, Silva, I gave you a chance."

Silva sprawls on the broken tiles where Mikelo shoved him down. I stand over him with my knife out.

"He was listening," Mikelo says. "I came back with water, and he was down a few walls, making his way toward the horses. I hate to say it, Kyrra, but you might have been wrong."

"I wasn't coming to steal your horses!" Silva says, kneeling upright. "I was coming to tell you that the Prinze have got the city shut off. If you try and ride through the gates, you'll be captured for sure."

"And how are we to trust you?" Mikelo says. "Why didn't you just make yourself known?"

"I was waiting for a good moment! Do you think I wanted to surprise *her*?"

I bend down next to Silva and hold the knife up to his face. "You had better be telling the truth."

"I *am* telling the truth," he says, violet eyes flashing. "After that speech about my sister, do you think I want to cause her more pain?"

"Did you tell her what I told you to?"

"Yes. But on my way down to the Youth—the streets are full of Prinze."

I look to Arsenault. "You didn't bring them with you, did you?"

"No. I left Geoffre's spies in Liera."

"Your time to choose," I say to Mikelo. "What kind of game do you think Geoffre is playing?"

He runs his hand through his hair. "How should I know? How are we going to get out of the city?"

"I can help you," Silva says quickly. "I know the woods and the gaps in the wall. If we follow the spring and wrap around Murderer's Ridge, we can make it."

"The spring? But it's clogged with men!" Mikelo says.

Arsenault frowns thoughtfully. "We might be able to lose ourselves in the crowd," he says. "It's a good choice."

"It's your only choice," Silva says, "as far as I can see."

"You said *we*," I point out.

"I can't get hired again in Karansis, and I don't want to make Meli work harder or longer to support me. I told her I was going with you. She argued with me, but in the end, she let me go. If you're against the Prinze, I'm with you."

I rise from my crouch and put the knife away.

"All right. You can help us out of town and we'll see you off at the crossroads. That's as far as you can follow. Did any of the Prinze see you?"

He scrambles quickly to his feet and shakes the dirt from his clothes. "Wouldn't matter if they had. They're not looking for me."

"As long as you haven't told them anything."

"I *told* you I didn't."

"Arsenault, are you sure you can sit a horse?"

"No," he says. "But it's my only choice, isn't it?"

There isn't any arguing with that. Mikelo has already gone to the packs and dug out the rolled-up clothing. He sorts them out and hands a new shirt and a pair of trousers to Arsenault, then my dress to me. I bundle it in my hands and turn to Silva.

"Can you ride?"

"If it gets me out of here."

"Good enough." I shrug the peasant blouse over my head and shove my skirt down to my ankles. The air immediately cools the sweat on my bare shoulders as I stand there in my shift.

"Stop gawking," I tell Mikelo and Silva. "You've seen women before, haven't you?"

❧

THE TOWN OF KARANSIS FORMS A SHIELD BUTTING UP AGAINST Murderer's Ridge. The wall that fronts the town spreads out from the narrow spike of an entrance forming the handle of the shield, and then the town spills wide against the hillside. The founders must have considered the hills protection enough on the back side, because the wall ends slightly upslope in dense woods of oak, chestnut, and beech.

Or perhaps it was only that the founders thought no one would be fool enough to cross a ridge crested with black basalt monuments marking the sites of past murders.

Silva clings to the reins of an older chestnut stallion with intention, his face white as we jangle through the milling crowd of the marketplace. He doesn't know how to ride. Mikelo continually catches at his mount's bridle to bring it back into line.

We lashed Arsenault to the saddle so he wouldn't fall, and I'm riding in front of him so he can lean on me. Having his arms around me, his chest at my back, and his thighs against mine is a strange and comforting feeling, though I'll be the one doing the protecting if it comes down to it. Right now, he's in charge of the reins, but it will be easy for me to take them if I need to.

I glance over my shoulder at him. His hood shadows his face, but the lines of stress at the corners of his eyes stand out clear.

"How is it?" I ask.

"A little pain," he replies.

Mikelo brings his horse up close to the mare that Arsenault and I ride. The horses bump haunches, dance away from each other, and Mikelo leans over slightly in his saddle and murmurs, "Silva says we veer off on the path behind the bordellos, but he can't lead. He can barely sit his saddle."

"I'm going to keep an eye on both of you," I say.

Mikelo's brows hitch, but he nods and reins his horse away, ahead of ours so he can ride with Silva.

Battle is different from escape. I've spent many dull days quietly waiting for enemy troops to ride through a pass. But this isn't waiting. Instead, we must look so normal though the town bristles with Prinze. Silver and blue spike through the crowd. It isn't just the town Guard, barring the gates; it's a whole damn detachment sent to find us.

I lean back and Arsenault's head dips down beside mine so he can hear me when I whisper, "What is Geoffre doing? Is he just trying to keep sight of me? Or is he going to take Mikelo back and kill me right here?"

"I don't know," he says, in an exhalation that sounds as if he's trying to breathe his pain out. "Geoffre liked Mikelo on a short leash. Maybe he's making a move to get him back."

"You think he wants me to kill Cassis? He can't be stupid enough to think I was telling the truth, taking his offer."

"He may want you to kill Cassis. But if he does, he won't let you get away with it."

I frown, trying to sort that out. But my thoughts fly away from me again as we ride past a gavaro lounging on the side of the road, the sky-blue armband of Prinze service prominent on his gray shirt.

We're almost past when Silva pulls his horse into a great looping turn. His foot slides out of the stirrup, and Mikelo lurches over the neck of his own horse to catch the chestnut's reins. We cause a commotion in the glutted street, and someone calls out: "Ho, there, keep your mount under control!"

Whinnies, snorts, and the resounding ring of ironshod hooves on brick sound off on all sides. Arsenault tightens his legs against our mare's sides, and she barrels her way through a hole in the crowd to get to Silva. We brush legs and boots on our way past. A spur rakes my dress, tearing the hem. I snatch it up, cursing, and a man who also wears a blue armband turns to look at me.

"Have a care for your boots, sir!" I shout at him.

"Have a care for your dress!" he shouts back at me.

I hate riding without reins in my hands. I want my hand on my sword, but my sword is wrapped tightly to my leg so that I can't sit the horse properly, and with every swing and sway, I feel in danger of losing my seat. I can feel the tension that's wiring Arsenault together behind me, and the gavaro is still watching me...

Then we're out. Mikelo leans against the neck of his horse and mouths to Silva, "*Ride.*"

Silva is shaking, but his sky-blue shirt is an answer to prayer. He collects the reins in his hands, and his knuckles stand out from gripping them.

He hangs on and rides.

We hit the path that curves behind the inns at a fast walk.

Gravel crunches under the horses' hooves and then becomes hard-packed dirt when we find the path to the spring. When the path climbs into the woods on Murderer's Ridge, the dirt turns loose, black, and thick with leaf litter.

We ride in a silence full of sound—Arsenault's heavy breathing, the wind in the trees and the chirping of birds, the snap of twigs and the huffing of the horses and the gurgling rush of the river in the distance.

Arsenault's grip begins to loosen and he slumps forward against me. I reach for the reins and he pulls on them too hard, readjusting.

Finally, the tall basalt markers lining the crest of the hill loom up against the spring blue sky like soldiers from another age, square and black. The sunlight traces the writing carved on their surfaces and makes them glow.

Murder markers. The territory of the dead.

"We'll stop on the other side," I say in a low voice.

Arsenault dips his head and gulps in air. It's not quite a nod.

"Kyrra—" he gasps.

I open my mouth to tell him to be quiet, but a flash from out in the open, near the murder markers, catches my eye. Silva starts to break from cover, and Mikelo is about to follow him. I snatch under my dress to pull my sword at the same time that I shout, "*Ware!*"

In that moment, the men hiding behind the markers break their cover—five, ten, twenty—Gods, I can't count them—running straight for Silva and Mikelo, their silver and blue flashing in the sunlight spilling down the bare crest of the ridge.

"Take them alive!" someone yells.

"Silva! Mikelo!" I shout. "*Run!*"

BATTLE.

This is the chance the magic has been waiting for, and it leaps to take it.

It rushes through me like too much liquor—a burning euphoria that sets my vision askew. Until the light winks out and I can hear, or I can see but there is no sound. Or blackness drowns everything except the brief feeling I've done something.

Arsenault leans over me, barely hanging onto the reins, and Mikelo backs his horse into the trees. The Prinze swarm toward him, weapons drawn.

Mikelo has a knife I gave him, but he has his hands out, open. "Stop!" he shouts.

"Get off the horse!" one of the gavaros yells.

"No!"

They pull Mikelo down, twisting and fighting, but without his knife.

I knock Arsenault's arm away from me, slide off the horse, and smack it in the flank. Its hooves churn in the dirt as it leaps forward.

"Kyrra!" Arsenault shouts. Out of reflex my sword sweeps down to meet the flat of another blade. I shove the man to the ground with my boot and rake him across the thighs as I bring the sword back up to parry another blow directed at my head.

If they want to take me alive, they've not denied themselves the taste of blood first.

"Arsenault!" I cry. "Get Mikelo!"

The sound of hoofbeats is all that answers me, pounding out before I'm even done speaking.

I stop trying to be aware of anything else, and with a shout, devote myself to battle.

※

THE BATTLE RAGE BUOYS ME UP LIKE A PIECE OF FLOTSAM IN A storm. Both my sword and my arm flare blue light as the runes catch and fire, and I run into the enemy, laughing that high-edged lunatic laughter that is the true mark of Ires's Chosen. Faced with the sight of me, the men hesitate and break, trying to run, but too late. I take them one by one, hewing into them as if I'm clearing a path.

The first one dies when my sword slices across his throat. Blood gushes out in a fountain. The man next to him slips in the old leaves, and I take him with a diagonal cut into his neck that sends him flopping to the ground. The next man gets the point of my blade in his gut, and then I whirl to take the fourth with a cut across his hamstrings, leaving him writhing in the dirt, unable to walk.

Eventually, some of the men conquer their fear of me. I can't figure the odds, except that the men I kill seem to be replaced as soon as I kill them. I smash a man in the face with the knuckles of my right hand. Chips of bone jut up through his skin, and a fine spray of blood leaves its salt tang on my lips.

I lick the blood away, and my arm burns. The only way to relieve that sort of pain is to swing it, so I do.

But my blade meets more metal than flesh, and I look up wildly for Arsenault, breaking my trance.

A hilt slams into my stomach; the rage falters as I buckle over, still clutching my sword. Another hilt comes slamming down into the back of my head, and light sparks bright and hot. I lash out with my sword before I lose my grip on it and—

"*Arsenault!*" I call.

"Never here when you need him, is he, dove?"

The sword lies in front of me. I'm on my knees in the dirt. I can't see for the pain, but maybe my eyes are closed. I end up looking at boots, blurry around the edges.

I tilt my head up, and a face swims in my vision. Blue-black hair, dark eyes, a raven's profile... Surely, I'm dreaming.

"Lobardin?" I say.

He squats in front of me so I can look at him eye to eye. "I took a liking to your father's estates," he whispers.

He wears a blue armband. I struggle to push myself forward,

to close my metal fingers around the hilt of my sword, but Lobardin grabs my wrist and holds it up before I can.

"So, the stories are true?"

I snatch my hand back. "Where is Arsenault?"

The crack of a gunshot takes me by surprise. The squeal of a horse and the *thud* of its body hitting the ground.

Lobardin winces, but then he grins. "There he is, dove. Just there."

"Gods *curse* you, Lobardin—"

I yank one of the hatpins from my hair and throw myself at him. But he steps away from me with a quick, languid step, and his sword is out and coming down toward my head, hilt-first, in a blow that is going to slam me into the dirt.

I drive the pin into his forearm, but too late.

I am in the dirt, part of the dirt, swept over by blackness.

I keep going down, down, down for a long time.

CHAPTER 28

"Fetch more water!" a man shouts. "That can't all be her blood, can it?"

Lobardin. I groan and open my eyes.

I'm looking up at a cloudless blue sky punctuated by the spearheads of cypress trees. I must be on the road, on the other side of Murderer's Ridge.

I try to sit up and ropes pull taut at my wrists and ankles. I'm on a pallet. I blink my eyes to clear my vision, but the blur remains.

My head is one heavy, lumbering mass of pain.

"Lobardin!"

My voice comes out weak, and a pain lances through my left temple. I close my eyes against it. The wind pushes beneath my loosened bodice. The folds of my dress cling wetly to me where they've tried to wash me. I pull at my ropes, but the movement just makes sick waves in my head.

I open my eyes again and Lobardin's face takes the place of the sky.

"So, you are alive. I was beginning to wonder. I thought I might have to flee the country yet again, take up another commission."

"How did Geoffre catch you this time?"

He laughs. "You think I'm working for Geoffre? You always did think so little of me, didn't you?"

You give me no cause not to.

"Kyrra."

I try to focus again, and he leans closer, looking concerned. A white rag is wrapped around his forearm, but there's no other indication that I managed to hurt him.

"I didn't mean to hit you so hard, in truth."

I laugh. Weak laughter, but it's mine, not the magic's. Still the wrong response, to judge by Lobardin's frown and the way he pulls back.

"Bring water," he says to someone as he stands. "Make sure you wash that wound well."

What wound?

Cypress trees swing crazily as I try to lift myself up off the pallet, then fall back, retching.

Where is Arsenault? I want to shout. But the pain is too much. Darkness falls on me like a stone.

❧

I'M IN A COACH. EAGLES CRY OUTSIDE, BUT ALL I CAN SEE IS rose-colored velvet. I'm lying on my stomach, on a bench cushion. The velvet crushes against my cheek, soft and warm.

My arms are bound behind me, and my ankles are bound too.

Some of the pain is gone, but not all. I smell less like blood and vomit, but there's another familiar smell in the coach with me.

Kacin smoke.

A man sighs and the other seat creaks. Smoke tickles my nose, cloying and sweet. I hold my breath so I won't breathe it in, but my need for air betrays me.

I cough and booted feet thump down on the floor. In an instant, someone pulls my head up by my hair, and I'm staring at

Lobardin again. His pupils are so large and black, they almost swallow the color of his eyes. He puts his face too close to mine and breathes the over-sweet scent of kacin onto me.

I cough again and try to twist away, but the movement makes my head hammer.

"Kyrra," he says, smiling. Then he leans back from me hesitantly. "Are you going to vomit any more?"

"If you blow your smoke in my face. Gods, Lobardin."

He chuckles. I hear a *clack* when he picks up his pipe again, smoke still swirling out of it. He draws on it deeply, swaying with the motion of the coach, then blows the smoke out above my head.

"Where's Arsenault?"

"Behind the wagon. I wouldn't have recognized him if you hadn't called his name. A master of disguises, our Arsenault."

"He should have killed you while he had the chance."

Lobardin grins. "His mistake, eh?"

"Where's Mikelo?"

"Mmm. Mikelo." Lobardin's eyes are so glazed, I'm amazed he can even speak. It's hard to gauge the emotions running over his face. "Mikelo is riding in front. Best keep him alive and well for the moment."

I try to remember who Lobardin said he was working for, but can't.

"Geoffre will want him whole."

Lobardin snorts. He's turning something that glints in the light over in his hands, and I realize it's my other hatpin. Metal gleams on the seat beside him, and I think it's the knife I was keeping in my stays. The familiar feel of all my other hidden knives is gone, too, as well as the gun. But it was useless without shot.

"Geoffre wants the world handed to him on a platter," he says. "Let him try after it. He's made a mistake this time, and I hope he knows it. His son's finally gotten some balls."

Which son? I wish Lobardin's tongue was just a little looser.

He takes another pull from the pipe, and I shift my head so I can look around better.

A plush carriage, a bit fragile for the mountain roads, even if they are Eterean-laid in this part of the foothills. No colors or symbols hang in its interior to tell me whose coach it is. The curtains are velvet, like the cushions, but aside from that, the interior is devoid of the trappings one might expect.

"Devid put you up to this, did he? He wanted Mikelo?"

Lobardin opens his mouth. The words seem ready to slide out, then he clamps his lips shut and squints at me.

"I don't think I should divulge that information right now. Why don't you go back to being comatose?"

"You'd have to hit me again for that."

He puts the hatpin down and it rolls into the crack of the seat against the side of the carriage and then slides off onto the floor. Lobardin, his senses smoothed by kacin, doesn't notice. Instead, he leans toward me again, reaching out for my head. I jerk away and pain slams me, leaving me gasping for breath.

I lie as still as I can while his fingers probe the back of my head. Finally, they rest on a tender spot.

"Gods," I wheeze. "*Gods*, gods."

"The chirurgeon assures me you'll heal. But you need to rest. You'll need your strength."

"Where are we going?" I gasp.

"You'll see soon enough."

Then he grasps me by my hair and shoves his pipe in my mouth.

The pipe feels like it's going down my throat. He pinches my nose. I gag and struggle, pain battering me like swords on a battlefield.

"Breathe. Kyrra, damn you, *breathe*," Lobardin mutters over and over again, and gods save me, but I can't help breathing.

I fight for breath, and with it comes a rush of the purest kacin smoke I've ever tasted, sweeping down my throat.

When he takes the pipe away, I shout at him, "I hope you rot, Lobardin!"

He tries to jam the pipe in my mouth again. I roll away, but he catches me and shoves it in. "Just be quiet, Kyrra," he says. "Would you? For both our sakes."

The kacin unpins me. I rise in its arms like a bird.

"The eagles will eat you, Lobardin," I hear myself whisper.

He starts to laugh, but it's a mad laugh. Like mine.

"Let them," he says.

THE SLAMMING OF THE COACH DOOR WAKES ME UP. IT'S NIGHT. I flop around, disoriented, before another face peers down at me. A man's face. Mikelo.

Metal flashes—Lobardin holding Arsenault's sword at Mikelo's back. The runes stand out in the moonlight.

"They let me see you," Mikelo says. "Just for a moment. Are you all right?"

I try to nod, but it makes me queasy. Kacin dreams can turn about on you, and I've not had good ones. Battle mostly, and Erelf's ravens circling around the eagles.

"Did they hurt you?" I ask. My voice is raspy from the smoke and my throat hurts.

"Not much."

"Have you seen Arsenault?"

Mikelo starts to answer, but Lobardin lays the blade against Mikelo's back. "I said you could see her. I didn't say you could have a conversation with her."

Mikelo glares at Lobardin. "This is ridiculous. If my uncle sent you—"

"He didn't," I say quickly, somehow, finally, making the connections. "Cassis did. Didn't he?"

Mikelo looks at me, startled, and Lobardin grabs him by the collar and yanks him away.

"I was wondering when you'd figure that out," Lobardin says, still pressing the blade against Mikelo's back. His teeth glint in the moonlight as he smiles.

"Cassis?" Mikelo says. "How could he know—"

Lobardin's grin grows wider. "He heard it from a raven."

I go cold. "Jon told him, didn't he?"

"Do you still want to see Arsenault?" Lobardin asks.

The hatpin still gleams on the floor. It's rolled toward the door now.

I shove off with my toes against the side of the couch and shoot forward, off the bench. I land on top of the hatpin, jerk myself forward until I can grab it with my hands, and launch myself into Mikelo and Lobardin. And then—

Everything's a muddle. Cursing and pain, a tangle of arms and legs under me, I stab into flesh with the hatpin as hard as I can and hope to all the heavens I've hit Lobardin. He swears, loudly, in pain, and all of a sudden, I'm heaved up by my hair and Mikelo hits the side of the coach with a heavy thud. Lobardin takes his foot away from Mikelo's ribs, and my hands spasm open with the pain that shoots through my head and I drop the hatpin.

Mikelo makes a wheezy sound as he tries to breathe. Lobardin yanks my head back and rests the sword against my throat. Blood drips dark through the white bandage on his arm, but it doesn't seem to affect him much.

"That's Arsenault's sword," I gasp, through the red wash of anger and pain.

"And if you ever want to see him again, you'll *be still*. If Jon hadn't pleaded their case, they'd be dead by now. It's you Cassis wants, and it's you who's going to be keeping those two alive. All right?"

I'm trembling. The blade presses cold and hard against the skin of my throat, and the runes flash light in my eyes.

"Yes," I whisper.

"There, now," Lobardin says. "That's a good girl." He shoves me down on the bench again. I bite my lip and it bleeds. The blood tastes like salt and copper.

"Geoffre won't stand for it," Mikelo says.

Lobardin shrugs and sheathes the sword. "Geoffre may not have a choice. Now up and out."

Mikelo glowers at him for a moment, but we're surrounded by a detachment of guards. Finally, he gets up and Lobardin begins to lead him away.

"How many men did I kill?" I call out to Lobardin on impulse.

Lobardin stops and turns his head slightly but not enough to look back at me.

"Seven," he says. "And wounded three."

The numbers should give me some satisfaction, but they don't. "Put Arsenault in the coach," I say. "And keep Mikelo well. Or I start hurting myself. Who knows how much I'll be able to take with this head wound."

"Kyrra!" Mikelo says. But I know what I'm doing.

Lobardin faces me. His eyes are dark like the night so I can't see into them. "You would," he says after staring at me for a moment. "Wouldn't you?"

"Death doesn't frighten me."

Seven men and three wounded. I hope he takes my words for truth. The Rojornicki always did.

He watches me a moment more. His voice wavers when he says, "If I put Arsenault in here and you try to escape, you have my word that I will gut Mikelo and string his entrails up for those eagles. I'm not beholden to Jon for anything. If Mikelo's life means nothing to you, then I promise Arsenault will have no mercy." His teeth flash in the darkness as he smiles.

"And this time, I think he'll break for good."

In a few moments, I hear thumping and men's voices

behind the coach, then nervous laughter. I strain to filter Arsenault's voice from the din, but I can't. Steel rings against the stones, and I jump, then lay still, shaking.

In another moment, the door opens and Lobardin shoves Arsenault inside.

He hits the floor of the coach on his shoulder, hands bound behind him. He gasps and grimaces, then opens his eyes and looks up at me.

The tatters of his dirty shirt flutter in the breeze. He smells like blood and sweat and earth. Lobardin stands behind him, on the ground, and he hasn't shut the door of the coach because Arsenault's feet still hang out of it.

"Kyrra," Arsenault says in barely a whisper.

I make some noise—nothing with words. Lobardin shouts, "Get in if you're going!", and Arsenault slowly gathers his knees underneath him and rolls sideways, drawing his feet inside the coach.

"Help him sit up," I tell Lobardin.

Lobardin sighs. "Now, tell me," he says, "who's in charge here?"

But he grabs the top bar of the doorway and swings himself up and into the coach, then grasps Arsenault's arms and pulls him into a sitting position on the floor, wedging him against the other side of the coach.

The front of Arsenault's shirt is a mass of blood and mud.

"Your wound," I whisper.

"It holds."

"How charming," Lobardin says. "Such a reunion."

I glare at Lobardin. "I'll cut off your balls and feed them to you, Lobardin, I swear. Get me up."

"That arm hasn't improved your disposition," Lobardin says, but he pulls me into a sitting position. I lean back against the wall of the coach and close my eyes for a moment to get my bearings.

The coach creaks as Lobardin sits down beside Arsenault.

"Now. We're all together again, heading back to your father's lands. Except this is rather more the way *I* left it, isn't it?"

"My father banished you, Lobardin. You vent your anger on the wrong person."

Lobardin stops for a moment. Then he stretches his boots out in front of him and leans back. "Well, your father's dead, isn't he?"

The knowledge makes no more than a flick of impact on his face. I wish I could see if his eyes betray any of his true thoughts. He was ever this way, and it stirs a fury in me I would do better to hold back.

"Admit you're working for the wrong man! Do you think Cassis will prevail against Geoffre for long? You think you'll avoid the Prinze jaws by working for his son, on the basis of an old grudge?"

Lobardin laughs. "I'll take a lot from you, Kyrra, but spare me the hypocrisy. You came all this way to kill Cassis, didn't you?"

"It was my child and my arm. And I didn't turn coat to my enemies because of it."

"And it was my *life*." Lobardin's boots *thunk* on the floor as he leans up. "Cassis stands against Geoffre now. You'd do well to let your own grudges go."

"Enough," Arsenault says. "I don't remember, but I think she speaks true. I never had the power to banish you. If Jon wanted you on the Aliente estate, why would I send you away?"

"Were it not for Jon, you'd have killed me and been done with it in the first place."

"Maybe. I don't know."

Lobardin gives a short bark of laughter. "You're not endearing yourself to your captor, Arsenault."

Arsenault tugs on his ropes a little. "We both know that would be impossible."

Lobardin smiles. There is more cruelty on his face than I ever saw before. It makes me shiver, like a wind walking up my back.

CHAPTER 28

"He was trying to escape, you know," Lobardin tells me, putting his elbows on his knees. "He had Mikelo and was just going to abandon you."

"I told him to protect Mikelo. I can handle myself."

Lobardin's eyes grow hooded. "Obviously. That arm is most ingenious." His gaze slides over to Arsenault. "He gave it to you, didn't he."

No use keeping it secret now. "Yes."

He leans back again and crosses his arms over his chest. "One of your last great feats as a magician, was it, Arsenault? Keeping that information from Geoffre?"

A muscle in Arsenault's face tics. I can see that in the moonlight, but I can't read the emotion in his eyes or tell if this is one of the memories he's kept. He doesn't say anything for such a long time that I wonder if he's hurt more than I thought. Finally, he says, "Don't bait me, Lobardin."

Lobardin goes still. Then he puts his hand on his sword.

Except it isn't his sword. It's Arsenault's sword. The sword Arsenault passed on to me.

"That's an interesting threat, from a dead man."

Arsenault doesn't move. He stays where he is, his head against the side of the coach, his legs bent in front of him. But there is a tenseness that hangs in the air like a line of ominous clouds.

Lobardin shoves the door open and backs out. After he closes it, there's a screech and the door shudders. He pushed something through the latch to keep it from opening. His boots crunch in the stones as he walks away.

"Hie on, boys," he says. "The horses have had their rest. Time to press on."

In a moment, the coach lurches to a start.

"What did he mean about Geoffre?" I ask Arsenault.

He doesn't answer. His body sways with the motion of the coach, as if he's finally succumbed to exhaustion.

The air of threat remains long after, until finally I sink into my own sleep.

⁂

Our journey lasts four days because of the mud. The coach gets stuck more than once, and Lobardin presses Mikelo into helping shove it out of its ruts, but he never unties Arsenault or me. The ropes cut a deep, bloody groove into my left wrist. Both my arms feel like dead weights, except for when my left awakens in a stinging mass of needle-like pain.

After a while, I piece together what I think Mikelo wanted to tell me—that Silva got away. But I don't put much faith in a rescue attempt undertaken by a courtesan shepherd-boy, not against a company of well-armed gavaros and Lobardin.

I know Arsenault and I could fight our way out. I don't know what other magic Mikelo is capable of, or how he fights with a sword, but I think the three of us could make it.

Except that this coach is taking me exactly where I want to go.

On the fourth day, the road grows steeper. Lobardin and Mikelo ride inside with Arsenault and me now. The coach groans as the horses pull it uphill, their hooves clopping on the remains of old Eterean bricks. Out the window, deciduous trees return to skeletons. Firs and pines become the only green. The air inside the coach grows colder. Lobardin lets us have our cloaks, in a gracious gesture.

When the road changes, I lean forward to mark our progress out the window. I haven't seen this road in five years, but I remember the markers well—the gray stone pillars covered in winter-dead vines, the shattered statuary that forms gray lumps in the brown detritus of the forest floor.

Every path to the hunting lodge is burned upon my heart. I know the way Arsenault and I came, together, and I know the way he left and I left, opposite each other.

CHAPTER 28

The coach creaks to a stop. Patches of steaming, melting snow scar the ground, and the forest is awash with fog. Lobardin grins and rises from the bench before the coach stops moving. "Finally," he says, and pushes the ropes down the handle so he can open the door. When he does, Arsenault and I are both jerked forward, but then Lobardin shuts the door and Arsenault, Mikelo, and I are left alone inside.

I flex my fingers, as much as I can. My metal hand obeys, but not as easily as I would wish. I've been unable to examine it since we've been in the coach, and then my head seemed the more important part of my anatomy.

Arsenault looks out the slit the draperies leave of the window. Four days in the coach have done him some good.

"We have a welcoming party," he says.

I clench my right hand into a fist. Then the door jerks open and Lobardin grins at me. "Time to go," he says, and pulls me out of the coach by my arm.

The step makes me stumble, and I hastily right myself. Mikelo is next and then Arsenault, and finally we're all standing in a huddled group, staring up at my father's hunting lodge.

Calling it a lodge is misleading. It was our country estate, but it isn't like the unwalled, unfenced country estates of the lowlands, mere pleasure holdings for rich city householders. My father's lodge is Eterean-built, as all our important holdings were. It sprawls across the lip of a granite bluff, gray stone and brown cedar timbers, with towers on either end from which blue-and-silver Prinze flags fly. Its huge pine doors are barred with black iron and studded with nails, and a short wall flanks it on all sides.

The whole fort is carved of granite block. The valley it defended has long since given up its population, but the lodge remains—defensible, impregnable.

Except with guns and gunpowder. What I heard is that my father sent all the Aliente women and children, including the serfs, up to this lodge while most of the men remained below to defend the mulberries and the worms. But Geoffre sent a detachment to attack the lodge with cannon. Cannonballs obliterated sections of the wall, and men with guns picked off the gavaros manning the towers. Archers took down some of Geoffre's gavaros, but mainly, it wasn't even a contest. The Prinze overran the lodge, took the women, and that was that.

I don't know if my mother was here or not, because I haven't heard what happened to her. And I only pray that Verrin got Etti and his children out.

Now it's just Cassis waiting inside with Driese di Caprine, and Jon waiting for us out here in the courtyard.

He stands half a head taller than any of the other men, so he's easy to pick out. He gives a short nod to the men to whom he's been speaking and walks toward us. Cold-brittle leaves crunch beneath his boots. He keeps the hood of his cloak up against the chill, and his hands are encased in matching brown leather gloves. Arsenault's cloak rustles as he moves behind me.

Jon seems to ignore him, but I'm not that stupid. "I think you might tell Cassis you've arrived," he tells Lobardin. "And get a wash."

"And leave you out here alone with them? I know you'd have no problem leaving Kyrra to us, but Cassis wants Arsenault and Mikelo, too."

I must have made a noise. Jon looks at me from under the fringe of his hood.

"He speaks truth, doesn't he," I say.

There is sadness in Jon's eyes. "You stand in my way, Kyrra. I try to tell you to get out of it, but you stubbornly insist on blocking my path."

Arsenault shifts closer to me at his words, which is some comfort.

"Go tell the Mestere we've arrived," Lobardin tells one of the men offhandedly, still focused on Jon. To Jon, he says, "The Mestere wants her alive, and alive he'll get her. You're at cross purposes with the other two, and don't think I won't point that out."

Jon watches him for a moment, then smiles. It's something I've seen before, that wide, laughing grin. He claps Lobardin on the back. "Do that and see how far you get."

Lobardin tightens his grip on the hilt of Arsenault's sword. I flex my fingers again, back and forth, gritting my teeth against the pain in my left hand.

In that moment, the big doors to the inner court begin to open, winch cables shrieking in the cold. When they finally part, my heart skitters.

Cassis stands between them, his breath clouding the air.

Just as carelessly beautiful as he always was.

He wears a fine coffee-colored cloak over sienna silks, and his brown hair blows free in the wind. The jeweled hilts of his swords jut past the edges of his cloak, but they're dull in the gray light of the afternoon.

He lifts his right hand and bends his fingers in a summoning gesture.

"He acts as if he's a king," I say through my teeth.

"He acts that way," Jon agrees, and walks ahead of us, his cloak snapping behind him.

Lobardin gives me a gentle shove to get me going.

Cassis looks us over briefly when we reach the doorway, but he doesn't look in my face. "Put them in the old mews. Strike their bonds. I'll hear them later."

"But, Mestere," Lobardin says.

Cassis's gaze flickers over to me, then he says, "No, do it. Strike their bonds and give them food and water. Bring Mikelo to me first."

He turns his back and walks down the stone hallway before we can say anything, the sound of his boots muffled by the tapestries on the walls—tapestries I recognize.

All the tapestries from my father's villa line this hallway. They billow with the wind swirling in the open door, their edges flicking out toward Cassis's legs as he walks away and keeps walking, down the hall his family plundered from mine.

I could trace my finger over every pattern and I would know it, the way I know the twists and turns of every hallway Lobardin makes me walk, and the old scent of birds that still hangs from the rafters when we reach the mews and Lobardin opens the door and has his men push us inside.

But there are no birds here now, no straw, no falconers. There are only the memories of fall hunts and summer retreats, and the misplaced hope of a girl.

Lobardin slices the ropes away from our wrists with his knife. I think about charging him, but what good would that do? I have no blades, no gun anymore, and I can barely lift my metal arm. Lobardin still gives me a wary look as he moves away, grabbing Mikelo.

"Someone will bring you food," he says.

Arsenault rubs his wrists. "What a good servant you've become, Lobardin."

"Did it do me any better to honor my contracts to the Aliente?"

My arm creaks as I lift it, and my knuckles shine dimly in the thin light. "Don't tempt me."

He backs away. Jon takes Mikelo's other arm, and they walk Mikelo out the door. Mikelo glances back at us, looking young and scared.

The door thuds shut. Then the iron sound of a bolt slamming home echoes through the room.

Arsenault stretches. "Fifty thousand astra, eh?" he says.

His wrists are as bloody as mine.

※

I'VE NEVER BEEN GOOD AT WAITING. I PROWL THE MEWS LIKE A cat, letting my metal hand trail past the empty wooden cages, thumping the bars. My right shoulder and upper arm awaken painfully.

"If I can find a way, I'll kill him tonight," I say. "Then we can all ride to Rojornick. The new Seroditch heir might welcome me back."

"You're not thinking, Kyrra," Arsenault says. "You're only angry."

"I have every right to be angry!" I say, stopping to face him. "He plundered my father's house and uses our lands as a stronghold against his father—"

"*Against* his father."

Arsenault rubs his arms as he watches the door. "That's the key. The Prinze are divided. If you really want to topple them, you'll let them tear each other down."

CHAPTER 29

Arsenault's words finally make some inroads into my anger. "That's what Jon's trying to do, isn't it? Why you were trying to kill me, to get me out of the way?"

"Let the Prinze tear each other apart, Kyrra."

"It's too risky. Besides, what's going to become of you and Mikelo? Is Jon just going to throw you into the pit? Cassis wants to kill you, and I bet he'll toss Mikelo in on the bargain, if he knows half the things about Mikelo you do. Would you lay your life down for Jon? Does he mean so much to you?"

Arsenault looks troubled.

"Do you even remember who he is?" I say.

He shifts and looks around. Kicks at something under the straw, like a dog trying to find a place to lie down. "We rode the caravans together. Fought some battles... I remember his boys, the ones who died. I remember when the slavers dragged me off that ship. Jon was young then."

I stop. "I always thought you and Jon were the same age."

Arsenault laughs. It's a painful sound, especially as it echoes in the dim, empty mews. "I perpetually never live to grow old. When I die, I just go back to where it all began. Over and over again."

"And that's why you seem younger now?"

"Did I seem old to you then?"

"At first...not old. But not young, either. *I* was young. But you look closer in age to me now than when I met you. How old are you, really?"

"I don't know. Some memories are lost forever, I guess. Sometimes I live long enough to get some gray in my beard, but mostly I always seem to be the same age I always am."

"But if Jon was young then and you weren't, does that mean Jon knows about you?"

"He knows. Otherwise, I'd still be drunk in an alley."

"Then why didn't you tell me?"

The words come out through my teeth and expose a lot more pain than I meant to, the way an unlaced shirt accidentally exposes flesh.

Arsenault sits down in the old, moldy straw and leans back against the frame of a falcon cage, draping his arms over his knees. "I didn't tell Jon. I'm forbidden from telling anyone. Jon knew because he saw it happen. As you did. Except there was no Mikelo." He gives me that sideways look again. "Did you really believe I was dead?"

I rake my hair with my left hand as I prowl about the room, wishing I could comb the thoughts and emotions from my mind along with the tangles in my hair. But none of them want to budge.

"If I did, I wouldn't be here. An Aliente gavaro I didn't know made it to Kavo and told me no one could find you. The first thing I did when I came back to Liera was find Jon and ask him if he knew anything about you. And he lied to me."

Arsenault rubs his jaw. He hasn't shaved in nearly a fortnight, and one might almost call his stubble a beard now. It makes him and that gesture look much more familiar.

"Trying to protect us both, I guess. Keeping you out of it and making sure the Prinze didn't get wind of who I was, either. I don't think that situation would have gone on forever."

"Really? And how was ordering you to kill me protecting me?"

"I'm not Jon's wind-up machine, Kyrra. Getting you out of the way was my idea, not Jon's."

That hurts. More than I'm willing to admit, even though I know the reason behind it. I take a deep breath and try to focus again on the issue at hand.

"But why would Jon do something so cruel? To let me keep believing that you'd died—and to let you keep believing that *I* was dead? Even if he didn't tell you to kill me, he would have let the Prinze hang me before he told you who I was."

Arsenault falls silent for a moment, thinking. Then he says slowly, "Maybe he would have seen you killed if it came down to it, but he wouldn't have wanted you to fall into the hands of the Prinze. If he really thought you were a threat, he would have shot you outside the prison, taken Mikelo back, and tried to convince me you were nobody."

"That would have been ironic. Since I've spent the past five years using Nothing as my family name."

Arsenault stretches out his legs. "By that time, I'd seen you with my sword, though. I knew you had some connection to me, but I didn't know what it was."

"I suppose..." I say thoughtfully, "that when I took Mikelo, you might have threatened me with your blade. Not just your hilt."

His mouth hooks up in a sardonic smile. "Ah. A declaration of love the poets will write about."

I smile in spite of myself and throw myself down in the straw beside him. "I could beat the door down," I say.

He looks at me strangely. "With your arm? You use it as a hammer?"

"I use it however I need to. They've got a bar on that door, but I might be able to beat through it."

"There are guards on the other side for sure."

"I said I use my arm however I need to. It's also a weapon. You know how to fight with your hands, don't you?"

"And when we're out?"

"What do you think Cassis is going to do with Mikelo?"

"Hard to say. First, I imagine he'll test Mikelo to see if he really is Geoffre's creature. When he finds out he isn't, Cassis may try to recruit him to his cause."

"Which is?"

Arsenault's brows shadow his eyes, and he scratches his beard again. "It can't just be Driese."

"I wouldn't have pegged Cassis as the ambitious sort. Do you really think he has the courage to defy Geoffre?"

"It may be less courage than firepower that makes the difference," Arsenault says. "But Geoffre wasn't treating him well."

The memory of Erelf's voice slides through my head again. *Ask Arsenault about those entertainments...*

I shiver involuntarily. "Did Jon know that Geoffre and Cassis knew who you were?"

He looks at me, startled. "What?"

"You didn't tell him, did you?"

"But how do you—"

"Did you forget I See, too, Arsenault?"

He lets his breath out. "I hoped you didn't See *that*."

"Not all the details." I could have told him I'd had it from Erelf, but I thought this was enough for now, as shaken as he looked. "Why didn't you tell Jon? If the whole reason he had you with the Prinze was to hide you in plain sight?"

"I don't think Geoffre knows who I am. But..." He leans his head back against the wall and closes his eyes. "Kyrra, it's been so hard to move. To get up again. Jon seemed hopeful, like he had a plan, and I didn't want to ruin it by telling him the base was rotten. So, I just took it. Liquor and kacin...it wasn't so hard."

Anger starts to grumble up in me again. "You're lying," I say. "You never thought it was easy."

"Does it matter?"

"Of course it matters. If Jon was as loyal to you as you are to him, it would matter to him, too. You're sitting here in the mews, not doing a damn thing to escape, not even looking around, and so I know you must either be planning something or you've just given up. Which is it, Arsenault?"

"I thought you wanted to be taken to Cassis."

"I'm not talking about me."

"Geoffre's moving troops. He's got a detachment of gavaros on their way here—and if he let that slip, it means more than one. Probably with cannon."

I stop for a moment to absorb that information. "So, he does want me to kill Cassis. And then Geoffre will destroy his troops."

"It's the way I'd do it."

"But why did he try to poison us in the bathhouse?"

"He didn't send the poison in the bathhouse. Devid did. I found that out from Madame Triente before I left to track you."

I ignore the flare of jealousy Madame Triente's name provokes. "So, Devid is on Cassis's side?"

"I wouldn't say that."

"What, then? Jon's not working with Devid, is he? Devid captained the fleet that sailed to Dakkar. He's the one—"

Arsenault shakes his head. "No. That was a ruse. Geoffre didn't trust Devid to captain the fleet on that kind of voyage, but he didn't want the other Houses to capitalize on his absence. So, he worked an illusion, left Devid at home, and led the fleet to Dakkar himself. He's the one who killed the B'ara."

"Geoffre...worked an illusion?"

"It's why I could never get close to him. I didn't know what was happening then. They kept the house locked up. Sent Devid in his disguise out only under heavy guard."

"But surely, the gavaros knew?"

"They weren't exactly gavaros. They were the men Geoffre had been collecting."

"Like Lobardin?"

"Lobardin would probably have been one of them, yes."

"But you said...then...you said that Geoffre would have had you. That he had a way of using people. As if you'd *Seen* him."

"It got more dangerous when Geoffre came back."

"But couldn't you have Seen through the illusion when it was just Devid?"

"I could have, if I had gotten close enough. But I wanted to stay out from under the eye of those gavaros. And there were enough times that one of them would show up around the docks, trying to sniff me out."

"Why didn't you try to infiltrate their ranks?"

"Because the illusion was Erelf's. And if I had come that close..."

"Can you really hide from him?"

"I can stay...quiet. The way deer hide in the open, in the grass. I'm forbidden from using my magic except for small things, like the writing, and in self-defense, so as long as I keep that under wraps..." He shrugs. "Kacin helps veil my actions, but it's not foolproof."

"So, Devid has even more cause to hate his father. Is that why he wanted to stop us? To give Cassis a chance to attack Geoffre?"

"Maybe. He and Jon had been talking alliance."

I try to dig the heel of my palm into my forehead. "Jon again," I mutter.

"Jon didn't put him up to using poison, Kyrra. Even Jon can't control everything."

"Damn near, though." I flick some straw off my metal arm. "I could take them both down."

"Both Geoffre and Cassis? How would you get to Geoffre?"

Kill Cassis, then sneak out dressed as a man. Find Mikelo and let him go. Blend in as a gavaro in Geoffre's army and get close to him that way. I could do it.

"I'd find a way," I say.

"No," Arsenault says, shaking his head definitively. "Geoffre wants *you*. He falls into black moods and upbraids Cassis for losing you and the child. He thought you were dead for years, so he didn't look for you, but now that he knows you're alive... Don't try to finish your commission. Cassis will trade you to his father in a heartbeat for his own freedom if he catches you, and if you kill him, you're just doing what Geoffre wants."

"Do you know *why* Geoffre wants me, Arsenault? As far as I know, the conjure magic is still working within me; I wouldn't bear them any heirs."

Arsenault runs his thumb down his trousers like he's smudging out a stain and keeps his eyes carefully on the line it leaves.

"For your magic, Kyrra. He's always wanted you for your magic."

Something is amiss. What could I be but a magical curiosity to Geoffre? Better as an assassin to take care of his son without it being traceable to him, but he wouldn't *want* me then; instead, he'd have me killed as soon as I'd committed the crime.

"You're not going to convince me to run away again," I say. "I won't let Geoffre have you, either."

Arsenault's gaze roves over my face. "If I hadn't seen you fight, I might take that less seriously."

"But this is what you did to me. It's my arm."

He didn't know. He had Seen the battle magic that pulled at me, but he didn't know how his arm took the magic and honed it like a blade.

"Is that really my fault?"

The words sting. "It's not a *fault*, Arsenault."

For a moment, he's silent. Then he rubs the place where his scar should be with two long fingers that aren't as nicked-up as they used to be. "No," he says. "You're right. I'm sorry."

"Sometimes, I wonder if it's you in there. If you haven't become someone new."

"Kyrra. I died at Kafrin Gorge."

The words take all the air out of me. I thought I understood before, but maybe…it's just beyond my ability to understand.

"It was your father," he goes on, without my asking for once, as he rubs his blood-crusted wrists. "I've been putting things together. I remember I got there late. Geoffre left me alone in the tent with a silver spoon in his tea service. It was careless, unless he did it on purpose. I Shaped the spoon and cut my ropes. He'd told me he was moving his troops up the other side of the gorge and going to parley with the Aliente troops, but by the time I got out of the tent, the Prinze were already setting it on fire. It wasn't as Silva imagined. I remember walking down into the mouth of the gorge. The flames were hot on my skin. I tried to Fix them, to push them away from me, but my talent weakens when it comes down to something like fire, and Geoffre had kept me…" He swallows, then smiles bleakly. "Well, let's just say to cut the ropes, I needed something metal. I could work with my talent, but anything else required too much magic. I wasn't in any condition to direct it, and when I tried to work the flames, the magic overran me completely without doing a damn bit of good."

I put my hand on his leg. "Arsenault—"

But he goes on. "Your father was ahead of the flames. It took a while for me to reach him. He held a white truce flag in his hand."

When I look up, Arsenault is studying me, trying to gauge my reaction. I can't help but hold his gaze, though I don't want to. Because what I see in Arsenault's eyes is a complicated mix of concern for me, bitterness, sadness, anger…and resignation. Perhaps it was inevitable that my father's devotion to the law would in the end become the sword he fell on. But that he dragged so many down with him…

"A truce flag," I say wearily. It makes so much sense now. "Because he expected Geoffre to abide by the same rules he did."

I've mourned my parents for a long time now. But talking

about it brings the pain up fresh. I rub the join between my arm and the flesh of my shoulder.

Arsenault takes a heavy breath and turns away. "Regaining my memories is like fighting a battle. Trying to outsmart the enemy. Erelf takes as much as he can, leaving me only what he thinks will torture me most."

Finally, I understand. "Your book," I say.

He nods. "It's an idea I keep having, I guess. But the book has to survive. And someone has to keep it for me."

"You should have given me one of your books."

"I'd planned on it. But there was no time for plans at the end. When I came back, I told everyone you were dead. It was easy enough for them to believe, although Geoffre took some convincing. But when I woke after Kafrin, nothing stopped me believing it, too. I still had a memory of *you* but separate from your name. As much as I tried, I couldn't remember your face. The god twisted everything so it was just a giant muddle. Mikelo's actions filled in the gaps."

"With what?"

A trace of warmth lights Arsenault's eyes. "I suspect it was some kind of memory."

And then he is looking at me, and I know. The scar on his chest is me. That's why he's recovered some memories now but not others. It's a trick of Fixing, making memory real.

"I'm not the way you left me," I say. "I'm not the way you remember me."

"I'm not the way you remember me either."

He touches my right hand and I flinch. But instead of drawing back, he tightens his fingers on mine and pulls me closer to him, lifting my metal hand to his lips. For some reason, when his lips brush my knuckles, it doesn't feel like dull metal anymore.

"Erelf is playing a long game, Kyrra, much longer than any of you can see. Geoffre's ambition is such that he makes a perfect tool for the god. I can't let him have Mikelo, and I won't let him have you."

Looking up at him, seeing the fierce earnestness in his eyes, I wonder if he knows about Erelf's offer to take me instead of him.

But then he pulls me toward him. I slide into his arms and tip my face up to his. For a moment, he remains still, and the look in his eyes changes. He leans closer to me by a fraction, and then a fraction more when I don't move away, and finally he brings his lips down warm and soft to touch mine, making a sound like something long tied has been loosed within him. His other hand rounds my hip, pressing me against him, his fingers solid and real against my body, and five years are erased.

And then the door rattles.

Both of us scramble to our feet in an instant. My hand goes to my side in a futile quest for my sword. I speak quickly. "I meant what I said about Geoffre. If you and Jon have other ideas, I'm going to stand in the way."

"Kyrra—" he says, but then the door creaks open and Lobardin stands there, his hand on the sword that should be at my side. Or Arsenault's.

Whose sword is it now?

"Well, Kyrra," Lobardin says. "You've an audience with the prince. Cassis requests that both you and your paramour be made ready to meet him, so I suppose that involves a bath."

"A bath?"

He looks me up and down. "I was as surprised as you are. But you certainly look like you need one."

CHAPTER 30

For the first time in eight years, I am bathed and dressed by a small group of women—chambermaids for Driese, I'd assume, though she's nowhere in sight. The dress Cassis provides fits well enough, and as far as I can tell, it isn't one of my mother's that was left hanging in the closets by mistake. The watered blue silk hugs me just a bit too tight, and the square, lace-scalloped neck dips down uncomfortably low. I guess this is the fashion now. Ungloved, my right hand gleams in the candlelight as Lobardin locks the manacles on my wrists. A small group of guards flanks him, their hands on their weapons.

"Where's Arsenault?" I ask as Lobardin pulls me up and sets me walking.

Lobardin doesn't look at me. "He'll join us."

"Mikelo?"

"Let me worry about the details, won't you?"

I study my own details, remembering the way the halls link together, refreshing my memories of iron sconces and peeling frescoes lining the walls—images of Ransi and Adalus, Tekus, Ires, and Erelf, the Doomed God, the god of Sight.

In the Eterean pantheon, Erelf is nameless because he traded the life of his brother Adalus for the ability to See. The Etereans hid his name and regarded his magic warily, like a double-edged blade. They knew that like water, magic seeks the easiest courses instead of the best. It becomes a handle for the gods to grab in the games they play and the wars they wage against each other.

Erelf's face haunts me all the way to Cassis's chambers—my parents' bedchamber. The artist captured a good likeness; I wonder if he was a Seer too.

Then Lobardin opens the door to the bedchamber and Cassis sits there, waiting for me.

My eyes have been opened too well to think the setting isn't well planned. The dress he gave me is the same color as the dress I wore the day we met. He sits on a gold brocade chair that used to grace the drawing room, and the huge oak bed upon which my parents slept looms behind him, draped in a canopy of rose-colored silk.

I have to remind myself that he doesn't know about the chair. How could he? He rises from it and stares at my right hand with the shock of a man who didn't know what to expect and only half-believed the stories, and I find myself beginning to grin, because at least this is something he didn't plan, something none of his family ever could have foreseen.

"It's true," he says. "What Jon said."

Jon again. I let my gaze rove over the room before I answer him, taking in the positions of all the candelabras, the furniture, his weapons.

There's a sword on the wall, in a rack. I turn my gaze back to him. "Where's Arsenault?"

He puts his hand on one arm of the chair and starts to sit back down. "That's nothing you need to worry about."

"I should have known not to trust you. Where did you put him? Back in the mews? In his own little cell in the towers, perhaps?"

Cassis leans back in the chair and lets his hands slide down the fabric of the arms. "We've renovated the old prison compound, actually. You didn't know about that, did you? We had to excavate the foundation." He props his head with a finger. "It was fairly clear what it had been used for."

I struggle to recall a prison compound...and then I remember the mound of earth and broken walls in the woods. When I was a child, I used to run away to climb through its rubble. I was always scolded severely, but I kept going back.

"You rebuilt it?"

Cassis smiles, and I can see the ghost of his father in its lines, but Mikelo, too. "Somewhat. A prison can't be too comfortable, you know. But it wouldn't do to have it look too much the part, either."

"Your father can't know you've turned this place into your own private fortress."

"No." He looks up, catches Lobardin's eye. "You can leave us now," he says.

Lobardin straightens. "But, Mestere—to leave you alone..."

"Her hands are locked, aren't they?"

"Yes, but—"

"Do you have the key?"

Lobardin tightens his mouth and nods.

"Then take it away. I can defend myself."

"I told you how she fought," Lobardin tries, one last time. But Cassis frowns at him.

"I said I can defend myself."

Against her, I read in his eyes. Are they really so arrogant, these Prinze? I hope so.

Lobardin bows. "So be it, Mestere," he says, and throws me a dark glance before he retreats out the door and closes it.

Cassis looks up at me. "Why don't you sit? I must apologize for what passes for dinner here. We have to be careful with our rations."

I sit. They manacled my hands in front, not back, so I clasp my fingers together, metal and flesh, and notice for the first time a stand and tray placed beside the brocade chair. Cassis is apologizing for a bottle of Imisi white with a vintage stamp and what smells like stewed rabbit in a bowl with bread. I would have killed for such a meal when I was campaigning.

"Why do you want me here?" I say, before he can speak. "Jon told you about me. That's the only way you could have known we might be in Karansis."

He smiles bleakly as he pours a glass of wine and hands it to me. "So, you really were on your way to kill me."

I accept the wine but don't drink it. "Did you expect otherwise?"

"From you?" He ladles out two bowls of rabbit. "I suppose I shouldn't have, though I was surprised to learn you were alive and in a position to be hired as an assassin. I don't know what disturbs me more—that the Caprine hired you to kill me or that my father sent you here knowing that." He pulls the stand in between us so we can both use it as a table.

I put my wineglass down and wait for Cassis to take the first bite before fumbling my spoon with my manacled hands. It just smells like rabbit, though, and the last thing I ate was a road biscuit early this morning.

"You're building a fortress out here," I say after I eat enough to stop the hunger pangs. "Is it any wonder your father wants you dead?"

He pales slightly and stops with his spoon in midair, dripping broth back into his bowl. Then he takes the bite and swallows. "I thought I might have to torture that information out of you," he says, wiping the corners of his mouth with a napkin.

"It's only a guess. Why would I hide it?"

He leans back in his seat and folds the napkin onto his thigh again. "I don't know, Kyrra. We've both been caught in the net our families wove."

I'm not sure I've heard him right. "Are you calling yourself a *victim*, Cassis?"

His face twists with distaste, and he hides it with a drink of wine. He sets the glass down firmly before he speaks. "Did you think I wanted to do what I did? That I didn't feel dirty every time I lay with you and knew what my father wanted? My father used me, too."

"I suppose it was too hard for you to tell your father you weren't interested before we even got started?"

"I can see you don't know my father very well."

"I only wonder how you managed to carry on with something that disgusted you so."

"It was the purpose that disgusted me, Kyrra. Never you."

"How do you expect me to believe that?"

"I suppose I don't. I could tell you what really happened, and you wouldn't believe that, either."

He refills our wineglasses. I spin mine between my manacled hands. "Try me," I say.

He sits back in the brocade chair with his wine, resting his arms on the armrests, rubbing the polished oak curl at the end with the fingers of his empty hand. "All right. I came to negotiate the silk in good faith. I didn't know you would be there. My father had nothing to do with the first dance. It was just some idiotic thing I took advantage of because I was there and you were there. I knew nothing would come of it because of your Caprine ties. I didn't know what my father was doing, treating with yours, but I didn't have any say in that matter and I didn't *want* to know any more."

I watch him carefully, the way his hand rubs back and forth over the wood knob. "But you came back," I say.

"I had to come back because we had to pay you for the silk. But I had been careless at home. I had spoken of you. My father heard me, realized who I was talking about, and told me I needed to…take advantage of the situation."

"That's a polite way of saying it."

"It wasn't supposed to happen so fast. My father just thought you'd be ruined and Pallo would cast you out, and then we'd sweep you up. He knew about your mother—about the magic that comes down her line. But you made it so damn *easy*, Kyrra."

I run my fingers down the handle of the spoon like it's the

hilt of a knife. "Because I thought you were going to marry me," I say, trying not to speak through gritted teeth.

"Most girls don't take a tumble in the bushes that fast, no matter what they think."

"It's my fault, then? I should have said no?"

"Well, why didn't you?"

"Why didn't you? You could have had me legally for the Prinze. All you had to do was ask for my hand in marriage."

"And then the Caprine would have thought we were threatening them. They would have sent assassins for both of us and my father, too."

"Oh, so you were protecting me?"

"I was doing my duty to my House, dammit! What I wanted had nothing to do with it. It was just my father using me to get to you."

He does sound disgusted now. Part of me wants to be sympathetic. To understand. To respond to the face I once found so pleasing, the voice I knew, the body I pressed hungrily against mine.

That part is submerged by my anger and drowned. I stand up.

"Let me have this clear, Cassis. You've abandoned your wife and left her at the mercy of your father, built a fortress for your mistress, and now you want me to believe that you found it impossible to say a few words behind the lilacs, such as *How can we find a way out of this, Kyrra?*"

"You don't understand—"

I slam my metal elbow down on the tray. The bowls jump and clatter, and my wineglass wobbles and tips over, shattering when it hits the floor. Cassis looks up at me in surprise but not yet fear.

"Did you lose an arm, too?" I ask.

"You seem to have acquired a new one."

I throw a bowl of stew at him.

He jerks backward, letting go of his wineglass. It falls to the floor, spattering wine everywhere when it breaks, and the pottery bowl hits him in the jaw. The stew splatters his face and hair and the back of the chair.

I hurl the table out of the way and raise my clasped hands to use my metal fist like a club. A neat shot to his temple will put him down, then I can run him through with that sword on the wall and make my escape.

He raises both his feet and kicks me in the stomach. I stumble backward, my boots crunching on broken glass, and grab the other bowl off the table. I toss this one at him, too, like a discus, but he's ready; he ducks, and the bowl hits the floor and shatters.

I run for the sword on the wall. But five years of war have turned him into a warrior, and he has both his hands. Before I can make the sword rack, he grabs me by the neck of my dress and hurls me down on the floor, into the leg of the bed.

My head bounces back against it. Pain blinds me, immediate and overpowering, and when I finally open my eyes, I have my hands up on my forehead and I'm staring at my own lap.

Damn that head wound Lobardin gave me.

I look up and Cassis is wiping blood from the corner of his mouth. I try to scramble to my feet, but he pulls a dagger from his belt and falls to his knees to lay the point of the blade to my throat.

"Kyrra," he says, hoarsely. "Don't make me do anything else to you."

I laugh. "You say that as if you mean it."

His hand begins to shake. The blade shudders against my skin. "It's easy for you to be righteous, isn't it? But where were you when our armies stormed your land? Were you among the women we took away? No? Your mother chose to put a dagger in her breast rather than go with us, but you, you simply *ran*."

He spits the words as he rises. Then he throws down the dagger. It clatters on the stone floor. "Arsenault would never say where you were, either."

CHAPTER 30

Out of the corner of my eye, the blade glints on the floor, a temptation just to look at it. I steel myself to look at Cassis. "Why did it matter?"

He looks down at me. "You didn't have to drink the potion, Kyrra."

And so it comes down to that. I hurl myself across the floor to grab the knife, but his foot comes down atop my hands. The bones in my left hand pop as he presses his boot down harder and harder. I try to move my right hand, but whatever is wrong with my arm has seeped some of my strength away; it starts to groan, as if it had muscles to tear. I give up, gasping, and stare up at Cassis through pain-watered eyes.

"My father is generous to bastards," he says, scowling. "He might have taken the child in, raised him up as mine—we could have had an heir. We couldn't have said he was Caprine, but I might have had an heir. Gods, Kyrra, do you think I like what I'm doing now? I hate hurting Camile, and I love Driese. But when it comes down to it, the Caprine are the only fertile family left, aren't they? Even my father hasn't found a way to change that, no matter what magics he uses to twist the innards of our women."

I stare up at him through a haze of increasing pain. "What?"

"We need Fixers. To heal our women. To subjugate the rest of you." He doesn't take his foot off my hands, but he leans down to speak to me. "My father told me your mother could See and so could you. He wanted that baby, do you understand? He wanted it much more than he wanted me."

Oh, gods. So much of this is starting to make sense now. My mother wasn't worried that Geoffre would take our lands. She didn't want him to take my child.

Did my brother meet the same fate?

"Get off my hands," I gasp.

Cassis takes his foot away, something changed in his expression, then sweeps up the dagger. I clutch my hands to my breast and hold them there like a child guarding a favored toy.

"My father is coming to kill me," he says. "Now that he has Mikelo, he won't need me."

"My mother understood." I wheeze out the words. "When she gave me the potion." My left hand aches. I massage it with the fingers of my right hand, but metal does a poor job and my right arm hurts. More than it ever has.

He stops. "What do you mean?"

I take a deep breath and flex my left hand. It burns for a moment, but I don't think it's broken. "She knew what Geoffre wanted."

Cassis's eyebrows arch. "Are you saying that your mother *made* you drink those herbs, Kyrra?"

Even I cannot avoid the irony in that statement. Did she make me drink it?

"No," I say finally. "No, she didn't make me."

Cassis stares at me for a moment. I can't name the expression on his face. Pain—yes, I see that in his eyes. Disgust—well, I expected to see that, too.

What I don't expect is the muddle of fear and relief, perhaps that I haven't shifted the blame, that I've let it lie where it belongs, buried close to my heart. Or maybe he believed, before, that my mother poured the potion down my throat... Maybe that's where the fear comes from.

I move and the pain in my head makes the moment go black, a small splinter of lost time. When my vision returns, disgust seems to have won out over his other emotions, and Lobardin is standing in the open door. He looks down at me with an expression of unguarded surprise.

"Take her away," Cassis says, turning his back to both of us, with the briefest glance at me over his shoulder. "I've heard all I care to know."

CHAPTER 31

MARRIAGE HAS ALWAYS BEEN A WOUND THAT LIES CLOSE TO MY heart. Sometimes, I still find myself woolgathering, wondering what my life would have been like if I had married Felizio di Caprine. How many children would I have borne in eight years? What sicknesses would we have weathered, what childhood falls and accidents, what joys and sorrows? Or would I have suffered his first wife's fate, dead in childbed, my soul on a farther journey?

They're old thoughts now, but five years ago, while we were preparing for my father's second marriage, they bore a brighter pain. In spite of Arsenault. Or perhaps because of him.

We would never have cake. Never wine, or white linen tablecloths, or dancing in the evening. No well-wishes and charms hurled upon us as we walked beneath flowered arches, no fresh-faced young girls standing beside us with their arms full of roses.

At the time, those thoughts ached like the ghost of my right arm. After my father issued his commands at our private dinner, I was relegated back to the combing house and my undyed guarnello and apron. Ilena was there when I walked in the door. In her black eyes there was nothing but hate.

Living in the barracks for the past year had helped me avoid her, but the estate was a small place. She hadn't given up on Arsenault after her first blackmail attempt. He was always polite to her but certainly not encouraging, and I wondered why she kept coming back. As time went on, I began to see Lobardin watching their interactions, but it still surprised me when he began walking with her in the evenings. It was hard to tell with Lobardin sometimes, but it seemed to me that he was trying to set her in his pocket in case he needed an ally against Arsenault.

I didn't know if Ilena knew Lobardin had hidden motives, though, especially the way she looked at me when I entered the combing house. Lobardin had been ridden off on the back of Util's horse that morning and deposited in the dust beyond the gates, and it looked as if she thought I was involved. I ignored her as best I could while I traded my own clothes for a woman's. Ilena's gaze made my skin burn, but I kept my back turned and asked another girl, whom I didn't know, to tie my apron.

I could ignore Ilena, but thoughts of Arsenault were more insistent.

That first night, after doing a hundred menial chores—scrubbing floors and hauling water and stirring silk—I lay on the rough straw-filled mattress, my body stiff and sore. I listened to the unfamiliar breathing of other women for a long time, unable to sleep. Finally, I gave up, belted on my dagger under my shift, and walked barefoot out into the night.

As the wedding approached, my father posted guards on all the silk buildings night and day, fearing whatever it was that he feared from the Prinze. But I knew, from being lately in the barracks, that Verrin had drawn guard duty for the combing house, and I didn't think he would stop me.

His silhouette moved in the courtyard when I cracked open the door. I pushed it open slowly and slid through the smallest opening. I had taken two steps when he turned around.

I raised my hand. "Verrin. It's only me. Just pretend you never saw me."

He came toward me quickly, gripping his sword hilt. "Pretend

I never saw you? Kyrra, your father pulled me aside this morning and warned me—he said if I were to let anything happen to you, he'd have my ballocks on a plate."

My eyebrows rose. "He said that?"

"Not in so many words, but it's what he meant." Verrin looked nervously over his shoulder at the wind-rustled trees, then back at me. "I know what you're doing."

"If you know what I'm doing, then why are you trying to stop me?"

He stared at me with a torn expression. I shifted onto my toes in preparation for a sprint into the trees, but then he suddenly relaxed.

"Ah, go, then," he said, turning around. "I'm not looking at you; I don't know which way you went. If you do get in trouble, Kyrra—have the decency to do it on someone else's shift?"

I grinned. "You're a good man, Verrin." I squeezed his arm. He grunted, and I didn't spare him another glance as I ran.

❧

I TOOK THE SAME PATH I HAD WALKED THE NIGHT I discovered Ilena with Arsenault. Pebbles and broken pieces of beechnuts bit my feet as I ran, but I didn't stop. I flew over the path like a hind running from a hunter. I ran until I came to the small grotto where the spring poured out of the rock and the armless statue stood guard.

And Arsenault was there, waiting for me.

In the dim spangle of moonlight, I could only make out his outline—the way he prowled the grassy area in front of the wall like a wolf. And then as I slowed, I saw the glint of moonlight on the pommel of his sword and the white slash in his hair. Then he came to meet me, taking my mouth with his kiss.

He smelled of sweat and smoke and earth and metal, and the calluses of his fingers caught at my shift as he ran his hands from my shoulders down my arms.

"Kyrra," he said, raggedly. "You should have stayed in the combing house."

"I know," I said.

"Gods curse me, but I'm glad you didn't."

I smiled, but I felt like crying. My voice was like a gate holding back my tears; if I spoke, they would spill, and I wasn't sure then that they would stop. So, I didn't speak. I pressed my lips against his and brought him down with me into the grass.

※

Afterward, we lay on the damp, cool earth, charting the stars through the gaps in the leaves above us. The moon had passed its zenith already, but it wasn't close enough to dawn that I needed to go back. We clung to that sliver of time the way we clung to each other in the darkness.

I lay beside him, my head pillowed on the curve of his left arm, his hand a warm weight on my hip. The stump of my right arm nestled in the space between us, but it didn't bother me. I traced the line of his scar and he shifted his head to look at me.

I wanted to ask him any number of questions. How he would disguise himself at the wedding, if he had told any of the other gavaros…if Geoffre would notice him anyway, with that glamour of magic sparkling in his wake. But somehow, in the dark, none of that seemed as important as it once had. Less than a month and whatever would happen would happen, but would I go to meet my fate without knowing anything about him? I'd known him for three years, but I still felt as if I knew less than nothing, and I wanted to know everything. Knowledge would be a tether, tying us together.

"The cut that made this scar might have killed you," I said.

He turned his head toward my hand so that my fingers stroked through his beard. "It happened a long time ago," he murmured.

"But you know about my arm. You know everything about

me. And what do I know about you? Just some stories about caravans and your childhood. I don't even know where you come from, exactly."

"Where do people say I come from?"

"From all four points of the compass, if you listen to the stories. I know it's somewhere north, but I've looked at maps and I think your home is off them." I scooted up a little so my head was propped.

"I suppose you're right," he said, "if all you're looking at is Lieran maps. We called it Frøna, but I doubt you'll see that name anywhere. The Qalfans label it Tule."

"Frona," I repeated, rolling the word around in my mouth, and he laughed.

"That Eterean *r* makes it seem like a woman's name," he said and repeated it, *Frøna,* slower this time, with a soft *r* that wasn't rolled and a closed-off sound in place of our long, round *o*'s that made it seem like a different letter. Hearing it, I could understand now why he said my name the way he did, so much softer than the aggressive way native Etereans pronounced it.

"Tule," I said, "is only a place in stories."

"Been a while since I've been back."

"Were you scarred before you left home?"

He rubbed my arm absently. "Yes. It was something of a test."

"Like the one you told my father about, for sorcerers?"

"You make it sound as if I have another life huddling in a purple cape and casting spells over pots of boiling spiders."

"Do you?"

He sighed. "Your problem is that it's too hard to tell when you're serious and when you're joking."

I snuggled closer against him. "Your problem is that I've learned to tell when you're trying to divert my attention."

"Mmmm." He was quiet for a moment, and the singing of grasshoppers and cicadas in the warm dark filled the gap. When he spoke again, I felt it as a rumble in his chest. "It was that kind of test," he said. "I passed it and failed it all at once. So, I was scarred. And if I ever tried to return home...people could read it. Like a sign."

"Your family," I said.

"No," he replied in a soft voice. "They're long gone."

"Your children, too?"

"Fostered out. Across the sea."

"So, the scar makes you an outlaw."

He sighed heavily. "In a manner of speaking."

I hadn't meant to make him sad. I reached across him to stroke his hair away from his face. "Tell me a good memory, then."

"All of them have a bittersweet edge," he said, pressing his nose and lips into my hair.

"So do mine. But surely, it's not wrong to hold on to some of them?"

He kissed my temple and remained silent for so long, I thought he was ignoring me. Then he said, "I remember the grass."

"It rolled for miles on the highland until the land grew rougher and colder. When we were children, we'd jump out on each other with rocks and swords of twisted grass. There were so few trees, the farmers made their houses out of turf. And the further inland one went, the colder it got until nothing grew, and it was just high peaks and snow, even in the summer. It was a little like your underworld—with giant rifts in the ground where steam and sulfur smoke poured out. Some of the springs would boil you alive. And back from our bay, there were huge cliffs, nearly like the ones down the coast at Iffria, where we hunted for bird eggs on the ledges."

"It doesn't sound so unfamiliar," I said. "We have volcanos and hot springs, and you said yourself your cliffs were like Iffria."

"Yes," he admitted. "But then again, everything was different. The food, the people, the grass..."

"Do you miss it?" I asked.

CHAPTER 31

It took him a long time to answer.

"It's the innocence I miss most. The feeling that the world would just keep going on like usual. I remember an afternoon..." He shifted beneath me, pulling me in closer to him, but looking up at the stars at the same time. "We packed a picnic into a basket and took the boys and Pippa out into the grass for an outing. By that time, there were signs that everything was crashing down. But I was blind to it. I was so bent on the knowledge I was pursuing that I barely saw the boys or Pippa or Sella, even when I was in the same room with them. Then one summer day, Sella came into my workshop and thumped a picnic basket down on my workbench in front of me. I was elbow-deep in a project, probably covered in grime, but she didn't let that stop her.

"*We're going on a picnic*, she said. *In the grass. You are coming.*"

He smiled. "I didn't realize at first that I'd been given an order. At first, I tried to get out of it. But she just stood there with the blood running high on her cheeks and her hands on her hips. For some reason, it reminded me of when we were much younger and I used to watch her from the boys' practice yard—trying to pretend I wasn't." That heavy sigh returned. "It was only then that I realized how little like herself she'd seemed lately. I couldn't remember the last time I'd heard her laugh."

It made me uncomfortable, hearing him talk about his wife in this way. But at the same time...I wanted to hear more. I knew he didn't talk about her to anyone else, and being given this story felt like being handed a gift that was both precious and rare.

"I took her orders. I went out into the garden to collect the children. The boys were having some game that involved a great deal of mud and complaining. Pippa was about two then, but already trying to join her brothers in everything. When I announced that we would be going on a picnic, the complaining stopped instantly. The boys ran about cheering, and Pippa had no idea what a picnic was but leapt into my arms anyway. She was covered in mud." I felt his low, quiet laughter as a rumble in his chest. "Which meant I was too, instantly.

"We walked up into the hills and ate cardamom buns and picked blueberries. Sella showed the boys how to make daisy crowns. I made Pippa one and she crowned me with it. I wore it all that afternoon and into town that evening. Pippa sat on my shoulder, and my two boys ran in front of me, whacking at each other with swords of twisted grass. Sella walked next to me. Laughing. I loved to hear her laugh. It didn't come easy to her, so when she did..."

He tightened his arm around me and tilted his face down against my hair.

"When we got to the house, my brother was waiting for us. He poked fun at me for wearing the crown. He wasn't married. He had no children. I ignored him. I put the crown on a windowsill to dry, thinking if I could just hang on to that afternoon..."

I raised my head briefly. "But you have, haven't you? The memory remains."

He let out a long, gusty breath. "Tainted by everything that happened after. Tell me your memories aren't the same."

I couldn't. And could I say that I would wish him back there, among the grass and the daisies with his family?

I couldn't say that, either.

"What happened to the crown?" I asked. "Do you know?"

"I broke it apart on the windowsill before I ran. I stuffed the flowers in my pockets. That was all I had to my name for a long time—just my cloak, my sword, and the flowers my daughter gave me. They crumbled, but I couldn't let them go. So, I Fixed them. They're made of gold now, but it's hard to look at them without thinking of what a great failure I have been."

I went still, remembering the night I'd stitched his leg, the golden daisies I'd found in the bottom of his chest.

His daughter's daisies.

"I thought I would only be sacrificing myself," he said,

looking back up at the night. "But instead, I sacrificed everything."

⁂

For the next few weeks, the estate was a buzz of excitement and tension. Servants and serfs worked round the clock, putting in the work with an expectation of enjoying the reward—celebration out from under the eye of the Householder. But I could tell that the gavaros had other things on their mind, and sometimes, as I walked across the courtyard, I heard Arsenault's voice raised in the practice yard: *"Get those shields up and pikes at ready! Quit making yourselves targets!"*

As the day approached, I grew increasingly more glum, thinking on the promise I had made to Arsenault and to my father. I didn't see how I could honor such a promise, if it came to war, and yet I had given my word. It was like a knife driven into my flesh: no matter which way I twisted, it cut me.

The nights after the first, Arsenault himself came to the combing house and waited in the shadows just beyond the building, practice swords in his hand and his own at his side. We went together to the grotto, to take up arms against each other while the armless centurion looked on. And then with that impassive stone gaze behind us, we flung our weapons down into the dirt and took each other there on the ground. I still can't smell the scent of crushed grass without thinking of those nights and his sweaty, leaf-speckled skin against my own.

One night, Arsenault came to me with news.

My parents meant to show the Prinze that I had been debased, that they had conformed to the letter of the law. So, on the day of the wedding, I would be part of a drama staged just for Geoffre di Prinze.

"You'll be out back of the kitchens, carrying a platter," Arsenault said as he paced along the stone wall in the little grotto. I had done my sword practice and earned a huge purple knot on my forearm for my lack of attention, though Arsenault had pulled the blow. I'd barely slept since moving back to the combing house. My mind was a clock, marking the time left until the wedding.

I sat on the wall, wanting to rub my left forearm. As a sort of stopgap measure, I rested my arm carefully in my lap as I listened to Arsenault.

"Someone will come into the kitchens to give you a signal, to tell you when to carry out the platter, because you must be within sight of the Prinze. When you can be sure that Geoffre is looking at you, you'll drop the platter—or let the food slide off, whatever you like—and then another serf will come up behind you and clout you on the head for your stupidity."

He'd reached the point in his pacing when he was closest to me. I could tell he didn't like the idea. Neither did I.

"And am I to cringe and gather the bread out of the dirt? Perhaps kiss his toes in the bargain?" Though my arm throbbed, I couldn't remain still at such news, so I scrabbled a loose stone out of the wall and hurled it into the spring. It plopped and sank, invisible in the darkness.

Arsenault scrubbed a hand through his hair. "I can't reason with your father, Kyrra. He still thinks the best course is to appease Geoffre. I don't think he accepts that Geoffre wants all his land, even after all the spying I've done for him."

"My father lives by an old code," I said bitterly, propping my head up on my fist. The action made me wince, but I felt as if I must do something with my good arm, and nothing felt right. "He refuses to believe that everyone doesn't abide by its rules."

Arsenault leaned on the wall beside me. In the moonlight, the light streak in his hair stood out stark against the black, but I couldn't read the expression in his eyes. "It will be his downfall."

I bit my lip and picked up another stone and turned it over in my hands. It glinted in the dim silver light, veined with quartz. I had never realized how much like quartz my father was. Brittle

CHAPTER 31

and crystalline, admired for its color...but not a stone to make buildings. In the end, quartz had little use.

I pitched it into the water as hard as I could.

"Kyrra," Arsenault said. "We'll find another way. Your father is wrong to have you humiliated like that."

I raised my head. "Do you think I worry about being clouted for the sake of my family?"

"No," Arsenault said. "But the only thing having you grovel in the dirt is going to save is Pallo d'Aliente's pride. It won't do more than that."

I tried to work up a sense of outrage. I wanted to tell Arsenault that it was untrue, that my father loved me more than to use me to uphold some doomed code of honor maybe he only half-believed. But my name didn't even belong to me anymore. So, what purpose would I serve beyond that of a scapegoat for spilling the bread?

I hardly knew what I felt.

"Do I have any choice at all?" I asked Arsenault.

He stared at me, silent. I held his gaze. Then that muscle stood out rigid in his jaw, and he turned toward the statue that stood guard over us.

"I didn't think so," I whispered.

We were quiet for a time. I listened to the gurgle of the spring and the shifting whisper of the wind in the beeches. A branch fell to the earth somewhere, and we both looked up, watched, waited. No one came. It was only the wind.

"You'll go soon," Arsenault said.

"I want to stay."

"I know."

"Does Isia's magic still work within me?" I asked.

His warrior's mask crumbled, just for a moment, and let me see the man inside.

I turned away from that, to stare at the lumpy, severed outline of the stone statue. Then I felt his magic.

It was like the touch of his hand: strong, sure, a little bit rough, but not in a bad way. It made me shiver, wanting him to touch me. But he just watched me, the shadows etching his face until it became like the statue's, gaunt and worn.

"You know that it does," he said, his voice pitched low.

I reached out for his shoulder. "Then there's no possibility of me passing on my blood. There's no reason for me to leave—"

"That isn't the only reason for you to go," he said in a low, intense voice, pulling me down off the wall so I stood in front of him. "You have a magic of your own. You know that. If you stay here, Geoffre will want it. And his patron will want it too."

"His *patron?*" I laughed. "Since when does the most powerful man in Liera need a patron?"

Arsenault looked at me askance. "Everyone has some kind of patron."

"Who?" I asked.

"You know. Why do you think he changes all the statues?"

Erelf. Goosebumps ran over my arms with the next breath of wind, and I shivered. "Geoffre dedicates himself to—"

Arsenault covered my words with his hand and pressed me close to him. His palm tasted and smelled like singed metal. "Shh," he said. "Don't say it. Don't think it. It's enough that you know."

He took his hand away. "But what does that have to do with me?" I asked. "Is it because of you?"

He flinched. "No. Not only because of me, but if you were to stay... Kyrra, I've led you into deep-enough waters already."

"I'd rather die with you than live knowing you're dead."

A peculiar expression passed over his face, as if he wanted to tell me something but couldn't. He moistened his lips, then tightened his hands on my arms. "If I live, I'll find you. You have to believe that. And if I haven't found you and it's safe...I hope you'll look for me. But my dying—that's not enough reason for your death. Dying is easy. It's living that's hard."

"Arsenault, my existence has been dishonorable enough."

"You could at least do a dead man the favor of allowing him

to think you're alive. If you fight with your father, you're doomed. If you go elsewhere...there's a chance you'll live, and your House name and your magic will stay alive too. I meant what I said to your father; there's a man in Vençal I want you to see, and I can put you on a boat or send you overland. He'll be able to guide you and answer any questions you might have and see you employed, too. And then"—he paused—"and then you'll be alive to seek revenge in the end, won't you? If you die, who will seek vengeance?"

He watched me for a reaction. I narrowed my eyes at him. "You don't mean that. You're only trying to get me to agree with you."

He let all his breath out in a rush. "Gods, Kyrra—isn't it enough to know that I can't bear the thought of your death?"

I tilted my head so I could look him in the eye. "And isn't it enough to know that I can't bear the thought of yours?"

He stopped and stared at me. In his eyes, there were secrets waiting to be read...wanting me to read them. Magic swirled around us. But before I could say anything—before I could grab on to it and See what it wanted to show me—he tore himself away, walked into the clearing, and picked up his sword.

"Arsenault!" I called. "Arsenault, wait!"

As he walked into the brush, I ran after him. I bent and grabbed the hilt of my own sword from the ground as I ran. "Do you think it all goes one way?" I shouted. "You can't treat me like this! Don't I deserve some answers?"

I stepped on a rock. Its point dug into the soft flesh of my bare foot, and I fell heavily into a tree, wrapping my left arm around it to keep from falling. I cursed as Arsenault's back disappeared into the trees.

"Arsenault!" I yelled after him. "ARSENAULT!"

But he just kept walking. I cried out, in wordless pain and frustration, and hurled my sword after him as far as I could.

But it was a paltry throw and, like our words, resolved nothing.

My lack of sleep began to show.

Combing stopped a few days before the wedding, and the combergirls were given linen napkins to embroider with the initials of my father and Claudia d'Imisi. Their long nails sometimes made it difficult for them to grip the needle and, sometimes, to see what they were doing. The task of helping them fell to me.

Most of the mistakes the girls made were honest ones, and I didn't mind picking up their dropped needles. But Ilena sought only to humiliate me.

"Hand the needle to me right this time, Kyrra. How do you expect me to hold on to it when you give it to me that way? Can't you do anything properly?"

It was the sixth time she'd dropped the needle while working on the same napkin. Mistress Levin wasn't around and most of the girls were off collecting their bread for the midday meal. Ilena stared at me, her black eyes oily with hate, the napkin resting hardly stitched in her lap. She settled her hands atop it and her fingernails clacked together.

I gritted my teeth. "You're doing this on purpose."

I'd spoken quietly, but the remaining girls in the room stopped their stitching and looked up at us. Ilena tightened her hands on the napkin and leaned toward me. "Pick up my needle. Now."

I thought about picking up the damned needle and ramming it straight through her palm.

Instead, I grabbed her by the laces of her bodice and yanked her forward to the edge of her chair. I noted with satisfaction the way her face turned a pasty beige. But she still glared at me, not backing down.

The few girls around us gasped. Chairs screeched, and I thought I heard the door open and running feet scuff the dirt floor. I shut it out. Nothing existed except me and Ilena, and this pent-up anger I hadn't had an object for in a long, long time.

"I am not going to pick up your damn needle!" I said. "You'll get down in the dirt yourself—and tell Mistress Levin, for all I care. I won't be treated like this!"

Ilena's eyes narrowed. "You're an armless girl and a gavaro's whore," she whispered. "You ought to be crawling about in the dirt."

I wanted to hit her, but I couldn't hit her without letting her go, so I shoved her back in the chair as hard as I could. The chair tottered with the sudden shift in weight and started to fall. Ilena's eyes grew round with fright and she cried out, flailing so that she smacked one of her hands against a small wooden table. The chair and Ilena made a great clatter, but Ilena had already started wailing, "My nails!" before she hit the floor.

Two of her three perfectly trimmed oval nails lay sheared and white against the brown dirt floor, leaving her fingertips ragged and bloody. She kicked the chair off her legs and crawled over to her torn fingernails. She picked up the broken tips, closed them in her hand, and cradled her hand against her chest.

"My nails are more useful than you are," she said. Her eyes were watery with tears, and her dark hair had pulled out of her braid and floated in fuzzy mussed tresses around her face, which was smudged with dirt and already turning blue-green where one pole of the chair had caught her in the cheek. "It should be you lying in the dirt," she said. "But you still think you're the Householder's daughter. You and Arsenault, running off Lobardin because he didn't grub after Arsenault like a worm. It should be you in the dirt!"

Ilena began to weep. Her tears made little black wells in the floor.

I stood perfectly still. The anger, quick as it was, leaked out of me just as fast.

I had nearly forgotten about Lobardin, with everything else

to worry about. Would Ilena try to avenge him by striking back at me? Or Arsenault?

I was nothing. I wished Arsenault and my father could see that. But Arsenault was my father's captain and his spy, and Geoffre di Prinze could not be allowed to discover him there, on my father's land.

I wondered, briefly, if Arsenault realized just what sort of danger he might be in with Lobardin elsewhere and not under his nose as Jon had intended. Probably, he did.

Cursed man.

I hauled Ilena to her feet.

She looked up at me in surprise. "What are you doing?" she said. "Are you going to hit me?"

"Only if you look like you need it," I said, and dragged her outside.

⁂

I GOT ILENA OUT THE DOOR BUT THEN SHE STARTED KICKING. My grip slipped and she tried to run away into the trees. I ran faster than she did, though, and I caught her by the arm and yanked her down into the dead leaves scattered on the ground. The heel of her foot dug up a fine spray of pebbles and dirt as she twisted, trying to get away from me, and by the time I'd struggled myself on top of her, my mouth tasted like forest.

"Ilena!" I gasped. "I just want to talk!"

She wriggled but I pinned her with my knees. I unsheathed the dagger from under my dress and spat the dirt out of my mouth.

"Are you going to run away again?" I asked.

She looked at the knife, and then she looked at me. Most of her hair had pulled out of its braid, and flakes of dead leaf burrowed in it like large brown lice. She had a scratch on her left cheek to match the bruise on her right.

Finally, she shook her head. Tiny lines of anger radiated from the corners of her lips.

"Mistress Levin will take you away regardless of your father," she said.

"Maybe, but she's not here now, is she? Look—Arsenault had nothing to do with having Lobardin banished. If you want to blame anyone, blame my father. It was his idea."

Her lips trembled. "Do you expect me to believe that?"

"It's the truth. Arsenault said my father dumped Lobardin on the road. Lobardin begged my father but my father wouldn't reconsider." What Arsenault had really said was that Lobardin had begged my father to kill him rather than set him free for Geoffre to find, but I didn't tell Ilena that.

"Lobardin said he would come back for me."

I found that hard to believe, considering it had already been a month, but I didn't say it. Instead, I said, "How much did Lobardin tell you? About what went on in the barracks?"

"He told me that Arsenault hated him and was going to make life hard for him. He said I should watch out in case anything happened to him. He said that Arsenault had gotten his magic into you, too, and you would just follow him like a faithful dog."

I scowled. "You mean the same way you kept after Lobardin? How are you not with child by now? Are you infertile?"

My cursed, cursed mouth. Ilena made a noise of pure fury and managed to wrench one of her arms free of my knees. She brought her hand up quick and hard to slap me.

I didn't mean to cut her, but my body reacted as Arsenault's teaching had trained it. My left hand came up with the dagger in it to block her, and the blade sliced her knuckles in one neat bloody crease.

She screamed and withdrew her hand with such speed that I hardly got a look at the wound before her hand was in her mouth and blood was trickling down her chin.

"You cut me," she gasped, taking her knuckles slightly down from her lips, rouged red with blood. "You *cut* me."

"I didn't mean to, Ilena— Gods. Here, let me see—"

I got off her and reached for her hand, but she jerked it away from me. "No!" she hissed. "Householder's daughter lording it over the rest of us. Violating your sentence!"

"I don't have anything you'd want, Ilena. It's useless to be jealous of me."

"You think I'm jealous of you?" She laughed, but it was too high-pitched. "I'm not *jealous*. What the Householder is doing, what Arsenault is doing, is an injustice. Arsenault threw Lobardin off the estate, and now where does Lobardin have to go? He'll be at the mercy of Geoffre di Prinze! Your father wouldn't even throw you to the Prinze, and what does he do to Lobardin? And how much more useful was Lobardin to him? He was a man, and he had both his arms!"

"I keep telling you, Ilena, Arsenault had nothing—"

"He took Lobardin away! I was watching!"

"But he didn't order it; my father—"

"Yes, *your father*. Your father does everything that Arsenault wants, doesn't he? But does he know that Arsenault is working for the Prinze? And you, following Arsenault around like a dog."

She raised her nose in the air and my grip on the dagger trembled.

Lobardin knew about Arsenault. I had tried to determine how he knew, but I had never been able to find out who his "little bird" was. He had contacts in Liera, and I thought that maybe on his off days, he had been able to use them for information.

But now with Ilena smiling one of her dark little smiles at me, I wondered.

Did she make a habit of hiding in the brush and listening?

Did she want more than just for Arsenault to notice her?

"I imagine that Geoffre di Prinze might like to have that bit of information, don't you think?" she said.

I shoved her back to the ground, then moved my blade to her throat. "Do you know where Lobardin is, Ilena?"

Her eyes squeezed shut. "No," she said, voice trembling. But then she opened her eyes and the smile returned, a little shakier than it had been. "But perhaps he'll go to the Lord Prinze. Or his son. Or perhaps I will. You won't be able to stop either of us."

The dagger blade trembled. Voices and footsteps approached, the thumping of scabbards and the jangle of metal —not just Mistress Levin but a contingent of gavaros, more than one.

"You never mean to use that dagger, do you, Kyrra," Ilena said.

Contempt filled her voice. I looked at her face and then she moved, taking courage against an armless girl with the gavaros almost here, I suppose—reaching up with her cut hand to claw me in the face with her ragged fingernails.

I jerked my head back. Then I plunged the knife into her neck as hard as I could.

Her eyes bulged. She opened her mouth to scream, but nothing came out, only a small upwelling of blood that spilled down her chin and dripped onto my hand. She writhed and thrashed so hard that I was thrown to the ground beside her.

Then she stopped. Just stopped.

I stared at her. I sat there beneath the oaks and beeches, dappled in their shade, their lost and old leaves tangled in my hair, smeared with the dirt they had created. I sat there knowing that the gavaros could see us through the gaps in the branches, that the men had started shouting and running toward me.

I heard my name. But nothing seemed to make any sense. Least of all the dead girl on the ground, wearing my dagger in her throat like a jewel.

I lurched upright and threw up at her feet. I began to run even before I was done, wiping my mouth with my hand, stumbling over roots, stepping on rocks and twigs—hardly noticing. The afternoon light seemed filtered like the light sifting through the murky water of a pond. Sounds and images reached me as if I were underwater.

My only thought was to warn Arsenault. But I'd started running too late. The gavaros were on me in a moment. And I'd left my knife in Ilena's throat.

I kicked and beat with my fists, clawed them with short, stubby nails. I fought like a cornered animal. I didn't think. I didn't remember Arsenault's teachings. I just fought. And fighting, I was strong, even with only one arm.

There was a lot of yelling. Finally, I looked up to see Verrin's face inches away from mine as he hugged my arm behind my back. His hand locked around my wrist so hard that I realized it hurt. The hurting was sharp, and it brought me back.

Sweat dripped off Verrin's brow and stained the black curls that hung down in his forehead. It dripped onto my face, too. "Kyrra. I said, *Don't get in trouble*, didn't I?"

"Arsenault—" I said. My voice came out hoarse and raspy, as if I hadn't spoken in months.

"Arsenault can't save you now," Verrin whispered. "There wasn't time to get him. I sent someone to tell him, but—"

"No," I said, shaking my head. "No, tell him Lobardin—"

I looked up. The other gavaros had crowded around.

"Lobardin what?" one of them said, a man with a crooked nose and pale blue eyes whom I hardly knew.

I closed my mouth and hung my head.

Verrin glanced at them, then sighed. "Come on, Kyrra," he said. "We'll have to lock you in the caves until the Householder can talk to you."

※

IT SHOULD HAVE BEEN ARSENAULT WHO HANDLED MY CASE, with my father involved in last-minute wedding details. Arsenault's justice was swift, sure, and fair when he practiced it on other people. Making him judge my case would be a hopeless predicament, but since Verrin said he'd sent a runner, I hoped I at least got the chance to tell Arsenault why I'd killed Ilena.

There was no doubt in my mind that when Ilena spoke of going to the Prinze, she was not bluffing. And maybe Lobardin had *not* gone to the Prinze, and what then, when Geoffre rode onto our estate sometime in the next few days?

You could have taken her to your father to find out. To let him take care of her, the small voice in my mind insisted on adding, allowing doubt to crawl in anyway, like a worm in a peach.

I could still see the way the blood burbled out of her mouth. I could feel the skin of her neck on my hand as I rammed the knife in. Her skin had been soft there. Thin.

I hoped, as I had not thought to hope while I was stabbing the blade into Ilena's throat, that Sight had something to do with my actions. It was strange how you could hate a woman when she was alive and then realize, when it was your hand that delivered her death, that the feeling you'd borne her in life didn't run deep enough to be hate. Ilena had been like the needle she'd dropped on the floor—small, irritating. Except that in the end, she'd revealed herself less a needle than a dagger.

No. I'd had no doubt.

I kept expecting Arsenault to overtake us on the path, but he didn't.

The caves were not where anyone awaiting justice was routinely kept—only those who committed serious crimes, like the Forza captain. Whether they were natural caves or holes in the rock hollowed out by the Etereans—or a people even older —no one knew. They might even have been tombs, but if they were, the bodies that once lay in them had long since turned to dust.

I had never actually seen these caves. They were near enough to the villa and the barracks that a number of gavaros could be called there quickly in case of emergency, but far enough away that the prisoners couldn't bother the main house. In any case, prisoners in the caves usually hung within three days.

Three days from now would be my father's wedding.

As we walked down the path, I kept a lookout for opportunities to escape, but there were none. I was unarmed in more ways than one and surrounded by three gavaros, two of whom watched me warily and bore marks on their faces from my struggles. Verrin just looked worried and gripped my left arm so hard that my bruised forearm ached.

The path led through the trees, then uphill, where the trees became increasingly sparse and finally gave way to stands of tall yellow grass and purple thistle. The villa loomed up before us, its windows like eyes watching from across the ravine. The servants who swarmed around it, readying the grounds for the wedding, were as small and stick-like as if a child had drawn them, all out of proportion to the house. Four gray horses pulling a mahogany coach clattered up the drive while we stood there watching, catching our breath before the descent into the ravine. Its flags glinted in the sun—silk flags, woven of the bright, soft fibers on which our family had built its fortunes.

The flags were blue and silver.

Prinze.

A shiver laced my spine. I stood hardly breathing as four people disembarked from the coach: one of the men was Geoffre, but the other man could have been Devid or Cassis, except that the younger woman had dark hair.

Devid's wife was blonde. Therefore, the woman must be Camile di Sere. Which meant that the man at her side, the man I couldn't recognize from this far away, was Cassis.

"So, they came," Verrin breathed.

"The Mestere's let a viper into a nest of chicks," the other gavaro murmured.

My whole body seemed to harden at once. I might have been made of wood.

I barely noticed as Verrin cast me a worried glance, then tugged me forward with a sigh. The rocks and sand slipped beneath my feet, and the villa and its guests disappeared over the ridge of the ravine that held the caves, lost to the silk-blue sky.

CHAPTER 31

Inside, the caves were cool, dank, and dark, a maze of small rooms, most of them big enough only for one person. When Verrin struck a flint, you could see the string of these rooms leading up into the bowels of the hillside, many, many more than I had ever imagined. The walls were smooth yellow stone stippled with bands of ochre and black near the floor. Faint outlines of ancient paintings marched along the length of the narrow passageway—the stiff, brush-like mane of a horse, a man wearing the head of a bear and dancing among faded orange flames. Gooseflesh lifted its bumpy heads along the length of both my left arm and my stump, and then Verrin nudged me into a room near the entrance.

It had a bench carved into the wall, but it was barely big enough for one person. Verrin had to bend over to stand in the doorway, and he wasn't tall. A pile of small bones lay in the corner, mice perhaps, and the knob of a bigger bone jutted out from the stone itself. It looked like a man's leg bone, and it unnerved me that stone could bear such a resemblance to something so human. I sat down on the other side of the bench, as far away from it as I could get.

Verrin glanced over his shoulder at the entrance, where the other gavaros milled about restlessly. "What did you want to tell me about Arsenault?" he whispered, hunched over so his head wouldn't hit the ceiling.

I moistened my lips. "Ilena wanted to expose him. The work he was doing for my father. That's why—" My voice faltered, and I cursed myself for a coward. Verrin watched me out of concerned black eyes, his gaze unwavering. I swallowed and went on. "It's vital that the Prinze not discover Arsenault here on our land. Ilena would have exposed Arsenault to the Prinze if I hadn't killed her. Lobardin put her up to it, I think."

Verrin's eyes widened. Then he nodded. "I'll tell him, Kyrra. Maybe you'll be out of here soon." He smiled at me, a little ruefully. "Arsenault was with the Householder. Your father will know."

I wasn't sure what that would mean for me, but it made me uneasy. Surely, my father wouldn't punish me in the way that those usually incarcerated in these cells were punished. Surely, he would see that I had acted only to preserve the integrity of our family.

Verrin backed out of the cell without saying anything else. Then he slammed the heavy wood door and locked it. The light winked out; there was a small crack of a window in the door for guards to peek into, but that only let in a sliver of dimness from the entrance.

Verrin's footsteps faded into the distance, leaving me alone with the steady *drip-drip-drip* of water somewhere far away and the silence of rock.

I sat on the bench for a moment, but then I had to move. I wanted to pace, but the floor was too small. I waved my arm instead to keep warm but also out of sheer frustration. Surely, Arsenault and my father would come soon.

I shoved on the door, testing it. It held fast. It was an old door but unrotted, and on the way in, I had noticed that the locks were all made of iron. So, there was no immediate way out.

When I thought I couldn't wait anymore, I heard voices.

I looked out the small window, but in the faint light from the entrance, all I could make out were the black shapes of men.

"I put her in the first cell..." That was Verrin.

Someone said something; I couldn't tell what it was. It might have been Arsenault, but it didn't sound like him. Then keys jangled.

"I'll talk to her myself. Alone."

My father. I stiffened and moved away from the door just as he jammed the key into the lock. The door opened with a screech, and the flame of the candle he held fluttered in the wind. Its light illuminated both of us.

CHAPTER 31

My father's lips pressed together in a thin, pale line. The candle made it all too easy to read the rage in his dark eyes.

I don't know what he saw in me. Ilena's blood dried black on my hand—my dirty dress, my bare, brown feet. He pushed the door shut while I was looking over his shoulder for Arsenault.

"Sit," he told me.

I lowered myself to the bench without looking away from him. The stone was cold against my legs. "She was going to expose Arsenault to Geoffre di Prinze. Lobardin had figured out that Arsenault was spying for you. I don't know if Ilena had been spying on Arsenault and told him, or if it was the other way around and Lobardin just figured it out."

The candle trembled. "Has Arsenault told everyone on the estate what he's been about?"

"He told no one!" I said, my chin jutting upward in the way Arsenault chided me for when I was fighting. "Ilena liked to hide in the bushes and eavesdrop on conversations. And Lobardin had seen Arsenault in Liera before. You sent him away for such long stretches, it probably wasn't hard for Lobardin to piece things together. Ilena had it in for Arsenault because he snubbed her."

For me, I thought, but of course I didn't say so. Wouldn't it just look like a lover's spat if I did?

"*Dammit,* Kyrra. Stop being so smug. You just killed a girl." He ran a hand through his hair, then looked around for a place to put the candle. He found one near the ceiling, a ledge with a shallow depression in it. The candle leaned against the wall and cast grotesque shadows of my father and me, but we did not look like people.

When I looked at him again, he was watching me as if he wanted me to speak.

"What do you want me to say, Father? I told you why I did it."

"And you have no remorse at all?"

Did I? I looked at my hand lying there in my lap, still

speckled with blood. My first death. Did gavaros feel remorse when they cut men down in battle?

I clenched my hand into a fist to stop its trembling. "Would you rather I'd left her to do her damage?"

"That wasn't my question. My question was, *do you feel remorse?*"

I shoved myself off the bench. "I'm not a demon, Father! How do you think I feel?"

The muscles of his face sagged. He looked, for a moment, like he wanted to touch me. But he didn't. His fingers twitched against his side, but his hand remained where it was. "I hardly know anymore, Kyrra," he said.

I dug my nails into my palm. The stump of my right arm throbbed in time to the beat of my heart, and the missing half of it ached. "What do you want from me, Father?" I asked, in a voice so cold, it surprised even me.

He flinched. It didn't give me any satisfaction. There was an empty place inside me, a place that had always been there but had at one time been no bigger than an egg—a small, hollow eggshell where there should have been something fertile, something that should have grown warm and large. But instead, it was the emptiness that grew, and now it was so big that it threatened to consume me. Until all I became was emptiness.

I tried to beat it back. Tears pricked my eyes and I beat them back, too.

My father straightened up, his face suddenly flat and expressionless. "You disobeyed my rule that serfs are not to carry edged weapons. You killed a girl in cold blood, without real evidence."

"But, Father—"

"Hush!" He put up his hand to stop me and closed his eyes, turned his head so he wouldn't be looking at me when he opened them. "You did it, Kyrra, and you know you did."

"I haven't been arguing about that, Father."

"I could let you go," he said, as if I hadn't spoken at all. "I

CHAPTER 31

could let Arsenault take you out of here right now. But—may the gods forgive me, Kyrra—I need you."

I blinked. "For what?"

"Verrin told you that you were to perform for Geoffre di Prinze, didn't he?"

I bit my lip. "Yes," I lied. Arsenault had told me, but I didn't want my father's trust in Arsenault to slip any further.

"I've opened negotiations with the Prinze on the price of our silk thread, and also about selling off a small parcel of our lands. He's more concerned with the Caprine than us—"

"Father!"

He was attempting to pace, turning in brief circles to touch the walls, to look at the ceiling. He stopped and looked at me instead. "This wedding," he said in a level voice, "will bankrupt us otherwise."

Now it was my turn to flinch. I looked down at the floor, at the head of the bone that jutted out from the wall. Then he surprised me by going down on one knee before me.

I looked down at him, startled and horrified. "Kyrra," he said, "as your father, I have no right to ask this, and no desire to, either. As your father, this will—" He swallowed and glanced away from me, then he reached out and took my hand.

I stared at his hand on mine. Hadn't his hand seemed larger once? Stronger? Now it was thin, and his fingers tightened hesitantly on mine. I looked up, into his eyes.

"Kyrra, as your father, I will rot in the deepest pit of the underworld for what I am about to ask you to do, but as the Head of your House, I must ask you—I *must*, do you understand?"

"What is it?" I could hardly bear to speak. I knew what he wanted. I could see it in his eyes.

"We can't give Geoffre any more ammunition than he already has. He can't be allowed to have any legal footing to attack us. And he can't be allowed to take you, either."

His hand tightened on mine.

"Kyrra. Will you give your life for your House?"

The nothingness that had only moments before threatened to overwhelm me broke like waters behind a dam. It swept me up and swirled me away.

"Yes," I whispered.

My father hugged me. He put his arms around me so tightly, I could hardly breathe. I had felt like crying moments before, but now all I could do was shake.

My father was shaking too.

※

HE STAYED FOR A WHILE LONGER. IT WAS AS IF WE COULD finally talk—could share a brief, bittersweet laugh over the fopperies of tailors and lutists—now that the pretenses between us had been chipped down. My father didn't look at me when he talked, but I felt half-hidden in dream anyway. It barely occurred to me what I had agreed to.

Then my father left and took the light with him. I remained sitting on the cold stone bench, alone with fragments of old paintings I couldn't see in the dark and a handful of rat bones in the corner. It was only then that the weight of my decision pressed down on me, like a rock too heavy to lift.

Outside I heard Arsenault talking to my father. The door and the stone muffled many of his words, but it seemed I could hear them clearly anyway. Only Arsenault's words, and none of my father's replies.

You're keeping her in there, Mestere? Why?

She told you why she killed Ilena. It's what I would have done in her place; would you lock me up, too, for doing your work?

He was angry. So was my father. I couldn't make out my father's words, but I knew his tone of voice.

The conversation grew more distant until it was as faint as the sound of water far back in the caves, and I got a twisty ache in my chest.

Surely, I could speak to Arsenault one last time. Surely, I might touch his hand or his face before I died. Otherwise, my last memory of him would be his back retreating into the trees and the sight of the sword I'd hurled after him.

"Arsenault!" I shouted.

Running footsteps echoed off the stone walls.

"Open the door," Arsenault said.

"The Mestere said—"

"Open the door."

Suddenly alarmed, I got up off the bench and stood on my tiptoes to look out the window, pressing my hand against the clammy wood. But all I could make out were shadows.

I pressed myself harder against the door. "Verrin! Let me talk to him!"

Verrin's silhouette didn't move. Nor did Arsenault's. "The Mestere says you're to have no visitors. No one, even Arsenault."

Not even Arsenault?

"But just to talk to her, Verrin…"

"Arsenault, don't make this into a struggle. He'll probably let her go in a couple days. She'll be safe here, and—"

Arsenault yanked his sword free of its scabbard. The runes on its blade sparked so bright, I flinched away from the window, and Verrin flung an arm up to protect his eyes, his own sword hanging useless at his side. The white light lit up Arsenault's face. His eyes gleamed as silver as his blade. He pointed the sword at Verrin, and Verrin stepped back, letting his arm drop to his side.

"I know you're following orders," Arsenault told him. "I wish you no trouble. But if any harm comes to her and you're a party to it, this sword will be the least of your worries."

Verrin blanched. "I—" he began.

I clenched my hand and let my forehead rest against the wood, slimy with mold as it was.

I couldn't let this happen. What had I been thinking, calling out to him? Of course my father would have left orders to keep him away.

"Verrin!" I called out, without looking up. "If Arsenault is still here, tell him I've changed my mind. I've no wish to talk to him anymore. Tell him to go away!"

The light that poured in through the window faltered. "Kyrra?" Verrin said.

"You heard me! Tell him!"

The light winked out. Arsenault cursed, loudly, but he didn't leave. Instead, there was a scuff against the floor, followed by the sound of a body hitting the wall.

"Arsenault—" Verrin gasped.

The door rattled against me as Arsenault tried the lock. The wood grew suddenly warm as if he might be using his magic on the iron bar, and I jerked backward in surprise.

"Arsenault!" I cried out in alarm. "Leave Verrin alone! Think about his children!"

"Kyrra, what game are you playing in there? What did your father say to you?"

"You know you won't be able to make it out of here with me. And then everything I've done will be useless. They'll all know, Arsenault, and my father will be forced to throw *you* in the caves—or put you to the sword. Dammit, Arsenault, stop!"

Smoke curled into my small space from the hot door. I raised my arm to my mouth and began to cough.

There was silence for a moment. Then Arsenault uttered a deep, strangled cry, and a slamming, clanging blow rang against the iron, echoing off the rock and making the door shudder as if an earthquake was going to pull down the walls.

I threw my arm over my head and cowered in the corner.

"I know he said something to you," Arsenault said through the bars at the window. "And I'll find out what it was."

The tattoo of his boots on the stone let me know how angrily he walked away. Then I heard Verrin say, "Dammit, Kyrra."

I slid down to the ground with my back against the door.

The ache in my chest held me tight in its fist—worse than I expected. I rested my head on my knees.

The sound of my tears was only another *drip-drip-drip* in the dark.

<hr />

THE TWO DAYS I SPENT IN THE CAVE I WOULD HAVE SWORN were the longest in my life. But that was before I left Arsenault and knew what living is like after your heart dies. Waiting for death isn't as hard as that.

But there was nothing to do, and not even Verrin talked to me. I made a game of feeling the bone in the wall, trying to determine what sort of man it had come from. I knew something of anatomy from helping gut pigs and sheep, and I knew something of human bones from illicit forays into my tutor's sketchbooks. I thought this bone had probably belonged in someone's leg. But it was so big that at first, I thought it might be a bear's bone. I spent a lot of time running my hands over its cool, smooth surface, my fingers finding every little scratch, every worn-down groove.

It was a man's bone, no doubt about it.

I started wondering how he had died. Had he been condemned like me, his bones cast aside, not even buried in a pauper's grave? Had he cornered a bear or a lion in this cave, this giant of a man, only to find that he had trapped himself?

It disturbed me to think of the man as an animal's kill. It seemed so random and unnecessary a death. If a man had to die, let there at least be a reason behind it.

I let my fingers wander away from the bone and discovered old paintings on the wall, ones I couldn't see but that I could track with my fingers. The artist had first carved lines into the stone, then brushed paint into the depressions. If I closed my eyes, I could imagine the paintings in my head: fanciful and grotesque combinations of human heads and legs and arms and animal bodies, teeth, tusks, antlers.

Perhaps the man that belonged to the bone *was* the artist. Maybe the earth shifted, dropping the rock on top of him.

Every little noise afterward seemed to me the trembling of the earth.

On the night of the second day, I let my fingers linger on a painting of a deer with the head of a man. Perhaps it was a centa, those half-hind creatures that bounded through old Eterean tales, kidnapping travelers and goring them with their antlers, then roasting them over their cook-fires.

I stayed awake as long as I could, fearing the quiet time before sleep. While I lay curled on the cold stone floor, all my fears ambushed me. But I couldn't fend sleep off forever. Eventually, I succumbed to exhaustion and dreamed about the man-deer on the wall.

His whuffling hot breath filled up the close space of the cell. When he moved, his antlers clicked against the ceiling and his hide scrubbed the walls.

It didn't seem possible that he could fit in the tiny cell. Enough light trickled in that I could make out the ruddy gold of his hide, the blunt shape of his head, and the luminous black ovals of his eyes—eyes that stared at me with far more intelligence than any deer's. Like the elk on the seashore I'd dreamed so long ago, this stag watched me with the eyes of a man.

"What do you want?" I asked. "Why are you here?"

The deer didn't answer. Instead, he bent his forelegs and lowered his head until his muzzle touched his chest. His antlers scraped against the wall as he brought them down toward me. I looked around wildly for an escape, but there was none. The tips of his antlers split my flesh like knives, sliding easily through skin and muscle, pinning me to the cold stone floor.

I writhed and thrashed. But with my every movement, his antlers punctured me more thoroughly.

Sacrifice, he whispered.

CHAPTER 31

The pain was hot and wet and filled me up. It transformed me into more of itself, an alchemical reaction that left me something less than human, a mass of blood and bone and skin and nothing else.

"Please," I gasped. "*Please.*"

The deer jerked his antlers. I howled like a wounded wolf, and the pain bore me off, spiraling down into some black sea. I bobbed on its waves until I found myself standing high atop a cliff, surrounded by the tossing silver-green foam of grass.

I couldn't breathe. My chest felt as if it had closed. I patted my hands over it, feeling for wounds. But my flesh was as sealed and perfect as it had been—

Before my arm was severed. I had two hands. I raised them both and stared at them, turning them over so I could examine the lines on their palms, the ridge of their knuckles. I flexed my right hand and it moved for me, as solid as it had been before my mother buried it beneath a cork tree.

It was only then that I realized I was dreaming.

When I looked up, the man who had been the elk in my long-ago dream stood before me, his long gray hair braided down his back like a tail. This time, he wore a shirt and trousers of soft, tawny gold. A polished bone horn hung from his neck on a leather thong. He stroked it and cocked his head, studying me.

"You toy with me," I said, "making me think I have two arms."

"I toy with you?" He raised his eyebrows. "Your arm exists. Flesh is more malleable than you suppose."

I clenched my hands into fists and took a deep breath. "Who are you?"

"That is a question not easily answered, I'm afraid."

"Try."

He gave me a look. "Let's just say I patronize sacrifices. You seem lately determined to become one."

"How else can I serve my family?"

"Another good question. How else *can* you serve your family?"

"Surely, I am in the only position—"

"Death is not the only route to sacrifice. Though perhaps," he said, with the ghost of a smile, "sometimes it is the easiest."

The corners of my mouth tugged down tight. "You make light of it."

Abruptly, his smile disappeared. "No, I don't make light of it. But if you continue to allow pieces of yourself to be carved off, you will cease to be the Hunter and become instead Prey."

The night pressed down around me, filled with the crashing of waves against the shore. Water eating away sand, whittling off pieces of the beach, devouring them in its belly. A gust of wind aroused the grass to a fury. It sounded like an angry crowd.

"When have I not been prey?" I asked. "My whole life, I've been used, my only value in how I could best serve the interests of my House or someone else's House. I failed in that purpose once. Now I only seek to make amends. I have to do this thing for my father because he asks it of me."

The man frowned. "Leaving yourself blind to the wider world. Walking through a forest like a human, blunt and big-footed, crashing and breaking twigs along the way, never realizing what's under your feet."

"And what would that be? To what am I blind?" I said crossly. "Your riddles make my head hurt. Can't you speak plainly?"

"If I did, I fear you wouldn't listen. There is more to the world than what you think you know. You have more use than as a corpse."

"Show me how to avoid it, then," I pleaded. "Show me any tomorrow in which I don't die, and Arsenault doesn't die, and my father and my House live on."

The truth was, I didn't want to die. But I couldn't see any other path that made me more than a coward. I was an armless serf girl convicted of murder, the unwed lover of a man who shaped the world with a magic I barely comprehended...but I would not be a coward. I owned nothing except my pride.

When the man didn't answer, the hope died within me, the

pain of its passing more intense for its short bloom. I turned, unable to face him.

But then he spoke, wearily. "Hunter," he said. "And Sacrifice. In you, the two are combined. You choose which road you follow, with which vision you will see. Your heart will always be your own."

"No," I said softly, shaking my head. "I've given that away."

The man went still, as if the prospect frightened him. Then he let out his breath. "A gift," he said. "To bestow where you wish."

Not wherever I wish. My heart resided with Arsenault, and if Arsenault died, they would bury my heart with his body. I didn't know how I would go on, heartless.

"Come." The man motioned to me. "Look."

I hesitated. He walked to the lip of the cliff and lay down prone, fingers curling around the crumbling edge. He looked down onto the beach below.

I followed him in spite of myself. And saw Arsenault.

It was like a continuation of that other dream, the one I'd had after I'd stolen Arsenault's silver wolf. But this time, Arsenault knelt on the beach beside a man with an arrow protruding from his chest.

I glanced at the deer-man, but he shook his head slightly without saying anything. Below us, Arsenault bent over the man on the sand, and the wind carried the sound of his weeping.

"Who is that?" I whispered to the deer-man. "Did Arsenault kill him?"

The man didn't answer me. I clenched my fingers on the rock in frustration and looked at Arsenault again. From this height in the luminous semi-dark, I couldn't make out the colors of the clothes he wore, but the cut of them was strange. His hair gleamed black as the sand on which he knelt—a trick of dreams, to see him so well, I thought—with no white to mar it. The dead man seemed to melt into the sand; his hair must have been black too.

"Listen," the deer-man whispered.

I frowned and listened as hard as I could. I heard nothing but the whistle of the wind, the crash of waves, and Arsenault's weeping. I wanted to go to him, but the man put a hand on my arm as if he could hear my thoughts.

"The ravens. Do you hear them?"

And then I could. Their cawing made my stomach clench. On the beach, one dove out of the night to alight near the dead man's head. Arsenault shouted and lunged at it.

"His battle is bigger than you know," the deer-man said. "You're part of it. *Kyrra*. Fortune."

"I've brought him nothing but ill fortune," I said. "Why doesn't he just walk away from this fight? He's a gavaro. He bears us no allegiance. We could leave—"

The deer-man turned to look at me. His black eyes were level. "Would you do that?"

I let out my breath. "No."

He turned back to watch Arsenault. "This is but one battle in a much larger war. As well call you Destiny."

I snorted. "Is there really such a thing? Fortune is fickle. I may be a pawn, but I know why. It has nothing to do with gods."

"Jaded, are we?"

"Somewhat," I agreed. Then I sighed. "What war are you talking about?"

"He's beset by ravens."

There were ravens all around the body now, swooping down out of the sky—not to eat from the body but to peck and claw at Arsenault. He waved his arms, drew his sword, but little by little, they chased him away. He stumbled down the black beach, shouting something that sounded like a name.

Sella!

He was calling his wife.

Before I knew it, I had risen to my knees. But the deer-man pushed me back down.

"Don't make me watch this anymore," I said, "if you're not going to let me do anything about it."

"But you can do something about it. From here, the dead man looks as if he is the Sacrifice, but I tell you—he is not. He is merely the tool, the wedge of Fortune."

I began to grow angry. "And where, then, is she? Where is the goddess for whom I am named? Does she do this to all men, then, arrange their lives for them and walk away while they mourn?"

"Your Fortune is an elusive goddess," the deer-man said in a low voice. "But do not cast aside her patronage so quickly. The other gods may try to pull you in other directions, but you belong to her. And she will make use of you as she sees fit."

"But for my heart, of course," I said, unable to keep the sarcasm from my voice. "Which is yet mine to give."

"A human heart may make all the difference."

I pushed myself up. "Talking to gods makes my head hurt. I'm going to die in the morning; what will you tell me then?"

The deer-man climbed to his feet and put a hand on my shoulder. I looked up at him in surprise. "Follow your heart where it leads. The path may be rocky, but the road will be right."

He squeezed my shoulder, the way a father would. Then he stepped back and brought the bone horn to his lips.

The sound that poured out of it swallowed me. I closed my eyes, gasping, and opened them to the rattle of keys at the door. The painting of the deer-man glowed red in the dim sliver of light. Then Verrin threw the door open and that vision died in the yellow glow of his candle.

"Your father sends for you," he said, his face somber. "I'm to escort you to the courtyard."

CHAPTER 32

ADALUS'S WORDS FROM THAT LONG-AGO DREAM RING IN MY head as Lobardin leads me to my old chambers. Even while I was fleeing across the countryside with Mikelo, I could pretend I was still Hunter. But now I must admit that I have become Prey.

Both my hands hurt. Which scares me.

"Will you gloat now?" I ask Lobardin.

Lobardin winds a rope in his hands as he walks. His hands still and his eyebrows lift in surprise, which isn't the reaction I expect. "While I must confess a certain curiosity about what went on in that room," he says, "you've blood on your shoulders, Kyrra."

Damn.

"From the wound you gave me."

"If you hadn't fought so hard."

"What did you expect me to do? Collapse in a simpering heap at your feet?"

He gives me a sharp, black glance. "No. I don't think I expected that. But must you throw yourself at everything so mindlessly?"

I lift my arms to wipe the nervous sweat from my upper lip

with my sleeve. "This from the man who pursues his own vengeance without thought."

"Oh, I assure you," he says, smiling but with his teeth gritted and his lips drawn too tight, "I pursue my vengeance very thoughtfully."

He opens the door to my old rooms and gestures me in like a gentleman. I keep my gaze on him the whole time. My legs are shaking and I want nothing more than to sit, but there is something in his tone that makes me nervous.

How deeply am I involved in his quest for vengeance? I've elaborated my own fantasies of revenge often enough that I know what I'd do if I wanted to injure Arsenault, if I were in Lobardin's shoes.

"Is Arsenault really in the old prison?" I ask abruptly as we pass through the sitting room—a blur of purple—and into the bedchamber, where he maneuvers me with a hand on my back. I shift away from him and sit down in a chair. Not on the bed. These are my old rooms, but I barely look at them.

"Would I tell you if he wasn't?"

I move my head too fast and the pain makes me grit my teeth. My vision skews and realigns, and Lobardin is kneeling down next to me, the rope coil slung over his shoulder, reaching out to gather my hair in his hand.

"No," I say, pulling away from him. But that just brings fresh pain and more vertigo. The saliva that pools in my throat warns me I'm going to vomit. I try to swallow it, to keep it down with my hand on my mouth, but it shoots out through my fingers and spatters the skirt of my dress, my shoes, the orange-and-red Tiresian carpet that softens the stones of the floor.

My rooms used to be azure blue.

As if I've just opened my eyes, I see the room in one quick, dizzying sweep—the blood-orange curtains swept back from the bed, the carmine satin bedspread, the Rojornicki pillows with their hunting scenes of stags and pheasants.

Lobardin kneels beside me, watching me.

"I'll get someone to clean this up," he says softly.

I don't say anything. He stops and digs something out of his pocket. For a moment, I think he's drawing a knife, and I flinch.

But it's a rag. He pours some water into the washbasin beside the bed, dips the rag, and wipes my mouth with it. The roughened tips of his fingers brush my lip.

"Why are you doing this?"

His mouth quirks as he wads the rag up, dirty side in. "I thought you might want a clean mouth. Though after listening to you curse me in a number of different languages, I do realize how difficult that might be."

"Why should you care, though? You didn't care when you hit me over the head. You didn't care when we were in the coach."

"Kyrra," he begins, then stops and glances over his shoulder at the door. Then back at me. Thoughtfully. "The Prinze trod on you."

"What should that matter? You've thrown your lot in with them."

He shakes his head, vehemently. "No," he says. "It's not like that. Cassis has genuinely changed. Would the Cassis of years ago defy Geoffre? You of anyone should know what that means."

"And you expect me to believe that Cassis isn't going to crumble as soon as his father marches up that hill? That he's going to risk being put out of the inheritance, cast off, and stripped of his titles, without recourse to the Circle? Do you honestly think Cassis could live that way, Lobardin?"

"Why hasn't Geoffre done that already? Why let Cassis escape to fortify himself in a castle like this? Why send you to take care of the problem?"

I flex the fingers of both hands and stare at my knuckles for a moment. "Because he wants to keep it quiet; that's why. Because he doesn't want to disgrace the name of his House with such scandal, or invite rumormongering—and he probably knows Cassis will break once he sees Geoffre arrayed in force."

"Ah." Lobardin grins, not one of his long, jaded grins but one lit with hope. "But Cassis holds the high ground. Or have you remained ignorant of tactics?"

He baits me. I draw in a deep breath to still my tongue. When I have it under control, I say, "What does it have to do with me? And why do you care now?"

"In the coach, there was Arsenault. Here, it's just you."

I go still. Once again, I feel the tips of Lobardin's fingers against my mouth. I can almost taste the salt of his blood, from that long-ago time when he kissed me to retrieve Jon's letter.

"And what should that matter?" I say.

"I've never blamed you, Kyrra. It's just war that makes us do things we don't want to." He looks up at me from beneath his lashes. "I didn't mean to hit you that hard. Truly, I didn't. Surely, you can understand battle rage."

"What do you want from me, Lobardin?"

He laughs, softly. "You're so wary, Kyrra. Like a cat."

"Should I be otherwise?"

He sobers. "But you've changed too. I can't begin to predict you anymore. The things you do aren't rational. It's more than that arm."

It is the arm, a voice whispers in my head. This won't do. I try my best to keep my gaze on Lobardin's face.

"So says the man who's gone over to his enemies. What did Geoffre do to you, Lobardin?"

He stumbles to his feet. "I am not Geoffre's! How many times do I have to say it before you believe me?" He hurls the rag to the floor. It bounces and rolls on the soiled carpet.

"I side with Cassis because Cassis will bring Geoffre down—haven't you been listening? Gods, Kyrra!" He paces, runs a hand through his hair, whirls to confront me again. "If you think I would sell myself to that bastard—"

"You tried to sell Arsenault to him."

That brings him up short. "I never tried to sell Arsenault."

"You and Ilena. However it was that she discovered Arsenault was spying on the Prinze, you convinced her she ought to go to Geoffre. To give Arsenault away."

I rise from the chair. My first steps are unsteady, but I keep walking and my dizziness evens out.

"Ilena was only a toy to you, like a doll. But she felt much more strongly for you. If it weren't for her, Arsenault could have kept his secret, and who knows what he would have been able to do. Maybe even kill Geoffre the way Jon thought you could."

Lobardin stares at me as if he's never seen me before.

"Kill Geoffre?"

"That's what Jon planned. When the time was right. Both Jon and Arsenault thought you could be an assassin. But my father wanted to avoid war at all costs—any war, even one that Geoffre didn't lead. That's why he sent you away."

Lobardin's mouth pulls down. "She did it, then? She really went to Geoffre?"

I want to hurl something at him. But there's nothing at hand. "How can you be so thick-headed? It wasn't Arsenault's fault!"

"He never thought I would live if I killed Geoffre. He and Jon were going to send me on a suicide attempt. You know it's true, or Arsenault would have just done it himself."

"He didn't have the chance."

"Well, he didn't have the chance to set me up, either, did he?"

Lobardin takes a deep breath and musses his hair, then leans against the door and folds his arms across his chest.

"All I wanted to do was for Ilena to have a bit of blackmail. Which was much more her style...although you must admit she would have made a good householder. I had my suspicions about Arsenault from my time on the Talos, and I knew she liked to eavesdrop. It wasn't hard to see how she felt about Arsenault, and how furious it made her that he chose you. She jumped at the chance to find him out. I thought it was because she wanted to coerce him into her bed. But good for her if she took it further. I guess having a serf girl expose all his plans would have taken some of the smugness out of Jon."

"She didn't," I say. "I killed her."

Never have I managed to take Lobardin so completely by surprise. All the artifice strips from his face in an instant. "You...what?"

"I said, I killed her."

I fake a grin. Lately, I've begun to make myself sick.

I've never been proud of killing Ilena. I did it only to protect Arsenault. But if I can get Lobardin away from that door, I can run past him. So, let him see something else in me, anything that will get me to the door.

I take a step toward Lobardin. "Did you hear me? I said, I killed her. I killed her so she wouldn't tell Geoffre. She said she was going to do it because she loved you, but I loved Arsenault more."

My throat tightens before all the words are out. Have I ever admitted that to anyone? And to say it to Lobardin now—

Lobardin is staring at me, aghast. "She was just a nattering titmouse; she didn't mean— Gods, why did she have to take me so seriously?"

He is still standing in front of the door. I won't be able to shove him out of the way. Frustration drives my next words out. "You threw away the life of a girl and all because of lies?"

It's the wrong thing to say. Anger burns out all the other emotions on his face. I try to dodge out of his way, but damn this head wound, I wobble, and he grabs me up by both my arms and jerks me to him.

"Arsenault's lies killed her," he hisses viciously into my face. "Not mine."

I drive my manacled hands upward toward his crotch, but he propels me backward and tosses me down on the bed. Then he climbs on top of me.

I dig my elbows into the mattress, but he has a rope.

He bends my arms up and leans on them though I thrash and kick, and then he binds them to my chest. My legs he drives apart and keeps useless with his knee.

"Do you want to know what Geoffre did to me, Kyrra? Do you want to know what he made me?"

There is nothing in his black eyes that I recognize. Not the Lobardin I knew, not even the kacin addict. It's as if he's just been erased. Is it the magic taking him over, or did Geoffre do something that horrible?

"Geoffre took me in a room," he says. "There was a mirror there, a silvered mirror. Smooth and perfect. And he said, *Look down into the mirror, Lobardin.* When I asked why, he wouldn't tell me, but it was just a mirror, so I did it.

"And do you know what I saw? I saw myself doing things too horrible to ever tell anyone. Murdering men in cold blood was the best of it. I even saw myself betraying my House. My *House,* Kyrra. They never approved of me, but they never disowned me. I still have my name. But in the mirror, my family died, one by one, and all because of my betrayals.

"Then I said to Geoffre—I said, *No, it's not true, I will not do any of that; what do you think I am?* And do you know what he said?"

Lobardin pauses, as if expecting me to answer. I try to throw him off but he just presses me down harder into the mattress, and my right arm is no use with this dent and this pain in my head, no use at all.

"No?" he says. "I'll tell you, then. Geoffre di Prinze said, *I think you're mine, and I think you'll do anything I tell you.* And do you know what he did, Kyrra?" He shakes me by the shoulders when I don't say anything, and pain rattles my head. "Do you know?"

"No," I rasp, trying desperately to think up some way out of this.

"He had four of his guards hold me down on the floor. And then he took me. He kept me in that room for six weeks. *Six weeks.* He used magic to do things I had never dreamed of. Things I cannot describe to you and will never be able to tell anybody. And at the end, he was right. I did anything he asked. For all the good it did him. It turns out that the magic I have wasn't the magic he wanted after all. All that—for nothing. Just to be thrown away like a broken pot."

He looks as if he wants to spit, as if he still has the taste of Geoffre in his mouth.

"And you gave Arsenault up to that?" I say, pulling upward against his hands until my face is just a breath away from his. "Geoffre held him prisoner for *three months*."

Lobardin makes a noise deep in his throat and lunges forward to smother my mouth with his own. I can't breathe. I thrash and struggle, but it's no use. He pushes me down into the bed. I try to bite him, but he's wise to my tactics now and he tears away before I can.

And laughs. A dark, helpess chuckle deep in his throat that sounds almost like it's going to turn into a sob. "Oh, Kyrra," he says. "I saw you in the mirror, too. In this very room. And this was one of the things I swore I would never do."

I look up at him, into those black eyes I could never decipher—and all I can see is that he is drowning. Broken.

In spite of myself, I can't hate him. I want to, for the chain of events he set in motion that saw Arsenault into Geoffre's hands, but what I see in those eyes, what I know of Geoffre—I can't. All I can remember suddenly is that once he tried to bring me orchids.

"Then don't," I say. "Lobardin, you don't have to be the person Geoffre made you. You don't have to fulfill every prophecy the mirror showed you. Fate isn't set; you have a choice."

"A choice?" His laughter is harsh. "Is that truly what you believe? Or are you just parroting Arsenault's lies?"

"I don't know that I ever heard Arsenault say that. He seemed to think we were locked into the game. Let me up, Lobardin," I say. "Please."

"Kyrra. You don't know how it burned me to see you with Arsenault, how much I wanted you—how it terrified me..."

"Let me up, then. Just let me up."

I lie very still. Because I can See.

It's a nauseating double vision, but it shows me true. What a tangle this is that I have gotten into. What broken pawns Geoffre has lined his road with.

"Lobardin," I say again. "Let me up. I haven't decided what to do about Cassis. Has he really changed?"

Lobardin looks down at me, confused. Then he shakes his head, as if a muzziness has taken hold of him. He looks down at my shoulders, at the crumpled lines of my dress beneath his hands as if he's seeing them for the first time.

I stretch my metal fingers, thinking that maybe I can grab his shirt and unbalance him enough for me to get out from under him—just for a moment.

And then, before I can move, he lets me go and rolls off the bed. His boots sink into the carpet with hardly a sound.

I lie frozen on my back on the bed.

"Here," he says hoarsely, head half-turned. "If you want to know about Arsenault."

My head moves of its own accord, finally, to look at him. He yanks open the drawer of my nightstand and throws something heavy on the end of the bed. I flinch and draw up my legs. But he's already walking through the sitting room to the door. The door creaks when he opens it, and he lets it slam behind him. The sound echoes, the way everything echoes in my mind.

I bring my knees to my chest to meet my bound hands. I ball my hands into fists beneath my chin and start to shake. My clothes all smell like Lobardin.

I lie on the bed for a long time. Maybe the rest of the night. But when I'm finally able to unbend and sit up, I see what Lobardin gave me.

It's Arsenault's book.

༺༻

OVER THE COURSE OF THE THREE YEARS I KNEW HIM,

CHAPTER 32

Arsenault filled more than one book with writings and sketches. The books he preferred were sturdy, leather-bound volumes like this one, square and small enough to slide into a pack or a pocket but large enough to draw a map that could be read without a magnifying lens. The pages were rough, so they would take his metal stylus, and always coated with the dust he ground from burnt bones or sometimes marble if he could get it.

This book doesn't have the look of one of his finished volumes, which all developed thick, wavy edges. Instead, it looks as if he tried to destroy it. Black burns stretch in fingers on the covers, and one charred corner looks as if something took a bite out of it. When I open it, gray flakes of ash crumble onto the bedspread along with the puff of bone dust I expect.

The pages aren't empty. They're full of sketches. Women, children, men. Some of them I recognize—a brief glimpse of Margarithe just above where the book has been burned, Jon standing in a Dakkaran shirt behind an enormous heart-shaped leaf—and some of them I don't. A man who shares the shape of Arsenault's brows and nose, who could be his brother. Two solemn-looking boys with dark hair, and a young girl with a mane of wild curls and a daisy crown on her head. A woman turns up over and over, with a sweep of hair hiding half her face and a mysterious smile.

And me. I'm there too.

For a moment, I think maybe Geoffre took the book from him before Kafrin and Cassis got it that way. But as I work to turn the pages with my bound hands, I realize that this is a new book.

Not all the sketches and writing are done in the strong, confident hand I remember. Instead, their lines skew and fall off the page, go crooked and unconnected at odd moments. Brown spills spatter across the pages and buckle the paper, and I remember he said he'd decided to drink himself to death. A few of the sketches are actually done in chalk or ink. And then he's drawn me mostly in poses where you can't see my face.

Me, sitting against the stone wall with the armless statue above me. Me with my head down and my hair in my face, stitching his shirt. Me, standing over Etti, tickling the baby's toes.

It's too hard to keep looking at these pictures. Even working from memory and half-drunk, Arsenault had a talent for catching gesture and personality. I wonder if his Sight ever subsides or if it's simply the way he sees the world.

But why didn't he hide these sketches with a glamour? Why did he try to burn them? Was it too hard? Were they too painful?

I have to lie down and keep the book up against my face to turn each page. I smudge Etti's baby girl and wince. But then I'm looking at a page full of his writing, the letters slanted with feeling, the silver metal point tinged with burgundy. The words begin in Eter, then switch to Vençalan and modern Eterean, a mix almost any householder could read.

Dear Tavi,

I know this letter won't find you well. It's a silly thing, to write a letter to your ghost. But I've had most of a bottle of rum and no one to talk to but myself, and the bums have already told me to shut up. I've seen you following me more than once in the last few weeks...months... I don't know. Time's a hopeless muddle and the liquor just makes it worse. But I know you're there, because you're always there. You're the one constant in my life. The thing I can count on when everything else goes to hell.

How many lives have I lived since you lived yours? I can't count them, except that I feel as if many men inhabit my skin. Since last you lived, I have committed murder, adultery, betrayal. I have burned villages and executed innocent men and women, struck them down in cold blood as ordered. I have loved and deserted women, and women have loved me and I have failed them, again and again. I have done everything I saw myself doing when Calden took me up to the glacier and made me look into the ice. But every memory I have might only be a dream—or a nightmare—vague as it is, and in the end, meaningless. My only vivid recollection is of the act that set me on this road of exile.

Your death. And Sella's.

I lie awake nights and wonder how I could ever have been so arrogant, so blind. So jealous. How I could have let my anger overcome every other emotion I had ever felt for you, my brother. I loved you. I loved Sella. That's what makes it so much worse. The anger was over in a moment. But the love went on, for both of you. Only, it couldn't rewrite that one moment when I thought I could take the place of Justice.

Then again—I'm drunk enough, I can say this, Tavi—you always did live ahead of yourself, assuming I would pick up the slack and the blame. I'm sure it didn't occur to you that even though I was a rotten husband and father, ignoring everyone around me as I went ever deeper after Erelf's knowledge...I loved my wife and I wouldn't want to share her. Maybe you thought so much of me that it never occurred to you that I could let the magic get out of hand. I know you didn't understand Sella enough to understand that she would intervene. She trusted both of us and didn't know how far down the path we had both gone in opposite directions, each of us chasing the magic that called to us like those monsters the Etereans talk about, the ones that sing men to death with their songs.

I saw one once, you know, a beautiful woman with a beautiful voice who sang me right into the back of her cave. It was a painful death but sweet, too, in a way, and what I don't understand is why I can remember that but I can't remember who I was six moons ago before I walked out of that gorge.

It was like being born from hell, but that's the way it always feels.

So, Erelf keeps me turning around. I wouldn't join you and

he never foresaw that Sella would act as she did, trying to save both of us, and now you're both dead and I keep this godscursed ability to See and Shape, to find the metal in people's souls. I always think I'm going to redeem myself, but in the end, I make them less than human. That's the knowledge I gained. You would say it's not so different than yours. I thought I would be an Artisan, a worker of miracles. But all I have become is a Smith, battering people with the hammer of my will.

Some day, perhaps the god the Lierans call Adalus will have mercy on me and step in to end this feud his brother carries on. Then maybe I'll be able to sink into the soil and grow back as something mortal. In every life I live, I become convinced I can change things, but it always seems to end with hardened metal and a sword. I wake out of the battlefield and can't remember anything but you and Sella, the way you both lay there on the beach with the blood leaking out of you, and the waves spilling over you, washing it away. I remember your eyes, fading like the green sea overtaken by gray water, and Sella trying to reach out for me. Nothing is enough to redeem that act. Nothing will ever be enough.

Now I write letters to your ghost, begging for forgiveness, knowing you shouldn't give it, regardless. Because in the deepest hours of night, I still blame you for her death, Tavi, and I can't forgive that. You lured her away from me and then you put her in harm's way.

But I can't forgive myself, either. I was the one who held the magic. I was the one who held her secret. I was the one who gave her away.

And now I am the one who's afraid to die. All these years and I'm still afraid of death—real death, afraid of facing you and her, afraid of meeting Erelf on his own ground.

War isn't so bad when you know it won't affect you.

Now I'm sitting here in this alley with the other casualties, those of us still walking even though we died inside a long time ago. We've got our territories all mapped out. I've got my corner and I'll defend it against anyone who threatens it. You stay away from me, Tavi. I can't help feeling that I lost too much, last time, and if you step over this line while I'm drinking, I'm likely to get mean. I don't think the bums would like that. We'd have to have our own little war over the alley, and I'm tired of fighting.

I'm tired, Tavi. Go away, and leave me alone.

❦

MY METAL FINGERS SPASM AND CRINKLE THE PAGES. THEY crunch like dead leaves. I try to get up, and that only wrinkles them worse. I don't know what to do, but I have to get away from this godsdamned book.

His wife. Did he kill her or was it an accident?

Did I ever know him at all?

I cross my hands, palm down, in front of my chest and heave myself up without touching anything. Then I slide off the bed onto the carpet, taking deep breaths and looking up at the door, trying to think. For the moment, I push aside all the secrets I have just learned about Arsenault, things I should have heard from him, and all the questions and fears they've spawned within me. For the moment, I must think about the circumstances of the letter.

Arsenault wrote it after Kafrin but *before* Jon found him, sitting in an alley. Maybe he was too drunk to use his glamour, and when he realized what kind of information he'd been putting in the book, he'd tried to burn it. Somehow, one of the Prinze had found it and rescued the book from the fire.

But why bring the book here? Cassis couldn't have known that Tonia di Sere would hire me to kill him. So, why would he have brought the book here and put it in my old room?

The carpet's smell makes me nauseous, so I get up and walk into my old sitting room. The combination of colors strikes me as garish, unworthy of such a high-ranking house; the purple clashes with the autumnal oranges and reds of the bedchamber. It's as if these rooms are only a display of wealth. As if Cassis wanted to crush my memory by taunting me even in my absence.

Maybe Cassis is trying to tell me that he knows who Arsenault is and can use him against Geoffre.

I lean my head back in the chair and stare up at the ceiling, whose fresco has been newly refreshed. I expect to find it changed, obliterated, to reflect Prinze ownership but the fresco remains as it always has.

Ekyra stares back at me, golden hair streaming in the wind.

She stands barefoot on a wooden platform above a crowd of men. The artist painted her in deep blue, which is why my chambers were all varying shades of that color. Her dress ripples in the wind. You can tell it's silk. No other fabric shimmers like that.

In her left hand she holds a sheaf of wheat. A bag of coins hangs from her left wrist. Children play on her left side, laughing and cherubic, amid coffers from a dozen foreign ports.

Her right side is different. Her right side is coated in shining silver plate. Her right hand holds a sword, and instead of children frolicking at her feet, there are skeletons. Dancing.

Ekyra is Fortune. She isn't Justice.

But what must I now be?

All those rumors of Prinze soldiers, all those soldiers in Karansis...and Geoffre letting me live in order to send me here... He was preparing to deal with his son in a way much more ruthless and efficient that merely disowning him. Geoffre wanted Cassis's powerbase snuffed out and him with it.

And Cassis knew it.

In the war of spies, perhaps he and Lobardin had ferreted out the information that Arsenault worked for Tonia di Sere. Since Jon wanted to support Cassis, might he not have made that information available to Cassis? Cassis would then have known that he could split Arsenault away from Geoffre, that Geoffre didn't even know who he was. Perhaps they expected Arsenault to receive Tonia's directive to kill Cassis. And when Arsenault got here...then what? What was Arsenault supposed to do?

Jon bears no love for the Prinze after what they did to his country. He won't support Cassis for long. What he wants, I think, is for Geoffre and Cassis to kill each other on the field of war, leaving only Devid to pick off so that Mikelo can take the chair. But if Jon wants that, why has he let Arsenault and Mikelo become hostages?

To use Arsenault as bait?

The thought makes me sick. I want to put my hands on my stomach. I clench my fingers against the silk of my dress instead.

Why would Jon let Arsenault fall into this kind of pit?

I know the answer to that as swift and sure as I know I'll leave Cassis and Driese here to fight out this battle however they please.

Jon is a prince. Jon would sacrifice men, women, and children for the good of his country.

He'd sacrifice Arsenault, too.

A muffled bang draws me from my thoughts. It's like the bite of an insect. I bring my head up from the back of the chair and listen, trying to discover its source. The sound comes again, followed by a rumbling crash.

I lurch out of the chair too fast and pay for it with vertigo. There are no windows in this room, which makes it defensible, but I curse the walls for what they keep from me. Another loud bang pops the air.

Cannon fire.

I'm to the door before I even realize it. Throwing my right elbow into it.

"Lobardin!" I shout.

Every thud sends spears of pain into my head, but I keep at it, whacking the wooden door until splinters fall at my feet like pine needles. Dimly, through the rush of blood in my ears, I hear more whining and crashing, pops and thuds, and I fill in those sounds with the screams of men, screams I can't possibly hear.

"Lobardin!" I yell again, and he finally flings open the door.

I stumble out into the hallway, into Lobardin's chest. He catches me by the arms and holds me there. His eyes have a hunted, haunted look in them, and his hair hangs down in them in unruly black spikes, as if he's been running, or as if he never thought to re-braid his hair after our struggle in my bedchamber.

"It's Geoffre," he says, breathing hard. "Geoffre's attacking."

CHAPTER 33

I could lay the blame for Geoffre's seizure of Arsenault those many years ago at Lobardin's feet, for planting the seed of revenge in Ilena's mind. Or, if I wanted to, I might lay that blame at my father's feet, for presenting me with a decision I couldn't back out of honorably.

Or I could bear the blame myself, for failing to see the consequences of that decision. I sought only to do what was best for my House. But in truth, my House was made of cards, and it was the single breath I took to utter the word *yes* that sent them tumbling down.

Yes to Cassis in the conservatory.

Yes to my mother's potion.

Yes to my father, when he asked me to give my life to appease Geoffre.

But there was no appeasing Geoffre, then as now. I should have known that Arsenault wouldn't stand by and let me hang. But I thought it would all happen too fast. I thought that the gibbet would be guarded, that he wouldn't be able to overpower the guards to reach me. I thought that perhaps my father would have sent him away.

Verrin led me out of the cave in the gray dawn light and

bound my left arm to my waist with a length of rope. He knotted it loosely at first. "Please," I said. "Let it press into my skin a little."

He looked up at me, a shadow of suspicion passing over his face. He'd spent the past two days sitting outside the caves, guarding me, so he had news from only the servants who brought him his meals, and those servants were undoubtedly instructed in silence by my father.

"Why?" he asked. "I'm to take you to the villa. The only reason you're tied is because the servant said you were supposed to be. Otherwise, I'd leave you loose. You're going to see your father."

I nodded. I couldn't tell him I wanted my hand tied tight so I wouldn't try to claw the rope from my neck—if hanging was indeed to be my death. I'd convinced myself of it, sitting in the caves, but in the dim morning light, I experienced a moment of panic. What if it wasn't the rope? What if it was something else, something more horrible?

I didn't think I could stand dismemberment. Not after my arm.

Verrin put a hand on my shoulder. "Kyrra. Maybe the ropes are too tight already."

"No," I said. "Tighter. Please."

He eyed me askance. "All right," he said. "And once you're on the burro, the boy brought tea for you to drink. To improve your constitution."

I almost laughed, it was so like the prelude to the execution of my arm. Except this morning would do away with the rest of me. Abruptly, I sobered. "My father is kind," I murmured, casting my eyes down at the ground.

"Your father didn't send it," Verrin said. "Your mother did."

"My mother thinks much of me, then." I wondered what was in the tea...but then it struck me: did it matter? If it killed me before I hung, that would only be a blessing.

"You're acting strangely this morning, Kyrra," Verrin said as we walked to the little donkey tethered near the cave's mouth. It stamped its front foot and brayed. "Not like yourself."

"It's just the time I've spent alone. And killing Ilena."

"I hadn't thought it affected you that much."

"I'm still a woman," I snapped. "Not a monster."

"I didn't mean it like that. You had to kill her, Kyrra."

Truthfully, I hadn't thought of Ilena much when I sat in the caves. How could I, when there was Arsenault to worry about? I worried that if I saw him, I would find some way to claw the rope from my neck, that I would scream and struggle and fight...

For nothing.

My throat clutched at the thought.

"Kyrra," Verrin said. "Are you all right?"

I nodded, not trusting myself to speak. Finally, I said, "The tea?"

Verrin watched me instead of his hands as he fumbled about in the burro's pack. The donkey shifted and bumped against him, swiveling its long ears, then laying them back flat against its head. Verrin held the skin with the tea in it almost under my nose before I realized he was offering it to me.

"Thank you," I said. He tipped it to my lips. I braced myself for a taste like the potion my mother gave me to miscarry Cassis's child, but when the warm liquid slid down my throat, it tasted mostly of honey marred only by a slight bitterness.

I drank it all. When Verrin took the skin away, there wasn't a drop left. He lifted me onto the donkey, which put back its ears, and then he took the lead rope and we set off. As the little donkey lurched along, picking its way with sure hooves up the rocky path and eventually over the top of the ravine and through the long grass, I began to grow lethargic. I felt as if my limbs slowly separated from my body like a boat slips from a mooring. Verrin had to catch me and shove me back onto the burro more than once, so I knew what had been in the tea.

Kacin.

She must have used a lot for it to have affected me so quickly.

But I remember weeping. I remember Verrin holding my shoulders to keep me on the burro and looking into my face in alarm. I remember the way the first real light of sunrise appeared like a slash of blood on the horizon. I remember saying to Verrin, *There is going to be a war and you should take Etti and the children away.* I remember saying, *My father is going to hang me for Geoffre di Prinze.*

I remember his look of horror, too. *Your father wouldn't do that to you, Kyrra,* he said. *What father would?*

But he wasn't from Liera. He couldn't be blamed for not knowing.

After a little while, the blur of the world began to be swirled with people, their faces peeking out at me from beneath lace veils and rough-spun hoods like the faces of pansies. They turned this way and that as if they were blown by the wind, and I began to laugh. The people turned toward me when I laughed, and their mouths were all slashes in their faces as if their petals had been torn, and now their jaws flapped like the tatters. I sank down against the burro and closed my eyes, breathing in his dusty burro scent, but that just made me queasy and reminded me of Cassis in the hayloft, and I wanted to cry. My face got sticky and I could feel the stiff prickles of donkey hair pasted to my cheeks, but I couldn't wipe them off. Verrin pushed me up and wiped them off for me.

"Thank you," I whispered to him, loud enough for anyone to hear, I'm sure. "You've always been nice to me, Verrin."

"What is this talk about?" he said. "What was in that tea, Kyrra?"

But I just shrugged. When I turned my head, it swung like a gate on a fence. I imagined that my muscles creaked, but then I saw the gibbet kneeling like a penitent in the dirt, its arms raised toward the sky.

Verrin grabbed my left arm. "No," he whispered. "The Mestere couldn't be so cruel! You— His daughter!"

CHAPTER 33

"Let me go, Verrin," I said—or thought I said, though even in my own ears, my voice had slurred. "I said, Verrin."

"You said what, Kyrra?" He still had his hand on my arm, holding me up but also, as I began to realize, pulling me away with him into the crowd.

"Come with me," he said softly. "Come with me now, before anyone—"

"No!" I shouted and put all my strength into stopping. In his surprise, he let me go and I staggered sideways, falling to my knees.

"Kyrra!"

I looked up at him. "No! I said I would for my father!"

I can remember the horror on Verrin's face. And then the crowds closed in like a tide, awash with the noise of voices. The two gavaros who'd been with Verrin when I killed Ilena seemed to come out of nowhere. They grabbed my arms.

"The Mestere passed judgement," the one with the hooknose said, gesturing over his shoulder with his head. "It's to be a hanging."

"It doesn't make any sense!" Verrin yelled at them, still holding on to me. "Why?"

"Mestere's orders," the gavaro said, and they both began pulling me away from Verrin, who cursed and yanked back.

I felt like a rag doll.

"Let me go, Verrin!" I yelled.

Verrin looked at me helplessly. The other gavaros tugged me away from him. He reached for me, but I pulled away.

"I told my father I'd do it. It's what I want."

I started laughing—mad laughter, kacin-sparked. My feet thunked on the wooden steps of the gibbet, but I didn't stop laughing. Not even as they settled the noose around my neck.

Then my father stepped up onto the platform.

Everything grew quiet. Even me. My father came closer and I waited for him. Tears pricked my eyes, but I fought them back.

It was hard, with the kacin. The gavaros behind me had to hold me up. "Steady, now," one of them murmured.

At those words, my father stopped and looked at me. He didn't stand next to me or touch me. He simply watched me for a moment. His gaze glittered with tears he didn't shed. For a brief moment—one I might have imagined—his face twisted and he looked as if he'd lose his resolve and reach out for me.

The kacin made it hard to be cold. But I willed my face stony and I turned away from him, shrugging off the gavaros who held me up. I stood upright on my own in the noose.

When I glanced back at my father, he'd turned his head, too. He looked old now, older than I ever imagined he could be. The skin on his face hung gaunt on his cheekbones.

"It is unfortunate that our festivities are marred with such proceedings, but justice is justice," my father said. "This serf girl broke my proscriptions on edged weapons and killed another girl. My will is that she die by hanging."

His expression was hard as a blade when he said it. I was proud of him. But maybe that was the kacin, flooding me with elation that, at last, I would do what was honorable and true.

I looked over the crowd as the gavaros behind me checked the noose and adjusted my feet over the trapdoor. My gaze snagged on a row of pansies in the front—Geoffre and Devid, staring up at me with their fierce blue eyes; Cassis, his eyes wide and dark and brown.

My vision blurred and I stumbled. The noose pulled against my neck and the hooknosed gavaro cursed and bent to shove my leg back where it should go.

When I looked up again, I saw Arsenault.

He stood at the edge of the crowd, wrapped in a beggar's brown robes. His hood fell back a little when he looked up at me.

My heart wrenched.

Then there was a thump as a gavaro kicked over the lever for the trapdoor. I moved my head, but the door flew open too fast and the noose caught my neck and yanked me up, hard.

The sensation of air beneath my feet and the blinding crush of pain from the rope were the last things I knew.

※

I FELT LIKE I WAS FLOATING. *DEATH, FREE FROM PAIN.* I looked down on myself from somewhere above: my body hanging limp like that doll torn between the gavaros. The noose creaked as it slowly twisted.

I remember everything so clearly, as if I were just another bystander eager for spectacle. I remember the way my hair hung down in my face in wild golden curls sparking with the new day's sunlight. I remember how the sky rolled itself out like a bolt of blue silk, shimmering with morning. I remember the way the crowd leaned forward as a whole, as if it were a single animal.

Was I dead? Had the rope snapped my neck? These questions meant nothing. I simply *was*, floating free, restless to be away.

Then someone shouted my name.

KYRRA!

The word boomed in the stillness, and the day, so silent, fell into pieces and slammed into me. I tried to dodge the power of that voice, but something in it skewered me and wouldn't let me go.

Kyrra! it came again. *Kyrra kyrra kyrra KYRRA*

Until it ceased to be my name and only a word, a sound, a hook in my flesh.

What? I cried out. *Oh, let me go—*

It was Arsenault.

I saw him suddenly, standing in a space all his own with his hood thrown back, staring up at me—not my body, but *me*—his eyes wild. Wind whipped his black hair away from his face, and his cloak had fallen askew so I could see the hilt of his sword jutting from his hip. It flashed silver in the light of the sun. The silver, the gleam of metal, fascinated me. My gaze was drawn to it like a flitting moth.

Hold on, Kyrra!

Arsenault, it was my choice! No one forced me.

And it's my choice to bring you back, he said in a determined voice. *My love.*

My heart felt as if it had been clawed in two.

I was dead. I would never see him again.

Kyrra!

The sound of my name was a sharp snap, like a slap in the face. I turned toward it, and there my clarity ends. Pain lanced me from every direction, molten and hot, dripping down my spine.

I screamed. Everything was a muddle. I thought I saw my body lift up out of the pit on its own, surrounded by a nimbus of silver. The noose loosened and twitched its tail as if it were alive. It untangled from around my neck like a snake, its frayed ends like fangs, hissing, spitting.

My body thumped to the wood like a carcass of meat. Still. Dead.

Let me back in! I screamed.

I beat at it, consumed by pain, but I could find no way back. A moment before, I had wanted to die for my House, but now I did not; Arsenault had set that hook in me and it drew me back like a fish. In my heart, I didn't want to die. And that was what Arsenault had seized on.

He stood there, on the platform. He'd thrown off his cloak and pulled his sword. I heard screams. There were thumps on the platform like bootheels and he gathered up my dead body and ran.

My head bumped against his chest. He whispered words I didn't understand, and then—

How shall I explain this? It can't be explained.

I was dead, my soul was in the air, and then—it wasn't. Then

CHAPTER 33

I was opening my eyes and opening my mouth to cry out, but when I did, something hot and scalding flooded out of it and burned my chin.

Not vomit. It wasn't vomit.

I thrashed, trying to free my left arm. I choked, tried to draw breath and couldn't—

Kyrra, oh dear gods, it has to come out of you now...

I opened my eyes again and I was on the ground in a copse of beeches, lying on my stomach. Arsenault's boot was next to my face, his hand twisted in my collar, holding me up so I wouldn't drown in whatever was pouring out of me. I coughed again, spewing out more and more of the scalding liquid that burned me inside.

The pool sparkled in the light. Almost, I wanted to touch it.

It was silver.

"Arsenault," I tried to gasp, but the word wouldn't come out —only a rasping croak that died in another fit of retching.

I felt his hands at my back, then my arm sprang free. I would have fallen on my face, but he caught me and gently wiped away the silver liquid from my chin with his sleeve. He shook it out onto the ground, where it ran away in little drops, then hardened in the dirt.

"Arsenault?" This time, I managed a hoarse whisper. I turned my head weakly so I could look at him.

He pushed my hair away from my face. "Forgive me, Kyrra," he whispered. "But I couldn't let you go." Then he glanced over his shoulder and picked me up again, heaving himself to his feet.

The movement hurt. I cried out, but Arsenault rolled me so that his chest muffled it. "Into the brush," he whispered, "and I'll be back for you."

I stared up at him, wide-eyed. "Arsenault, you can't—"

He didn't answer. He kicked some briars out of the way and laid me down in a thicket, then covered me up with brush. "I'll be back," he said.

He brushed his lips against my brow before he left.

I DRIFTED AWAY, THOUGH I STRUGGLED TO STAY ALERT AND watch what happened. All I could see were boots, anyway—the flash of brown and black as Arsenault fought off the men who chased us.

"Leave her be!" he shouted once, sword flashing. I closed my eyes as pain shot through me, kin to the silver in his sword, and when I opened them, someone else spoke.

"Arsenault—don't make us kill you! We're only following orders!"

"Then, dammit, if you don't want to kill me, stand with me— the Prinze will be here soon enough."

"She's dead, Arsenault—let the Mestere have her body."

"She's *not* dead, and anyone who hurts her will get a stomach full of my sword."

"Traitor!" an unfamiliar voice called out. "He's betrayed you all and us, too. Give him up!"

My heart went cold. I recognized that voice. It was Federico, Cassis's gavaro.

I bit my lip. The taste of metal seeped again into my mouth. I wanted to spit it out, but I dared make no sound. I swallowed it instead.

Leave him to me.

Cassis's voice, joining the fray, venomous and cold.

The sound of struck steel reverberated in my head. I imagined them circling each other, swords out, until one struck a blow...

A man cried out. Then a hand swept away the gorse that kept me hidden and male arms picked me up, threw me heavily, but not ungently, over one shoulder.

It had to be Arsenault, but I didn't have the energy to notice.

Everything went black.

CHAPTER 33

I WOKE TO THE SOUND OF HORSES.

Not the *clop* of hooves, as if we were riding, but simply the sound of them—snorts and whickers, the ring of a shoe tapped against a rock, the heavy stomp of an impatient foot in the dust. For a moment, I thought we were in the stables, but then someone shoved me up and over his shoulder onto a horse, and when I slitted my eyes open in surprise, I realized we were in the middle of the woods.

The movement and whirl of vision made my head reel. I closed my eyes again. More hands tugged me from the other side, and my face scraped horsehair. I tried to help, to clutch for the reins, but I was too weak. The black tide rushed in again, washing me out with it when it receded.

When I woke again, I was still on the horse, but there was a man mounted behind me now, and air wafted past my face. My head rested in the crook of his arm.

"You know the path?" a woman's voice asked.

Isia, the strega. Why was she there? I struggled to open my eyes, but they were so heavy.

The man who held me moved. His shirt rubbed against my face, and his stomach muscles moved beneath it, lean and warm. My head bumped something hard in his cloak, something heavy. A gun? I fought to open my eyes, seized for a moment with the fear that it was Cassis who held me, not Arsenault.

"I know it," the man said, breathing hard, and I wanted to weep with relief; it *was* Arsenault. He settled me on his lap more securely, the reins falling over my stomach.

"I'll ride with you," another man said. Verrin. Had Verrin run to get Arsenault? Was that why—

I realized I didn't know what happened. I wanted to wake up. I wanted to ask my questions. But it took too much effort, just wanting all that. I sank down again, and the sounds of conversation grew distant and muddled, though they never disappeared.

"No," Arsenault said. "Go back to the villa. They'll need all the hands they can get. Everything is unraveled."

"Arsenault, if I had known he would sentence his own daughter to death..."

"I'll hold it against him, but don't you. The Prinze brought enough gavaros for a fight, and they'll all be looking for me. The Mestere will be putting them off. He'll need help."

"And what if they find you? They're not that far behind. Whatever it was you did—"

"They're occupied," Isia put in, sounding somewhat bemused. "And Arsenault is right, boy; the Aliente need someone they can trust back there. The Messera didn't send us out here to allow her daughter to be captured again."

My mother sent Isia with a horse?

"I made a vow," Isia said in a low voice, which seemed to be directed at Arsenault. "I vowed that Carolla's children would live. Now that vow becomes yours, too. Do you swear it? Will you uphold them?"

"I will," Arsenault said. I felt him reach out his hand, as if to touch Isia.

But I wanted to shout, *I am Carolla's only child!* How could Isia not know that my brother was dead?

"Ride, Verrin," Arsenault said, "and I'll be back within a fortnight."

Damn the man. He was going to take me somewhere and leave me. I fought to move, to open my eyes and pound at his chest until he let me go, but all I could manage was to slit my eyes open and clutch at his shirt.

For a moment, his eyes met mine and a worn, sad smile curved his lips. "Hold on, Kyrra," he said.

"Arsenault," I choked.

But he'd already touched his knees to the horse's side. The horse bounded forward, legs churning, and all I could do was hold on.

"May Fortune ride with you!" Verrin called out.

CHAPTER 33

I wanted desperately to laugh.

※

I don't know how long it took to ride to the lodge. I knew that's where we were going, because when I roused myself to look around, we were often traveling uphill. But I don't remember much of the ride, just that sometimes I would wake and we would be tucked into the trees at the side of the road, Arsenault sleeping at my side with both of us covered up in his black cloak.

One night after my strength had returned a little, I reached out and touched the corner of his eye, where something glimmered and caught the light. "Arsenault?" I whispered.

He said nothing but took me in his arms and rocked me back and forth, his lips pressed into my hair. I could feel him weep, but his tears were silent and it was only his chest moving. I didn't know what to do, so I held him, too, until I fell asleep, and then in the morning, we were moving again, all uphill.

If the Prinze made any attempts at us, I don't remember them.

But I remember our arrival at the lodge. Night had fallen already, but we'd pressed on. I woke to moonlight and the song of nightingales in the trees, and Arsenault humming an artless little tune above me. When I looked up at him, his eyes were focused straight ahead and gleamed with an odd, hard light. The moon picked it all out.

And the moon picked out the lodge, too, when we stopped on the ridge before it. The pale white glow made the whole place seem like something out of an old story, a fortress where Eterean ghosts roamed. I wondered, in a new way, how many had died there, in attack or defense. As Arsenault clucked to the horse and we started down into the valley between the black volcanic buttes, I even imagined I could see the ghosts, thin and silver as old blades.

Arsenault tightened his arm around me.

"Don't heed their call, Kyrra," he murmured. "It's only that you're so new."

I looked around, wide-eyed, at the shades that scuttled in the grass, wrapping themselves around the tall stalks bending in the wind. *Kyrrakyrrakyrra*, the grass seemed to say as it rustled against itself. I watched as a man passed under the horse, knife in his mouth, then disappeared into the night.

I closed my eyes, feeling sick. "Was I dead?" I asked.

Arsenault was silent. Then he let his breath out, a puff of air over his lips. "Perhaps. For a moment."

"It wasn't long enough to suffocate," I said.

"No. It wasn't."

"Was it my neck, then?"

Another pause. "Yes."

"How—"

"Later," he said, looking around us like a wolf scenting men. "I'll tell you everything later."

He lied, of course. He didn't tell me everything. Only enough.

❦

We clattered into the courtyard, and I managed to hold myself on the horse while Arsenault dismounted and led it to the stables. Then he pulled me down and set me outside the stall so he could see to the horse. When he was done, he came out and lifted me in his arms.

"Put me down," I said. "Let me at least try to walk."

He smiled, briefly, a flash of white teeth in the darkness. "There's some spirit left in you after all, is there? I was beginning to wonder."

"Arsenault."

"You're not well enough to walk, and you know it. I'll put you down on a bed inside. Then you can ask me as many questions as you like."

I bit my lip. He was right and I did know it, but it felt odd to be carried. I had spent three years proving to myself and everyone around me that I was not weak. And now he carried me across the threshold like the bride I would never be.

The lodge was empty, its hearths full of ashes. A year before, my father had pulled back the servants who'd seen to the running of this house. Somewhere in the night, wings flapped and an owl hooted in the emptiness.

Arsenault cursed the dark as he carried me down the great hall, trying to find a suitable room. His breathing had a strain in it, and I wondered—probably for the first time—what he'd done to save me, how much of himself he'd spent.

"Did you kill Cassis?" I asked.

"I thought I told you to wait to ask questions."

"Is it a gun in your cloak?"

"Would that I had a gun. But no."

"Then what is it?"

"Kyrra—you aren't as light as you look."

"You could let me down. I could try to walk."

"You're not ready yet." He took a deep breath. "Shall I take you to your chambers?"

"They're upstairs."

He cursed. "I can hardly see where I'm going."

"Put me down in the drawing room. It shouldn't be far—to your right."

A draft billowed a tapestry. Its fringe rustled against the stone like the susurrus of the windblown grass outside. Arsenault hissed and jerked away from it, so fast he nearly lost his balance, and I had to grab tight onto his shirt.

"Arsenault," I whispered. "It's only the wind."

"I know," he said raggedly, in the kind of tone that said he did not know but was trying to convince himself. He took a deeper breath and adjusted the arm that supported my knees as he carried me into a doorway that yawned beside us, dark as a cave.

I shivered.

"Kyrra?" He stopped.

"I'm all right. There's a chair; put me down."

It was the gold chair. He set me down gently and I sank into its cushions, closing my eyes and wondering how I could be so tired when Arsenault had done all the work. I tipped my head against the chair's back and thought of how my father had often sat in this same chair after a hunt, in this same manner. Head tilted back, eyes closed, feet stretched out before him, while the servants stoked the fire and brought him hot apple cider on a tray.

Something hit the table with a *thunk*. I startled and opened my eyes. It was Arsenault's cloak.

"Damn," he said. He leaned past me and took a wrapped-up lump from the cloak—a bag, since I heard the flap open. He hunched at my feet, fumbling in it, and then with a scraping noise, light flared.

A match. I remembered them, from the house in Liera with Jon. Arsenault touched it to the wick of a candle, then shook it out, set the candle in a holder, and looked up at me.

I hadn't seen his face clearly before. Now I did. Dark circles, not just shadows cast by candlelight, cupped his eyes. Lines of strain fanned from the corners.

For the first time, I realized I didn't know how old he was. And I hadn't known how much it cost him to save me.

I started to cry. It embarrassed me, but I couldn't stop. I reached out and touched his face.

His eyes lit up in alarm. He put a hand on my arm and tensed as if he might stand.

"It's nothing," I said, letting him go and shaking my head, wiping my eyes and my nose with my sleeve. "Nothing. I'm not myself. I'll be better soon."

He shifted onto one knee and leaned forward to run his

hands down my arms—both of them. "You were never as brave as when you stood up there. But it wasn't your time. Even if it had been, I couldn't let you go."

"I did it for my father," I said, willing the tears to dry up. "He asked me to. Ilena—"

"You were trying to protect me."

Tears suddenly changed to anger. "Yes," I said, leaning forward, "and you ruined that, didn't you? You should have let me die, Arsenault. Now Geoffre knows who you are!"

For a moment, there was a hurt glint in his eyes, then he chuckled and began to smile. "So, it's all my fault?"

For some reason, my mouth wouldn't smile with him. "It would have been better if you'd left me dead, Arsenault. Then Geoffre wouldn't know about you, and you could kill him in his sleep."

The humor on Arsenault's face snuffed out. He rubbed his brow. "I know," he said. "I know that."

I waited for him to say more. Anything more. When he didn't, when he just sat there with his hand shaking on his brow, his head bent toward the floor, I let my breath out. I took his hand and lowered it.

He looked at me in surprise.

"I sent you away at the cave because I didn't want you to hurt Verrin. And I wanted to spare you my death."

"Nothing could have spared me that."

"I wouldn't have returned for anyone else."

He stared at me for a moment. Then he lurched forward and caught me up in his arms. "We're both fools," he said, his voice muffled in my shoulder. "The biggest fools."

I couldn't speak. I clutched him to me, as hard as I could.

And over his shoulder, in the candlelight, I saw the glint of silver in his open bag. I stretched a little to see what it was.

A hand gleamed back at me.

I drew in my breath. Arsenault raised his head and his eyes searched my face. "What is it?"

"What is it?" I said angrily. "In your bag."

"You saw the arm."

"Why did you make me another one? You said the last one was dead. You're going to try and leave me here, aren't you?"

He rocked back on his heels and stood, then ran his hand through his hair. "Kyrra, you've got to think for once."

His words stung. "All I want is to do what is honorable and right for my family—"

He rounded on me. "But your family kills for honor, Kyrra. They kill their own. And that isn't right."

"To save my House," I said in a strangled voice. "He only asked me to do it to save our House."

"Did he?" I had never heard as much viciousness in Arsenault's voice before. "Saving your House by killing your daughter? I saw my daughter sent away with strangers, but at least she was alive. I'd rather let my House burn."

"My father did what he had to," I said, and cursed my bottom lip, which wanted to tremble. "Geoffre left him no more choices. And now *you*—"

Arsenault's jaw worked. He paced away from me. "I've been giving him choices. For three years. But has he ever listened to *one* of them?"

Quicker than I could see, he loosed something from his hand. It flew across the room to the hearth, a blur of silver, and buried itself in the wood of the mantel.

His dagger.

He ran both his hands through his hair and stared at the still-quivering dagger. "I thought when he sent me to spy on Geoffre that I would be an assassin, but the orders never came. I could have killed Cassis—more than once. I could never get close to Geoffre, but maybe...once or twice...though I probably would have died doing it..." He took a deep, ragged breath and faced me. "That's why I didn't tell him about Lobardin. Jon and I thought we could do something with him ourselves. If that didn't work—well, then, we'd think of something else. I'd slink back to

Liera and use my own knife, if I had to. Then your father sent Lobardin away and I got word you'd killed Ilena and he had you shut up in the caves and wouldn't tell me anything. When he wouldn't tell me anything, I knew he meant to kill you. I knew he meant to show Geoffre just how debased he was."

"You make him sound like a coward," I said. I sat stiff in the chair. As if by doing so, I could provide myself some defense against Arsenault's words.

"There's more to it than that, though. Your mother told me his plans. Plans he didn't see fit to share with me."

He paced to the mantel and levered the dagger out.

"Your father planned to trick Geoffre into seeing that he no longer favored you at all. To lure Geoffre into believing that the Aliente had switched alliances to stay alive. He knew the Prinze wouldn't care, that they'd go through with their attacks if they were expedient—which they are, Kyrra, in more ways than you know. Your father's land is important, not just for its silk. I told your father that, but..."

He toyed with the dagger in his hands. He was wearing the same black gloves he wore when he had Fixed the silver rod to treat his leg wound long before.

"Your mother convinced him that Geoffre would try for the land no matter what they did. I wanted to kill the lot of them, with stealth, but the Mestere said that if such an assassination were discovered, the Aliente would be the target of all the Prinze allies and the heirs to the Householdership. Killing Geoffre wouldn't matter."

Grudgingly, I said, "He might have been right, Arsenault. A House isn't a snake. If you cut off its head, the rest of it's still dangerous."

"At least we'd have stood on better ground. The pieces would need to regroup after we cut off the head. They might have lost their monopoly on guns, and we'd be better prepared. Your father wanted to plan out the whole war right there when he was already losing the battle."

"Maybe he was just farsighted."

"Tripping over the snare set in front of him?" Arsenault held my gaze for a moment, then snorted and shook his head. "No. None of the other candidates for Householdership is capable of half the damage Geoffre is. Not even his sons. Especially not Cassis," he added as he caught my look. Then, more softly, he said, "He's still alive. I didn't kill him."

"Did you have the chance?" I asked.

He shook his head. "You were more important."

I flushed and looked away from him. "What did my father plan to do?"

"He planned to enter into a merchant agreement with Geoffre. The Prinze would carry and sell Aliente silk, and the Aliente would receive a portion of all profits. He knew it wouldn't matter to Geoffre, but set up that way, he'd have the legal backing of the entire Circle when Geoffre did attack."

I chewed a nail. "So, when he struck the betrothal agreement with Claudia d'Imisi...he was hoping to invoke their distant kin ties with the Prinze?"

"I imagine."

"But my father couldn't have known that I would kill Ilena."

"Of course he couldn't. Initially, the plan was just what I'd told you before—he would exhibit you to the Prinze as a downtrodden serf. But then you killed Ilena, and it was as if the fates had signed sanction to his plan."

I bristled. "And my mother told you all this?"

"As soon as she heard you'd been taken to the caves, she suspected your father. She came to me and told me about the negotiations he'd been carrying out with the Prinze. Then she arranged with Isia to have a horse on the trail to the lodge. Verrin came of his own accord."

"He had no idea what I'd agreed to."

"I should have known you'd do it voluntarily."

I shoved myself out of the chair and wavered, standing. Arsenault shot to my side, but I pushed him away. "What else was I supposed to do?" I said, out of breath already. "Any other answer and I would only have been a coward. How do you know that his plan wouldn't have worked?"

"Because it involved killing you!"

I steadied myself on the arm of the chair, praying my dizziness would leave me. "It's all so much clearer."

He made a frustrated noise deep in his throat. I made myself look up at him, and he looked as if he wanted to throw something again. The dagger was still in his hand. He shoved it back into its sheath.

"I told you," he said, very quietly, "that I would not betray you. I would do anything to rid the world of Geoffre di Prinze. But I will not give you up. Do you understand?"

When I looked into his eyes, I did.

"Why do you want to kill Geoffre?" I asked. My voice was barely a whisper. "Why do you fight our fight?"

He stared at me for a moment. The anger and determination blanked out of his eyes to be replaced by a momentary surprise, as if he had expected me to say something but not that. He reached out and took my arms, gently. "I fight Erelf. Always."

It startled me to hear him say the god's name. I must have swayed, because Arsenault's grip on me tightened again. He pushed me back down into the chair, and I wasn't strong enough to resist.

"You said I could ask as many questions as I liked," I said, cursing myself for sounding like a child after all of this.

He let out his breath. "I did. But I must sit down if you won't."

He lowered himself to the floor in front of a couch next to me, then crossed his legs and leaned back against it, closing his eyes. "You want to know about Erelf," he said, without me even asking.

"I do," I replied. "I want to know why you fight him. I want to know—"

I want to know who that man was on the beach in my dream is what I wanted to ask. But the words sat awkwardly on my tongue and Arsenault was rubbing his scar.

"Gods strive for territory, the same way humans do. They wage wars with each other because it gives them something to do. They think of humans as their playthings—like they're arranging us on a board in order to win games with each other. Even in the best god, there is darkness. But in some gods, the darkness has grown."

"Erelf killed his brother," I said. "Is that the reason for Erelf's darkness?"

"Not the reason. The result."

"Then why—"

"Maybe knowing such darkness is in him has driven him a little mad. Having given himself over to it." Arsenault rubbed his thumb along his temple. "In my homeland...before you are allowed to use your magic, you must first go to see your reflection in a huge cliff of clear glacier ice that we call the Wall. It shows you back all the good and terrible things you're capable of—no one knows why. If magic is like water, maybe the Wall is a place where a spring bubbles up to the surface. The people of my land are often born Fixers, and they discovered the Wall and its use long, long ago. In order to control such a power, we go through apprenticeships. We learn our art, and then we See ourselves. If we can't deal with what the Wall shows us, if we succumb to the kind of madness it can provoke, then we aren't allowed to Shape, to become Artisans."

He licked his bottom lip nervously, a brief flick of his tongue. I narrowed my eyes at him.

"How not?" I asked.

"The masters kill the weak. Because to be weak and in charge of a great power is a dangerous thing."

There was something torturous in his eyes. "The body on the beach," I said, without thinking about it. The words popped free of my mouth like chicks hatching from an egg.

For a moment, there was silence. In it I heard again the

sound of beating wings from somewhere far away. Then Arsenault said, "A body... what are you talking about?"

I pushed myself against the back of the chair. "I had a dream," I said. "When I was in the cave. A painting of a deer turned into a man. He showed you to me, and a body on a beach."

Arsenault went pale. I had never seen him so affected by anything. "Just one body?" he said.

"Were there supposed to be more?"

"A man or a woman?"

"A man. He looked like you."

"My brother," he said, turning away from me to face the empty hearth. "You See so true and yet you can be so blind."

I wasn't sure if he'd meant to speak the words aloud or not. They stung me like the prick of a nettle bush. But perhaps—I thought about my father—perhaps he was right.

I hung my head to cup it with my left hand. "I'm a fool," I said. "Not you, Arsenault."

I heard him let out his breath, then the rustle of fabric and the sound of his boots on the floor as he rose and walked over to me. He pushed my hand away from my head and put his fingers under my chin, tipping my head up so that I had to look at him.

"I should have killed Geoffre long ago and been done with it," he said quietly. "But I talked myself out of it. I wanted the time with you."

"Are you really going to give me that arm?"

Candlelight flickered on its surface, turning it almost gold, the same color as my hair. He sank down onto his knees before me.

"Gods help me, Kyrra, but I am."

※

First, we ate.

Hard bread, hard cheese, and a few cookies Arsenault saved

from the kitchens, crunchy and heady with vanilla. He let me have one of them and some bread. He said I should have had broth and wouldn't let me have any cheese.

"You remember how to snare a rabbit?" he asked as he dusted the crumbs from his cloak, upon which he'd set out the food.

"Arsenault. I could do it in my sleep."

"And you know the little mushrooms, the ones that are good to eat."

"My mother taught me that," I said.

"And the wild asparagus and arugula and—"

"Why are you leaving me here? I could use that arm as a bludgeon."

He cringed. "Gods, Kyrra, I hope not. It isn't like the wooden one."

I frowned, wondering what that meant. But then he began rummaging in his pack and went on. "Go north to Rojornick. I'll leave you what coin I have, but it's not much. You'll have to seek employment. From Rojornick, you should make your way west and south into Vençal to the town of Orienne. Ask for the family of Sereaux, and a man named Enri. Tell him I sent you. I'll find you when I can."

"Arsenault."

He stopped and looked up at me. "Why am I sending you there?" he said. "Because this is my battle, not yours. If you died—"

"That doesn't—"

He put up a hand to stop me. "No. That's most of it but not everything. Geoffre wants all of the Aliente. Go north. Continue your House."

"But my titles were stripped, Arsenault, I can't—"

"You're of an old blood, Kyrra. Survive so that you can take back your land one day. Survive so that your Sight may be..."

Passed on. That was what he wanted to say. But before the words could pass his lips, his gaze fell on my belly. I placed my hand over it self-consciously, then stared at my grubby knuckles resting on the dirty and torn dress I'd been hanged in. I had few curves anymore. My hand pressed the fabric flat against my skin.

"Did Isia know?" I asked.

Arsenault shrugged and looked away from me, a flush lining his cheekbones. "I don't know. The first time I met her was on the road with you."

There were two strands of magic inside me, twining around each other. Three now, with whatever Arsenault had done to me. I could feel it sliding up and down my spine.

It wasn't a pleasant feeling. I shivered, closing my eyes for an instant. When I opened them, Arsenault had packed up the rest of the food and was on his feet with his hand on my head.

"How did you move so fast?" I murmured. His face swam in my sight.

He cursed. The magic moved in me again as he brushed the wayward strands of hair from my forehead with his thumbs. "Kyrra," he said, his voice tinny and distant. "I have to give you the arm now. The metal needs somewhere to go."

"What metal?" I blinked at him. The whole room wavered.

I wondered if he'd put kacin in the cookies.

"The metal I pulled to the surface to save you. You've a bone shaped out of it, just here."

He touched the back of my neck briefly with two gloved fingers. Heat sizzled through me. I sucked in my breath and pulled away from him.

"There's no metal in me," I said. "It just hurts.

"Metal—mettle, it makes no difference. I'm a Smith, aren't I?" He slid one arm behind my back and the other under my legs, then hefted me up.

The room spun. "Put me down," I said, though I barely knew what I was thinking with all this movement inside me. It felt as if there might be a war going on, a strategic choosing of positions, tactics discussed and discarded. I wondered which magic had the high ground.

I thought it might be Arsenault's. I didn't know whether to feel assured or frightened by that.

"You never spoke of Erelf before," I murmured as he laid me down on the carpet. "Why do you speak of him now?"

"Because I've already chosen to give myself away," he whispered.

Then he leaned over and kissed me. I lifted my hand to his hair, but my fingers only slid through as he straightened up and reached for the bag with the arm in it.

"Go north," he said as he unwrapped the rest of it. "Trust that the fates will weave your pattern true. Switch sides if you have to."

A gavaro. That's what he wanted me to be.

"And you?" I said, struggling to beat back the tide of magic that washed through my blood. "What about you?"

His jaw tightened. He drew another, smaller bag out of his packs and emptied it on the floor. The blades he'd given me, so long before. He arranged them on the carpet like a chirurgeon's, his mouth a grim line. "I have to fight Geoffre. And Erelf. But trust me, Kyrra—I'll find you when all of this is done."

I forced the words out of my mouth that I knew I had to speak. "My father will give you up. If his plans were to trick Geoffre."

"I know," he said. "But it's a chance I'll take. And you must go north and then to Vençal," he added, forestalling my protests. "Enri Sereaux. Remember his name. You can't let your Sight fall into Geoffre's hands. He'll warp it, and then all the deaths of your household will have been in vain."

I frowned. "Am I that important, Arsenault? Or are you merely trying to get me to leave you?"

He glanced at me from the corner of his eye, then laughed. "Don't you think I should know better by now? I'm telling you the truth."

I smiled, too. But, dammit, there were tears in it again.

"Close your eyes," Arsenault said softly, scooting over to sit closer to me. He brushed a tear away gently with his thumb. "It's going to hurt."

❦

I never wanted anything save honesty. If I thought he'd lied to me before, this at least was true—it did hurt.

He had a bowl in his pack and a few skins of water, which he set out beside me. A bottle of imya. And the blades. The first thing he did was to rub one of them with imya and slice through the end of my puckered stump.

It was a deep cut. It hurt. I bit my lip hard and tried to ignore the sound of my blood spattering the bowl. "Hold on," Arsenault said. He breathed in deep, then breathed again. The feeling of the room changed around us.

Whatever was in my spine began to slither and buck, to move with agonizing but determined slowness up my back and over my shoulder blades. I writhed, trying to get away from it. Arsenault held me down as the silver squeezed out of me, molded itself to me, wrapped itself around the arm that Arsenault held to my stump.

Knives sank into my flesh, deep, writing their runes on my body, in my blood. I heard myself screaming. But it might have been somebody else lying there. It could almost have been a dream.

Except even now, I can feel the knives tearing open the seams of me as if I were merely a dress to be altered. The knives opened me up and I poured forth, bone, blood, flesh, magic, metal—because Arsenault was right, there was metal in me, and that metal flowed into the dead arm he forged to my body and made it live.

Once, I opened my eyes and I saw his face, slick with sweat, taut with strain, eyes closed, but smiling.

After that, the pain didn't seem so bad.

In the end, though, my body couldn't take it. I don't remember anything else clearly until I woke up eight days later.

Everything else is a dream. A dream of Arsenault holding me, rocking me when the pain took me too hard. Of my lips on his mouth and his hands on my skin and the salt of sweat and tears on my tongue. Of the way he tipped the water glass so I might drink when I was fevered. The weight of his hand on my stomach, his breath soft and light on the back of my neck as he slept.

And then on the morning of the eighth day, I awoke and he was gone. I lay by myself in my own bed in my own chambers, with a new silver arm growing out of my flesh, Arsenault's sword beside me, and a suit of men's clothes hanging in the closet.

I got up and looked for him, but I knew he was gone. I looked everywhere, and then I went back to my room and sat down on my bed. I wrapped myself up in the black cloak he'd left for me, with the comb and the wolf in the pockets, and I wept.

And then I went north. Just as he'd asked me to.

PART VI

CHAPTER 34

Now it's come full circle. Once again, I'm alone in my rooms, Arsenault is gone, and Geoffre threatens the walls. Except this time, I'm in the thick of the battle. This time, I fight in the trenches.

But first I have to get out of here.

I take a quick inventory of the room. Someone swept these chambers clean of sharp edges, and I'd wager it was Lobardin. Since I can't find anything sharp, I'll have to make it.

I have a washbasin, a pitcher, a few cloths, a candle—burned low now—and a bottle of imya. I think Lobardin intended to wash out my wound before I distracted him from his purpose.

So, it's merely a question of timing. The washbasin is made of porcelain. The key will be to push it off the stand when the next cannonball strikes the wall.

A muffled whine issues from outside. I close my eyes and count silently, *one, two, three...* then I give the basin a hard shove with my chin. It topples off the stand and onto the floor. The crashes of porcelain shattering and rock falling are almost perfectly timed.

I learned a few things about artillery while I was in the

north. But I don't fool myself that no one can hear outside the room.

"Everything all right in there?" a guard calls. Not Lobardin.

"Was that more cannon fire?" I shout. I fall to my knees. Every movement I make to use my hands is laborious, contorted, and slow. But I've got what I wanted—a host of wicked-looking porcelain shards. I lean over and pick one up without letting myself think about how I'm as like to cut my own throat as I am to cut the rope. I don't have much time.

The guards scuff about in the hallway outside the door to the sitting room. Cursing, I curl my metal fingers around the shard and hide it in my palm, then drag the bedspread off the bed with my left hand and my elbows. I step on the puddled fabric to help it onto the floor, and I'm still kicking it under the bed—dragging the shards along with it—when the door opens.

Two guards come through the sitting room into the bedroom. Both are young, one with auburn hair, the other dark-haired and dark-eyed. The redhead approaches me, hand on his sword. They both wear guns.

"That noise sounded like it came from in here."

"I heard nothing save the cannons. Are we in immediate danger, or is this to be a siege?"

He circles me warily, gaze flitting over the room but never leaving me for more than an instant. The other guard backs off and steps over to cover the other flank. The shard grows warmer in my hands.

"We're not in immediate danger, no." He ducks his head. "What's that?"

I turn. A bit of red shows underneath the bed. "I don't see anything," I say, swearing in my head.

He gestures at the floor with his elbow. "That. Tallou, hold her a moment."

Damn.

The dark-haired guard steps toward me as the other crouches

down to look underneath the bed. "What's this?" the red-haired guard mutters, pulling out the bedspread.

My guard—Tallou—slides his fingers between the rope and my left arm. In the same moment that the auburn-haired man opens the bedspread to find the shards, I spin toward Tallou. Tallou stumbles into the point of the shard I hold upward in my right hand.

He cries out in pain as he jerks his hand free and puts it to his face. Blood wells up through his fingers and drips down his hand.

"Tallou!" the other guard shouts. Tallou is on his feet again in a moment. I careen backward into the nightstand, on purpose. The bottle of imya rocks and topples over, rolling onto the stone floor, where it shatters. Glass and imya splatter everywhere, and a large puddle of clear liquor spreads toward the bedspread.

The lit candle in its holder skitters down the top of the table but doesn't fall off.

The guards look at me with sudden comprehension, right before I sweep the candle off the nightstand with my right elbow.

The imya catches immediately. Flames race greedily over its surface, orange and blue, onto the soaked edge of the bedspread, which flares up in the other guard's face, catching on the imya-splashed patches of his trousers.

He roars, beating at the flames.

"Deppe!" the dark-haired guard yells. "I'll bring you water!"

"No—her! Get her!" Deppe yells back.

But I've already jumped the flaming imya and I'm running for the door.

It's closed, of course, and I ram it hard with my shoulder, dropping my elbow down onto the handle. The door latch clicks open. I stumble out into the hall.

Tallou's boots clatter over the threshold.

And I'm running.

I know this building better than any of them. This lodge was the site of my childhood summers and autumns, a childhood spent evading my nurses and wriggling through close and empty spaces in the walls. I have a map of this place in my head.

"She's out!" Tallou cries behind me. "Ware!"

Who is he warning? The servants? Most of the fighting men are out on the wall. But just off my father's chambers used to be a set of large guest chambers; my guess is that Driese is there, along with most of the servants. I turn right down a narrow, ill-lit hall to avoid them, just in case.

Tallou is gaining on me. I can hear his breathing just behind me, and his blade flashes in the torchlight. Down the hall I go, down the twisting, turning spiral staircase. I stumble and careen off one wall, trip down three or four steps at once, and hit the bottom running.

"Stop," Tallou says, breathing hard. Then he starts to laugh, a wheezy kind of laughter. "You know you're going to be killed anyway! We were supposed to bring you out at noon!"

"Noon!" I call back. "Why so late?"

A doorway yawns before me, off to the right. The room I've been looking for.

I keep going straight until the last possible second, then I jag through the door. It brings Tallou up short and gives me an instant to get into the room without him.

It's a large room and nearly bare. My father called it the War Room. In Eterean times, the lords of the fortress would gather here with their officers to plan their defense. Frescos of death and dismemberment in all their gory wonder line the walls, every one. The Etereans had a deft touch for detail.

The room is also supposed to be haunted.

As a child, I was intrigued by the ghosts more than by anything else. I used to go exploring for them, trying to excavate their bones from the cracks in the stones.

One afternoon, among the cobwebs in a forgotten closet, I found a passage.

I dart inside the closet and throw myself at the wood door,

making sure I hit with my right elbow out. The door splinters as Tallou clatters into the room. "Where are you?" Tallou shouts, and I kick the rest of the door in—cursing women's soft slippers. I grit my teeth against the pain and launch myself through the hole, into the dark tunnel it reveals.

The air stinks of damp. Cobwebs cling to my hair and face. The chipped contours of the carved stone floor shove themselves up against the soles of my slippers. It's like walking barefoot and blind, and Tallou's behind me, standing in the closet.

"Dread gods," he breathes.

I hear a ratcheting click behind me. "Come out or I'll shoot," he says shakily.

He can't see me. If I'm quiet—

"I said I'll shoot! Do you want me to kill you?"

My eyes are adjusting to the darkness, but I don't see the way the ceiling starts to slope. My forehead scrapes the rock, and I let out an involuntary curse.

The sound of an explosion behind me sends me scrambling down on my knees, throwing myself immediately prone. Lead shot crashes into the wall beside me, scattering chips of rock into my hair, biting my face. I press my face flat to the floor—slimy with mold and damp. For a moment, everything is just an echo of the shot; smoke hangs acrid in the air and the ball rolls around the tunnel like a memory you wish you could forget. I start inching myself forward on my elbows before the smoke clears. Behind me, the sound of hesitant footsteps taps itself out against the stone; he's coming to see if he killed me, I guess. If I can make the first turn-off, I might be able to hide—

But I can't move fast enough. He's upon me in a moment.

He reaches down to feel my leg, and I kick out as hard as I can.

He yelps—an undignified sound, but then again, this room is supposed to be haunted. I shove myself forward with my toes, and the sound of my dress ripping fills the tunnel. Then I try to scramble to my feet, but Tallou grabs my legs and brings me down to the floor again, hard.

Pain blots everything hot and black for a moment. I kick, twisting around onto my back, but his fingers scrabble over the rope and then he hauls me back toward him, grunting, breathing hard. The lines of his face appear out of the darkness like a ghost's, eyes wide and scared.

But when he gets close, I do what I have to do. I don't want to do it, because he's too young and he's just following orders. It's different from being in a battle, but the same, too. Sometimes, you look at the other man's face and there's a space where both of you become more than toy soldiers.

In the middle of a fight, the space blinks out and you just act.

He leans down over me and I have the shard sticking up through the fingers of my right hand. When he gets close, I kick his feet out from under him and I shove the shard upward with a flick of my thumb.

He cries out in surprise as he's going down, but his cry ends in a high-pitched, gurgling scream when the shard pierces the skin under his chin. Blood pours down over me in the instant before he collapses, kicking and thrashing for a moment before pain and blood loss rob him of consciousness. Then I heave him off with a twist of my shoulders and wriggle out from under him.

There's blood everywhere. I can't see it, but I can feel it and I can smell it. The tunnel smells like a battlefield with the gun smoke still lingering in the air.

I feel for my discarded shard on the floor. It slides out of my fingers when I try to pick it up. Tallou moans, then makes a choking, gurgling, whistling noise that lets me know he's dying. I struggle to my feet.

"Why couldn't you have been scared of the damn ghosts?" I whisper as I take his knife. He had wide doe eyes. Somebody probably loved him.

I vomit all over the floor and then I start walking.

CHAPTER 34

The old prison used to be a tumble of sheared-off slabs of black basalt and big stone pillars standing like the stumps of lightning-blasted trees. But now there are walls, built up out of re-chiseled basalt blocks. I don't know why anyone would spend so much work on a prison.

The passage comes out near the smokehouse and the slaughtering pen. I stick to the trees and manage to stay hidden. But I don't know how I'm going to get into the prison.

Four guards on the door, and all I have is Tallou's utility knife. I managed to cut my ropes, but it's still just me and my arm in this damn silk dress that's soaked with blood.

Well, and the manacles.

I make a decision and take a deep breath, stumble out of the trees and into a run. I make a lot of noise. The guards turn around. One of them says, "Hoy! What are you doing there?"

I throw myself onto the ground, trying to make it look as if I tripped. It's not too hard. I fall to my knees and then down into the mud.

"Well, you better go see who she is," another guard says.

"Probably a camp girl somebody used up."

"Dammit, why do I always lose the flip?"

The guard who yelled at me comes walking cautiously across the yard. He doesn't pull any of his weapons. "Where did you come from?" he says in a tense voice as he comes to loom over me. "Well, quick—answer!"

Instead, I wrap the chain of my manacles around his ankle and give it a good yank.

He windmills as he falls backward, then hits the ground hard on his hip. I lunge forward, knife out, which I drive into his throat.

I leave the knife and pull the sword from his swordbelt, just as the other three guards run up to me. A quick slash at the nearest drops him, but the other two have time to get their own weapons out. A blade clangs against my right arm.

"Fucking hells, it's *her*!"

A fist crashes into my jaw.

Damn that head wound Lobardin gave me.

The sword falls from my hands and I drop to the ground.

A middle-aged man with crow's-feet and dark hair hauls me to my feet, and my head spins.

He grins. "If you thought you were going to find your man here, you're going to have to look harder. They've already taken him down to the wall."

※

Inside, the prison is dark and cold. Smoky torches burn in iron sconces every few feet. Light shows through the chinks in the walls where the stone is ill fitted. You can tell they were built in haste.

The commander drags me down the hall, his sword out. Two of his subordinates walk behind me, the points of their swords against my flesh. I struggled once, and the man with the crow's-feet sank the tip of his sword into my left arm. Not enough to do damage, but enough to hurt. Enough to know what he'd do to me if I were to run.

"We'll put you in here," he says. "That way, we can watch you better."

"Why are you so worried about me going anywhere? If Arsenault's already gone, I can't do much here, can I?"

He grins. "Just keeping you for the executioner."

I decide I don't like him.

"I've been killed once already," I tell him. "I came back."

"Maybe the second time will do it, then." He opens the cell door and shoves me inside, not gently.

I stumble, then whirl around. But the door's already closed.

"Damn," I mutter. "Damn!"

My voice echoes off the stone. The cell is no bigger than the cave my father held me in and filled with moldy straw.

I kick the door. "Damn!" I say again, louder this time, almost a shout. It does me no good—just makes my head spin and hurts my bruised toes. I sit down on the floor in disgust.

Something scratches inside the wall behind me, and I stand up in a hurry, thinking of rats. But then a voice whispers through the gaps, "Kyrra?"

"Mikelo? Is that you?"

"Me or my ghost," he says in a low voice, then laughs. It's a bad laugh. His voice is hoarse, too.

I bend down near the wall. There's a hole in it, almost big enough to put my fist through. "Why are they keeping you here?"

"Your guess is as good as mine. I thought I might be for ransom, but...I think he's going to kill me."

I chew my lip. "I would. If I were in Cassis's place."

"That's comforting, Kyrra. To know that."

"You know what I mean, Mikelo." I pause. "Have they—"

"No," he says. "I've not been treated well."

I can hear it in his voice. The hoarseness can only have come from screaming.

He coughs. "Arsenault's gone. Jon came and got him."

"They put you together?"

"I think they were trying to break him. But I don't know why he would be so important to Cassis."

I rest my face against the cold stone wall. "He's not important to Cassis. Or he's only important for the worth he holds to Geoffre."

"What worth would that be?"

I rub the fingers of my left hand down the smooth metal fingers of my right. "It has something to do with the god Geoffre worships and Arsenault's magic. I think Jon wants him to draw Geoffre out." Then, reluctantly, I add, "Perhaps to fight him. If Arsenault remembers..."

"If Andris remembers who Arsenault was, you mean," Mikelo says. "He's a Fixer."

"Yes. Geoffre held him captive for a while." I hesitate a moment, then I ask, "What did Geoffre want from you?"

"From my magic, you mean? I'm not exactly sure. I studied a lot of anatomy. He had me do...dissections. And I spent some time learning how to heal small cuts and injuries on..." He stumbled. "On animals. But we had not yet come to the most important part of my training. He said."

I let my breath out. "The scrying. You haven't passed your test yet, have you?"

"He never mentioned scrying. I'm not sure what that is."

"Arsenault says all Fixers must be able to look into themselves and face what they see. Their darker corners. You haven't done that yet, have you?"

Thick, impenetrable silence from the other side of the wall.

Finally, I hear him take a long, ragged breath. "I think," he says, so quietly I can barely hear him, "that scrying was what— was— Gods, Kyrra, the things I saw in that mirror, the monsters, the *demons*—"

"Hush," I say. "It won't do you any good to dwell on it now. We have to get out before they kill us. I need to get Arsenault. I can't let him die. He'll let Geoffre kill him again and again, for Jon or whoever asks."

Mikelo takes another long breath. "All right," he says. "I'm with you. If you want to kill my bastard of a cousin—"

"I don't know if that's the fight anymore. There may have been some worth in what Jon and Arsenault wanted, to let him live until Driese conceives..."

"I want my revenge." The viciousness in his voice surprises me. "I want my revenge against Cassis."

It's like looking in a mirror, hearing those words. How often have I said them? How often have they seemed to form the core of me?

Except they were false, all those years. But it's only now that

I see how incidental Cassis was. Is. He's like an arm. Sever the arm and the body still lives.

All these years, the man I've wanted revenge against most is Geoffre.

Fifty thousand astra be damned, but I want Geoffre.

"Kyrra?"

There is a hesitant, almost childlike quality to the way Mikelo says my name. I've heard it before, out of men older than him. It's that seeking for someone in the dark.

"Are you strong enough to use your magic?" I ask him.

"If I have to be. What do you want me to do?"

"Is it only flesh you Fix?"

"I don't know. I'm untrained. You said it yourself. I don't know what I can do."

I chew on my lip again while I think. In states of siege, I've gnawed my lip bloody.

"You could try to make us a hole out through the rock."

He doesn't say anything. Then: "Can I do that?"

"I don't know. But you could try."

He laughs, a soft outflow of air laced with bitterness. "Gods. It might have been that easy."

"I don't know if it will work, Mikelo. The walls are basalt—they might revert to molten rock."

"Then we'd be scorched by lava," he says. His voice is grim. "What are our other options?"

"The door is wood. I don't know what its true nature might be. I don't See into things, only people. The tree it once was? Something dead? If it was something dead, it might fall away into rot—except we'd have to deal with the guards. There are two of us now, so it would be easier, but—what kind of shape are you in?"

"After I use my magic? Probably not good."

I want to pace, but if I do, Mikelo won't be able to hear me. I shift my feet in the straw and it releases a fetid stench into the air.

"You could try to Fix the guards," I say slowly.

"How?"

"Fixers have talents, like any other artisan. Arsenault's talent is for metal."

Mikelo lets out his breath. "And he Fixed you." He pauses. "But you're flesh. How could he—"

"He forged my arm. Then he turned the part of me that was"—*basest*, a voice in my mind says, but I clench my jaw against it—"*strongest*," I say, "into metal. Into a thing." I sigh. "Don't ask me to explain it. I'm not really made out of metal, but there's metal in me. And that's how my arm is a part of me now."

For a moment, he sits in silence. I fight down my impatience. He has to think this through or we won't get anywhere.

"I saw myself Fixing men," he says finally, in a low, strained voice. His words stick in the hole between us, and I have no time to absorb what he means.

"Then this is what you must do. This is how we'll escape."

"But, Kyrra, I saw myself *twisting* them."

"Mikelo, Geoffre has a god on his side. And Arsenault will die. And then he'll come back and he won't remember. If he falls in with the wrong people, they could convince him of anything."

"Is that meant to cheer me?"

"It's meant to light a fire under you, dammit! Do you want your uncle to win?"

Quiet for a moment. Then he says, "No. No, I don't."

I let my breath out. He's with us now.

"Wait," he says. "I'll have to get the key to your door. How will I do that?"

"You'll think of a way. I can't tell you how to Fix, only how to See. You learned that, didn't you?"

"Yes," he says. I hear him take a deep breath. "We'll be dead in a few hours anyway, won't we?"

"If you fail," I say.

He laughs. "If you'd have said anything else, I would have begun to suspect you. You've been far too nice to me."

I blush. I don't know why, and I'm glad Mikelo can't see. "Just do it," I whisper.

The scratching of grit against stone lets me know he's moved. I put my ear to the wall to hear better. Straw rustles. I can't tell what he's doing.

In a moment, though, a series of thrashing, fevered kicks beats against his door. I rise in alarm. Purposeful kicks are more rhythmic; this sounds like a struggle.

Then the guards start yelling.

"What's going on in there? We're not going to open the door—"

"Curin, gods damn you, it sounds like there's something wrong; get the key out— Now, Curin, now!"

The door screeks open. Boots impact with flesh; one of the guards cries out, "Dread gods!"—then scuffling, rustling fabric, straw rattling, the sound of flesh against stone...

I don't hear Mikelo at all.

And then someone screams.

I've never heard such a scream before. I try to bring my hands to my ears to shut it out, forgetting my hands are chained together. So I have to listen to it. Its shrill, inhuman wail. Until abruptly, the scream dies.

A man sobs.

"Unlock the door," Mikelo says. "The other one. That one— now, now, now!"

A key slides into my lock. I move back from the door and put up my hands, ready to fight. The door flies open and light spills in.

Mikelo stands there, silhouetted in orange. And one of the guards.

Except you can't tell anymore that it's a guard. I stand back for a moment, staring, because it's all I can do. The guard is bent, shriveled, shrunken, like a golem from a story. Humps stick out of his spine. The flesh has drained from his fingers, leaving them skeletal and dry.

"Kyrra," Mikelo says, through gritted teeth, in a voice with tears in it. "Kyrra, come."

He did this. This golden-haired boy.

I start to walk forward, a little hesitantly.

"I did what you wanted," the guard lisps, in a voice like the rattle of dead branches. "I opened the door. I did what you wanted."

I give him a wide berth as I step around him. But in passing, I can't help but look down at his eyes.

Black eyes, with crow's-feet. In their depths I can read his greatest wish and that is *Kill me*.

It's the guard who caught me. I glance up at Mikelo in—astonishment? Horror? I don't know what he sees on my face.

"Do it," Mikelo says.

His own face is set. He's talking to me.

I look at him, then at the stooped, misshapen guard. I nod, a slight dip of my chin. I move forward as if in a dream and take the guard's knife from the sheath at his hip.

When I find the gap in his ribs where his heart lies, he doesn't even scream.

CHAPTER 35

I AM TIRED OF WATCHING PEOPLE DIE.

During my time at Ilichnaya working for Markus Seroditch, I learned a few things about Sight and Fixing. Mostly because Markus wanted to curb my impulsivity and thought six weeks of guard duty for his dying wife might do it.

The Lady Serodnaya suffered a wasting disease that might or might not have been the result of a curse. The lady saw evil everywhere. I don't think her Sight ever left her. She was constantly on the lookout for threats to her husband—of which there were many. By the time Markus brought me to her bedside, her magic was eating her alive.

She told me that most Fixers only work objects. In her eyes, I was an abomination and what Arsenault had done to me was a crime. I learned that when a Fixer alters a thing, he picks and chooses among the qualities he sees within it. The Lady said that Arsenault had remade me into an image of me that was not truly myself but only a reflection of what I *might* be. She told me that the runes glowing on my arm were what made me into the killer I became, all because Arsenault wanted me to live by any means necessary.

Before she died, after I attended her for six weeks day and

night, out of her sight only when I pissed or she slept, she finally managed to exonerate me in her own mind. It wasn't my fault that I drew death to me like flies to meat, she said; it was Arsenault's. Her only wish was that I draw death away from Markus, and I tried. I tried my best.

But in the end, he was in his bed, up in the house, and I wasn't on guard shift. An Amoran assassin, hired by the Rojornicki Grand Prince himself, somehow infiltrated the serving staff and poisoned Markus.

I never made it to Vençal the way Arsenault wanted me to. Instead, I got caught up in Rojornick, trying to repay Markus for his kindness by hunting down his killers.

But now I've had enough death.

And I'm tired of playing the prince with Mikelo. Forcing him to do crimes that the Lady Serodnaya would would have called abominations and worse.

He Fixed the guard. Not with love, as Arsenault Shaped me. With hate and fear.

"His servile nature," Mikelo says as we stand, looking down at the bleeding, shriveled body. "The man never questioned his orders. He was cruel. I pulled it out and made it flesh."

Mikelo's face is a desert, bare of emotion.

He pulled something out of himself, too, something that was good and kind. It's lost now, perhaps forever.

I'm struck with a sudden longing to be far away from here, to awaken from all of this as if from a dream. But the dream nears its end now, and I must see it through.

"You only did what I asked," I say.

Mikelo doesn't answer.

"I'm going to take his swordbelt." I watch Mikelo's face carefully all the while. "And his boots. Find a hammer—something hard and heavy—and you can break my manacles."

He nods and strides away almost angrily. Stronger than I would have thought.

I bend down and take the swordbelt without looking at the

man's face. It seems wrong to call it a man. It seems wrong to call it anything.

When I get the swordbelt off, Mikelo is back with a hammer.

"Are you all right?" I ask.

Again, that short nod.

"Put your hands out," he says.

I kneel and lay them on the floor. He swings down as hard as he can—once, twice, three times—and the blows ring so loud, it feels as if he's splitting my head. The manacles give way with a sharp *crack*.

I gasp and draw my hands out, twisting and turning them, rubbing my left wrist, before I sit to pull on the boots. When I look up at Mikelo, I notice the thin purple bruise around his neck for the first time.

"What is that?" I ask in surprise.

"They didn't take my belt," he says. "It was the only way I could think to get them to open the door."

"Hanging yourself?"

"What would you have done?"

I bite my lip.

"Let's just go. Get out of here."

I rise and put my right hand on his shoulder. He flinches, but I don't think it's because of the metal.

"You don't have to come. If you don't want to. I—I thank you. For what you did."

"No," he says. "I have a responsibility to my House that overrides blood. And I will rid it of men like my uncle and my cousins."

"But, Mikelo—you'd be Head of House."

"I will," he says with some conviction. "If Driese isn't already with child."

"Let's hope she is, then." I lever myself to my feet. "I'd spare you that fate, Mikelo."

He looks up at me, startled, and I put my hand out—my right hand—to draw him to his feet.

It occurs to me, as we run from the prison that was once my childhood playground, that I'm the Head of House Aliente now.

I'm all that's left.

※

I know I must look like an old painting of Ekyra as I run. Clad in my blood-stiff, once-blue silk dress, the guard's swordbelt clanking at my side, his too-big black boots on my feet, I am the epitome of ill fortune.

I hope Geoffre will see it that way too.

We keep to the trees as we run to the wall. Both of us are running on sheer determination, but I always feel better after the waiting is over and the battle is about to begin. It's as if something takes over inside me, and I labor gladly, like a horse racing for its master.

Mikelo looks less good, but there's a glitter in his eyes. I don't like it, but it keeps him going.

The blunt wedge of trees narrows until it disappears entirely. We stop at its edge, near the side yard. Men toil back and forth, hauling rubble and earth to shore up the wall. At the wall itself—which looks like a shattered bone, sheared off and jagged—men shout to each other and trowels scrape as they scramble to repair the biggest holes. The muzzles of three cannons jut out through the wall.

Does a man escape with his lover to a fortress he expects to be soon under siege?

None of this makes sense. And if there is one thing I can't yet puzzle out, it's Tonia di Sere's role in all of this.

Did she simply not know, or was she in league with Cassis all along?

"What shall we do now, Kyrra?" Mikelo asks. His words come out as mere edges to his hard breathing, and he presses a hand to his side as if his ribs hurt.

"I need clothes. To blend in." I take the guard's knife out of its sheath and walk forward in a crouch to the edge of the trees.

The next time a smallish man walks by with a barrow, I step out of the brush and bring the hilt of the knife down heavy on the back of his head.

He falls to the ground in a limp heap.

"Mikelo," I hiss, and Mikelo lurches up to join me. Together we haul the man's body back to the trees and strip him of his clothes.

Getting my clothes off takes longer. I need help with all the pins and hooks and laces of gown and stays, front and back. Mikelo stares at me in horror and I have to laugh.

"You've seen far worse things today than my naked body, Mikelo."

He blushes, fiercely, then bends his head to fumble with the pins and laces. My gown comes off in pieces, then my skirts. My stays go next. I shrug out of them and yank off my shift.

It's cold. I'm instantly shivering, and I hold a hand out to Mikelo. "Shirt," I say, trying to keep my teeth from chattering.

He's staring at me.

I give him a lopsided grin. "I really am a woman, you know."

"I always wondered what your arm looked like," he says as if I haven't spoken.

I look down at it. It's the same, the silver melting into the lightly freckled skin of my shoulder. Except now you can see the dent, long and deep.

Maybe it makes sense that only Arsenault could have done me this damage. And only Arsenault will be able to repair it.

I bend down quickly to retrieve the man's shirt myself and slip it on over my head. It's a relief to be in a man's shirt again. A relief to wrestle on the trousers and belt a swordbelt at my hip, even if it isn't mine.

I've never had a sword of my own, anyway.

When I'm dressed, I feel almost like myself again. The clothes smell of unwashed male and dirt and gunpowder, but the cloak is warm, my feet are protected from rocks and mud, and I have two hilts on which to rest my hands, gloved in warm leather.

"You look like the Huntress," Mikelo says, watching me with a funny expression, and I suppose I do, in the man's brown clothes.

"Let's see if I can sniff out Geoffre, then." I grin and Mikelo's expression grows even stranger. What does he See in me now?

"Come on." I gesture over my shoulder. "Let's go."

That breaks the moment. He follows me out of the brush, looking everywhere like a hare hopping into the open. I take a deep breath so I don't do the same.

I want to look like I belong here. As if this estate is still my own.

I put my hand on the hilt of my sword and try to swagger in these damn too-big boots. We thread our way through the men with their barrows until a man standing atop a pile of blasted rocks calls out, "You there! Grab a shovel!"

Mikelo glances at me and I nod, just enough that he can see. The man hands us each a shovel, and we start hefting rocks into the quarter-full barrow beside the pile. I'm too weak to shovel big piles the way he is, and so is Mikelo. I hope the man doesn't notice.

"How long you think this break will last?" I ask.

The man glances up at me. "You're new," he says as he turns to dump a heap of rocks into the barrow.

"We're from the prison," Mikelo says quickly, before I can answer. "We've been rotated."

The man grunts, banging the edge of his shovel down into the rocks until it rings. "Didn't see you on the way up."

I wipe the sweat from my brow. "We didn't come with the bulk of the force. We came up secret."

"Secret," he repeats, eyeing me skeptically.

I dart a glance out the hole in the wall. The land falls away beneath us, a tumble of rocks and the tops of trees. There's an

CHAPTER 35

army encamped in the valley, milling around. The black lines of earthworks come about a quarter of the way up the hill. A line of cannons rest atop them, with their muzzles propped up on rock cairns. Cannons with good range. But Geoffre didn't do that overnight. He must be taking advantage of the remains of his attack on the Aliente. Or he's been preparing for this battle with Cassis for a long time.

"We're to take up our positions right away," I say. "But I wanted to have a look first."

"Well, you better look quick then."

I stare up at the wall. In the spots that have held, Cassis has archers up. But this is a sparse force. I look through the hole again.

Geoffre has an army. Tents, earthworks, cannons, horses...though what he thinks he can do with horse on this terrain, I can't imagine. Perhaps he thinks he can lure Cassis down from his walls and then overwhelm him on the flat. But to do that, he'd have to play dead.

The sound of a shovel sinking into gravel snatches me out of my thoughts. I turn, just quick enough to see Lobardin striding up from behind the man. The man sees Lobardin too. But Lobardin has his head down.

Mikelo looks at me in alarm.

I back down off the pile. Mikelo follows me. "I think it's time we took up our positions."

"Commander!" the man calls out suddenly. "I've two of your recruits here!"

Under my breath, I curse whatever gods are listening. Lobardin flings his head up and his eyes go wide. There's no good way to extricate ourselves from this situation. Free will is supposed to be a man's right, but there must be gods at work here, shuffling us all like cards.

I cross my hands over my hilts, preparing to draw. But Lobardin hides a blindingly quick grin beneath a military scowl. "It took you long enough to get here, didn't it?"

The man on the rocks blinks. Obviously, he didn't believe our story. My hands itch, wanting to be set down. Instead, I withdraw, slowly.

"We ran into some trouble," I say carefully. "At the prison."

Mikelo's gaze slides over to me; he thinks I'm mad. Even Lobardin looks a little surprised.

"I don't want to hear about any trouble. Just get your asses moving now."

I duck my head. "Yessir," I murmur, and Mikelo echoes it.

Lobardin whirls on his heel and starts walking back the way he just came. When I move to follow him, Mikelo bends down and whispers, "Why are we going with him?"

"If he wanted us," I whisper back, "he could have taken us right there. It would've been a bloodbath, but why should he care?"

"Why should he help us?"

I gnaw on my lip. It's a bit bruised now. "It's a feeling I get."

Mikelo scowls. But how can I explain it? Call it Sight. It was in Lobardin's eyes when he left, as if he'd woken from a dream.

Lobardin falls back to walk beside us.

"You're a sight," he says.

"No thanks to you," Mikelo replies. His eyes burn hot.

"I laid nary a finger on you while you were in my care," Lobardin says to Mikelo. "Don't blame me for crimes I didn't commit."

"You acted in concert with agendas which can only be to the detriment of Liera. Had you not aligned yourself with those forces, none of this would have happened."

Lobardin looks theatrically—lazily—to the left and right. "You blame me for this little war, do you? Have they now become *my* uncle and *my* cousin?"

Mikelo lunges. I fling out my right arm to stop him. It hits his ribs and he crunches up with a little cry, then looks up at Lobardin red-faced. "Not *this*, you idiot," he gasps. "Not this war. If you'd left us free, we would have been free to act, and now—"

CHAPTER 35

"And now," Lobardin says, stepping forward, all trace of amusement erased from his face, "you've served as a fine distraction while Jon Barra and Kyrra's precious captain go to do the real dirty work, haven't you?"

I let my hand drop. "What?" I say.

Lobardin nods in the direction of the wall. "Arsenault's gone. To Geoffre's camp." He looks me up and down. "What did you do to my guards, Kyrra? One of them came running to the wall with his eyebrows singed, shouting that you'd escaped. The other one—where is he?"

"Was Arsenault alone?"

Lobardin's eyes narrow. "No. Jon went with him. Where's my other guard, Kyrra?"

I look up at the wall. The bare trees on the other side are speckled with black shapes.

Ravens.

I put my hands on my hilts. "Your other guard's dead. Give me your gun, Lobardin. I'm going after Arsenault."

He sighs. "Somehow, I knew you'd be determined to do that. Cassis sent them. There's nothing you can do."

I grit my teeth. "I'm not going to stand here. Do I have to draw steel?"

"Damn you, Kyrra, you don't understand. *Cassis sent them.* Jon and Cassis had an argument, and Jon told him he was being stupid for keeping Arsenault in the prison when he could be using him instead, and Cassis finally told Jon to get Arsenault out of the prison, but that he didn't want to see him alive at the end. So, Jon went."

"And you were privy to all this?"

"Of course not. I was listening at the door. They went down to Geoffre's camp and they're not planning on coming back. Arsenault passed me something to give you on the way out."

He reaches into his pocket and pulls out the silver wolf.

"Your parting gift looks somewhat less this time."

I'm on him like lightning. I grab his collar with my right hand

and yank him down to my level. His eyes are hot. So are mine. "He hasn't abandoned me. He's fighting a battle he can't possibly hope to win. And he's probably as much a prisoner of Jon as he is anyone else."

I grab the wolf and then push Lobardin away in disgust, trying to hide the shaking that has suddenly overtaken me. Did I expect Arsenault to storm the fortress, looking for me? Or did he come here knowing he was going to die, thinking to spare me—

Dammit.

"How does Jon expect him to do anything?" Mikelo says, frowning. "He wasn't in the shape to fight. Not Geoffre."

Lobardin smooths his shirt and glances between us, somberly. "I don't think that was Cassis's point. I think what he means to do is throw Arsenault to the wolves, while he sets upon Geoffre's flanks." He looks anxiously over his shoulder, then back at us. "I should be at my post now, awaiting word. But I had to come looking for you, Kyrra, because I knew you'd foul things up."

"And I've a sword at my side now, Lobardin, and if you think you're going to take me again, you'd better start thinking something else."

"Gods help me, but that is *not* what I was thinking." The broken, wounded look returns to his eyes. I set my jaw. I have my hands crossed, fingers wrapped tight around my hilts. Lobardin sighs.

"Just go. Don't jeopardize what Arsenault is doing. Much as I dislike the man, he's doing a brave thing, and it may bring us a quick victory rather than a lengthy siege. Driese isn't here. Just go."

Trust Lobardin to casually drop a load of truth on your foot.

"*What?*" says Mikelo.

Lobardin smirks. "Did you really think that Cassis would endanger the mother of his heir by bringing her *here?*"

"It doesn't matter what I thought," I say. Then I look up at Lobardin, struck by what he called her. "The mother of his heir?"

CHAPTER 35

Lobardin's smirk becomes one of his long smiles as he nods. Then, abruptly, he sobers. "She's with child. Cassis has sent her somewhere to be safe, but that all depends on whether or not her party can maintain secrecy in the face of Geoffre and Devid's spies. And whether or not this battle succeeds."

"He can't want to unite the Houses," Mikelo says.

"Of course not. He wants someone who can avenge him, if this doesn't work." Lobardin cocks his head at Mikelo. "You shouldn't wave it around that you've escaped," he says. "That won't fit into Cassis's plans at all. How did you manage it, anyway? Did you kill the guards at the prison, too?"

Mikelo stiffens. I step in quickly, wondering just how much Lobardin knows about Mikelo. "They're tied up in the prison," I say. "I got Mikelo out."

"You didn't kill them?" His voice is curious but bitter, too.

"I was feeling some guilt," I lie, "even though your guard tried to shoot me. I thought to practice mercy."

"Mercy." Lobardin lets the word out with his breath. "I suppose that's what I'm giving you, isn't it?"

"Why?" Mikelo says.

Lobardin laughs. "Oh, I didn't mean *you*, Mikelo. Cassis would have me swinging from the nearest tree if I let you go. I meant Kyrra. I'll let Kyrra go if you come with me. It's too late to save Arsenault, anyway."

Mikelo backs up, glancing at me. The muscles in his jaw ripple as he clenches it. "Very well," he says, straightening himself. "I'll go."

"Fucking martyrs," I mutter.

I slam my right hand into Lobardin's face.

He doesn't see it coming until too late. Blood erupts from his nose and he staggers back. As my hand drops, I lunge to snatch the sword at his side. It rips free of the leather with a hiss.

Arsenault's sword.

Runes flash in the sunlight, writhing like silver snakes from guard to tip. My right arm sings with them.

"Go!" I shout at Mikelo. "*GO!*"

Everything becomes a blur. None of the men around us were prepared, and Lobardin is still trying to struggle up out of the dirt. We get a good head start, running for the hole in the wall behind us. Ahead of me, Mikelo dodges a shovel wielded like a sword and knocks another man out of his way with his shoulder. By the time the man gets to me, he's pulled his dagger, but I take him with my sword. He falls behind me.

And we're running, hurdling the rubble at the foot of the wall, skidding down the boulder-strewn slope, and from behind us I can hear Lobardin's voice bellowing, "Get back into your positions! If you chase them, Geoffre will think we're attacking! Let his gunners take care of them!"

And so, we're out and we're running, half-falling, and I'm laughing that battle laugh and Mikelo gulps air beside me.

"Where are we going?" he pants.

"Where do you think?" I say. "We're going to get Arsenault."

※

If I had been commander of Cassis's small force, I would have opted for the long, slow siege. What is Arsenault going to do that will give Cassis's far smaller force a chance? What would be deadly enough to make Cassis give up the high ground in the face of Geoffre's cannons?

Before we're halfway down the hill, shots crack from behind Geoffre's earthworks. Not cannons but arquebuses.

Cursing, I throw myself prone on the patchy, thin grass. Mikelo hits the ground beside me a little too heavily, and I look over at him in alarm.

"Tripped," he whispers. Sweat drips from his forehead, even in this cold.

"Get up," I say. "*Now.*"

They have to reload. We both scramble to our feet and run a zigzag line for the trees, hunched over as far as we're able until the next shots ring out. It's a long process of throwing ourselves down and heaving ourselves back up, but we finally make it, only to fling ourselves down in the leaf litter for a moment to rest.

"They'll do a man some damage," I say, breathing hard, "but only if they can hit you."

"Why bother, then?" Mikelo asks.

"Because you can sit behind that damn wall and still kill people. It'll be worse than longbows if the gunsmiths can sharpen their aim."

"Why is Arsenault in Geoffre's camp, Kyrra?"

I take a deep breath. "He's bait. Cassis knew who he used to be. Jon must have convinced Cassis that Arsenault can use his magic to help them win, but if I know them...that isn't the case. They're trying to trick both Cassis and Geoffre. But I don't know exactly how they're going to do it—how they're going to bring both of them down at once."

"So, you're not going to give it a chance? He can't *really* die, Kyrra."

"Just because he hasn't doesn't mean he won't. It doesn't mean that dying doesn't hurt. And if he forgets everything... would you really want to have him fighting on the other side?" I push myself up. "You don't have to come with me, Mikelo. You can run."

He stands up, too. "I'm not a coward."

"Neither is Arsenault. But that doesn't mean I should leave him to die. It's too great a sacrifice."

"You wouldn't let him give himself for the good of all Liera?"

"He wouldn't let me do it. And what is his death going to serve? Then Devid will be householder, Cassis will be disowned, and Erelf—"

I look up, scanning the sky for ravens. A few black shapes wheel far above the treetops.

"If he has help, maybe he won't have to die. Will you help him or do I have to do it myself?"

Mikelo gives me a small smile. "Can't you just say that you love him?"

I don't have time for this. My throat clenches.

"All right," I say, tightening my hands on my hilts. "I love him."

"Sometimes, love is greater than truth," Mikelo says softly. "Let's go. I'll give you whatever help I can."

CHAPTER 36

LOBARDIN SAID WE WERE TOO LATE. HE'S ALMOST RIGHT.

The cannons begin their booming cadence before we're halfway to the camp. Mikelo and I skim close to the line of earthworks to avoid them, but sometimes balls go astray. One crashes into the trees, splintering a tall pine with a loud *crack*, and the crown topples with slow, frightening grace, ripping through its own branches on its way to the ground. Its impact shudders through the forest, startling hundreds of birds into the air—ravens, eagles, hawks, kestrels, and falcons—a strange, disturbing mix of birds to see decorating the evergreens and leafless oaks like midwinter ornaments.

"Kyrra," Mikelo says suddenly, grabbing me by the arm. "Look."

He points downslope to Geoffre's camp. At Arsenault.

Geoffre leads Arsenault by a rope tethered around his neck. His arms are bound, but Jon walks beside him, free.

I make a noise through my teeth and pull forward.

"No, Kyrra," Mikelo whispers, tightening his hand on my shoulder. "Wait."

He's right. Arsenault waited until I dropped through the trapdoor on the gibbet. But it's so hard to stay calm.

Geoffre jerks the rope around Arsenault's neck and Arsenault drops to his knees in the mud. Jon stands by, impassive. I creep forward to see better.

"How close do you have to be to Fix?" I whisper to Mikelo.

"I don't know. I've never tried to do it without touching."

"Keep an eye on Arsenault."

"What—" Mikelo begins, but I'm already gone, running low in the brush with my knife out.

Geoffre's words float to me on the wind, in the intervals between cannon fire.

"This coward, this dog, has betrayed us all! I sent him to kill my treacherous son—to make sure the killing was done well. But he lost track of my assassin, and when he fell into the hands of the enemy, he betrayed his knowledge of our strategy! This dog doesn't deserve the death I'm going to give him!"

A whip-snap makes me stop and peer out of the brush. There are a few shouts at Geoffre's words, but most of the men watching this spectacle only look mildly interested. They're gavaros; they've heard it before.

Arsenault kneels in the mud, his head hanging down, shirt rippling in tatters in the wind—his right eye swollen and half his face crusted with blood.

"The punishment for treason is to be drawn and quartered, the pieces of his body scattered in the four directions. We'll make him a sacrifice for our god, for our victory—and we'll lure my snake of a son down here to cut off his head! Victory will make your fortunes!"

At this last, a huge roar of a shout goes up.

If Jon and Arsenault are planning anything, they'd better do it soon.

I stop cold, my hands on my hilts.

But what if *this* is what they've planned? What if it's only Arsenault's sacrifice?

Cassis has Geoffre's plan of attack. Cassis thinks Arsenault is going to perform some feat of magic that will distract Geoffre and cause hundreds of his gavaros to desert in fear. But what if Arsenault simply dies? Cassis's flanking maneuver will generate enough confusion to give his forces a chance, and Arsenault's death gives Cassis time to maneuver his men into place. Then Jon remains to see that Cassis and Geoffre both die in the charge. Taking Geoffre away from Erelf.

"*Fucking* martyrs," I mutter.

The worst thing is, Arsenault probably told Jon it was nothing, dying to fight Erelf. Maybe it was even what he wanted, on the off chance that the gods would have mercy on him and release him from his eternal turning around. I wish I could blame Jon, as I have so many times before, but it's starting to become clear to me what kind of partners these two men are.

I see the guard at the same time he sees me. For a moment, we both freeze. Then I rush him, drawing Arsenault's sword as I run.

We meet in a flashing clang of metal. But I was the first to react, and I've got him down on the ground and I'm pulling my sword out of his gut in an instant. I wipe the blade on the grass and jam it back into its scabbard, then I take the gun slung across the gavaro's back and grab the bag that holds the shot, powder, and wadding. I sling both over my shoulder and hoist myself into the nearest tree, climbing as fast as I can, startling ravens into the air. I settle myself into a crooked gnarl of branches just as a host of men run into the woods and find their fallen comrade.

"Tie him to the horses!" Geoffre is yelling.

"Which way did he run?" one of the men below me shouts. "Spread out!"

I pour the powder into the pan, then take the ramrod out of the bag and jam the shot down the barrel. Ravens caw and flap their wings, and I wave the gun at them, shooing them off my branch before I pull out the wadding and light it with a match.

Across the yard, Geoffre stands beside Arsenault while four

men begin the process of binding him spread-eagled to two horses.

I push the lit wadding into the pan and settle the gun against my shoulder. Arsenault cranes his neck to look up, in my direction. Can he see me in the tree? Does he know I'm here?

I pull the trigger.

The gun kicks back hard against my shoulder, almost knocking me out of the tree. A horse squeals and a shout goes up among the men. When the smoke clears, I see why. The first horse is down, bleeding and floundering, just like I wanted. But Arsenault's right hand is still tied to it. The horse dragged Arsenault down but didn't roll on him.

"Where did that shot come from?" Geoffre roars. "Find the sniper, gods damn you!"

I reload as fast as I can and sight straight down the line of the barrel.

At Geoffre's head.

Men bob in front of him. The men who were looking for me in the woods are coming back, having heard the shot and smelled the smoke. I can't wait much longer.

Geoffre flashes back into view.

I take the shot.

It cracks in a pop of smoke and noise that shoves my back against the tree trunk. I can't see Geoffre, but that doesn't mean I hit him.

I sling the gun over my shoulder and clamber down, until I'm low enough that I can swing to the ground.

But now there are men below my tree.

I pull my dagger and drive my hobnail boots into their heads. Two of them fall, giving me time to hit the ground and bring my blade up in a slash that leaves another man bleeding. I whirl and rip the other man shoulder to hip.

I'm running before I've even pulled the blade all the way out of his clothes, crashing through the underbrush and out into the yard...

CHAPTER 36

Among all the men who are running the wrong way.

Bodies hit me in their haste to escape whatever stands in the circle with the dead horse. I use my right arm like a battering ram until I see what everyone else has seen already.

Geoffre stands over Arsenault with a gaping hole in his head. *Dread gods.*

Bloody, ragged, and smoke-charred, the hole makes no difference at all. It's like I hurled a pebble at him, not a lead ball.

Birds of prey dive on the army, tearing at men's faces and arms as the men push each other down in their haste to leave. Ravens swoop down upon eagles and hawks, trying to drive them off. Birds knocked from the sky thump to the ground, and men trample them on their way past, adding the sound of crunching bones and eagle screams to the cacophony.

"Here's one of Cassis's men!" a man yells.

"Damn him to his own hell!" another man shouts back. "This isn't worth the pay!"

"Betrayal!" yells another, and I'm stuck in a forest of men and birds and blades, fighting me, fighting each other, fighting ravens and goshawks... Talons rake my cheek and I swing my right arm at a raven only to have it smash into a man's face. I lose the gun, and it's too close for swords. Just the thud of bodies, the slap of wings, and the smell of blood and mud, trying to tear my way through the kind of jungle that would grow in the underworld.

"You think you can win against me?" Geoffre laughs, loud and wild. "Have you ever been able to win against me, Ari Gunnarsson?"

"It's not about me, Erelf," Arsenault says. "I promised I'd finally cooperate with you if you'd leave her alone, so why don't you get it over with?"

Geoffre/Erelf laughs again. "Yes," he says. "Let's get it over with."

A man thuds into me and propels me backwards, knocking me down. Boots pummel me as I struggle to find my feet again, kicking me in the head, the back—

Magic swirls in the air. Another boot to the head and my Sight jars in.

Arsenault's ropes turn into snakes.

He tries to remain still, but he can't. Not with snakes coiling around his arms, twisting along the line of his shoulders and curling around his neck, flicking their pink tongues against his chin and collarbone. More snakes slither up his legs from the ground, twining around his knees and thighs.

I drag myself forward over the ground by my fingernails, kicking at men's ankles to knock them away from me.

Arsenault grabs the snake around his neck and digs his heels into the ground, trying to push himself away. But the horse has the rope that binds his right arm pinned under its body, and Arsenault can't stand up.

A man hooks his foot in the crook of my knee and falls on top of me. "Damn you, get *off!*" I shout, and shove him away.

Jon has been trying to stand by impassive, but now he breaks. "This isn't what we planned, Arsenault!" *he calls, and runs to Arsenault's side with his sword pulled, striking out at the snakes.* "I'm tired of watching you die, brother!"

"No! Jon!" *Arsenault shouts, just as Jon is about to cut the rope that holds him to the horse...but it's too late. The horse lurches upright just like Geoffre, in spite of the ragged red hole blown in its side. Glistening blue loops of intestine droop from the wound, but it begins to walk anyway, and the rope that binds Arsenault to it sings taut and drags him away from Jon, scraping and thumping through the dust. One of the snakes sinks its fangs into his chest and he cries out, scrabbling at its scaled muscles with his fingernails. The other snakes stretch and grow, anchoring themselves on Arsenault's limbs and slithering to the horses that waited for his ropes.*

I'm almost to the edge of men. Almost to the point where I can see what's happening with my physical eyes...

Jon whirls his sword down, but bright silver shoots over the snakes like armor, and Jon's sword bounces off the way swords bounce off my arm.

"You talk me into letting you die all the time," *Jon says, trying to hack another rope, only to have it strike at his foot.* "But this is too far. How is it going to help anyone if you give yourself up to this god? It's not honoring any of your promises!"

"I'm honoring the most important one -- the one I made to Kyrra," Arsenault rasps.

"What shall I do to you this time?" Erelf says. "I don't think you've ever been pulled apart, have you? Do you think I could put you together again?"

"As long as you honor our agreement," Arsenault grinds out through gritted teeth. The snakes are wrapped tight around the legs of the other three horses now. The horses stamp and shift, pulling him in different directions with every movement. With my Sight, I can see the strain on Arsenault's face.

"Of course," Erelf says. "But when you come back—however you come back after you die in pieces—and I take your memory...then I can do whatever I want, can't I? I mean, I'll have *you* do whatever I want, because that was our deal, but perhaps I'll just rob her from you forever, too. If you can't remember what we agreed, you won't care what I do, will you?"

Arsenault growls in rage and yanks against the snake-ropes. Metal cracks down their lengths, screaming as it pulls apart. But then magic slams him back. The horses, startled, shy in pairs in opposite directions. The sound of Arsenault's rage turns into an animal cry of pain as his limbs are pulled to the edge of their sockets.

Jon hurls his sword to the ground and darts to catch the horses that are tearing Arsenault apart. He throws all his weight into stopping them and speaks in a soothing voice, pulling them back.

I thrust my way up out of the muddle of trampling feet, using my arm like a club. "Leave him, Erelf!" I shout. "I'll fight you!"

Geoffre—Erelf—turns around in amazement. The wound in his head is like a window into the structure of his skull—blackened and red flesh underlaid with chips of white bone and gray brain matter. But it's already starting to heal, the edges of the wound groping together like wriggling worms.

His lips twist into an expression like a smile but devoid of human emotion. "And here you are. Little bird. Right into my hands, in spite of what he's done to prevent it."

"Kyrra! Don't!" Arsenault shouts.

"Kyrra," Jon says softly, trying not to startle the horses. "Perhaps you can talk some sense into him. Or into this god."

"I know you had it all set up," Arsenault says. "But this is something I have to do."

I draw my sword—Arsenault's sword—and rock back on my heels in front of Erelf. "I don't know what you're talking about, Arsenault."

"Erelf," Arsenault says weakly. "We still have a deal."

"The terms will be null and void if she tries to attack me," Erelf says in a bemused way that surely owes at least as much to Geoffre as the god inside him.

"The terms were terms. No exceptions."

"Neither of you has the right to bargain for me," I say. "Especially since I don't know what you're bargaining for."

"Go ahead," Erelf says. "Tell her before the poison begins working on your vocal chords."

"He wants you as a bride," Arsenault chokes out.

For a moment, I can't be sure I've heard him right. But then Jon groans and my surprise turns to fear and revulsion.

I adjust my grip on my sword and look Erelf—Geoffre—up and down.

"I've had better suitors," I say.

Erelf shrugs. "I've had better brides. But you have all the abilities I need. And the right genealogy."

"I told you," Arsenault says. "There's more to your father's lands. More to you."

"Why didn't you tell me the whole story?"

"Took me a while to figure it out. If I told you...he would

CHAPTER 36

know. I didn't want him to know. Where you were, that you knew about him."

"Oh, I knew about you." Geoffre dusts off his sleeves. His wound is still knitting itself. If I'm going to have a chance against him, it has to be soon, before that wound heals entirely. "After all, we did have some interesting conversations, didn't we, Kyrra?"

Arsenault curses without opening his eyes and laughs in that helpless, defeated way exhausted men have. "So, everything I did...it was for nothing?"

I step forward, settling my sword into guard. "You're a god of lies. You left me alone for five years until I entered your temple to buy a knife. If you'd been able to carry me off, you would have, so there must be something stopping you. Is it Arsenault? Me? Something else? Ires maybe, or Ekyra?"

An emotion flickers in the god's eyes. It's not exactly fear, but it tells me I'm on the right trail.

"I never lie," he says. "Sometimes, I don't call attention to the entire truth, but I never lie."

"Never? You killed your own brother. The stories say it was an accident, but you knew it was him. You shot him on purpose."

"Have *I* ever said otherwise? It only comes out different in stories. Mortals need to wash us clean. It's too hard otherwise for you to imagine a god."

He runs his hand over the flank of one of the horses bound to Arsenault. Its muscles shiver underneath the skin.

Jon tightens his grip on the bridles. "It's too much, what you're doing, even for a god. Aren't there some rules about this sentence of his? Can't we make another agreement? I'm sure Kyrra would weigh in on the bargain."

I'm going to have to apologize to Jon. I've gotten him all wrong.

Erelf looks bored, then flicks his hand in Jon's direction. The horses' bridles melt into brown patches of paint and dissolve into the horses' hides. Jon is left holding nothing. He lifts his hands, startled, and Erelf leans forward, lips pursed, and blows Jon into pieces on the wind that scatter and disappear.

"Erelf!" Arsenault shouts.

My left hand starts shaking.

It's easy to be fooled into treating Erelf like a man when he looks like one, but he's a god. How can I defeat a god?

Maybe if I distract him enough, Mikelo can make it to Arsenault.

I step forward.

Erelf's fingers scritch down the line of one long muscle on the horse's rump...then stop, knuckles up, as if he is going to give the horse a smack.

"Your beloved Arsenault also killed his brother," he says, then pauses, his expression hardening. "And my daughter, too,"

I stop, in spite of myself, frozen in surprise. "Your...daughter?"

"His wife." Erelf gives me Geoffre's cold, twisty smile, but his eyes smolder with anger. "Did he not tell you that? Did he bank on your love without telling you how he murdered his own? Do you think perhaps he was trying to keep you away from me for his own reasons—trying to push down your magic because it threatened his?"

"No," Arsenault says hoarsely. "No, it wasn't like that."

"Wasn't it? Do you deny that Sella died at your hand, then?"

"She died because I gave up her secret. She only wanted to be free of you, and I let it slip to Tavi, and then— Damn you, Erelf, he took her to bed!"

He pulls against his bonds in his anger, and the horses stamp and shy without Jon to calm them. Is Jon dead or is it only illusion? Is Erelf telling the truth about Arsenault, or is it only more lies?

Arsenault bites his lip on a whimper as the horses start to pull him apart, then, as the horses come back together, lessening the tension on his limbs, he takes a shuddering breath.

CHAPTER 36

"You knew you could turn Tavi. And you couldn't turn me. So, you made him into a snake."

"See how he twists?" Erelf says to me. "See how he turns the fault away from himself? It's not about Tavi at all. It's about you. You killed my daughter. My only daughter."

"Erelf! You know her death was an accident!"

"So, you've always said." Erelf's voice drips sarcasm. "When you found your brother being the man you weren't?"

"I didn't know Sella was so lonely. He took advantage of her!"

"Because you failed her. And you want me to believe that in your anger—"

"My anger at Tavi," Arsenault says, trying to keep his voice reined in tight, the muscles of his arms taut as the ropes in his attempt to remain still, "She threw herself between us. I tried to turn the blow but I couldn't. You *know* this. I told it to all the gods at my trial!"

"And after you killed her, you hunted your brother down," Erelf says. "You'd like to pretend you're on the side of light, but you let that darkness into yourself. The darkness you say you've always fought. But when you killed Sella and Tavi, it spread like a blight into you, and from there it spreads into everyone you come into contact with."

"Tavi embraced it," Arsenault says, his voice shredded with the effort of holding still between the horses. "He thought it was the only way to make a difference in the world."

Erelf raises an eyebrow in one of Geoffre's cold expressions. "And have you shone so brightly since?"

Arsenault sags in his bonds. "You know I haven't. But use what you can. Just leave Kyrra alone."

"Quit tormenting him," I say.

Erelf whirls on me. "You think you shine bright, but the darkness burns within you, too—oh, so dark, doesn't it, with mad Ires calling you? How many years have you spent living only for revenge? How many years have you lived only to spill blood?"

I can't refute that. I can't refute the way the metal turned me into a machine for killing.

"If you had left Arsenault to me, perhaps things would be different."

"Was it my fault or was it his? Little bird. He never told you the truth, did he? About anything."

I open my mouth to tell him he lies, but the words won't come out.

Arsenault never did tell me the truth. He never told me about his brother. He never told me why he hid from Erelf.

He never told me about his wife.

And yet...with his every action, Arsenault *showed* me truth. He showed me what it was like to love someone.

"Kyrra," Arsenault says, his voice rough with pain. "I'm sorry. I was afraid of what you would think of me. Of losing you. If you knew I killed my wife... Please, Kyrra. Go. Don't let him take you. I don't mind dying."

I take a deep breath and raise my sword.

"Liar," I say.

His face twists like I just put a spear in him.

I swing the sword around into guard. "You do mind dying. I'm not going to let you do it again."

"Kyrra!" he yells, like a curse or a warning or maybe just in relief, but I'm already turning to face Erelf.

"You made a game of stealing my light and leaving me only darkness," I tell the god. "And now I will have it back."

❧

I BRING MY SWORD AROUND IN A TWO-HANDED SLICE AT Erelf's neck.

He laughs. He puts one hand out and the metal of Arsenault's sword bucks. I stumble forward, and he steps neatly away from me. With a movement too quick for me to follow, he has knives in his hands, and he cuts me in a big X across the chest.

CHAPTER 36

I gasp in pain and go down on my knees, gripping my sword in desperation. Erelf stands over me with one hand holding his knife and the other hand raised over the horse's rump.

"I am a *god*," he says, his eyes glittering and terrible.

In that moment, a crashing wave of magic pours over us.

Mikelo.

He waited. Just like Arsenault did.

One of the metal snakes shudders and tugs so hard that the horse swings its hindquarters. It pulls Arsenault so viciously, I'm sure it's just dislocated his shoulder. He shouts with the pain. But the horse knocks Erelf off balance.

Mikelo! I shout. *Use me!*

He knows what I mean. He's Seen it in me.

Kyrra, I could kill you!

Now, while he's off guard!

Mikelo doesn't hesitate anymore. He turns his magic on me with all his strength. It grabs me by the throat. I feel as if I'm being lifted off my feet and throttled. I can't breathe. I'm burning. My sword feels like it's welded to my hand. Metal ripples up my shoulder and shoots down my entire right side.

Kyrra, Ekyra, valkyr.

I can't fight a god as myself.

But Fortune and War can fight him.

I climb to my feet and raise my sword. The runes flash down the blade and my arm, over my whole right side.

"Kyrra," Arsenault breathes.

"I can't let you go either," I tell him, settling my feet. "And now I'm going to ruin all your plans."

Erelf laughs. Long and hard. But he drops his hand from the horse and puts it on the hilt of his sword. "Very well. Come at me with your sword and see what happens. If you lose, I'll have both of you."

"And if I win?"

"You won't win."

"But if?"

"I'll give you Ari back. For now."

"Pick up your sword, then, old man," I say, grinning. "And we'll see which of us is stronger."

A flicker of unease passes over his eyes. But he lifts his sword. And swings it.

I charge into his attack, laughing.

❧

I DON'T ONLY FIGHT FOR ARSENAULT. I FIGHT FOR EVERYONE caught up in Erelf's lies.

I fight for my mother and my father. For my dead son. For Arsenault's wife and his brother who betrayed him, and Mikelo, betrayed by his family too. I fight for Lobardin, broken and warped. I fight for Jon and his country and his murdered wife and sons, and Silva and Meli and everyone who hides in Charri's house. I fight for Cassis, manipulated by his desire to win a father's love. For Driese and her unborn child, the child who might unite Liera.

For Vadz and Razi.

And for that girl I used to be, broken and bloodied and set adrift.

But mostly, I fight for the man who found me. The only person who saw not what I was but who I might be.

Erelf hurls Geoffre's body into my strokes with complete disregard of the wounds I deal it. His sword rings against my body, leaving big cuts and dents, but I charge again and again until he begins to stumble.

I disregard the pain. I disregard the blood. I disregard the life that begins to slip through my fingers.

"Give. Up," Erelf pants as we lock swords again.

"No," I say, and throw myself against him, everything I have: my sword, my body, my life.

For Arsenault.

CHAPTER 36

I feel his magic at the end. Behind me, shoring me up. Jon, too, fighting back from wherever the god tried to put him—his sword swinging into birds and men, carving out a space for both Mikelo and Arsenault, letting me battle the god.

Until finally, the magic breaks and the world rushes back in.

My sword sticks out Geoffre's back like a skewer.

His sword sticks in me the same.

We fall together.

CHAPTER 37

It's like a dream. I hear my name, but it's more like the wind. And I see her standing ahead of me, beside the river Ransi. Her golden hair floats around her in a fuzzy nimbus of light, like a halo around the moon. Her skin is icy white, smooth as new-fallen snow. She hails from colder climates. She wears black armor, plate, but her gauntlets are silver steel. Two golden eagles sit on her shoulders, twisting their heads as they watch the trees.

Ekyra stares into the foaming, roiling waters. The plummeting current of the river breaks up any reflection that might form there, so she isn't watching herself. It's something else, swirling and hidden beneath the water.

I walk up behind her, my blood-rusted metal arm hanging at my side, pocked with dents. I'm as full of holes as Geoffre is, but like him, I keep walking.

Ekyra looks over her shoulder at me. Her eagles ruffle their wings and duck their heads to pluck at errant feathers. Their golden eyes trap my reflection.

"Sister," she calls me.

Fear makes my heart pound. "Have I come into the afterlife?"

Her lips pull up into a half-smile. "No. This is too peaceful to be your afterlife."

CHAPTER 37

"Why have you called me here, then? Am I dying?"

She spreads her hands. "You asked me for help, and here I am." The eagles swivel their heads, and she cocks hers, like the birds. "I have something to show you."

She beckons me toward the river and kneels again on the bank. I sink to the ground beside her, cradling my metal arm against my chest. I find myself looking down a slope of tangled roots, slick with the white mist that hides the river. I can't see the other bank for the fog.

"Watch," she says.

The mist boils up into shapes that arrange themselves into people wearing white robes and flat leather sandals, reclining on couches, walking through frescoed rooms...

Etereans. I lean closer and watch as a man detaches himself from the general swath of images. He is tall and well made, his burgundy robes swishing against bare ankles as he walks, alone, down a long, brown stone hall. Arches pierce the hall at intervals, allowing sunlight from a garden courtyard to spill through, sliding in spears across the burgundy robe as it moves with his stride. He wears a short sword at each side and a crown of gold-gilt olive leaves atop his curly blond hair.

He walks the hallway to its end, where it opens to a wide balcony from which he can see the ocean, distantly, like a silk ribbon of blue.

I give a start. I know that view, though the hallway is unfamiliar to me. "My father's house."

"The land is old. It's trapped its share of souls."

"Who is he?"

Ekyra waves my question away. I look down into the fog again and watch as the man leans on the stone railing, looking out over a different view: Liera, more resplendent than I have ever seen it, the Doge's alabaster palace as white as the purest block of kacin from Dakkar.

Out in the harbor, a fleet sets out, not the mismatched shapes of Lieran caravels with their House colors. No, this is a *fleet,* a hundred warships rigged with sails striped gold and dark.

Burgundy.

"Eterea," I breathe.

"He's dreaming," Ekyra says. "His name is Attrasca. Not that it matters. It's only a dream."

"Eterea existed, though. We see it on our walls, step on its shards underfoot..."

"To him, it's a dream. My father intended it as such." A bitter smile creases her face. Her skin isn't as smooth as I thought. There are lines at her mouth and eyes, the lines of one who has seen many campaigns.

Her blue-gray eyes are old, older than stone.

"Do you know the story?" she asks.

"I know history," I say. "My father taught it to me, how the Etereans collapsed into their own decadence and opened their borders to the hoards."

"That isn't the story I'm talking about. Do you know the story of how Eterea came to be?"

I shake my head.

"My father gave it to Attrasca, encased in a pearl. He meant it to tempt Attrasca, and tempt him it did. It tempted him so much that he shattered the pearl and loosed his vision of Eterea upon the world. And then he could not call it back. His dream seeped into the heads of all around him, until they began to see it too. Eventually he inflicted this dream, this shattered pearl, upon the whole world, and all men and all the gods were called into its defense or its damnation."

I frown. "Which side were you on?"

She laughs. "You, a gavaro, ask me this. Does it matter which side I was on? Perhaps I stood in the middle so I could see both sides of it."

"It was beautiful," I say. "The city."

"And it was dark and ugly, too. Men killed for it. Men kill for it still."

CHAPTER 37

She rises, and the fog begins to seep away. I lever myself up after her.

"You've a brave heart, Kyrra," she says, laying her hands on either side of my face, brushing away my hair. "I have need of it yet."

She bent down to kiss my forehead, and the world rushed back into me.

※

"She's awake!" someone shouts. Male. Young. "Awake, awake!"

I have my eyes open. But I can't see. Not quite.

Dull, unmagical colors surround me. Browns mostly. A ceiling, with beams. Walls.

I'm lying on a narrow bed. A man who's little more than a boy leans over me, his barley-brown curls and dusky violet eyes familiar.

Silva.

"How—" My voice croaks out of me. Barely recognizable.

"Don't talk," Silva says. "Arsenault says if you ask one question, you'll ask a thousand."

He grins.

"Arsenault is here?" I rasp.

"Did you think I would leave you?"

It's Arsenault's voice.

I shift my head. Now I can see him standing behind Silva. His old scar jags down his temple, the metallic silver-white streak startling to see again in his dark hair.

He looks so much like his old self that at first, I think I've just changed my dream of Ekyra for one of Arsenault. But then he sits down in a chair beside the cot and leans forward, smiling at me, and I realize I can feel him and smell him, and so it must be him, really him.

He has another scar, new and pink, on his other cheek, but

it's smaller. Maybe it's the mark my dagger left, back when he didn't remember me and shot Razi.

"How?" I ask. "What—"

Arsenault glances at Silva. *I told you*, his eyes say.

I try to glare at them both.

"I followed the gavaros who took you prisoner," Silva says quietly. "And when you came to the lodge, I joined Geoffre's army. I thought it would be the best way to get back to you."

"Why—"

"Because of what you said about Meli." He lifts his gaze to mine. "And because it would have been easy for you to kill us both, but you didn't. I didn't find you until it was late, though."

"Cassis made the charge," Arsenault says. "But by then, most of Geoffre's army had disintegrated. Cassis had no trouble dispatching the rest."

"Jon." I clear my throat. "Is Jon alive? Jon didn't want—"

Talking hurts. I wince and let my head sink into the pillow.

Arsenault frowns. "Let us tell it. Silva, get her a drink, will you?" Silva nods and spins away, walking quickly for the door. Arsenault puts his elbows on his knees and leans closer to me.

"Jon's fine," he says. "A little shaken up, but that kind of illusion magic is only permanent if you accept that it is. He fought his way back, set me free, and gave Mikelo the space to keep backing you up with his magic. He's with Cassis right now, trying to figure out where to go from here. Technically, Devid is Householder, but no one's quite certain what happened to Geoffre after Erelf retreated, and it isn't clear if Devid will strike a peace with Cassis or if Cassis will accept one if he does. And there's still Mikelo to be reckoned with... Neither Devid or Cassis know exactly where Mikelo stands on this matter. Which is probably a good thing, considering the conversations I've had with him over the past eight days."

He rubs the bridge of his nose. "Whatever happened in that prison...he's determined that neither Devid or Cassis will sit in that chair. So, that leaves him. For better or worse."

I open my mouth to comment, but Arsenault raises a hand to stop me. "So, no, it's not an ideal situation. It would have been much easier if Cassis and Geoffre had killed each other on the field of battle, leaving only Devid to deal with."

"Is Jon angry with me?"

"Hah," Arsenault says, with his old hook of a grin. "No. He's angry with *me*. I'm the one who made a mess of things. Which, frankly, he ought to be used to by now. It's not the first time I've taken it on myself to do something and thrown a wrench into the works. He put me with Tonia, thinking I would be the one she hired to take care of Cassis. He kept trying to put her off your trail. Dakkarans don't take promises lightly. Their whole society is built upon them. And he promised me, long before Kafrin, to keep an eye on you. He had contacts inside the prison and was planning on springing you, after I went on to the lodge in your place. I wasn't supposed to be in that contingent of guard that caught you at all. Just like I wasn't supposed to try to assassinate you."

"Was that why Jon came north? During the wars? To keep a promise to you?"

"One of the reasons. Not the only one. It solved a couple of problems. Jon was headed out of Liera anyway so he could run his smuggling rings out from under the eye of the Prinze. The Rojornicki had an interest in keeping your Houses destabilized. But mostly, I asked him to go because Erelf wanted you and I wasn't sure that I'd done enough to keep you hidden."

"You knew? That he wanted me as a bride?"

Arsenault sighs raggedly. "I didn't figure that out until later. But I knew there must have been some reason for him to claim you even after Ires's magic took you. Sella's death tortures him. I think he loved her after his own fashion, and what does time mean to a god? It never passes to heal wounds. The wounds just keep bleeding. But maybe...he's come to the point where he would like to have another child. I think...he misses her."

I turn my head to see Arsenault better. "Do you miss her?"

He threads his fingers together and looks at them. "She was my wife."

I think maybe we're done with secrets.

His fingers draw apart and he takes my left hand in his, running his thumb gently over my fingers, avoiding my knuckles. They're all over red and purple, bruises, cuts, and scratches.

"I didn't know how much it would hurt to have you gone. It's been so long since I was able to love anyone. Since I let myself love anyone. The gods know how much I fought it and for how long. I sent Jon to Vençal first, hoping you were there. Enri knows who I am and could have told you everything, but you never went. So, Jon went to Rojornick to see if he could find out what happened to you."

He looks troubled, like he wants to ask me why but he doesn't want to cause me anymore distress.

"You—remember?"

He smiles. A wounded, sorrowful sort of smile. But a smile. "Everything," he says, tightening his fingers on mine but not enough to hurt. "You won me a reprieve."

"But your scar—"

"It's Erelf's mark. Knowledge. Memory." He pauses. "Magic. That's back too, in full. Though I don't know if I'm still forbidden to use it except in self defense or not. My reprieve has...boundaries. It's not forever, but I don't know how long it will last. That's up to the Tribunal, and they're still discussing the parameters. Erelf is regrouping, and it's not clear what he'll do next."

"The gods are having a discussion about you?"

"An argument, more likely."

I try to laugh, but it comes out too quiet. Then I try to rub his fingers, but I can't. My fingers won't grip.

He notices me trying, though, and he curls them up around his for me.

"Mikelo saved you. For a while, we weren't sure it worked."

"Ekyra—sent me back. I had a dream..."

CHAPTER 37

Gods, it hurts to talk. I swallow and try to lift my arms to look at them, but I can't summon the strength to move.

Arsenault looks troubled again. "The metal receded," he says. "All on its own. Except for your arm. It's still there."

Something in his eyes looks bad. "Let me look," I say. "Please."

The trouble in his face deepens. But he pulls back the covers and lets me look.

My right arm is a hopeless mangle of metal. It's no wonder I can't lift it.

I catch my breath. It sounds like a sob. "It might as well be cut off."

Arsenault leans forward. "Kyrra, I can Fix it."

"No," I say. "Let me be for a while. Just let me...be. Here. Together, with you."

With my head on this pillow and his hand in mine, among people who care.

I try to move my fingers again, and he reads my intent and squeezes them gently.

"But just one more question," I say.

"Only one more?"

"In that story about Udolfo and the pirate, the one I read to you...who were you? The pirate Udolfo's betrothed loved? Or her faithful fisherman, the one who saved her from drowning?"

He looks surprised. Then he grins.

"The fisherman, of course."

APPENDIX: MAJOR LIERAN HOUSES

Note: The final "e" is pronounced in all Eterean names, usually as /ay/, "r" is rolled, and "i" is generally pronounced /ee/.

- Aliente
- Caprine
- Forza
- Garonze
- Imisi
- Prinze
- Sere

APPENDIX: ETEREAN GODS

- **Tekus** — Father God and god of the sea
- **Ahra** — wife to Tekus
- **Adalus** — son of Tekus, the Dying God; god of springtime, sacrifices, and harvest
- **Erelf** — exiled son of Tekus and brother to Adalus; god of knowledge, secrets, and magic
- **Ekyra** — daughter of Tekus; goddess of fortune, also called the Huntress
- **Ires** — insane god of war; shackled deep within the volcano Kosemi
- **Cythia** — daughter of Tekus; goddess of love
- **Pana** — daughter of Tekus; name means "willing".
- **Lusa** — daughter of Tekus; goddess of the moon

APPENDIX: GLOSSARY

- **allaq** — Qalfan body robes falling to mid-calf, usually worn with trousers beneath.
- **arquebus** — long matchlock gun, comparable to a rifle.
- **astra** — gold coin minted by the Lieran Circle.
- **cato** — copper coin minted by the Lieran Circle, of lesser value than the astra.
- **conjure-woman** — a woman experienced in the use of conjure magic, a variety of magic used specifically by women and having to do primarily with the body and fertility.
- **dikkarro** — a hand-held wheellock pistol, named for Dakkar, its country of invention.
- **Eter** — the language spoken and written by the ancient Etereans, who unified the peninsula and ruled an empire many hundreds of years before the story takes place.
- **fila** — supernatural, godlike beings native to Dakkar.
- **Fixer** — a magic user who can use magic to **Shape** (or **Fix**) objects according to their will. Depending on

the material a Fixer operates upon, a Fixer may also be called an **Artisan** or a **Smith**.
- **gavaro** — a mercenary or sword-for-hire. Gavaros form the bulk of the fighting forces among the city-states of the Eterean peninsula. They are also hired as guards, assassins, bounty hunters, and debt collectors.
- **guarnello** — the common dress of peasant women in the Eterean peninsula. A long jumper worn over a lighter underdress. The bodice laces up to provide support in lieu of stays.
- **Head of House** — the lead householder of a House, who makes decisions and rules everyone of that House name.
- **householder** — any member of the noble Houses of the Eterean peninsula. When capitalized (**Householder**) this refers to the Head of House.
- **Ibuu** — the ruler of Dakkar, male or female.
- **imya** — clear liquor imported from Rojornick.
- **indij** — card game favored by gavaros in which the jester is the strongest card.
- **kacin** — powdery, white drug formed by drying and grinding berries from a plant grown in Dakkar. Can be smoked or taken orally. Induces sleepiness, functions as a pain killer. Addictive. The leaves of the plant can be chewed for a milder effect.
- **kai dahn** — dice game imported from Saien and favored by sailors.
- **Messera/messera** — In its capitalized form, the title for the first wife of the Head of House. Uncapitalized, it functions as an honorific for any female householder. (Equivalent of "mistress")
- **Mestere/mestere** — In its capitalized form, the title for the Head of House. Uncapitalized, it functions as an honorific for any male householder. (Equivalent of "master")

- **Mistiri/mistiri** — the plural form for the man and woman who are Head of House, or, uncapitalized, householders in general. (Equivalent of "masters").
- **Nezar/Nezari** — member or members of an elite Qalfan fighting order who often hire out as mercenaries.
- **sanval** — the spring wind from the south that often brings violent storms.
- **See/Sight** — the magical ability to see the truth or underlying nature of people or things. Not always able to be controlled.
- **ser** — honorific for male members of the free merchant class, who are neither nobles or serfs.
- **sera** — honorific for female members of the free merchant class, who are neither nobles or serfs.
- **sontana** — afternoon nap.
- **sweetweed** — mild drug imported by Qalfans, usually smoked.
- **urqa** — the headcloths used by Qalfans, especially men, to cover their heads and faces.
- **vota** — religious artifact, usually carved of wood and imbued with life-like attributes by conjure magic. Used in religious ceremonies in place of live sacrifices or to satisfy different needs of the owner – luck, health, love, etc.
- **whiteskin** — somewhat derogatory term used by Dakkarans, Vençalans, Qalfans, and darker-skinned, southern Etereans to refer to people with fair skin from northern regions.

ACKNOWLEDGMENTS

This book was written in two different periods in my life, separated by many years and the addition of many children (six added to the three I had when I finished the first draft).

For reading the earliest drafts and listening to me yammer on about characters and ideas, many thanks go to my old writing group, the Sporks, but especially to Sue Glantz, Karin Lowachee, Helen Vorster, Roger Eichorn, Elizabeth Glover, and Mike Dumas. (Mike — *requiescat in pace*, my friend, because you are very missed.)

Nancy Proctor, you get all the thanks times three for reading *all* the drafts — early, middle, and late — the ones with giant holes and the ones with way too many words. Everybody needs a friend to tell them when they wanted to throw the book at the wall.

When I pulled the manuscript out of my closet after a thirteen or fourteen year hiatus, I thought maybe I was going to have to go it alone — a thought which terrified me. Thankfully, this was not the case. To Krystle Matar, Stephen Coey, and Fiona West, my intrepid beta readers, who slogged through all the later drafts when I was trying to patch the holes and get the sequence of chapters right — you have my undying gratitude. If the book is any good, it's largely because of you.

John Anthony Di Giovanni did an amazing job of taking the vision of my book and my characters and turning it into gorgeous art. Shawn King took the art and turned it into a fantastic cover. I can't emphasize enough how much I love it.

Richard Shealy at SF/F Copyediting did a monumental job of sorting out all the commas in this very large book. He probably deserves a medal.

Clayton, Nick, Justine, Luke, Dave, and Krystal — you keep me laughing and help me stay sane... or insane, which is the preferable state. And to everyone in the Indie Fantasy community on Twitter — thank you for accepting me into the fold, for your humor and your support, and for all the crazy gif threads, too.

And finally, thank you to my kids, who put up with a mom who spends way too much time at the kitchen table, hunched over her computer, mumbling at characters who won't behave — and to my husband Andy, who knew what he was getting into when he asked me to marry him and went ahead with it anyway.

ABOUT THE AUTHOR

Angela Boord published a handful of fantasy short stories in the early 00s, then had a bunch of kids and took a long break from writing. She lives in northwestern Mississippi with her husband and their nine kids, plus two dogs, a cat named Mouse, and varying numbers of chickens.

She is currently at work on more books and stories in the Eterean Empire series, as well as a portal fantasy series set in a different universe.

Look for Eterean Empire 2, FOOL'S PROMISE, coming in mid-2020!

Subscribe to Angela's mailing list at Angelaboord.com for information on upcoming books in the Eterean Empire series and to receive your free copy of the short standalone Eterean Empire novel, SMUGGLER'S FORTUNE!

Printed in Great Britain
by Amazon